WHAT BECOMES OF THE FUTURE, IS A QUESTION
OF WHAT BECOMES OF THE DISTANT PAST

■ ■ ■ ■ ■ ■

BEYOND
OUR HORIZONS

M. H. FROGGATT

Ark House Press
arkhousepress.com

Cataloguing in Publication Data:
Title: Beyond Our Horizons
Series: The Horizon Series - Book One
ISBN: 978-1-7641051-3-2 (pbk)
Subjects: FIC042080   FICTION / Christian / Fantasy; FIC042100   FICTION / Christian / Contemporary; FIC042020   FICTION / Christian / Futuristic.

Design by initiateagency.com

Dedications

To my younger brother, Aaron—
an inspiration beyond the horizons you can see.
You have overcome many challenges,
and you never give up.

I also dedicate this work to those who journey
with mental health challenges—
who suffer, endure, overcome, navigate, and traverse
the painful, frustrating, confusing,
and yet often character-building terrain that it is.

To all who support and understand:
the friends, the whānau and family,
the pastors, teachers and kaiako,
the youth workers, social workers, support workers,
medical practitioners, counsellors,
and all who champion freedom and quality of life
for those affected.

And finally, to those who did not make it through—
whose journeys ended too soon.
I honour your lives.
You mattered. You still do.

"Let us run with endurance the race God has set before us."
Hebrews 12:1

CHAPTER 1

**"There is nothing new in the world except
the history you do not know."**
Harry Truman (33rd U.S. President)

C had sat in the living room of the apartment he shared with three others, zoned out after a long day of feeling distant in the doldrums of his current predicament.

When he snapped out of it he could hear his flatmate Zack in the kitchen doing something. Probably waiting for his irritating girlfriend Emma to arrive home. Unfortunately, also Chad's flatmate. At which point he'd disappear into his room for default fellowship with his Xbox or go off for another walk.

The evening news was on, formerly in the background. Now his ears had attuned to the name of his older brother... "...leading historian Tim Harison, who grew up here in New Zealand," the newsreader said, "comes to us live from the remote western Sahara town of Ouadane in the middle of Mauritania.

Tim's cheery face appeared on the TV screen with a dry and dusty backdrop on a hot sunny day. He wore a white Ripcurl surf cap and a baggy white cotton shirt.

"Tim, you've been on site with archaeologists from Australia, Britain and the US for a little over a year now," the news anchor began the interview, "yet up until now, the dig at the Mauritanian location has been particularly secretive. How much can you tell us about your work there so far?"

"Right, so—we've been here over a year now, working under tight security. Our team includes researchers from Auckland, Yale, Oxford, and Queensland Universities. It's been a massive collaborative effort. What we've found... it's unlike anything we've seen before. The scale alone is staggering. But it's not just the size—it's what it implies.

We're looking at the remains of an ancient city. And based on early analysis, this site could date back thousands—maybe tens of thousands—of years. That's well beyond anything in the established historical record. Some scholars are calling it the 'Parahistorical period.' It's a term used when there's no formal documentation, but the evidence is too compelling to ignore.

This discovery challenges everything. The timeline of human civilization—the one we've relied on for centuries—is no longer complete. What we've found suggests it's about to expand in ways we couldn't have imagined. Not just a few missing pieces, but entire chapters we never knew existed."

"That sounds interesting and very exciting," the anchor responded, "are you able to reveal any of the details of this ancient city or any aspects of significance that this discovery may entail?"

"As I say," Tim continued, "we are under high security, due to the nature of such an archaeological breakthrough. The exact specifics of the city itself are classified top-secret by the Mauritanian government, who have been incredibly accommodating and hospitable to us. But what I *can* tell you is that its centre alone, is around twenty-six kilometers in diameter. The full extent of the city is potentially far greater at forty-eight to fifty kilometers and that's larger than Lake Taupo or Singapore for example—

you could fit all of Auckland within that. And up until now, we've had little substantial knowledge of lost civilizations like these."

"So, this may give us more insight into human history before Ancient Egypt and Rome?"

"Exactly. There is potential for many of the missing links between civilized and prehistoric mankind to be uncovered here, and it's our intention that we complete a thorough search for whatever treasures this site has to offer up, and document as much as we can."

'Well that sounds interesting.' Chad thought to himself as his mind began to wander.

Chad and his brother Tim had always been opposites—like chalk and cheese.

Chad loved gaming; Tim preferred books and ancient history. Chad played chess; Tim—rugby. Tim was a committed Christian, while Chad had distanced himself from church—a can of worms he refused to reopen. Religion was the last thing he needed amid the chaos of his life. To his surprise, Tim had once agreed with that sentiment, but their conversation had been cut short.

Their last real talk had been over Skype, not long after Chad's breakup with Sonia Tallay—his celebrity tennis-star girlfriend after three years. Their relationship and her career unravelled after a drug scandal. The fallout took its toll on Chad, triggering a mental breakdown and the start of his journey through its challenges.

Fortunately, he had a brilliant counsellor, a loving family, and unwavering friends—some from his old church, others elsewhere. His half dozen loyal mates were the real deal.

Yet, to Chad, everyone around him seemed to have perfect lives. He questioned that often, unsure. In his valleys of doubt and frustration, he struggled to grasp what was real, uncertain of his own thoughts.

Long walks helped—music playing through his ear buds, he often wandered the quiet streets at night—fewer people, little traffic and noise—less to fuss with.

He glanced at his phone. Half six.

"Goin for a walk man." He said distantly to Zack on the way past the kitchen, through the ranch slider and out onto the deck.

"Sweet as, bro. You all good? Want me to save you any?" Zack was making some kind of chicken dish.

"Yeah—all good, just need a walk. And yeah if ya want—cheers."

Zack watched Chad step onto the deck—something was definitely off. He wasn't convinced his flatmate was 'all good'. Chad stared at the sky, plugged in his ear buds, and shuffled his long-walk playlist—a mix of metal, rock, and Charlotte Espanzia. Charlotte, Tim's fiancée, was skyrocketing to fame, both locally and internationally, with her unique fusion of hard rock and metal dance—a style Chad had grown to appreciate.

The rest were all that remained of his music collection after a purge, his therapist had suggested. Anything negative or antagonistic that fuelled his anger or fed his anxiety—gone.

Around him, friends were thriving, chasing dreams, while Chad struggled in the wreckage of his catastrophic breakup with Sonia. The fallout messed with his heart, mind, and studies. Once, a top law student at Waikato University, he had everything going for him—his family was successful, wealthy yet grounded.

His father, Ken Harison, founded Hurricane7, a booming snow, surf and street retail brand. His mother, Dr. Leanna Harison, a distinguished university lecturer, ignited a passion for history in his brother Tim. She made up bedtime stories when they were little for he, Tim, and their sister Celesta, who turned that inspiration into award-winning creative writing and her first novel at eighteen.

Chad had it made—until Sonia. Catching her with her drug dealer shattered everything. He never saw it coming—her secret addiction, much less her betrayal. She'd been his closest friend, fun, athletic, a rising tennis star. That ended when headlines exposed her steroid abuse and ties to a notorious drug lord.

The emotional toll was relentless. As Sonia's world crumbled, Chad was dragged down too—hounded by paparazzi, drowning in unanswerable questions. Celesta lost Sonia's friendship, the disgraced athlete severing ties in shame. Friends took sides, and Chad fled from the wreckage of Sonia Tallay's downfall.

He walked alone in the aftermath, going from a straight-A student and top team leader at Hurricane7, to failing two papers and quitting his role in the family business. He put his studies on hold, vowing to retake the failed courses and return to his father's team once he was in a better headspace.

Ken, whilst a hard man, refused to let his son suffer under meaningless pressures. He'd wait for Chad to find his feet again. Though Chad initially distanced himself, frustrating them both, Leanna helped Ken understand—his son needed space. Ken had been raised to prioritize people over anything else. No matter the circumstances, family came first. That principle changed everything between them. For the first time, Chad felt truly close to his father.

"It's ironic," he recalled Tim saying, when the two of them had discussed as much, *"that when the hard times hit, it's often then that a lot of stuff that needs to, is made right, it comes together."*

Chad missed his big brother. They'd grown closer in the weeks before Tim's latest expedition.

Chad wandered aimlessly down River Road, lost in thought, his music drowning out the troubles in his mind. The streetlights illuminated his path under an overcast sky that mirrored his mood. After walking several kilometres, he decided to see a movie, texting his friends Kate and Mitchell, who worked at the theatre. Their response lifted his spirits. As rain turned to a heavy downpour, he hurried toward the mall, cutting through a servo forecourt. A lightning flash followed by thunder startled him. Soaked but relieved his phone was dry, he entered the quiet mall, heading for the elevator to the theatre.

After Kate's initial shock and amusement at how drenched Chad was, she printed him out a ticket as Mitch found him a dry change of clothing. He changed while the other two finished their shift, gathered popcorn and drinks, then the three friends sat back and enjoyed the movie.

As the credits rolled, Chad let Kate and Mitch's off beat banter wash over him—absurd hypotheticals and sly jabs softening the edges of his day. Between laughs, they shared a quiet moment of truth. "You've got us," Kate said simply.

"Always there for you, bro." added Mitch.

Chad appreciated the reassurance—it meant more than he could say.

~~~~~~~~

The sun streamed through Chad's window, breaking through the morning clouds of an overcast sky. Light filled his room, waking him gently to a brand-new day.

He stretched and yawned, then heard a buzz on his bedside cabinet.

He rolled over and grabbed his phone to answer.

It was his father...

"Hey Dad." He greeted sleepily, almost yawning again.

"Hi son... did I wake you?"

"Hmm, nah—the sun did that... I'm awake."

"It's nearly 10:30am! Whatta you doing in bed still?" Ken demanded.

"What? How did you know I was still in bed?"

"Never mind. You got plans for lunch?"

"Eating food, I guess..."

"Hmm, right. Well you can eat it at Foundation Bar at 12.30pm. My shout."

"Sounds good." Chad loved the huge gourmet Pizzas they cooked there.

"Great. Ya need a lift?"

"Ah, nah, thanks. I'll bus it."

"Good boy. See you then, shall I?"

"Sure."

"See you, son."

"See ya."

Chad showered, dressed in jeans, a grey T-shirt, and a black Billabong hoodie, then grabbed his phone and headphones before heading downstairs. With everyone at work or Uni, he locked up and walked to the bus stop.

Settling into his seat, he received a blunt text from Emma demanding a flat meeting about rent and chores. He rolled his eyes, ignored it, and put on his headphones.

At The Base shopping Center, another text arrived—Zack reassuring him not to take Emma's mood personally. She was having a bad day, nit-picking everything.

"Crazy lady," Chad muttered, and browsed the shops across from the mall.

With time to kill before meeting his father, he visited friends working nearby, browsed EB Games, and eyed the latest Assassin's Creed game. Seated outside Subway and a sushi bar, his phone pinged with an email—from Tim, wanting to call him.

Hey bro!

When are you free for a phone call? I have something I want to run past you. Let me know the time and day and I will match that up with the time zone and give you a buzz. Talk soon, Tim

"Interesting... I wonder what he wants to discuss?" Chad pondered.

He wandered back over to Te Awa mall and made his way toward Foundation Bar.

Ken stood outside the mall. Near the entrance to their family's favourite place to eat, looking at an LED advertising fixture.

Chad walked up to his Dad whose eye was caught by his son approaching him.

Ken greeted him with a smile and a hug. "Let's go eat." He said as he put an arm around his son's shoulder.

The waitress led the two of them to a booth, and they took a seat.

"Good day?" Chad asked his Dad.

"Yeah." Ken replied as if some thought had distracted him, then corrected himself. "No, actually, sorry. I've had those idiots from Sydney. Photon Gear, with us all morning." He frowned at Chad.

"Oh, the 'opportunistic system jockeys with their heads up their behinds'?" Chad grinned.

Ken paused, returning the grin, "that's right." He chuckled at his son's spot-on recollection of his description of the Australian wholesalers who'd rubbed him the wrong way over the phone.

Ken couldn't and wouldn't tolerate arrogance and had little time, or the patience to pretend otherwise, for types who bowed to 'the system'. Who operated according to the philosophy where dog-eat-dog—walk-over-people—immoral business tactics, and 'the end justifies the means' is 'just good business'.

Ken was a sharp, principled businessman who rejected questionable market trends and practices, no matter how legal they seemed. If an approach was unethical or exploitative, he'd walk away. He'd be unyielding and see red if challenged on it.

Photon Gear were known for exploiting their workers. Their company was riddled with problems and "their products are rubbish", Ken had ranted while telling Leanna, Celesta and Chad over dinner the other night.

"I told them they could take their arrogance, rotten business and sub-standard wares back to Australia and don't waste any more of my time. The snot-rags didn't just intend to sell us rubbish, they wanted to buy into Hurricane7 and proceeded to lecture me on my naivety and how we would be much better off with them."

"I would have ended it there too." Chad agreed.

Ken was amused and laughing it off now, but a few hours earlier he was fuming.

"Ah well, I was certainly happy to get out of the office, away from the madness of business negotiations with the likes of them and have lunch with my boy." He looked at Chad with affectionate eyes on a time weathered face.

The waitress returned to take their orders.

"You haven't had breakfast yet?" Ken told Chad rather than queried as the waitress walked away.

"Nah, was saving room for a this."

Ken laughed, "pizza for brekky." He shook his head and took a sip of his drink. "Enough about my hoo-ha and your questionable breakfast options! How are ya?" Ken had a way of asking how you were, with sincerity in the question, yet, the only response one could imagine, or would be comfortable with giving was at most, along the lines of "yeah good mate. Yaself?" which Ken would understand as "Unequivocally fantastic; couldn't possibly be better." Otherwise, there was "yeah alright." The latter, which to Ken, meant something was up. But you wouldn't feel easy sharing anything deep with a bloke who had the rough exterior and confidence Ken Harrison had.

Chad could confide in his mother—she was strong but gentle. He'd also opened up to Tim during his last visit. His brother had walked the same road, battled depression and anxiety, and emerged wiser, understanding the world beyond heartache.

"Getting there, I guess. Day at a time."

"Good man!" Ken applauded Chad.

Chad never resented his Dad's gruff demeanour—he knew Ken was always in his corner. While deep conversations weren't his strong suit, his Dad's unwavering commitment to fighting for those he loved proved his sincerity. Ken's skills in empathy were non-existent, but his passion for doing right and ensuring others were cared for spoke louder than words.

With Ken, work, rugby, and humour replaced heartfelt talks. Yet his hard-man persona paired with a loving heart inspired Chad to keep pushing forward. Tim once said, 'The journey is one of passionate fighting as well as passionate caring,'—wisdom Chad suspected came from experience.

Their meals arrived and the two of them thanked the waitress. Ken blessed the food, which was always a mix of awkward and reverence for Chad in public, then they ate.

"A couple of things, son." Ken began after the two of them had shovelled in a few mouthfuls each. "Your brother is trying to get hold of you is the first."

"Yeah, I got an email from him earlier."

"Right. Good. Did he tell you what it was regarding?"

"No, he's keen to discuss over the phone."

"Hmm, makes sense. It's the kind of thing you need to talk about over the phone."

Now Chad was fully focused on the what. What was it Tim wanted to talk to him about?

"What's it to do with?" He asked, putting his pizza eating on hold, too distracted now.

"Eat your lunch—breakfast. You'll have to wait till you talk with Tim to find out."

Chad had a mix of worry and annoyance on his face.

Ken paused from his carbonara and looked surprised at Chad.

"Don't look so worried, son." Ken frowned. "It's nothing you need be concerned about, any more than... I dunno, going to Disneyland." He'd no idea where that example had cropped up from.

"Disneyland? What?" Chad was confused.

"I dunno, it was the first thing that came to mind. Anyway, stop asking questions and listen. Tim will explain everything to you."

'Likely a good idea too!' Chad thought to himself, then remembered his dad could be terrible at these kinds of conversations. Simple, light-hearted things would be accidentally communicated heavily and complicated, leaving the other person confused and wondering if they'd done something wrong or were in trouble.

There was something Leanna had recently said to Ken, after he'd put someone on the spot, it'd all gone down like a lead balloon and Ken wondered what on earth he'd said wrong. Something about how to make things right, he couldn't recall half of what she'd said, but he suddenly remembered the words "You are not in trouble." He told Chad clearly.

"Yeah, alright. I didn't think I was."—awkward silence—"Don't worry about it, Dad." He reassured, amused at the irony of the shoe now being on the other foot.

Ken shook his head and went back to his carbonara.

"Tim has a proposal for you, and I want you to take him up on it." He told Chad with a serious look.

"Alright." Chad replied positively. He still had no idea what was going on.

"It'll be the best thing out for you at the moment."

"Sure..." Chad agreed, smiling and nodding.

"And don't worry about a thing, son." Ken smiled, "It will be exciting, I'm positive. Get you outta the house and away from all the hoo-ha o'Hamilton."

Chad now had his suspicions but opted for finishing his pizza while it was still hot.

Polishing off his carbonara, Ken brought up Chad's living arrangements, prompting Chad to brace for awkward news. Instead, Ken surprised him. He and Chad's mother, with his Uncle Conner, had bought a family rental home for his cousins whilst studying at Waikato, and for anyone needing a place to stay. He offered Chad a room, rent-free, to ease his struggles.

Touched, Chad considered the offer. Ken reassured him, emphasizing the importance of stability while he found his footing. He also noted Zack was a good flatmate, though Emma—he wasn't sure of.

As Ken ordered dessert, Chad opted for hot chocolate, reflecting on the unexpected lifeline. Later, they'd visit the new house together.

Later that afternoon, Ken dropped Chad off at his apartment after showing him around the most impressive house he'd ever considered living in.
The new property rivalled the elegance of his childhood home. Perched
on a hill, it boasted stunning views of the Waikato region's rolling green
pastures, the distant Kaimai ranges to the east, and city skyline southwest.

Far from typical student housing, it featured six bedrooms, a pool, a
BBQ—entertainment area, and even a cinema room. An orchard of fruit
trees in the backyard ensured fresh produce year-round. For Chad, it was a
perfect escape from city chaos and painful memories. Without hesitation,
he told his dad he was in.

Back at the flat, Chad was ready to leave, eager to escape Emma's relentless
nagging over rent and responsibilities. He'd miss Zack and Kal—the latter
who was barely around, off scaling skyscrapers and the like in his high-altitude window-cleaning job.

As Chad arrived home, Zack greeted him from the kitchen, immersed
in preparing a Moroccan lamb dish. Emma, however, watched him in
silence, disapproving. Chad hesitated before telling Zack about the new
house his family had bought, outlining its perks. Zack was instantly supportive, urging him to move.

Emma joined them.

"Chad's moving out Babe. He's leaving us… he doesn't love us anymore!"
Zack joked, feigning a distressed, betrayed look... he and Chad laughed.

Emma smirked, but her mood quickly shifted. She demanded he find
a replacement tenant. Zack's recollection Chad wasn't on the lease, subtly
aggravated Emma further. Her frustration grew until Zack assured her he
had someone lined up.

Emma, moments away from losing her temper, exhaled in frustration
as Zack calmly folded his arms, silently urging her to relax. As the tension

simmered, Chad was relieved—his exit was imminent, and the messy flat dynamic would soon be behind him. He was grateful for Zack—always the peacemaker, had smoothed things over, leaving Emma without leverage.

Chad had won this round, and a fresh start was finally within reach. He left before tensions escalated, not in the mood for another argument. He headed to the carport, jumped into his Toyota Hilux, and drove to a look-out on the western edge of town.

Having parked his vehicle, Chad stood at the lookout on a hill near his parents' place. It offered breath-taking countryside views—the perfect escape to watch the sunset paint Mount Pirongia in fiery hues and momentarily disconnect from city life.

Parking at the street's end, he climbed the hill, responding to Tim's email as he walked the winding path. He'd waited long enough. Whatever his dad thought best, he'd hear it from Tim himself.

He told Tim he could take a call as soon as Tim was free.

The sun was low in the sky, steadily approaching the horizon hills between Hamilton and the coast.

Moments later, Chad's phone started buzzing in his pocket.

"Hey man, how ya been?" Chad greeted.

"Doing great; all good, man! How about yourself?"

"Not too bad, doin' fine today. We'll see what tomorrow's like," Chad replied, a hint of caution in his tone, as always.

"What are you doing with your days at the moment? You've taken a break from Uni, right?"

"Yup. Nothing much else."

"Good, so you don't have to be at work or anything?"

"Nope."

"Well then, do you want to pack your bags, ready to travel with Charlotte to Auckland airport and fly over here for a break away from everything?"

Chad paused for a second, that was hardly what he expected his brother to come out with.

"Are you serious?"

"Straight up. Flights are available—three days from now—Charlotte's locked in, you simply have to say yes."

"Oh man! I'd love too! Yeah, fully keen," Chad said to Tim excitedly.

"Awesome! Good man! Honestly bro, this place will blow you away, it's a lot different to Hamilton, anywhere in New Zealand in fact. I want to show you some things that are seriously gonna make the last few months feel like a distant memory. Plus, it'll be great havin' you over here. I can't wait to introduce you and Char to the crew and show you guys around."

"This is, wow! I dunno what to say."

"Nothin', ya already said yes. I'm flicking you the tickets and flight info as we speak."

"I dunno what to say," Chad repeated, distracted and blown away.

"Yeah you said that." Tim chuckled as he filled in the last details needed on his laptop to secure two seats on an evening Air New Zealand flight across the globe and emailed it to his brother. "You'll see it all come through soon. Put me on speakerphone when you're ready, and we can go over the plan."

"This is so cool!" Chad hadn't known what to expect, but this meant a lot. He'd always admired Tim's rise as a historian, even if they'd never been particularly close. Ironically, their shared struggles—Tim's past battles with depression and Chad's current turmoil—now drew them together.

Chad had often dreamed of escaping for a break but lacked the mental clarity to plan it. His wealthy family would have gladly helped. Yet when overwhelmed, such solutions rarely seemed obvious. Tim, understanding this, anticipated what his brother needed and acted.

Chad read Tim's email. Then they chat a while—their conversation confirmed the value of time away—and the healing it might bring. He opened the attached ticket info on his phone and put it on speaker.

"It's gonna be one hang of a long trip. You'll get here and if you want to do anything but sleep, I'll wonder what you've taken."

"We're flying into Paris?" Chad observed, as he scanned the tickets and attached information.

"Yup. Can't fly from Auckland direct to Mauritania, so Paris is it, and the trip itself is twenty-two hours long."

Chad had been to Australia, and the Pacific islands multiple times and those flights had all been four or five tops. Twenty-two left him speechless as he tried to grapple with that.

"It's set to be a long drive to where we're staying too. Once ya here, there are things I can't wait to show you and Charlotte that are gonna blow your minds right outta tomorrow. Seriously, I'd tell you now, but that'd take a while and honestly, you actually have to see some of this to believe it. It'll be your reward for surviving a grand total of twenty-eight hours travelling time." Tim laughed.

"Wow… You kidding me!"

"Nope, but you'll get a sleep on the plane—likely on the way to Paris—dunno about from there to Nouakchott. You guys will be flying in luxury in a private jet, on the connection from Paris to Nouakchott, which'll stop shortly, for a refill in Madrid on the way. That leg of the journey will be about six hours. Oh, and you'll be in business class from Aucks to Paris too—should be a pretty comfy ride for the most part.

I've emailed you the details for where to meet Rod Chandler. He's a colleague and good friend of mine, great guy, Australian, and give him grief about the Bledisloe cup." Tim joked.

"Sure." Chad laughed.

"That'll certainly get a reaction, he'll likely threaten to kick you off the plane and make you walk." Tim joked again. "He'll meet you at international arrivals at Paris Charles de Gaulle Airport—carrying Red Sword Security (R.S.S.) I.D. You guys'll get in at about 8.45am the same day—yeah going backwards around the world messes with the time of day a bit. Now that's gonna be the really trippy part—you're not really going to see night. You'll get hours of sunset as you chase the dusk westward. Then from the Indian Ocean it'll turn to sunrise as you approach the Mediterranean and Europe."

"Wow, that's a little different!" Chad tried to picture how all that worked.

"Rod's in Paris at the moment with family and will be coming back to Africa with Crouton Bull from Red Sword Security Services."

"Crouton Bull? Interesting name..."

"Yeah long story... truly fascinating guy too, great man. His actual name is Collin Ericson—looks like Santa Claus, if Santa was from West Auckland, rode a Harley-Davidson and was a bogan," Tim laughed, "I think you'll enjoy Crout."

"Right!" laughed Chad.

"When you get to Nouakchott at around 4.20pm, I will meet you and Charlotte at the airport there. Nouakchott is the capital of Mauritania and one of the largest cities in the Sahara. And if you think there's nothing there, then wait till you get to Ouadane, the town our base is located several k's out of. This place is truly a different world, you'll see what I mean. You're in for the experience of a lifetime."

"How longs the trip from Nouakchott to where you are?"

"Ever driven non-stop from Auckland to Wellington?"

"I have, once."

"Yeah, it's pretty much the same distance, but it's more like driving across some random part of Tatooine. And the difference is NZ has well-made roads—we'll be travelling cross-country through dessert and along mountain roads. So instead of it taking around seven or eight hours, it'll be more like fifteen to sixteen."

"Oh wow!"

"Every few hours you come across something completely odd, that shouldn't be there... a rusted out old ship or the skeleton of a whale."

"Wait—what?"

"Yeah stuff like that, there's another long story... you'll hear a few between Nouakchott and the Richat. We'll do some sightseeing, hole up near one of the external dig sites overnight, then push onward come morning."

"Alright," Chad said thinking, "I'd better gear myself up for this... that's... like what—forty hours of travelling?"

"Yeah, you up for all that?"

"I think so." He had a distinct feeling he'd no idea what he was in for, but he was more or less going to go with it and make it work.

CHAPTER 2

C had hadn't seen Charlotte in over a month. She'd been touring across New Zealand and Australia with her band. Now back, she was unwinding at her parents' holiday home in Whitianga.

Excited about their upcoming adventure and reunion with Tim, Chad called Charlotte while taking in the last view of green hills west of the city. She had arranged to leave her car at her brother's place in Manukau, and he'd drive them to the airport. Chad agreed and filled up her sporty little Mazda 3 before leaving town.

Tim had been with Charlotte for three and a half years before proposing after the Corinth excavation in Greece. To Chad and Celesta, she was family already. Venezuelan-born, Charlotte had lived in New Zealand since childhood, along with her brothers—Kael and Dominic.

They hit the Waikato Expressway early in the afternoon three days later, and spent the hour-long drive catching up on everything.

"How was the tour?" He asked after filling her in on how he'd been, answering all of her many questions full of genuine care and interest.

"Oh, my goodness! Awesome! And *so* much fun."

Charlotte treated Chad like a brother she genuinely admired—always kind and understanding. She talked non-stop. Even if firing off endless questions, she somehow still dominated the conversation.

She hated how things had ended with Sonia but never spoke ill of her, careful to offer Chad only compassion. Though she mourned the loss of friendship and missed her, Charlotte wisely moved on, not letting Sonia's self-destructive choices affect her.

"I bet you're looking forward to seeing Tim?" Chad asked.

"Yes!" she beamed with great enthusiasm in her reply.

"Absence makes the heart grow fonder," Chad quoted, not having a clue who it was who said that, and frowned at how cheesy it sounded.

"Yes!" Charlotte repeated in the same manner as her first.

"I can't wait to see him either," Chad said, pondering how much he'd missed his brother over the past few months.

"He is seriously excited you're coming to visit him, he's missed you too. He's been worried about you."

Chad nodded silently, emotions overwhelming him. Lately, they had a mind of their own—crying himself to sleep, breaking down over everything, or nothing. He longed to regain control.

Charlotte understood; she'd seen Tim navigate the same dark road.

"Brothers are incredible, Chad," she said. "Sometimes, you don't realise it until the right moment."

She spoke his language, and he felt it. Chad was deeply grateful—Tim had Charlotte, and he had her as a friend. Their strength, forged through struggle, gave him hope. Charlotte faced anxiety with emotional strength and mental endurance, while Tim embodied resilience. Together, they reminded Chad he wasn't alone.

Later that evening, Chad and Charlotte arrived at her brother Kael and sister-in-law Katerina's home, dropping off her car before settling in for cold drinks and stories on the sunlit deck. Childhood memories mixed with laughter, sibling banter, and Charlotte's tour tales filled their catch-up.

After an early dinner and warm farewells, they cleared customs by 6:20pm and boarded their Air New Zealand flight.

Onboard the Paris-bound Boeing 787 Dreamliner—settling into business class, Chad marvelled at the luxury. This flight would be unforgettable.

"Wow this is cool!"

"It is eh." Charlotte agreed. She'd been getting used to travelling to and from Australia as well as half a dozen other international flights via business class.

"I'm used to economy and..."

"And your height is always a challenge with legroom?" Charlotte finished for him as he put his legs out and leaned back in the comfy chair that seemed to sink with him into an oblivion of relaxing.

She bounced on to hers and leaned over the modest barrier between their booths.

"Now you two are not going to be any trouble, are you?" said an intriguing looking gentleman seated behind Charlotte, wearing a dark grey Milano felt fedora, with a black overcoat folded next to him and peering over the top of a copy of The Herald. He had a serious expression, struggling to hide a grin.

Charlotte glanced at the man, looked back at Chad who wasn't sure what to say.

Mouth open with a broad smile and a cheeky spark in her eyes, she told the stranger, "We're gonna make the next twenty-two hours *very* interesting for you." She joked, mostly to see what kind of reaction he'd give.

"Good!" he said, to Chad's surprise.

Charlotte looked back at Chad, less surprised and still grinning.

"Otherwise," the man continued, "I was going to have to entertain myself with this absolute load of complete and utter garbage." He roughly folded his newspaper and flung it aside like it had personally betrayed him. Folding his arms, he muttered, "A waste of two dollars-fifty! I could've bought a block of chocolate for that." He glanced at each of them, wide-eyed.

Charlotte laughed.

"Honestly, I could have sat down and concocted all that drivel on my own, drunk." The man shook his head in disapproval. "That's what happens when the tabloids start cost-cutting by not proofreading, checking for accuracy or authenticity of what's being written and wait for it, borrowing stories from gossip magazines! The tabloids have really taken a dive when it has to acquire content from a gossip magazine."

Charlotte was nodding and smiling as he ranted and Chad, with furrowed brow and a smirk, figured this guy was a hard case.

"My Apologies," realizing he'd not introduced himself. He reached over to shake Charlotte's hand. "Charles S. McPherson, at your service." He had a relaxed British accent, and a warm sophisticated demeanour.

She shook his hand, as did Chad, and they each introduced themselves.

"Well it's lovely to be sharing the trip to Paris with two young people, such as yourselves." Charles complimented them cheerfully.

Charlotte asked where abouts he was from. He informed them he was originally from Bristol, but had lived most of his life in South Africa and New Zealand. "I work for a security company in Auckland, and I'm heading to Paris on a business trip." Charles shared intriguing details but never revealed which security company—a question Chad forgot to ask as they bonded over common interests.

Soon, the jet engines hummed as the aircraft taxied toward the runway— the fasten seat belt sign glowing. Soon, the whir intensified, and they surged down the runway, lifting off.

From above, Chad and Charlotte admired the Manukau Harbour and the Waitakere Ranges, bathed in the soft glow of dusk. Once the seatbelt sign disappeared, Chad joined Charlotte, continuing their conversation with Charles, who enquired of Chad what he did with his days. Chad and Charlotte shared with Charles their recent life events.

They went on to explain that they were both heading to Mauritania to visit Chad's brother and Charlotte's finance, Tim. And that he was working on a large archaeological dig site there.

Charles's demeanour changed as he learned about their purpose for travelling to the remote parts of nowhere.

After quickly scanning the cabin cautiously, he leaned closer to them and calmly suggested they "keep your volume down when speaking of what it is Tim is working on in Mauritania." He gave them a number of other warnings and aspects where discretion should be observed.

Charlotte was nodding, taking everything in and matching it up to what Tim had filled her in on about Mauritania. There were huge risks involved, travelling to a politically unstable region full of dangers and uncertainty.

"There are those who oppose what is going on in Mauritania, some who want it shut down." Charles warned.

"Why?" Chad asked, "Why do they oppose it?"

Charles paused, thoughtfully. "Because, it opens up a storm of controversy—setting in motion a great deal of things that will change nations, history, the future. And if the common issue of people having difficulty dealing with change, under current circumstances is a point of contention, this will blow that right out of the water," he said with seriousness in both tone and expression.

"You seem to know a lot about this, then...?" Chad probed.

"That's why I said the newspaper was a waste of my time and a complete load of garbage." Charles transitioned from serious to smiling again.

"They haven't a clue what's really going on in the world. They resort to opinion pieces and borrowed gossip magazine articles. If you actually begin reporting the *truth*, in this day and age, you start getting people outside of their comfort zones. Or bore them with the mundane, or the non-sensational... the average reader is as bad with a hunger for the dramatic, as the tabloids are to jazz it up."

It sounded to Chad as if Charles had a bit to say about the press media. More than just a gripe—something of genuine complaint... a knowing of matters, in order to speak of such things the way he did... a conversation for another time perhaps.

"Sounds interesting..." Charlotte remarked, not fully sure what to make of Charles's account of what was 'going on' in Mauritania.

Chad mulled it over, once again wondering what they were getting themselves into.

"Alas, for the likes of you and I, there's actually nothing to worry about. When you seek truth, and live by it... when you find it, it is no burden, for you are people of 'the real McCoy'. It is when one attempts to twist the truth or turn it into an optional extra, to go alongside, or diminish it to another type of opinion, that's when it gets complicated. When things like raw, unbiased authenticity and absolute truth arrive, well, it becomes a little harder to deal with. It's akin to being caught with your trousers down in public."

"This is getting deep," Chad said, without much expression.

"That, actually makes a lot of sense... and is reassuring," Charlotte thought out loud, "...in a complex, yet simple kind of way"

"Indeed!" Charles chuckled, "Reality can often be a paradox."

Though Charlotte clearly had the inside scoop on the Mauritanian dig, Chad stayed focused, quietly collecting questions of his own.

After take-off, meal service arrived—Charlotte and Charles opted for chicken, while Chad chose beef briskets and a Speights Gold. As they ate, Chad and Charlotte entertained themselves with a couple of movies. Charlotte drifted off near the end, and Chad gently covered her with a blanket.

Uneasy about the Sahara's dangers, Chad slowly convinced himself Tim had it handled.

After sleeping soundly for roughly five hours, they enjoyed desserts and a few laughs watching reruns of Big Bang Theory.

Curious, Chad asked Charlotte more about the Richat structure. She shared details Tim was able to disclose—an ancient ringed city with a mysterious dual spring of hot and cold water at the centre, was once devastated by a massive wave. Chad couldn't shake a familiar sense about it... it reminded him of something...

Meanwhile, Charles vanished after a quiet exchange with a flight attendant, heading toward the cockpit. Charlotte thought little of it, yet Chad's suspicions about the dig—and Charles—continued to grow.

He was gone for about half an hour—occasionally peeking through the business-class curtain. Chad and Charlotte sensed he was up to something but felt reassured by their trust in him.

Distracted by the mystery unfolding ahead, Chad barely glanced at the in-flight magazine he'd attempted to start.

Instead, Charlotte animatedly relayed more of Tim's tales about Mauritania and the Richat structure.

Charles returned. They exchanged smiles before he settled in to watch a movie.

They landed at Paris Charles de Gaulle International Airport at 9.15am local time. Charles wished them a safe journey to their final destination and an unforgettable adventure in Africa. Having cleared customs and collecting their luggage, they parted ways. He vanished into the bustling crowd.

"He was an interesting sort," Charlotte said, frowning.

"Yeah... he was." Chad wasn't overwhelmed—just momentarily lost in the crowd's volume and the sheer size of everything compared to Auckland Airport. For a brief moment, he missed New Zealand... until the excitement kicked back in.

Charlotte had a look of suspicion on her face as she subconsciously scanned around the crowds, half expecting to see Charles again.

"You alright?" Chad asked, thinking they should work out how to find their contact.

"Yeah—I'm all good. I can't help wondering about Charles, he seemed—I have no idea—never mind." She snapped out of it and gave Chad her full attention again. "We need to find—Rod Chandler, is it?" She asked, trying to recall the name Tim had given them.

"That's the one."

"Alright," Charlotte said, lifting her carry bag onto her shoulders. She swept her long dark brown hair over to one side, letting it drape softly across her shoulder and settle in front of her left arm. "Let's find a trolley for our bags and make our way to the arrivals lounge."

They found their way to the bustling arrivals lounge beyond the baggage collection. Charlotte scanned the crowd to see if she could see any obvious sign of which one of thousands was Rod.

"How the hang do we know what he looks like?" Chad asked. "Other than he's Australian."

"Don't worry, Tim sent me the deets."

Meanwhile, not far away, Rod had been scanning the crowds too.

He'd seen a photo of the two of them and knew who he was looking for.

Two individuals who seemed to match their description were standing about ten meters away with bags on a trolley and looking his way.

A medium-built young woman, dressed in black jeans, white hoodie, skate shoes. Petite, but carried herself like she owned her space. Dark eyes flicked with warmth and mischief; high cheekbones caught the light. Her smile was grounded, effortless. Hair in soft waves framed a face that felt both familiar and striking.

A taller gentleman wore baggy blue jeans, skate shoes, and a grey iLab hoodie. He moved with quiet charm, casual but focused, and bore a faint resemblance to his older brother. His well-kept short beard framed a relaxed smile, while wavy, shoulder-length blond hair brushed gently against his collar.

Back with Chad and Charlotte...

Chad squinted at the guy in the Brumbies jersey. The age felt right—maybe mid-forties—and he looked just Aussie enough to be their man. The guy concentrated with a slight frown as if he was trying to figure the two of them out.

Charlotte tilted her head, sizing up the man in the rugby attire. Rugged yet charming, sure—but was he Rod? Before she could ask, Chad had already clocked someone else.

His attention suddenly caught by the glare of a second, riled yet focused man with dark hair and beard. The man wore denim jeans black military style boots and a brown overcoat. He frowned, just as Charlotte speculated the guy in the rugby jersey might be Rod.

She glanced at Chad and, wondering what'd distracted him, followed his perplexed gaze to the creepy man making a bee-line for them, and narrowed her eyes.

The man's stride caused his coat to open a little in the breeze, exposing a hidden fire arm, his hand moved to.

To Chad and Charlotte's relief, airport security had spotted the same thing. Responding with haste they rushed to the scene—apprehending the man—removing the weapon and putting him in handcuffs before the two of them could ask what was going on.

The man, a total stranger, kept his gaze fixed on them—his expression now frustrated, and still hostile.

"The hang...?" Chad asked, he and Charlotte looking on in bewilderment. Passengers and onlookers either moving out of the way or as puzzled as they were.

While this had been eventuating, a second man in similar attire and appearance came up from out of sight and firmly took Charlotte's right wrist—pulling her away from Chad.

No push over and unfazed, Charlotte acted swiftly with a quick sharp punch to the man's face with her free fist—it'd leave a nice bruise.

Her would be assailant staggered back letting her go, his left cheek red, he rubbed it appearing surprised.

He looked daggers at her; she knew she needed to press her advantage. Taking a fighting stance, she followed the strike to the face with a swift hard kick to the man's stomach.

Chad'd turned to see what was happening, still trying to figure out the first man, in time to see Charlotte take a second down. The man doubled over in pain, and before he could look back at her, airport security had apprehended him too.

"Are you okay?" one of the guards all dressed in black with a red and white logo on the front of his polo shirt asked, sincerely.

"I'm fine." Charlotte assured, calm and collected, letting out a breath of relief.

"What? ...huh?" Chad shook his head, struggling to keep up with it all.

"Would you like anyone to debrief with you?" the guard offered.

"I'm great, thanks. Thank you for checking though." Charlotte responded appreciatively, rubbing her knuckles.

The man in the Brumbies jersey had been speaking with some of the guards, and made his way over to where Charlotte and Chad were.

A startled laugh escaped Chad. "What was that?" he asked, eyes wide with curiosity.

"No one messes with me," she joked. "I've taken self-defence classes and I have two brothers. I work out a lot too, so, yeah." she shrugged.

"Wasn't expecting that!" Chad both impressed and uneasy.

"Yah, well, now that it's done, I admit I'm a little unsettled."

"You managed to handle that pretty well," said the man in the Brumbies top, smiling.

"Thanks." Charlotte smiled, both her and Chad assuming he was most likely Rod.

"Chad Harison and Charlotte Espanzia?" He asked in an accent that gave them a comforting reassurance. He produced a retractable 'Red Sword Security Services' ID tag—the same red, white and black logo as on the guards polo—reading 'Agent Rodney Chandler'.

Proper introductions were made and the three of them warmed to each other instantly—discussing the flight from Auckland, and what there was to look forward to.

They followed Rod toward the exit, their chatter light and casual. Three more guards—armed but approachable in black Red Sword Security polos—joined them, offering genial smiles that contrasted the weight of their holsters.

"Don't worry, you're safe. Your friend with the bruised face was about to get a dart in the shoulder if you hadn't taken him to task," Rod motioned upward on a mezzanine level, to another security guard in the same black polo to the ones who apprehended the two strange men moments earlier. Chad and Charlotte looked up. The guard smiled and nodded to them. "There's detail all over the place, as well as airport security, and we'd been tracking those two since this morning."

"Who were they? The guy who tried it on with me smelt weird." Charlotte screwed up her nose.

"Pretty sure they work for a Sudanese billionaire who disapproves of what we're doing?"

"And that'd be?" Chad queried him.

Rod smiled as one does when the answer is about to be awesome. "The greatest discovery in all of history."

"This is getting serious—still, very exciting." Charlotte grinned.

"What are we getting ourselves into?" Chad asked, concerned.

"Have no fear mate, you're on the greatest adventure of your life. Serious, do not worry about a thing, you are safe. Your brother's placed a lot of trust in us to get you two, unharmed, to Nouakchott where we'll meet him."

Although apprehensive, they both knew Rod was a good friend of Tim's and could trust him.

~~~~~~~

They loaded their luggage into an impressive sleek yet solidly armoured black Humvee and climbed in before Rod shut the door and got in the front. The driver steered away from the main terminals toward private hangars.

Charlotte and Chad, with Rod, discussed how Kiwis and Aussies, despite their sports rivalry, tend to bond abroad—feeling at home in each other's company. Chad was grateful to be travelling with Charlotte—her experience eased the journey. Then meeting someone from their part of the world made everything feel slightly less foreign, especially being on the farthest side of the globe.

The driver parked the Humvee inside a massive hangar and the three of them piled out. Rod helped them with their gear and took them over to a smaller plane—a Lear jet—nose pointed toward the runway.

"The flight to Nouakchott is the better part 'o five hours long, and we'll be making a quick stop in Madrid to refuel before continuing." Rod told them.

They climbed the stairs and entered the Lear jet, where Rod gestured for them to place their bags on a nearby two-seater sofa. The sleek cabin, featured a kitchenette, bar fridge, two facing sofas, and four single seats flanking a central table.

Rod briefly greeted the pilot and co-pilot in the cockpit, exchanging jokes before handing over a tablet. Returning, he introduced them to a towering, burly man seated at the far end—mid-fifties. Built like a granite sculpture, he had the warmth, cheer and appearance of Santa Claus.

"Crout, this is Chad Harison, Tim's brother and his lovely fiancé Charlotte Espanzia." Crouton looked up from his laptop, wide-eyed with a big smile, peering over the tops of his reading glasses at the two young people. He set them on the table and got up to shake their hands.

"Chad, Charlotte, this is Crouton Bull. Head of Red Sword Security Services and the co-visionary behind the entire project in Mauritania."

"Great to finally meet you!" Crouton said with a deep booming voice in an accent neither of them could place as he shook Chad's hand with the biggest Chad'd ever seen and the firmest grip.

His expression changed when he shook Charlotte's and glanced at Chad.

"She has a firmer grip than you!" he said, jokingly. He looked back at Charlotte and the two of them laughed, Chad frowned with a smirk.

The big man's look was unforgettable: baggy black-grey camo pants, heavy boots, and a plain black tee mostly obscured by his thick white-grey beard. His kind eyes and disarming smile shone beneath a hairstyle reminiscent of a younger Sean Connery.

CHAPTER 3

The jets roared to life as Rod returned and took his seat opposite Crouton. He gestured for them to buckle up as the craft taxied toward the runway. Departing at 10 am local time, they were headed for a brief refuel at Madrid-Barajas Airport—a two-hour, fifteen-minute hop.

"Once we leave Madrid," Rod noted, "it'll be another four hours."

Chad marvelled at the day's journey. Charlotte, used to shorter flights with breaks between shows, realized she'd nearly doubled her typical flight time. Crouton laughed—his response to their dawning exhaustion and quiet awe—no grin, no flicker, just a series of guttural grunts. Chad and Charlotte exchanged a glance. Despite the polished smile, Crouton's laugh was raw—more animal than human, somewhere between hog and hiccup.

Rod smirked. They'd get used to that.

"That's why we fly this way, eh boy?" Crouton nudged Rod.

"On tough assignments" Rod explained, "travel becomes the R and R."

"We invested in Lear jets, a fleet o' Humvees—comfortable as a king-size bed, but packed with the fire-power of a small tank," Crouton added.

"Will we be taking one from Nouakchott?" Charlotte grinned.

"Aye," Crouton replied.

"Yuss!"

"Awesome," nodded Chad.

The two of them took the opportunity to offer their sincere thanks for the arrangements.

"Tim Harison's been a true friend to our team—principled, respected, wise beyond his years," Crouton said.

Charlotte beamed. "That's my fiancé. That's why I love him."

Crouton nodded. "You're a lucky woman... and Tim's a blessed son-of-a-joker to have you."

Rod handed them drinks. "Cheers—to you both, and for supporting him in Mauritania."

Glasses raised. Chad smiled, momentarily lost in thought.

He reflected on Tim's work—the Richat Structure, the ancient city beneath, and its potential impact. It was clear he'd missed a lot. Tim had been swept up in a whirlwind of archaeological discovery, powered by satellite imaging and digital exploration. Tools like Google Earth had revealed hidden landmarks, triggering expeditions and debates. Historians and archaeologists, armed with tech, were unlocking ancient worlds with new eyes.

Chad listened as Rod and Crouton spoke, curious about Red Sword Security's purpose. Why a security firm for a dig site? Questions began to stack without end.

Charlotte shared experiences of her music career, and Chad played her album through the jet's sound system. The cabin filled with her electrifying fusion of rock, metal, and dance—every beat a reflection of the passion she lived.

"Nice... that's good," Rod said—convinced, nodding to the rhythm.

"Thanks," Charlotte replied modestly.

"Quality stuff, lass," Crouton added. "Not my usual style—different generation and all." He chuckled with his grinless laugh, then softened into a smile. "But I like it. Metal guitars, dance beats, hard rock. Talk of Jesus... spiritual, but not stiff."

They listened to 'Way Beyond the Typical', drawn in by its unexpected force:

"Somethin' gonna catch ya
Like a raging fire
Like a passion of the heart, the mind, the deepest part of who ya are
Someone's gonna catch ya
When ya least expect the freedom
When you thought ya knew religion, knew my God 'n knew all how it works
He's gonna blow ya mind away, like a hurricane
Like a giant wave, ya swept away in freedom so legit, in grace 'n love 'n ecstasy
divine."

The beat hit hard. The lyrics caught hold. Rod and Crouton didn't expect it—but they were hooked.

Chad was stoked. Charlotte glowed, reminiscing about her final Brisbane show, energized by the life she was living.

"Ya got a lotta passion," Crouton said, beaming. "Makes a difference— makes the music real." He glanced between Charlotte and Chad, then back at the speakers. "You and Tim... you're doin' it right. Livin' loud, livin' with heart. That kinda fire's contagious."

Later the jet touched down in Madrid for refuelling, Crouton turned to them.

"How much do you know? What's Tim told you about his work in Mauritania?"

What once may have been an unsettling question—now felt like a door, not a wall needing to be pushed through, or it's secret entrance otherwise discovered. After hours with Rod and Crouton, trust had been earned. It echoed the easy confidence they'd felt with Charles earlier in the journey.

Charlotte shared what Tim had disclosed—his work at the Richat Structure. Most of it focused on his friends, his team, and the lifestyle surrounding the expedition—not much more than what he'd revealed during the TVNZ exclusive earlier that week. She spoke without hesitation and with genuine sincerity.

Crouton nodded attentively.

"I see you have questions... I've got some too," he said, voice low and thoughtful. "I want you both there—alongside Tim, Rod, myself, and the others—when we find the answers. Let's ask together. Seek truth as a team... and as individuals."

Crouton was a man forged in fire—deeply revered, fiercely protective, unwavering in loyalty. Though untouched by religion, he lived a sacrificial creed, scripture etched into action. Wealth followed, but devotion defined him: the kind of leader who would bleed for his people and never speak of the scars.

"When it comes to Tim and Rod," he continued, "I care only where their hearts are. Good intentions can mean little. 'Ere's plenty distorted views on what's 'good.' I don't give a rip about credentials or status—only trust. I care what the people I trust say about you. That's what gets your foot in the door. Both of 'em, to be fair."

He leaned forward, studying them. "You can read the spirit of a person—the mouth and eyes give it away. Words reveal the heart."

"Well, that's easy with Charlotte," Chad teased.

She narrowed her eyes at him.

"What about me? I don't talk much."

Crouton smiled. "A quiet person is the longest story. It speaks volumes without words."

"Nice," Chad nodded.

Crouton's tone deepened. "I tried taking my life five times at sixteen. Back then, no one understood the pressures o' the mind the way they do now." He tapped his temple gently.

"Years later, at my lowest, fate—or God—led me to a monastery in the Himalayas. That changed everything. I learned about my ancestry... and I found direction—via one heck of a unique adventure..."

He looked toward Chad. "Tim told me a bit about your journey. About how things fell apart with your missus and all. I've been there—it's brutal."

He nodded, kindness flickering in his eyes, then leaned back.

"Tim vouches for you both. And everyone vouches for him. I'm more than happy for you two to join with us and—see everything Tim's involved in while you're here with him."

A quiet pause settled, filled only by the hum of jet engines.

Crouton leaned in again. "Mauritania's a long story. Tim invited you here so I'll let him do the telling of it. The Richat—it's not just a dig site—the story requires careful telling."

His expression shifted—now charged with promise. "There's far more waiting for you. Tim's eager to show it. And we're all just as excited to uncover the secrets of the Richat."

A beat passed. "Security is of the utmost importance... trust even more-so. If I'd had any doubts, you'd be halfway back to Auckland by now. But you did well. We knew you would."

He smiled again.

Soon they'd finally landed at Nouakchott—Oumtounsy International Airport at 4.20pm local time.

~~~~~~~

Moments later, Tim and Charlotte disappeared into each other's arms, the world narrowing—all else fading out around them. For a moment, nothing else mattered—who was with them, where they were, or why. What silence and space couldn't diminish, reunion amplified. Four months of longing collapsed into one breathless embrace.

"Absence makes the heart grow fonder—and all that guff," Crouton chuckled.

Chad smiled, stacking the last equipment crate beside the Lear jet's boarding stairs, the black tarmac warm beneath his boots. He was stoked for Tim and Charlotte. And, he was grateful to be reunited with his brother—someone he'd missed more than he'd realized. But most of all, he felt joy. After nearly twenty-five hours in the air, they'd finally touched African soil.

From the jet's exit, a pilot descended the stairs—their first time seeing him. Behind him came Charles—not whom they'd expected.

"Good morning, Chad," Charles greeted with a grin. "Charlotte."

Still wrapped around Tim, Charlotte hesitated before snapping out of their reunion. She and Chad exchanged curious glances.

"Oh! Sorry," Crouton said, catching himself. "You haven't met our pilot yet!" He made the introductions, and a round of handshakes sealed the moment.

Then Crouton gestured toward Charles. "You met Charles on the Paris flight. He handled your security for that part of the trip."

Tim and Charlotte looked at each other, intrigued.

"Precautions," Charles said warmly. "This project is high-security. We couldn't afford risk and needed your travel to remain discreet."

"Right..." Chad nodded.

"That makes sense," Tim agreed. "Thanks, Crout. Deeply appreciated."

"So, you were our bodyguard?" Charlotte asked, flashing a smile at Charles.

"Indeed," he replied. "And I must say—you were both excellent company."

"I see." Chad stroked his beard. "That explains a few things."

He and Tim embraced—firm and brotherly.

"Great to see you, bro!" Tim said.

"Yeah, man. So good to see you too," Chad smiled.

Crouton shook Tim's hand and embraced him warmly, then checked, "Everything all set for the road trip?"

"All sorted," Tim replied. He took Charlotte's hand and led the group toward a nearby hangar, where two Humvees waited by the entrance.

"We'll move one of those over to the jet and load up the gear," Crouton grumbled, feeling the weight of the day. "No sense lugging crates more than I'm bothered."

"We've got some serious catching up to do!" Chad smiled at Tim. "Thought we were here for a holiday—to see what you do. Seems there's a bit more to it."

Tim laughed. "That we do! Once we reach the Richat, security won't be an issue—Crouton's team has it locked down. Still, we'll stay cautious. But you'll relax. Trust me—you'll love the pool. It hits 42 degrees out here in autumn."

"Oh great," Chad muttered.

"Ouch," Charlotte agreed.

"No worries. Every building and vehicle's air-conditioned. The site feels like a small town crossed with a summer festival. The rest of Mauritania's another world—mostly empty, nothing green. I'll fill you in once we're moving."

Rod and the other Red Sword agents finished loading the second Humvee.

Crouton rode point in the lead Humvee. Charles manned the wheel of the second, carrying Rod, Tim, Chad, and Charlotte all ready to roll.

Charlotte checked her bag then tossed it into the back. Chad dropped his pack on a seat and glanced around.

Crouton approached Tim's Humvee, scanning the group he'd begun calling 'the young ones.' A slap on Tim's shoulder. A nod exchanged. Everything was ready.

"You'll get them up to speed on the drive, eh, son?"

"Absolutely," Tim replied. "I've got a few places in mind—might be fun to add some visuals to the tour of ancient history."

"Aye," Crouton nodded, climbing into the lead vehicle.

Charles hit the gas, tires screeching as he wheeled the Humvee left racing Crouton toward the exit. His focused grin met Rod's raised eyebrow.

"You haven't driven in a while, have you?"

"Four weeks!"

Rod shook his head.

"This thing's awesome!" Chad said, grinning at the engine's roar.

"Red Sword Humvees are beasts," Tim agreed. "Titanium-alloy armour, mine-resistant, double-glazed bulletproof windows, fire and blast-proof tires. Guess how much each tire costs…"

Chad looked at Charlotte. She smirked—already knowing.

"Couple grand?"

"Six and a half."

"You're telling me this thing has twenty-six-thousand dollars' worth of rubber under it?"

"Yup. Custom blend of titanium fibre and gold-tungsten mesh."

Chad glared at him. "You made that up."

"Which is pretty much what I said," Charlotte added.

"And Crouton's fine with that conclusion," Charles chimed in.

Chad frowned. "Titanium fibre rubber sounds fake—and gold tungsten mesh? What even is that?"

"Welcome to the Sahara, little bro." Tim flashed a ridiculous grin.

"Right," Chad said, turning to face him fully. "Tell me everything—starting with the tires and why an archaeological dig needs high-end security."

Charles chuckled from the front seat.

Rod straightened, eyes scanning the horizon.

Something struck the roof—like a rock. Charlotte jumped, startled by the thunderclap of an explosion behind them. A flash of light burst from behind.

"Hold on to your hats, ladies and gentlemen," Charles said coolly. "You're about to meet President Rutherford's finest."

"His black ops boys," Rod added, "still trying to pass as angry locals—grenade launchers and all."

Charlotte dug her fingers into Tim's leg. Chad stared wide-eyed, torn between disbelief and feeling like he'd stepped into an Xbox game come alive.

Charles and Rod exchanged simple but urgent words—no panic, no raised tones, just calm threading through the tension.

Tim tried to steady his fiancée and brother. Crouton burst from the top of the lead Humvee, beard whipping in the wind, manning a concealed M420B machine gun now blazing. Orange blasts flared to the left as both Humvees tore down the battered road at 140 kph.

Crouton in action was like a crazy man—mouth stretched into a mad grin. Out the left windows, two hostile desert Humvees bounced across the dusty terrain. Each carried three men—the driver, one with an automatic, the other firing RPGs.

Two projectiles struck—one per Humvee—but ricocheted off. They detonated harmlessly, ten to thirty meters behind them at full speed.

Rod smiled confidently and turned excitedly to Tim and the others.

Tim was wary but composed—unlike Chad, glued to his seat, and Charlotte, clinging tight to Tim. He'd faced this kind of chaos before. He knew how it played out.

Chad watched in stunned awe as another grenade slammed into the lead Humvee—only to appear as if caught and flung one-eighty at blistering speed before exploding. His mind spiralled. Quantum engineering? Alien tech? Bizarre thoughts whispered from the edges of his imagination. He dismissed the latter, but the former lingered.

Then the gunfire stopped.

Crouton's relentless defence had obliterated the first hostile vehicle— its front crumpled, flipping end over end before crashing in a tangled heap. The second smashed straight into the wreck, stopping with a catastrophic crunch.

Crouton thrust his fist in the air, shouting something completely inaudible.

Rod rolled down the window, both arms flailing as he celebrated, "YEAHH! WOOHOO!"

"These guys are crazy!" Charlotte said finally.

"You have no idea," Tim grinned.

"Now I'm awake!" Chad declared, shaking his head.

"You two okay?" Tim checked.

"I think so?" Charlotte said, heart still racing.

"Yeah... or I will be," Chad answered, wide-eyed.

"What the hang was that all about?" Charlotte asked.

Rod turned, calm now. "What all that was, is exactly why Red Sword Security's involved with the Richat Project. Those were black ops—likely U.S.-orign—trying to shut the expedition down."

Chad and Charlotte exchanged bewildered glances.

"A network of corrupt power players—billionaires, politicians from the Middle East, UK, France, Russia, Sudan—they'd love to kill this project," Rod continued, smiling. "But they're outmatched. Crouton commands a fiercely loyal army. Our tech? They haven't even begun to dream of it. While they play catch-up, we stay untouchable."

"Why would they want to stop this?" Chad asked, turning to Tim. "And those RPGs—how did they bounce off? They're supposed to explode on impact! And the tyres—" He looked around, desperate for answers.

"Trampoline steel," Rod said, straight-faced.

Chad glared at him. Then looked at Tim. "Seriously?"

"I'm not kidding," Rod replied. "Was an accidental breakthrough—tungsten-alloyed steel, forged via hot isostatic pressing. Phase-tuned for elasticity. The microstructure absorbs impact like coiled springs. Cryo-tempered, layered, and refined—it redirects kinetic energy. Reveron steel. Engineered to rebound bullets."

Chad blinked, speechless.

"Crazy..." Charlotte whispered. "Why accidental?"

Holden wanted to create a safe friction-free steel, but it worked far too well and far too expensive to mass produce.

Holden's board, unhappy with the soaring costs, scrapped the project. Before anyone caught wind, Nathan O'Conner—chief sponsor of the Richat Project and Red Sword co-founder—stepped in. He acquired the tech quietly and handed it off to Crouton for our vehicles.

"One man's trash is another's treasure," Tim said thoughtfully. "I'll give you a demo when we stop."

"Sweet!" Charlotte grinned.

"Okay," Chad nodded, still reeling. "The tyres..."

Tim met his eyes. "Made by a manufacturer that doesn't exist. With technology that doesn't exist, but exists anyway. They're virtually indestructible. Won't show wear for two hundred years."

Chad shook his head, unable to find words. Only breath escaped.

"That's insane," Charlotte muttered.

"My dear," Charles chimed in, "you've entered the realm of the ridiculous. And Red Sword's tech? Just a drop compared to what Tim's about to reveal."

"What do you mean?" Chad asked.

The vehicles began to slow, pulling over.

They'd been on the road for just under two hours. The horizon burned low, sun slipping into sand, painting the desert in dusky gold. Shadows stretched long and languid, and the sky—half dark lilac, half soft flame—seemed to hold its breath as evening crept in.

"Come check this out," Tim said, opening the passenger door.

Charles and Rod joined him. Crouton followed.

Tim crouched, searching—studying the ground. Chad and Charlotte awaited what he had to reveal.

He lifted a seashell, turning it slowly in the light before passing it to Charlotte, then found another and handed it to Chad.

They examined the shells, glancing toward the area Tim illuminated.

The desert floor was littered with them.

"Wow, where..." Charlotte started, confused.

"...did they come from?" Tim finished. "The ocean. This whole area—thousands, actually tens of thousands of square kilometres—was once underwater."

"That's amazing," uttered Chad, sweeping his torchlight across the shell-strewn ground. He'd vaguely heard about it before, but never truly considered it.

Tim fetched a medium-sized rock near the Humvee.

"Watch this." He hurled it at the vehicle.

The impact echoed—but the rock rebounded at startling speed.

Charlotte squinted. Chad shook his head slowly, stunned. They both examined the point of impact—not a scratch.

"Seashells in the Sahara aren't the only surprises on this adventure," Tim smiled.

Rod and Crouton got the gas cookers humming—cooking from the back of the second Humvee. Their laughter drifting into the warm evening air as burger patties sizzled in pans. The scent of grilled beef and toasted buns cut through the dry heat, drawing Tim and Charles over with easy smiles.

They layered their burgers—lettuce, tomato, pickles, a generous dollop of sauce—and settled near the Humvees, eating while standing or leaning against vehicles. Half-curious talk of ancient oceans filled the air, as if the words themselves had ferried them into another world.

Crouton handed Rod a burger. "Not bad for roadside dining."

Charlotte nodded, mouth full. "I could get used to adventures like this."

Twilight cooled the sand around them, shadows softening into memory. The day's haste had folded away, and for a while, they were simply adventurers—gathered by torchlight, sharing a meal beneath a sky slowly turning to stars.

"You ready for some off-roading?" Crouton asked.

"Let's do it," Tim grinned.

Over the next hour, Tim explained—among other things—how, many deserts were once ocean floors. Formed and transformed by tectonic shifts, ice ages, and fluctuating sea levels.

"What's fascinating," he said, "is the evidence showing northern Africa was completely different ten to twenty thousand years ago."

He described a Sahara without deserts: lush jungles, expansive grass-lands, massive lakes rivalling the Black Sea, and coastlines reshaped into islands.

"Wow, that's amazing to think about," Chad remarked.

By now, darkness surrounded them. Nearly 10.30 pm. local time. The Humvees rolled to a stop, beams of light piercing the dark. Their spotlights swept over the sand, fixing on a looming silhouette—vast and ancient, shrouded in mystery, its contours barely outlined against the star-lit void.

Chad and Charlotte stepped out—Crouton joined them.

Before them lay something surreal: the wreckage of a decaying tall ship, tilted on its side.

Its timbers groaned with the memory of storms and silence, half-swal-lowed by earth as if the land itself sought to bury its secrets. The figure-head—weather-worn by sand storms—still bore the noble lines of some forgotten herald, lips parted mid-cry. It felt less like a wreck and more like a relic caught mid-transformation—from vessel of commerce to mythic tomb.

"Oh, my goodness!" Charlotte gasped, wide-eyed.

"Pretty cool, eh?" Tim grinned.

"This is insane!" Chad exclaimed, approaching the towering vessel. "Ya weren't kidding about things that shouldn't be in a dessert!"

"It's magnificent," Charlotte whispered. "And it's just... sitting here. In the middle of the Sahara."

"Yes—and this is only the beginning," Charles said with a knowing grin.

Crouton stood beneath a massive hole in the hull.

Tim pointed out key details: the remnants of two lower decks, evidence of a missing centre spar.

"This was likely a five-masted East Indiaman tradeship," Tim explained. "Origin unknown. Carbon dating's maddeningly inconsistent—some samples suggest the 1600s or 1700s, others say much older." He frowned.

"Interesting," Chad muttered, narrowing his eyes.

"We've explored it," Rod added. "Aside from a few cannons—too risky to move—nothing gives us clues. Shifting them could collapse the ship."

Chad ran his fingers along the barnacle-covered exterior—solid, but coarse and powdery.

"Like much of Mauritania," Tim said, "it's desiccated and semi-preserved. The real threat is erosion from sandstorms."

Charlotte and Chad stood in silence, awe-struck. The idea that the sea once reached this far inland felt unreal.

"The risk posed by further investigation is frustrating," Tim admitted.

"It's like something from another world," Charlotte breathed.

"I don't get it," Chad said. "This ship should be, at most, four hundred years old." He paused, staring at the wreck. "But the fact that it's here—so far from the Atlantic—must mean there was... sea, right here?"

"We don't know yet," Tim replied. "We're just beginning to uncover the Sahara's past. My team searches northern Africa, the Middle East, and Europe for clues. Records only go back a few thousand years—mostly Greek and Roman. Further back? Things get hazy—shaped by politics, culture, and speculation."

"History becomes legend," Rod said. "Then myth."

Tim nodded. "Islamic history often records events without dates. So, we build timelines in reverse. Western historians have had limited access, but satellite tech's revealing new secrets."

Crouton noted that astronauts had seen the Richat structure for decades—but dismissed it as natural formation.

The Humvees roared to life once more, heading northeast.

Chad and Charlotte kept their eyes locked on the desert-stranded ship, longing for more time to explore its decks and secrets.

"The scientific community widely agrees," Tim began, "that northern Africa was lush jungle and grassland just five thousand years ago—supporting people, wildlife, even massive inland seas. Evidence shows megalakes larger than North America's Great Lakes, rivalling the Caspian and Black Seas. If Lake Chad hadn't shrunk, it would be the world's largest inland water body. Archaeologists found the Nile had once flooded over 67,000 square kilometres of northeast Africa—at one stage flowing west, not south."

"Wow," Charlotte said.

"Great name for a lake," Chad smiled.

The others grinned.

"Ancient riverbeds cross what's now desert," Tim continued. "They run through Mauritania and beyond. And each bit of evidence sparks a new hypothesis—opens possibilities. It's led to discoveries I'm still trying to wrap my head around."

"This is so cool, babe!" Charlotte beamed.

They travelled for hours, the sand stretching endlessly around them, lost in conversation about lost worlds and mysteries newly unearthed—fragments of ancient history waiting to be pieced together.

"Mankind hits plateaus," Charles said. "By the 1800s, most maps were drawn—people thought discovery had peaked. Similar with philosophy and belief. Knowledge stalls, assumptions harden, and politics or conspiracies fracture understanding."

"That's historical estrangement," Tim added.

"Exactly," nodded Charles. "Gutenberg's press revolutionized Europe, but Arabic printing was banned in the Ottoman Empire for centuries—to protect tradition. Islamic scholars led in medicine, astronomy, engineering. But Catholic Europe ignored it. Arabic medical texts eventually shaped European universities, yet the credit went to the Greeks. And by the seventeenth century, the Ottomans rejected Copernicus— the Sun at the centre of the universe, Earth and other planets orbiting it—still clinging to outdated models. Instead of merging knowledge, both worlds turned inward... and progress stalled."

"Interesting," Chad said.

"Very," Charlotte added.

"Are you familiar with the term 'philosophy breeds methodology'?" Charles asked.

"Rings a bell..." Chad said thoughtfully.

"The way people think determines what they do," Charles explained. "Governments, rulers, organisations—everything flows from their core values and world-view."

"If it doesn't align," Tim said bluntly, "it gets side-lined—forgotten."

"Or tossed into the black hole of conspiracy," Charles added. "And once it's in there, it'll take no small miracle bringing it back out."

~~~~~~~

Tim had just begun outlining the Richat Project when Charlotte suddenly clutched Chad's arm.

"Wait—what's that?"

They looked ahead.

Two vast arcs rose from the desert—whale bones, polished white by sandstorms, shaped like cathedral ribs. Moonlight bathed them in a silvery hush, casting soft shadows across the dune-etched ground. As the Humvees rolled to a stop, headlights cut through the dark, lighting the towering remnants like stage curtains drawn back. Crouton pulled over, knowing Tim wouldn't miss this.

"These," Charles said quietly, "are Alagra and She'ul."

The wind stirred.

Tim stepped forward, scanning the bones. "According to legend, they were lovers," he began. "Caught in the crossfire of war. After they sabotaged the Atlantean fleet, Poseidon was furious. Set—the Egyptian god of secrets—warned them. They hid in the ocean's farthest depths. But Poseidon's wrath stretched further than anyone could imagine. His wave that swallowed Atlantis reshaped Africa. These two were left behind—stranded when the oceans receded."

No one spoke.

Moonlight cast long shadows beneath the ancient rib cages.

"That's unreal," Chad whispered. "Like finding ghosts with names."

"They were in love," Charlotte said softly. "Now they're just... left here."

Tim nodded. "A Tuareg storyteller connected their story to historical seismic shifts and coastline changes. Locals have known about these bones for generations. Oral maps never forgotten."

"Makes ya wonder," Chad muttered, eyes lingering in the mirror as they returned to the vehicles.

Crouton rested his chin on his fist. "Hmm... 'bout a few different types o' things."

Back in the Humvees, the silence lingered.

"What'd Crouton mean by that?" Chad asked as they drove.

Tim paused. "Discovery brings the unknown. Some chase facts, others chase meaning. I think truth has a shape—embedded in the world, not imagined. Even mystery follows order."

Chad studied his brother's face with quiet respect.

"Some people fear the unknown," Tim added. "It threatens their way of life."

"Or their wallet," Rod suggested.

"Humans fear what they don't understand," Charles said.

Rod smirked. "We've already unsettled some powerful folks with deep pockets."

"For three decades," Tim explained, "Red Sword has operated publicly as a reputable firm. But underneath? It's a coalition of adventurers. A group preparing to uncover secrets—many buried beneath this desert. Till now, every time research gets close, someone shuts it down. Especially when sacred truths start coming into focus."

"Like what?" Chad asked.

"Babe, this sounds serious," Charlotte said, uneasily.

"It is," Tim replied. "But I wouldn't have invited you if there was even the slightest risk to your safety. Red Sword has a flawless track record—unmatched security, airtight operations. Crouton and Nathan O'Conner lead the Richat Project with elite researchers and scientists. Red Sword operates independently, outside any government or corporate control. Their agents aren't just employees—they're deeply invested, driven by something... seraphic."

Chad and Charlotte listened intently, inwardly scrutinising and being blown away.

"Nathan and Crouton foster loyalty that money can't buy. He and his closest allies built a system that keeps governments honest. Most know interference isn't in their best interest. Opposing forces are blocked—gridlocked by politics or fearful of exposing corruption. Their networks are skilled... but they're always one step behind."

"Seriously... that's nuts," Chad said.

"And it's all above board," Tim added. "Transparent. Legal. No under-handed tactics. No one's ever dug up dirt on Red Sword—because there is none to be found."

"Wow, that's almost..." Chad began.

"Unheard of?" Tim offered.

Chad disappeared in thought... *If Nathan and Crouton's loyalty is beyond price, and Red Sword's safeguards can't be replicated... it almost feels far-fetched.*

"The Richat Project must be massive?" Charlotte asked.

"Monumentally bigger than anything," Rod called back.

"What's coming will change history," Charles said bluntly. "It'll cast new light on everything—from religion and democracy to World Wars, politics and the creation of the universe."

Silence.

The weight of his words sent chills through Chad and Charlotte.

Chad wanted to say, *"You know what you're looking for—and you know where it is"*, unease held him back.

Charlotte considered asking what they were hoping to uncover—but part of her wasn't sure she wanted the answer.

Instead, they let the gravity of it all settle in. Whatever this was, it had frightened the comfortably corrupt—and taken thirty years of preparation just to reach this moment.

Tim noticed their unease. He gently took Charlotte's hand. "You know me. I wouldn't be here if anything felt off."

Chad nodded, grounding himself amid the mental whirlwind. Charlotte felt a peace—a reminder of love, faith, and the thrill of discovery.

As the road dipped and rose, Chad reflected: he wasn't in New Zealand any more. His safe places, his routines, his distractions—they were behind him. He braced for the anxiety, expecting it to seep in like gas through a door left ajar. But it didn't come.

Had the shock of new reality burned it away?

He glanced at Tim and Charlotte—genuine, warm, uncomplicated. Then at Rod and Charles—enigmatic but seemingly solid. He'd stay cautious... but he trusted Tim and Charlotte without hesitation.

His thoughts drifted back to the Richat. The elite security. The black ops mercenaries. Tim was unfolding everything like a story—carefully, intentionally.

A sudden realization sent goose bumps down his spine—just as the vehicle jolted over a sandbank.

Charlotte had nearly nodded off before snapping awake at the bump. Tim checked on her, while Charles apologized for the rough patch.

"We're off-road again," he said. "That town down there to our left is Atar—the largest in the region. We bypassed Akjoujt earlier. Atar has an airport, but we steer clear due to local opposition groups."

They began ascending toward the Adrar Mountains, aiming to skirt the slopes before crossing the N1 highway and avoiding urban areas.

Rod recalled a previous stop in Atar—locals had confronted them, stirred by unseen influences.

"Law enforcements stretched thin here," Charles said. "Western governments usually advise against travel to Mauritania."

"And here we are," Chad laughed.

Later, after crossing another highway, they continued off-road toward one of the excavation sites.

"We're only halfway to the project camp," Tim announced, surprising the new arrivals.

"Once we're there," he added, "it'll feel more like a subtropical resort."

At the base of the Adrar Mountains they pulled over once more.

Tim guided Chad and Charlotte to the rim of an ancient riverbed—its dramatic channels now fractured and sunken across the foot-hills. Erosion had etched elaborate contours, tracing forgotten paths through stone and silence.

~~~~~~~

They arrived at their first destination—tires crunching quietly along gravel as they rolled through manned gates flanked by steel mesh fencing.

"Welcome to the Chinguetti Sub-project section—one of several excavation sites outside of the main Richat Project territory," Tim announced.

A long building with a wraparound verandah emerged from the dark, floodlights brushing soft light onto its eaves. Across the way, a three-bay marquee waited with a line of parked Humvees out front. In the distance, five front-end loaders and several massive earthmovers loomed like sleeping beasts.

Stepping out, Chad and Charlotte zipped up hoodies against the crisp air. Tim rubbed his hands together.

"At this time of small hour oblivion, it feels like the desert forgot it was a desert," he joked.

Charlotte smirked and Chad chuckled.

From the verandah, a stocky round-faced man with a booming drawl emerged.

"Howdy be, Tim Harison?"

"Alive and in one piece!" Tim grinned. "Could go for a hot chocolate and a soft mattress though.

Texo, meet my fiancée—Charlotte, and my brother—Chad. Guys— this is Texo, unit leader for this dig site and head of Red Sword's operations here."

"Well I'll be!" Texo said, warm and booming. "Pleasure to meet y'all. Welcome to Mauritania! Rooms are prepped—all ya need and warm as a preacher's handshake. Now then, let's get a batch of hot cocoa bubbling for ya already."

Hot chocolate steamed in thick ceramic mugs. They each gathered around in a spacious sitting area on comfy couches, quietly sipping and reflecting on the journey. Yet after long travel and star-fed silence, even laughter felt muffled by the hour. One by one, they peeled off to their sleeping quarters.

~~~~~~~

By mid-morning the compound hummed outside with activity. Archaeologists, Red Sword Personal, service crew and Geologists moved about tasks and mostly heading in and out of the huge marquee across from the main building. Which, had come alive with the scent of sizzling bacon and toasted ciabatta. Sunshine slanted in from the east, as they moved about in half-alert states.

"Grub's up—get it while it's hot! Or it's still there," called a towering Pacific Islander who could've passed for an All Black lock.

"Tim!" he boomed.

"Apia!" Tim answered, embracing him with a solid, blokey hug.

"This is Apia," Tim told Chad and Charlotte. "He handles logistics, resourcing, and hospo here."

Apia greeted them both with hugs as big as his grin.

As Tim and Apia caught up, Crouton gestured toward the buffet spread nearby.

"Morning's feast: bacon, eggs on ciabatta, hash browns, mushrooms, chorizo snags, and enough chilled orange juice to baptise a camel," Crouton declared. "Tim, bless the food, if ya'd be so kind?"

Tim appeared beside Charlotte and Chad, mug in hand and gave thanks, blessing the food.

They all filled plates and settled around couches and outdoor tables. The marquee glowed with food smells and excited anticipation for the day ahead.

"Welcome to breakfast at the edge of the middle of nowhere." Rod smiled.

"Everything here's massive," Chad noted, eyeing the eighty-inch screen mounted behind the bar... and watching Crouton stack hash browns like bricks.

"Wait till dinner," Tim joked. "Crout does New York cut steak you could land a plane on."

Charlotte smiled, "This is so good!"

They wrapped up breakfast, and Tim glanced toward Crouton and Charles. "Let's move. There's lots to see and we've a bit of travel left yet. Then later tonight, one of Crout and Rick's epic barbecue feasts?" Tim checked, glancing at Crouton.

"Yup."

Rod nodded, already picturing it. "Assuming Rick's still walking and Chaiyala hasn't maimed him..."

"He's my best sniper and barbecue chef," Crouton grunted.

"I wouldn't put it past him to hit targets with one arm, though" Rod shrugged.

Chad chuckled. "Rick and Chaiyala... are they a couple?"

Charles joined the group, eyebrows raised. "You're talking about Rick Henderson and Chaiyala Mizrah? Oh, they're... entertaining."

"Definitely," Tim said. "They're nuts together. Hard to tell if it's love, rivalry, or some kind of blood feud."

"Rick's a hard case," Crouton added. "Only takes sniping, cooking, and whiskey seriously."

They stepped outside into the furnace blast, crossing the dusty avenue as supply trucks rumbled past.

"Rick's climbed Everest six times," Tim noted, shaking his head. "Also vanished twice—once in the Amazon, once at the Vatican. Both times, he just popped up in Sydney. No one knows how."

"Hmm, he's an enigma," Charles mused. "And no, they're not a couple—not officially anyway. Chaiyala's ex-Israeli police. Tough as steel, loyal, smart... but sweet, once you earn her trust."

"Rick once impersonated a monk," Crouton added, chuckling.

"She's a third-dan blackbelt ninjutsu," Rod said.

"Interesting," Chad noted, eyebrows lifted.

Tim burst out laughing. "Rick did what?"

"They sound like the life of the party," Charlotte grinned.

"Very much so," Charles nodded.

"You'll meet them soon," Tim said, pausing at a corner of the compound. "But first... come take a look at this."

CHAPTER 4

A sea of ancient artefacts stretched before them, unearthed from beneath the desert sands at the excavation site a hundred meters away.

Pots, jars, arrowheads, and weapons lay alongside unique marble tablets. Each inscribed with symbols—a strange fusion of Egyptian hieroglyphs and ancient Greek.

The room was filled with towering statues and strange machines—massive, intricate, and unlike anything they'd ever seen. Their presence gave the space an eerie, almost sacred feel.

"Wow... this is like some kinda strange museum," Chad remarked, gripped by curiosity and uncertainty.

Charlotte nodded slowly... impressed.

The artefacts rested on trestles, plinths, and platforms—ready for examination, yet utterly out of place.

Some were especially intricate, cast in gold, silver, or copper. One object, resembling a refrigerator, sat beside something that looked like a rotary hoe.

"This is the examination centre," Tim explained. "Everything here was recovered from ancient mud or pulled from the partially intact structure nearby. These are remnants of a civilization unknown to history—until now."

"This is so awesome," Chad said, wide-eyed.

"Yahuh!" Charlotte agreed, captivated.

Chad glanced around, still stunned by how cool and fresh the air felt inside a tent pitched under the Saharan sun.

"It's like... there's aircon," he said. "But gentler. Drier."

Tim grinned. "Not aircon." He motioned toward the far corner of the lab. "It's an ancient method."

Charlotte tilted her head. "Oh, interesting."

Tim knelt beside a low intake vent and ran his hand along the frame. "This is built on a geothermal drafting system—passive cooling using pressure gradients and buried ducts. The ancient city we're studying—most likely used it to keep entire stone halls temperate."

"But this isn't just passive air flow," Crouton added. "There's tech we still don't fully understand. Clay and copper chambers that somehow regulate moisture and redirect wind currents. Feels like an engineered breeze."

Charlotte leaned closer, eyebrows raised. "You're telling me people from thousands of years ago cooled desert halls without electricity?"

Tim looked over at Crouton, Rod, and Charles. "Well... the mystery is this—Atlantis may have had electricity too."

It hit Chad like a wave. They'd definitely entered the realm of the unbelievable.

Charlotte stared at Tim—puzzled, thrilled.

"This system though?" Tim gestured. "It doesn't require power. We've reverse-engineered it. Scaled it up. It's working right now."

Chad blinked at the ceiling. "That's... nuts."

"Welcome to the paradox," Charles said from behind them, arms folded. "None of this should be possible. And yet—here we are."

A car-sized device caught Chad's eye—hundreds of cogs, discs, and panels spinning his thoughts as much as they did the machine.

"Looks like some kinda old-school navigational... star-chart... thingy-ma-hooza-watzit," Chad guessed.

"Close," Tim said. "We believe it mapped stars and planets. Recovered records suggest it may have belonged to an ancestor of one of the magi who visited Jesus at His birth."

"Wait—what?" Charlotte blinked.

"Whoever they were," Tim said, "they studied a celestial anomaly resembling the Star of David—forecasted its rise through prophecy, time and astronomy."

"In short," Rod added, "they grasped the science behind the signs."

"That's nuts... wow," Chad gasped.

"Beyond cool," Charlotte agreed—just as an excited commotion erupted at the far end of the marquee, drawing their attention.

Several staff stepped away from their tables and gathered under a wall-mounted screen, chatting excitedly.

Tim and Crouton stopped everything and hotfooted it over too—the others close behind.

On the screen, live footage from the canyon at the other end of the dig site showed workers clearing debris from the entrance of a half-buried structure—tilted in the earth, angled toward the sky.

Without a word, Tim and Crouton raced for the vehicles like schoolboys at bell time on the last day of school, waving for the others to follow.

They piled into the Humvees—Crouton behind the wheel of the first, Charles in the second—and wasted no time.

"So... what's happening exactly?" Charlotte asked.

"The excavation site we're heading to," Tim explained, "is a major architectural complex. We're almost certain it originated from the city once built upon the Richat. A massive structure, long buried and tipped on its side, has finally revealed its entrance."

"This has been decades in the making—decades!" Crouton beamed, his beard bristling with excitement. Charles and Rod shivered with anticipation. Tim looked like it was Christmas morning—and he was twelve.

"Yay! This is so exciting!" Charlotte beamed.

Chad remained quiet, wide-eyed, waiting for Tim to continue.

A wild thought flashed through Chad's mind—once more—*Nah... no way. That's insane.* He shook it off.

"I can't believe we're finally here," Crouton whispered to Charles and Rod. "Pinch me."

Rod back handed him in the shoulder.

"Yeah, this is happening!"

Crouton slammed the brakes. The Humvee skidded a meter. He opened the door and moved like a ghost—fast, surreal, eyes locked on the structure ahead. His mind darted between awe and a practical procedure. Rod and Charles followed, cross-checking protocol with on-site staff.

Technicians bustled past, hauling equipment toward a vast entrance that loomed like a neoclassical sentinel—evocative of the Auckland War Memorial Museum. Its columned façade, built from interlocking red, white, and black stone, whispered of ancient mystery and solemn grandeur. Above the threshold, a triangular arch echoed the Pantheon's timeless geometry. Dust clung to the stone like memory, and the air buzzed with the quiet urgency of discovery.

"What's up?" Tim asked Chad, spotting the frown on his brother's face.

"Not sure yet," Chad replied. He thought it might be how fanatically driven Crouton and the Red Sword crew seemed—like they'd been born into this job—destiny hard-wired into their DNA. But it wasn't that. "... Can't place it."

Then it clicked.

Chad's law-student mind seized on something he couldn't shake. Disbelief collided with logic. He froze—speechless.

And then, slowly, he spoke.

"You've discovered Atlantis."

The words landed—conclusive, absurd, electric. Everyone—including Chad himself—felt the delay. Heads turned. Eyes locked on him.

"... Haven't you? You've discovered the lost city of Atlantis."

"Sorry... what?" Charlotte asked, her mind suddenly rapidly connecting the dots.

Tim's eyebrows lifted. Then came the grin.

Crouton stared daggers—mind racing, weighing, measuring, cautious but impressed. Tim had laid groundwork. Chad, a budding lawyer, had assembled the puzzle.

"He is indeed as sharp as his elder brother," Charles decided.

"Aye," Crouton said. "We have discovered the lost city of Atlantis."

Tim beamed, electric.

Charlotte frowned, caught in a whirl of realization.

"Very good indeed! Highest marks, young man," Charles said with pride.

Rod looked between Crouton, Charles, and Chad. "How in the heck did you come to that?"

"It has to be," Chad said, half certain, half wondering if he'd lost the plot. "This region of northwest Africa was once underwater. Ancient riverbeds in the mountains... the Richat's concentric rings—it all echoes

Atlantis. I remembered Charlotte mentioning eroded circles. And last year, during a study on Solon—Plato's ancestor—I came across Plato's writings. He described Atlantis as a city of concentric land and water rings.

As we left the plains and travelled through the mountains, I kept thinking... could this have been an island in the Atlantic?"

"You have a brilliant mind, young Chad," Crouton commended.

"And an open one," Charles added.

"Thank you. Solon and Plato were revered thinkers," Chad went on. "Plato's account was incredibly detailed. He credited ancient records from Egypt's Temple of Sais. I brushed over that—my study focused on law and democracy."

"Nice! I'm impressed," Tim said.

"Wait—so who are Solon and Plato?" Charlotte asked.

"Solon was a Greek lawmaker and poet, lived around 630 to 560 BC. Plato—a philosopher from the fourth century BC—was distantly related. The only known source of Atlantis comes from Plato's dialogues— 'Timaeus' and 'Critias'—which have preserved the legend for over two millennia."

"Interesting," Charlotte said, eyes narrowed. She found herself replaying old conversations with Tim. Bits and pieces, once scattered, now began to align.

"The temple where those records were kept—didn't it sink into the Nile Delta?" Chad asked, looking to Tim.

He smiled. Crouton and Charles did the same.

"That temple," Tim said, "has been located. The problem is—it sits smack in the middle of political unrest. A diplomatic mess."

"We've been negotiating," Crouton interjected, rolling his eyes, "with the Egyptians. As expected, they've been 'unable' to offer the same freedom Mauritania has."

"Hence why we're here—and not there," Tim said. "Exploring. Excavating."

"Egypt is a work in progress," Charles added. "Our access here, reflects the political web—some strands to untangle, others to cut. Mauritania may have instability, but it's less wrapped up in fragile treaties and disputes between the Middle East and the West."

Crouton gave a sharp chuckle. "We sort of, caught a few people by surprise with Mauritania. Egypt, though? That's a..." He paused. Sighed. "A different story."

Tim smirked.

Chad and Charlotte frowned at each other.

"All the same," Charles said cryptically, "the Richat Structure is the ultimate prize in a platter of very revealing locations of ancient interest."

"I... I can't get my head around this!" Chad muttered, both stunned and elated.

"I know! Oh my goodness!" Charlotte added, eyes wide. "Seriously?"

Tim had rarely seen his fiancée so utterly baffled.

Crouton and Rod grinned at Chad and Charlotte's bewilderment. They turned their attention toward a pair of technicians emerging from the structure. They'd connected thick electrical cables to a generator.

"We should be ready to go in shortly," Rod advised.

"Atlantis..." Charlotte whispered.

"I feel like I'm dreaming," Chad said. His mind wrestled with the notion that Atlantis was mythology. But now? He'd seen too much. His law-student logic and outside-the-box thinking had carried him past the point of no return.

"Yahuh," Charlotte related, her voice distant. "Something like that..." She laughed gently, half dazed.

Tim handed them hard hats and hi-vis vests as the crew suited up. Rod did a quick scan for boot sizes and came back with steel-capped pairs.

"You guys okay?" Tim checked.

"Yeah, bro..." Chad nodded, intensity in his eyes. "This is gonna take a while... this—this is way, *way* beyond next level." They both laughed.

"I can't believe," Charlotte said with a grin-frown combo, "that with everything you told me... I didn't figure it out."

"If I'd just said 'we discovered Atlantis' over Skype," Tim asked, "how would you have responded?"

Charlotte paused, considering. "I don't really know."

"I think I'd have said, 'I need to *see* this.' To understand— *'believe'* it," Chad added.

"Exactly," Tim nodded. "I planned to introduce everything gradually. There's a world of dynamics at play. I wanted to reveal it step by step. But I think we just skipped a few chapters and dove straight into the deep end."

"Yeah, that sounds about right," Chad joked.

"You jumped," Charlotte said, serious now. Like he'd personally cracked open their mental vault and tossed their understanding of Atlantis into chaos.

Charles and Crouton moved with the archaeologists and technicians, managing access to the newly exposed structure. Most of the preliminary work complete—now the teams combed through its layout, tested its stability, and flagged any lurking risks.

Charlotte and Chad sat nearby, trying to absorb the scale of what Tim had described. Five rugby fields' worth of excavated terrain stretched before them—carved into steep, benched cliff faces. Scientists paced through the site, examining relics. The interlocking red, black, and marbled stone slabs stunned them—each fit like Tetris pieces, holding the structure together.

"Look how the brickwork's like some kinda jigsaw puzzle," Chad observed.

"The colours are incredible too," Charlotte added, eyes scanning the stone.

"Good catch," Tim said. "The interlocking slabs share traits with Inca and Maya stonework, but they're different in key ways. This civilization mastered precision engineering. That's why their buildings have held up so well."

"Are we ready?" Crouton asked, addressing Tim, Charlotte, and Chad.

"More than ready!" Tim replied, excitement bubbling.

Four archaeological technicians entered first, followed by Crouton, Charles, and Rod. Tim led Charlotte, Chad, and a camera crew followed them.

Inside, floodlights lit the vast chamber in harsh relief. The twenty-five-degree tilt made every step feel precarious—like climbing a slanted ramp while weaving around jagged floor fractures.

To their right, a towering promenade stretched from the outer entrance under a cathedral-like ceiling.

The initial dig hadn't seemed significant—just debris from a corner. But as more earth was removed, a second doorway and wall had surfaced, revealing they'd already broken through. Now, into something much larger.

To their left, the hall vanished beneath mounds of mud washed in from the main, or the first entrance.

"Look at *that!*" one of the archaeologists said, pointing to a huge wooden door—half still hanging from its hinges.

"Where's the other half, I wonder..." Charles mused, studying the massive arched frame.

"I've never seen anything like it," said another archaeologist. "What kind of wood survives this long, buried in mud?"

The first archaeologist knelt for a closer look.

"It's definitely extraordinary timber, that's for sure," she said. "One side looks preserved—protected by mud. The other seems petrified. Very brittle. Odd contrast. Let's get samples from both sides and run tests."

"It looks like the other half broke away," one archaeologist said, studying the doorway. "Probably during the initial cataclysm, when the mud poured in. Judging by the slope of the flow, it solidified enough to breach the inner chambers—but didn't flood them completely. Like this section here..." He pointed toward the dusty floor where the outer hall disappeared into the earth.

Large floodlight frames had been pegged to the floor of the vast room they entered next.

"Oh wow... check this place out," Charlotte whispered in awe.

"Look how structurally intact everything is..." Tim remarked, pausing to scan a mound of broken relics—ceramic pots, stone tables, chairs. All shattered, scattered across one end of the room like debris hurled by a massive quake.

"It's as if a giant picked this place up and bowled it across the countryside," Charles mused. "Everything inside shaken loose, then gathered in one corner as it came to a halt."

The room stretched nearly a hundred meters long, forty to fifty wide. At its centre stood a colossal, floor-fastened table—sixty meters long, ten across. A fractured black glass panel ran the length of it, its surface cracked and cratered from violent collisions as the building toppled and objects flew, bouncing off the table.

"My goodness..." Charles whispered.

He viewed, as the others beheld it too. At the far end—fifteen monumental statues leaned against each other at a steep angle. Ten were distinct. Five at the centre—two women between—were taller. The figure at the centre towered above the rest, arms stretched over the other twelve.

"Oooh yeah," Crouton nodded, eyes locked. He turned to Tim, Charles, and Rod. "This is definitely Atlantis. Possibly one of the central government buildings."

"Incredible," Tim breathed. "The ten rulers of the Atlantean empire... and the one in the middle? Poseidon—Father to all ten. But the man and women at his sides? That's a mystery... at least one may be Cleito—Poseidon's wife."

Charles smiled mysteriously.

Charlotte's gaze lifted to the vivid murals covering the walls. In the closest left-hand corner, a spill of mud had crept through a collapsed entry. Yet beyond it, rows of strange script ran horizontally across the walls, beginning about a meter and a half above the floor.

"I can't wait to see that script translated," Tim said.

Before the nine towering murals, Crouton, Charles, and Rod stood in silence—like pilgrims before relics. Their expressions carried the quiet relief of belief confirmed. Charlotte, stood nearby—spellbound, drawn in by the murals' haunting beauty and layered mystery.

"These guys aren't just security..." Chad wondered. *"No security detail has this much passion for archaeology or ancient relics. Who are they really?"*

Tim caught the question in Chad's eyes. His look said: *"I know"*. Chad's reply. *"Keep going—I'm ready."*

Charlotte stood before the first mural. It radiated primal energy—evoking Genesis, the creation of the world. Light and matter emerging from chaos. Gases, atoms, and energy forged by perfection, passion, and cosmic will. The depiction stretched back before history... and forward into timeless futures.

The second mural cast a celestial war. A supreme being—The Almighty One—battled a deceiver cloaked in false light, masquerading as fun, freedom, and friendship. The entity bore the likeness of serpent and angel.

In the third mural, the serpent-angel was revealed as the deceiver—flung into a blazing abyss with his loyal followers. Dark gods from many cultures tumbled from the heavens like lightning, cast out as emblems of ruin, sorrow, and decay.

The fourth offered a counterpoint: divine emissaries dispatched to Earth—not to dominate, but to guide, protect, and bind what had been broken.

After that, the fifth depicted filth and damnation. The fallen angels served the dark one, gathered, tethered to him in chaos. On a mountain, a lamb was slain. From a tomb, a lion rose—light exploding across the cosmos, bringing peace, justice, and finality. Then came the lake of fire—the abyss reopened only to cast the fallen into flame.

These five murals lined the right-hand wall, stretching inches above the ancient script and towering toward the ceiling.

The wall adjacent—in the massive hall, five more equally majestic frescos continued the saga.

Charlotte observed at a depiction of Poseidon descending to Earth—light shrouding him like a divine mantle. It sent a chill through her.

The mural continued—Poseidon's family arriving. The birth of his first son—Atlas, first emperor of Atlantis. His name etched in ancient maps, North African mountains, the Atlantic and the name Atlantis itself.

The next panel glowed with the rise of Atlantis—a golden age. A thriving culture, humanity flourishing, cities rising in brilliance. Poseidon's sons ruled distant realms, loyal to Atlas and bound by shared origin.

Expansion followed. Cities multiplied. Technology soared. The final mural glowed with machines and knowledge—each one strange, brilliant, and beyond understanding.

Atlantis stood at the height of its existence. With progress complete, the empire turned inward. Thinkers gathered in amphitheatres, exploring life, morality, and the divine. Wisdom grew. Belief shifted. The soul of the civilization began to change.

Then, a shift—depicted in vibrant detail. Atlantis began to reach beyond its borders. Atlas's sons ventured north, south, and west—encountering distant oceans and undiscovered continents. Trade missions took months by sea... but far less by air.

"Correct me if I'm imagining things here," Chad said slowly. "But are those objects in this mural... ancient aeroplanes?"

He tried to shape the thought without sounding absurd.

They all stared, each carrying a thousand questions. Rod and Crouton simply nodded. Tim and Charlotte voiced the same wonder that flickered in Chad's tone.

The tenth and final mural marked a turning point.

Global trade boomed—but so did conflict. A rival empire across the sea rose to equal power. Tensions flared. War erupted—between Atlantis, its foe, and Kekropia (Athens), and its eastern allies.

Then Poseidon, enraged, reached to the sky—pulling a star from the heavens and hurling it between the warring nations. What followed was global catastrophe. Civilization crumbled. Memory faded. Only vague myths survived.

Tim stood frozen—lost in the imagery. This place... this moment... didn't resemble any known chapter of human history. The colours and architecture vaguely echoed Ancient Greece and Egypt—but neither pantheon nor papyrus. This felt older. Deeper. The twilight of prehistory.

"You know," Charles said softly, half entranced, "it's such an odd thing to prepare your entire life for something—only to find it's beyond anything you imagined."

Crouton nodded, glassy-eyed. A rare sight for anyone who knew him— yet here, entirely fitting.

The group fell quiet, each absorbing the moment. The space was stuffy, smelled of mud. But the magnitude of the discovery eclipsed discomfort.

Crouton and Tim circled the stonework of the central table. Rod counted hundreds of fixed seats—once reserved for the esteemed. They studied the shattered black glass strip running down the table's centre, each wondering silently...

"Why does it look like a twenty-first-century flat-screen?" Rod finally asked.

"There are more," Charles called from a corridor wrapping around the main chamber. "Two more over here—set into the walls."

He pointed to two glossy black rectangles.

Chad felt his thoughts blurring, his heartbeat spiking—it was too much. Thankfully, he'd remembered his meds that morning—despite the travel and timeline chaos.

"I need some air," he told Tim and Charlotte.

Tim caught his tone.

"You okay?" Charlotte asked gently.

"Yeah... yeah. Just gonna sit outside for a bit."

He stepped through the massive entrance, feet grateful for horizontal ground. He found a wooden table, sat down, closed his eyes, and placed his forehead in his hands.

It was mild. But real. The kind of anxiety that required stillness. He recalled what his counsellor had taught him 'presence of mind'— 'Mindfulness.'

In panic, he sought the quiet. The ordinary. A leaf's shape. A sparrow's flicker. The grain in a table's wood. One tiny detail—holding his focus—detached him from the spiral. Breath slowed. The rush subsided.

It worked. Just like it had before.

The meds helped. As did good diet, exercise, sleep, and company. He loved walking. Miles of it. Along with inspirational quotes pinned to the wall or saved on his phone—he had a roadmap.

Tim and Charlotte joined him soon after. Crouton approached but stayed respectfully back.

Tim sat to his right. Charlotte to his left.

"You all good, bro?" Tim asked.

"Yeah... all good now," Chad replied, smiling.

Tim nodded. Charlotte smiled quietly.

"Just admiring the woodwork," Chad said, running his hand along the rough slab of four-by-two.

Tim chuckled. He recognized the technique.

"I used to carry a bunch of little trinkets," Crouton began, eyes sweeping across the sunlit dig site. Activity buzzed around them—oblivious to the terrain of mental health being navigated.

"Called it my bag o' tricks," he said. "Kept 'em on me everywhere I went. A Donald Duck figurine. A Salvation Army pen. Somethin' that looked like a gargoyle in a tutu—meant to ward off evil spirits, though I never believed in that part. And this wind-up lawn mower... drove my wife crazy."

He laughed—full and free.

"They snapped me out of it, those wee things," he said. "By the time I finished focusin' on 'em... I'd come back."

Crouton had been through anxiety, depression and suicidal hell. Tim hadn't known the extent of it, but the big bearded man could relate to Tim's past experiences, and Chad's present predicament alike. He knew a thing or two.

CHAPTER 5

C routon looked to Tim, "Bart's taking a chopper to the project Camp in fifteen, did you want to take the Humvee back up and get him to give you guys a birds-eye of the Richat?"

"Oh yes!" Tim loved the idea.

Charlotte lit up and Chad wearily came back to the world of the living—both keen.

Crouton flicked Tim the keys to his Humvee—wasting no time, they got in and sped off back up to ground level.

~~~~~~~

The helicopter pilot was an amusing character—Bartholomew (Bart) from Germany—introduced himself as "Bartman" in a rough, throaty voice. He had a thick German accent, and seemed to be entertaining himself more than anyone else, grinning broadly as he gestured for them to hop in.

Chad frowned then shrugged. Charlotte liked him—random, but likeable.

Tim discussed with Bart circling the Eye of Africa as he climbed into the front seat beside him. The three tugged on headsets, adjusting mics as the rotor thrum began to swell. With introductions made, Tim settled himself, his fiancée, and his brother for what would normally be a five-minute flight—straight-line from the dig site to the project camp and the Richat structure.

"But this time," Tim explained, "we're going to view the Richat from way up above."

"I shall take dis baby high as I can get her," Bart declared.

"It's only at high altitude where you can truly grasp shape and size of the Richat. It's around twenty-three kilometres across, and from ground level—even from the highlands—it just looks like rows of rolling hills off in the distance," Tim explained as they darted across the desert in a sleek black helicopter.

Bart pulled the craft higher. As the altitude climbed, the view became nothing short of incredible.

From this height, the earth stretched out beneath them. Chad and Charlotte both began to notice a vast and undeniable curve bending across the horizon.

"Wow, look at that," Chad said, pointing.

"The Adrar highlands at a glance," Tim narrated. "It took us hours to thread through those mountains. Funny how a view can change in a minute, depending on method and angle."

"It's incredible," Chad replied, eyes wide as he gazed down at the dusty, barren peaks far below.

Charlotte was first to notice the sudden transformation in the land—a broad expanse, distinct from the sparse wilderness all around, the Adrar highlands running like a spine through its centre.

"There's a huge area that rises up out of the desert. Everything else is flat," she observed.

"Good observation. Now look—behold—the Eye of Africa—The Richat," Tim said, grandeur threading through his tone.

"Oh, my goodness... wow," Charlotte breathed.

Chad simply stared through the window, silent and wide-eyed.

"Amazing, eh?"

"It's breath-taking... and kinda haunting," Charlotte said. "It's way bigger than I imagined. Kinda eerie."

"That's pretty different, I'll give you that," Chad added.

"Dis as high as we can go," Bart chimed in. "Otherwise it pulls da power cord outta da back of the chopper—den we're toast."

Chad and Charlotte burst out laughing. Tim shot Bart a confused grin.

"Where do you come up with this stuff?"

"I joke!" Bart laughed. "I'll fly us around da structure so you can get a good view of how it looks."

Chad sat quietly, thoughts spinning. Everything Tim had said during the news interview... the ancient catastrophes around this region... it all began to link up in his mind.

"So, this whole area's being excavated?" he asked.

"The biggest excavation project in the world," Tim replied. "Largest in archaeological history. Imagine the city of Auckland buried under mud for thousands of years. New Zealand as an ancient lost civilization. It'd be like examining something that size."

"Crazy," Chad muttered, shaking his head. "And this is really the site of Atlantis?"

"That's the most likely possibility. Based on all the evidence so far. Once we decipher the script of the civilization that once called this place home, we'll be able to confirm it. We're fairly confident it's a foregone conclusion. The evidence matching Plato's details is incredibly compelling," Tim said. "Just waiting for the hard proof."

"Very interesting," Chad replied.

"It's enormous," Charlotte whispered, her eyes sweeping the terrain below. "Four concentric circles..." She recalled Tim's earlier description. "Do you know how many people might've lived here?"

"Hard to say for sure," Tim said. "But possibly over a million—similar to Auckland's population today."

"Seriously..." Charlotte breathed, mesmerized. Her eyes tracked the mountains rising to the north—now desolate, barren, eerily quiet. It didn't look like a place anyone had ever lived... let alone a million people.

"Those northern mountains," she said. "Looks like rivers used to pour out from them." From here, ancient riverbeds cut faint lines through the terrain.

"Can you imagine those peaks were once covered in forest?" Tim asked. "Waterfalls everywhere, carving down through the stone. The city's edge would have reached the foothills."

"Oh yes," she replied. "This place would've been stunning."

"Incredible," Chad said softly, shaking his head in quiet awe.

Bart took them lower, tracing the inmost valley of the structure. On either side, hills rose like ancient waves—etched as though carved by water long gone.

"I can't get over this..." Chad said, shaking his head. "This is nuts! So—the Atlanteans built this Richat structure?"

"Not entirely," Tim replied. "In fact, that's highly unlikely. No evidence so far points to that. That said, we haven't unearthed everything. We've barely scratched the surface."

"The Eye of Africa has long baffled scientists," Tim continued. "Very little geological research has been done—'til now. One theory suggests a meteorite impact, but the lack of shock evidence or supporting formations rules that out. More likely, it was an ancient volcano—an eruption that never fully happened. Molten rock surged upward and receded, possibly multiple times, creating the rippling terrain. If it had erupted, the crater might rival Lake Taupo. Now, geologists, archaeologists, and historians are investigating together—finally bringing scientific rigour to the mystery."

"Nice!" Charlotte nodded, surveying the valleys and ridges shaped by what now appeared a natural phenomenon.

"As you observed earlier", Tim said to Charlotte, "Plato described rivers flowing from northern mountains—forming three water rings within four land circles. Atlantis was likely built upon the rings of land, using its natural layout and water sources as a strategic, fortified capital."

"That is magnificent," Chad said, trying to picture it.

"So that's the Richat structure—The Eye of the Sahara," Tim concluded.

"This place is insane. Truly breath-taking..." Charlotte said. "Thank you so much for inviting us to see this, babe." She hugged Tim tightly.

Tim laughed, kissed her on the head.

"And thank you," she expressed to Bart, "for taking us up high!"

Chad echoed her gratitude.

"You're most welcome," Bart said with a smile.

"Now that you've seen it," Tim said, "there's even more at the Project Camp—how it was formed, how Atlantis might've been built on it."

"For now, let's head down," Tim said. Bart lowered the helicopter, descending toward the Richat's outer edge—a little off from the old town of Ouadane, toward a semi-fortified compound sprawling across the desert floor.

~~~~~~~

At four o'clock, they touched down at a small airfield—still partially under construction. Two hangars stood side by side, and a large marquee served as the secure arrival terminal.

"That is a beast of a security fence!" Chad observed— "it's insane!"

"Wow!" Charlotte joined his gaze as they stepped away from the helicopter—walking toward Crouton, Charles, and Rod—already approaching to greet them.

"Surrounding the entire Richat Project area," Tim said, "is a 245-kilometre zinc–titanium alloy galvanised steel fence. Its twenty metres high, with a five-metre-high–foot-thick base wall. It's lined end-to-end with infra-red, seismic, and real-time surveillance."

The mesh between towering steel uprights resembled thick iron ropes.

Chad and Charlotte shook their heads—speechless.

Bart completed post-flight checks and climbed out a few minutes later.

Crouton smiled. "Back, at last."

"Yeah. Always good to be back," Tim replied. It had been a long day—everyone ready for a break.

"Barbecues at six," Crouton announced.

"Come," Tim said to Chad and Charlotte, "let's get you checked in and sorted. Rod and I will walk you through the process, then show you where we're all staying." They moved toward the marquee.

The airfield was secured by high fencing lined with razor wire—similar to the compound they'd seen earlier.

"This is the high-security arrival centre," Tim explained. "It includes mini customs, a visitor lounge, an admin HQ for flights and arrivals, and accommodation for Red Sword staff managing the airfield." he pointed out as they passed the hangars.

"There are three checkpoints spread across the perimeter. It encloses the Richat, the northern mountains, and the camp."

"Everything here is huge!" Charlotte remarked.

Two security guards greeted them, shaking Tim's hand. Bart exchanged jokes with one. After introductions, they passed through a tunnel lined with several kinds of sensors. Their bags ran through a parallel conveyor scanner.

"Heya, Tim," said a small, stocky female guard with a Mediterranean look.

"Maria," Tim smiled. After quick introductions, she and a colleague processed clearance, issued photo IDs, and welcomed them officially. As Tim handed Chad and Charlotte their bags, he recounted their journey from Nouakchott.

"Well, enjoy your stay at the Richat," Maria said warmly.

They joined the rest of the Red Sword team waiting near the visitor centre entrance.

"This place is actually pretty awesome," Chad said, looking around. "I mean, for a marquee in the Sahara? You wouldn't guess you're in a tent—or the desert."

One might've thought they'd stepped into an upscale arrivals lounge or a sleek conference centre.

"We like to do things well here," Charles said. "Everyone, and every-thing is treated with the highest regard."

"I like that," Charlotte said thoughtfully.

Crouton led them into the lounge—a tranquil, air-conditioned retreat. The entry framed by staggered wall panels forming twin openings. Inside, a long refreshment table stood between entryways, flanked by water cool-ers and glasses. Soft lighting, potted palms, and cushioned sofas created a warm, welcoming atmosphere.

"Darn! Wasn't expecting this!" Chad exclaimed, caught by surprise.

The spacious room, divided into three sections, featured a central reception area where Charlotte quickly made herself at home.

"Hmm, this place is nice! I think I'll stay," she said dreamily, flopping onto a sofa.

Crouton explained the lounge's purpose—an oasis for guests and their families. Many were here for safety, protected within the camp from rising external threats. His offhand but sincere remarks revealed a team culture built on loyalty and care, echoed by the unity between staff.

Two adjoining sections branched off from the lounge—one a library, the other an information centre. Suspended from a rafter overhead, two Perspex panels displayed enlarged excerpts from Plato's Timaeus and Critias.

"The library spans many genres," Charles explained, "but its heart lies in the Atlantis archive—a vast repository of myth, mystery, and archaeological inquiry, focused on Mauritania and the greater Sahara."

Beyond the hangars, aviation buildings, and the marquee, the scenery shifted dramatically.

"Welcome to the Project Camp," Crouton boomed as they walked along a dusty path flanked by grassy flats. "Population: three thousand, three hundred and twenty-four."

"Sorry—what?" Chad recoiled, surprised.

"That's eight hundred and twenty Red Sword personnel," Rod began, "thirty-five on Tim's historical team, including himself. Six hundred and eight archaeologists. Two hundred and eighty geological staff—including all scientists, technicians, and admin. Then one thousand, four hundred and fifty-seven family members and camp staff. And one hundred and twenty-four short-to-medium term visitors."

"Well done!" Tim smiled.

Charles and Crouton laughed at how precisely Rod rattled that off.

"That's a small town where we come from," Chad said, as they passed several large buildings on the left and a bustling gas station on the right—complete with vehicles and customers.

"About two-thirds of that population have been here nearly two years," Rod noted.

They wandered through a space that reminded Chad and Charlotte of The Village at the old Parachute Music Festival back home.

"If you can resist the smells and mouth-watering sights along this stretch," Crouton said, "we've got a barbecue feast fit for kings waiting at your accommodation."

On their left were several food outlets with crowds lining up, wooden tables filled with guests. To the right, a large open marquee housed a café at one end and hundreds of tables where people ate, socialized, played cards, or milled about.

"Remind you of Parachute days, eh?" Tim said.

"It so does!" Charlotte said. Chad nodded.

"The Parachute Music Festival was one awesome summer tradition for us back in the day." Tim recalled fondly. "It was the largest summer festival of its kind in New Zealand and the Southern Hemisphere, attracting twenty-five-thousand festival goers, with over one-hundred bands. It had a variety of artistic expressions and worship in a largely Christian setting.

At its heart was The Village—a bustling marketplace strikingly similar to the setup we have here."

"Interesting," Rod said, intrigued. His view of Christianity hadn't ventured beyond church and Bible studies. He was still wrapping his head around the festival vibe and context Tim described.

"Did you perform at Parachute?" Crouton asked Charlotte.

"Nope. Parachute was before my time. I wasn't doing anything seriously back then. But I've performed at festivals that now happen in the same spot at the same time Parachute used to."

"Ahh cool," Crouton acknowledged.

"On the other side of the café eatery," Charles began, "you'll find international food outlets—reflecting the cultures of the people working here."

"These outlets," Tim added, "lean heavy into meat—burgers, pizza, roasts."

"Except that darn vege place down the end," Crouton muttered. "Vegetarians—everywhere. Even here. Didn't know that was gonna happen."

"Must've slipped through security," Charles said dryly.

"Hey! I'm vegetarian, thank you!" Charlotte protested, as Tim and Chad burst out laughing.

"Well, that ain't good for you, eh Tim?" Crouton said, shaking his head. "It's alright, young lady—you can't be completely perfect."

"I'm not vegetarian," Charlotte smirked. "But I'll take that as a compliment!" She beamed.

Crouton frowned.

"Gotchu!" she laughed.

"She did—she got ya good!" Tim chuckled.

The others laughed. Crouton unleashed his familiar, unsettling laugh.

Tim grinned. "You fit in just fine," he told Charlotte. They kissed, and the group strolled past shaded pools, the water glistening beneath leafy palms. To the right, beyond a cobbled courtyard strung with party lights, a lively restaurant and garden bar—The Richat Bar and Grill—welcomed guests escaping the Sahara heat.

"This place has everything!" Chad said.

"There's a lot to do here," Rod told them. "Three-theatre cinema, a library, gymnasium—you saw the eating precinct. Sports competitions. Motocross, BMX and mountain bike tracks were recently expanded. And there's a high ropes and adventure sports centre."

"Wow—serious? Nice!" Charlotte blinked, clearly impressed.

"You didn't think I invited you to the other side of the world just to hang out in the desert, did you?" Tim laughed.

"There are palm trees, gardens... grass—everywhere." Chad paused, the realization landing. "This shouldn't be possible—not in this part of Mauritania. How's that even possible?"

"Now this is cool," Tim replied. "Legend has it, Poseidon created both hot and cold springs in Atlantis' central precinct. Amazingly, before we arrived, locals had already dug a well confirming freshwater exists here. An oasis thrives at the site—and both hot and cold water are now pumped all the way here."

"What about the salt water under the surface?" Chad asked.

"The well at the centre of the Richat is quite literally the only freshwater spring in the entire region."

"Crazy." Chad stared at Tim, impressed.

"That is pretty cool," Charlotte remarked, intrigued by the Poseidon connection.

Chad's thoughts wandered through a terrain of bewilderment, until one surfaced—deep, sudden, and quiet: *Is God trying to tell me something?* It didn't seem far-fetched—not after a day that had blown his mind five ways from Friday. And he wasn't convinced it was over. His thoughts drifted far beyond himself, beyond Hamilton, into terrain he'd never imagined.

What was all this about?

Everything he'd seen and heard in the last twenty-four hours was beyond ordinary. And it was making him think.

The sun dipped lower in the sky. Evening had begun to settle, but several hours of light still remained. The group left the village market precinct, following a dusty road up a gentle slope beyond the pools and restaurant.

A lush jungle of palms, succulents, and desert-thriving vegetation covered the hillside. At the top stood a lone palm, silhouetted like a sentinel. To the far left rose newer, sizable buildings—warehouses and administration facilities.

"My team's offices are that way, at the Central Hub," Tim gestured. "Alongside Red Sword HQ and the archaeological and geological bases. The science labs rival those of top universities and government programs. My office is in the historical research centre—home to an extensive library open to everyone in the camp."

Chad nodded. Interested. Thoughtful. His curiosity and questions increasing by the minute.

Nestled among tropical fauna, half a dozen simple yet elegant houses situated about the gravel road veering left at a fork, climbing a gentle slope before ending in a cul-de-sac. The righthand road descended into a lush basin, where a vast, flat grassy expanse—nearly three rugby fields wide—unfolded, framed by gentle grassy slopes.

Behind the restaurant and market, the road curved along the longer slope, leading to larger buildings beyond.

"The large structures you can see—between the village marketplace and the slopes down to the grassy basin," Tim directed, "are the cinema, gym, and community centre. That's a popular retreat from the heat, which takes some getting used to. You'll drink more water than you ever have... yet weirdly, fewer bathroom stops."

"Evaporates right outta ya," Crouton added.

"...and if you don't like New Zealand's humidity," Tim smirked, "you might change your tune after a week of this killer dry heat."

Chad and Charlotte stopped, eyes drawn to the huge stage set up at the far end of the grassy flats below.

"So, that down there," Tim pointed, "is the venue for concerts and shows. Every couple of months, we bring in a few bands."

"That's way cool," Charlotte beamed.

"Nice stuff. Who've you had?" Chad asked.

"The Evergreen Riot, Ashwell Drive, Filament Ghosts, Iron Psalm... those are the main ones since I've been here."

"Gettin' Uprise and Ferrosaint soon," Crouton added.

Chad shook his head, half convinced he was living inside a dream—Atlantis discovered, and now this oasis-town in the heart of the desert.

"How many people even know about this place?" Chad asked. "This camp—it's more like a small town. And you must have a ridiculous irrigation system to keep everything this green..."

Crouton and Charles chuckled. He tapped his boot against the turf. "It's all fed from below," Crouton said. "Subsurface drip irrigation. A grid of lines buried just under the surface—slow release, no waste. Keeps everything green without a single sprinkler in sight."

He looked out over the lower field. "Efficient. Quiet. You'd never know it's there unless you dug."

"Wow—nice," Chad nodded.

"The location and purpose of this site aren't entirely secret," Charles said. "Locals have known about the structure for thousands of years."

He glanced toward Crouton. "Red Sword secured excavation rights through strategic diplomacy—and Nathan's long-standing friendship with President Amani Darafed. That connection helped us move faster than most. And the local Tuareg people have been exceedingly welcoming."

He paused, letting the context settle.

"Some explorers have revived interest in the theory that the Richat Structure might be Atlantis. They weren't the first to suggest it, but their expeditions drew fresh attention by comparing its features to Plato's account. Their work sparked real consideration.

We secured access to protect this site—and the truth—from being buried under financial schemes and conspiracy theories.

Guests here respect the mission. The discovery belongs to the world. But if Atlantis is truly beneath us, it's unearthing could disrupt political, financial, even moral interests. Not everyone is ready for what lies below."

Chad listened carefully for the tremor beneath the surface—what some feared, what others buried. He sensed the real answer lived in another chapter, one not yet open to him. But for now, he pressed gently, deliberately.

"So, what sets Red Sword apart from the others? The ones who shut things down, bury the truth before it breathes. You've got loyalty, precision, systems that don't follow the usual play book. What's the core of it? What's the thing that makes it all hold together?"

"Some institutions," Charles began, "use classified narratives, threats, and treaties to control information. We've chosen a different path—one that won't leave a toxic legacy. They use an approach of ultimatums. We have opted for the power of a better; deeper attraction." He looked at Chad and Charlotte with quiet sincerity. "So, we figured... we'd try being nice to people. Tends to go a long way."

"Really? That simple?" Chad asked. "Nowhere in all my experience or studies as a law student does that sit right—especially not at this level. As terrible as that sounds..." He privately lamented humanity's pettiness—that cynicism and mistrust had become the default, rather than the kind of approach Charles had just described.

"To be exact—a very long way," Crouton continued. "Respect, honesty, and fairness create the strongest alliances. When people know they are highly valued, with nothing to fear—that sense of freedom and trust becomes an unstoppable force. What conventional intelligence agencies call naïve... is our strength. Trust and solid friendship outperform any currency, shutting out opposition. And when those agencies—or the people behind them—trip over their own corruption, we don't stand in their way."

"You've got dirt on all of them?"

Crouton chuckled. "They walk around with enough mud on their faces to do the job themselves. You could write a new volume on that hoo-ha every other month. They've mastered the art of self-sabotage—ignorantly so—gets 'em tangled in their own webs, while we keep moving."

"Nice," Chad muttered warily.

"There's such a gridlock of respect for Red Sword now," Charles continued, "that our adversaries won't break through. For every enemy, we have ten allies—not just because of our mission, but because of personal trust. Nathan O'Conner's a skilled diplomat. His reputation buys more than protection—it buys breathing room. Room to operate freely, to chase the bigger picture while others are still playing catch-up—stuck waist-deep in the mud of needlessly complicated details, all fallout from a need for classified secrets and protocol that hamstrings and takes many a toll. We stay out of headlines and politics to keep our focus—because the Richat project is just one piece of a much larger strategy.

Another goal is to disrupt corrupt agendas—those who twist truth, rewrite history. In doing so, we elevate our standing. Governments and corporations start relying on us."

"In fact," Crouton added, "without us, a lot of good—and a lot of sensitive dynamics—would be at risk. Political stability, reputations, regional peace."

Chad shook his head. "How is that even possible? This is starting to feel far-fetched—excuse the term. I'm trying, but..."

"Take U.S. President Jackson Rutherford," Charles offered. "Huge influence. Several of his businesses filed for bankruptcy, but banks bailed him out, believing his brand too valuable to lose. Despite corporate failures, his name kept things afloat. It's sparked plenty of debate—about the true source of his wealth."

Crouton frowned. It was a harsh truth, but fair. When branding outpaced substance, collapse was inevitable.

"Would be a decent wake-up call if they sank with his ship," Crouton muttered.

"One can dream," Rod smirked.

"Thing is," Charles said, "it works both ways. Sometimes, admirably."

"You guys are more than the average security company," Chad decided. "I figured as much."

"We're 'way' more than your average security company," Crouton confirmed, grinning. "We exist to make sure the right things get done. That people stay honest. That moral compasses don't veer off true north just because cash and temptation come knocking."

"Who keeps *you* honest?" Chad challenged.

Crouton paused. "Each of us—Rod, Charles, Nathan, Chaiyala, every Red Sword agent—has sworn an oath to our purpose." He hesitated. "Hmm... one thing at a time.

That purpose," he continued, "is simple: freedom and well-being for all. Our creed isn't strictly religious—but it's rooted in humanity's best virtues. Strip away the noise, and it's respect, kindness, compassion. That's it. We don't overcomplicate it. If it echoes Christ, the lives and work o' Mother Teresa, 'n' William Booth—it's because their lives reflect what it means to walk the walk."

Rod added, "We've all reached a point where conflict and self-interest are endless distractions. Whether through personal loss or seeing others suffer—we're done with falsehoods. It's time to put people first. Before things, beliefs, or politics."

Crouton glanced at Chad. "You asked who keeps us honest? That oath does. The creed does. And each other. We hold the line together."

"The only fools still aiming at us," Crouton muttered, "are clueless mercenaries hired by corrupt politicians and tycoons. Still stuck in those outdated black ops games."

"Still enjoy Black Ops," Chad said casually. "Fun for the most part."

Charles, Crouton, and Rod frowned, confused.

Tim smirked. "Been a while since we fought them Nazi zombies together."

He and Chad grinned. Charlotte caught the reference instantly.

"Ahh... 'Call of Duty'," Rod remembered.

Charles and Crouton smiled.

Chad and Charlotte were still turning over everything they'd just heard as they approached one of the houses that would be home for the next several weeks. Chad felt as though a raft of questions had just been answered—and now, a whole new tide was rising.

CHAPTER 6

T he Richat Project Camp felt like something pulled from home for Chad and Charlotte.

An oasis that stood in striking contrast to the stark desolation of the surrounding terrain. A place that, while sun-scorched and dry, felt no harsher than the hottest New Zealand or Australian summer. Within its dusty borders, it had become a second home for Tim. He'd grown close to Crouton, Chaiyala, Rod, and Charles, and had built strong bonds with several historians, archaeologists, and geologists he'd been working alongside.

"This is good... this is good," Chad said, relieved to finally arrive.

"Welcome to my place," Tim said as they passed through the roadside gate.

They ascended the timbered terrace—a communal space shared by Tim, Chaiyala and their housemate Rick with Crouton and his housemates, and Rod with his wife Kristie. Tim's house, furthest from the village, had a direct view of the bar and grill. Crouton's and Rod's residences sat opposite across the deck, with Rod and Kristie's place at the far end.

At the lowest level of the spacious vestibule area was a refreshing pool. Further away from the street-side edge stood a wood-fire pizza oven and the 'mother of all barbecues'—all three—Crouton's culinary pride and joy.

The three houses were comfortable, expansive yet simple. Surrounded by palms on what appeared to be the slope of a hill overlooking the grassy green before the concert stage, it felt almost like a luxury resort.

"Wow—this place is beautiful, Tim!" Charlotte admired, tempted to jump straight into the pool.

Tim smiled and put his arm around her shoulder as they and Chad moved toward Tim's place.

Crouton headed to Rod's house with him to check in with Kristie before the evening barbecue welcoming the guests. Rod and Kristie's elevated home overlooked the Central Hub, administrative precinct, and science labs a hundred meters away.

Crouton shared his place with Antonio Calanardi—a mild-mannered Italian in his mid-thirties. Along with Rhys Harvey, a New Zealand-born Scotsman in his mid-twenties whose thick Scottish accent often caught people off guard, especially given his distinctive Māori appearance. Raised north of Edinburgh—Scotland, after his whānau immigrated when he was seven years old. Rhys embodied a vibrant blend of cultures—equally at home with Highland reels, and kapahaka, salt air and sacred whenua.

"I thought you get back at midday?" called a blond-haired woman about Tim and Charlotte's age from the top terrace. Her dark sunglasses masked her expression, and her accent was hard to place. Then Chad and Charlotte remembered she was Israeli.

"We would've," Tim began, "but I wanted to take our time and show Chad and Charlotte some of the sights."

"Chad, Charlotte, this is my flatmate and good friend, Chaiyala," Tim introduced. "Chaiyala, this is my brother Chad, and my fiancée Charlotte."

"Is so lovely to meet you both, really!" Chaiyala said as she came down the steps. She hugged Charlotte warmly, shook Chad's hand with firmness and grace, offering a soft smile.

She wore little more than a swim top, small denim shorts, and Oakley sunnies. Her presence was quiet but fierce—stunning yet elusive, strong yet wounded. A warrior at heart, a friend in spirit.

Her build, attire, and manner reminded both Charlotte and Chad of Sonia—though for very different reasons. For Chad, it hit instantly. He glanced away, distracted, suddenly just wanting to know where he could dump his bags and take a break.

Part of him craved solitude, especially if being around the Middle Eastern version of his ex-girlfriend was going to mess with his head. He inwardly scolded himself for being so judgmental—even if the reaction remained internal. He sighed. Maybe he was still dealing with the legacy of Sonia.

He offered a polite smile. Nothing more.

Charlotte, sensing none of this, returned the warmth and figured she'd get along fine with Tim's flatmate. In truth, there were echoes of her old friend—before the drugs and everything else changed Sonia. In some way, it felt like encountering who she used to be.

"Where's Rick?" Tim asked Chaiyala as they moved indoors through a large concertina ranch slider and into the living area. Their other flatmate was nowhere to be seen.

She rolled her eyes with a sigh. "I do not know—he's probably with Rhys, fooling in the eatery or what. That lazy schlemiel, not doing dishes, underwear on the kitchen floor—*again!*"

"Sounds typical," Tim said. "When I'm not here, he's only got you to annoy. And because he avoids annoying me—since I don't want to kill him or, as you said the other day... what was it? Cut him up and put him in a casserole? He acts out."

Chad and Charlotte laughed.

Chaiyala planted her hands on her hips, face twisted in exaggerated scorn—though her smirk couldn't hide how amused she was by Tim's recollection.

"I thought he was scared of you..." Tim said, feigning confusion as he led Chad and Charlotte down the hall to their rooms.

"I wish he scared of me," she muttered. "He should. But he is not. If he were, doing what I say—no questions, no trouble."

"Chaiyala loves Rick..."

"Loves to hate."

"Kinda like an annoying little brother?" Charlotte suggested.

"Hmm." Chaiyala considered. "Maybe..."

"This is yours, babe." Charlotte's spacious room overlooked the deck, sharing an ensuite with Tim's room further down the hall. It featured a queen-sized bed and the comforts of a five-star hotel. Her bag rested at the foot of the bed.

Chad and Tim's rooms were similar—though Tim's was fully established after a year of living there. Chad's, across the hall, offered a north-facing view of the Richat hills framed by palms.

Outside, the heat had dipped into the low thirties—making the evening more bearable. By the time showers were done, the sun had sunk behind the rooftops. Chaiyala, now wearing a sleeveless hoodie, curled up with a book in the living area. She stood as they entered and offered cold drinks.

"Yes please!" Charlotte accepted, yawning. She stretched and exclaimed how good it was to be clean again.

Chad and Tim welcomed drinks too. They gathered around the island bench between the dining and kitchen areas, talking through the day's events—Chad and Charlotte's epic two-day journey from Auckland to Nouakchott, then to the Richat. Compared to that, Chaiyala's day had been quiet.

"Rick's not back still." Tim noted.

"He show up when meat starts cooking," Chaiyala said. "Never pass up free feed."

Charlotte and Chad were enjoying her soft, exotic accent. She was lovely to listen to—but there was a sharpness beneath it that suggested messing with her was a very bad idea.

Chad caught himself staring a little too long, which got a suspicious glance.

"Crouton's barbecues are on another level," Tim said. "He's passionate about food. Doesn't do things by halves."

"What's the time?" Chad asked, stomach beginning to protest. "Dinner's at six?"

"Yup, that's it... knowing Crout, it'll be ready fifteen minutes early." Tim moved to the fridge, pulled out a handful of limes, and began slicing them on a chopping block. He transferred the wedges to a bowl.

Truth be told, Chad couldn't shake the feeling that what he'd heard about Red Sword, Nathan, and Crouton sounded... too good to be true. It gnawed at him—an internal itch for answers.

Chaiyala lifted a box of Coronas from the fridge.

"And it's five forty-five—the meat's on. And, nice! Rhys is here."

Chad looked out the ranch slider to see Crouton, a tall Maori guy about the same build as Crouton sporting a stylish afro, and Rod loading slabs of beef, drumsticks, and ribs onto the enormous barbecues. Chaiyala grabbed a bottle opener, uncapped four beers, and Tim dropped lime wedges into the necks.

Distracted by his thoughts, Chad grabbed a second Corona... then, noticing Chaiyala, reached for a third.

"You okay?" Tim asked. "You thirsty or something?"

"Yeah... I'm fine," Chad muttered.

Tim and Charlotte exchanged a quiet look—agreeing silently to keep a gentle eye on him tonight.

The four stepped onto the deck.

"Aye brother! How was the road trip?" The Maori gentleman greeted Tim warmly—the two embraced. Chad and Charlotte were introduced to Rhys Harvey, dressed in a loose white collared shirt and navy-blue shorts. Tall, athletic, striking—and his bushy hair added to the effect. His distinctly Māori appearance made Chad and Charlotte feel instantly at ease.

Until he spoke—with a thick Scottish accent.

They turned to each other, wide-eyed, as Tim and Rhys laughed.

"Every time," Tim chuckled.

"Those are barbecues?" Chad asked, stunned by the scale.

"Oh wow—those steaks are huge!" Charlotte cried.

"Remember those New York cuts we used to barbecue at Parachute?" Tim reminisced.

"Sure do," she smiled.

"Those were two or three kilos. These beasts?" Tim grinned. "Five."

He led them to the lowest level of the shared terrace where the barbecues smoked away.

Kristie arrived from hers and Rod's house. Rod wrapped his arm around her—they kissed. He introduced her to Chad and Chaiyala. Kristie wore a stylish blue-and-white summer dress, had a tall, elegant build, and long dark auburn hair. She greeted Tim's guests warmly—with hugs and kisses on the cheek.

Charles and Jacqui came next. He introduced his wife Jacqui. She carried the same youthful energy as he did—despite the couple being older than most present, Crouton excluded.

Jacqui welcomed Chad and Charlotte like old friends, curious about their journey.

"Looks like half a cow!" Chad said, eyes wide at the sight of the steaks.

"You want finish it and dessert?" Chaiyala advised "Eat slow—between drinks."

"Wait... can you eat one of those?" Charlotte asked.

"I can."

"Woah, you're doing well!" she said, eyeing Chaiyala's lean, toned stomach.

"I have fast metabolism. Work out often. Sahara heat do rest."

"You're in the same boat, Angel," Tim said. "You burn off a meal in no time."

"That's true." Charlotte nodded. "But if I didn't dance so much... not sure if I could eat a steak that size!" She laughed.

"You'd be mountain biking and rock climbing more," suggested Tim.

"Oh—you climb and mountain bike too?" Chaiyala beamed.

"I love it."

"Chaiyala's an awesome mountain biker—and she loves rock climbing," Tim said to Charlotte. "You two are gonna get on great."

"And dance, also?"

"I do. Love dancing. Been doing that all my life—well, since I wrapped up gymnastics as a kid."

The two women chatted briefly about their histories with gym sports.

"Tim tells me you are a rock star. Yes? That so cool!" Chaiyala complimented.

Charlotte modestly shared that she'd "done a few shows, and I've released two albums with my band. We're like hard rock/metal dance—a four-piece with three dancers. We're currently on a break after touring New Zealand and Australia. And, hopefully I will start writing a third album soon."

Crouton vouched for her talent from the barbecue, encouraging Chad to play one of her tracks over Bluetooth. Charlotte agreed with a smile, and curiosity rippled easily through the group.

Dusk settled in, casting a soft glow across the terraced decks. Citronella torches and braziers flickered as Charlotte's second album played—now on its third track. The atmosphere was vibrant but relaxed: beers, dancing, and a spread of epic food—home-kill steak, pork ribs, chicken—from Rod and Crouton's French visit—and Rhys's pasta, seafood, and garden salads.

Rick arrived with Antonio, followed by more of Tim's friends. New introductions were made, and Chad and Charlotte were soon entertained by Chaiyala and Rick's sharp banter—their trash talk amplified by Corona-fuelled energy. Rick buzzed quickly while Chaiyala stayed just shy of tipsy.

Around ten, Tim dipped a toe into the pool—finally making good on his plan to soak after getting Chad and Charlotte settled.

"Seriously, this thing holds the heat of the day. Might as well be heated."

"You got that right," Chaiyala said, removing her shorts—swimwear underneath—and leaping in.

Tim, Rhys, and Rick ditched their tops and followed suit, one after the other.

Chad and Charlotte headed to their rooms to change.

Rick raised his stubby with a smile and nodded as they returned.

Chad smiled back. Rick had scraggly light-brown hair and big, mischievous eyes like someone perpetually cooking up another joke. He rarely took anything seriously.

"Tim, your girl's gorgeous," Chaiyala whispered, eyes tracking Charlotte's stride. "She has striking Latin beauty."

"Venezuelan," Tim said with a grin. "It's not just the looks—it's the fire, the grace, she's the whole deal." He shot Chaiyala a look. "I'm just trying to keep up... and keep your hands off... Chad's single, though"

"Good," she said, watching Tim's reaction with discrete amusement— he couldn't quite tell what to make of her response.

Charlotte looked skyward through the torchlight. The night sky glittered, constellations rearranged and scattered differently than back home.

"What a beautiful evening," she said, joining Tim and Chaiyala at the end of the pool farthest from the road.

Nearby, Chad, Rick, and Rhys chatted about New Zealand and Australia, swapping stories from home. Crouton and Rod sat quietly two levels up at a wooden table outside Crouton's house. Antonio, not far away, was nodding off.

"Before bed," Tim and Chaiyala had suggested to Chad and Charlotte earlier, "we'll take you up the Sky Hill. It's a little rise tucked in the bush— the highest point in the camp. From the top, you can see the horizon stretch south, east, and west. And the mountains to the north, just beyond the Richat. It's breath-taking at night."

"We hauled a picnic table up there last year," Chaiyala had added. "It's good place for sitting, relaxing... you see everything."

Chad didn't linger in the pool. He excused himself quietly, dried off, dressed, and sat alone at the far end of the top deck's terrace.

Tim noticed and was glad his brother had chosen solitude with others nearby.

Shortly after, Charles joined Chad and offered him another Corona and lime.

"Cheers," Chad said softly.

They looked out together across the lower levels of the terraced deck. The temperature dipped gently into desert stillness.

"Little bit on your mind?" Charles asked, tone gentle.

"Hmm... yeah." Chad admitted, grateful for the quiet company. Charles felt easy to confide in—careful, grounded.

Tim would've been great, but Charles, Rod, and Crouton seemed privy to deeper layers. Of them, Charles felt the most approachable.

"I keep wrestling with the idea that this all seems too perfect," Chad said, voice low and deliberate. "Red Sword Security feels too perfect. I can't think of a single example in history where something like this has worked—or even *could*."

Charles remained silent, listening.

"In my experience," Chad said slowly, "from law school—and even the Bible—I've never seen a time in human history where everything aligned this flawlessly." Saying it aloud cast his thoughts into the courtroom—an untested conclusion, uncertain but firm in his mind.

Charles nodded in silence, letting the notion settle in Chad's mental debating chamber.

"Are you sure?"

"Nope... and that's good." Chad felt a strange but welcome sense of relief.

Charles nodded again, impressed by the young man's thoughtfulness.

"I wonder," he began, "how vast is the scope of your experience and understanding?"

He let the question simmer.

"Thinking, intelligent, reasoning, civilized humanity has existed for— what we now believe—over twelve millennia. And yet the average human lifespan is barely seventy years... maybe a bit more than a hundred. That's what—less than one percent of twelve thousand?" Charles paused, running the numbers mentally.

"Even then," he continued, "we've only had five or six thousand years of recorded history. Passed-down knowledge. And half of that's a jumble—debates, theories, educated guesswork. At best, history and its lessons are hard to preserve in the twisted maze of human nature.

I wonder how often our expectations are capped by our experience and understanding. Regardless of however limited and open-ended they might be."

"Ooh! I like that! That's good!" Chad snapped out of his internal fog, energized by the thought.

"Yes, I thought you might." Charles smiled. "You have an amazing and inspiring mind, son. That's exciting."

"Cheers," Chad said, almost caught off guard. His thinking had cracked open—revealing the genesis of something new.

"Push past what you've seen, stretch beyond what you know, and suddenly the horizon expands. That's faith—not just the spark, but the engine, the scaffolding, and the blueprint. It's the design that makes the journey possible."

From that platform—or in your case, Chad—from that courtroom... may the trial begin."

Chad nodded with quiet understanding.

"So where do we go from here?" Charles continued, adopting Chad's metaphor. "The prosecution argues: 'This all sounds too perfect.' And the defence begins its final address...

Why does it sound too perfect? Why does it *have* to? Consider the parameters: if they're limited to personal experience and understanding, then the findings are confined to those limits.

But once we've looked beyond personal limits—once we've examined the facts, the histories, the evidence outside our own experience—then the foundation is set. The recap is complete. The precedent reviewed. The defence is ready to speak."

Chad nodded once.

"We're standing in a wider frame now—the record stretched, the evidence louder, the story changed. Insight has deepened, new paths have opened, and the future awakens—ready to be rewritten.

So why, when human knowledge is so finite, and the ancient world so vast and unexplored, must what we've seen and heard be dismissed as 'too good to be true,' 'fictitious,' or 'too perfect'?" Charles let that hang.

"Why is the ideal—or near-perfect—deemed unattainable? I don't believe human perfection is completely, and entirely possible... but why not aim for it anyway? Why not come as close as we can? And with careful thought, precision, maybe even divine assistance—who's to say perfection *can't* be achieved?"

Charles paused again.

"So... will your verdict be confined to the limits of your experience and understanding? Or will it reflect a journey beyond those limits—toward a broader, more freeing perspective? One that embraces possibility, unshackled from personal constraint?"

Chad was unexpectedly at peace. "You were a lawyer once, weren't you?"

Charles gave a nod. "Barker and Sons, of London."

Chad knew the firm.

"I won ninety-four cases over twenty-two years. Unfortunately, I regret two-thirds of them. I made compelling legal excuses for the scum of the earth. The remaining third? Half turned out to be vindictive rat bags I wished I'd pawned off on rookies—maybe they'd have lost."

Chad frowned, considering a side of Charles he hadn't expected to glimpse.

"Chad," Charles said gently, "as perfect as Red Sword might seem, each of us—especially those at the top—carry sacks of slain demons. If not that, we've got monkeys on our backs we haven't quite trained to get down and get lost... or figured out how to pit against each other until they kill each other off." He grinned wryly.

Chad's law-student bliss was tempered now by stark reality—Charles' truth.

"I'm happy now—happier than I've ever been in my fifty-two years on this crazy rock," Charles said. "But if Red Sword seems perfect, it's either by God's grace... or because we're just faster runners than our flaws."

They both smiled.

"In all honesty," Charles continued, "as excited as I am about what we're doing here... I'm a recovering racist. A recovering religious bigot. And—on top of that regrettable nonsense—I'm a recovering conspiracy theorist.

Until something changed. Unbelievable encounters. Unexpected events. Over time, Jacqui, Nathan, Crouton, Rick, and Chaiyala, entered my world—and turned it inside out."

"In the space of three months," Charles said, "I turned my back on God, had a nervous breakdown, became an alcoholic, closed the door on my legal career... and then, as the tide turned, I got help, made peace with God, and joined Red Sword.

Most of the others you've met—or will—have their own underdog stories, barrel-bottom moments that changed everything. Except Nathan O'Conner. He's worth watching. Bit of an 'Aslan' figure in this outrageous tale."

"He certainly sounds intriguing." Chad felt there was more on his mind about Nathan, but the words never seemed to come.

"I think you'll really like him. He's looking forward to meeting you and Charlotte."

"So I hear."

"Hmm. You might find him challenging, too," Charles added, raising his eyebrows.

"Right." Chad furrowed his brow.

"Either way," Charles said gently, "I think you'll both be blessed to meet each other... might be quite the gift from above."

Chad narrowed his eyes—unsure if Charles was speaking in riddles.

"Which reminds me—few movements in history were as unexpectedly transformative as the early church.

Despite immense challenges, it spread across the Roman world and reshaped society in ways no one could've imagined. It emerged amid prejudice, oppression, and brutal politics—where populations were wiped out, cities razed, and women and the poor lived without protection. Losing a husband in battle could mean destitution.

Then came the church—with hope, unity, radical social change.

Today, institutions and human rights groups and the UN Security Council aim to uphold justice. Atrocities like the Holocaust still stir global outrage.

But Christianity deeply shaped the moral foundation of the modern world—compassion, dignity, mercy. The love of Christ—radical, sacrificial, inclusive—breathed life into those values. In a world once ruled by might, His love introduced a higher way. It transformed empires. And it still transforms hearts.

Before the coming of Christ and His teachings—civilizations vanished through war and purges—lost to time. Before His rule of compassion rose, the forgotten were abandoned to the gutters.

Rome ruled with force, yet it preserved culture. As the empire began to falter, Constantine embraced Christianity—not just to unify, but to inspire. Its message of justice, peace, and enduring hope reshaped history and echoed far beyond Rome's final days.

Despite persecution, the early church practised radical unity. Believers shared possessions; none went without. Women and children gained rights-unthinkable in that world—greater even than in later Western contexts. In parts of the Middle East, inequality persists today. Back then, it was worse—until Christianity redefined how people lived."

Charles paused.

"Too good to be true? Maybe. But the record speaks for itself. It *was* real. Resilient. Transformative. As true as the one who began it."

"You certainly know your stuff—and the way you've presented it definitely helps put a few things in perspective." Chad said, impressed.

"Wonderful, Chad. I've spent many evenings around the brazier with your brother, Rod, Crouton—and Nathan, when he's here. The conversations run deep. They leave you filled with wonder for the universe. Hungry for understanding."

Chad nodded, lighter and clearer.

"Thanks, Charles. Fully appreciate it." He sat straighter now—energized, encouraged, free to imagine how things might unfold without needing to worry.

"You're very welcome, Chad. Your brother brought you here to experience it all. So, sit back—and enjoy this new world." Charles grinned, glowing with enthusiasm.

Rhys picked up his guitar, strumming softly into the night.

It was 11:30 p.m. and Chad was surprised he was still awake.

He downed a litre of water and found Tim and Charlotte—who hadn't called it a night. For them, it was the excitement of simply being together again.

Chad figured, as did Chaiyala, they'd likely be up till the wee hours regardless of the day's events—and probably sleep late tomorrow.

"... no, you won't!" Chaiyala snapped at Rick, who was grinning like an idiot as Chad stepped into the room.

"Yes, I will! You'll enjoy it too. Ooh, just like old times, baby—and then we can do it all over again."

Chad had no clue what they were arguing about.

Tim and Charlotte were locked in an embrace across the counter, oblivious to Rick and Chaiyala's antics.

"I do your face in again," she growled, "and *then* you see if you enjoy that!"

"Hey," Tim called out, catching Chad stepping down into the living area. "Shall we head up to the Sky Hill?"

"Yes—keen," Chaiyala said, abandoning thoughts of Rick's demise.

Rick agreed, went along—he rarely found anything boring.

Charlotte was keen. Chad was open to something interesting—his thoughts of turning in disappeared at the thought of the view Tim has described earlier.

Tim led the way, hand in hand with Charlotte, guiding the group with a flashlight through a narrow gap past Charles and Jacqui's house. Chaiyala followed, Chad and Rick bringing up the rear with a flashlight.

They navigated dusty bends, winding around rocks, palms, and shrubs, until they reached the summit—a flat clearing with a wooden picnic table at its centre. A lone palm stood beside it, marking the trail's end. Beyond, the hillside dropped steeply into shadow.

"Welcome to Sky Hill," Tim said to Charlotte and Chad.

Chaiyala hopped onto the table, leaned against the trunk, and tied her hair into a ponytail.

Rick sat at the opposite end, he and Tim switching off their torches.

The five of them scanned the dark horizon—an awe-inspiring 360-degree view beneath a canopy of stars, palm leaves silhouetted above them.

"This is beautiful," Charlotte said, beaming as Tim wrapped his arms around her from behind.

"It's pretty amazing," Rick agreed.

Tim and Chaiyala were first to notice a faint glow—thin as a cord—on the southeast horizon. It pulsed low and dull at first, then they were drawn upward by the star-speckled sky.

The glow intensified.

"What is that?" Charlotte asked.

It looked big. Significant. Nobody was quite sure.

A fiery orange began to emerge above the horizon, carrying a quiet sense of mystique.

"Wow... that's the moon!" Tim said, as intrigue gave way to awe.

"It's enormous!" Chad exclaimed.

"Ah yes—full moon tonight," Chaiyala remembered, having seen it marked on a calendar earlier.

"Whoa... so cool," Charlotte whispered.

Chad was amazed—and puzzled by its massive size. He recalled seeing the moon appear twice as large back home, and wondered about it again.

"It's just on the horizon it appears much larger," Chaiyala explained. "Watch—it shrinks as it rises. It's an optical illusion. Known since ancient times by many cultures. But the cause? Still a mystery. Still debated."

CHAPTER 7

C had slept like a log, barely remembering going to bed—let alone resting his head on the pillow. He woke at around half ten the next morning.

Tim and Charlotte had drifted off in each other's arms after hours of catching up, despite months of constant calls and video chats. Rising early, they headed to the Richat Bar and Grill for breakfast. The place had a relaxed indigenous African vibe—exotic, yet cosy.

"This place is lovely, babe," Charlotte said appreciatively to Tim.

"It's neat, eh? Right in the thick of the action and crowds—and yet there's something about this spot that's... calming. It's like this paradox. You're appreciating the distance," he glanced toward the mountains beyond the Richat on the horizon, "the sheer scale of it all, and still being part of it."

Charlotte smiled, leaned into Tim, and rested her head on his shoulder. They took in the view before sitting down.

A waiter handed them menus. They browsed the options.

"The French toast always reminds me of our first date," Tim said, grinning.

"I know! Same! That little café on Mount Eden Road."

"That was such the best day."

"So special."

They set their menus down and took each other's hands.

The waiter returned, and they both said, "The French toast, please," in unison—then laughed.

"Sure," the waiter smiled, amused, and disappeared into the kitchen.

When their breakfasts arrived, they thanked the waiter, bowed their heads to bless the food, and spent the next hour chatting about life back home in New Zealand—Tim's work, the friends he'd made at the project, and the success of Charlotte's recent tour across Australasia. Most of all, they savoured finally being together again.

~~~~~~~

Chad reached the entrance to the kitchen, dining, and living area, standing at the top of three steps from the passage. He spotted Rick on one side of the island bench with an excessively cheeky grin, and Chaiyala on the other side, looking like she was contemplating murder—ready to leap over the bench and tackle him.

"Good—morning—what'd I miss?"

"Rick is about to get his butt whooped! Happens many times."

Chad laughed.

"I'm playing hard to get," Rick said, hands splayed in mock surrender. "She wants me so bad, and I want her—but where's the fun in making it too easy, right?"

Chaiyala sighed and refused to give him the satisfaction. She turned to Chad with a calm, unaffected smile.

"Good morning," she greeted. "I put a hurt on him later—when I feel like it."

Chad laughed again. "You guys remind me of some friends back home."

"Really? She already kill him, no?" Chaiyala asked with a smile.

"Nah. They just mess around. He cracks all the smart-aleck jokes, she makes all the threats, and they're a great couple at the end of the day."

"Ah... Rick and I—we are not. Definitely not..." Chaiyala began slowly, shaking her head.

"Sounds exactly like us, honeybunch!" Rick cut in, grinning with infuriating cheer.

She despised how he called her 'honeybunch', but she'd grown annoyingly accustomed to it—much to her displeasure.

Chaiyala snarled as she tensed again.

"What did you do?" Chad asked Rick between laughter.

"This is the point where we gotta get outta the way and run," Rick joked, grinning. "She's about to go postal!"

"Is homicide a crime in New Zealand?" she asked with a casual bite, her Israeli accent cutting through the syllables like dry heat.

"Yeah, pretty sure it's still frowned upon—legally—and morally." He grinned.

"Damn it." She narrowed her eyes menacingly at Rick. Then turned to Chad. "You sleep alright?"

"Slept great—really awesome. Dun'even remember hitting the sack, to be honest."

Chaiyala frowned, puzzled by the phrase.

"'Hit the sack' means 'go to bed,' ya sack," Rick explained, doing his best to wind her up.

She wouldn't give him the pleasure. Instead, she stared at him blankly—expressionless in that spooky way he hated—and asked, "I kick you in the sack, yes?"

Chad shook his head, laughing.

"Oh, I know you want that," Rick teased. "But let's keep it to the bedroom, honeybunch!"

"Damn!" Chad laughed harder.

Chaiyala glanced at Chad pleadingly, "You see what I have to deal with?"

She turned to Rick, "You want I drop you—like sack of potatoes? I do it now."

Chad frowned thoughtfully. Minus the accent, it sounded suspiciously like a Tim-ism.

"Pleasure me, baby," Rick replied with an infuriating grin.

"Dude, you know I beat you." Chaiyala threatened, raising her right arm, flexing.

"Wow... that's so hot," he drawled in sarcastic monotone.

"I put you in headlock—you scream like little girl, yes?" she countered, trying hard not to smile.

"I wouldn't mess with her," Chad chimed in, grinning.

"You see? Man with brain." She caved to a grin. "You can learn something—not be annoying boy."

"You love it!" Rick insisted, to Chad's amusement and Chaiyala's ongoing tedium. He leaned back on the sofa, hands behind his head, closing his eyes.

"I hear you're a ninja," Chad said, grabbing his water bottle from the fridge.

"That's the *only* way she can beat me!" Rick sat up dramatically to plead his case. "She cheats."

"You mean she can actually beat you up?"

"I can," Chaiyala said with a smug smile aimed at Rick.

"She comes outta nowhere using those cheating ninja moves—gets me when I'm not ready!"

"Not my fault you slow," she dismissed.

Chad had been laughing for the past few minutes, it almost hurt.

"Chad, you are hungry, yes? Come—I take you to market for breakfast." Chaiyala suggested. Then, before he could answer, added, "Actually, yes. You are."

She wasn't wrong. He agreed without protest.

"Otherwise I'm gonna drown this toad in the pool," she grimaced at Rick.

"Then you can come back and do the housework... housewife." Rick stirred, he couldn't help but laugh. Chad laughed again as Chaiyala threatened to put Rick in a little dress and hurt him, then left through the ranch slider. "Catch you up later," he said, following her.

Rick raised his eyebrows and said, "See ya later, man," still chuckling to himself over the exchange.

They walked down the terraced decks toward the main road leading to the camp's centre, where the village marketplace and eatery buzzed with activity. Chad had learned—no jeans in the Sahara—and dressed accordingly: white singlet, matching O'Neill bucket hat, and smoky blue cargo pants.

Chaiyala wore a pink sleeveless hoodie and white denim shorts—a look that momentarily unsettled Chad, stirring memories of Sonia. Yet Charlotte dressed similarly without issue. Neither she nor Chaiyala were Sonia... and Chaiyala wasn't seeking attention. Was she? He caught himself. That was a baseless assumption. He barely knew her. Besides, in this heat, minimal clothing was more practical than anything.

"He's one hang of a cheeky beggar—Rick," Chad remarked.

"Complete dork, he is. Smart aleck like no other."

"Was there ever any... like..."

"Oh no! Definitely not." She laughed, immediately dismissing the idea. "He be dead already—and I be gone from prison, broken out, living in mountains."

Chad laughed.

"Okay, maybe not quite like that. But no, never in million years, yes? He is so infuriating. With him—it's wrong thing. Totally."

"So—does he have a thing for you?"

"Yes, yes—then no. Who even knows?" She shook her head. "Either way, he's a total moron with this. I tell him no—many times. Maybe he stop now? So, he torture me with this boyish, dorky... Rickish thing he does."

"He's a stereotypical guy, then." Chad laughed.

"Yes, yes—he's funny. Too much." She glanced at Chad. "You never tell him I said this, okay?"

"Hey, you know I won't mess with you."

She gave him a wry smile.

"You guys are friends all the same?"

Chaiyala sighed. "Yes. He's funny... occasionally. Often. But mostly he makes my blood boil." Her voice softened. "We are friends... many years now." Her words held weight—half history, half surrender.

"And you beat him up."

"Yes, I do. Not seriously. He laugh too much. Then I get serious—and he tap."

"Tough girl, eh?"

"I am. I must be. Not because of Rick—he is harmless. Silly boy. No... I have lost too much. Too many things happen..."

"Good morning, you two!" Tim called out, unaware of his interrupting. He and Charlotte were walking hand-in-hand toward the café in the middle of the market.

"Heya!" Chaiyala greeted.

"Hey, man. How are you guys?"

"Good. We've just come from the bar and grill," Tim said.

"Tim took me out for breakfast," Charlotte beamed.

"Cute," Chaiyala smiled warmly.

"Where are you guys headed?" Tim asked.

"We get breakfast. Need break from Rick—he doing my head in."

"As always," Tim laughed.

Chaiyala shook her head.

Tim and Charlotte grabbed iced chocolates and planned to enjoy them under the shade of the marquee stretching down the middle of the eatery. They invited Chad and Chaiyala to join them after they'd settled on something.

Chad ordered a huge breakfast roll—upon Chaiyala's recommendation.

She picked up a tropical fruit smoothie. Earlier, she'd demolished a huge bowl of Nutri-Grain, a cereal she'd become hooked on after meeting Tim, Rod, Kristie, and Rick. It was one of several things she was glad to have inherited from Kiwis and Aussies.

They joined the others beneath the café marquee, close to one of the cold-air generators humming gently nearby.

"That looks beast!" Charlotte said, eyeing the size of Chad's breakfast.

"Those are so good," Tim nodded.

"It's a 'Big Breakfast Roll,'" Chad said between bites. "Bacon, scrambled eggs, chorizo, hash brown, and hollandaise sauce."

"Not good for abs... unless you work hard day. Or run after, maybe." Chaiyala suggested with a smirk. "But actually? Always very good."

"Hmm," Charlotte mused, feeling the heat spilling in from the marquee's sides. "I think I'll go for a run in the cool of the evening."

"Wise, yes? Full sun run—crazy." Chaiyala agreed. "Here, sport is indoors or evening."

"Do you ever run in the heat, though?" Chad asked.

"Yes."

"'Cos Chaiyala's hardcore. Action woman," Tim joked.

"I was going to say... suffered, yes? Should have brought water. Stupid."

Chad swallowed the last bite, satisfied. His mind drifted back to yesterday—staggering beauty, mysterious relics, and discoveries that seemed to whisper through time. He knew exactly where he was and who he was with, yet today felt strangely ordinary. Only the camp's lingering quiet reminded him it wasn't all a dream.

He turned over the shifting dynamics in his mind—how they made him think differently, feel differently, see differently. Relaxing with friends, he and his brother shared jokes over food and entertaining topics that had nothing to do with anything they'd witnessed and heard over the past twenty-four hours.

A breath of calm before Atlantis breaks open the world's deepest secrets.

"What is this? How did I get here, of all places?" A rush of concepts—huge ones. Not just a paradigm shift, but something far more disruptive. *"What the heck do I even do with all this?"*

Tim had spent months adjusting—getting familiar with lost civilizations, abstract ideas, and ongoing debates like the recent discoveries in ancient Corinth in Turkey. This was his dream. His domain. His new reality.

Chad knew his brother had mastered the art of compartmentalization—keeping life's pieces in their places to avoid overlap or stress. Charlotte, meanwhile, had gradually accepted the strangeness through months of calls and video chats. But seeing it first-hand? That was different. This was mind-blowing.

Chad's experience was starkly different—an isolated life dropped into epic immersion. It still felt like he was wandering through someone else's dream.

A Red Sword agent had struck up conversation with Tim and Chaiyala while Chad stared into space.

"You okay, man?" Charlotte asked gently.

"Yeah…" he replied, his mind was elsewhere—suddenly preoccupied by two Greek men who'd been dead for about two and a half thousand years. Plato and Solon—he needed to know more.

What struck Chad most was how nearly everything he'd seen over the past forty-eight hours—combined with the staggering organisation, preparation, and fervour of Crouton, Charles, and Red Sword Security—seemed geared toward proving one thing: that the Richat Structure was, in fact, the lost city of Atlantis.

Short of definitive proof, Chad was hard-pressed to see how it could be anything else.

The sheer scale of the unearthed structure he'd been privileged to enter alongside his brother and the others the previous day was hard to get past.

The Richat's design mirrored Plato's description, and the debate surrounding it ran deep.

He had to build a clear picture—from ancient history to modern digs, and most of all, Plato's dialogues.

He was impressed—stunned, even—by the strength of the case now laid before him. What he couldn't reconcile was the fact that conventional history dismissed Atlantis as pure myth. That there were those actively working to prevent serious excavation of the Richat, to shut down any attempt to investigate it as Atlantis.

Why?

He needed to know everything.

"I might go for a walk," he said to Charlotte. "Get some time to myself, maybe."

The Red Sword agent'd moved on.

Tim nodded. "Yeah, all good, man. I'll catch you later?"

"Sweet."

Charlotte smiled at him as he headed off toward the events field.

"Thank you," he smiled at Chaiyala with gratitude for the company and breakfast suggestion.

She returned the sentiment with a warm smile-come-smirk. Her eyes conveying just enough to suggest she wasn't finished getting to know him—the moment had been paused, would be later revisited.

~~~~~~~

Plato, the Greek philosopher, was born around 428/427 BC into an aristocratic Athenian family. His father, Ariston, carried noble lineage. His mother, Perictione, was connected to influential Athenian circles. Details of his early life remain uncertain, but his writings profoundly shaped Western thought—especially politics, justice, and social structure.

His ideas, along with those of Socrates and Aristotle, became the backbone of Greek philosophy. Their influence extended through the Alexandrian and Ptolemaic empires. Later, Rome integrated much of Greek philosophy, and after its fall, those foundations shaped the intellectual evolution of Europe—impacting empires like the French, German, Dutch, and British.

During his law studies, Chad had briefly encountered Plato's 'Critias' and 'Timaeus', but never explored their depictions of Atlantis in depth. Tim had mentioned them before, sparking casual curiosity. But now—as Chad walked the ridge bordering the camp's bustling village marketplace— the relevance struck entirely different.

'Funny, the things you never really think about when they're right in front of you... until you're given reason to consider them properly. Then they demand all your attention,' he thought.

Seeking relief from the heat, Chad ducked into the community centre, passing the gym and cinema. He walked by the shops and made his way to the visitor's centre, drawn back to the ancient texts, hoping to reconcile them with the compelling evidence he'd seen—and was still seeing.

A flat-screen played the documentary Tim had mentioned. It followed some of the first explorers to seriously investigate the theory that Richat Structure might be the lost location of Atlantis.

Nearby, sat a detailed display of history, geology, and science from the Richat region, all connected to the enduring mystery of Atlantis.

Chad immersed himself in books. He delved into the region's history—getting lost down rabbit holes on a literary adventure. He wanted to investigate as much as he could.

Eventually he got hungry and helped himself to snacks, fruit and juice from the table near the entrance to the larger lounge area.

What caught Chad's eye were the large Perspex-encased prints of Plato's 'Critias' and 'Timaeus', arranged like the Treaty of Waitangi exhibit at Te Papa museum in Wellington.

Skim-reading, as he often did, Chad bypassed the verbose intro and honed in on the sections describing Atlantis's war with Athens, dated 12,000 years ago.

The dialogue described how the gods divided the earth among themselves. Though long-winded, Chad appreciated the philosophers' precision—their structured clarity.

He read for hours, immersed in Atlantis's intricate layout, pausing whenever a piece clicked into place. Something had begun to stir. He pulled out his phone and started making notes—pieces of a puzzle long dormant, suddenly alive with relevance. The mystery had weight now. And perhaps... answers.

- At the heart of Atlantis lay three concentric rings of land and four of water, forming a perfectly symmetrical city spanning roughly twenty-three kilometres in diameter.
- The central acropolis, sparsely populated, was encircled by towering walls atop cliffs dropping into the first water ring. Here stood the royal palace, the temple of Poseidon, and his legendary gardens. Two springs—one hot, one cold—bubbled from the centre, supplying the royal elite and the city at large.
- The second ring housed a large priesthood, tending to Atlantis's religious and spiritual life.
- The third ring served as the military and naval hub, with 1,200 warships moored in underground docks. It reportedly accommodated over 240,000 soldiers and sailors, along with weapons, provisions, and war machines. A circular thoroughfare cut through this ring— used for troop movement and horse racing, which drew spectators from across the empire.
- Beyond the military district lay the city's largest harbour, a bustling merchant precinct where boats and ships transported passengers and goods. Causeways spanned the harbours, linking each ring of land.
- Atlantis stretched fifteen kilometres past the outer water ring, surrounded by a perimeter wall. The area between the harbour and the city's edge was packed with homes and buildings—probably a mix of downtown and suburbs, with over a million people living there.

To the south, the city faced the open ocean, which fed into the outermost ring. To the north, towering mountains sheltered Atlantis, with rivers and waterfalls cascading down their slopes.

"The country immediately surrounding the city of Atlantis was a level plain, itself surrounded by mountains which descended toward the sea."—Plato

Chad replayed the helicopter ride in his mind. Everything surrounding the Richat Structure matched Plato's words—a level plain, or what remained of it after the destruction. And, encircled by mountains to the north. Goosebumps. The Richat had three major circles of raised hills, with valleys between, before the land climbed again into mountain foothills.

Something jarred him. A law-student's instinct. A contradiction:

"Atlantis is supposed to be myth... legend. But none of this reads like a myth..." he realized. He had expected tales—narratives, not architectural schematics. "This reads more like a city profile. A list of features... almost factual?"

Suddenly, cracks appeared in the traditional narrative. He needed to find out why. He'd have to quiz Tim—or Charles—on why Plato's texts are considered mythology when they lack the archetypal structure and flourish of myth.

He read on.

"The stone which they quarried was white, another black and a third, red. The main city was constructed with red, black and white rocks."—Plato

Chad sat back. He remembered the dig site—stones piled everywhere: red, white, black. The large building they'd explored? Constructed entirely from those same stones.

"That's very interesting," he muttered. "...they've discovered Atlantis."

Only now was it starting to settle—how slowly his mind had been working through the weight of it all.

"There was an abundance of metals—copper and gold."—Plato

Chad was sure Tim—or maybe something he'd read—had mentioned Mauritania's primary exports: iron ore, gold, and copper.

"Funny, that," he smirked.

He reread the text, focusing now on the Atlantean royal family—how Poseidon had fallen for Cleito and raised five sets of twins. Each would rule one of ten kingdoms across the empire.

Chad leaned back again, diving deeper.

"There's that 'gods interacting with humans' thing," he mused, "as if they weren't too different from us."

But what *were* they?

Spiritual entities? Angelic beings? Or some kind of human no longer around?

He recalled past conversations with Tim. They'd both pondered similar questions.

Some theories suggested the gods might be extra-terrestrial—beings from other planets. Chad didn't want to jump to that. But he couldn't discount it without proper exploration.

His Christian tradition offered another angle. Maybe they were angels. Or spiritual figures—described in ways that varied through time and culture.

Either way, something was beginning to shift in Chad's thinking—and it was tied not just to discovery, but to identity.

Chad paid close attention to Plato's remarks about the Atlanteans. They were advanced in thought, technology, architecture and art. This, he suspected, was what led scholars—without hard evidence—to assume Plato's account, myth. A utopian ideal, invented to inspire his contemporaries. *"But what's the point in the specific details—measurements etc.—what's so inspirational about all that?"* he thought.

"Well, that's all good and well as a theory," Chad muttered aloud, "but where's the solid evidence to back that up?" He read on. Plato here is recording a dialogue of **"a tale which, though strange, is certainly true. It was attested by Solon, who was the wisest of the seven sages."—Plato.**

Chad recalled Tim's frustration with sceptics. When people fixated on single details while dismissing the broader evidence pointing to the Richat Structure being the location of the lost city of Atlantis.

"How can anyone call this a myth when Plato explicitly states it as truth?" Chad shook his head. He reflected on how easily people overlook critical details lost in narrow debates—missing the forest for the trees.

He spent the rest of the day combing through the visitor centre's library, studying everything he could get his hands on and his mind around. This was structured detail—key factors and information—not just storytelling.

He wrestled with the paradox: Plato explicitly framed the tale of Atlantis as true, reportedly passed down from Solon—yet history had largely filed it under mythology. Why?

"Because the idea of Atlantis as myth is a flaky theory that hasn't been thought through correctly," Chad told himself. "In fact, I don't even think this has been thought about at all. But why? And when did the concept of Atlantis become myth? Again—why? For what reason?"

Big questions. Hypotheses born of gut instinct.

He had a sense that Crouton, Nathan and previous explorers and researchers had already opened that particular can of worms—flipped the lid into the bin. The worms, no longer hiding, were smiling eagerly at passers-by. Demanding answers. Big questions. Real ones.

"The quality of the questions you ask determines the quality of the answers you get."—Derek Arden

Until recently, Chad had thought the questions about Atlantis were pretty poor—had any real ones even been asked? Perhaps they had, and the answers were inconvenient, so their recipients chose to treat Atlantis as fiction, reshaping history to reflect that view. Or maybe the answers were simply too old, lost over time—especially given the circumstances already mentioned.

He focused on the Exploring Atlantis documentary. It had sparked more interest in Atlantis than anything else in recent years—especially the theory that the Richat Structure might be its real location.

Chad finished the documentary in stunned silence.

It covered the basics: Atlantis, the Richat, the evolving theories—things he was now becoming familiar with. But it raised two new ideas that struck him deeply.

The first: how history, over time, becomes legend—and legend becomes myth.

What if, in ancient times, mythology didn't exist—not categorised as fiction—but only what is, or what was? What if what we now call myth was simply historical account, without any intent of fiction? When did fiction become a thing?"

The second: If an entire civilization were wiped out completely... how would anyone in the future ever know it existed?

In Atlantis's case, Egypt may have once been a colony—and that's why records remained, buried in archives at the temple in the city of Sais, known to Plato and Solon.

The documentary engaged and challenged Chad. It wasn't a court case—but it built one. A case for Atlantis's factual existence. Or what remains of it. It exposed research gaps and flawed questioning.

"Ahh," Chad sighed. "That's the thing!"

Chad understood that scientists, like lawyers, chase truth. But lawyers face moral trials—truth tangled with motive and consequence. Good lawyers uphold integrity, wrestling with human nature's darker undercurrents. Scientists, by comparison, tend to walk a cleaner line: the evidence either exists or it doesn't. Until proof arrives, a theory remains a theory.

Within the Richat Project, archaeologists, geologists, and Tim's team were working to tell Atlantis's 'real' story. But Chad had seen it before—in law. Some scientists were pressured, paid, or manipulated to distort facts. Truth pushed into the realm of fantasywhere questions weren't asked—and real answers went begging.

Neither Crouton, Charles, nor Red Sword Security entertained conspiracy theories. Least of all Tim—a historian who longed for a time when truth mattered more than life itself. Not that Tim would sacrifice lives for accuracy—but he loathed modern assumptions that Plato's era thought like the twenty-first century.

Chad snapped back when his phone buzzed. It was Tim.

"Howzit?" Chad answered.

"Yeah good. Good day? Where you at?"

"Great thanks. At the visitor's centre. Been researching Plato."

He heard Tim relay that to the others, like someone had just won a bet.

Tim laughed, then said, "We're firin' up the barby if you're keen for a feed. You've been gone most of the day!"

"Yeah… sorry. I got deep into this whole Atlantis/Richat structure thing. Been reading—trying to wrap my head around it. You know me," he laughed, "I can spend all day in a library and forget the world exists."

They both laughed.

"Anyway, I'm about done. I'll see you shortly."

"See ya soon then."

CHAPTER 8

Tim, Rick, and Rhys were already in the pool, when Chad returned to their accommodation. Charlotte and Chaiyala were soaking up the last warmth of the sun on deck loungers, while Rod and Crouton tended to the grill, beers in hand, sharing laughter.

"Chad!" Tim called.

"Hey, hey! The scholar returns!" Rick shouted, raising his drink.

Chad grinned. "I'll grab a towel and join you guys."

"There's your competition, Rick. What do ya think?" Chad heard Chaiyala tease.

"I don't have competition—what's the point in that?" Rick scoffed, frowning, absurdity thick in his voice. Laughter followed.

Chad smiled, shaking his head. These two were a handful. Mental note: stay clear of entanglements.

He tossed his singlet and towel onto the table, flicked his jandals underneath, and jumped into the pool—a blissful reprieve from desert heat.

"Busy day?" Tim asked.

"Yup. Been diving into Plato's account of Atlantis—from a legal perspective."

"Interesting," Tim replied, brow raised.

Rod and Crouton glanced over, nodding. Making notes—both of them in agreement Chad'd be one to watch.

"Ah, Plato," Rick blurted, "the Greek bloke responsible for all this crazy," gesturing with his beer. "Gone... long time ago."

Rod passed Chad a drink.

"Cheers."

"Good bloke, Plato. Great cook too, apparently!"

"What?" Tim frowned.

"True story," Rick nodded, a tipsy grin betraying the tale.

"How much have you had?" Rhys asked, thick Scottish accent in tow.

"Yeah, sure," Tim said. "And Chaiyala's gonna have your babies."

"What?" came the protest from the loungers.

"Make my day honeybunch!" Rick stirred.

"I make you tasty knuckle sandwich, yes?"

Laughter rippled across the deck.

"I've got questions about the 'myth' around Atlantis..." Chad began.

"Fire away."

"Plato insists it was real—straight from Solon's account. Why do historians still call it a myth?"

"Originally the word myth," Tim explained, "which comes from the Greek word 'mythos' simply meant 'story' or 'record', not fiction as it is known, now, in the twenty-first century."

Chad got goose bumps. He nodded, "exactly along the lines I was thinking as I researched." He paused, "then, originally, myth was actually history."

"In a sense, yes," agreed Tim.

"Talk about lost in translation," Charlotte reflected, thoughtfully.

"By Plato's time, mythos was still respected—but logos, meaning reason and logic, was gaining ground. Mythos became seen as less rational, though still meaningful. No other ancient scholar mentioned Atlantis, so lacking parallels, it was downgraded to 'myth'—a term that, over time, became synonymous with fiction and falsehood.

After Plato, Aristotle didn't touch it. The Romans brushed it aside. Renaissance thinkers brought it back, but by then, scholars had shifted toward archaeology and source-based history. The 'myth' label stuck."

"Wow... that's how it became fiction," Charlotte felt satisfyingly enlightened. She hadn't thought about it like that before. And now, somehow, she'd been handed a surprisingly complete answer to a question she never asked.

"So, the truth about Atlantis was shelved in the wrong part of history's library—until now," reflected Chad.

Tim leaned back. "Yeah that'd be about the size of it."

Chad smiled. "Explains why the wrong questions have been asked for so long."

"Exactly."

As Charlotte and Chaiyala climbed into the pool, Chad found himself admiring Chaiyala more than he intended, an unanticipated cheer and calm—happy she was there—it surprised him. Tim and Charlotte noticed. No one else did.

The girls had just finished doing their hair, weaving long French braids with practised ease. Chad had to admit—Chaiyala might be hard to resist. His better judgement hoped it wouldn't become an issue. He sighed, muttering to himself, "More steak, less beer."

"Yeah," Tim said, grinning over his drink. "Dinner shouldn't be far off."

Charlotte leaned against the side of the pool, smiling at Chad. They exchanged a few words, quiet and warm.

"So anyway," Tim began once the others were caught up in separate conversations, "tell us more about the house Mum and Dad bought with Uncle Conner."

Chad filled them in—he'd decided to accept. He spoke about Emma's drama and how eager a change.

Soon, Charlotte and Chaiyala climbed out of the pool, wrapped in towels, heading inside to grab plates, cutlery, and condiments. Chad and Tim joined them, the four friends prepping dinner and chatting about siblings back home. Tim asked about their sister, Celesta.

"She's a riot," Chad said with a grin. "Smart, hilarious... and surprisingly grounding on rough days."

"She's got a good heart, our little sis."

"She does. Full-on with studies though."

"What she study?" Chaiyala asked.

"Journalism," Chad replied.

"Still fed up with the circus that comes with that?" Tim quipped. Cynical as he could be about modern news, he spent more time focused on what mattered than what frustrated him.

Chad chuckled. "As much as you are with historical ignorance."

"Good on her. She'll do well—she knows the value of real investigation. Knows the difference between digging for truth and chasing ratings." Tim nodded.

"How old, Celesta is?" Chaiyala asked.

"Almost twenty-one," Tim answered. He was set on making it back to New Zealand for her birthday—no matter what.

"Oh, I loved that age," Chaiyala said, her accent rounding the vowels into something soft and nostalgic. Her cheer trailed off, caught mid-sentence by a memory she hadn't invited.

Chad, and Charlotte—particularly—both noticed the shift. She clocked it and quietly vowed to check in with her later.

"She's writing when she can," Chad added. "Otherwise buried under the study pile."

"Still working on 'Alexa the Adventurer'?" Tim asked.

"Yep. It's solid stuff—great read! Girl's got talent."

"She sent me some of it," Tim recalled. "I need to catch up on those emails."

"She's gifted," Charlotte added. "Her stories are so vivid."

"That's awesome!" Chaiyala said—genuinely excited to meet Celesta.

"Still leading youth at church?" Tim asked.

"She is—mentoring a half-dozen kids. Loves it."

"Sounds like she's doing great."

"She is," Chad nodded, grateful—for the blessing, chaos and fun of family, and the grace that kept them close.

Kristie arrived with Charles and Jacqui, plus a few others Chad and Charlotte hadn't met yet. Two were Tim's colleagues, the rest friends of Rod and Crouton.

Rod greeted Kristie with a kiss and wrapped an arm around her. With Charlotte and Chaiyala's help, Rod and Crouton laid out platters of grilled meat down the length of three adjoined wooden tables.

Chad and Tim tucked into slabs of sirloin and ribs alongside mouth-watering salads, while Chad continued to fill Tim in on New Zealand life and got to know Tim's team.

Charlotte and Chaiyala broke from the group and sat talking alone. Charlotte shared how her family had migrated from Venezuela to New Zealand when she was seven, about her music career and her family living in Auckland.

Chaiyala's story, though, had very different beginnings.

"I was born into endless feud," she said softly. "Neighbours always in old war. My mother and father—they were police. My brother, he still is."

Charlotte tilted her head at 'were' and 'is.'

"My father was killed first—terrorists," she said plainly. "My mother... captured. Tortured. Raped. Killed."

Charlotte froze. Her fork lowered. Her eyes searched Chaiyala's face, finding distance and the discipline of composure.

"I'm so sorry. That's—dreadful."

"Don't be sorry. Yes, it's dreadful. They should be sorry. What the tabloids say, what the news shows—it's distortion. Our enemy hides behind lies. They kill their own and blame my people."

Anger shimmered beneath her words. But it was contained.

"Media lies. The world's friends—they shake hands with shadows. Israel stands alone more often than it should. We have, America, some others. But how long they stay?"

She looked to Tim and Charlotte. "Evangelical church—our strongest ally. Politics, weapons—never enough. What we need is miracle. Your faith—this is where it works. I believe in God. For hope. And for vengeance."

Her eyes locked with Charlotte's—fierce, honest, exhausted.

Chad and the others had re-joined the girls' conversation around the table. At the far end, Jacqui and Kristie chatted about other things. Those near Chaiyala leaned in—drawn by quiet gravity.

Rod, Crouton, and Tim were already familiar with her story. Chad and Charlotte were just beginning to grasp its weight.

"Everything I do—survival, preservation," Chaiyala said. "Is miracle my brother and I still alive. At least dozen times, we should not make it. But... we did. For that—I thank God."

She looked down, voice steady.

"I didn't care about God before—or religious things. My brother and I, we didn't follow old customs. Not like our parents, not like grandparents. But now..." she paused. "I don't know how we survived when they didn't. Must be help... from somewhere. I hope God will avenge our enemies— like He did, long ago. Hatred—I run from it every day. I fight it. In here," she tapped her chest, "and here," pointing to her head.

Silence held the space. Every word. Every pause. Fully felt.

"Hope and hate—they don't live together forever." Her voice dropped. "Some days, I feed anger. Some days... hope."

Crouton looked out over the pool. "Reckon you're getting better at feeding the latter, my girl," he said, flat and sincere. He turned back to her and smiled.

"Agreed," Tim added warmly.

"This is why I am tough girl, Chad." She said, looking his way—revisiting an unfinished conversation. "I must be. Life shaped me this way. I may look strong—pretty even—but I am who Hashem (*Hebrew—God*) made me. Who world made me become."

Rick nodded. He'd heard her story before. He always listened with the same quiet respect. Tonight, was no exception.

"Rick and me, we joke," Chaiyala said, a smile tugging. "We never actually hate. He drives me mad. I drive him crazy. But we mess around and forget what doesn't matter—and hold tight to what does."

Rick smiled.

"What matters most to you?" Chad asked gently.

"Friendship. Fun." She smiled, nodding toward Tim, Rhys, and Rick. "Loyalty. Family." Her gaze swept to Crouton. "Staying alive. Fighting for every good thing—what's worth living for, enjoying. And fighting off anything that tries to take it."

Chad nodded. As did others. A pause settled over the gathering.

Eventually, Chad looked up and spoke, "Thank you, for sharing your story." He paused, "Life throws hardship our way. You do what you must to survive those seasons. But it also highlights the value of joy, greatness, even happiness."

They shared a smile.

He placed a hand on Tim's shoulder. "If my brother hadn't dragged me into this wild adventure in some forgotten corner of the world, I'd never have met everyone here."

He raised his drink. "Cheers—to each of you, for being here, for being who you are. And to you, Chaiyala—for being strong and beautiful when it mattered... and still does, no matter what. Because here we are—laughing, sharing good food, and holding onto each other."

"Aww... thank you, Chad," Chaiyala said softly. "I appreciate that."

Crouton sat forward, "I think you'll find most of us—everyone here on the project—were somehow invited, roped-in, hand-picked. Often, it had little to do with Nathan or me. It's the strangest thing—coincidence, fate, divine will? There's always a story to how we all wound up here."

He stroked his long beard, glancing toward Rod and Charles, who nodded.

"Not always dramatic," Crouton added. "But always interesting. What an incredible thought—thousands of stories converging, intersecting... here."

"That's a crazy one to think on," Tim remarked softly.

"Dat's deep, boss. Real deep," Rick grinned, still very much tipsy. He grinned then laughed stupidly—no longer able to hold it in.

Rhys and Chaiyala frowned at him.

"Rick's had far too much to drink for this conversation," Charles chuckled.

"Have not!"

"Go home, Rick. You're drunk," Chad teased as laughter broke out.

"Am not!"

"How many's that?" Charles asked.

"Err... dunno..."

"Fifteen stubbies, give or take," Tim said, counting the empties in front of Rick.

"He he." Rick chuckled, stupid grin intact.

"Alright. Let's get you to bed." Tim and Charlotte hauled him up, guiding him inside.

"Yep. I'm about done too," Crouton announced, standing up. "Oh! Nathan arrives in the morning."

"Indeed," Charles chimed. "And no doubt with more intriguing stories of his adventures abroad."

"Both political and outrageous... not excluding the chaos and nonsense of Hamet Albarad, I'm sure," Tim grinned.

"Albarad—halfwit, imbecilic muppet," Crouton muttered, walking off to help Rhys and Rod clear the table.

"Nice!" Tim said, reacting to the news of Nathan O'Conner's pending arrival. "You and Nate are gonna get on real good." He called to Chad, who nodded with intrigue.

"Wait—who's Hamet Albarad?" Chad asked, racking his brain—trying to place the name.

"A skilled and manipulative con man," Rod replied darkly, shaking his head. Clearly, the man wasn't popular among these friends.

"Face like a twisted outhouse," Crouton added, "arrogance of a politician with a crop of carrots stuffed where the sun don't shine. He's a liar and a moron."

Charles offered a more balanced take. "Hamet Albarad is Egypt's minister of archaeology and antiquities. He is a fraud in every way—a master of concealment. Anyone who challenges him is reduced into the realm of conspiracy theorists. He's also Crouton's arch nemesis."

"Clearly," Charlotte whispered, eyeing Crouton.

"The fool is but a creature gaunt of spirit," Crouton continued, slipping into poetic venom, "eager to flatter with desperation... long divorced from the scent of integrity. I await the day his stitched illusion collapses under the quiet weight of long-suppressed revelation."

"Wow..." Chaiyala said, wide-eyed.

Rod, Rhys, and Tim laughed and shook their heads.

"Settle down, Crouton," Charles chuckled. "You're gonna have Chad up all night deciphering riddles."

Chad frowned in agreement.

"No, he won't," Chaiyala said slyly. "Something else, I give him to think about."

She stepped forward and planted a subtle, affectionate kiss on Chad's cheek. "Goodnight, Chad. See you in the morning." She didn't smile, not fully—just that half-tilt she used when flipping someone's certainty upside down. Her accent sharpened the tease, making it clear: the chessboard had shifted. She slipped inside, her glance over her shoulder warm and playful.

Rod and Rhys whistled. Charlotte did a double take and smirked. Tim and Rhys exchanged silent looks. Rick, of course, was already in bed.

"Well, that was interesting," Charlotte said.

"Hmm, true," Tim smiled.

Chad's first thought: *"What in the hang was that?"*

Second: *"Clever move. Kiss equals distraction. No more thinking about Egypt's archaeology minister—now it's all about that kiss."*

After a long mental pause and some goodnight greetings, his third—the conclusion: *"Forget it. Not losing sleep over either."*

He went straight to his room, stripped off his boardies, and collapsed starfish-style across the double queen.

~~~~~~~

It was just shy of midnight—Chad had been asleep no more than ten minutes when the explosion shook the ground.

Chaiyala had just stepped out of the shower.

Tim and Charlotte were curled together. Chatting and drifting toward sleep.

Rod and Kristie had just climbed into bed when Rhys and Antonio spotted a flash out the kitchen window in the distance. Crouton and Charles, still out on the deck, sprang from their seats and raced for the nearest Humvee. In one fluid motion, Crouton reversed and was headed down the road, around the corner and proceeded with haste to the Central Hub.

Tires screeched as they halted in the front car park.

Rod—living nearest—had already dashed through the back gate, sprinting past the warehouses toward the central hub, seeking answers from the night watch.

Kristie and Jacqui hurried to Tim's to offer reassurance.

Chaiyala and Rick tore off in another Humvee, urgency mirrored in their posture and speed.

"Tell me the story," Crouton requested as Rod joined him at The Hub.

"Geo sensors and sonar picked up something big—moving fast, one-eighty tops. Central hub flagged it as hostile. No comms, no bio signatures. We launched rockets, took it out. Infra-red never saw it, so probably another ice-clad."

A handful of black ops teams had been retrofitting ice trucks. Unmanned. Explosive-packed. Rigged for collision—barrelling them toward the Project Camp like battering rams.

Helicopters were in the air now—two, already locked in with live gunfire.

"Righto," Crouton said, already moving. "Let's find out where the shots are coming from and join in."

Rod and Charles followed close behind.

After helping Chaiyala and Antonio run a weapons and ammo check on both vehicles, Rick and Rhys climbed into the front of one of the Humvees. Rick pulled out a tablet linked to the central hub, scanning live coordinates for helicopter and Humvee units already engaged in defensive manoeuvres.

~~~~~~~

Tim and Charlotte jolted from her bed and dashed out about as quickly as Chad—meeting him in the living room just as Kristie and Jacqui arrived in nightgowns, checking on the younger guests.

"How often does this kind of thing happen?" Charlotte asked, as Kristie draped a protective arm around her.

"Not often," Tim replied, "not quite this dramatically at least," tone shaded with cautious intrigue. "But it's the second time in as many weeks."

He and Jacqui moved to a cupboard to the right of the entrance to the passage—built into the living room wall. They ensured its contents were quickly accessible in case the situation escalated toward evacuation.

"What's all that?" Chad asked.

"S.P. cupboard," Tim said, retrieving an inventory notebook. "Secondary protocol. If everything goes pear-shaped and the camp's breached, we evacuate to seven fall-back sites deeper into the Richat, then helicopters get us out."

Inside were eight go-bags packed with essentials.

Chad frowned.

"Oh goodness," Charlotte whispered.

Tim quickly reassured them. Camp breaches were improbable. "Red Sword has spent the past year repelling black ops and mercenary attacks—all retreated in failure. Crouton and Nathan have reinforced every weak point." Not a single breach to date.

~~~~~~~

Crouton stood through the Humvee hatch Rhys was driving, beard whipping sideways, both hands gripping the M240B machine gun mounted overhead. Antonio piloted the second vehicle beside them.

Gunfire zipped past from the dark. Crouton swung the barrel toward flashes and unleashed rounds with rapid fury.

Something exploded—flames burst skyward. Smoke billowed through night like ghost shadows.

Antonio's Humvee slid into position five meters away. Then, overhead the rumble and whir of a helicopter before its spotlight illuminated two tanks rolling in from the distance.

"Ohhh-hoho, this hoo-ha's gettin' real now!" Crouton roared.

Rod manned the semi-auto on the other Humvee. Chaiyala crouched at the rear, ready to leap—nimble, calm, lethal.

"Ninja woman," Crouton muttered. Half prayer. Half amusement. She'd always made it back.

"What's the plan, boss?" came Antonio's voice through Crouton's earpiece.

Crouton ducked down and sealed the hatch. "All units pull back—send in the ninjas."

Rhys and Antonio peeled off. Helicopters circled back. Ground units curved homeward. The shadows advanced.

Four stealth Red Sword dune buggies—anti-sonar, anti-infra-red—raced silently across the sand, lights off, engines whispering.

"Find Chaiyala," Crouton added. "She's probably already there."

"Cheating again," Rick muttered.

"Don't be a sook, Rick," someone shot back.

Four Red Sword agents sprinted as shadows. Starlight faintly brushed the horizon. The moon hid behind clouds—like it didn't want to witness this night.

The five figures—Chaiyala among them—switched to night vision.

Buggies parked behind a dune, twenty meters from idle tanks.

Chaiyala joined the others and whispered her briefing.

"Tanks are ready. They expect a breach—but it's not happening. Their ranks sound confused."

They focused in, ears sharp.

"Fifteen hostiles. Twenty-three meters to tank one, then ten more to second. Three Humvees. They speak Farsi or accented English."

"Affirmative," the team leader replied.

Chaiyala outlined the plan: "Five-pronged attack. Hit Humvees first—take tanks last. Terminate only in self-defence. No prisoners. Disarm—release them on foot. Destroy Humvees. Seize the tanks—drive them home."

The five split up. Chaiyala veered far left, zigzagging through shadows toward the Humvees. Her team-mate crept behind one, slashed the rear tires, thumped the back windshield, then vaulted onto the roof without a sound.

Two black ops grunts poked their heads out. One exited; the Red Sword shadow dropped, legs locking around him, arm snaking to his throat. The grunt fired twice. A third shot cracked as the second grunt rounded the rear—only to have his aim redirected by swift manipulation.

Chaiyala arrived just in time, sweeping the driver's legs as he exited. She rolled beneath the Humvee, and ankle-tapped another sprinting grunt trying to find cover on the other side.

They fired wildly into darkness, unaware they were being played. The five hadn't fired a single shot. Their loadout: six explosive packs, a few backups, hand-helds, hidden wrist blades, piercing knives, eight-inch combat daggers.

Chaiyala wheeled back beneath the Humvee, caught sight of the driver she'd tripped—he aimed again, blindly. She drew her dagger, flung it— embedding it deep into his gun barrel just as he fired. The weapon exploded. His scream rang out, buying Red Sword shadows room to advance under cover of agony.

She pivoted—but too late. The other grunt grabbed her leg, dragged her from beneath the Humvee, pistol aimed at her.

A blade flew from the dark, knocking the gun loose. As he cursed, Chaiyala rolled to the side, evading a bullet to the face, then to her back now free, launched herself with her hands, and roundhouse-kicked him across the head. He stumbled, then came swinging with his uninjured hand.

"Rookie," she muttered, taking his arm, spinning him to his knees. She whipped her legs over his shoulders, locking his neck in an iron vice. His hands clawed—but she squeezed until he crumpled.

The vehicle had been cleared of hostiles, now was her chance. Chaiyala commando-crawled beneath the Humvee, slapped an explosive pack onto the chassis, activated the ten second count, and sprinted.

Sixty meters away, she hit the deck.

The blast shook the terrain. The Humvee lifted, slammed down again as a second explosion lit the sky. Fireballs flew from its rear, flinging shrapnel across the battlefield.

"Blast!" she hissed—hadn't checked the vehicle's condition first. Whatever was in the boot was volatile, amplifying the explosion and increasing the risk to her and her team.

Molten rubber skimmed overhead. Burning stink filled the air.

She lifted on elbows, scanned the wreckage. Three grunts lay dead nearby. Her team had stayed low—smart.

The second Humvee—crippled and crammed with panicked black ops grunts—sputtered and jerked as a Red Sword ninja beat down the driver, both feet planted on both accelerator and brake. The engine screamed in protest. Twin plumes of sand erupted behind the back wheels.

Chaiyala spotted blood running from a gash on her shoulder. Her entire sleeve was gone. Her hidden blade now visible. She didn't know when or how it had happened.

Lucky. From the look of the tear, something had tried to take her arm. It settled for only fabric.

A team-mate fifteen meters away smiled at her through firelight. She returned it, catching her breath.

The others finished subduing those who'd tried escaping in the Humvee.

But the tanks were on the move—rumbling toward Chaiyala and her companion.

They exchanged a glance. Her team-mate grinned madly and charged the nearest one, zigzagging to avoid gunfire.

Chaiyala shook her head, amused. He was enjoying this far too much.

She pointed at the tank rolling toward her and beckoned it forward. She smirked at how ridiculous this was—adrenaline had subsided now—calm and focus had taken over. Machine gun fire sliced across the sand. She zigzagged, calculated its speed against her own, then leapt and spun around the barrel of its primary gun, landing on the tank's front like it was meant to be.

Gunfire ceased. She heard scattered shots in the distance—hand-to-hand combat near the second tank and the last Humvee. She climbed the beast's body, expecting a confrontation.

"These guys are slow," she thought, crouching near the hatch. *"Their mistake."*

A gun barrel edged into view—peering over the top of the tank's hatch.

"Seriously?" she whispered.

She pounced, seized the weapon mid-rise, flung it aside, and slammed the grunt's head against the rim of the hatch.

He growled, gripping the rim with both hands, climbing up. His mistake. She pulled him out, flipped him into a reverse headlock, and squeezed until his resistance faded.

Two more appeared—better prepared. One landed a punch to her cheek, but adrenaline dulled the pain. She returned fire, striking his temple. He slumped, dazed.

The second attacker tried a headlock from above. She jammed her arms inside, lifted him off—same size, same grit—but the momentum tipped them sideways and landed hard on the tank's flat surface.

They scrambled side by side, wrestling for position. Chaiyala propped against a sloped panel, kicked him off the platform. He crashed to the tracks, rolled onto the sand. She bounded after him like a cat.

He staggered to his feet. She crept behind him, low like a shadow, and kicked him square in the back.

"Ughf," he wheezed, spinning and swinging a haymaker. Missed.

She delivered a crisp uppercut, staggering him again. A second swing grazed her cheek—just knuckles.

Another uppercut. He reeled. Then, desperate, he lunged.

Her boot met his chest. He slammed into the tank's steel wheel.

She seized the moment—grabbing his collar, striking several times, ending with a nasty knee to the groin. He dropped to the sand, beaten and breathless.

Panting, she looked up. No more emerged from the hatch.

She climbed the tank again—three hostiles. All subdued. All stranded.

Across the battlefield, the second Humvee exploded—fire lighting the sky fifty meters away.

Her team-mate stood atop the other tank, raising a triumphant fist. "Yeeha!"

Chaiyala lifted her own, exhaled hard. It was all she could manage.

It was finally over.

Crouton radioed Tim and reported the all clear—Chaiyala and her team had neutralised the threat.

~~~~~~~

Jacqui brought hot chocolates from the kitchen, setting mugs on the coffee table. A sweet contrast to the sudden awareness of worst-case scenarios.

"I'm looking forward to meeting Nathan O'Conner," Chad said, accepting his mug. He thanked Jacqui.

"You will," Kristie nodded. "He's a lovely man—big heart, thoughtful manner. Second to none."

"His reputation precedes him," Jacqui added, "but no one's truly prepared for Nathan."

"How so?" Chad frowned.

"Bit of a mystery man," Tim said.

Jacqui continued. "Some say he's tapped into something—otherworldly, maybe divine. But he's never confirmed, never denied being religious."

"Crouton's similar," Kristie added, her thick Australian accent mellow but sharp.

"Difference is," Tim began, "Nathan doesn't fit any stereotype. Don't let appearances fool you—he's unpredictable. In politics, strategy, and conflict, he's always ahead of the curve. He spots patterns others miss." Tim paused, then grinned. "He's very weird. But in a good way."

"Oh yeah, definitely," Kristie nodded slowly.

"Charles calls him Red Sword's version of Aslan," Tim chuckled. "He calls Crouton 'The Bull.'"

"Narnia!" Charlotte beamed.

"Aptly named, sounds like..." Chad mused. "Hmm. The plot thickens."

CHAPTER 9

Charles and Crouton found a less-than-happy Chaiyala around four in the morning. They met at the halfway point between the skirmish and the Project Camp as the two unmarked tanks rolled steadily toward the southern main gates.

She was satisfied with the outcome—less so with her own part in it. Crouton knew as much without needing to ask. He and Charles said nothing.

She should have checked the Humvee's cargo. It was a human error. She'd been in this business long enough to know when she'd slipped—and everyone knew that rarely ever happened.

The risk factor had been high, and the potential for casualties very real. As far as Crouton was concerned, what was done was done. Chaiyala was already beating herself up over it, and he could see she was torn. She'd need time to wind down, evaluate and come right.

Crouton wasn't one to dismiss someone on principle—what would that accomplish? He trusted every hand-picked member of his team with his life. They were human, capable of errors, but never of deliberate carelessness. There was always room to improve and move forward.

More importantly than all of that, Chaiyala was practically family.

So, they left her alone. Crouton made a point to check in with her the next day.

~~~~~~~

Tim was up before dawn and found Chaiyala reclining on one of the outdoor sofas above the pool, staring into the distance. Her expression suggested she was even farther away inside than her gaze.

"Mornin'," Tim greeted.

No answer. She was somewhere else entirely. For all he knew, she might've imagined his voice—she didn't notice.

"I'm surprised you're awake. Thought you guys got back about an hour ago."

"Sorry? ... Yes. Yeah, something like that," Chaiyala replied, sleepily distracted.

She had her reasons for sitting out on the deck in the hours prior to daybreak. A thin line of light was appearing on the horizon. Tim understood the need to find space, to be alone and soak in the quiet for whatever purpose. Hence, his being there—he didn't rush her for conversation.

"You all good?" he eventually asked.

She replied slowly, solemnly, with sleepy pauses. "Hmm... maybe. Dunno... yes," she smiled at him.

He smiled back and looked toward the horizon.

"Charlotte's still asleep?"

"Yeah. Took her a while to get back to sleep after last night's fireworks."

"She okay?"

"Yeah, just took her a while to settle. Still coming to terms with it all," Tim replied. He paused thoughtfully. "Bit of a paradox, ya know? You try to make the here and now work with the bigger picture and..."

"...you spend forever trying to make them match. But then... you look at now—and you see, this is how the big picture builds."

"There you go again, reading my mind."

They both laughed.

"You have done well with Charlotte," Chaiyala said, sincere. "She is beautiful. So many ways." She looked out toward the horizon.

"Thanks! She's an angel," Tim reflected, relishing the blessing inside.

"How do you make most of now", Chaiyala asked, more personally now, "to shape the big picture?"

Tim thought on that, wanting his answer to do justice to what was in his heart.

"People are the most important thing ever. Otherwise, why would God create them and make such a fuss over them—more than anything else in the world? I try to keep it simple. As complex as people are, I think what matters to them is crucial to understanding them. Understanding, knowing... there's a word back home in Te Reo Māori: 'whakarongo'— deep listening. Hearing each other before we let our preferences and beliefs prejudge. From there, life happens more amazing, richer, and better than if you try to do it all on your own."

Chaiyala smiled warmly.

"Doing what you love—what makes you come alive—is what truly matters. Otherwise, what's the point? I've always believed life is about connection, and the better we relate to others, the richer our experiences become. Good friends amplify joy."

As Tim shared, Chaiyala's scattered senses, came to rest in a welcome calm.

"Saint Irenaeus said, 'The glory of God is mankind fully alive.' It's simple—life is meant to be lived, loved, and enjoyed, not endlessly analysed and argued."

They watched the horizon in silence for a moment, the sun's first glow rising in the distance.

"The glory of God is mankind fully alive—life, freedom, and yeah... enjoying it, and enjoying it with each other." Tim concluded.

"Thank you, Tim. That, I needed to hear," Chaiyala said sincerely, gratefully. "I needed reminding what it's all about," she realised.

They bid each other a good morning and Chaiyala finally found her bed.

Now alone, Tim sat back at the other end of the outdoor couch, watching the brilliance on the horizon intensify. The sun was almost ready to flood the dusty world around, with full light. Once up, the temperature would soar and barely ease until evening.

He was deeply grateful for the shade sails stretched over the outdoor spaces, softening the sun's bite.

As he sat there, appreciation filled him—thankful for his friends, and most of all for Charlotte, now by his side. For Chad, finding relief from burdens back home.

Still, he missed home—the gentler climate, his parents, Celesta. More than once, he fought the urge to retreat inside, to Charlotte's room, to hold her and wait for her to wake. But he knew he needed space—a moment to reset. With chaos, action, and adventure all around, stepping back was crucial. Catching his breath. Slowing his mind. Regaining perspective.

Without that, he'd become overwhelmed.

He'd overcome depression and anxiety, discovering they weren't just chemical imbalances or external triggers. In hindsight, the struggle seemed simpler. It had been needlessly complex—philosophically and medically. At its core, it came down to neglecting health: poor diet, sleep and exercise, a lack of meaningful company, and quietly shelving his dream.

Correcting those was all it took to move past survival—into thriving. Charlotte had helped him through all of that—valiantly.

He leaned back on the couch, exhaling, watching the sun rise over the Sahara in tranquil silence.

The thing about the desert was, there were next to no birds. Not like New Zealand or Australia, where the morning chorus greeted you with the melodic calls of Tūī and sparrows. Or in Australia, where you were woken by a bizarre avian jam session that sounded like Bohemian Rhapsody played on broken kitchen appliances—off-key, out of time, and completely chaotic.

Here, wildlife was sparse. Much less inclined to sing. But it did make for an incredibly peaceful atmosphere.

Tim's mind drifted to life's simplest and most meaningful joys—friendship, love, the beauty of simply being alive. He savoured a moment free of the enormity of discovery. Unburdened by mercenaries and black ops, he allowed himself to recharge.

He slipped into quiet communion with God, listening as He spoke back.

"Hmm," Tim breathed.

He let the silence and morning warmth saturate every part of him. He truly relaxed—Sabbath rest—seeing the world within and around him with peace, purpose, freedom, and fresh perspective. He thanked God for the day and the season he'd found himself in, almost floating with his soul toward the embrace of the Divine.

Then he opened his eyes again.

The sunrise exploded on the horizon, magnificent in colour, painting the morning with brilliance and the feel of an endless summer he'd grown accustomed to. And yet, something shifted—suddenly, something felt odd.

He glanced down at the deck, across the pool, barbecue, outdoor furniture... then at the beer crate at the end of the couch— someone had used as a table the night before.

On top of it sat an icy cold, 500ml can of Blue Nectargy.

Tim did a double take, frowned in disbelief, then realized with delight that what he was seeing was real. He picked it up. Cloaked in a thin layer of ice and condensation...

"You weren't here a minute ago... and where did you come from, anyway?" he wondered.

Someone had placed it there. But who? And where on earth had they gotten Blue Nectargy—a citrus-based energy drink only sold in New Zealand and Australia?

Tim turned around to find none other than Nathan O'Conner seated at a table behind him, wearing Oakleys and watching the sunrise with a slight grin on his face. He wore a white Adidas hoodie, his tufty greying brown hair a little bushier than usual, and he had his trademark bright blue tablet set in front of him.

Tim burst out laughing—for the answer to the mystery, and for the joy of seeing Nathan sitting there, casually sneaking his favourite soft drink into his morning.

"Nathan!" Tim exclaimed excitedly, wheeling around in his seat.

"How's it going, Tim?"

"Great. Could not possibly be better! I have my fiancée and my brother with me. Now you're here! And now I have Blue Nectargy? I haven't had one in months—my dozen ran out ages ago. Thanks!" He got up to properly greet Nathan. "Great to see you, man!"

"It's great to see you too. And no worries, my friend," Nathan smiled. "There's a dozen more in your fridge—and the same amount of Raspberry

Nectargys for Charlotte. I'm sure those used to be her favourite... I was certain of it," he said, feigning second-guessing himself.

Tim was stunned, grateful for the Nectargys, and gave a distracted, "Thank you... what?"

He paused, mentally tracing the puzzle. Yes, he knew Raspberry Zs were Charlotte's drink of choice—but they'd gone out of production years ago, long before they'd started dating. So how did Nathan know?

The guy was full of surprises. Most of them? Way out left field.

Tim's next question: "Where'd you get them from?"

"Picked them up on a stopover in Auckland the other week. On route from Lima to Bangkok."

"Right... cheers for that. So—they've started making Raspberry Nectargy again? That's pretty cool. That stuff was always great!"

"Nah... that took a little more work to come by, actually," Nathan began to explain—then got interrupted.

"Brother!" bellowed Crouton from inside his ranch slider.

Arms outstretched, his heavy boots stomped down the steps and levels of the terraced deck. Nathan stepped forward to meet him.

The two were inseparable in spirit, bound by a shared passion for unlocking the Sahara's secrets. One: a rugged warrior with a Santa-like presence and a heart for people. The other: a diplomatic mastermind, trusted by world leaders, royals, and even the most unlikely and unloved.

"It's great to see you! You're doing well, then?" he asked Crouton.

"Couldn't be better!"

"I received reports there was another attempt on the camp last night."

"Yeah—tanks this time! They were confiscated and brought on site. Minimal casualties all round, and all taken care of by Chaiyala and her team."

"Excellent. I look forward to seeing her, Charles, and everyone else once they're awake." Nathan's tone shifted. "As for the tanks—I know who gave them tanks."

"Who?" Crouton asked.

"Your best friend on the other side of the Sahara," Nathan replied with a smile.

"Argh..." Crouton groaned, shaking his head. "Moron... why do I have to share the desert with that abominated salmon?"

"The tanks are old, out-of-date models the Egyptian military were set to dispose of. Albarad pulled a few strings and got them to our friend Mohammad Saurashan. Which is why our visitors last night were likely black ops hailing from Iran."

"Hmm, Chaiyala mentioned they'd heard Farsi."

"Those desperate to stop us hail from many places," Nathan reminded, gazing out toward the sun risen over the horizon.

A silence settled between them. The three men let go of political matters for a moment, choosing instead to take in the serenity of their desert oasis. They opted to enjoy the peace and quiet of first light—before the hijinks of Rick and Rhys, and the ostensibly endless banter between Chaiyala and Rick, inevitably kicked off.

"It's always so good to be back here," Nathan smiled. He remembered the bacon, eggs, hash browns, and brekky sausages waiting to be cooked once everyone surfaced. Crouton decided that'd be the perfect way to wake the others.

Chad, followed by Charlotte, slowly stirred. No one expected Chaiyala, Rick, or Rhys to surface any time soon after the previous night's fireworks out yonder.

~~~~~~

Chad could hear Tim, Rod, Crouton, and Nathan talking out on the terraced deck about Egyptian pyramids as he made his way into the kitchen, satisfied with the amount—more-so the quality—of sleep he'd had. They'd all gotten back to bed around two in the morning, and it was now eight.

He refilled his water bottle from the fridge dispenser, helped himself to a peach, and while waiting for his H2O, noticed two dozen cans of Nectargy—Berry, and Blue. He furrowed his brow, about to put down the fruit and grab one of the red Nectargys, but was distracted.

He was pretty sure Nathan had said something to the effect of, "After Atlantis had its own Chernobyl—directly following the failed attack on Athens and the disasters that came after—the colonies shut down all the pyramids across the empire, one by one."

Chad made his way toward the ranch slider, intrigued.

"... prior, though, enraged and furious with their arrogance, Poseidon returned to the heavens—and that's when everything went royally pear-shaped for them," Nathan was finishing as Chad stepped out onto the deck.

"That was pretty much hitting the reset button on the progress of human civilization," Rod surmised, piecing together concepts and legends in his mind. He wasn't the historian Tim was, nor as well-versed in the parahistory of Atlantis and the world beyond 10 to 12,000 BC as Nathan and Crouton—but he knew enough to grasp the significance.

"Well, that was the thing," Tim added. "And because the last of the records were lost shortly after Plato's time, there was literally nothing to go on. Then modern thinking got structured in such a way that its ethos doesn't leave room to accommodate even the remotest possibility of Atlantis's true story—its legacy or destruction—as actual fact."

"Egypt and Athens were let off lightly too, really," Nathan said. "Thankfully for us. Without Egypt's record keeping, we wouldn't have known a thing about Atlantis."

"Morning, bro!" Tim greeted Chad.

A series of greetings followed, and a sleepy Charlotte followed—stepped out onto the deck in boxers and a singlet top, rubbing her eyes. Her hair was all over the place.

"Hey, beautiful," Tim beamed at his fiancée as she sat on the arm of the sofa beside him. She smiled sleepily at Tim and the others as the two exchanged a hug and kiss.

Crouton was about to make introductions, but Tim beat him to it.

"Chad, Charlotte—this is Nathan O'Conner. Our very good friend, Crouton's business partner, and co-founder of Red Sword Security Services. Also, co-visionary and benefactor of the Richat Project. Nathan, this is Charlotte Espanzia, my fiancée, and my brother Chad."

Nathan stood to shake their hands.

"It's seriously a pleasure and an honour to finally meet you both," he said sincerely. "Tim's told me so much about you, I almost feel like I know you already. But then—how often are first-time acquaintances merely friends who haven't met yet?" He smiled warmly, disarmingly.

Charlotte suddenly felt incredibly underdressed and regretted stepping outside in her pyjamas with her hair a mess.

Both she and Chad were caught off guard. They'd expected someone who looked more the part of a multi-billionaire political diplomat. They hadn't anticipated a regular bloke in shorts, hoodie, and sunnies. And they certainly hadn't expected a New Zealand accent.

Still, both were genuinely pleased to finally meet the 'man of mystery' everyone had been describing.

"This guy's like your typical average Kiwi bloke—just a bit more sophisticated, but still easy to relate to," Chad thought after only a few minutes of conversation.

Nathan could see that while Charlotte was trying to be polite, she was clearly self-conscious. He set about disarming that.

"Tim, you are a very blessed young man," he began. "It's genuinely so refreshing to be around people who are free and real!" He spoke thoughtfully, regarding all present with warmth and respect. "We are very blessed, aren't we, Crout? Rod?"

They both agreed.

"You are very, very blessed," Nathan repeated, nodding toward Tim and Charlotte with sincerity. He sighed. "I might have to fend off jealousy," he said, light-heartedly, with a cautious smile. "You're living your dream—in the beauty of loving family, good friends, and great things yet to come. Have the two of you set a date?"

"Thirty-first of January," Tim replied.

"Excellent! Very exciting."

Tim and Charlotte were moved by the sincerity in his eyes. There was sheer happiness beaming from him—for them, for meeting Chad, and for being back in Africa.

"Yup, I've been very much looking forward to returning to the Richat," Nathan continued, "to be with my brothers and sisters, and refreshed by the likes of young Rick, Chaiyala, and Rhys... and all the fun and laughs they stir up."

A few laughs and smiles were exchanged. The atmosphere around Nathan was magnetic. Energetic. Uplifting. Every sentence carried life and love.

"I've spent the last couple of months surrounded by people either pretending to be someone else—or wishing they weren't who they are," he said. "Some regret entering politics; others regret their actions yet see no escape. You wouldn't believe how many genuinely good people feel trapped in lives they despise—caught in a system they once hoped to change, only to be ensnared by its deceit and sickness. It's heart-breaking."

He shook his head.

"You need a higher power—God, or whatever you believe in—to lean on. Just to survive and stay sane in the world I navigate daily. Otherwise, it's overwhelming. And, it *must* be something constructive, positive, real—not self-serving, vengeful, or about earning divine favour. That's just more of the same."

His tone sharpened, warm but firm.

"Christianity—genuine Christ-likeness," he emphasised—continues to grow faster than any other movement on Earth, not through force or spectacle, but through the quiet power of hope and love. It offers freedom without conditions, purpose without pretence. Even in Western nations like New Zealand, the light of heaven is rising, while empty religion and fleeting spirituality lose their grip.

His eyes met theirs again.

"True Christ-likeness—supernatural freedom—flourishes wherever there's oppression, devastation, hopelessness. That's why ISIS is failing. Why tens of thousands in China, the Middle East, and North Africa turn to the way of faith, hope, and love every week! It's why empires, imperialism, and corruption are crumbling. Cancerous systems have short lifespans—death's nature is to die. But love, community, and friendship endure. That's *real* life."

He looked directly at Chad, Tim, and Charlotte as he finished.

And that smile...

It made them feel as if they were sitting with someone who'd been hanging out with Jesus Himself.

"Youth isn't a countdown that ends at thirty," Nathan laughed. "It's more than a mindset. It's a state of being. No matter your age, you never truly grow old—so long as love, community, and friendship outweigh pride, success, and possessions."

Charlotte stopped caring what she looked like after all that.

And Chad? He had no clue what to say or think any more.

Rod and Crouton sat back, relishing the friendship and the love they had for their brother. They both thanked God for the honour of knowing someone who inspired others, spoke life and acceptance, and possessed almost otherworldly wisdom about the world the way Nathan did.

"And so," Nathan began, "as we witness another spectacular sunrise on the distant horizon, so to do we welcome new horizons approaching our lives. Even now, we draw closer to crossing borders humanity has long viewed only from a distance. Those distant lines are now upon us!"

He grinned suddenly.

"Who's up for a trip to Jamaica?"

"Ahh," Crouton laughed. "Alesandro?" he asked, clearly unsurprised if it turned out he was correct.

"Yup. Alesandro," Nathan smiled. "It was him... and I let him tell me the whole story at his own leisure."

Crouton chuckled and nodded.

"Who's Alesandro?" Chad asked, as he and Tim wondered the context.

"... what story?" Tim added.

"Alesandro Karahalios," Crouton began, "is a joker Nathan and I met at a rare antiquities gallery opening in New York a while back—good, solid, no-nonsense Greek historian."

"Oh, that guy!" Tim recalled Crouton speaking of him in relation to Nathan a couple of months earlier. He frowned, trying to place the significance. Then, "Oh! *That guy!*" he repeated, wide-eyed, now with sudden clarity.

"Yes—the man we suspected knew something about Solon and Plato. You literally wouldn't read about." Crouton confirmed, grinning.

"We will soon though," Nathan smiled.

"The guy we knew was hiding something when Nathan mentioned the Eye of Africa," Crouton informed.

"With good reason," Nathan continued. "Turns out he's a direct descendant of Solon and Plato. And he lives in Jamaica."

"You're serious?" Tim felt goose bumps wash over him. His eyes lit up like headlights on a freight truck. He sat forward, burning to know more. "This guy is descended from the great Greek sage and the philosopher? Obviously, you were able to verify all that."

"It all checks out," Nathan went on to explain, "and the reason he was cagey about Mauritania is that he has a whole lot at stake. His family archives contain Solon's own account of Atlantis—far more than that which we already know."

Something in Nathan's tone made Tim pause. *"That which we already know... last I checked, there's very little known about Solon's take on Atlantis beyond what Plato wrote. What am I missing here?"*

Nathan grinned like a cheeky schoolboy.

Chad and Charlotte exchanged glances, both anticipating clarification.

"Cast your minds back to Athens—the hidden archives under the city library in 2015..." Nathan prompted.

"The discovery of the Solon diaries... that's right. And the controversy and conspiracy around it all—it was a mess. A real shame," Tim recalled.

"The diaries went missing, correct?" asked Crouton.

"Yes..."

"We have them," Nathan revealed.

Tim was stunned. Even Charlotte knew what that meant.

"What's the deal with these Solon diaries?" Chad asked.

"Nathan!" Tim looked like he'd seen a ghost. "You have to be kidding me! How the...?" He didn't know whether to laugh or be aghast.

"Hmm. Very mysteriously," Nathan replied, eerily. "Gifted, actually... Anonymously."

Tim, Crouton and Rod exchanged puzzled looks.

"Apparently, someone—a 'friend'—found them," Nathan continued. "All five, sitting in a briefcase outside the Pyramids at Giza. They were sent to me with a simple, mysterious note reading: *Here they are—the diaries of the sage, Solon. Use them to reveal the truth. Change the future by uncovering the secrets of the past.*"

"Who was the friend?" Tim asked.

"We've no idea," Nathan replied.

"We completed the usual investigation process—but nothing came up," added Crouton.

"No fingerprints, forensic red flags, postal tracking...?" Chad checked.

"Not a sausage."

"What were they doing in Egypt, I wonder..." Tim was baffled, barely able to process what he was hearing. "So, you have in your possession one of the most precious artefacts in history—and you didn't say a thing?"

"Oh, sorry Tim—I failed to mention. To be fair we only received them two days ago. Which is half the reason I'm here. And I want you and Crouton there when Alesandro opens his family archives for us in Jamaica."

"Okay... my apologies. Sorry, that kinda blew me away," Tim admitted, feeling a little silly for assuming something had been kept from him. Reassurance gave way to renewed bewilderment. "When he does what?"

"I know," Nathan smiled. "You heard correctly."

"As peculiar as the disappearing and reappearing of the diaries is," Chad began, "this has all worked in your favour, right? What if they hadn't gone missing—then found by this mystery friend? They sound like an incredibly valuable source of information. They need to be in your hands—not out in the open, only to be hidden again, their secrets buried by those who oppose what you're doing here in Africa."

"Excellent, Chad. Very good," Nathan applauded.

"And that's exactly what we suspected had happened to them," Crouton said. "So ,we set out in search of them—not knowin' they were comin' to us."

"And you have no idea who the friend was who sent you the diaries?" Charlotte double-checked, clearly puzzled.

"Correct," Nathan replied. "That's a mystery still unsolved. Working on it though."

Chad's questions about the pyramids remained. He figured they could wait. Tim had more questions about the Solon diaries and was eager to see them.

"So, Jamaica then," Chad said.

"Yes. You keen?" Nathan asked again. He looked at Charlotte as well. "I'm assuming you'll both be keen to tag along with Tim, seeing as he's the reason you're here. I've got rooms booked at the Caribbean Paradise Resort."

"Really? We can come?" Charlotte beamed at Tim. "That sounds amazing!"

"Sounds like a plan," Tim smiled. Chad nodded in agreement—he and Charlotte expressed thanks.

Crouton turned to Nathan. "When do we leave?"

"When's good for you guys?"

"Got a few things to get sorted," Crouton considered, "couple o'days?"

"Nice," Nathan nodded once, "I'll get things sorted."

"You and Charles'll have the run of the place while I'm off then," Crouton said to Rod. Then, reconsidered— "Or you wanna come?"

"Nah, nah, you guys go ahead. I'd love to, and thanks Nate—appreciate it—but I'll have to decline."

Nathan nodded.

"I've got a lot to catch up on here since France, and I'd really like to spend some time with Kristie for a change. Might be pushing my luck if I jet off to Jamaica for a luxury resort stay without her."

They laughed and agreed.

"Why don't you bring her with you?" Nathan suggested.

Rod paused. "I'll run it by her."

"All good," Nathan smiled.

"Everything's running fine here," Charles reported. "All going well. We'll update you with progress and any events."

"Good man," Crouton commended.

"Today we'll take you to the Chinguetti dig site," Crouton told Nathan. "Rod and I—so you can see the interior of the building entered on Tuesday."

"Oh yes! I've been looking forward to that." Nathan turned to Tim, "I assume you're chomping at the bit to get your hands on the Solon diaries?"

Tim smiled, "That's like asking a fish if it swims!"

They laughed.

"What's the story with the diaries? They here?" Crouton asked Nathan.

"Yup. Indeed, they are—secured at The Hub," Nathan smiled.

"Well, son, you and your team can get stuck into those as soon as you're ready. In the meantime," Crouton grinned, "let's fire up the barbies and cook up some brekky."

The guys set to it, and Charlotte went off to shower and get dressed.

Tim returned to the kitchen while breakfast was cooking. Rod, Crouton, and Nathan caught up on things. Kristie had joined them, and Rhys had surfaced too.

Tim opened the fridge, remembering the treats Nathan had stashed there for him and Charlotte. He puzzled over the Red Berry Nectargy until Charlotte came back out, tying her hair into a ponytail, wearing black shorts and a white backless halter top.

"Babe, can you sunblock my back?" she asked, passing him the bottle—then paused, distracted by the red can in his hand.

"Oh, my goodness... seriously? No way!"

"Yeah..." Tim replied, still trying to figure it out. "Flip, this guy's got some mysteries about him..." He shook his head, referring to Nathan.

"What? Who? ...how?" Charlotte asked, spotting another eleven red cans in the fridge alongside twelve blue ones. She looked outside toward Nathan, completely bewildered.

"I know... he managed to source these and..." Tim trailed off, distracted mid-sentence. "...and surprise us with them. Look at the date on the bottom of the red cans..."

Charlotte leaned in. The date ended in "09."

"It's 2019 now. That's... are these cans ten years old?" she asked.

"Dunno. They look like they could've just come outta the fridge at a local dairy down the road in Hamilton."

"But Berry Nectargy's been out of production for nearly ten years..."

"Who knows? He's Nathan O'Conner. He does this kind of thing all the time," Tim said, still baffled. "Mind you, if two Kiwi comic legends once engineered their own flavours of Nectargy—and sealed a mate's car keys inside a can at the factory—all for the sake of national comedy and the most over-engineered prank you've ever heard..."

Charlotte frowned at Tim in disbelief, then smiled—unsurprised but highly amused by the antics of the New Zealand comic duo.

"...then I'm pretty sure Nathan could get some limited-edition Red Berry Nectargys made. He knew the berry kind was your favourite."

"That's pretty amazing... but how'd he know it was my favourite flavour before they stopped making it?"

"Well, that's the thing—I've no idea. The only explanation is that I must've mentioned it when he was here last. But I have no idea why... I don't recall talking about Nectargy, or my favourite being blue, let alone that my fiancées was berry before being discontinued.

I must've said something..." Tim muttered, searching his memory.

"That's cool though—mysterious—but I'm *so* not complaining!" Charlotte smiled.

"He can do all kinds of background checks and investigations to find obscure details about people," Tim said, shutting the fridge and grabbing the sunblock. "But to know something this hidden about you? That's pretty out-of-it—even for Nathan."

Charlotte turned, letting Tim gently rub and massage her back as he applied the cool ointment.

They set the breakfast table outside, planning to enjoy the morning sun. Tim decided to have his team translate the Solon diaries from Greek to English for the journey to Jamaica, freeing up the day to spend with Charlotte and Chad.

Everyone arrived for breakfast, gathering around a generous spread of bacon, eggs, hash browns, breakfast sausages, grilled tomatoes, and lizard fillets. Crouton had even grown field mushrooms in a repurposed fish tank. Despite their praise, he dismissed the effort with a chuckle, calling it far too much trouble and swearing he wouldn't do it again. Charlotte, in particular, found herself increasingly charmed by his quirky, food-related eccentricities.

Nathan engaged Chad and Charlotte in lively conversation, eager to hear first-hand about their lives. Tim had told him plenty, but nothing thrilled Nathan more than hearing people tell their own stories—where they came from, what truly mattered to them. When asked about his low profile despite his vast wealth and influence, Nathan explained he preferred to operate in the quiet space between visibility and secrecy—free from entanglements, able to move swiftly and do good without distraction.

Nathan's phone rang. He glanced at the screen and excused himself.

A gap settled in the conversation as everyone focused on eating.

"Nathan," Rod began, for Chad and Charlotte's benefit, "is, without exaggeration, the richest—and possibly one of the most influential people in the world. He has more wealth than the Elon Musk and the Vanholms put together. Every charity across the globe, every nation in need or teetering on bankruptcy, has a major benefactor: Nathan O'Conner, who tactfully flies under the radar."

"Are you kidding me?" Chad snapped, disgusted. He'd missed Rod's latter sentence, snagged on the former. "If he has more wealth than half the world, then why is most of the world suffering in poverty while the rich couldn't care less?"

Tim and Charlotte froze, stunned, as Chad realized what had slipped. He leaned back, embarrassed, eyeing Nathan on the phone. Rod had struck an unseen nerve, shaking Chad to the core. His brain-mouth filter had failed, exposing a wound he himself hadn't known existed.

"I'm sorry..."

"Take a breath, Chad," Charlotte said gently, placing a hand on his forearm.

Crouton wasn't fazed—nor were the others from Red Sword. They were used to it. It was usually like water off a duck's back. He'd been waiting for an outburst and was impressed it had taken this long. Based on Chad's personality, a few things discussed, and a couple of subtle reactions, Crouton figured his young friend was prone to this—especially when confronted with the more extravagant attractions in the theme park of crazy they lived in.

"Clearly," Rod continued, "all the wealth in the world doesn't cure poverty. Poverty, primarily, is a mindset—it has little to do with money. Curing poverty financially alone is about as effective as curing depression with antidepressants alone."

Chad nodded, understanding.

"There's little point going deep," Rod added, "but governments worldwide—if we're brutally honest—are about as useful as a condom machine in a monastery or a chocolate teaspoon in a coffee mug." His crude analogy made the point clear. "Yes, democracy has its place, and it's better than dictatorship. But real power and impact lie with local initiatives—aid organizations and movements working at ground zero, tackling the roots of societal challenges. Frankly, regardless of belief, the work that embodies Christ's heart has done more to end real poverty over the centuries than any government policy ever could."

Rod leaned back, then continued.

"Now, about Nathan—yes, he's a mystery. He comes from Paeroa, New Zealand. About forty minutes' drive from Hamilton, if I'm right."

Chad, Charlotte, and Tim exchanged baffled looks.

"Locals there say he has a nice yet modest house overlooking the old racecourse, owns the Goldfields dairy there, and is wealthy enough to travel the world year-round. But beyond that? Nothing. He's the humblest man any of us have ever met, and his wish to stay out of the spotlight is respected by all who know him."

"Who does he work with—other than yourselves?" Chad asked.

"He's an independent advisor to twenty-six world leaders—including New Zealand's, Mauritania's, and Egypt's Prime Ministers. He's a major benefactor to World Vision, UNICEF, the Red Cross, and the Salvation Army. He's responsible for the removal of Osama bin Laden from the Middle East—along with a dozen key Al-Qaeda operatives and leaders. Without bloodshed. And yes, he's good friends with Osama, who is very much alive—and goodness me, that's a whole other world of story to tell."

Rod paused, then added: "If you so much as think about placing Nathan O'Conner on anything resembling a pedestal, he'll know, and he'll leave faster than your next breath. He's rejected several Nobel Peace awards and UN requests to take over its leadership."

Silence.

Rod pushed aside his plate—food now cold—and looked at Chad intently.

"Here's the real kicker," he said, looking earnestly at Chad, then Charlotte, then Tim. "And I cannot possibly stress how serious I am being right now: Nathan O'Conner is on record—more than once—as being in two or three locations at the same time."

A wave of goose bumps hit Tim and Charlotte like a storm. They looked at each other, eyes wide with bewildered excitement.

Chad, stunned for a moment, pulled himself together... and hoped to God he never had to face an opposing lawyer who resembled Rod.

He sat back in his chair, utterly relieved—and bothered by how relieved he was. How did he know he wasn't being had?

He knew full well he wasn't.

He looked Rod directly, then Tim, Charlotte, and Crouton. Crouton didn't joke. Rod's gaze was drilling holes through any sliver of doubt still lingering in Chad's mind.

"Great," he thought. *"Now, on top of everything else, I gotta square with the paranormal?"*

Chad stared at his empty plate. After the stunned silence had taken its toll on everything that had preceded it, he finally spoke.

"If I ever come up against a lawyer in any court of law who delivers anything quite like that—the way you just did—I'm going to quit my job and come work for Red Sword Security."

They all laughed. And kept laughing.

Until Crouton was in hysterics—and it got weird. Disconcerting even.

"What'd I miss?" Nathan asked, smiling through a frown. "You guys were completely quiet the whole time, and then, an eruption of raucous laughter."

Everyone laughed again.

"Nothing to worry about, old friend," Rod chuckled. "Young Chad here was finding himself... educated."

Given the chaos of the previous night—and with no pressing need to be anywhere—they all took it easy for the rest of the day. Chad and Charlotte welcomed the cruiser, less eventful interlude in their adventure.

Charles and Crouton had planned a trip back to the Chinguetti dig site to show Nathan around the newly unearthed, awe-inspiring Atlantean government building.

CHAPTER 10

The following morning, Chad came racing along the top of a straight ridge, flicking through gears on his mountain bike, trying to catch up with Tim, who'd passed him at a spot his older brother knew well—one with tricky turns a first-timer would take longer to handle. Speed wasn't an option for Chad. And Tim had gained a healthy advantage down a winding dip that preceded the ridge they were now racing along.

Chaiyala was way ahead of them, and Charlotte had been taking it easy, sticking a meter or two behind Tim until he surged past his brother. The four had decided to get out before the heat fully set in and check out some of the mountain biking tracks set up on the edge of the Project Camp.

Charlotte was hot on Chad's heels—closer than he'd realized.

"You've got to be kidding me!" he heard her say from behind as they approached the next slope. She thought she was more out of puff than she actually was.

Chad knew she was fitter and definitely lighter, but he hadn't anticipated her accelerating past him as fast as she did.

"Yeah... okay," he muttered to himself, watching her speed off up the rise. He gave up trying to race the others, lowered his head, and pushed up the hill. At the crest, the view was breath-taking—the Adrar Highlands stretched westward, the northern Richat ranges curved into the distance, and rolling hills framed the structure below. To the southwest, the Project Camp, and the security fence faded into the desert haze behind the ranges.

Once they'd all arrived at the end of the track, Chad found Chaiyala seated on the ground, leaning against a rock with a "took your time" grin.

"Dude, it is nearly lunchtime, no?" she hassled... it wasn't.

"I was taking in the view at the top," he replied.

"Sure, sure."

Tim and Charlotte lingered close, trading notes on the track's turns and terrain. Tim wore only boardies, his shirt tied around his head for shade and to purge the perspiration. Charlotte, now in activewear shorts and sports bra, had shed her singlet to stay cool. Everyone was soaked in sweat—the early heat already biting.

"Gee, this'd be an extremely hot day back in Hamilton!" Chad said, amazed at the heat—it was only nine in the morning.

"It's thirty-two right now—about to get hotter," Tim warned.

"Better we head back now, before it gets worse," Chaiyala suggested.

They made their way back along the dusty path winding through the low hills. Chaiyala explained how workers and residents had carved out the track in the early months of the project, and since then, it had been well-trained and extended.

"We have twelve things to do outdoors—if you want something more than just the pool," she informed, eyes flicking between Chad and Charlotte. "Mountain biking, of course. Timed for early morning—we're pushing it today—you need strong legs and stronger coffee—lucky you had some of your Nectargy."

High ropes adventure—is also early morning. You want to feel the wind before the heat comes, yes?

Rugby, soccer, and cricket—play those at twilight, or under lights at events arena. The ground holds the day's heat, but the air is cooler. It's very alive then.

There's an orienteering trail—you follow the clues, find the markers. Archery under the acacias—the light there is golden, very cinematic.

She stopped to fix the ponytail below her helmet. "Tim is a master at the sand boarding—he makes look like flying," she smiled at Charlotte. "Camel treks go to the central oasis, where the pump station for all water and irrigation is. There's a Tuareg village there—they make a cultural tea that tastes like stories.

Low ropes course also under the acacias. Evening desert volleyball— when sand is cooler, easier to run. Like beach volleyball, but with stars instead of seagulls.

Rock climbing—that, and volleyball, are my favourites.

The teens and kids—they love the wide-game night missions. Torches, glow sticks, capture the flag. It's chaos, but beautiful chaos.

And Amazigh games, storytelling around the fire-pit. You sit, you listen, you forget the time. It's very special."

"Nice! That's pretty cool," Charlotte remarked.

"Timed well too by the sounds of it all," Chad observed. "Working with the dessert heat, not against it."

"Exactly," said Tim.

Making their way at a slower place, Chad finally remembered to ask Tim, "Hey, so what's the story with the pyramids in Egypt? You and Crouton were discussing it with Nathan and Rod when I came out to join you yesterday morning before breakfast."

"The pyramid saga—it never ends," Chaiyala said, her voice clipped and dry.

"The pyramid plot..." Tim began. "Chaiyala's right—it goes on and on, like a bad smell you can't find the source of. It'll only end when it's finally forced to. And this is why Crouton can't stand the Egyptian Minister of Egyptology."

Chad listened intently, while Charlotte had already heard it all before arriving in Africa.

Chaiyala eagerly awaited the day excavation would finally settle the long-standing debate.

"In short," Tim continued, "traditional Egyptology has serious blind spots when it comes to the Great Pyramid at Giza and others. The problems are obvious—yet still ignored. So-called experts cling to their theories, even as the contradictions pile up. From an investigative historian's view, it's maddening."

Most people don't care. They shrug it off or dismiss it outright. Only a few politically jaded revisionists push for full disclosure. Some physics and electrical experts have flagged problems in the mainstream theories—but they've got bigger things to worry about.

Honestly, we wouldn't have cared either—until we stumbled on theories worth testing.

Then came the moment we couldn't ignore: evidence suggesting the cataclysm that destroyed Atlantis was triggered by the explosion of a 'working pyramid'. That changed everything.

Chad looked up at the sky, momentarily stunned by the phrase 'working pyramid'. *"There I go again... can't help myself,"* he laughed inwardly. *"Opening up yet another door... another whole new world of strange and unorthodox. What on God's good earth is—was—a working pyramid? What work was it doing, and how does that result in an explosion?"* He listened on.

"There's a dig site north of here that's turned up some strange evidence," Tim said. "If the theory holds, it has serious implications for the pyramids in Egypt. Pyramid technology came from Atlantis—but after the disaster, it was abandoned."

Tim glanced at Chad, now fully hooked.

"Now that I really have your curiosity and attention," he continued, riding side by side with Chad while the girls pedalled ahead, "let me begin with the traditional aspects of the history of the pyramids at Giza:

Chad recognised this as part of the unfolding narrative Tim was carefully building. His unpacking needed solid groundwork before any real conclusions could be drawn.

"The Great Pyramid was built over a period of twenty years using stone hammers and bronze chisels, and consisting of about 2.3 to 2.5 million limestone and granite blocks. Intended as Pharaoh Khufu's tomb, it housed three burial chambers.

The mathematical precision of its architecture is staggering—so much so that Egyptologists agree it would be difficult to recreate even with today's technology. And yet, it was built in the Bronze Age, without wheels, long before they were even invented."

Charlotte couldn't help but smirk.

Chaiyala rode on, indifferent.

Chad was immediately confused. "Okay, so that all sounds problematic and contradictory right from the beginning," he remarked.

"Precisely," Chaiyala called back, her tone laced with bored annoyance.

"The precision of Egyptian craftsmanship is remarkable."

Chad listened closely.

"Look at the statues and pottery. They raise a striking question: how were they made so perfectly? Achieving that level of detail with hammers and chisels alone seems implausible—maybe even impossible. Today, we use laser-guided tools and computer-controlled machines to reach similar accuracy. And even then, it can take days.

Tim let that settle, as Chad mulled it over.

"Egyptologists argue that the Ancient Egyptians had access to advanced mathematics and techniques we still don't fully understand. Yet, in the same breath, they insist these feats were accomplished with nothing more than Bronze Age chisels. It doesn't add up."

Chad frowned, "sounds about as much fun as cutting grass with a pair of scissors when you could be using a lawn mower."

"Makes you wonder what's the deal, eh?"

The prevailing theory—that limestone and granite blocks were cut using stone hammers and bronze chisels—has been tested, with disastrous results. Experiments show the chisels snap after a dozen strikes, and every alternative method takes hours just to leave a mark.

The hammer-and-chisel explanation raises serious problems. If the blocks were shaped this way, millions of tools would've been needed due to constant wear and breakage. Yet no vast cache of discarded bronze chisels, nor evidence of construction debris has ever been found to support the claim.

"Hmm, it's not till you actually stop to think about that..." realised Chad.

"Theories on how the pyramids were built vary widely, but all have serious flaws. Some suggest massive stone ramps were used, with slaves hauling blocks to the top using long straight logs. Others propose water-based methods—floating stones up inclined surfaces. However, no trees suitable for rolling logs ever existed in Ancient Egypt. Much less wood anywhere in the world sturdy enough to hold the weight of the blocks without being crushed. And no archaeological evidence supports the floating theory.

While some theories seem plausible at first glance, none have solid evidence. The lack of physical remnants—tools, ramps, or materials—casts doubt on conventional explanations."

Chad's mind was blown. He was keen to hear more.

"The maths is staggering—2.5 million blocks in twenty years? That's one every two and a half minutes, day and night, for two decades straight. And that's just the cutting—never mind hauling and stacking them with Bronze Age tools."

"Wow!"

"What's even more troubling is the absence of definitive evidence explaining how the pyramids were built. No Egyptian records describe the construction process—only speculation and circumstantial theories.

That's a glaring omission, especially given Ancient Egypt's meticulous scribal tradition. Scribes documented everything: royal achievements, religious rites, administrative minutiae. Papyrus enabled a centralized bureaucracy and a cultural obsession with legacy. So why the silence on their greatest architectural feat?"

Chad, eyes narrowed, found himself far away down a rabbit hole—he might as well keep going... these rabbits though, smelt more fishy than ancient relics and strange conspiracies.

"Still, there were exceptions," Tim continued. "Records were often selective, leaving out failures or politically sensitive events. Many documents were lost to decay, looting, or time. Periods of instability—like the Intermediate Periods where there was disruption to the flow of bureaucracy. And because scribes came from elite circles, everyday lives were rarely recorded unless tied to taxes or labour.

"What were the 'Intermediate Periods'?" Chad queried. "Egypt had three Intermediate Periods—times when central rule collapsed. Local leaders rose, foreigners invaded, records thinned out. It was both decline and transition. Power shifted, culture adapted. So yeah, gaps exist.

Religious upheavals like Akhenaten's radical reforms—led to censorship and the rewriting of earlier texts.

For all its reputation for precision, Egypt's record-keeping was shaped by power, ideology, and circumstance. Gaps exist, and they continue to intrigue historians."

"I see..."

"But even with those inconsistencies, the absence of any record detailing how the pyramids were built doesn't fit. It's more than a missing piece—it's the absence of decades long events, in a culture obsessed with documentation."

"That's very interesting... that their greatest achievement left no trace..." Chad thought out loud, "...if they documented everything else... why not that—why would something so monumental go unrecorded?"

"Well, that's the million-dollar question. Or, the twelve-thousand-year-old question." Tim left that hanging there.

"Because even in the worst of Egypt's periods, they still recorded grain tallies, temple repairs, priestly lineages. Bureaucracy didn't vanish—it just fractured. But the Pyramids? They were *supposed* to have been built during the Old Kingdom, Egypt's most stable era. No wars, no collapse. If ever there was a time to document something monumental, that was it."

Chad frowned.

"Sounds like the silence wasn't just neglect?"

Tim nodded. "It's deliberate. Or lost. Or worse, perhaps never even featured in the timeline to begin with. Either way, it's more than a missing page—it's a missing chapter. And that's what makes it so strange."

"So, they tracked how many loaves went to the temple kitchens, but not how they built a structure that's still standing after four thousand years? No record... over decades, this is hugely significant—it makes no logical sense—it doesn't fit. It's like someone wanted it forgotten... or, like they never built them..." Chad got the chills.

"And so, the plot thickens," Tim said with a grin.

He went on, "The idea that the Great Pyramid was Khufu's tomb rests mostly on some graffiti in an empty chamber—just a scribble translated as 'friends of Khufu'—and records of building materials arriving near Giza during his reign. But unlike actual burial sites, it's missing the usual hieroglyphic prayers and funerary texts. Egyptologists chalk that up to a shift in religious practice. Maybe. But that's speculation, not evidence—like the construction of the pyramids and who built them—no records."

Chad listened on, each of his brother's words like bronze nails sealing shut, the sarcophagus of doubt.

"The Great Pyramid is said to have housed mummified remains. Yet there's no solid evidence those bodies were placed there intentionally—or that the structure was even built for burial. At this point, the theories are so speculative, they might as well have been invented without considering the pyramid's architecture or its religious and cultural context.

Yes, mummified Pharaohs have been found in *some* pyramids. But conventional Egyptology often sidesteps the above unanswered questions."

The principle of 'Ma'at'—truth, justice, and cosmic balance—made Pharaohs divine, unquestionable rulers. Their egos towering high as the pyramids themselves. And they weren't above rewriting history to suit their image, erasing inconvenient truths to preserve their legacy.

Pharaohs embodied 'Ma'at', maintaining harmony between gods, people, and nature. To challenge their rule was to challenge the gods themselves."

"Wow. There's a lot of room for truth to have been reshaped..." Chad reflected, seeing the depth of the issue. "... and along those lines, a lot of room to repurpose a pyramid or two, given the size of some of those Pharaoh's egos," he speculated.

"What a weak case—in a legal context, the claim that they were tombs simply wouldn't stand up in a court of law." Chad was as puzzled as he was in awe. That this whole world of strange—seemingly fabricated or altered history, whatever it was—had been going on, even existed... it was a tad unnerving.

"Exactly," Chaiyala agreed. She and Charlotte had dropped back and rejoined Tim and Chad. "Endless possibilities. The tension between truth and legacy—that is the real story. What survives is not always what happened. It is often what someone *wanted* remembered."

"Okay... so, why then, are the pyramids considered tombs—where'd that begin?"

"Much of modern Egyptology rests on the writings of Herodotus, the Greek historian who relied on second hand accounts—many of them unverifiable. As a result, his work introduced errors that still demand serious correction. Coupled with the Ma'at problem and the fact that some mummies were found in pyramids. Of course, with no verifiable records, only speculation."

"Actually, that's the part that puzzles me the most," Chad began. "Why would an Egyptologist be happy with all of that; with the tomb theory? They should know what constitutes an Egyptian tomb of the Pharaohs? And I would have thought cross-referencing and verification would be paramount before presenting guess work and theory as fact? And, why would they be comfortable with the claim it was the Egyptians who built them, when an ancient people who were painstakingly thorough with record keeping left absolutely no record of their construction?" Thoughtful silence lingered a moment.

"What it really says to me, is there is way more to Egyptology than maintaining and preserving historical legacy... something much bigger at play here. More than a cover-up—more than conspiracy theory..." Chad paused. "The plot's now as thick as porridge..." he smiled.

"Brilliant way to sum it all up!" Tim grinned.

Chaiyala frowned and Charlotte smiled and shook her head.

"You see how the more you *actually* investigate everything—the more your conclusion becomes apparent," added Tim.

"Alas, you can only get so far with that. There are eighty archaeological scientists working at the Richat Project now who've been shut out of Egypt, deported, or targeted with attempts to discredit and slander their reputation in the scientific community because they challenged the system.

From a building engineer's point of view, the traditional time frame and proposed methods of construction are ludicrous. Yet such experts are routinely ignored—as are physicists who've broached the issue. From an investigative perspective, the facts and figures don't add up. The conclusion? Something smells fishy."

"This feels like textbook conspiracy—but it's too precise to be made up. That's what's messing with me." Chad shook his head—frowning, trying to make sense of it all. "I'm a law student, for crying out loud. Motive means opportunity—I've been trained to find truth behind illusion...

The alternative theory is feeling increasingly more grounded than the textbooks back home."

Tim nodded. "When my team visited the pyramids last year," he continued, "and the area where obelisks and blocks were shaped, "we discovered unusual rock cuts. Weird, like scoop, marks, holes, and surfaces that looked like they'd been shaped with modern machinery—some resembling laser-cut, half-finished stone blocks or discarded off-cuts. As we photographed and recorded, police arrived, questioned us, confiscated our cameras, erased the footage, and warned us of charges and deportation if we continued. What does that tell you?"

"Far out! ... that's crazy!" Chad replied, shaking his head.

"Hold onto your handlebars, bro—it gets worse. And more interesting. There's the mathematical aspect of the pyramids, where—throughout its measurements—you find the value of 'pi'."

"What?" Chad looked at his brother as if he were crazy.

"Yet Egyptians in that era weren't supposed to know about 'pi'. Whether conventional Egyptology accepts that or not is irrelevant," Tim explained with a grin. "Mathematical experts have made the calculations, using the structure of the pyramids, and are currently asking huge questions of Egyptologists—who can't give them any answers and don't want to know about it. The same experts are working here on the Richat Project as we speak."

"Seriously..." Chad gazed into the distance—mind blown—needing to hear more.

Tim continued, "There's one archaeological dig site—made famous in more than a couple of black-and-white movies from the early twentieth century—that's been shut down and fenced off by the Egyptian military. They're using it as a rubbish tip. It's made a lot of people furious."

"So why are they doing all of this, exactly?" Chad muttered, narrowed his eyes, frustration creeping in.

"A mess of convoluted reasons, is the short answer," Tim told him.

"There's a quiet tension between Egypt's modern religious identity and the ancient deities and customs that shaped its earliest civilization. While not always acknowledged, this contrast adds complexity to the ongoing debate over Egypt's true history. And despite decades of excavation, the Egyptian government has often been selective in its support for pyramid research—leaving many questions buried beneath layers of time, politics, and silence."

Tim paused. "Now we come to the most controversial theory—so radical, it's often dismissed as pure conspiracy.

It blows everything else out of the water, yet it's built on everything I've laid out so far. And it touches on the biggest unresolved question in Egyptology.

Nathan and Crouton won't waste time debating it until they've got hard evidence—irrefutable proof. But they believe the theory holds weight. Especially now that we know more about what happened with the exploded pyramid north of Atlantis."

He glanced at Chad.

"Here's where things get controversial. Some believe this is why black ops and mercenaries have opposed the Richat Project:

A growing number of historians, scientists, and electrical engineers argue that the Pyramids at Giza—and others like them—may have once functioned as colossal generators of ancient electricity.

The stone obelisks scattered across Egypt? Allegedly, they acted as receivers, forming part of a wireless energy system. The materials, design features, mathematical precision, and structural engineering all seem to support this theory—hence the rising interest from electrical experts and engineers."

"There we have it! The motive for the crimes." Chad's law-student mind had reached the precipice of a wild journey—rummaging through pieces of the unhinged, and the story Tim had been methodically unfolding over the past few days. "I can see now why you didn't begin with that."

"Exactly—you need all the background first—to really grasp how huge, how crazy, and how controversial it all is."

Crouton and Chaiyala—like most of Red Sword Security—have grown weary of how all this keeps getting brushed aside. It's the very reason they're constantly dealing with mercenaries and black ops teams, yet it's tolerated... for now.

"If there's nothing big with the Pyramids," Chaiyala began, "and the Richat structure—then why are some so desperate to stop the project from revealing their secrets?"

"If the theory is proven," Tim continued, "it could trigger a domino effect—exposing long-buried advancements in energy technology. Innovations that were ignored, downplayed, or outright suppressed by those who couldn't monetize or monopolize them once they surfaced.

And that's just the beginning.

This includes the suppression of Nikola Tesla's research, which led to him being cast out of the scientific community and dismissed as insane."

"Tesla—the guy who was researching wireless electricity," Chad recalled. "But history paints him as a mad scientist, maybe even dangerous. Some fringe theories say he was sabotaged... or worse."

"That's the one."

"Oh, how convenient," Chad remarked sarcastically.

"So, there's the big 'conspiracy theory' everyone's made a circus out of," Tim concluded, racking his brain for anything he'd missed.

"That's... huge!" Chad remarked, not sure what to think. "I think I've heard everything now... that's not just off the hook—that's off the planet! If reality had a disclaimer, I'd be reading the fine print right now."

They both laughed.

"Seriously though—I give up. I've got nothing on that, bro... dang!"

The bike track led Chad and Charlotte into a strikingly different part of the camp. As they ascended a small rise, the path curved alongside a fence—desert sand sloping down on one side, houses and green lawns on the other. It reminded Chad of home in Western Heights, resembling suburban Hamilton.

They passed the concert stage rising above palm groves and exotic vegetation. The sky hill now visible as they skirted the grassy fields—the stark contrast between greenery and desert was unmistakable.

CHAPTER 11

- -

After rinsing off the sweat and dust from their morning ride and feeling fresh again, Tim and Charlotte began prepping lunch for the group.

Chad and Rick lounged indoors, escaping the heat. Chaiyala soon joined them, fixing Rick with her signature intense stare. She knew threats no longer fazed her rival, even if occasionally used to vent. What truly unsettled him was her piercing gaze, silence, and the unspoken promise she could strike at any moment. She relished teasing him just as much as he did her—always in good fun, though rarely in ways anyone else would notice.

Chad appreciated how they could go from scrapping like over-competitive siblings to engaging in mature conversation about something work-related or of mutual interest. A sign of good friendship—as much as they drove each other up the wall—they were weird in the best of ways.

~~~~~~~

Later that afternoon, Nathan and Crouton stood around Tim's kitchen counter with Tim, Charlotte, and Chad, discussing the layout of tomorrow's trip across the Atlantic to Jamaica—when Charlotte's phone rang. It was one of those moments where conversation had, coincidentally paused, everyone between things to say.

Charlotte glanced sideways at her phone, unsure who'd be calling at that moment or what it might be about. It was her road manager, Tyrese.

"Hey dude!" she greeted.

"Hey, hey! How's the desert?"

"Hot, dry, exciting—and fascinating."

Tyrese laughed. "Whereabouts are you again?"

"Tim's working in Mauritania, North Africa. There's a pretty legit camp set up where all the excavation site workers live. Well, it's like a small town here actually... it's pretty cool, kinda like a summer festival vibe. Like the hottest summer ever! Zero humidity, and it's killer out in the direct sun."

"Ouch. Hope you've got a pool then."

"Yah, we do."

"Good. Hey, I've got some excellent news..."

"Yeah?"

"You sitting down? This is breakthrough stuff..."

"Okay, tell me..." Charlotte insisted.

"Jacob McKenzie wants to meet with you and discuss touring options next year."

Charlotte's eyes went wide with disbelief. "NO—WAY! OH—MY—GOODNESS!" She looked at Tim with the biggest smile, running the hand she wasn't holding her phone with through her hair.

Crouton gave Tim a puzzled frown, and Tim looked at her quizzically.

"He wants to know if you're able to meet with him and his roadie while you're in Jamaica at some stage...

"For sure! Wait—what? How?"

Nathan was grinning at Charlotte, and she gave him a pleased look of disbelief.

"I got a call last night from Mountain Goat Records—asking when you're free next year. Jacob's keen for you and the band to join him on the

'Deep-Unto-Deep' tour. A friend of his caught one of your shows in Aus. earlier this year and urged him to check out your sound. He did—was convinced and impressed. Jacob's with family in Jamaica and keen to meet if you're free. I've held off booking flights until speaking with you."

"Wow, that is so legit! Thanks so much, Ty!"

"You're welcome. It'd be nice to find out who it was who recommended you—this is pretty huge for us, Char..."

She cut him off, "Oh, I think I know who that friend could be."

"You do?"

Tim, Chad, and Crouton were all completely curious now, looking to Nathan for answers—or Charlotte, once she was off the phone, whichever came first.

"Yah. Friend of Tim's. Met him this morning."

All eyes snapped back to Nathan. Crouton chuckled, looking at the floor, then out into the distance—amused and delighted by his friend's ability to make people's day. Not that he knew what Nathan had pulled off this time, but it was a pleasant quality of his, and it always brought a lot of joy.

Chad and Tim exchanged a glance, highly intrigued. Tim was beginning to put two and two together—and got goosebumps. Jacob McKenzie was one of Tim's all-time favourite musicians.

"... It's a long story, but I'll tell you everything soon! Hey, so—email me the detes and let Mountain Goat know I'm super keen. One moment..."

She looked at Nathan and Crouton. "What's our schedule while we're in Jamaica?"

"We'll make it up as we go along," Nathan smiled. "Jacob knows we'll be there from tomorrow, so you and he pick a time—and we'll work around you either way."

"Thanks so much! You're amazing!" Charlotte beamed, returning to her conversation with Tyrese. "Do you want to suggest any day and time after tomorrow evening? Then let me know what they say. We head over from Africa early tomorrow morning."

"All good, my friend. I'll get back to Mountain Goat and let them know."

"You're amazing!"

"Cheers. I'll email you everything you need to know shortly and then call to discuss. Did you want me there, or will you Skype me in?"

"Yes! Absolutely! Oh—either, really. Up to you."

"Hmm... I'd love to be in Jamaica, but I've got so much post-tour work to do. Skype it is."

"Oi, you make sure you take a break, right?"

"What's a break?"

"If you haven't had one by the time I'm back in New Zealand, I'm making you take one."

"Yeah, alright... cool. Then we'll talk soon."

"Yes! Thanks—see ya!"

They hung up. Charlotte squealed loudly, then hugged Tim, jumping up and down before announcing, "WE'RE GONNA MEET J-Mac!"

"Serious?" Chad asked, smiling.

"Wow! Crazy! That's seriously insane!" Tim celebrated.

Charlotte looked at Nathan, her smile growing, then jumped at him, wrapping him in a tight hug. "Thank you so much!"

"You're very welcome!" Nathan laughed.

"You didn't tell me you went to see this lass's concert..." Crouton grinned.

"You didn't tell me you knew Jacob McKenzie!" Tim protested.

"Oh, didn't I?" Nathan feigned absent-mindedness. "Must've slipped my mind," he added indifferently. Then, looking seriously at Tim and

Crouton, he said, "...all the same, what have I told you both about asking? Neither of you asked, so neither of you found out, did you?"

Crouton shook his head with a grin, sighed, and said, "You're a hard case."

"Yeah, I'd be there forever and never get anything done if I asked you questions every time I thought one was needed," Tim replied. "Then half the time I wished I hadn't asked." They all laughed.

"So, which show were you at?" Charlotte asked.

"Gold Coast Arena. I had meetings nearby several weeks ago, and if I hadn't walked past the front gates and spotted ads and your name on the upcoming events screens, I wouldn't have known you were performing there. I recognized your name—Tim's told me much about you. So, out of curiosity, I grabbed a ticket and went.

From what Tim shared, I knew this was part of your first big tour, and I also knew Jacob had been looking for someone new to partner with for touring and ministry. You're incredibly talented—no doubt about that."

"Aww! Thank you so much!"

"Actually," Nathan said, turning to Crouton, "is Charlotte slated to perform here? The festival, I mean. We have Uprise, Element, and Kayla Breeze all booked?" He trailed off, caught mid-thought, trying to piece it together aloud.

Crouton followed the train of thought and figured it'd be a great idea. He wondered why he hadn't considered it already.

"End of the month we've got those guys and a bunch of local acts happening," Crouton confirmed, thoughtfully, then asked Charlotte, "You keen?"

"Heck yeah! Keen as!"

"Excellent!" Nathan celebrated.

"Local acts? In Mauritania... I'm intrigued now," Chad said, fascinated.

"Local as in inclusive of most of Africa, the Middle East, and France," Rod clarified.

"Riptide. Starfish, too," Crouton recalled. "They're booked with Uprise and co."

Tim and Charlotte looked at each other wide-eyed with excitement.

Chad struggled to process—his mind swam as he studied his brother, amazed at how effortlessly he handled the absurd and unpredictable.

He recalled a guy he used to work with. Someone who'd overcome anxiety and depression by learning to let overwhelming thoughts, simply fade. The guy had made a conscious choice to recognise that some thoughts are too much and need to disappear.

Chad had often thought about that, wondering if he truly understood it... could it actually be that simple?

Right now, he did. It was a mental health survival mechanism.

~~~~~~~

The house had settled into a kind of quiet hum—sunlight slanting through the blinds, the occasional clink of a mug in the kitchen, and the low bustle chatter of Tim and Charlotte in the kitchen. Chad let the stillness wrap around him like a weighted blanket. He didn't need to solve anything right now. Just breathe.

Rhys and Antonio wandered in around mid-afternoon, dusty from the road and mid-conversation about something involving solar flares and goat migration. Antonio was animated, gesturing with both hands, while Rhys looked like he'd been listening for hours and had no idea how to stop. He gave Nathan a nod and a half-smile, then collapsed onto the couch with theatrical relief.

Chaiyala was already there, curled up with a book and a cup of something herbal. She looked luminous—fresh-faced, relaxed, and entirely at home. Chad noticed the way she'd tucked her feet beneath her and tilted the book just so, like she'd done this a thousand times before in a thousand different places.

Then, in true random Rick style, he emerged from the passageway with both arms raised, wearing giraffe sock puppets on his hands. He made a loud noise that sounded like a pig being slaughtered, while moving around the lounge room in much the same way a chook would.

Tim and Chad frowned and laughed—girls shook their heads, grinning.

Nathan was highly amused—unsurprised. He'd been looking forward to Rick's unique brand of humour.

In a booming, dramatic voice, Rick declared, "And there were an abundant number of elephants on the island of Atlantis!"—followed by more dying pig noises.

"What in blazes are you doing, son?" Crouton demanded.

"I'm quoting Plato?"

"Why?"

"Cos there were lots of elephants in Atlantis... It's from the writings of Plato," Rick said, almost disappointed that Crouton didn't know this.

"I know that! But why are you walking around like a goose with a carrot up its rear, sounding like a hog in a slaughterhouse, and what's with the giraffes? Heck, son! What's all that got to do with Plato?" he bellowed.

Everyone laughed.

"Giraffes! They're bloomin' elephants!" Rick corrected indignantly.

"Elephants? Eh-eh. No chance." Chaiyala dismissed.

Rick's tangled retelling of Plato's elephants in Atlantis had them all in hysterics.

But beneath the humour, it stirred real curiosity—especially about the six sites where elephant remains had been found.

~~~~~~~

The afternoon was spent in the pool. Tim and Charlotte only got out to crack open ice-cold Nectargys savouring the rare blue and berry flavour while soaking up the sun on the deck's bean bags.

Chaiyala read a book, curled up on a sofa until just before dinner.

Crouton, Rod, Kristie, and Rick prepared another culinary masterpiece. Eventually they fired up the barbecues, commencing the burning of meat.

"Actually, I've changed my mind," Crouton said to Rod as he moved spicy chicken drumsticks around on the hot plate. "I want you with us in Jamaica—and I want Chaiyala and Rhys as well. I need your input and experience; I need at least one ninja and a couple extra muscle. Rhys and Chaiyala work well together and get on great with our new friends. Again, Kristie you're fully welcome to come, as always. There—we're looking a whole lot better for the trip now."

Kristie looked up at Crouton from what she was doing and smiled at Rod.

"Was it bothering you, prior to that decision?" Rod asked.

"Hmm... not so much bothering me. Sometimes things just feel incomplete, and I don't like a strategy with loose ends."

"Honestly," began Kristie, "I was a bit disappointed for you, that you weren't going. You need a break from the usual, Honey—just something different for a change. I'm fine—I'm not too fussed about coming along this time. We've got a decent amount of leave owing, we can wait till then—when we can enjoy a few weeks, just the two of us, up some snowcapped mountains in Europe skiing and doing other cold activities to compensate for the heat here."

"That sounds so good!" Rod breathed.

"Brilliant!" Crouton chuckled.

He paused, looking over the top of the barbecue. Rhys and Chaiyala were engaged in an arm wrestle in his line of sight. Neither seemed to be taking it seriously, yet both were going hard at it—back and forth.

"When we return, you and Kristie should definitely get outta here for a month or so—get some proper R and R and time alone. God only knows you've earned it."

"Cheers, man. That'd be perfect," Rod replied, nodding.

"We can always fly you back if something really exciting is unearthed," Crouton added, then called out to Rhys and Chaiyala, "Oi, you two—holding hands—keen for a trip to Jamaica?"

"Aye! Yup, I'll do it!" Rhys called back in his thick Scottish accent. But his enthusiasm caused a lapse in concentration, and Chaiyala pinned his hand.

"YUSS! I don't believe it—I actually did it!"

Chad, Tim, and Charlotte were in hysterics.

Rhys protested, "No you didn't—I was distracted!"

"Excuses, excuses... I can beat you at arm wrestling," Chaiyala teased.

"Alright then, Miss Muscles—let's go again."

"Hmm... you really think your ego's got the stamina to lose again?"

"You cocky cow!" Rhys laughed.

Chaiyala poked her tongue at him and flexed. "Another time, yah? I'm busy celebrating."

Tim and the others laughed, then began grabbing plates and migrating toward the barbecue.

"Don't worry, mate," Rick said, arriving just in time to witness the end. He slapped Rhys on the shoulder. "This is the same kinda poppycock I have to deal with from her over and over."

"Oh come on, Rick! I beat you, two seconds flat. You know it," Chaiyala joked.

"See what I mean? Never-ending. I blame H..."

"No you don't..." Crouton cut Rick off before he could get going. "Don't start with that. There's no need for that hoo-ha. Here—take the biggest piece of steak you can find and stuff it in your trap. There we go. That steak'll save ya life, ya crazy wombat."

Rick went and sat back down.

"Young man's brain-mouth-filter needs servicing" Crouton muttered under his breath.

"Woulda' gotten more than a servicing if he'd have finished his sentence," Tim joked.

Thankfully, Chaiyala hadn't heard a word of what Rick had said... or was gearing up to.

"And that's getting off lightly," Rod added, eyeing Rick—who was clearly oblivious to how badly he was about to put his foot in his mouth.

All the while, Rhys and Chaiyala were preoccupied with a different topic of discussion.

Chad frowned, not having a clue what on earth was happening.

"Don't ask, bro," Tim warned. "You don't want to know. Not right now. I'll tell you later."

Chad gazed at his brother blankly a moment... "Right..."

After a hearty feast, they sat around—some in the pool, others on bean bags or deck chairs—chatting the evening away.

"Take it easy Rhys, no hangovers from anyone flying outta here in the AM!" Crouton declared as the clean-up concluded and another box of Woodstocks was cracked open around 10 p.m.

"Aye boss!"

Nathan, Crouton, Charles, and Jacqui relaxed in the outdoor loungers outside Crouton's place, while Chad and Tim sat by the water with drinks, feet dangling, farewelling Rick and Rhys around half ten. Down the other end of the pool, the girls chatted away, while Rod and Kristie had left earlier to enjoy a quiet evening alone.

"Hey, I think I'm gonna head up to the sky hill," Chad said to Tim. "Keen to come?"

Tim hadn't made any plans. "Yeah, why not," Tim agreed.

~~~~~~~

Chad was glad he'd invited Tim along. He hadn't remembered the way through the palms and ferns up to the sky hill and figured a short trip during the day would help get a proper feel for it—each step and every corner looked the same in the dark.

Then suddenly, they were there. The lonely wooden table with the silhouetted palm next to it stood against the navy-blue sky, lit spectacularly by the stars. Toward the west, the last sliver of dusk light from the sunset was vanishing beyond the northern end of the Adrars.

The pristine sound of pure silence was broken for a split second when the two brothers cracked open cold cans of Blue Nectargy.

"To new horizons beyond the ones we know," Tim said, raising his can in the dim light just as their eyes were adjusting.

Chad knocked his can against Tim's. "And to brotherhood."

"This stuff is dangerously good," Tim groaned after his first sip—chilled to perfection. They marvelled at Nathan's love for creating meaningful experiences—whether through small gifts or grand events that brought joy or even transformed lives.

"You're doin' all good? Like, with the trickier things of the mind..."

Chad knew what Tim meant. "That's why I wanted to come up here. Was trying to detach my mind from things, but I can't do that when there's lots of people around."

"That's why I come up here every other night or so. Chaiyala's the only other person I know who comes up here regularly. It's a great spot to clear the head... look at the sky—remember how much bigger and more awesome the better things of life are...

It's good to come up here and get away from it all. Honestly, I'm really looking forward to flying out to Jamaica in the morning. Get a break and a change of scenery."

Chad was silent.

"Yeah... I'm the same." His tone carried weight. He took a deep breath as his eyes began to fill...

"Yup. Breathe easy, man. Take your time—I'm here."

"Cheers," Chad sobbed.

"You're doin' the right thing coming up here, bro," Tim thought to himself.

That was the thing about their relationship, Chad thought. He had others, of course—some who understood, some who knew first-hand. But Tim was different. He'd watched his big brother suffer through depression and come out on top. That gave Chad courage. Reassurance.

Plenty would see Chad suddenly in tears—sad beyond return—wondering what had brought it on, unable to understand. What made things worse, is he couldn't explain why.

Or they assumed something had happened, or they'd put it down to his breakup with Sonia. That last part he utterly loathed. It wasn't that simple—there was more to it than that. He hated how some had to attach it to a thing—rationalize it and make it about something it wasn't.

It wasn't always automatically about anything.

At first, Chad had no idea what was happening—then the anxiety attacks began. He feared losing his freedom, either in a hospital or life itself. Both possibilities terrified him. Rationalizing it never helped.

As he navigated it—much like Tim—he *sometimes* traced it to a specific issue or experience, but not always. It was rarely as simple as a breakup or a tough day that left him vulnerable. No, that would've been too easy. He was beginning to understand it ran deeper—something was unsettled in his mind and inner world. Often, hunger, exhaustion, isolation, or lack of physical activity triggered it too.

Tim never trivialized anything. He didn't rush to solutions that had nothing to do with what Chad was dealing with. Tim sometimes knew it was just what it was—depression. That was it.

Understanding that the issue partly stemmed from chemical imbalances in the brain helped.

"Let's be honest," Tim once told Chad, "the human mind is an intricate machine—still beyond full neuroscientific understanding. If a single brain chemical misfires—one that regulates everything from fear to reasoning—it's like a human short-circuit. Not beyond repair, but it takes patience, understanding, and care."

Tim exercised all three immaculately.

He sat there quietly, sipping his Nectargy for about five minutes. Still—completely present—watching to keep at Chad's pace.

His younger brother let out a long breath of release in the shadows. The two of them, along with the table and palm tree, were mostly silhouettes—the moon rising late tonight.

"What's the first thing that comes to mind?" Tim asked.

"Thankfulness. Thanks that you're here." Chad felt a smile from Tim in the darkness.

Tim paused. "What's the next thing?"

Chad took a moment... "This place, right here It's incredible... calming, peaceful."

Tim waited again. "What about after that?"

"My head feels like it's going to explode with everything racing through it."

"What does it look like inside your head right now, bro?"

Chad paused, searching for words, but the complexity of it all pushed him to the edge of a panic attack. He stopped, focused on his breathing, then on the patterns in the stars—distracted for a few minutes by thoughts of ancient explorers who navigated the world using constellations.

Tim took the opportunity to reflect on how he dealt with head traffic when it got too much.

"It's... all, it's all so frustrating—crazy!" Chad shook his head. "It's overwhelming, all at once. I don't know where to start with all this new information, what the heck I'm supposed to do with it. And on top of that, the controversy—the attacks on the way here and the other night, the government conspiracies—it's all so heavy..."

"That's okay," Tim said kindly and casually.

"Plato's description of Atlantis, the library at the visitors' centre, the documentary—that's all fine—maybe I'm more comfortable in a library researching things." Chad struggled to speak, to understand himself or what was actually doing his head in. "I dunno, man. Everything's getting so intense, and it's messing with me."

"I fully get that, bro. I hear ya—and it's completely fine to feel that way," Tim reassured.

Chad thanked Tim inwardly. He didn't need words for Tim to know.

A few moments passed before Chad asked, "How do you stay above it all? This is world-changing—you clearly get the gravity of it—I'm in the deep end here."

Silence.

"Don't get me wrong though, brother," he added. "I'm truly grateful you brought me out here—it's amazing! Your friends are cool, and this is exciting stuff. I guess I just gotta slow down... but my mind can't. Ya know the infuriating thing? In the morning I'm gonna be fine—and it's so darn infuriating, knowing that right now!"

"I know," Tim laughed. "It's so irritating eh."

Chad breathed out, frustrated—then nodded, calming. "Cheers!"

"Ironically, the fact that you know you're gonna be okay soon is the biggest key. It's worse when you don't."

Getting all of that off his chest had done Chad the world of good.

"This might sound funny," Tim began, "but the Richat project, black ops mercenaries, and pyramid theories—none of it really matters. I love my job—the excitement, the adventure. I love history and discovery, both as a scholar and a man of faith. But, I love my family, Charlotte, my friends, and God more than anything in life. Conspiracy theories come and go—the pyramids were power plants, or they weren't—the Richat was Atlantis, or it wasn't. What's undeniable is the incredible story here—something truly significant.

Yes, I'm a historian, but more than that, I'm your brother, Charlotte's fiancé, a child of God. Seeing you and Char here, going back home to Mum and Dad—that fulfils me more than unearthing lost civilizations. I'm excited about history, but I'm even more excited to stand beside Charlotte at the altar and live the life we've dreamed of. I'm one of the crazies living in a high-tech desert camp that's grown beyond what Nate and Crout imagined. And we have rock concerts here—simply because it's fun. It's flipping ridiculous!"

They both laughed a while.

"I mean seriously!"

Tim paused.

"I take stock of all the intense, serious, or stressful stuff and say— literally say— 'That's enough. Forget it. I'm going home. I'll deal with it tomorrow. I've got better things to do.' Something like that.

Crouton's funny with it too—does something similar. He jokes, 'Tomorrow I'm outta here. Gonna open me an ice-cream parlour at the beach and retire a happy, ice-cream-peddling old man with nothing but ice-cream to worry about.'"

Chad laughed, then paused. "Was Crouton married?"

"Yeah... Natalie. Killed by black ops, before the Richat project began."

"Oh... gutted to hear that."

"Yeah. Really sad. I never got to meet her, but, Chaiyala, Charles and Jacqui, Rod and Kristie were very close to Natalie—still are to Crout, obviously. Natalie was like a mum to Chaiyala. It hit her hard... Crouton has two sons and a daughter. All work for Red Sword as well. His sons head up Red Sword in Canada and South Africa. His daughter works undercover when she's not leading strategics and intel—providing Red Sword with vital information about any opposition."

Chad nodded.

"Kids are like their dad..."

"Much like a blender with no lid?"

They both laughed.

"...but it's one way of keeping them protected—at least you know someone's got eyes on them when you can't."

"Wow, that's pretty cool then," Chad said thoughtfully.

"I'm extremely strict about what goes on in my mind too," Tim shared. "The Richat project is just one small part of my life. Even my friendships with Crout, Rod, Chaiyala, Rhys, and the others matter more than work—which stays compartmentalized in its own box."

Thought grouping was something Chad's therapist had been guiding him through—a method he struggled with, despite reassurances he was making progress.

He was glad he'd committed to the process before realizing how bad he was at it... otherwise, he might never have tried.

"Anything that fuels anxiety goes in a separate box." Tim shared, "then there's my family box, my faith box, my Charlotte box, and others. The work box stays separate from the chaos and controversy box—and both stay far away from the boxes with the things that truly matter."

It's a mental strategy I work—not always easy, but conditioning my thinking this way keeps me from going stir-crazy. Things get overwhelming; too much at times. People turn to different things for stability—sport, religion, whatever keeps them grounded. For me, it's God—His comfort and peace. Not everyone's approach, but I believe He helps people in ways as unique as they are.

"Interesting thought..."

One of Tim's biggest turning points in his mental health journey—something only Charlotte knew—was learning to say 'no' to anxiety and depression itself. He wasn't sure if it was something someone said or a realization that hit him, but suddenly, he saw how much he'd used them as a crutch.

"Something else, bro. I've only told Charlotte about this, actually. I realised I'd been using anxiety and depression to avoid people, to not make an effort. If I couldn't cope at a job, I'd quit and blame my anxiety and depression. I even tried to push Charlotte away, convinced she'd eventually get fed up with me—that I didn't deserve her. But she wasn't having it. She can be stubborn sometimes, funny thing is—the timing's often perfect..."

He sighed. "Backing out was easy. Telling myself, 'That happened because I'm depressed, and that's okay,' was easy. But eventually, I had to face the truth—it wasn't okay. And I saw how much smaller my world had become because of it. Praise God I had Charlotte!"

"Far out, man! I had no idea," Chad said, shaking his head—part of him wishing he'd known more back then, another part grateful he did now.

"I couldn't live that way, eh. It had to have been divine intervention. It was such an epic answer to prayer, whatever it was. Once I knew what was going on, it was like the light had been turned on. Then I was passionate about doing something about the real issue. The rest is all history."

What Tim had shared made a lot of sense to Chad. There was far more in what Tim had disclosed about his own mental health journey than Chad had ever known—it gave him a great deal to ponder.

"Thanks—thanks heaps, man," he said.

"All good, bro," Tim replied, taking another sip of his Nectargy.

Chad hadn't touched his since taking a few sips before their deep and meaningful. "I might leave that, if that's all good. Appreciate the thought though..."

They heard voices coming from below, in the trees. It was Charlotte and Chaiyala.

Eventually, the flicker of their LED lantern could be seen weaving up through the gaps in the ferns and palms along the track.

The two girls arrived to join Chad and Tim.

Tim and Charlotte kissed as she sat beside her fiancé, opposite Chad. Chaiyala settled next to him, setting the lantern on the table near the palm tree.

"How are you doing?" she asked. The other two giggled about something.

"All good..." Chad said, nodding—as if he'd just made a decision and agreed with it.

She looked at him keenly, her face lit with shadows from the eerie glow of the lantern. "You guys having deep talks, maybe?"

"Yeah, pretty much," he replied casually.

"This drink—what is it?" Chaiyala asked, examining Chad's nearly full can of Nectargy.

"That's Nectargy—you can try it if you want. Have the rest. It's an energy drink, and I really shouldn't be drinking it anyway."

"I see." Chaiyala put the can to her lips and took a sip. "Wow—dang! That's sweet. Like sherbet... in liquid form."

"It's good, huh?" Charlotte asked.

"Yes! That's sweet," she said, taking another swig. "Fruity, like... peach? Passion fruit? Cherry? I don't know. What's this flavour?" she asked Chad.

"Blue."

"What's blue?"

"No idea. That's part of the deal—you're not quite sure exactly what the flavour is. It keeps you guessing."

"Interesting fruit—so it's blue-looking—like, really?"

"Huh?" Chad didn't follow.

"No, no, no. Blue—the colour. It's not a fruit," Charlotte giggled. "The can is the only thing that's blue. The drink inside is more of a yellow-green."

Chaiyala was puzzled... then clicked. "Wait... ohh! Got it. That's funny!"

They all laughed.

CHAPTER 12

Without meaning to, Tim and Charlotte drifted into their own conversation, tuning out the others.

Neither Chad nor Chaiyala minded. They let the couple chat and turned their gaze to the huge full moon ascending gradually over the western horizon, just left of the Adrars.

"It is beautiful," Chaiyala stated softly, jadedly, holding onto the sight like it was the last good thing in a world weighed down by exhaustion and turmoil.

"Yeah... pretty awesome," Chad replied, equally distant.

Both sat in silence, minds heavy, seeking relief. Both knew the view was incredible, yet couldn't appreciate or enjoy it.

Chaiyala leaned against the palm trunk next to the end of the table, settling in her usual spot on top of it. Chad sat behind her on the bench. They spoke no more—letting the quiet stretch and settle between them.

Everything Tim had shared earlier, before Charlotte and Chaiyala arrived, had landed deeply. Chad clung to every word. His heart wasn't the issue—his mind was a battlefield. Exhausted by the world: its greed, corruption, and selfishness. He longed to switch his heart off to everything that didn't matter. His thoughts churned beneath the night sky, shadowed and tired.

Chaiyala, too, desperately needed a break. Physically, she was sharp, even at her peak. Mentally, it was the opposite. The morning's mountain biking trip had been her first in weeks—she hadn't been running at sunrise or dusk like she used to. She'd confined herself to the gym, sprinting on treadmills because it was easier. Lately, her frustration was poured into weights and punching bags, battling ghosts of the past and fury at mercenaries increasingly getting under her skin.

Should she walk away? Find a quiet job in New Zealand or Australia—somewhere removed from unrest? Or stay with Red Sword, the only family she had? They were past the point of no return—quitting wasn't an option. But would she reach the finish line whole... or barely holding together?

At the other end of the table, Tim and Charlotte chatted about life. Wedding plans, and the mysterious Red Nectargy. Their lives were full of light and laughter—a contrast to Chad and Chaiyala, who craved something to brighten their own worlds.

A phrase entered Tim's mind, clear as crystal—as though spoken aloud:

"Speak life into the vision and the hearts of your friends—speak now."

He glanced at Charlotte, wondering if she'd heard it too—but no. Then he clicked—he knew exactly Who it was. Especially when his gaze fell upon Chad and Chaiyala.

"Hey, you guys alright?" he asked gently.

Chaiyala didn't respond—barely registered his words.

"Stop the world. I want to get off. I'm sick of it all," Chad muttered, finally looking over at Tim and Charlotte.

"Sorry... what?" Chaiyala blinked, snapping out of it—wondering if she'd imagined something.

"Bro, I feel like I'm stuck on one side of a chasm—surrounded by the world's lies, corruption, and hypocrisy. I can hardly stand watching the news—can't even focus on it any more. It just makes me angry... I'm fed up with people."

He wiped his eyes and continued.

"Everything you've said tonight is incredible—wise, true, and inspiring—but I've no idea how to make it real... it's all on the other side of the chasm. I can't get to it. What good is kindness when I feel so weighed down by hatred and deceit?"

Chad broke down and sobbed.

"Oh man—" Chaiyala breathed. Her heart shattered for him—but she had no energy left. Not for her own stuff, let alone anyone else's. She felt bad she couldn't do more.

"Aww, Chad," Charlotte said tenderly as she shuffled along to hug him from behind. Chad leaned into her and Tim shifted to sit directly in front of him.

"Now we can really deal with the stuff that needs dealing with," he began. "I love you, bro—Charlotte does too. You're with family and friends, and we're gonna get through this together. Okay?"

"'kay," Chad whispered—exhausted.

Chaiyala turned around to face Tim and Chad and Charlotte moved to give him their attention.

"Sometimes," Tim said, "there are moments for sorting out what matters from what doesn't. But sometimes we get hit with so much of the latter—trying to trick us into believing it's important."

He sat forward, calm and grounded.

"Let me share something a wise woman of God once told me: 'we stand in a room with two windows, one at each end. Through one, evil and corruption creep in—bringing burdens, bitterness, distraction. Through the other, righteousness and freedom pour in—bringing purpose, joy, peace. You can only focus on one at a time. If you choose the first, fear and anger consume you. But if you focus on the second—you're lifted by hope and inspiration."

Chaiyala liked that—it gave her something positive to hold onto. She wasn't battling anxiety and depression like Chad. She was just drained... and in need of renewal.

Chad nodded. "That's awesome. But how do I focus on the good instead of the bad?"

Tim met his gaze directly. "That's the best and most simple part: you just focus on the good—and shut out the bad. Some would call that naïve—unrealistic. But you can stay aware of the world's issues without letting them consume you.

What should consume you is the good. And trust me—there's a lot of it. You just have to know where to look. Once you find it, focus on it above everything else. Let that positivity fuel your strength to confront the rest."

Tim glanced at Chad and the girls. "So, here are a few good things that all happened recently—around the world."

"For starters, Nepal's wild tiger population more than doubled in under a decade. From 121 in 2009 to 225 in 2018."

Salt Water Brewery in Florida developed edible beer rings—safe for turtles and marine life.

The town of Collecchio in Italy passed a law allowing only silent fireworks, helping protect dogs and animals that are normally terrified by the noise.

"Aww that's so cute!" Charlotte beamed.

Chad nodded, impressed.

"In 2018, global literacy rates hit an all-time high—95 percent. In 1960, it was 42 percent, climbing by 4 percent every five years. That's the opposite of what media often leads you to believe."

He continued with a calming rhythm.

"Tree growth over the past 35 years has more than offset global tree loss.

Honeybee populations are rising.

Giant pandas are no longer endangered. China's building a $1.5 billion panda conservation park, bigger than Jamaica or even Israel."

"Adidas partnered with Parley for the Oceans, selling over a million shoes made from ocean plastic."

"Nice!" Charlotte expressed excitedly, "Cyrill Gutsch founded Parley for the Oceans on the idea that creative collaboration—fuelled by imagination—could inspire people to care about our oceans. I read about it in an inflight magazine during my Australasia tour. Super cool."

"Adidas are making shoes from plastic cleaned up out of the sea?" Chad clarified.

"Yup," Tim confirmed. "And guess who helps fund the Ocean Clean-up Project?"

"Who?" asked Chaiyala.

"Our friend—Nathan O'Conner."

"I'm not surprised," she smiled knowingly.

"Oh man, I feel like a real jerk for what I said the other morning." Chad shook his head.

"What did you say?" Chaiyala asked.

Chad sighed. "I need to remember that just because someone is rich doesn't automatically make them an elitist gatekeeper."

"Oh..." Chaiyala said gently. "If that's the worst you've said, you're fine. Worse has been said of him."

Tim silently considered pointing out the irony—Chad's family weren't exactly middle-income. And Chad clearly had no idea what Nathan and Crouton paid Tim annually.

"Rural doctors in Rwanda can now order medical supplies via text—and receive deliveries via drone."

"Awesome!" Charlotte beamed.

"Looking at success stories from aid organizations—truly brightens your day. Good things are happening worldwide. Constantly."

Chad nodded slowly. Charlotte smiled wide. Even Chaiyala seemed comforted by the reminder.

"Soft drink sales in the US dropped for the twelfth year straight due to consumer education and sugar taxes. Portugal banned the use of wild animals in circuses—joining a growing list of countries where it's illegal."

"Julia—Sesame Street's new character with autism—is helping parents recognise early signs in their children."

"Oh, that's real cool," Charlotte added.

"Some of this stuff is just pure creative genius," Chad remarked.

"Is common sense. Very refreshing, honestly," Chaiyala added.

"Single-use plastic straws are being banned globally and replaced with wax-lined paper ones—including at Buckingham Palace," Tim noted.

"Interesting," Chad pondered.

"Yes, I saw that in parts of Australia," Charlotte recalled. "It's begun in McDonald's restaurants."

"Nice!" Chad nodded.

"In 2017, the ozone hole over Antarctica shrank to its smallest size since 1988.

The border between Ethiopia and Eritrea reopened this year—ending twenty years of war and resentment."

"Rats are protecting elephants," Tim smiled. "They're being trained to sniff out land mines on migration routes across Southern Africa—mines too small for the rats to trigger."

"Aww, that is so adorable! Seriously!" Charlotte beamed.

"That is so!" Chaiyala agreed warmly.

"Saudi Arabia lifted its ban on women driving—allowing women behind the wheel for the first time in history.

Global breast cancer deaths have dropped 39%, saving over 322,000 lives.

The Netherlands now has the lowest prison population in Europe. Some prisons have even been converted into homes for Syrian refugees."

Chad looked astonished, feeling better than he had in days. "How do you even remember all this?"

"It is reminding me of Rod," Chaiyala said with quiet smile.

Tim shrugged. "I'm used to memorizing historical events, dates, and global trends—part of the job."

"Global tobacco use has declined. Especially among women," he continued.

"The world added nearly 30% more solar energy capacity in 2017.

California banned beauty products tested on animals.

France banned five pesticides linked to bee deaths—and they now prohibit supermarkets from throwing away excess food. All surplus must be donated or face a fine.

And ISIS is losing control in the Middle East due to internal disillusionment. The regular horror and trauma witnessed is fracturing their ranks."

"And back home—in New Zealand," Tim added, "the government passed legislation allowing victims of domestic abuse up to ten days paid leave to relocate into safer housing."

He paused.

"I think that's all I recall off the top of my head... and, this year is not alone. Positive stuff has been happening year after year, and on the increase."

A hush settled over the group—thick with encouragement, stillness, and relief.

"That is a whole lotta seriously cool," Chad said quietly.

Charlotte smiled. "It's so important to focus more on the good in the world than the negative... there's so much of it out there."

"Is true—especially when having negative to face head on," added Chaiyala reflectively.

"Studies show constant exposure to negative news is linked to mental health issues," Tim said. "But when we shift our attention to the bigger picture—the good in the world and in each other—it calms the mind, brings clarity, and stops fear from stealing our peace."

The air had softened. The sense of freedom gently erased frustration—for Chad, and especially for Chaiyala. They sat in quiet serenity, letting the night breeze move through them as the full moon bathed the terrain in gentle glow.

Chaiyala no longer felt disillusioned. Chad's mind had stopped racing—no longer spiralling toward anxiety.

"Thank you, Tim," she said with a genuine smile. "Thank you for reminding what matters—and for helping us to keep the balance."

"You're welcome," he replied. "I had a sense something was up."

"My mind feels emptied out," Chad admitted. "All the whinging, frustration, and negative noise... it's gone. And better things replace those."

He exhaled slowly, tired—but at peace. "Thanks for a great chat," he added.

They exchanged weary good nights.

Chad and Chaiyala walked back through the bush track down Sky Hill. Tim and Charlotte followed soon after—moonlight guiding their steps.

~~~~~~~

Tim awoke to a burst of laughter and a sudden weight pressing down on him. Charlotte had landed squarely on the bed, knees pinning the duvet over him, her eyes sparkling with mischief.

"Good morning, my handsome historian," she grinned, her face inches from his.

Tim blinked against the sunlight, registering her presence just as she kissed him.

"Good morning, my rascally rock star," he replied.

"I'm not rascally!" she protested, narrowing her eyes. "How about stunningly sexy singer?"

"Someone's woken up super confident," Tim laughed.

Charlotte held firm, giggling as he squirmed. His thrashing finally dislodged her, and she tumbled backward with a squeal, sliding down the bed in a heap of tangled sheets and laughter.

"We're going to Jamaica! We're going to meet J-Mac and relax at a luxury resort!" Charlotte bounced gleefully with an excited grin.

"I can't wait! It's gonna be awesome," Tim said, shaking off sleep to match her infectious energy.

He couldn't wait to meet Alesandro Karahalios and J-Mac—and was just as eager to dive into the Solon Diaries and soak up everything ahead.

But starting the day with Charlotte's grin and kiss? That was the perfect beginning to an unforgettable adventure.

~~~~~~~

Chad packed a few changes of clothes, checked his passport, and tossed essentials into his day pack. Still in the boardies he'd slept in, he threw on a light t-shirt, leaving his hair messy.

He paused at the window, breathing easy as he gazed through palm trunks toward the hills of the Richat. The subtle tension of past mornings—barely noticed before—was gone, replaced by calm. A mindset shift from the night before had helped.

Suddenly, he was in holiday mode. Relaxed. Present. He hadn't realized how distant he'd been lately, but now he felt lighter. *"Amazing how easily life slips away—rushed, caught up in maintaining some illusion of logic between what's liked and disliked,"* he thought. *"What a waste, battling over things that don't matter. All it does is leave my head aching."*

"Good morning," came a soft, lilting voice from the doorway.

Chad felt himself starting a journey—sorting what mattered from what didn't. One indefinate, and not too dissimilar to his brother's.

"Hello..."

"That'd be interesting... easy to think on. Easy to see realized, maybe..." He paused in thought. "The good thing is I've had my head cleared of rubbish," he muttered aloud, "so... where do I go from here?"

"Sorry?" Chaiyala asked.

"What?" Chad blinked, realizing she'd overheard.

Still in her gym gear, she'd already accomplished in a few hours what Rick might in twelve.

"Are you... alright?" she asked.

"Oh—sorry—couldn't be better," he smiled. "Slept beautifully. Like I haven't in a long time."

"Same," she said, arms folded, leaning on the doorway, relaxed and smiling.

"You just come back from a run or something?"

"We snuck to the gym earlier, me and Charlotte," she replied.

"Nice. I'm all sorted for the trip," Chad said.

"Good. Trip should be nice... I hope. Business is business—even when we pretend it's not. We enjoy the resort, yes?" she smiled, unfazed by the likelihood of encountering black ops.

"Definitely!"

"Oh, Rhys and me—we're assigned to protect you, Tim, and Charlotte. We're your bodyguards now."

"Oh, right... sounds good," Chad said, happily intrigued.

"So—you're okay, yeah?" she asked, uncertain.

"Yes, actually," Chad replied, checking two lists he'd made on his phone. "That's not as silly as it sounds."

"You think me as your bodyguard sounds silly?"

"What? No—sorry, that's not what I meant."

"Explain, please—what was it meant to sound like?" she teased, feigning annoyance.

"Nothing... I'm pretty sure you and Rhys will make perfect bodyguards," Chad said with a reassuring smile.

She tilted her head, smirking, eyes narrowed.

They headed toward breakfast.

As they passed the bathroom, Chaiyala shook her head and Chad chuckled—the shower was running—Rick's voice rang out: "Rubber ducky, you're the one... you make bath time so much fun... rubber ducky, I'm awfully fond of youuuu!"

~~~~~~~

Crouton had baked two loaves in the pizza oven, and the aroma drifted across the deck, luring the others to breakfast. Chad and Chaiyala entered the living area just as Tim and Charlotte followed their noses outside.

A simple meal, done in style—toasted freshly made bread—Crouton's homemade butter, and raspberry jam. Marmite courtesy of Nathan, and Vegemite for Rick, Rod, and Kristie.

Once fed, Nathan and Crouton outlined the route from the project camp to Nouakchott. Showers were taken, gear packed into Humvees, and Charles and Antonio drove the team to the airfield.

Two helicopters awaited—blades already spinning—ready to carry the eight-person crew across the scorching Sahara to Nouakchott. From there, phase one would end, and the long-haul flight to Jamaica would begin.

The two-hour flight to Nouakchott was a stark contrast to their previous full-day trek across Mauritania in the Humvees. Swifter, but no less captivating. As they passed over the Chinguetti dig site, the massive, enigmatic Atlantean government complex came into view—finally under proper study, thousands of years after the catastrophe that reshaped the world.

Crouton, Tim, Charlotte, Chaiyala, and Chad rode in one helicopter; Nathan, Rod, and Rhys in the other. Bart flew the craft carrying Chad and Charlotte, greeting them: "Guten Morgen. You're still here? Not dead or otherwise gone nuts?"

Chad and Charlotte blinked, confused, then remembered Bart's odd sense of humour—and laughed.

They followed the southern foothills of the Adrar highlands, tracing the shape of what would've been the main island of Atlantis long ago.

"That's incredible..." Chad whispered, eyes wide. Both he and Charlotte tried to picture the world below as it once had been—before the disaster filled in the sea between Atlantis and the African continent, extending the land mass westward.

"There's the shipwreck," Tim pointed out the window.

"Wow..." Charlotte murmured as the remains of the ancient sailing vessel lay in the middle of desert sands. From up high, its isolation seemed even more haunting.

When they landed in Nouakchott, what they found was not at all what any had expected. Crouton and the other Red Sword Agents—less surprised. Bart and the other pilot landed them in a field a distance away, instead of the helicopter pads closer to the private Learjet hangars. Two Humvees, armed with M240Bs, greeted them. Two Mauritanian police vehicles sat nearby.

As they touched down, Crouton and Rod stepped out cautiously, followed by Rhys, who hurried toward Bart's helicopter.

Two police officers and two Red Sword agents emerged from their vehicles.

"What's going on?" Tim asked as Chaiyala reached back and tightened her half-ponytail into a knot.

Charlotte instinctively followed suit—tying her hair out of the way. The air had shifted—tense and electric.

The political climate was already volatile, and this felt like a spark.

"The airport's been compromised—mercenaries, I think," she said, eyes scanning the distance. "Sounds like Red Sword agents are holding them off beyond the hangar."

Bart kept his engine running, as did the other pilot in the first chopper—ready to evacuate if needed.

"Let's go!" Rod shouted. Tim passed gear through the open helicopter door.

Within seconds, they piled into two armoured Red Sword Humvees. Police cruisers flanking them, they transitioned toward the jet. Overhead, helicopters hovered—rotors thundered above, pilots waiting for the call.

Crouton briefed the others: "Our adversaries got wind of our Jamaica trip. Ten mercs are tangling with a dozen Red Sword agents on the far side of the hangar. The Learjet's safe on the tarmac here, but the situation's volatile. We need Nathan, and the three of you," he motioned to Tim, Chad, and Charlotte, "on board safely—without damage to the jet."

Rhys and Chaiyala acknowledged affirmatively.

He paused as a loud explosion erupted—a fireball consumed a small shed past the hangar.

Chad and Charlotte froze. Reality had shifted.

"Yonder's what we're dealin' with," Crouton said calmly. "Stick close to Chaiyala and Rhys. Your lives depend on that."

M240Bs rattled to life, adding to the noise of rotor blades. A hostile vehicle closed in. Shells clinked to the floor. The Humvee absorbed gunfire as rounds pinged off its sides and the diver hit the accelerator.

He veered around the attackers. After a brief exchange, he looped back on course. The hostile vehicle fell behind—no movement inside.

They reached their destination: the Learjet parked fifty meters from the southeast corner of the hangar. One Humvee sat fifteen meters from the jet, another parked to its left as a barrier. A third sat ten meters beyond, shielding the aircraft from the hangar's far side.

Crouton and Rod tossed the last of Tim, Chad, and Charlotte's gear up to Rhys and the pilot. Nathan was already on board.

The other four—Tim, Charlotte, Chad, and Chaiyala—were closer to the Humvee they'd exited.

"Get in! Inside the Humvee, now!" Chaiyala shouted as bullets cracked past, striking the tarmac just meters away.

Mercs sped toward them in a Ute, pursued by a Red Sword-armoured Impreza. Three M240Bs atop the Humvees locked on, roaring to life as the

Ute's windshield shattered, tires exploded, and its fuel system detonated in a chain reaction of sparks and precision fire.

Two men jumped clear before impact. More enemies emerged from behind the hangar—something had gone wrong. Red Sword reinforcements tore down the tarmac, their vehicles flanking the Learjet to reinforce the perimeter.

Inside the Humvee, bullets pinged off armoured sides as tension peaked.

From above came a short, sharp boom-boom-boom as Chaiyala's teammate focused on repelling a wave of attackers. The fire fight had reached them.

Chad cursed under his breath, wishing he'd shut the door behind them—too late. A figure in black clambered into the Humvee and yanked Charlotte out with a scream.

Tim and Chaiyala flew out after her like synchronized defenders.

Tim was pure fury—he hurled himself at Charlotte's assailant, a blur of rage and desperation. The grunt swivelled, dodging, and Tim hit the tarmac hard as several bullets zipped past him, narrowly missing.

"Back...!" Chaiyala began, but stopped short. Charlotte needed her focus.

The attacker dragged Charlotte, knife to throat, struggling backward. She elbowed him repeatedly in the ribs, finally making him flinch. Chaiyala pounced, grabbing his knife-hand and striking the pressure point between neck and shoulder. He slumped, releasing Charlotte.

"Get her inside!" Chaiyala shouted, eyes blazing.

Tim helped Charlotte scramble into safety without hesitation.

Nearby, Crouton faced a towering brute charging at him with two haymakers. He ducked backward.

"Are you kidding me?" Crouton thought. *"They send this fumbling oaf just for me?"*

Around him, the others engaged smaller opponents who'd slipped through. Chaiyala and Rod moved in sync—she spun a fighter her size before Rod's roundhouse dropped him. Chaiyala pinned and knocked him out.

Another assailant swung a metal weapon at Rod. He caught their wrist mid-swing, swept the attacker's legs, and Chaiyala locked the fallen man in a chokehold, scissoring his waist. She leaned in.

"Goodnight," she whispered.

But Crouton's giant opponent was reserved for him.

The big oafs always were. Usually slow, dumb, and easy to floor. But this one surprised him—like a humanoid kumara on steroids. He switched from haymakers to side-stepping footwork, mimicking a boxer.

They traded punches. Crouton took two hard blows to the face, shook them off, and returned fire twice as hard before kicking the brute square in the chest, sending him stumbling backward.

They squared up again, then dove for cover as a grenade bounced across the tarmac, missing the Learjet's landing gear by ten meters.

It exploded—loose asphalt rained down around them.

"Damage! This is muckin' around!" Crouton growled, leaping to his feet. "Rod! Get 'em inside!"

The brute drew a foot-long dagger, eyes menacing.

"I don't have time to tarry..." Crouton began, reaching for his gun.

...but Chaiyala appeared, snapping the man's forearm in one swift strike. The dagger clanged to the ground. She wrestled him down, straddled his chest, and hammered him with rapid, machine-like blows.

Crouton hauled the dazed man up and sent him flying.

"No more muckin' around! Let's get the hang outta here!" he boomed.

Bart and the Red Sword pilot hovered overhead, shifting the battle's tide. Two almighty booms and a chain of smaller explosions tore through the far end of the hangar. Local police had joined the chaos.

Everyone was safely on board. The Learjet was ready to taxi.

Crouton pulled the stair lever. As the aircraft moved, the steps lifted to a closed position.

He turned to look at his friends, caught his breath—then grinned.

"Mornin', Caitlyn!" he boomed at the second pilot, seated beside Rod.

"Good morning, boss."

"Get us outta here. Let's go to Jamaica!"

Crouton grabbed his phone, instructing the choppers to escort the Learjet ten kilometres beyond the coast. He thanked them, sat down opposite Nathan and Tim, who were now poring over the Solon Diaries—translated and auto-analysed for key revelations.

"Well done, my friends!" Nathan beamed.

"Cheers. Never gets boring, that's for sure." Crouton wiped his brow with his shirt, then slipped it back on. "Almost expected that was gonna happen."

"Of course you did. So did I—that's why we've got that place covered twenty-four-seven." Nathan leaned in. "Still... someone's getting desperate."

"Clearly. But we won't let them ruin anything either."

Nathan debriefed Tim, Chad, and Charlotte. Rattled but exhilarated, they thanked Rhys and Chaiyala for their protection. Tim helped Charlotte double-check her gear—nothing planted, nothing stolen. Safe. Unscathed.

With eight hours in the air ahead, Tim returned to the Solon Diaries. Nathan arranged lunch: roast beef sandwiches, along with enough snacks to satisfy even Rhys's and Crouton's appetites.

Chad and Charlotte, now settled, melted into the couch and caught up on 'Doctor Who'.

Crouton and Rod discussed security plans for Jamaica while Caitlyn managed the flight solo. Everything according to protocol—nothing left to chance. When Nathan and Crouton travelled, plans were airtight. Nine times out of ten, mercs and black ops teams never even got close.

"You had fun, yeah?" Chaiyala asked Rhys.

"Nah—not enough dragons. Or explosions! The pirates' performance was a bit wooden today—bit of a disappointment," he frowned, deadpan—then smirked.

The cabin laughed.

The flight was off to a great start.

Rhys and Chaiyala, exhausted from the past two days, were first to nap—waking for lunch. Tim took a break.

After several episodes of the Doctor, Charlotte settled in to read. Chad dozed off beside her.

CHAPTER 13

C had stirred from his snooze, momentarily puzzled about where he was. Then he remembered—he had questions for Nathan.

"So, you're from Paeroa then?" he queried.

"Who's been spreading that awful rumour?" Nathan replied, shocked, frowning.

Chad looked at him for a second, then smirked.

Nathan reversed his frown. "Yes. I maintain a carefully crafted façade as the owner of the Goldfeilds dairy, with a secluded home in the hills above Paeroa's old racecourse. To outsiders, my frequent absences are chalked up to world travel. In reality, my estate—while technically my home—functions as a covert Red Sword base. Undercover agents operate as household staff, and security personnel remain as permanent, concealed guests."

"Fantastic work, on all that," Tim commended.

Nathan explained how small-town politics and gossip were deftly managed by the mayor, trusted staff, and locals.

"We've got friends who grew up in Paeroa—still have family there," Chad shared. "That place is a different world from Hamilton!"

"I love the relaxed vibe. Not so much the small-town politics," Tim added.

"Why Paeroa then?" asked Charlotte. "Wouldn't a large, impersonal city offer better anonymity?"

Nathan smiled. "While cities offer obscurity, they're more exposed globally. Small towns, for all their nosiness, can be managed with the right connections. Less can go wrong on a large scale. After living in Auckland and Sydney, I'd grown tired of city life. Paeroa offered charm and community—and it suited our needs."

"Oh, my goodness! I totally forgot to thank you for the Berry Nectargys Nathan!" Charlotte exclaimed, momentarily embarrassed. Awkwardness quickly made way for gratitude... and intrigue.

"Oh yes, of course. You're very welcome," Nathan replied, as if he'd just remembered too.

"How on earth did you come by Red Berry Nectargy?" Tim asked—curiosity catching up with him.

Nathan paused, looked at Tim, then Charlotte.

He took a deep breath. "Would you prefer a straight verbal answer to that question... or would you rather see it in person—the very means by which I managed to wrangle Berry Nectargy, despite it being out of production for a decade?" His tone held a quiet challenge, prompting them to lean back and wonder what obscure world of wonder either response might unlock.

Crouton looked over his reading glasses at Nathan, thinking to himself, *"What weird and abstract adventure have you been on this time... What have you gone and done now?"*

Tim sighed inwardly. "Why don't we wait until we've got fewer things on our plates before opening more cans of worms—from the distant past or the abstract realms of what used to be science fiction?"

He returned his attention to the Solon Diaries report open on his laptop, putting thoughts of Red Nectargy out of mind.

Crouton chuckled in admiration. "Very wise, Tim. Very wise," he grinned, looking back at his own tablet.

"Those cans were bought in 2009," Nathan said sincerely, "but they're as fresh as if you bought them yesterday."

Charlotte narrowed her eyes at him. She wasn't convinced he was joking. She was familiar enough with the oddities she'd seen in recent days—plus everything Tim had shared with her over the past few months. Anything felt possible now.

"Hmm," Chad thought. "Very interesting."

"Don't worry, young lady," Crouton said gently, his tone warm and reassuring. He continued typing as he spoke. "I've known Nate here for nigh on thirty som'n years, and just when I think there's nothing more to learn about him—boom—he drops something brand new and exciting. And, always worthwhile."

He glanced sideways at Nathan, over the top of his glasses. "Based on the coming days and such... I suspect it'll be something entirely worth waiting to see with your own eyes."

He anticipated Nathan's agreement.

"Yes, of course," Nathan nodded thoughtfully. "I was just thinking about how the human brain processes things that fall far outside its expectations. The mind relies on past experience to interpret what the eyes see—integrating sensory input with memory, logic, and subconscious assumptions."

He sat forward, "but when the brain encounters something completely beyond its frame of reference—something contradictory or incomprehensible—it can struggle to process it. In extreme cases, mechanisms like inattentional blindness or cognitive suppression might block conscious awareness... even if the eyes physically see it."

Nathan looked at the group calmly.

"The mind might instinctively filter out what it can't categorize—scrubbing it from perception before conscious awareness even registers. It could explain why one person sees the supernatural... and another, sees nothing at all."

Tim marvelled at how the man's mind leapt from canned energy drinks to neurological philosophy in seconds. Then, dismissing his surprise, he returned to reading.

"Eh? Right. I suppose that works," Crouton said, thoughts still ticking.

"That's incredible!" Charlotte exclaimed.

"Yes, I've heard of this," Chad said. "The brain's response to the unknown is fascinating. The region responsible for processing novelty—handling surprises and adapting to change—can be overwhelmed. When overstimulated, it may trigger a kind of perceptual shock. Instead of accepting the impossible, it might reject it entirely—wiping it from conscious awareness even though it's standing right in front of you."

"Whoa—dang! That's next level," Rhys muttered, impressed, before rolling over in his lazy boy flight chair. Sleep reclaimed him instantly.

A few chuckles followed.

"We've cracked the genetic code, built machines that whisper across galaxies, even taught metal to think," Nathan continued. "And yet, when it comes to the brain—the very architect behind it all—it's as if we've spent centuries polishing the doorknob without ever stepping inside. The discoveries and breakthroughs are phenomenal, no doubt... but compared to how little we've applied them? It's like inventing fire and using it *merely* to light scented candles and little else."

He stared out the cabin window.

"The human mind is beautiful... and sometimes scary, too." Charlotte's said softly.

"Very true. Most definitely," Nathan nodded. "The brain intrigues me endlessly, but two things remain baffling. First: despite its complexity, it wasn't properly studied until the 1990s—the aptly named 'Decade of the

Brain.' Medical and psychological breakthroughs since then have radically expanded what we understand.

Yet problematically, most of this knowledge hasn't made it into practice. Humanity keeps operating as it always has—slamming into truths we've already uncovered. We know how depression works... anxiety... trauma... and yet families, workplaces, and governments carry on as if none of it matters."

He paced slowly now, lost in thought.

"We know a lot about how the brain works—how powerful and delicate it can be. Yet media, businesses, and education systems still use outdated mental models that suppress human flourishing. Most of the time, they don't even realize they're doing it.

Social media could have been designed to nurture creativity and connection. Instead, it pulls people away from themselves."

There was silence. Heavy, reflective.

"Yet amidst all that," Nathan continued, "there are exceptions—incredible ones. One force disrupts the monotony of a suppressed world: compassion. Love dismantles every device that harms the human spirit—corruption, cruelty, confusion, despair. Wherever fear grows, love begins its quiet work of undoing."

He paused, letting that hang in the air.

"If the brain is the body's most underestimated tool, then love is its intangible counterpart. The brain governs thought, but love governs meaning. One is underestimated for its complexity; the other for its invisibility. And both are essential to human flourishing"

Nathan walked with purpose now—his words gathering speed, half sermon, half stream-of-consciousness, and all strangely captivating.

Tim managed to follow Nathan's words and read Solon's journal at the same time. His ability to process both at once was still a mystery to him—but one he was grateful for.

"Love reshapes neural pathways," Nathan went on, "influencing emotion, memory, and decision-making. Though widely studied, much remains unexplored. Love transforms hostile environments—lifting the weary, building resilience. Even in sacrifice, it leaves an indelible imprint on memory and perception."

He turned and looked squarely at them.

"And to be clear: I'm not speaking of romance. Not conditional affection. Love that seeks convenience or reciprocity isn't love—that's transaction. True compassion is selfless. It draws strength from something beyond the self. That kind of love dismantles even the deepest dysfunctions of society."

Then, with a shift in tone: "Which reminds me..."

Nathan glanced at Crouton. "Osama asked if, once the Richat Project is secure and established, we might channel more resources toward the Ark Project. Meant to mention it earlier—mind got sidetracked."

At the name 'Osama' and 'Ark Project', Tim, Chad, and Charlotte froze—exchanging looks like moths caught in a flash of flame.

Crouton, never one to tiptoe, saw their expressions and responded directly.

"Osama bin Laden—the mastermind behind 9/11 and Al-Qaeda—was taken by Red Sword Security in 2011. After extended talks, he agreed to ditch terrorism and work for us. The alternative? Being tossed to the dogs for his crimes."

"That was only part of it," Nathan clarified. "We offered him something his ideology couldn't give him. And something else—something so blindingly compelling that the man might as well have become a fish convinced it was a cow—now mooing and grazing in fields of green."

"You've got a fascinating way with words," Chad said, trying to mask his disbelief with humour.

"You've no idea," Tim muttered without looking up.

Nathan gave a half-smile. "Such is the absurdity and obscurity of his transformation—from international public enemy number one to director of one of Red Sword's major archaeological operations."

Tim, Chad and Charlotte had goosebumps thinking about this. All a mix of disbelief—wanting to check if they'd heard correctly.

"None of this exists outside Red Sword," Nathan said firmly. "Publicly, he's dead. Technically, presumed dead. The rest is swallowed by the black hole people call 'conspiracy theory.' He is dead to society—and it has to stay that way. His codename: Agent B."

"Wait... why is he still free?" Chad asked, genuinely baffled. "Shouldn't he be brought to trial?"

"Freedom is perception," Nathan replied. "If you ever meet him, you won't see a free man. You'll see someone haunted. Not by punishment—but by the ghosts of his own mind."

He looked darkly toward the corridor. "War veterans... prisoners. You've heard how they scream at night? I've never heard shrieks like Agent B's. It's inhuman."

"He's fully functional as Agent B—but due to his... history," Crouton cut in, "emotionally? He's one messed-up son of a beggar."

"He's spent almost a decade in treatment for post-traumatic stress disorder. The man's imagination is wild. He sees faces—victims—in his dreams... and even open-eyed visions," Nathan added.

"Goodness... that really is a living nightmare," Charlotte whispered, aghast.

It left the cabin quiet. Tim felt suddenly heavy, as though the weight of history had settled in his chest.

"He's in the safest possible care," Nathan said, "yet his conscience is his prison. Nothing any authority could do could punish him more than the terror he faces each night. Sometimes I wonder if he balances on the edge of madness—but somehow, he still leads. Still directs."

Nathan turned toward Crouton, brow furrowed.

"Boggles the mind," Crouton said, resting hands behind his head. Then more seriously, "The man's a wreck and a miracle. He's got a watch team made up of elite bodyguards, psychologists, and medical professionals. Always monitored. Always supported. But his battles are internal, and no amount of protocol fixes that."

"See this is why I try not to ask Nathan too many questions," Tim explained, "you end up with answers you're not quite sure what you're supposed to do with," he grinned.

Crouton chuckled.

"Pinch me," Chad muttered to Charlotte.

She smirked and flicked his arm.

"Oh great... I haven't been dreaming all this," Chad replied dryly.

They all laughed—breaking through the tension with welcome levity.

Nathan softened, looking Chad's way. "There's a lot that beggars' belief, my boy. Just remember: don't take everything too seriously—but whatever you do take, take it with sincerity and freedom of heart. Just don't take it so far that you lose it."

"Interesting thoughts," Chad said softly, chewing on the words.

Charlotte tilted her head. Nathan had a knack for being comically cryptic—yet strangely profound.

"These are interesting times," Crouton added.

"Speaking of interesting..." Tim chimed in, "Solon—not only did he visit the temple of Sais in Egypt, but also the Eye of Africa. Back when it was still lush—rivers, jungle. And while there, he met someone who told him the location of Atlantis's hidden wealth and secrets. They'd sealed it up during the war with Athens... but the government didn't know."

"That... *is* interesting," Chad echoed, eyebrows raised.

Nathan and Crouton didn't react with the excitement Tim expected. But from across the cabin, Rod shifted in his chair—smiling faintly—then turned back to face the sky ahead.

"Go on..." Crouton instructed.

Tim was used to Red Sword oddities... he looked back at his screen. "The first entry regarding this, reads...

"I have come upon a small town in the jungle near the Atlantis mountains where I've made some friends within the town's academy. They advise, as the story goes: there were those who came and went from up in the mountains after the flood and the destruction of Atlantis, and they kept to themselves. They seemed to materialise and vanish like ghosts and not one soul had witnessed any of them coming beyond the mountains.

"Moreover, giant machines were seen flying in and out, behind the mountains, yet these too, did not appear to leave the mountains. Scouts and champions were sent forth to locate said machines and those in the mountains and all came back with no evidence or proof of anything of the kind.

"I find this to be greatly intriguing and wonder whether or not if it has any connection with the empire of Atlantis. The story troubles me and I cannot cease to think of it."

"The next entry on the subject..." Tim continued enthusiastically.

"One of my new friends from the academy came to me today and advised we make haste for the village of Dachara at the foothills of the Atlantis mountains.

Upon our arrival I was introduced to a man who was the keeper of his family's archives, a scribe and one held in high esteem by his peers and elders. He told me the story of how the servants of the Ancient of Atlantis had been instructed to, in secret, save and conceal the knowledge and wealth of the empire in the sacred halls of Alastragah. Such a task preceded the fall of Atlantis and its destruction by no less than five years and also enduring beyond it by another three. Its last prevailing survivors concealing themselves within the sacred halls for long enough to safely venture abroad the mountains

once again. Almost a year did they remain hidden in the secret realm they had fash-
ioned—the salvation of their race.

Upon proceeding forth from Alastragah, they found that all the world had been
turned into ice, a frozen wasteland for as far as the eye could see. They returned to the
halls and then travelled by sky, day and night to survey the extent of the ice. They
learned that it eventually subsided before Athens, and the colony of Egypt where the
obelisks were being toppled and the caps of the carsakarisks were no longer illuminated.
The coastline for what could still be seen of it, was vastly different to what it was before
the explosion. Moreover, lands once known—those islands of former time—have van-
ished from sight, swallowed by the sea or scattered to silence. In their place, new shapes
have risen: peninsulas, unfamiliar shores, and terrains unmarked upon the charts of
Atlantis, nor upon those of Athens, nor any among the nations beyond.

I asked of him many questions. Alas, he was not able to give me any further expla-
nation for any of the details he had conveyed to me. Even the location of these sacred
halls of Alastragah seems to have been forgotten and lost. I was extremely grateful for
the hospitality of the scribe and for accommodating me on my quest to search for sur-
vivors and remnants of the lost Atlantis. I thanked him and returned from Dachara
wrought with wonder and laden with questions abundant."

Crouton stared at Tim, quiet with bewildered excitement.

Nathan was grinning and nodding, sharing in Tim's exhilaration.

Chad and Charlotte sat forward, intrigued. Chad's mind was already
at work—wondering about Solon, decoding the implications of this new
information and his ancient quest.

"Who... what is this from? Where?" asked a sleepy Chaiyala, stirring as
Tim's voice had nudged her back to awareness.

"The Solon Diaries," Tim replied. "These are the final entries written by Solon about Atlantis. Nothing else is recorded on the subject for

another three hundred years—until Plato wrote the dialogues of 'Timaeus' and 'Critias'."

"Oh wow!" Chaiyala blinked herself awake, wide-eyed and smiling.

"What's going on?" Rhys asked, groggy but curious as he joined the group.

"Tim is reading diary—Solon's lost writings!" she told him, voice warming with enthusiasm.

Now Rhys was wide awake and listening intently.

"So exciting, babe!" Charlotte beamed, squeezing Tim's arm.

"It is," Tim agreed, smiling modestly.

"This is... truly remarkable," Crouton said, unusually moved—his voice thick with feeling. The weight of Solon's lost insight left him floored.

"Until now, the idea that survivors of Atlantis hid away their wealth and technology was considered pure myth," Nathan added. "And not even a very well-known one."

"I was gonna say!" Chad nodded.

"That was the assumption without Solon's diaries," Tim said quietly. "Till now, so much has been concealed."

Rod and Caitlyn landed the Learjet smoothly at Sangster International Airport. It was a quarter past eight in the evening, local time—concluding their flight from Nouakchott to tropical Jamaica.

Red Sword Security (RSS) personnel met them on the tarmac, arriving in three sleek black armoured Humvees marked with the Red Sword logo on the doors and rooftops. They assisted with luggage and escorted the travellers to the arrivals gate. After clearing customs, Nathan handled security arrangements for firearms and restricted items. Once sorted, they reunited with the drivers and returned to the Humvees. Most gear was loaded into Crouton's vehicle, though Tim kept the Solon diaries close—never letting them out of sight.

They bid farewell to Caitlyn, who'd remain in Montego Bay at Red Sword's Jamaican base while Nathan and the others continued their mission.

"The drive between Sangster and the Caribbean Paradise will be about thirty-five minutes," Rod told them as they pulled away from the airport. "We'll head east toward Falmouth where the resort is located."

As they joined Jamaica's A1 highway, they passed the University of the West Indies.

"To our left is the northern edge of the Caribbean Sea, with Cuba just under 250 kilometres across the water. Also, to our left—Montego Bay. Slightly smaller than Hamilton, with a population of around 110,000. Major cruise ship port, popular beaches, resorts. Nice city—very touristy. I've visited a couple of times, all work-related.

East of here is Haiti and the Dominican Republic. Directly south is Colombia—right next to your country of birth, Charlotte," Rod recalled.

"Yes!" she smiled.

They passed a string of grand beachside resorts, their façades gleaming like palaces against the dusk light, as the city's sprawl gave way to open coast.

The sun was setting in the west, though from their route, the view remained mostly obscured. Rod assured them the sunrises from the Caribbean Paradise were something remarkable on a mild tropical morning. The sky across the sea glowed peach-orange. Jamaica was cooler than Mauritania, yet still warm—shorts and a light top were all they needed.

"Is the humidity here that makes difference," Chaiyala noted. "Heat doesn't dry you out like Sahara does."

"Now that I can contrast the two, I think I prefer a little humidity," Chad decided.

"Yup. Took me weeks to adjust to desert heat," Tim recalled.

They navigated Montego Bay's bays coastal suburbs. The scenery reminded the New Zealanders of coastal highways near Wellington, Paraparaumu, and the stretch between Auckland's North Shore and Warkworth.

Charlotte, now fully immersed in the excitement of meeting J-Mac, saw the opportunity as a major breakthrough for her band. Still, fatigue tugged at her, and she was close to dozing off again.

Chad remained in quiet disbelief at how drastically his life had changed since accepting the invitation abroad. First, he learns his brother is part of the archaeological discovery of the century—Atlantis. *"Seriously—what even is that? You wouldn't read about it!"* he thought. *"And now I'm in Jamaica, about to stay in the luxury penthouse suite of a tropical resort while meeting J-Mac and a direct descendant of Solon and Plato... how's that for a stretch?"*

He had to admit—God had a uniquely brilliant sense of humour. One that made him look sideways at everything he thought he knew about matters of faith or religion. All of this, just to get out of town and clear his head. He smiled, chuckling quietly to himself as they wove through urban pockets, parks, and seaside reserves.

Chaiyala and Rod discussed work aspects while Tim's mind raced with the flood of new revelations. Someone who'd only briefly appeared in classical history was now proving to be a pivotal figure. More significantly, this added to the mounting evidence that Atlantis—known as such in Solon's time—had once existed, and Solon himself had searched for it.

Questions crowded Tim's thoughts. Who were the figures spotted in the mountains? Solon mentioned them in his journal—were they near the northern shelter of what was once Atlantis? Regarding the flood of Noah, recorded across multiple ancient cultures and the Younger Dryas catastrophe circa 12,000 BC—could this be the same event shared across many ancient traditions?

Then there was the matter of flying machines, described by a mysterious scribe to Solon—had the Atlanteans possessed advanced technology? If so, why had no trace of these machines or their creators surfaced?

Tim didn't doubt the ancient sage's accuracy, but if they now held a trove of new information on Solon, why was there no supporting evidence? No records; no historical links to Dachara, no suspected location or even a vague hint of even the idea of the sacred halls of Alastragah... was it truly hidden in the mountains?

It was all unfamiliar terrain. He'd always relied on timelines, genealogies, and documented events to anchor his understanding. The Richat sites had their link to Atlantis—but this? This felt like something else entirely. Something history hadn't prepared him for.

Tim wrestled with the idea that the Solon diaries might be a gateway to an entirely forgotten era of human history—one so distant it lacked recognizable links to what followed. It had to make sense. That was the essence of the newly coined 'Parahistorical' period—a bridge between the prehistoric and historical.

But which questions weighed heaviest? The flying machines of twelve millennia past? The halls of Alastragah and the eight-year concealing of Atlantean society? Who was the Ancient of Atlantis? Or were the more pressing mysteries tied to Egypt's toppled obelisks? The obscure term 'Carsakarisk'? And the explosion—did the scribe, Solon met, reference the pyramid power station theory, which may have triggered the catastrophe that wiped out half the known world at the time?

"Goodness... was that the cause of the great flood?" he wondered.

The A1 highway cruised out of town for a few kilometres, bush on either side. Then the Caribbean in peach and turquoise twilight reappeared on their left, more urban area to the right. They passed several more resorts, each competing for size and high-rise views.

"These places are enormous!" Chad exclaimed, beholding what looked like something out of Las Vegas.

"There's a hang of a lot of money tied up in these resorts," Rod said. "They charge a small fortune to stay a night."

"May I ask the cost of a night at the Caribbean Paradise?" Chad asked.

"NZ$1,523 per night—standard. The penthouse suites, of which there are two, crown the top of the towers at either end of the main resort building. Right now, they're NZ$8,911."

Charlotte was visibly shocked. Tim was surprised. Chad was overwhelmed—having done the maths. The idea of spending $44,555 for six nights was almost incomprehensible.

He was torn. The extravagance felt excessive, but the generosity behind it was hard to ignore. Nathan O'Conner, the man footing the bill, was known for extravagant giving, done quietly—almost in secret.

Rod tried to help Chad understand. "Nathan never lends money—he gives it. And never less than $100,000 at a time. He lives by a spiritual principle that generosity multiplies, and his wealth continues to grow because of it."

Chad, still reeling, began to suspect Nathan might not be entirely human—more like a divine steward of practical blessing. It was generosity on a scale Chad had never encountered, and it left him speechless.

Still in Montego Bay's suburban area, they passed a shopping precinct on the left and the massive Montego Bay Convention Centre on the right. Then finally, they arrived.

The Red Sword Humvees rolled into the resort's expansive car park and followed an elaborate circular driveway, stopping before an enormous white high-rise—eight stories tall and stadium-sized. Two towers rose— one at either end, each with waterfalls cascading from the eighth floor into shimmering pools below. Tropical jungle pressed in—glowing in garden lights—merging with the resort's entrance grounds. Dusk had fallen, and the front entrance glowed softly in the fading light. The arrival of the armoured Humvees signalled business. This was more than just a vacation.

Red Sword personnel met them at the drop-off zone, assuming the roles of baggage handlers. Nathan and Crouton expressed gratitude, and everyone's gear was trolleyed inside.

Nathan and Crouton proceeded to the front desk with three RSS agents who could have passed for diplomatic security. They checked the eight of them in.

As they made their way toward the western tower penthouse suite—a five-minute walk from the front desk—the first-timers were impressed by 'The Grand Isle'—a long wide corridor resembling a luxurious lounge with dozens of sofas, low tables with device stations, bookshelves, and bean bags. Potted plants, sculptures, and a waterfall descending down a rock feature adorned with indoor ferns and palms. The 'Entrance'd' café bar sat behind the lobby at the start.

They veered left down an equally spectacular atrium, exiting the main building at the far west end into a small enclosed courtyard below the western tower. Lush tropical bush and birdsong surrounded them. To their left, the massive waterfall thundered down the building's side.

Nathan keyed in the room's security pin on the touch screen. The elevator doors slid open, and they piled in, ascending to the eighth floor. The levels below housed premier suites—similar in size and style to the penthouse, minus a dozen prestigious features.

Once inside their suite, the bags were placed beside the hallway leading to the bedrooms. The group thanked those who'd assisted with their arrival, wishing them a good evening.

Nathan and Crouton gathered the team around a large dining table at the centre of the suite. Rod and Crouton plugged in their laptops and began organizing for the work ahead.

Chaiyala, Crouton, and Rod had stayed in the penthouse before. The rest were amazed. This suite was the extreme end of luxurious—pearl white interior with high ceilings, gold trimmings, and furniture crafted from mahogany or polished pine. Some walls were entirely made of LED screens, displaying immersive scenery that responded to guest preferences—or transformed subtly as they moved from room to room...

Two sprawling lounge suites flanked the open-plan space opposite the dining area, anchored by an eighty-inch flat-screen mounted on the wall. A seven-meter concertina ranch slider opened onto a spacious balcony, while a gold-plated telescope stood elegantly in the corner near the gleaming full kitchen.

The penthouse suite was absent of exterior walls. Instead, thick, continuous double-glazed windows offered a panoramic view of the Jamaican coastline and the Caribbean Sea. The illusion of being outdoors came with luxurious insulation. Floor-to-ceiling curtains were electronically drawn from each corner.

Chad opened what appeared to be the mini bar—it was actually a large fridge freezer, generously stocked with desserts, local delicacies, and every beverage imaginable. There were more Blue and Berry-flavoured Nectargys too—the glass bottle kind.

"This is nuts," Chad grinned.

"It's unreal, eh?" Tim nodded, smiling.

"He thinks of everything, huh," Charlotte said.

"Yup." Tim agreed, still peering into the fridge's bounty. It looked more like a gourmet supply drop than a casual mini bar.

Nathan spoke up: "Well, here we are—make yourselves completely at home. Whatever you need, whether room service, mini bar, restaurants, spa—everything's covered. Put it all on my tab and don't spend a cent. If you do, I'll find out—you'll get a telling-off—and be reimbursed double." He added sternly.

Chad frowned and looked sideways at Nathan, then at Tim—who just smiled and shook his head, as if to say "that's completely normal."

Charlotte wasn't sure what to make of Nathan's odd mix of warmth and command, but everyone expressed their thanks. The Red Sword crew were used to Nathan's 'Nathanisms.'

Nathan sighed. "Rod, have you not explained O'Conomics to young Chad here?"

"I tried," Rod replied dryly. "But I might've started speaking in Turkish or Lithuanian by accident. It's been a long day."

"Aye," Nathan nodded, leaning his hands on the table. "That'd explain it." More laughter followed.

"There are ten rooms—sleep wherever you want. Some of the sofas fold into bed settees you won't want to leave. I use this suite as a home between engagements around the region. If you need space, take it.

I think between Charlotte, Tim, Crouton, and myself, we've got two work appointments while we're here. The rest is a break for now, for the most part. We head back to Mauritania in seven days—so enjoy this place. It's certainly one of my favourites."

"Right then," Crouton barked as if kicking off a mission. "Who's hungry? I'm darn crazy famished. Gonna head down to the Hereford Steakhouse. Best steak you'll find. Who's joining?"

It was closing in on 9pm. Everyone agreed.

"The Caribbean Paradise offers twelve restaurants and seven bars and cafes," Nathan told them. "All of them brilliant—a fusion of local and international flavours."

"Oh wow—spoilt for choice!" Charlotte said.

"This place is next level," Chad added. "Like some kind of fantasy world."

"Exactly," Crouton replied. "Pretty much the idea—a place to get away and disconnect. Recharge."

"It's awesome," Tim nodded.

"I love it here," Chaiyala said, smiling. "Was excited when I hear we come here."

Chad thought back—she hadn't seemed overly enthusiastic in Mauritania. But now she did seem happier. *"Probably exactly what she needed,"* he thought. *"A proper holiday."*

The eight of them took the elevator down to the ground floor and strolled across the polished stone pavement. Nathan and Crouton led them down the Atrium colonnade—a corridor lined with six fine dining establishments around the base of the main building. At the centre, The Place of Zen served Chinese cuisine. Down from that, The Tamarind specialized in West Indian fare. They passed The Round Robin Sports Bar & Grill, where a cricket game between South Africa and the West Indies drew a crowd of lively fans.

"The Caribbean Skillet is top tier," Nathan said, pointing to a standalone restaurant under a massive palm-thatched roof, surrounded by pools. "Won several culinary awards five years running—for good reason."

Chad liked the sound of that—he made a mental note.

Charlotte adored the look of Gringo Mexican BBQ, and Tim promised to take her there. They passed Poseidon's Garden, a Mediterranean restaurant that caught Tim and Chad's attention.

Nathan smiled quietly.

Guests lounged across the resort's expansive pool precinct, basking in the soft evening breeze. Pools shimmered under ambient lighting, guests soaking and chatting with cocktails in hand. Abstract sculptures depicted Caribbean themes, and lush tropical gardens added to the exotic charm. A reggae band played on one end, and a singer in a wide-brimmed fedora strummed country tunes at the other.

Nathan led them off the Atrium toward a thoroughfare of zigzagging bridges over water gardens near the resort's western pools. They passed Oishii Osara Japanese restaurant on its own island, then Trattoria Italia and Nectar of the Gods Café at the base of the eastern tower.

"Nathan O'Conner! What a pleasant surprise! Wasn't expecting you back so soon!" boomed a confident, sharply dressed man in his forties, seated outside Trattoria Italia with a stunning Jamaican couple and a woman whose makeup made Chad do a double take. Charlotte wasn't sure she was real, or if cut out from a Woman's Day magazine and enlarged.

The man's Eastern European accent rolled warm. "Truly a pleasure to see you again, my friend!"

"Maurice!" Nathan exclaimed. They embraced and shook hands.

"Meet my friends," Nathan introduced. "Chaiyala Mizrah and Rhys Harvey of Red Sword Security. And from New Zealand- Tim Harison, his fiancée Charlotte Espanzia, and his brother Chad—you've met Rod and Crouton before. Everyone, this is Maurice Chipolatto, owner of Paradise Hotels and the Caribbean Club."

Maurice stood and shook hands warmly. "A pleasure!"

"Likewise," Tim said. "Your resort here is fantastic—very, very nice."

"Thank you!" Maurice beamed.

He and Nathan chatted briefly and made plans to catch up later.

The group arrived at Hereford Steakhouse, a standalone venue nestled between the eastern tower and the shimmering pools. Nearby, the Hot Rocks and Roast, Shrimp and Marlin, and Caribbean Club Beach Bar hugged the rocky outcrops just shy of the shoreline.

They settled at an outdoor table overlooking the pools with the grand main building towering behind.

"This place is stunning," Charlotte said.

"I'll second that," Chad nodded. "Thank you for bringing us here, Nathan. This is incredible."

Nathan looked around. "It really is. One of my favourite places away from home."

Their waiter arrived, and soon their meals followed.

Crouton, Rod, and Chaiyala each tackled a half-kilo New York cut steak. Crouton and Rod washed it down with Dragon Stout. Chaiyala requested a full mug of grapefruit juice, which made Crouton wince.

Tim enjoyed a T-bone pepper steak with house-made lime sweet chilli sauce.

Charlotte impressed the group by finishing the Sirloin Twins of the Caribbean—two thick sirloin slabs marinated in honey lemon, topped with sautéed shrimp, mussels, and squid rings dusted in lemon pepper.

Chad had the Scotch Triple Stacker: three 100-gram scotch fillets layered with cranberry and Camembert mushroom sauce that dripped decadently over the edges.

Nathan leaned toward the trio. "Just over there," he pointed, "is the Lazy River—it winds through the resort's pools and tropical landscape, ending at a hidden, nautical-themed swim-up bar. Perfect for quiet relaxation."

Tim followed the line of Nathan's gaze. The river curved between palm trees and torch-lit paths like it held secrets beneath the surface. He said nothing—but he wondered what else this place might reveal.

CHAPTER 14

‑‑‑

Tim and Charlotte woke in the exact spot they'd fallen asleep the night before—curled together on the spacious recliner between the main lounge and the wide-open concertina ranch slider. Beyond that, the balcony overlooked the resort and the ocean. A tranquil tropical breeze floated through.

They'd spent the night talking, snuggling, and making out as the festive atmosphere below slowly dwindled to only those doing the same—lounging in pools or beach chairs. The moonlit ocean was a sight to behold, to fall asleep to, and to wake beside as the first light rose above the Caribbean horizon.

They stirred and decided to check out the Lazy River pool with its swim-up bar and lagoon, following Nathan's recommendation. The night before, they'd envisioned a morning drifting along the Lazy River before enjoying breakfast smoothies at the swim-up bar.

Just as they were heading out, Chad and Chaiyala appeared—surprisingly energized. Tim did a double take upon learning Chad had been up since before dawn, training in the penthouse suite's private gym with Chaiyala. His brother, working out? That was practically unheard of. He couldn't help but wonder what kind of spell she'd cast to make it happen. They invited Chad and Chaiyala to join their Lazy River adventure, and both eagerly accepted.

They slipped into the thirty-degree water at the far end of the Lazy River pool, having selected colourful, stylishly patterned fibreglass rafts.

"Hey, there's a current," Chad noticed, letting himself drift.

"I love this place!" Chaiyala exclaimed again.

They drifted and swam their way around the massive pool and courtyard precinct, passing clusters of palm trees and loungers, winding between the main pools and some of the restaurants and bars. Part way along, the current picked up and spun them about like rapids—before calming once more.

Tim and Charlotte drifted ahead of Chad and Chaiyala. As they did, Chaiyala's senses went on high alert. She felt they were being watched. Discreetly scanning her surroundings, she studied her peripheral vision—nothing obvious. A resort lifeguard and security officer stood nearby. No, not them. Trained observers were harder to read, though. Ordinary people were more relaxed, uninvolved.

Then there were single men—or those who should've been paying more attention to their partners—stealing lingering glances before looking away, thinking they wouldn't appear too obvious. Lately, her proximity to Chad had shifted perceptions. Assumptions made. She was off-limits?

She and her best friend, also a Red Sword agent, had often discussed the challenges of being too easy on the eyes while working. They'd tried downplaying their appearance, but results were mixed—sometimes it worked, other times it attracted the wrong kind of attention.

The old lady knitting on a lounger seemed out of place... but almost too much so. Her husband returned with takeaway coffees and joined her. The younger girl caught the old woman's attention, who threw Chaiyala a friendly smile and shrug as if to say, *"Isn't this place great?"*

Then a young guy, seemingly hiding behind a palm tree, caught her attention. He looked at his phone and walked away, greeting a woman, similar age with a polite hug and kiss on the lips. They moved to a table near The Tamarind.

Then she spotted him—almost sitting in one of the gardens bordering the Lazy River. He wasn't trying to hide. Who was this guy?

He seemed to be looking directly at her, but without the usual cold, vacant menace of an adversary. He moved carefully, walking around the garden and out of sight, no longer paying attention to her or her friends.

She frowned inwardly. That was definitely him—he'd given away all the right indicators. Yet strangely, her adrenaline had subsided. Concern transformed into curiosity. Did she know this guy? Or more, how?

Chad offered a kind yet subtly flirtatious remark about her gym performance that morning, momentarily distracting her. Smirking, she acknowledged him with a discreet flex. Charlotte turned to ask Chad about a similar pool in New Zealand he'd mentioned earlier.

Perfect timing, Chaiyala thought—just as the stranger came back into view, now standing beside a lamp post, observing peacefully. Watching her float along. Tim relaxed, taking in the sights, while Chad and Charlotte spoke.

She fixed her gaze on the man and gave him her intense stare, paired with the subtle, menacing smile that usually preceded a reckoning—mostly to see what response she'd get.

He smiled and chuckled silently, briefly... then his smile faded to the expression of someone with a heavy heart.

He went out of view again. She kept her eyes on the corner he'd moved from, and this time Chad and Charlotte caught her off guard.

She turned back, faced with their curious looks, still preoccupied. *Who is this guy? Do I know him from somewhere?* The possibility now played on her mind.

"You okay, hun?" Charlotte asked.

Chaiyala delayed her reply, still wondering. *"Damn, I wish I could've gotten a closer look at his face."*

"Yeah... I just, I think I saw someone I might know."

"Oh, cool?" Chad queried.

"Who? Any ideas?" Charlotte asked.

"No, none... but at first, I think someone suspicious may have been following."

"Right... but you're sure they're friendly instead?" Charlotte clarified.

"Yes. But I have no idea who... what..."

"What's the deal?" Tim asked, overhearing.

After a pause, she filled him in. Her gut told her to downplay any concerns, reassuring the others as they drifted along the Lazy River's twists and turns.

Still, she questioned whether disregarding this was a risk. The more she considered it, the more convinced she became—there was no threat. If he approached her directly, she'd get the answers she needed. Only then would he warrant her attention.

The Lazy River meandered past the two towering eight-story waterfalls, cascading into pristine rock pools surrounded by lush tropical vegetation. The first pool was shaded by birds of paradise and palms, while the second featured a vibrant orchard of peaches, pineapples, mangoes, and more. Swimmers were invited to gather fresh fruit for custom smoothies at the Lazy River bar.

Drifting further, they entered a man-made jungle, alive with colourful birds, before reaching a mini lagoon with a swim-up bar enclosed by tall, dense palms. Lanterns, reminiscent of shipwreck relics, hung from trunks as sunlight filtered through the foliage.

At the bar, an attendant collected their fruit baskets and rafts, while a lanky Jamaican bartender, his radiant smile lighting up the space, awaited their smoothie orders.

"This place is amazing!" Charlotte beamed.

"You got that right. I could seriously spend all day here," Tim agreed.

Chad watched a Macaw bobbing its way along the top of the palm-thatched bar shack with deliberate swagger, then spread its scarlet wings and ascended to the top of a palm tree to forage for grubs.

They spent a good hour in the lagoon before Chaiyala felt his presence again.

He made his way through the pool toward them, having placed his sandals, shirt, and towel on a rock at the water's edge.

The man, in his late forties, moved slowly closer. He had greying locks like stratus clouds and a weathered look. Eyes kind and friendly, yet tired. Slim, fit, tanned, wearing long white and purple boardies.

He and Chaiyala regarded each other. Her friends looked first at him, then at her, anticipating growing.

She knew there was a connection—but couldn't place it. *Who was this?*

He studied her face. Yes, it was definitely her. He'd finally found her.

"Mordechai?" she asked cautiously—surprised—narrowing her eyes, suppressing a flood of nostalgic emotion. *"Who else could it be?"*

"Chaiyala!" he said, almost in a sigh of deep relief, his accent akin to hers. "Yes, it is me—your cousin."

Water splashed between them as she leapt into his arms, holding him tightly, tears threatening to spill. She recognized him only from childhood memories—before he vanished.

He'd fled Tel Aviv, hunted by Hamas assassins for knowledge of his family's ancient heritage beyond the Hebrews of old. As a child, she hadn't understood his departure or the secrets he carried—only that he hadn't left by choice. Her parents had tried to explain, but the truth remained beyond her grasp. Mordechai was twenty-four when he fled.

She pulled him in for another tight embrace, struggling to control her emotions.

"Mordechai!" she repeated.

"Goodness girl, you've gotten strong!" he exclaimed, looking her up and down. They both laughed.

She struggled to know where to begin.

"Ahh, Chaiyala... so very good it is to see you again."

"Chad, Tim, Charlotte—my cousin, Mordechai," she introduced, voice almost shaking with disbelief. "We were close... before he had to leave Tel Aviv."

It had been about fifteen years since she'd seen him. They'd been close—he looked out for her like a brother. She was a tomboy who didn't fit in, fought with her brothers, and was a handful for her parents. But somehow, Mordechai brought out the best in her. He helped build a bridge between her, her siblings, and her parents—where healing quietly took root. Her parents had always been supremely grateful to Mordechai for the influence he'd had on their daughter.

Tim, Chad, and Charlotte were moved by what they'd heard. Beyond the reunion—it was discovering the foundational role Mordechai had played in shaping the woman her friends deeply loved and respected. His presence felt like another thread in the rich tapestry of who Chaiyala had become.

To their great surprise, Mordechai wasn't at all unfamiliar with the Richat Structure or the ongoing excavation work. Nor was he surprised by Red Sword Security or Chaiyala's role within it. In fact, he disclosed details that astonished them—insights into the Richat, Atlantis, the place of Red

Sword, and the heritage of their people stretching back long before the days of Isaac, Jacob, and Moses.

The five of them spent another hour at the lagoon before enjoying a flavourful West Indian lunch at The Tamarind.

The two cousins, reunited at last, shared secure contact details—quietly sealing the promise of future connection. Afterwards, Mordechai invited Chaiyala for a walk along the beach—they had a world of things to catch up on. The others returned to the penthouse suite to prepare for their meeting with J-Mac.

~~~~~~~

Reunited after years apart, the cousins strolled casually through the pool precinct, reflecting on their present working engagements in Jamaica. They discussed how things had unfolded across two decades—Chaiyala spoke of her role with Red Sword; Mordechai revealed his work as an agent of the Israeli government.

To their left, the resort's water park came into view, its towering hydro-slide rising above palms and tropical greenery.

"This place has something for everyone," Mordechai said. "I believe there's a wave pool as well."

"Yes, I love this place," Chaiyala replied. "I see why Nathan comes back so much."

The semi-deliberate small talk faded once they were out of earshot. Their conversation shifted.

"How much of our people's origins are you aware of?"

Chaiyala considered. "Probably far less than I will be... once we've finished talking."

He studied her with a slight, unintentional intensity—quickly replaced by a warm smile.

"You were always intuitive. Intelligent. Often beyond your years," he recalled. "Which is probably why you clashed with others your age. You haven't changed."

She smiled, appreciating his words.

"You know the Torah, yes?" he asked, tone measured.

"Is the first five books, yes? Moses wrote them—through inspiration, divine."

"And the lifespans recorded in Genesis?"

"Yes, longer—so very much longer than today's people live."

Mordechai's expression hinted that she likely knew less than she realized.

"What is it?" she asked.

"You see... sometimes, things very important—things that change everything we think—are lost in translation. Or... more often, bent by interpretation. Translation, that is simple—language to language. But interpretation? That is where meaning... shifts. Two people, they read the same manuscript—and each finds a truth. Very different. This, my cousin, is why we must read not only with eyes—but with understanding."

She nodded. He was setting a stage—she felt it.

"For generations, my cousin, they debate—six thousand, nine thousand years... or millions. But all are based on systems—systems that assume time has always meant the same thing. It hasn't."

"I have heard this, yes. Tim and Nathan—they spoke of it, just the other night. About Genesis, lifespans... the Earth's age."

"Yes... you take that formula, you apply it—and what you get is this: somewhere between six, maybe nine thousand years. That is what tradition tells us. Or, carbon dating says its millions of years old."

He paused.

"May I suggest—neither view holds full truth. One bends under poor translation... the other stands on theory that rests too comfortably on assumption."

"So, what's the actual age?"

"More likely? Somewhere in the range of eighty to a hundred thousand years. Not the figures they tell in schools... but the truth that hides beneath layers of forgetting."

"Interesting—go on..."

He resumed. "The Torah—it was first written in Paleo-Hebrew, shaped by how we, the Hebrews, saw the world. Later, it became Greek—the Septuagint. And the Pentateuch? It is five books, yes—but Torah... she is more."

His tone shifted slightly.

"Now, you must consider this. We have no record—none at all—of how Genesis, Exodus, Leviticus, Numbers, and Deuteronomy were given from Adonai to Moses. So then, I ask... could there have been writings before? Older records, from before Moses? From a time... even more ancient?"

"You mean... there were ancient writings with the inspiration of Genesis? Side by side?"

"Exactly. These writings... they could explain what was misunderstood. About the lifespans—yes—of the sons of Adam... and about those who lived before the Hebrews. Before Egypt, even. Who was there in the days of Enoch... of Noah? "And these... these are not stories, you understand. They are windows. To lives that came before our people even had a name. They held truths—buried truths—that were never meant to vanish. Not entirely."

Chaiyala felt the depth of what was about to unfold.

"You see... this is why I waited, Chaiyala. Because of what the Richat Structure truly shows. With your background—with how you see and feel things—you are ready, yes? Ready to understand how the lost pieces... they fit. Especially this—how the old Hebrews are connected to Atlantis." He looked out toward the sunlit horizon as if seeing time layered in stone. Then turned back to her—with eyes that held both wonder and burden.

"The plot thickens," she said, the warm breeze brushing past.

"Yes... the Richat, as Atlantis—this idea, it is not fringe any more. Some... they know. They truly know its story. But many—they still dismiss, ignore. And others? They fight. Very powerful factions... they do all they can to keep it hidden."

"They would bury it forever, yes?" Chaiyala said. "But we—we cover it only for now. For the right moment."

He nodded slowly. "If Red Sword Security is guarding Atlantis... then this Richat Project? It's only the first page, my cousin. Just the beginning of a much deeper story."

She gave him a look. "What is this you speak now?"

"I speak of the ancients... those who walked the Earth long before Eber, Isaac, Jacob. But tell me—Joseph, Moses... who were they, really? Were they just leaders? Or... did they have access to Egypt's oldest secrets? What truths did they carry that were never written? They were not only men of God. They were men of knowledge. Of power. And perhaps... keeper of secrets passed down from forgotten ages." The sea breeze tugged at his shirt as if echoing the questions he posed—unanswered, ancient, lingering in the sun-drenched silence.

"Now you sound just like Solon," she smiled—half amused, half intrigued.

"Ahh... Solon. The ancestor of Plato. He—he went to Sais, yes? Before it vanished into the Nile delta. Egypt... she guarded what was lost. And the Temple of Sais—it held the last records of Atlantis. The final accounts... hidden in stone."

"Do you remember the Solon Diaries? Found below Athens—under the old library. Then... gone."

"I do."

"We have them."

Mordechai's eyes widened, flickering with restrained urgency. "I'd like to see them, yes... but not now. Protocol, I'm sure—it applies. And truth is, I do not have much time."

"How come?"

He spoke quietly, almost as if to the wind itself. "You see... things have changed in Israel. The conflict with Hamas? That is surface noise. Distraction. The true shift—it breathes elsewhere. Washington, Europe... they hold to broken systems, and borrowed time. But when Atlantis returns—when it reveals itself... those systems will fall. The power... it will move. Like puppets dropped mid-performance—only to find the whole stage is no longer theirs."

"A whole new framework," she breathed.

He lowered his voice, the words almost cloaked in dusk, "I am a Shadow. I serve President Asaharif—yes. The details... they're not for now. But I will tell you this: when Atlantis rises... the old world fractures. East versus West? That war ends. What comes after... is something else entirely. It will be stranger. Deeper. As if the rules themselves become rewritten."

He turned the conversation back.

"Long lives, yes. But the meaning of 'year'—it is not fixed. Back then, 'year' could be a moon cycle... a season... the span of a king's rule. Even divine periods. We must read Genesis with the old eyes—not the calendar of today."

"This—shifts everything."

"You see... a number like four hundred years—it might mean thousands. Maybe more. If death came after Eden... then the early ones, yes—

they could have lived a hundred thousand years. Then ten thousand... then one thousand... and now?" He paused, voice thinning. "Now... it is decades. Nothing more."

"That's... insane," she blinked. "What does this have to do with Atlantis and Israel?"

"It is written. Shem gave us our roots. That Atlantis was never real. But myth... it is a mask. And behind it—truth lives, quietly."

"Go on..."

"Some accounts say Poseidon stood aboard the Ark. A boy. Not a god. His line—it goes from Japheth... to Javan... then Kittim.

Hebrew name. Greeks called him Kronos."

She stopped walking. "Kittim is Kronos? Poseidon. On Noah's Ark?"

Mordechai turned to her, eyes serious. "Same man. Different name. The Greeks, they remembered—but not exact. They made him a titan. But he was grandson of Javan. Great-grandson of Noah."

"So, Poseidon's from Noah's line?" Chaiyala frowned.

"Yes." He nodded again. "Noah's great, great-grandson. From Japheth's line. Not myth. Not marble. A boy. Flesh and blood. He stood beside Eber. They watched the flood together."

She kicked at the sand. "But the stories... they say he ruled the sea."

Mordechai smiled, just a little. "People forget. Or they remember too strong. They stretch truth into legend." He looked out at the waves. "Poseidon became legend. But before that—he was just a boy. From the Ark."

"And Atlantis?" Chaiyala looked out at the waves.

"Atlantis came from him. From his line. A city born from memory. From the sea. But its roots—they are in the Ark. In the silence."

As they walked, his tone deepened. "Poseidon... they did not just crown him. They sanctified him. His name echoed in temples, in dreams. Even as Atlantis sank—he remained. In symbols. In bloodlines. In power that moved beneath thrones."

"You're saying Poseidon lived... beyond his time? Even still?" she stopped to focus.

"Perhaps. Some believe—that Poseidon's presence lingers."

She nodded, storing it away—but something in his voice unsettled her.

"This is all working backward. The flood... it's meant to coincide with Atlantis's destruction."

"Not quite, Chaiyala. The great flood... it came long before Atlantis fell. That's why I spoke of ancient versus modern views—how we read old time through a lens of new eyes. The Torah? It doesn't list every soul aboard the Ark. Only Noah's sons... and their wives. Only the lineages of whence we came.

She paused thoughtfully, eyes narrowing just a touch. "Like the Gospels—five thousand fed, yes? But no mention of women. No children. The record... it's partial. Always."

"Exactly. The Book of Noah—it's in Enoch, yes? It hints that his world... it was larger. Far larger than known. The Ark? It might have carried hundreds. Not just the names we know—but many more."

"Where did you learn this?"

He smiled. "The Book of Noah."

She blinked. "Of course... that makes sense."

"The Book of Noah—it never made the canon. Vast it was, rich... like the Old Testament. But they forgot it. No—they excluded it. The councils, the scribes. Moses... he gave us the concise version. A pearl from the deep. But the full story?" He paused. "It is... far richer."

"So—great-grandparents from many generations... they lived to see great-grandchildren... from many generations." her voice trailing slightly—

final words stretching into thoughtful silence as the weight of continuity settled between them.

Mordechai saw it all coming together in her eyes.

"Poseidon... and Eber. The fathers—of Atlantis, of Israel. On the Ark, together. That vessel... it held more than survivors. It held beginnings. Hidden ones."

She nodded, finally gaining some mental relief, yet no less awed.

"One—wrapped in wave and storm. The other—in covenant and silence. Atlantis crowned Poseidon a deity. Israel remembered Eber as a man. But the flood... it bore them both. Real. Living. Witnesses."

"Interpretation can reshape history," she said softly.

"Exactly, he nodded slowly, voice low and deliberate. Our scriptures... they're not exhaustive. Far from it. If we gathered every authentic biblical text—excluding the corrupted, the false—the result? It would rival the greatest encyclopaedia ever published."

"Woah..."

He smiled.

"The most important link is this: Poseidon and Eber grew close as friends while aboard the Ark. That bond—born during catastrophe—endured long after the flood waters receded."

Chaiyala took this in silently. Her mind was racing, but her heart was still.

He slowed his pace, eyes tracing the dust where old footsteps might have lingered. "And what the Torah... and the Christian scriptures don't record, Chaiyala, are the layers. The hidden folds behind Moses... behind Joseph. Egypt was more than exile. It was intersection. With the priesthood of Sais. With what they preserved—quietly."

He glanced sideways.

"Moses, a Prince. Joseph, a Prime Minister. They weren't just rulers—they were readers. They had keys, cousin. To vaults that held knowledge... from before Egypt. From Atlantis. That's why your Solon Diaries matter. They aren't forgotten relics." He paused. "They are echoes. Echoes of a shared origin."

Chaiyala looked out over the Caribbean Sea. The horizon stretched like eternity before them.

She watched him carefully, her voice barely above the sea's hush.

"There is more to your visit, no? This is not just history lesson. Not just a walk by the shore."

Mordechai nodded, eyes deep and deliberate.

"I didn't come just to reconnect, Chaiyala. I came... because something is stirring. About to change. And you—cousin—you are part of what hasn't yet been written," his gaze held hers, unwavering. "It's not history we're reading. It's prophecy we're walking into."

CHAPTER 15

He spoke with calm precision, eyes scanning the horizon as if weighing every word.

"Israel... is a paradox, no? Political freedoms—and complications. We defend our sovereignty with vigour—yes. But we are tangled. Tangled in a dense web... of agreements. And adherences."

He turned to her, eyes fixed. "As you will know... Nathan O'Conner is in talks—with sixty-one governments. Across the Atlantic. Across the Mediterranean. To form... what may become the United Countries of Atlantis."

There was a pause. Chaiyala halted mid-step, mouth parted in silence, colour fled from her cheeks. For a moment, the words simply landed—like puzzle pieces aligning. Her breath caught slightly; composure intact, logic still grounding her. Then it shifted—something deeper, heavier. Possibilities bloomed, intoxicating and limitless. But underneath them... betrayal. Quiet, creeping, undeniable.

Pressure welled in her chest—not painful, but dissonant. Her fingers curled slightly, grounding her against the swirl in her thoughts. She looked toward the horizon, though didn't truly see it. Her mind was elsewhere—racing toward a truth unnamed.

She stopped cold. Breath escaped in a slow, broken exhale. Pulse hammering, she turned to Mordechai—no longer curious, but fierce. Something unreadable sat in her gaze, and the world felt slightly off-kilter beneath her feet.

"Chaiyala... are you okay?" Mordechai asked, uneasy.

She looked at him—her eyes cutting through him, chilling his blood.

"Chaiyala, you're scaring me."

She didn't answer right away, her gaze remained fixed on the horizon—her heart searching...

Nor did she know exactly where it came from, but a peace—not inward—something greater. It brought her a sense of calm and reason. She didn't question it... she knew it gathered peace of mind and logic together, allowing her to remember who Nathan was. His character. His record. An indelible knowledge that there was either a noble explanation for why she hadn't known about something this monumental. Or, there was something far greater than she, Nathan, or Mordechai at work—and that was reassuring in a way she could only describe as *faith with substance*. There was no other way for her to understand it. Explain it. Reckon with it.

The wind shifted, brushing warmth across her skin. Not comfort, exactly—but clarity. She blinked, slowly, as if waking from a dream that hadn't been hers. "I'm okay," she said at last, voice quiet but steady. "I think... I just needed to remember what's true."

Mordechai didn't press. He saw it—the way her shoulders eased, the way her breath found rhythm again. Whatever had shaken her had not broken her.

"I'll be okay. I promise. Just... shocked. But excited too." She steadied her breath, then smiled with effort—but sincerity—softening the air between them. "No—I truly had no idea Nathan was speaking with all those governments."

Mordechai blinked in surprise.

"Nathan O'Conner... he's more myth than man," she said gently but firmly, gaze steady on her cousin. "Enigmatic, yes. But the most trustworthy soul I've ever known. Transparent—genuine. Hundreds will vouch for him. So, if he hasn't told me?" She shook her head softly, "there's a reason. A good reason."

She continued outlining Nathan's character, his integrity, and his motives. Eventually, Mordechai accepted her word, though he looked forward to meeting the man himself.

"You'd like me to speak... with Nathan. About Israel—joining the union?" Her tone held clarity, but also a trace of curiosity—the kind that knew the answer but invited him to say it aloud.

Mordechai smiled, placing his hands on her shoulders and kissed her forehead.

"You are... as intelligent as you are beautiful, cousin." A small smile followed—pride in his gaze, affection in his tone.

"Yes, of course," she answered.

Mordechai laughed. "And so confident!"

"Not the compliment part—though it's true," she laughed softly. "But yes. I'll talk to him. Still wondering, though... why me? You're here too."

"Because I trust you—with more than just words. "This meeting... is no luxury. It is risk. High risk. If you weren't trained like you are, cousin—I would not be here. You're a match—for any adversary. But I must leave. Immediately. Under strict protocol. Very strict."

"I understand," she nodded. Such things were familiar territory.

"Thank you, Chaiyala. If Israel can break free... from these limitations—finally..." He exhaled slowly. "We may breathe easy. No longer looking over our shoulders. No longer... waiting."

"And why do you think Nathan—or Atlantis—can offer better than Washington?"

"No strings attached," Mordechai said, and the words carried a kind of release—like stepping out from under a long shadow. "For once, it means exactly that. No leverage. No compromise. Just a clean break from the circus—and a step into something better."

As they walked back to Caribbean Paradise, they shared memories of youth—lighter, simpler days—when joy wasn't tempered by politics and ancient history.

~~~~~~~

Charlotte, Tim, and Chad took their seats at The Oishii Osara we're they'd planned to meet Jacob McKenzie. Excited but nervous, they ordered drinks and pork and prawn gyoza. Charlotte opened her laptop and called Tyrese via Skype. He answered from his beach house on the Coromandel Peninsular back home in New Zealand, relieved she reached him before Jacob arrived.

Tyrese offered gentle guidance. "Remember, Jacob's not just about success—he's ministry-driven. He wants the music to resonate, uplift, create impact. Stay anchored in that, and you'll be fine."

Jacob arrived soon after, casual and relaxed, alongside his wife Melinda, and his manager. They were also in Jamaica on sabbatical—perfect timing.

Charlotte, thrilled to meet J-Mac, was especially delighted to connect with Melinda, herself Jamaican by birth. They hit it off immediately.

The meeting stretched over two hours. They discussed music, touring logistics, and their respective journeys. Jacob spoke fondly of his time with '90s Christian Pop-Rock band Amplified Exodus. They talked about Jamaica, Montego Bay, Tim and Charlotte's upcoming wedding, and Tim's work in Africa.

Charlotte and Jacob spoke like old friends with much in common—passionate, thoughtful.

"You've hit the ground running," Jacob noted. "From what I see, it's all legit. How've you stood out in such a competitive field so far?"

"I've developed a unique sound—hard-hitting lyrics that blend gospel truths with relatable storytelling. That's my niche."

"And her authenticity shines through social media." Tyrese added.

Charlotte nodded. "It's helped me connect deeply with fans. That strategy builds loyalty and amplifies reach—spreading the gospel's message of freedom and wholeness far and wide. With Tyrese's help and the band's input, I navigate industry politics. It's how I live this dream."

"What help?" Tyrese joked. Tim and Charlotte laughed.

"She's a natural, honestly" Tyrese smiled. "Hopefully I offer more guidance than annoyance."

Jacob chuckled. "You two work well—there's good chemistry, I can see. Keep good mentors close—and don't underestimate the value of a wise pastoral adviser."

Charlotte absorbed every word. Tyrese, quietly proud, basked in her big moment.

"If you ever need anything—tips, help—don't hesitate." Jacob offered with sincerity.

"I'd be truly grateful," Charlotte smiled, squeezing Tim's hand.

The mid-afternoon sun filtered through the palms, casting dappled light across the low outdoor table at Oishii Osara. They each settled in—Charlotte and Jacob at the centre, Melinda tucked beside Jacob—Tim and Chad relaxed on the opposite sofa, and Jacob's manager scrolling quietly through his notes. The last of the shared plates had been cleared, drinks refreshed, and the mood had shifted—still easy, but leaning into purpose.

Charlotte tapped her laptop screen, having moved her drink to the side. "Alright," she said, glancing at Jacob. "Let's get this down."

Jacob nodded, pulling up the draft. "We've talked it through. Now we shape it."

Tim leaned forward, curious but quiet.

Chad gave a low whistle. "Feels like something real now."

"It is." Melinda smiled, her hand resting lightly on Jacob's arm.

They reviewed the contract line by line, voices low but steady. No tension, just shared clarity. A few edits, a couple of affirming nods. Jacob's manager added a note about scheduling buffers—Charlotte adjusted phrasing to keep things flexible.

"Ready when you are," Tyrese's voice came through the speakers, sunlit from New Zealand.

Jacob signed first, then Charlotte. A soft ping confirmed Tyrese's signature. Then Jacob's manager.

All sorted, they had clarity. The tour was locked in, and momentum had already begun.

Before parting, they exchanged contact details. They talked some more, savouring the ambience, enjoying the food, and living the moment.

When the trio returned to the Penthous, Nathan asked how it went.

"Awesome! Hugely successful!" Charlotte beamed. "Jacob's keen. We locked in dates, signed contracts. Everything's done!"

Chaiyala hugged her. Nathan congratulated her. Crouton fetched champagne and flutes, and poured celebratory drinks.

"I'm thrilled," Nathan smiled.

Rod and Crouton nodded approval. Tim buzzed with joy—his fiancée was stepping further into her destiny.

Charlotte could hardly express her gratitude. Her grin refused to fade. Doors had opened—thanks to Nathan's orchestration.

More awaited Nathan, Crouton, and Tim.

Tim and Chad exchanged amazed glances, still reeling from the surreal journey their lives had become.

~~~~~~~

After cocktails by the pool, the moment they'd come to Jamaica for finally arrived. Nathan had secured a private lounge at the Caribbean Club for he and Crouton's second meeting with Alesandro Karahalios. Their first encounter had been fleeting—just long enough to leave an impression, not long enough to settle anything.

He'd secured exclusive rights through management, making sure Maurice was generously compensated—not just for the logistics, but for the trust and groundwork he'd laid. On top of that, he covered the cost of complimentary food and drinks at the second lounge and beach bar. It wasn't about perks. It was about setting a tone: open-handed, distraction-free, and quietly honouring the team behind the scenes.

No announcements. No spotlight. Just a gesture that reflected the spirit behind the work—intentional, generous, and aligned with the message they were carrying. A quiet way of saying: 'this matters, and so do you.'

"Generosity goes a long way to simplifying what is complex. It expands what's possible." Nathan shared.

Chaiyala and Charlotte went to the beach with Chad, while Rhys took a break. Nathan led Crouton, Rod, and Tim to the lounge—purposefully vacant except for Red Sword guards stationed discreetly, sniper rifles on the balcony.

A smiling Red Sword agent escorted them outside, where refreshments awaited. Soon, four men and two women in Red Sword gear entered. Tim noted the tactical attire—these were field operatives.

No words were spoken. Five of them exited quietly, leaving one behind. Nathan leaned forward, extending a hand.

"Thank you for agreeing to meet us."

Tim realized this was a clever VIP escort tactic—designed to avoid drawing attention to the central character.

"Rod, Tim—I'd like you to meet Mr. Alesandro Karahalios."

Both greeted their guest warmly.

"Alesandro, you've met Collin Ericson..." Nathan motioned.

"Great to meet you again." Crouton smiled—they shook hands firmly.

"This is Rod Chandler, head of security. And Tim Harison, chief historian for the Richat Project in Mauritania."

"An honour to meet those unearthing Atlantis's truths," Alesandro said, his Greek accent rich with reverence.

Tim's intuition sparked—something hidden between the lines.

Nathan nodded. "They're familiar with what we've discussed—your ancestry and Solon's invaluable, sensitive archives. The diaries have reached us."

"That was me," Alesandro said. "I took them from fools who would've shredded them into 'Greek mythology.'" He mimed sarcastic air quotes and made a goofy face.

"I have no time for that garbage. I think the five of us know full well, what happens to things like my Great, one hundred and seventy-fifth Grand Father's diaries if the 'wrong' archaeologists got hold of them? Hmm?" Alesandro paused. "I wasn't prepared to risk that."

Tim's mind reeled. "One hundred and seventy-five generations..." he whispered.

Alesandro didn't flinch.

"I know who you are," he said quietly. "Descendants of Atlas—risen twelve thousand years after Atlantis's fall. Here to uncover and rebuild."

Rod frowned. Crouton blinked. Tim recalled the moment at the Chinguetti dig site where Chad sensed something about the RSS agents, but couldn't place it. There was an awkward puzzled silence. Nathan waited, gauging the dialogue before speaking himself.

"You're the brotherhood of..." Alesandro began.

Nathan interrupted: "Tiki takasardin, syrem eto calabraxi iner mora tya kalaris hadi capalatle," Nathan said in a cadence both ancient and deliberate.

Alesandro's face lit up. "You speak Manuscrat!" he whispered, stunned.

Though he recognized only fragments of the sentence, he interpreted Nathan's words roughly: *"I have not yet explained the brotherhood to them."*

Rod stayed silent, brow furrowed deeper. Confusion hadn't left him. Then as if memory had been re-written, none of them remembered any of that, except Nathan.

"The Halls of Alastragah," Alesandro continued, "are where Atlantis stored its wealth, essence, and history. The Secret Service of Atlantis hid there—preserving its technology, virtues, and spiritual legacy."

Tim felt like he'd missed something, and Crouton felt like he'd zoned out momentarily.

Alesandro fixed his gaze on Tim. The intensity was unmistakable. Tim felt marked—as if singled out to carry something critical.

"The people of Atlantis live on," Alesandro said softly. "Read Solon's journals carefully—you'll understand how." Then, shifting: "The diaries, they're written in ancient Greek, yes?"

"They are," Tim confirmed.

"We ran it through a deciphering program," Tim said. "It scans the surface, picks out characters and oddities, then translates using pattern analysis. The output includes full English text and thematic breakdowns. We can flag anything strange—misaligned symbols, irregular digits, things that don't fit."

Alesandro leaned back, eyes sparking with approval.

"Did it highlight anything strange? Characters that don't fit? Dots, symbols...?"

"No. But I know what you're implying." Tim's concentration deepened. "Hidden messages. Null ciphers. Acrostics. Steganographic codes— embedded in the text."

Alesandro grinned wide and tapped a finger in the air. "Exactly!"

Tim smiled, momentum rising.

"That's how you unveil the sixth journal. The seventh... well, it's written in a Greek variant of Manuscrat. Nathan can help there."

Rod, Tim, and Crouton exchanged glances. A deeper layer had clearly just been revealed.

"I'll adjust the decryption parameters," Tim said, unlocking his phone. "Focus on the outliers. We should have access to the sixth journal within forty-five minutes."

Crouton nodded. "I like it."

Nathan smiled approvingly.

Alesandro reached into a modest satchel and retrieved a sleek device— steel-clad, gold-tipped, and cool to the touch. More fortress than flash drive.

"This contains everything," he said, his Greek accent lending the words a quiet gravity. "Solon's writings on Atlantis—outside the journals. Everything about Sais, the temple priesthood, the Exolothreftis. All my family archives. Sixteen terabytes. Yours."

Rod's eyes widened. Nathan accepted the device, surprised by its deceptive lightness. He handed it to Tim.

"Thank you," Tim said, sincerely moved.

"We're deeply grateful," Nathan added.

"You're welcome." Alesandro's stoicism was softening. "One last thing—Atlantis isn't merely a lost place. Its location was once common knowledge. Solon wrote less about where Atlantis was... and more about what was hidden and where within it."

"Like if New York or Tokyo vanished overnight," Tim mused. "We'd still know where they stood."

"Exactly," Alesandro said. "So it was with Atlantis. And with the rest of the ancient world—erased by cataclysm."

Tim nodded, deep in thought. "Fact becomes legend. Legend becomes myth."

"Hmm," Rod muttered. "There has to be a method—distinguishing truth from tale."

"There is," Nathan replied. "But not through conventional means. Modern historiography depends on proximity—eyewitness accounts, timelines, how long details remain unwritten before they're archived. That method works only when the chain of transmission stays intact." He glanced at Rod.

"But when catastrophe breaks that chain—when records are lost, voices silenced—what remains can't be verified by human standards." Nathan's tone deepened, not with dismissal, but with certainty.

"Pre-catastrophe civilizations weren't preserved by human hands. They were preserved by divine intention. Scripture doesn't survive because it was carefully recorded—it survives because it was never meant to be lost. That's why the New Testament stands inerrant," he added. "Not because it's close to the events—but because God ensured it couldn't be distorted."

Alesandro regarded Nathan with perplexed awe. What on earth did this man know to speak with such conviction?

Tim caught the frown on their guest's face, but his own thoughts were elsewhere. Nathan's understanding of the divine stirred something deeper—this wasn't just brilliance or theological fluency. It had to be more than knowledge. It felt lived.

"So, what we're facing is a loss of reference—history severed from verification." Rod considered.

Tim agreed. "Conventional understanding of history only spans five or six millennia. Beyond that—it's hazy."

"Solon's stretched that timeline another six thousand years," Crouton said.

"Correct," Alesandro affirmed. "And his older archives on that drive, begin with the start of his adventure—his reasons for searching for Atlantis to begin with."

"This is... phenomenal! Thank you," Tim expressed in deep sincerity.

Crouton checked his watch. "Dinner?"

"Shrimp and marlin," Nathan offered. "Gourmet fish burgers, caught and prepared the same day they dock. The chef's a purist—no freezer, no shortcuts, just the real deal."

Crouton "You've eaten here before?" Crouton suspected with raised brow.

"Let's just say I know the tides," Nathan smiled.

Tim chuckled, sensing the layers in that answer.

"I like it," Crouton grinned, already standing. "Great choice. I'm starving."

Alesandro lingered a moment, watching Nathan with quiet curiosity. There was something about the way he spoke—like he wasn't merely recommending dinner—there was something else to the man—only he couldn't place it.

"I'm in." Rod nodded.

"Alesandro?" Nathan asked.

"That's very kind. I'd be honoured."

"You've shared so much—thank *you*."

"I'm grateful to contribute," Alesandro smiled. "Solon's quest may have paused—but tonight, it continues."

Rod smirked. "He's getting better at smiling." Alesandro was warming to them.

As they rose and headed toward the beachside restaurants and bars, Red Sword agents moved with quiet precision—discreet but ever-present.

Rumours of black ops agents lurking nearby signalled a confrontation brewing. One that might erupt before the team's return to Africa. At the Montego Bay Red Sword Headquarters, Caitlyn and her agents kept vigilant watch over the Caribbean Paradise, their eyes trained on every shadow while the Richat team remained in Jamaica.

CHAPTER 16

T he hour was late—the final traces of dusk dissolving beyond the coast, blending into the western horizon. Below, the pool precinct buzzed with guests dining, laughing, and soaking in warm waters, while Chad, Chaiyala, and Rhys relaxed in the privacy of the penthouse spa on the balcony.

Charlotte sat at the outdoor table, a mug of hot chocolate in hand, unwinding after a long day. Her world felt surreal—meeting J-Mac, absorbing it all. Gratitude pulsed gently—deeply through her chest. Beside her, Tim had his laptop open, reviewing the extracted Solon diary report. His last ice-cold Blue Nectargy rested nearby as he studied the screen with measured excitement.

To their right, Rod lounged, feet up, lost in thought, savouring a tall glass of top-shelf Woodstock bourbon. At the far end of the table, Nathan, Crouton, and Alesandro discussed Red Sword, their work at the Richat structure, and Alesandro's career as an investigative journalist—as well as his role as the current keeper of his family's archives.

Tim studied the sixth and seventh journals, his focus steady.

Beside him, Charlotte stirred—half-asleep, warm and close. He reached for the ice-cold Blue Nectargy, cracked it open, and took a slow sip, the fizz sharp against the quiet.

Journal Six contained four entries. Using the decrypter, Tim had been able to piece together from over three thousand stray characters recovered from earlier translations. Once correctly ordered, the entries revealed themselves in full.

Then, almost instantly, Journal Seven emerged. Hidden within the sixth, unlocked through a layer of diacritic-based encoding.

Many of the ancient Greek characters bore faint shadow lines, subtle enough to go unnoticed. The decrypter recognized the anomalies and sorted the glyphs accordingly.

Tim now had access to Journal Seven.

A strange mix of excitement and nerves stirred in him as he scanned the list of key aspects—laid out like a digital table of contents, each topic embedded within the newly deciphered text.

He glanced at Charlotte, who gazed back at him, smiling sleepily.

"Hello," she said, as if he'd just returned from another world.

"Hey..."

They shared a quiet kiss. Charlotte rested her head on his shoulder, and Tim leaned his gently against hers. Then, as the ocean breeze gently curled around them, he returned to the journals.

Tim smiled, heart full, as he began reading the first entry of the sixth.

The trail ran cold as the stories ended, and at the same time as my duties in Athens required attention. Although my return home has not included the results I had originally hoped for, it has also not found me empty-handed. I have been enlightened to depths I had not anticipated. I suspect, having considered all I have learned while in the land of the Atlantes, that there is substantially more to the world than is obvious. What one beholds at first glance, it appears, is merely a fraction of the sum of its entirety.

Tim stopped, pondered that for a second, then continued reading...

On one hand there appears to be far more beyond our horizons than I once thought possible, an abundance of truly exciting proportions. On the other, I fear, that such an abundance—the depth of the unknown and unseen may evoke anxiety in those who fear what they don't understand...

Tim thought to himself, "So, that kinda thing is no new concept... funny that."

I hold reason to believe that, in the wake of Atlantis's fall, the King of Athens did commission a silent order—assassins sent forth to hunt what remained. Survivors. Relics. Any trace that might rise again against Athens and her allies. This act, veiled in secrecy, left no mark in the archives of our forebears. Yet the order bore a name: Exolothreftis—the Eradicators. Their charge: to extinguish memory itself. And so long as Atlantis lingers in record or recollection, so too shall they endure...

"Incredible," Tim muttered aloud.

The realization hit hard—an entire thread of Hellenic history, lost to time? It left him with a chill, the kind that comes when something familiar turns suddenly alien.

For a moment, unease crept in. But Tim pushed it back, reaffirming the truths he'd verified. This wasn't some revisionist concoction—it held weight, precision, lineage.

He exhaled deeply, only then realizing he'd been holding his breath.

... This, I have learned from Corineas, who is not a friend to the present aristocracy. He was happy to divulge its questionable history as passed down his line, from generation to generation since the days of conflict with Atlantis.

Why was all of this done in secret?

What did the king fear so much about Atlantis? What did he suspect they still carried—so dangerous, so enduring—that it must be erased with such haste, such totality?

There was the million-dollar question, once more. *"Hmm, no new concept indeed!"*

Charlotte curled up in her chair, sleep gently pulling her under. Chad, Chaiyala, and Rhys had already left the spa, though Tim—immersed in the unfolding mysteries of the journals—hadn't noticed. At the far end of the deck, Nathan, Crouton, and Alesandro continued their quiet dialogue, voices low and steady. Rod, half-lost in the haze of reflection, drifted deeper into drowsiness—soon to follow Charlotte into sleep.

Tim, now alone in his focus, turned his attention to the second entry of Solon's sixth diary.

It appears I have asked perhaps, one too many questions. I am being followed, day and night. Others have witnessed the like and my family grow concerned. I on the other hand, remain intrigued. Today I received a secret warning to abandon my research into Atlantis and leave it alone. Why is that? Why do those in the shadows, fear the knowledge of Atlantis or coming to me to discuss why? In addition to these curious circumstances are the reports given to me by Corineas, my wife and others of my family—in those I place great trust, and they in me. It appears I have a positive force at work, operating also in secret. Their sole evidences being the apparent thwarting of attempts on my life and the lives of those I love. Again, why am I and my beloved under threat? Why the need for protection? Why are the activities of these entities veiled, with scarce indication of their existence?

"Well, that's a long story," Tim thought. "We could spend all day unravelling that..."

His mind turned inward. Who protected Solon and his family?

And then—who was Corineas?

A trusted friend, perhaps. Maybe a relative. Someone with connections—high ones. Someone who knew enough, and dared enough, to warn Solon.

The plot seemed to be thickening as he read on through the next entry.

A curious turn of events has unfolded. Men have been arrested, it appears they are the ones who have been following and watching my family and I. It has reached me that the order of the Exolothreftis—an organisation of ill repute—has become aware of my research, and of my pilgrimage to Sais in Egypt. They have taken note, too, of my journey to the Atlantes in the distant southwest, where I sought the site of the old city and whatever remnants might yet endure. It seems they have moved to bring this exploration to an end. Do they mean to bring an end to me as well? This troubles my family greatly, yet again, I fear not the wiles of men and their futile efforts to conceal truth. For truth will endure throughout all the ages, unhindered by the deluded attempts of the worst of human nature. All the same, I must ask, once more, why? Why is this strange tale of Atlantis, a threat to some?

I learned all of the above from a man who travelled from the kingdom of Phoenelakai of the far side of the Mediterranean to meet with me, having heard of my search for Atlantis and the journey I had made several months prior.

"Phoenelakai..." Tim muttered.

As far as he knew, no historical or archaeological record confirmed its existence. It belonged to the same elusive realm as Hawaiiki, Hiva, or Lemuria—names tethered to legend. Just as Atlantis had once been.

He sat back, eyes wide, pulse steady with rising excitement. First Corinth, then Atlantis, now Phoenelakai—another door to a new world of possibility creaking open.

Something stirred beneath the thrill—a quiet alarm. The growing list of 'mythological' cities being uncovered felt less like coincidence, more like a pattern. A truth whispering beneath centuries of doubt.

"But then... myth wasn't always what we call myth today. Once, it was story. Record. Mythos." Tim blinked, brow furrowed. *"That changed—when record keeping shifted from memory and meaning to structure and reason."* He paused. *"And that shift... it reshaped everything that came before."*

Tim read on, *"This man was mysterious, of wonderful manner and conduct, with the appearance of a prince. He was dressed in a red robe with many different shades and patterns of scarlet embroidered into his cloak, tunic and cowl. He wished not to be known and requested I speak not one single word to any soul of his meeting with me. Instead, he has shown me a way to hide records within text, along with the art of apocalyptic writing, a new form of encoding, to ensure further security of that which he has entrusted unto me. The man in red paid rich compliment to me, stating there are few of such wisdom and fortitude who might receive what he was prepared to unveil. I was humbled by his regard. Yet, having heard all he chose to reveal, I found myself— then as now—utterly perplexed. It is as if, I have had the inner workings of good and evil explained to me along with greater knowledge and understanding so strange and extremely difficult to put into words. The details that are about to follow are both the undoing of the current thinking and paradigm of the world now and for thousands of years to come.*

There it was—the moment Tim had long suspected would arrive.

A paradox, exciting and unnerving: his work frequently unearthed knowledge so far-fetched it flirted with fiction—yet it wasn't. It shattered the illusion of perception—because it was real.

And now, he stood at the edge of something rarer still—a peculiar, untrodden road paved not with myth, but with the unveiled mechanics of a forgotten reality.

Coming to terms with that kind of truth was no casual endeavour—it demanded redefinition. Of history. Of belief. Of self.

The man in red began to tell me how the people of Atlantis came to both hate and revere Lord Poseidon. The monarchy had created a chasm between the citizens of the empire and the person of Poseidon. In a bizarre course of deception and confusion of facts and lies, the government turned Poseidon into an object of worship and Poseidon despised the king of Atlantis for this.

"Intriguing!" Tim expressed out loud. *"Poseidon was not originally a god... as legend has portrayed?"*

For the lords—called gods of the earth in the tongue of old—were not men, but messengers, teachers, and administrators from the heavenly realm. Their charge was to serve and protect, to teach the ways of creation, peace, and life-enhancement among the peoples. Poseidon, one of these originators, grieved deeply as he watched the sacred purpose of his kin unravel. Across Egypt, the Atlantikos Pelagos, and the Mediterranean, the distortion spread. The rulers—descendants of these heavenly administrators—began to exalt their forebears as gods, not servants. And in doing so, they weaponised reverence, using the memory of the originators to manipulate and control the common folk.

"Hmm... *Atlantikos Pelagos*—the Ocean of Atlas," Tim whispered, the words hanging in the air.

He paused, letting the thought settle. The issue wasn't semantics—it was structural. Context had collapsed. Definitions drifted. Connections eroded over time. What once held coherence had become something else entirely—something alien in shape and meaning.

What on earth was Poseidon, then? Tim pondered. Some kind of angelic being? Or... an alien, as certain schools of thought suggest?

He leaned back, unsettled but deeply intrigued. His thoughts drifted to the Parahistorical Period—an era older than history itself, untouched by archaeology or written memory. A time when the so-called pagan gods may have walked the earth—not as deified symbols, but as beings of divine or alien origin. Sentinels. Messengers. Architects of meaning.

Perhaps they were real. Perhaps they were corrupted—distorted by human hands, human hunger. Once messengers, now idols. Once luminous, now hollowed out by myth and worship.

Tim exhaled softly, returning from his deep excursion into thought. The page waited. And he read on.

He spoke also of the prophecies of Atlas, first-born of Poseidon and Cleito...

According to tradition, Atlas was the first emperor and high king of Atlantis. Cleito was the human woman Poseidon loved. The god Poseidon shaped the very location of Atlantis around her home—a divine act of devotion transfigured into topography.

The idea of Atlas as a prophet was new to Tim. And, absent from conventional Greek mythology, yet not entirely incompatible.

Filtered through time's distortions, history had become a mosaic: fragments of truth mingled with half-truths, legends sutured to forgotten facts. A pattern modern minds struggle to grasp, tangled in shifting world views and cultural bias, compounded by the vast corpus of literary and historical riddles that haunt the academic record.

[the prophecies of Atlas] ...*which are as follows:*

"At the height of our existence, the creators of the world will become scarce having been separated from humankind by their children. Conflict will follow and lead to the rearranging of the world. The things we have created with our hands and the knowledge imparted of heaven, having been perverted and used against each other will offend the earth and the earth will retaliate first with fire, then with water, then with ice." This *was the first prophesy.*

Tim had goosebumps. He shook his head, reigning in the rush—the urge to shout his astonishment. This first prophecy referenced the destruction of Atlantis: fire and water swallowing a city of grandeur. Then the ice-age, cold and slow, descending long after the echoes of ruin. Thousands of years—unfolding beyond the prophecy's delivery.

The scope staggered him. Tim steadied his breath. Eyes wide, heartbeat low and thudding in his ears, he leaned back in silence. And then he read on.

The second prophecy details the understanding of such things:

"Fact will become folly, history will become legend and legend will become myth—the truth of our legacy reduced to fantasies that offend, scare, and bring discomfort to those who enslave and are enslaved by the mind. The one they call the deceiver and the hinderer has climbed out of the abyss and seduced the minds of the rulers of the world with power and wealth, and they will discover the unending hell that is riches and rule without love and friendship. Gold, will become more valuable than human life, and they will consign cleaver mystics to distort all knowledge of our legacy."

"Truly awesome," Tim whispered—shaking his head, half in disbelief, a grin tugging at his lips.

The one they call the deceiver... the hinderer. Titles long associated with satan, he mused.

The description in the diary—it fit. More than he liked.

Charlotte was now sound asleep. Rod was also traversing the land of nod.

At the far end of the deck, Crouton and Alessandro seemed caught mid-motion—frozen, like images suspended between frames. And Nathan... Nathan was staring directly at Tim with a haunting expression.

Tim blinked. A flicker of light—had it flashed from Nathan's eyes?

He shook his head and rubbed it, breath held tight in his chest. Bewildered.

But when he looked again, Crouton was mid-sentence. Alessandro nodded along.

Nathan watched him still—but now with the familiar, warm smile that always grounded Tim's trust.

Tim turned back to his laptop.

"That was weird," he thought, brow furrowed.

Probably the dull deck lighting. Or maybe the bizarre content of the sixth Solon diary. Or the strain of intense focus twisting his perception.

Still... that feeling lingered.

Unsettling. Charged. Real.

He continued to read.

The third and final prophesy speaks of the distant future, of an Age of Enlightenment where truth and false are at war:

"Alas, the philosophy and inspiration of humankind will turn against unbelief and question all things. An age of revision will collide, in depraved deceit and disillusionment, with both truth and falsehood. The three will battle in the subtle places of

the world, rendering humankind tired and fatigued as the three continue to wage war on each other..."

Tim sat back again and thought about the ambiguity of that... it became less and less odd as he decided that sounded pretty accurate on the whole.

"... finally, on the precipice of love and friendship and by the sign of a scarlet blade, will all that has been hidden and concealed, be uncovered for all the world to see once more. In those days, myth will be reversed into legend and legend into history according to the legacy of our god and father, Poseidon, and the supreme will of his Creator, The Ancient of Days."

"Come on, now..." Tim breathed, elation and bewilderment escalating. The overload was staggering—mind-blowing, history-altering revelations stacked one on top of the next. He contemplated stepping away, taking a break before the momentum unravelled him entirely.

He refused to glance in Nathan's direction. His gaze settled on the cold can of Blue Nectargy instead. Tim tapped it lightly, fingers restless, as he tried to anchor himself. What in the world had he gotten himself caught up in?

Perhaps a walk would help. Clear the flood of thoughts, digest the revelations. *"Survive what remains,"* he thought.

He glanced over at Charlotte, curled and sleeping. Decision made, he stood—his legs stiff, as though he hadn't moved in hours.

Tim approached Nathan, Crouton, and Alesandro, setting aside any lingering images of flickering eyes or strange stares. "Just putting Charlotte to bed. I'll be back shortly," he said, voice low.

The three men nodded in warm acknowledgement. Nothing unusual.

CHAPTER 17

- -

C harlotte barely stirred as Tim carefully picked her up. Sleep clung to her like mist. Her arms looped gently around his neck, and as they passed through the doorway, she smiled briefly, dozily, before drifting off again after their lips met.

Tim laid her down on her bed, pulled a light blanket over her, and returned to the deck. He moved like someone sleepwalking through a dream.

He returned to the deck and to his laptop, blinking at the screen. The ocean beyond pulsed in darkness, mirroring the deep sea of intrigue he now bobbed inside. He felt out of depth—adrift in a free-fall of faith.

He'd crossed the threshold. The point of no return.

"Funny," he mused aloud, "how the point of no return is never sign-posted."

His heart turned inward, seeking the only constant he trusted: The One who guided his spirit. And so, he prayed quietly, the words etched into soul rather than air: *"Help me keep my head in all of this... help me stay grounded. Objective. Open-minded. Aware of Your truth."*

He sat again. Nathan caught his eye.

The older man smiled—not mysteriously this time, but warmly. Proudly. Like a father seeing something he'd hoped for bloom.

Tim felt a wave of reassurance wash over him.

He exhaled, then returned to his laptop.

The man in red continued, speaking at length about Poseidon—ageless, enduring beyond his sons and their sons, and the sons that followed. Over time, estrangement crept in. His descendants, enamoured with foreign rites and pagan customs, grew impatient with the old ways. They assumed Poseidon had grown irrelevant. Their interest waned, and with it, the values of Atlantis—love, friendship, fidelity—were quietly abandoned. Yet in preculiar irony, the monarchy still wielded his name like a blade, holding the people hostage with threats of divine wrath, as though Poseidon might still be provoked to punish what he no longer protected. Poseidon eventually seceded from the central island of Atlantis where his exquisite home and gardens dwelt. He found new residence in the mountains surrounding the north of the city where he fashioned the halls of Alastragah and summoned those still loyal to he, and the heart of what Atlantis originally was. These were the number who were the Posidean Guard, now also, the agents of the secret order of statesmen and women—valiant warriors whose hearts were not so easily corrupted by the fabrications of greed and selfishness. Known also by another name I was requested not to write down or speak aloud of. Alastragah, meaning "Place of Preservation and Restoration", was to be a haven of peace and reverence, untouched by the destruction Poseidon foresaw. Alastragah would serve as a place to continue the technology, knowledge and history of Atlantis in such a way, that when the time came, the city may be rebuilt and the empire remade as much as possible, both physically and philosophically.

That final revelation blazed like a beacon—an unexpected shift that struck Tim with greater force than anything preceding it.

So, Atlantis was meant to be rebuilt...

Until now, everything he'd uncovered had been buried history—past tense, sealed events, relics of ancient memory. But this... this was different. A change in narrative posture. The story was tilting forward, reaching into the present and beyond.

It carried weight. Serious weight.

Tim sat, baffled. In all their time working on the Richat project—in every sleepless night and speculative conversation—he'd never once considered that the tale of Atlantis might not be concluded.

That the final chapter had yet to be written.

The realization reframed everything.

My friend continued, turning to the darker chapters of Atlantis—those that followed Poseidon's departure, which the king welcomed with relief. In his absence, the king deceived the people, claiming Poseidon had ascended to a supreme, unseen existence: a god who watched from afar, blessing or punishing them based on their sacrifices or insolence. Without Poseidon's guiding presence, Atlantis grew volatile. Pride replaced wisdom, and arrogance eclipsed the values it once held—love, kindness, freedom, friendship. The empire expanded aggressively, claiming lands across the northern and southern Mediterranean. In response, the kingdoms of the far northeast united to defend themselves against the growing threat. This alliance was led by the great city of Athens. Atlantis, now drunk on conquest, waged war against both Athens and the distant empire of Hiva, far beyond the lands that lay past the Pillars of Hercules.

Solon's journal detailed Athens' war with striking clarity. Its chronicle aligning almost seamlessly with Plato's account. A familiar echo in Tim's memory.

But Alesandro had spoken of Hiva, that elusive land beyond the Pillars of Hercules. Across the Atlantic, into the Pacific.

Solon's knowledge of distant geography was remarkable. The possibilities were clear—he may have known of the Americas long before explorers ever set sail.

Despite canonical records, it now seemed Western society of Solon's era may have grasped far more than previously believed. Lands beyond Europe and Africa weren't just whispered legends—they were known, mapped, acknowledged. Or, at least it was known, yet kept in secret...

"Intriguing," Tim muttered.

All in all, Atlantis appeared to have lost the plot entirely. Its fall would later mirror those of Egypt, Persia, Macedonian Greece, Rome, and a dozen other ancient empires dragged down by their own grandeur.

"Pride and arrogance..." Tim sighed. *Sometimes I wonder what the point of history really is. If the world's leaders were historians—true ones—how many mistakes might have been avoided altogether?*

It was a beautiful notion.

And painfully elusive.

Atlantis had created weapons of warfare so devastating that they could summon the anger of the fiery depths far below the surface of the earth, as well as the power of the sun itself. This they inflicted upon Hiva and its entire continent was destroyed, sinking it under the sea in a storm of earthquakes, rivers of fire and giant waves below a sky of black clouds that could be seen from the western colonies of Atlantis. What remained of Hiva was a great many small islands stretching across a now vast ocean. The people of Hiva fled in haste to the lands that divide the new ocean from the Atlantic, as well as the subcontinent of Java to the west and to other large islands in the deep unexplored south-west.

Tim stopped reading.

"Wow..." he breathed, goosebumps prickling his skin. *"That'll rattle more than just the Egyptologists."*

Other large islands in the deep unexplored southwest?

The words struck close to home—he wasn't prepared for that.

"Goodness," he muttered aloud, eyes widening. "This gets crazier by the sentence."

The gravity of the revelation settled over him like a weighted blanket. So many theories—some deemed myth, others pseudo-history—were both confirmed or shattered in a single breath.

But this went deeper. Here, buried in ancient text, lay the first real clues to the existence of Atlantis's famed, enigmatic technology—not metaphor, not allegory—evidence.

Tim had always suspected the obsession around Atlantis wasn't about geography or grandeur—but tech. That was the lure. That was the legacy. And clearly, that's what the fuss had always been about.

He sat forward, the edges of his world tightening around the glow of his screen. And he continued reading...

The destruction of Hiva took a grievous toll on the navy of Atlantis. Time and distance compounded the loss, and the empire's fleet—once swift and indomitable— grew weary and diminished. Its efforts to suppress the uprising in the far east faltered. Athens and her allies, resolute in defence, prevailed against the invading Atlantean force. The triremes, once thought invincible, limped home—fewer in number, stripped of glory. Pride and arrogance had undone the empire's dominion across the Okeanos and the Mediterranean. Yet beyond its military might, Atlantis had been a cradle of astonishing invention. Its sages had unlocked deep truths in science and physics, mastering the fusion of light, energy, minerals, and gases. Foremost among these marvels were two: the relocation of matter—including living cells—and the transmission of electrical energy through the atmosphere. This latter breakthrough was made possible by the Carsakarisks—great pyramidal structures whose geometric precision and mineral composition enabled energy to move across vast distances.

And there it was. For the first time, the cat was truly out of the sack— irrefutable evidence that the ancient world had harnessed electricity. Wireless. Sophisticated. Real.

Tim sat back—his world suspended. Not surprise. Not shock. Merely the hush that follows revelation too vast for reason.

This was it. The core of the fuss. The spark behind every heated argument about the pyramids. And now he saw it plainly: this was exactly why Hamet Albarad wanted the Richat project shut down.

Albarad at least knew what the pyramids were used for. And he knew Nathan and Crouton were fast approaching the proof.

But what struck Tim most wasn't just the evidence—it was the way years of theorizing, speculation, and every day hypothesizing couldn't touch the force of raw revelation. This had passed beyond myth, and fiction. It was fact. Illuminated and undeniable.

Tim stared at the schematic.

Symbols pulsed softly with embedded light—etched like secrets into the screen. What shocked him wasn't only the technology itself—it was its timeline. Light, energy, minerals, gases... this was the lexicon of 21st-century innovation.

But the source? Twelve thousand years too early.

The ground beneath his understanding trembled. Either the dates were wrong—or the truth had waited, buried, for millennia. What he'd called civilization was only the surface.

Then came the kicker: matter relocation.

The concept bordered on science fiction. Something more advanced than quantum physics. Something whispered in theory papers, but here—on screen—it looked real.

Tim blinked hard.

"Is Atlantis's story what happens when humanity gets carried away with technology?" he wondered.

He'd long marvelled at society's ability to race forward in technological brilliance, yet lag behind in well-being, stability, and wisdom. The bottom line remained: if the Lordship of the land was foolish, no amount of progress could save it. Atlantis had proved that.

He shook his head, goosebumps bristling across his arms.

And read on.

Across the empire stood the great Carsakarisks and obelisks—one to generate, the other to receive. Energy moved through the atmosphere, drawn from afar and distributed with precision. This science, perfected in the eastern colony of Egypt, flourished where the minerals were pure and the conditions most favourable. But it was north of Alastragah, along Atlantis's northern coast, where neglect and depletion kindled disaster—as oil to flame. There, a Carsakarisk failed. Its destruction was swift and violent, echoing the ruin dealt to Hiva. That day, Atlantis tasted its own wrath. The earth tore open. The seabed split. Terrible quakes rippled across the main island and deep into the continent of Libya, reaching as far as the southern inland sea. The Mediterranean surged across the empire in one direction, the Atlantic in another—until land and sea alike were rearranged beyond recognition.

"Crazy... that's incredible," Tim whispered, the truth settling with quiet gradual force. Carsakarisks. A mystery no longer. The pyramids were being named outright, their purpose no longer veiled in debate or myth.

He recalled the investigation beyond the Adrars, north of the Richat. There, a theory—once dismissed as fringe—spoke of a functioning pyramid whose violent failure had scarred northwest Africa.

Now, Solon's account didn't just echo that claim. It confirmed it. The pyramids had been colossal energy generators. And Solon's words weren't symbolic. They were precise. Intentional. A record of what had been—and what had gone terribly wrong.

And then, that curious phrase: *"southern inland sea."*

Tim's eyes narrowed. It likely referred to ancient Lake Chad—once vast, shimmering across thousands of kilometres. Far larger than the modest basin known today.

The implications hit like a surge. Solon wasn't referencing architecture—he was charting the fault lines of a lost technology, a disaster encoded in the earth itself.

Tim saw it now: the pattern, the pulse. Cataclysm braided through aquifers, granite, and algorithms.

The use and function of the Carsakarisks and the obelisks of Egypt ceased abruptly, spared only by the swiftness of their shutdown before a terrible chain reaction could reach them. Yet the far north was not so fortunate. There, a similar fate unfolded—violent and unrelenting—and with the ruin of Atlantis, all lands west of Athens were swallowed by fire, quake, and the surging waves of the Atlantic. So vast was the magnitude of this disaster that the very atmosphere was altered, the elements themselves rearranged. The world became a barren waste of ice. The Libyan mainland, now enlarged, pressed outward. Atlantis, no longer an island, had become an impassable barrier of mud stretching far beyond the coastline where once its harbours stood. Its mountains were stripped and diminished, and the concentric rings of the old city—once vibrant with water and life—lay dry and hollow, the last remnants of a vanished world.

Tim sat back, impressed and blown away. He muttered to himself, "pretty much sounds like confirmation that their little tech malfunction was what ushered in the ice age... I understand why the king of Athens didn't want to leave anything to chance."

Not one single soul, save for those protected by Alastragah, survived the destruction that came upon the empire of Atlantis. They within Alastragah emerged to find the world frozen in an age of ice that lasted a great many years before subsiding.

"There we go!" Tim had his confirmation.

Though Athens and Egypt escaped the ice, they did not escape the cold. A perpetual winter settled over all lands not frozen outright, and every people endured a hardship so severe it stunted the growth of society for centuries to come. The notion of transmitting electrical energy through the atmosphere—once a marvel—became a warning. For as long as memory endured, each generation was taught to shun it. It was spoken of not with awe, but with sorrow, for it had brought ruin upon the world through the recklessness of its wielders.

Tim reached the fourth and last entry of the hidden content of Solon's journals...

Finally, my friend confided in me the utmost secrets requiring thorough and precise record and concealment, according to time frames which should match the ages to come, fittingly. The man in red explained to me that he was a descendant of one of the Posidean Guard who had each one, taken oaths to protect the heart of Atlantis and uphold its values and purpose. Their number began as two hundred and eighty, along with their families, a total number of eight hundred exactly, and it was they who had survived the cataclysmic days of destruction by fire, waves and ice. The remnant of Atlantis, prior to, and following the demise of their great city, completed the process of concealing everything dear to them, in the halls of Alastragah. All things from their origin story and history, to their discoveries, knowledge and technology, in order that one day, many years from then when the age does suffice, the city of Atlantis may be rebuilt. And the land from whence it exists restored to abundance.

He went on to explain that the remnant of Atlantis departed Alastragah, sealing up the most revered halls that had been purposed for the distant future. Proceeding, they did spread out across the world to begin new lives in different lands. They continued the lineage of Poseidon who would one day gather together again his children, and in accordance with the will of The Creator, uncover the halls of Alastragah then rebuild the ancient city. It was at this time a great brotherhood was born. They, cloaked under the guise of the priesthood of Osiris in Egypt, in the temple of Sais on the Nile delta, held the knowledge of Atlantis. Osiris had himself left his descendants to their own devices in much the same manner as Poseidon had done so with Atlantis, and for similar reasons. Their primary purpose, to house the knowledge of Atlantis, for a time, before it too, would be concealed by water. Such information to be passed on to the wise who would write it down, limited to the location, dimensions and details of the city and its culture, omitting Alastragah and that which pertains to it.

My friend had seen fit to travel to Athens to bestow upon me, the complete account of Atlantis and the world that once was, before the cataclysm of the age whence it existed.

He left with me two final pieces of key knowledge to be hidden accordingly, their meaning known only to they who would one day realize and perceive it—the apocalyptic writings of the first Emperor—Atlas, the prophet king. To those who are ready to discover the Halls of Alastragah, at the appropriate time, read carefully and see revealed, the path to Alastragah.

Tim stared at the screen of his laptop, then out to sea, for what felt like hours—though only minutes had passed—suspended in a sliver of time-lessness. He looked up into the night, seeing nothing of his surroundings for a moment longer. His mind reeled—not just from facts, but from a feeling he couldn't name.

What had he just read? Surely others knew some of this—Alesandro was Solon's descendant. Nathan and Crouton ran the Richat Project. They had to suspect something.

Tim's thoughts collided—questions, impressions, half-formed concerns. Uncertainty nagged him—fear of the unknown begged residence within. Thankfully, instinct kicked in. He yawned, stretched, and shut his laptop. He leaned back, mentally compartmentalizing everything to avoid confusion and dread.

He thought of Charlotte—his fiancée, his anchor. That thought alone slowed the chaos. In a few months, they'd be married. That calmed him. He thanked God quietly for her—for the love, for the grounding.

The Solon diaries could wait. Wisdom said: shelve it for now.

~~~~~~~

It was just past midnight. Parties had drifted closer to the beach establishments. Most bars remained open, though noise was strictly confined to the beach precinct.

Tim walked through the atrium, his thoughts clashing against reality like surf against stone. The far-fetched had begun peeling back to reveal something disturbingly real.

He passed tropical gardens and near-empty pools on a conflicted path of aimlessness. He needed a beer—two, actually.

The Tamarind's bar was still open. Tim ordered a handle of Kingfisher Premium and surprised himself by sculling it before the bartender had even turned away.

A Japanese couple were nearby, immersed in honeymoon romance. Another guest stood at a stool table, face lit by his phone.

"You alright, man?" the bartender asked, his tone gentle but concerned.

Tim took a breath, checked himself. "Yeah... that one was to wash out all the crazy," he smiled. "Same again. In a can this time."

As the bartender passed it over, Tim nodded gratefully. "This one's to process what's left."

"Take it easy, eh?" the bartender replied with a smile.

"Yeah. Bit of food, a walk, I'll be good." Tim was relaxed and distracted—but aware enough to know he needed to regroup.

He ordered Lamb Korma takeaway. "Good choice for a friend of Nathan O'Conner," the bartender beamed.

Tim thanked him, took the brown paper bag and headed toward the beach.

He sat on a rock at a quiet curve of shore, waves washing ancient sands with their repetitive chant. The sea whispered like a timeless echo. Stars shared the sky with moonlit haze. The crowd's subtle hum reminded Tim of a familiar world behind him, as he leaned into the unfamiliar wonder unfolding ahead.

As he ate, his thoughts slowed. The highway of his mind shifted onto a quieter path.

He remembered a conversation with a university friend—a staunch atheist Tim deeply respected. They'd landed on common ground: understanding shapes perception, and friendship matters more than winning arguments.

One day, that friend had asked, "Tim, what if you faced absolute, undeniable proof there was no God? That your entire belief system was just an old, elaborate fabrication—how would you deal with that?"

Tim had answered quickly.

"Well... I'd be blown away by the scale of such a performance," he admitted. "But beyond truth or fabrications, if what I believed gave me meaning, purpose, belonging—and more than anything, brought love and peace, no philosophy could fabricate nor deny—I'd still hold onto it."

His friend was stunned. Tim explained that concepts like truth and evidence would lose relevance. What mattered was the fruit—wholeness, peace, love, authentic community.

After some rumination, his friend had laughed. "Funny. My dad warned me never to associate with 'people like you.' Said if God doesn't exist, don't waste breath discussing Him. That it only leads to brainwashing. Back then I didn't get it. But now... it's like my brain just got washed. And it feels amazing."

Days later, Tim reflected: the answer didn't feel like it came solely from him—he never had to think about it... it felt partially divine. Faith wasn't built on arguments—it was carved from lived experience. A sound testimony of the Living Presence of the Divine, of Love, friendship, and peace rooted in something greater carried more weight than any debate.

He sipped his beer, gazing toward the horizon.

"This is how I'll navigate this upheaval," he thought. The Solon diaries had thrown not just the book—but the whole bookshelf—at both conventional thinking and conspiracy theory debates. Confirmations were colliding with ancient suspicions.

It was heavy... yet liberating. Scary and yet exhilarating!

Tim understood excitement about the discovery of Atlantis. But he couldn't help wondering: *"Has anyone realized the gravity of it?"*

He knew what such truths could do. People resist change, especially when it threatens core beliefs, pride and wallets. History was full of religious and political upheaval triggered by things like this. And now, in his hands, lay something equally volatile.

In the Sahara's unstable political climate, these discoveries could even provoke war. But deep down, Tim felt it wouldn't go that far.

He lamented the paradox. Real discoveries were met with scepticism, often buried under buzzwords like 'conspiracy theory.' Meanwhile, sound history was replaced with hollow trends.

No. He wouldn't spiral tonight.

Still... hiding it all? Pretending this was just a dream? It was tempting, but Tim had too many questions—too many mysteries now challenging normality with no regard for the ordinary.

He'd combed through every thread of knowledge. The fog had lifted. No confusion remained—just the still, eerie hush before the impact of revelation.

For now, Tim alone carried the finer details of the Solon diaries—except the seventh, still unread. He hoped the final entry would pivot gently. But as he sat beneath the stars, he knew: the future had grown irrelevant. What mattered were the constants: faith, Charlotte, friendship, peace. Those anchors were untouched by even Atlantis.

A sound broke his reverie.

Nathan approached along the rocky path, carrying a small canvas bag.

"Nathan," Tim greeted.

"Evening," the older man replied, taking a seat nearby.

"How's it going?"

"Good, mate. Everyone else has turned in. Alessandro's staying with us in the penthouse."

Tim nodded, unsurprised.

They sat peacefully. Behind them, music echoed faintly. But here—just ocean silence and starlight.

"Kingfisher," Nathan observed.

"Had it for the first time at a nice Indian restaurant in Hamilton. Charlotte and I had just started dating," Tim recalled fondly.

Nathan smiled and pulled out two large Blue Nectargys from the canvas bag. "You're a bad influence on me," he said, handing one to Tim.

"You're the one who keeps supplying it," Tim laughed. "I hadn't touched one in months until you showed up."

Nathan grinned. "How'd the sixth journal go?"

Tim blinked, exhaled.

"Good... I think. It's exhilarating—like reading Revelation. I sense where it's going. But I've still got the seventh to face. That's why I'm out here—getting some fresh air, food, and reflecting."

He paused. "It was less reading, more mental disassembly. Brutal, brilliant, and peculiar."

Nathan nodded.

Tim knew Nathan was holding something back. Or biding time.

"The content clarified so much. But it's heavy. Raises some big questions."

Nathan responded silently.

Tim continued. "Solon learned of two factions: the Posidean Guard—remnants of Atlantis who preserved knowledge in Alastragah in the northern Richat. He referred to 'land of the Atlantes—and the Exolothreftis of Athens."

Nathan's eyes sharpened. He gazed out to sea.

"Ahh... the Atlantes. So we should be exploring in the Adrar highlands. Specifically in the mountains sheltering the north of the Richat?"

"Exactly," Tim said, curiosity building. But unease flickered deep inside.

"And then—Solon had a secret visitor. From Phoenelakai."

Nathan showed quiet excitement. "Descendants of the Atlanteans. Where does he feature in things?"

Tim explained that after Solon's return to Athens, his life came under threat. Someone had been following him—possibly agents of the Exolothreftis, a secret order sworn to erase Atlantis from memory. It was after this that the man in red came to visit, having heard of Solon's pilgrimage and investigations.

"Very interesting," Nathan spoke softly.

"Yes," Tim nodded. "The King of Athens had commissioned the Exolothreftis after Atlantis's fall."

"Tell me more about the man from Phoenelakai."

Tim recounted everything—the ornate red clothing, the blade, the details shared. He deliberately avoided drawing links to Red Sword, opting to preserve mental bandwidth.

When he finished, Nathan sat in thoughtful silence.

"That's quite the story," he said at last.

Tim felt unease at first—but was reassured as Nathan continued.

"Phoenelakai was very real. And this meeting confirms a great many things." He paused. "This is brilliant, Tim. Well done."

"Cheers," Tim replied, expecting more but staying open.

"It was a lot to take in, wasn't it?"

"Profoundly stranger than I expected," Tim said. "You think you're ready—after all the speculation, the breadcrumbs and suspicions. But when the stark reality of it hits you—really hits you—it knocks everything loose."

Nathan nodded.

Tim went on. "I thought I'd be ready. But confirmation is different... it's both exciting and deeply unnerving."

After a moment, Nathan spoke softly. "It's rarely the truth itself that causes disruption—it's what truth replaces. What it displaces. That's what sends people scrambling to reassemble meaning in the aftermath.

We're not rewriting history. We're rediscovering it. What happened... happened. No legend or erasure can change reality. Reality is what it is and is not subject to human preference.

The trouble lies in how deeply myth has cemented itself into society's thinking. Atlantis as 'just a legend'—it's more than a label, Tim. It's a defence mechanism. A boundary. When new truth knocks on that wall, most minds instinctively push back. It's not always disbelief. Sometimes it's just defence, even if subconscious."

He paused, then added, "What you've experienced... it's like hearing about someone your whole life, then finally meeting them. The reality rarely matches the picture built from fragments. It can shake you—in wonder, or confusion, or awe."

Tim blinked, then muttered dryly, "I get it. Though it feels more like waking up with your ears tied to the backside of a galloping horse... charging through a swamp and jumping into an ice-cold pool."

Nathan burst into laughter.

Tim continued with quiet reverence, "You can talk about God, hear Him preached, discuss faith endlessly. But none of that compares to the real thing—an actual encounter with Him—His presence. That changes everything."

"There's a difference," Nathan reflected softly. "Between hearing something—and living it. Between thinking you know, and actually knowing. Hearing isn't the same as experiencing. Just like theory isn't the same as truth."

Tim nodded. "Exactly. And that's what it felt like. I guess I just didn't expect such a collision between speculation and conclusive truth."

"It does mess with the head for a while," Nathan agreed. "But you seem to be handling it."

"Took some time. Still taking some time."

"How?"

Tim recounted the discussion he'd had with his university friend—the philosophical curveball, the question about faith in a world without God. He explained the answer he gave, and the peace that followed.

Nathan listened intently, then smiled.

"Tim, that's some profound wisdom. Hold onto it. Live by it, speak from it, share it. That kind of grounding will carry you through whatever comes. It's why I think you were meant to be the first to read Solon's hidden diaries.

My concern's never been the content—it's been whether the minds receiving it could bear the truth. Most aren't ready. You are."

"Some barely cope with what's inside the box," Tim said.

Nathan chuckled. "Exactly. But maybe our journey—yours and mine, and this whole team—have prepared the ground. However long it takes."

They sat quietly.

Nathan finally asked, "Do you have any questions for me, Tim?"

They both smiled—Tim's thoughtful, Nathan's knowing.

"Some very big ones," Tim said. "But not tonight. It's nearly 2 a.m. I'm keen for sleep more than answers right now. We could talk from now to sunrise, then sunset and still not unpack it all... and I'd probably nod off halfway."

They laughed together.

Nathan stood. "Tomorrow then. Take your time. Read the seventh journal when you're ready. We'll decide together how to share it. For now, just enjoy this place. You don't want to leave a place like this too soon."

"Cheers, Nate. All good," Tim nodded.

Nathan smiled, glancing around at the night, the stars, the sea. "And Tim... thanks for the trust. For putting friendship, and this moment, before the need for answers."

Tim raised his nearly empty can in quiet tribute. "We're on the same page about what really matters."

They exchanged a final smile, then Nathan made his way back through the thinning echoes of the Caribbean night-life.

Tim followed not long after.

He stepped into Charlotte's room, slipped beside her quietly. She stirred, pulling back the blanket and tugging him close.

He snuggled into her warmth.

"Love you," she whispered sleepily.

Tim kissed her on the head. "Love you too."

CHAPTER 18

- -

N athan awoke with the sense that someone had gently nudged him—summoning him to something important. That's how his first thoughts of the day unfolded.

He sat up and checked his phone... eight thirty.

"Chaiyala..." Nathan muttered, her name weighing on his mind. He hadn't checked in with her lately, and the thought lingered with increasing urgency.

When he surfaced, he found Chad and Rhys in the kitchen, fixing breakfast. After exchanging greetings, he asked, "Do you know if Chaiyala is up yet?"

Rhys shrugged and shook his head.

"She left early," Chad replied. "Seemed distracted—said she needed some space and fresh air. She mentioned she'd be down at the beach if you needed her."

"Good, thank you."

Suspicions confirmed, Nathan made his way down through the Atrium, wove through the pools precinct, and toward the Shrimp and Marlin. He spotted Chaiyala seated at a wooden table on the rustic deck of the seaside café, her back to the resort, gazing out at the horizon.

He entered through the double doors and approached the bar, warmly greeting the young woman behind it. He placed an order of Mackerel

Rundown, with green bananas and roasted breadfruit—for two. He asked for it to be served outside, where Chaiyala sat.

Nathan found her leaning comfortably in a chair at a rustic wooden table on the deck, arms folded. She wore a hot pink hooded singlet and white denim shorts—frayed at the edges like they'd lived through a dozen summers. She liked the contrast: bold and bright, like she was daring the day to try her. Crouton never understood the appeal of stressed denim—paying more for less fabric seemed like a scam—but he'd long since accepted that fashion wasn't designed with his logic in mind.

A jug of tropical iced tea sat on the table between two tall glasses, one full.

"Boker Tov..." she greeted, flashing a quick smile before her eyes returned to the sea, serious once more.

"Boker Or," Nathan replied.

"Well, that's good," she said bluntly as he took the seat across from her, his back to the wall. "You've got a lot to explain. And after that—I've got a request." Her expression had that unnerving focus—the kind only Rick could tolerate without flinching, thanks to his strange humour or unique carelessness.

"Oh really? Story of my life," Nathan sighed. "I've honestly lost track of what I'm supposed to have explained but haven't, at least not adequately."

He raised his eyebrows matter-of-factly, unphased by her strong-willed tone.

"Gets that way, after a while... after you've been around as long as I have," he added under his breath—eyes drifting seaward.

Chaiyala frowned. Nathan's offhanded remarks often lingered in her mind—half-thoughts that made one wonder where, or when, he was referring to. This one made him sound older than he appeared... which made her wonder.

"I ordered Mackerel Rundown," he said.

"Yum!" Her mood lifted instantly. "Well, that's a start. But still—you explain to me why my cousin had to be the one to say you're taking over the world?"

Nathan's gaze remained steady, though his tone held the weight of a man untangling expectations not entirely his own.

"Just the North Atlantic," he replied. "Only the countries that existed in territories once part of the greater Atlantean empire before the fall." His voice was firm but weary—threaded with restrained resolve. "It's fascinating how my intentions are described, given they were never mine to begin with."

Chaiyala frowned again, her mind searching for something just out of reach.

Nathan exhaled, watching her carefully.

"Nothing is hidden, Chaiyala," he said. "Just like the rebuilding of Atlantis—it's no secret. Our deal with Mauritania still stands. We're restoring the land: the soil, the farms, the ecosystems. That hasn't changed."

She listened, brow furrowed.

"The United Countries of Atlantis, as people have started calling it," he said with a shrug. "I have to admit, I wasn't expecting this idea to snowball the way it has. And for the record—it's not happening overnight. First things first."

She studied him more closely, noting the tension in his jaw, the subtle downturn of his brow.

"Discovering Atlantis is overwhelming enough," he said, tapping the table before stopping mid-motion. "Turning it into a multi-state operation like people imagine? That takes years. Compared to that, the Richat Project is easy. And then there's the politics, the legal structure, the social impact. It goes from unbelievable to something that needs divine coordination."

The silence settled—not uncomfortable, but charged. Seagulls cawed faintly above the shore, as if eavesdropping. For a moment, Nathan's thoughts drifted—not to politics or restoration, but to simpler memories of sunburnt days and salt-stained maps. He glanced at Chaiyala, wondering if she sensed the paradox too—destiny and choice intertwined.

"Not the reply you were expecting."

"No," she admitted, curiosity peeking through. "Knowing you? I should've known better."

Nathan chuckled as their food arrived. Chaiyala poured him a glass of iced tea.

As they ate, Nathan explained his position. The surge of requests for inclusion in the United Countries of Atlantis had expanded far beyond his original vision.

"It was only supposed to be about restoring unusable lands—those impacted by desiccation and drought."

"Was the G.A.B. Project—Geo, Agri, Bio. Geological, Agricultural, Biological. That's what it's called?"

"Yes. It's remarkable how quickly things progress," he said calmly, nudging her thoughts forward. "The vision has expanded beyond expectation. Nations once thought disconnected are now reconsidering their place."

Her earlier certainty blurred. The rebirth, the restoration—it all slipped into the background. Instead, she found herself grounded in the present, in Nathan's presence, and in the enormity of what was unfolding.

He waited, letting the moment settle. For now, she would assume only Sahara nations were involved.

"What began as a focused mission has quietly expanded. Now, there's growing expectation that Atlantis will take charge of the whole region. It's snowballed into talk of recreating the empire as it once stretched—from

North Africa across the Mediterranean... even from Venezuela to Britain. Go figure."

"Britain?" She shot him a sideways glance.

"You would not believe the conversations I've had with the Queen and Prime Minister Allech Newton."

"You don't *really* sound so captivated—or convinced—by the idea," she noted, sensing a hint of hesitance.

"Oh no, don't get me wrong!" Nathan raised his hand slightly. "It's a fantastic idea—always destined to happen. I just had no idea how soon... or how it would look."

Chaiyala was surprised by his honesty—and the strange expression on her face showed it. Nathan ignored it for now.

"... And I'd sort of hoped it wouldn't be me who initiated the whole thing. But then there are the prophecies, of course."

Chaiyala stared at Nathan, hoping he would go on and bring some explanation, as opposed to a rabbit hole stuffed with more questions.

"That's the trouble with prophecies. Or more accurately—the twenty-first-century approach to them. It's a little imbalanced. Impatient. Like a toddler who knows she'll get to go outside when the rain stops—but throws a fit anyway because 'later' isn't 'right now.'"

He shook his head slightly.

"There are very, very ancient prophecies wanting to be fulfilled—and apparently, they want me to do the work."

"No way!" she said sarcastically, a small smile forming.

"I know!" He chuckled. "Do I look like God?"

"Well..."

Nathan sighed, rolling his eyes.

"Many times, you've come across like a miracle worker. Especially that one time—you were in more than one place!" she teased.

"Great, so maybe I'm my own worst enemy..."

He paused, his tone deepening.

"Contrary to popular belief, prophecy isn't always destined for fulfilment. Hollywood—and what I call the 'Church of the OTT,' where spiritual gifts go theatrical—have blurred mysticism with melodrama, pushing this illusion of fixed fate in a world governed by free will. Ironic, really.

Prophecy offers a path—not a guarantee. It's an invitation to align with something favourable. Just as easily, it can signal misfortune if one refuses to correct their course.

Some prophecies are sovereign and unchanging. Others are more like signposts than scripts. It's less about predetermined fate, and more about navigating possibilities that lead to fulfilment."

He paused meaningfully.

"Now that we've clarified that..."

She listened on.

"I'll tell you that sixty-one countries and states have approached me—in secrecy, under high security. Somewhere buried deep in the ancient history of their peoples, lie prophecies. Each one tied to the remaking of a great ringed city, once central to a long-fallen empire. Each seem to depict a time when society is far from ideal, needing revitalisation and the people are hungry for change. They all seem to include a figure—an administrator restoring the city and empire, making it a great and glorious improvement on the fallen version, with untold benefits, peace, and prosperity."

"Of course they do..." Chaiyala replied, not intending to sound dismissive.

"Yes indeed—peace and prosperity. Concepts that world leaders wander between, unsure whether to surrender to their impossibility or cling to them as distant hopes. The theme is simultaneously too good to be true, and the hope they hold onto regardless."

Chaiyala sighed in agreement. "The latter prevailed, so it would seem."

"—While doing as much as possible to ensure such a thing would never happen."

"Sure—world politics and irony, always together, no?" she quipped.

"And now, yours truly has to come up with something to deliver... on top of everything else we're juggling right now."

"Another miracle? I'm sure you've got it tucked up your sleeve," she smiled cheekily.

"Cheers." He sipped his iced tea. "It's not as if I don't enjoy the challenge, though."

Nathan straightened up, his tone and posture erasing any suggestion of *really* being caught off guard.

Chaiyala knew it was true. His ability to juggle countless roles—where others required teams just to tread water—never ceased to amaze her. Or anyone for that matter. He thrived under pressure: the Richat Project, major Red Sword initiatives, diplomatic and high-level advisory responsibilities... and yet, he remained fully present to those around him.

She admired the way he empowered others to share in his vision, freeing himself to focus on what truly mattered.

"So, what the heck, ah?" she said, struggling to fathom it all. "Sixty-one states—hardly knowing the Richat, let alone the Project—and they still picked Nathan? And came knocking on your door?"

"Hmm, pretty much how I think it's supposed to work."

She raised her eyebrows and smiled, shaking her head as she looked to the horizon. "I don't know what's more amazing—them, or how you handle the size of it."

"Hmm, try being me."

'No thanks!' she thought to herself. "Who else knows about it, ah?"

"Well, that's the thing. I haven't really had the chance to gather the full team and have a serious conversation. I've told Charles and Crouton—and now you. Crouton was about as baffled as you are, and once he came to terms with it, he said—" Nathan smirked, mimicking Crouton's gruff cadence—"'Well, tell them to beggar off until we've figured out what's what with the place before we start resurrecting an extinct empire and setting up a new political state, for crying out loud.'"

They both laughed.

"You know Crouton—he shook his head like he'd just woken from a surreal dream, then gathered his wits—transitioning to tactful and logical again. I was hoping to speak with Rod last night," Nathan continued, "but he nodded off early. And then you and Tim—he's almost finished reading the Solon diaries..."

"Wow. How he's going with that, *ah*?"

"Good. It's unsettled him a bit—mentally demanding, intense, and requires careful handling. But he's the right person for the job. I found him at the beach last night—sitting on a rock, taking it all in. No point overwhelming him further."

"You're sure he's okay?"

"Oh, he's certainly fine. His perspective and his faith afford him a bold yet healthy approach. I'm grateful for that."

"It is good," she said, relieved. Then queried, "And those calls—the ones from countries wanting to join—when did they start?"

Nathan thought for a moment, then replied, "I received the first a month before Chad and Charlotte arrived. Since then, I've been bombarded. I knew of Atlas's prophecies—but not the others. I assume they were embedded in forgotten folklore tied to these regions. The prophecies and the requests were half the reason I returned to the Richat Project in the first place—the other half being the Solon diaries and the meeting with Alesandro."

"My goodness... *zeh* is incredible. My head was already swimming after Mordechai explained the whole Hebrew-Atlantean connection."

Nathan's eyes lit up—bright, too bright—but Chaiyala didn't notice.

"Now *that's* a tale I'm more familiar with," he beamed.

"Oh?"

"Cousin Eber—he was on the Ark. According to Atlantean tradition, he rode the storm, cradled in covenant, carried in the hush between thunder and promise—Father to the Hebrews, the Middle East, and half the rest of the world."

"You know the connections then, yes? Between Eber and Poseidon on Noah's Ark... and Moses, Joseph—in Egypt, with Sais?"

"All of the above," Nathan nodded.

Chaiyala smiled excitedly, then looked out to sea once more. For now, she'd ignore the question— "how?"

She turned back to Nathan, her expression now formal—diplomatic.

She began revisiting Israel's political situation—its current alliances, and the limitations they faced.

"Mordechai—my cousin—he's with the Israeli Secret Service," she said, her voice steady but quick. "He reports straight to President Asaharif. And because of Eber's connection to Poseidon... Asaharif, he has asked—officially—for Israel to join the United Countries of Atlantis."

"Absolutely!" Nathan responded. "Far be it from me to begrudge the descendants of Eber a seat at the table of his cousin's descendants."

She smiled—relieved, excited, grateful.

"I'll call President Asaharif now to confirm," he said. The formal talks would come later.

Nathan activated Red Sword protocols—secure codes, layered encryption.

By the end of the call, Yosef Asaharif was ecstatic. The typically discrete and demure Israeli prime minister set down his handset, then leapt out of his chair with such force that it flew backward into the wall. He raised his fists skyward and shouted זְמ וּנתוא םתררחש! וְּוס פּו, ההא! הדות! ה! וּנלש םילבכה ("Thank you! Thank you! Ahhh, at long last! You have delivered us from our shackles!")

~~~~~~~

Tim awoke in the same position he'd fallen asleep, Charlotte nestled against him, her head rising and falling with each breath on his chest.

He checked his phone—almost ten. Wide awake now, and eager to dive into the seventh Solon diary, he carefully slid out from beneath her, letting her settle back into the bed's warm stillness.

He kissed her gently on the cheek. She gave a sleepy smile without opening her eyes.

He'd take a quick shower, then journal—no distractions.

A warm, soft tropical breeze wafted through the large open-plan living area of the penthouse apartment as Tim entered the kitchen and grabbed a tall glass of ice-cold juice to sip while reading.

He set his laptop down on the wide dining table and glanced toward the balcony, where Chad, Chaiyala, and Rhys were sprawled comfortably in morning ease.

"Good morning," he greeted.

"Oh, morning bro!" Chad sat up, peering at his brother over his sunnies.

"Heya," Chaiyala echoed, glancing at him briefly over the edge of her magazine.

Rhys, fast asleep, offered nothing in reply.

Tim settled in, opening the decrypted translation of the seventh Solon diary.

There were two entries in this journal. He proceeded with the first...

This is the account of Solon, Sage of Athens, of the oral tradition of Atlas, entrusted to me by the one who wears the scarlet robes and holds the scarlet blade. May these words be understood by the wise and hidden from the undiscerning. Understood by those who are pure of heart and dismissed as folly by those whose time or purpose does not voyage in unison with the architect.

Upon the waves of the mighty western ocean, Haskalaran glides as one with Serenea and Talakanis, the three of them favoured of Poseidon and most magnificent of their kind. Haskalaran leads the way as the western ocean is mapped out according to its length and width and the far distant coastlines of the continent in the west are explored. The days ahead for these lands are determined by Poseidon and his kin as he guides Haskalaran and her number from shore to shore, across the waters and around new lands. Great and glorious were the days she sailed across the expanse beyond the horizon where the world curves toward the future. Great will be the days again and most incredible will be the age in which she is set free to find the ocean once more. As she provides the children of Poseidon access to the place of peace and preservation whence ten thousand years and two thousand more of sleep, the knowledge and treasury of her people will exact a harvest of renewal.

Yet not before all the age of chaos and corruption. Not before the levelling out of the gardens of Poseidon and the planting of new seeds under the waters and the shaking of great rearrangement. Not before the long sleep, O great Haskalaran and your sisters Serenea and Talakanis, three greatest among the remnant of Atlantis sent to be destroyed—a sacrifice to appease the false gods of war and arrogance, pride and dissension. Two remain among the few to return to Atlantis before the end. They, in divine orchestration retire to their chambers before the shaking of the world; before the storm and the days are frozen in time, ten thousand years and two thousand more will pass before their tale is told. They have enjoyed the days of old; the days of peace and prosperity, the days of exploration where their people advanced across the expanse of ocean and terrain. They carried three thousand loyal to the scarlet blade, the rare metal that summoned the power of Poseidon in battle, his compassion and that of his Creator in the time of need and the abundance of heaven whenever petitioned. They carried three thousand on that ruinous endeavour to smite the eastern alliance to no avail. They did not join in the destruction of Hiva and suffered not, the fireball of heaven along the straits dividing the southern and western continents. They instead, anchored themselves in rebellion against the proud and the arrogant and marched in unison along the second ring in formidable defiance upon their glorious return.

They have and will endure much. Flanked by Serenea and Talakanis, Haskalaran waits along the grandest of voyages ten thousand years and two thousand more. When at last her heart will be unveiled and the keys to peace and preservation will be offered up to those still loyal to the scarlet blade and their place of residence revealed. Such keys dwell within her heart and shall not be bled until the proper time. Such keys, concealed by that which is easily dismissed, that which does not fit inside nor outside of their time or relevance at all. The seat of every tenth vessel holding a piece of the key, etched and crafted below and seen only in the first few seconds of the blazing light of a new day dawning, otherwise veiled from vision for another day and night.

Sleep, O beautiful and mighty Haskalaran, Queen of the sea. Await those who long to find you and bring about your renewal, that of your sisters and your people.

Tim was pleased with what he'd just read—pleasantly surprised, even.

"What a beautiful piece of ancient literature," he thought, nodding with modest excitement and a subtle grin.

This journal, unlike any of the others, had never been read by anyone since Solon himself.

The others—written in plain ancient Greek—had been skimmed and lightly studied by his team back in Mauritania, alongside their network of associated archaeologists.

This was something new. For the first time, authentic apocalyptic texts from a Helene philosopher were being read—works likely dating back to the same era as the Prophet Daniel's exile in Babylon.

With its symbols, cosmic metaphors, and divine codes, apocalyptic writing was never meant for the masses. It was written for those who could feel its pulse, while keeping its truths concealed from the uninitiated.

"So—" Tim pondered, *"This speaks of ships, would be my first guess... telling the story, past and future of three, one in particular, named Haskalaran... of which there is the greatest significance. Hmm..."* He inserted digital notes beside the details he understood and highlighted the ones that needed further revelation.

Tim was about to read the second entry when he recalled an update from Rod via Charles—three successful excavations near the Richat's ring hills, once the empire's military hub. He made a mental note to ask about it later.

He returned to the second and final entry of the seventh journal.

Following my meeting with the man who wore the scarlet robes and holds the scarlet blade, I had a dream that same night. I saw the way ahead was blocked by an obstacle created by the destruction of Atlantis, then it was blasted out of the way and I saw before me, the words "Proceed with feet of righteousness according to the sum total of your years." I stood upon a glass ocean of deep cobalt. The sky was of a lighter aqua blue and moving like water, and the sun was as if it could be viewed from beneath the waves, and I was walking within them.

Then I saw the gardener rise up from the waters below as well as descending from those above. He placed into a sifting pan, rock and dirt, plant and soil and all things grown according to the natural order and crafted by human hands. Life and death were separated as far as the east and west are divided by the storms and the shaking of the world. He moved water and stone, thought and desire with fire; then violence reacted causing all that is irrelevant to be washed away and covered in the mud of the distant past. This was the sifting of what is relevant from what is not—the sorting of wheat from chaff.

I saw his face, and it was fashioned of gold, his shoulders bore the burden of chaos and corruption, and they, as were his arms and hands, were composed of clay and metal. His chest was made of ice and the rest of him was an incredible combination of lush jungle, great lakes and dessert sands. He walked here and there, across the expanse of ocean and terrain, watching the world move from one season to the next. All the while, he held in his hand, hidden from view, a perfectly preserved portion of his masterpiece, the garden he'd fashioned long ago before the rearranging of the world.

Next, I saw him stand before an elaborate and beautiful mosaic of sculptures and structures that utilize light and time in order to reveal the place of peace and what has been preserved. He looked at the mosaic and I saw its entirety turn to gold. Then he bowed his head in sorrow for a moment and I saw the edges of it connected to a mighty empire and a beautiful city. When he lifted his head, the empire and the city were gone, and the mosaic had been blanketed in thick snow and ice. Yet, itself, had not been destroyed. Following this, I saw him wave his hand across the mosaic, melting the ice, then it was covered in jungle. He passed his other hand over it in the opposite direction and the jungle was replaced by a barren dessert. He waved his hand across it a third time, and it returned to jungle again, yet this time there were also parts of water in addition. He passed his hand across the mosaic once more, and it turned back into sand.

Finally, I saw rising out from within the mosaic, at its centre, a building with seven pillars. Four serving as cornerstones and the carsakarisk placed upon the top half of the structure. The gardener made his way through the sculptures on the mosaic towards the building in the centre, and he vanished inside.

Tim found the second entry to be quite cryptic indeed and figured it reminded him of the biblical book of Revelation even more so than the first entry had.

"Interesting... the gardens of Poseidon would have been located somewhere right in the centre, of the Richat... although that means nothing given the nature of the cataclysm that flung parts of the city hundreds of kilometres across the west of Africa." Tim discussed this in his mind, remembering *"two of the dig sites are near the coast south of Nouakchott—Chinguetti—one's out at sea... hmm—if this is, in fact, referring to the garden of Poseidon, how will we know where it is? ...there's likely to be more in that, that'd reveal where..."*

Tim shelved that one after making a few notes, accordingly.

The seventh and final journal wasn't as controversial as the sixth—less explosive, but just as exciting.

Journal six had been radical, challenging much of accepted ancient history and confirming theories that made people uneasy. It was the reason Red Sword Security kept fending off covert attacks from powerful private groups.

Journal seven, by contrast, was subtle and cryptic—more of a puzzle to solve than a direct challenge to historical narrative.

Tim was miles away in thought, pondering the last two entries of the Solon dairies when two tanned arms slid around his shoulders—firm, familiar, and unmistakably hers—a kiss was placed on his cheek.

"Good morning, my love." Charlotte greeted, embracing him.

"Hey—good morning Angel," Tim smiled, he snapped out of his daydreaming, rubbing his fiancé's arms affectionately.

"Have you had breakfast yet?" she asked Tim.

"Nope."

"Let's go find something yummy then." She suggested, excited and keen to go explore the resorts culinary options some more.

Tim stood, looking out across the sea with much on his mind. Most of him was fascinated and slightly perplexed by the last two journal entries, in a very different way to the previous five, yet the final two seemed to add to the size and puzzle of the overall mystery.

"Are you okay?" Charlotte asked with mild concern.

"Yeah—there's a lot to think about." Tim summarized the Solon diaries for her, capturing her full attention like a gripping novel. He kept it concise, resisting the urge to dwell on his own lingering questions. Charlotte was both impressed and unsettled but grasped most of it.

Once finished, Tim suddenly didn't feel right about something. He looked around; eyes narrowed lightly.

"What's the matter?"

"Where are Nathan and Crouton? Alesandro..." he asked, then looked directly at her.

Chaiyala had felt the same thing, had gotten up and was now standing—oddly, hands on hips, inside the ranch slider showing an ominous expression, she looked almost frightening.

"What is it?" asked Rhys, getting up to see what had disrupted the peace and quiet.

"What—what's going on?" Chad queried as he joined them.

"Where are Nathan, Crouton and Rod?" Chaiyala asked with disconcerting suspicion.

A couple of silent seconds passed as the odd sensation lingered and no one seemed to know a thing.

CHAPTER 19

The doors of the elevator opened—not fast enough. Nathan, Crouton and Rod were in a hurry.

"Where is Alesandro?" Nathan asked directly, almost sternly.

"No idea..." Rhys replied.

"We thought he was with you, no?" Chaiyala said, pulling a towel snug around her hips. Something in Nathan's tone made her stomach tighten.

"What's the deal? Has something happened?" Tim asked the older men.

Rod was swiftly making phone calls to other Red Sword agents on the island while hastily setting up a laptop on the dining table.

"Ahh!" Crouton swore out loud.

"Crouton..." Nathan said calmly as if redirecting an angry child from frustration to composure. In doing so, the two of them regrouped inwardly. Crouton took a deep breath then made his way briskly to where Alesandro had slept the night prior.

Tim, Charlotte and Chaiyala followed him.

"Dammit, Alesandro!" Crouton muttered frustratedly.

"If he left on his own accord, that's on him," Nathan advised, "but if something happened to him—we need to find out. Crouton, until we know more, we hope and pray he knows what he's doing."

"Sorry?" Chaiyala stood, distracted in her search for any clues in his room.

"What is going on here?" Rhys asked, keen for answers.

"Yeah—please explain..." echoed Tim.

Chaiyala, awaiting an explanation, tried to focus on basic detective work required to get any idea of where Alesandro had gone and what he may be up too.

Nathan began, "We assumed Alesandro was still asleep as the three of us woke up separately and went about our morning. Later, as planned, we met at the Caribbean Skillet for brunch—but Alesandro never showed."

"After ten minutes of him not showing, we got concerned." Crouton added.

"Okay," Chaiyala began, searching for what might help make sense of things. "What do we have—CCTV of him leaving? Anyone acting strange at the resort, maybe interacting with Alesandro?"

"Coming through now," Rod called out, hearing their conversation from the dining table where he and Rhys along with Chad stood around and focused on the laptop. Rod clicked on the file containing camera footage for the path which Alesandro would likely have taken from the penthouse suite elevator through to the main car park out the front of the resort.

~~~~~~~

Earlier that morning, about 2.45am...

Alesandro felt his phone vibrating under his pillow. Sleepily he answered.

"Ci aitountes." A female voice on the other end of the line began in Greek.

"Synkentrotheite." Alesandro replied quietly—waking fast—completing the Greek phrase that translated in English as 'seekers come together'—

reference to the crew from Red Sword travelling to Jamaica to meet with Alesandro.

"Sienna, good to hear from you" Alesandro greeted the woman calling him.

"Let's meet. I'm here at the resort, covertly. You'll find me at The Tamarind. Look for the cleaner, see you there in five."

He agreed, they hung up. He got out of bed quickly, got dressed and made his way through the penthouse without making a sound.

As the elevator doors opened, a chilling sense of hostility filled the Atrium between him and The Tamarind, he hesitated. The night was quiet, with only cleaning staff and a few lingering guests by the pools and tables, lost in conversation or resisting sleep.

Their presence gave him short-lived comfort.

It seemed as if all of them suddenly vanished in the space of a few quick moments. When, without any warning he was confronted by a balding, bloodshot eyed man with wispy blond hair who looked as if he hadn't slept in far too long. The man had a pale white complexion that made him appear disturbing and ghostly in his black attire.

"Good morning Mr. Karahalios," the man greeted in a tired drawling tone.

The man made Alesandro's skin crawl.

"Do we know each other?" he queried.

"You don't—but I know all about you," the man spoke like the devil itself.

There was a discomforting silence—coupled with uneasy anticipation.

"Hand over the piece of Atlantis, Mr. Karahalios," the man ordered, holding out his hand.

Alesandro frowned and looked at the man cock-eyed. *"Piece of Atlantis... I have no piece of Atlantis"* he thought... then both a chill of excitement and of panic ran down his spine as he connected the dots.

Alesandro had possessed it for years—a small aqua-blue glass prism, pyramid-shaped, just a couple of inches wide but impossibly heavy. A friend, an expert in rare antiquities, once spotted it atop a cabinet at his home and remarked, "That's Atlantium... incredibly rare. I thought it was either lost to time or purely mythical."

He'd had no further information, yet Alesandro suspected a link to Atlantis. Uncertain but intrigued, he stashed it in his safe house and eventually forgot about it. The weight was excessive—so much so that it nearly cracked a wooden bookshelf before he moved it to a sturdier cast-iron cabinet housing his family archives.

That had to be what this creepy little man was on about.

"Do not play games with me Karahalios, give me what I have asked for" he demanded, growing impatient.

"You think I have it on me?" Alesandro frowned—it wasn't exactly the kind of thing he'd carry around casually.

"I do, as you do the diaries of Solon the sage. You can hand those over too."

Alesandro couldn't help but laugh at the man's optimistic stupidity.

The man swapped his indifferent facial expression for a screwed-up nose and advanced upon Alesandro who decided to make haste and dash back to the penthouse as fast as possible. Only to find his path was blocked by a man who resembled a rhinoceros. The man's head and face were covered by a balaclava, revealing two mad, menacing eyes fixated on the seizure of Alesandro.

Alesandro backed away, and the insidious ghostly man lunged for him. A scowl twisted his face, mouth hanging open in a deranged way. The man hissed as Alesandro leapt to the side, almost stumbling over a couple of yakkas growing in the garden in the middle of the Atrium near The Caribbean Skillet. Evading capture, he steadied himself and dashed along the Atrium until beside the entrance to the Grand Isle.

Alesandro dodged the charging rhino man then sprinted down the Atrium; then the Grand Isle toward the lobby. From nowhere, a slim figure in tight black attire swung a haymaker—he ducked as a muffled curse, distinctly feminine, escaped their balaclava. Pushing his speed beyond his limits, he wove through sofas, sculptures, and tables, tearing past the Entrance'd Café at the heart of the resort's main building.

He ran on adrenaline now. Survival mode had kicked in and as he sailed past the café, he flung chairs and whatever furniture and objects he could between he and his pursuers. It bought him mere seconds as the lithe one in the black fitting suit simply leapt over and around them like cat woman and the rhinoceros bulldozed them out of his way as he followed his accomplice.

Alesandro kept running—it had finally come to this. He'd endured threats—letters, calls, texts—and six unsettling encounters in person, but tonight was different. This trio was the first to attack. He hadn't grown used to the danger, and it wore on his nerves. Yet he knew his duty. Solon's research had made him both guardian and keeper.

The piece of Atlantis remained on the archive cabinet. The Solon diaries—the originals were safely stored, where they should have been for centuries. Regardless, these fools were already too late. They were safe with Red Sword Security Services and their chief historian had reviewed the diary's key passages.

He couldn't get back to the penthouse, the route blocked by his assailants.

He dug in his pockets to find his phone and speed dial Crouton or Sienna as he ran, that'd at least raise the alarm.

"Dammit!" He'd left it on the bedside table after speaking with her. How could he have been so foolish! He scolded inwardly.

He kicked himself, for a moment—being angrier with that, than concerned about his current predicament. The latter prevailed. *"And where the heck is everyone else in this deserted resort?"*

Alesandro nearly collided with three men between him and a black Bedford van at the drop-off to the right—his planned escape route. As they moved toward him, he veered left and sprinted through the car park driveway.

"This is ridiculous!" he thought as he slowed and spun around to see what was happening behind him.

He heard shouting. Resort security had finally arrived on the scene. Arguing ensued and the brandishing of firearms.

Figures dressed in black were getting into the van and another vehicle—a black sedan—two of them holding hand held firearms fitted with silencers aimed in his direction.

He hastily made a decisive turn into the bushes and fauna to the left of the car park and practically dove in.

The sound of two or three small objects darting through the trees at immense speed made Alesandro extremely grateful he'd acted quickly and gotten out of sight.

The chase far from over, he pushed past his nerves, adrenaline driving him as he scanned his surroundings. Streetlights filtered through the trees, illuminating a safe path through the ferns beneath towering palms. Soon, he reached a familiar footpath—one he'd often taken from his house to the beach, passing the Caribbean Paradise before reaching the sand.

He wondered how acquainted his pursuers were with his own neighbourhood and had a hunch he knew it better. The chances were, they knew enough about him and knew where he lived, even if they'd not done their homework on the Atlantium. He picked they'd likely send one vehicle there and the rest would be searching for him between the resort and the beach.

He had no such intentions to go back to his home in the nearby suburb of Coral Spring. Certainly not on foot, while they had wheels.

As the beach came into view, he tore through a hibiscus grove, crashing past sprawling watermelon and pineapple vines that'd escaped a nearby fence.

He reached the sand and could see the headlights up the slope where the road was. Flash lights were being swung around, and he heard hurried exchanges between those who hunted him.

Alesandro stopped for little more than a second though, he kept low and followed a line of thick bushes and palm trees that formed a barrier reserve between the road about thirty meters up a gradual slope, and the beach. He would carry on along, as quickly as he possibly could. The Burwood public beach, past the smaller Sea Hawk Beach resort to where the sand ended, and he'd lose the grunts on the shore line and the boulders.

Amongst the rocks sitting between the sandy beach and the cover of trees, existed hidden tracks, of which there were several, if they could be found. But only one led to his concealed safe house nestled in the tropical bush high up on a hill on a small peninsular overlooking Coral Spring, The Caribbean Paradise and the ocean.

Still keeping low, Alesandro turned around, having bouldered his way over the rocks at the end of the beach. No sign of his pursuers, thank goodness! This meant he could safely enter the bush unseen.

Suddenly an almighty BOOM shook the neighbourhood, startling Alesandro who nearly toppled over backwards on the last rock at the top before the hill climb.

"What was *that?*" he muttered, perplexed.

Toward Coral Spring, flames from a fierce fire blazed among the trees and streetlights, casting an eerie glow over the dark urban landscape.

Alesandro didn't hesitate—whatever had happened wasn't good. He rushed into the bush, brushing past ferns toward one of three hidden tracks, which splintered into several. To a stranger, the maze was disorienting.

Most paths barely looked like trails—Alesandro had designed them to confuse or deter wanderers. His secret safe house lay deep within coastal bush on land once owned by an almost urban legend now—Captain Billy Barns.

Barns never existed. The eccentric hermit was pure fiction—crafted by Alesandro to deflect curiosity.

Coincidentally, a real hermit matching the myth *had* lived nearby and died quietly. Alesandro claimed the forgotten land, its history muddled by rumour and decay, using the confusion to conceal a safe house guarding humanity's most controversial secrets.

While trickier to move along the correct track in the darkness of night, Alesandro knew it off by heart and found his way through to the small front lawn that overlooked the Caribbean. Before him in the shadows, stood the simple shack with its one widow and door on the front wall under a triangled roof. The place appeared humble and modest yet was every bit as sturdy and invisible from afar as any miliatary bunker—with its steel reinforcing, blast and fireproof titanium granite compound cladding behind a facade of old grey weather boards and corrugated iron roofing.

Alesandro entered the security code and scanned his fingerprint—releasing the lock's mechanisms. The door's interior, previously meshed with the wall, clicked and parted—its dented knob merely decorative.

Inside, he secured the door with another fingerprint scan, sealing himself within the vault-like space. Exhaling deeply, he powered up his laptop, gazing across darkened ocean as he accessed CCTV to check on his home a few kilometres away.

Nothing had been compromised at the safe house—excellent—safe to turn on the lights. Blackout windows allowed light in while preventing it from shining out. As well as being equipped with exterior night vision surveillance cameras—giving him an advantage over any hostile trespassers after dark. Night was usually when he completed most of his work. The cover of darkness allowed more security and access to the house unseen.

He was bracing for the possibility the safe house might become his new home, given how the night was unfolding. Unless his fears were wrong and his Coral Spring home hadn't been destroyed in the explosion less than twenty minutes ago, he had little reason for hope. So far, CCTV and the sentinel had only confirmed smashed in front, side, and back doors—and nearly every room in the house ransacked.

From three different camera views he could see police cars outside of his house, what looked like guards positioned out the front and forensic personnel were moving about. Sienna was walking around with a woman who appeared to be a detective and another man in uniform. This to Alesandro's relief! He was glad someone he could trust was on the scene able to influence things.

"That girl moves quickly!" He said to himself. In the time he'd fled from the resort to his safe house, she'd achieved similar and was at his place.

He couldn't get a clear angle from the cameras out the front of the house, but it looked as though a fire truck was parked across the street.

"My goodness!" Alesandro remarked.

He looked swiftly to the top of the archive cabinet to where the piece of Atlantis was kept.

There it was. The apparent reason for the wee-small-hour chaos.

Alesandro retrieved the item from the cabinet. The last time he'd noticed it was, moving it to the safe house —proceeding his antiquities expert friend's remarks about it... they'd never discussed it further. He'd nearly forgotten it—having pulled it from a box of miscellaneous objects with unknown origins.

All he knew, was it was a rare mineral called Atlantium and the unsavoury man who'd accosted him an hour ago had referred to it as a 'piece of Atlantis'. Whatever that was supposed to mean... which piece?

He intensely lamented forgetting his phone. He could've contacted Nathan, Crouton, or even Sienna via his laptop, but hadn't memorized their numbers.

Alessandro eventually came to terms with the realization that he was going to need to get back to the resort in much the same way as he'd fled. If he left the safe house, the piece of Atlantis was going with him. It was pivotal he get it into the safety of Red Sword Security—he wasn't taking any chances, regardless of how secure the safe house was.

His gut was telling him something world changing hinged on the possession of the mysterious trinket.

Though, the thing must have weighed twenty kilograms at least! It looked like it should have merely weighed one or two. Alesandro needed both hands to remove the object off the top of the iron cabinet where it had been perched almost two meters from the floor. Even more effort was required to keep it from plummeting to the ground and putting a hole in the floorboards.

"Ughf! This thing is ridiculous!" Alesandro grunted, holding the small prism in both hands, fighting gravity.

"Now what am I supposed to do with it? How am I s'posed to transport it back to the resort?" He tried to remember how on earth he'd moved it the first-time round. He briefly had second thoughts, maybe there was another way...

"No. Dammit..." He'd little choice but to stuff it into one of half a dozen pockets in his cargo pants. Trusting the stitching could handle it— not tearing a hole in the fabric or otherwise pulling his trousers down.

It did neither! He praised the makers of cargo pants for the quality of workmanship and fabrics used, and the fact that he was wearing a sturdy leather belt in addition. Otherwise, it would have been an instant down trou.

Before leaving, he eyed the cupboard and the wide-brimmed fedora hanging on its door. Retrieving it, he paced awkwardly, adjusting for the heavy object in his pocket. Inside the cupboard, he found his smoky purple overcoat and yellow-peach Hawaiian shirt—both long unworn. He changed, donned the hat, and from a drawer, grabbed reading glasses, purely decorative but convincingly real.

Looking decidedly different, he hoped the odd gait caused by the weight in his pocket would add to the disguise. With luck, he could return to the resort undetected and slip back up to the penthouse.Neither of which was about to happen in quite that manner.

~~~~~~~

Standing around the laptop set in front of Rod, they were able to see everything from the point at which Alesandro exited the elevator at the ground floor of the western tower. Up until he dived into the bushes at the side of the car park in front of the resort when his pursuers began firing at him.

Nathan answered a call, paused, then said, "Come on up, Maurice."

In the living area, Nathan, Crouton, Chad, Tim, and Charlotte pieced things together. Rhys left to meet with resort security to assist or gather intel.

Rod and Chaiyala discussed the car explosion and home invasion in Coral Spring with Red Sword agents when Maurice and his head of security arrived.

Brief greetings were exchanged as Rohit Prasuad, the resort's head of security—a well-presented, distinguished Indian man in his mid-thirties—was introduced before Maurice advised "the news isn't positive my friends, yet it is not entirely negative either.

While Mr. Karahalios' house has been ransacked, for what reason, police have not yet determined, he wasn't at his home. The police have confirmed that much.

His vehicle, however, was found not twenty meters from his house—burnt out, with the remains of someone..."

Charlotte put her hand to her mouth in shock. The others hovered between anguish and anticipation—why was the news *not exactly negative?*

"...whose DNA matches a known criminal who's been at large for years—and is, of course, not Alesandro Karahalios."

There were sighs of relief and deep breaths released at the sound of that good news.

"For goodness' sake Alesandro! Where are you?" Crouton shook his head. He was quiet for the next few moments though—staring out across the ocean—the movement of his eyes indicating he was hard at work in thought. Eventually he took a deep breath and composed himself.

"Right then," he began, looking at Rod, Chaiyala and Rohit, "what do we know?" He then looked at Nathan and Maurice in case they'd anything else to add.

Chaiyala had retrieved Alesandro's mobile phone earlier and all she could find, of interest were three phone calls from a private untraceable number. "The first of three calls went through. The remaining two... did not."

"Interesting."

"Okay," Rod began, his tone firm and assured. He and Rohit had completed the background checks on the individuals who'd accosted Alesandro before dawn... "The first man who approaches Alesandro, is Egyptian fugitive Kiaos Tilabetti. Wanted by Egyptian police for alleged theft of national antiquities."

Crouton sighed and shook his head.

"Kasandra Murdoc. She's the one who takes a swing at Alesandro and now that we know who she is and what she's capable of, either Alesandro had divine intervention, or, she's become slack since her days in the British S.A.S. before she went rogue and tried to blow up Stonehenge."

"Just... let me near the cow," Chaiyala whispered.

"Interesting." Maurice frowned.

"She what?" Charlotte asked, shocked, checking she'd heard correctly.

"I remember this..." Tim recalled, "that was her? They never caught the culprit."

"Sounds unhinged." Chad suggested.

"Indeed." Agreed Nathan.

"The big thug," Rod continued, "is a black ops grunt connected with our friend Albarad, also Egyptian."

"Typical." Said Tim.

"Surprise, surprise." Crouton concluded cynically.

"Conicho Cadavid is former US special forces, same deal as Murdoc, went rogue, along with his girlfriend Lacy Jax, wanted terrorist with suspected connections to ISIS, formerly CIA."

"Righteo then. A band of textbook misfits with bad attitudes and 'kick me' signs taped to their behinds." Crouton said comically.

Chad and Charlotte grinned.

"Sums it up." Rod replied. "But what strikes me as odd is how Alesandro seemed to get away so easily... is there more to this guy than we know of?"

"What would you suspect?" Nathan enquired in a curious tone.

"No, no. I mean, he has the appearance of a middle-aged man who's spent his life in study, yet... maybe he has some kind of training, perhaps..."

"You wouldn't be wrong." A woman spoke, her voice carrying a trace of a South African accent.

A tall woman wearing a black Red Sword Security Services polo stood before of the elevator doors. Her long red hair was pulled into a ponytail, and she hugged an armoured plastic file case. Dark green eyes and a subtly cheeky smile said more than words could.

"Darling!" Crouton beamed—was first to greet her.

"Hey Dad!" she smiled.

"Sienna!" Nathan said pleasantly.

Chaiyala stood and walked over, embracing her warmly—it had been months since they'd last seen each other.

Crouton quickly introduced Tim, Chad and Charlotte to his daughter—Sienna after he scooped her up in a warm hug.

"Sienna," Crouton began, "while being amazing in every way, as well as the joy of my life, is Red Sword's director of intelligence, covert operations and special tactics. She is every bit the genius I am not and, she gets her stunning smile and beauty from her lovely mother, and her height from me."

She's been handling a special short-term assignment related to our missing friend. And—she's single, too," he added, glancing subtly at Chad.

Tim and Charlotte shared a subtle knowing grin.

"Shut up, Crouton." Chaiyala muttered.

He shot her a look of confusion.

"Let's not get side-tracked here..." Rod intervened.

Sienna smirked again "Yes, agreed."

"Indeed," Nathan concurred. "While it is very nice to have you with us again Sienna, to what do we owe the pleasure of your arrival?"

"It's been a busy night." Sienna smiled, having thanked Nathan. "Alesandro will be fine, don't worry, I have trained him well."

"Good! Well done." Crouton commended.

"Yes, Daddy, I've ensured my assignment is safe. He's terrible in hand-to-hand combat but excels at staying hidden. He's likely in his safe house or on his way back, so we should begin searching for him. If he's at the safe house, he's fine. Let's hope and pray they haven't found him before we have." she said—glancing at the faces of those on Rod's laptop.

Chaiyala held up his phone in her hand, Crouton shook his head slightly.

Rod remembered hearing their guest speak of the safe house before he'd nodded off the previous evening.

"It's state-of-the-art and not far from here," Sienna explained, "where he keeps his family archives and a number of other interesting items of historical significance. Including, rumour has it, an Atlantium prism, or, a piece of Atlantis."

"A what?" Crouton asked.

"*Very interesting!*" Nathan remarked, a little too eager in his curiosity, with a look of haunting fascination.

"Alright, crazy eyes," Sienna teased Nathan, "don't get too excited yet... we need to find Alesandro first."

"You're right, Alesandro must be found, Atlantium can come later."

"Sorry, what's the story? What's Atlantium and this, piece of Atlantis?" Tim queried, pulling himself away from acute observations of Nathan's weirdness.

"Atlantium is an extremely rare mineral that has the capacity to transfer and project energy at an incredible rate. It is supposed to be pure pseudo-science..." Nathan explained, "...with claims it could be used as a weapon of mass destruction, rumours suggest the Christchurch earthquakes of 2011 were caused by terrorists testing out a similar concept. Regardless, it's supposed to be a myth. Apparently though, our friend Alesandro may be about to put an end to that myth, perhaps..."

"Hmm," Chad thought, *"myth... interesting concept."*

"What's your plan?" Sienna asked Nathan and Crouton.

Rhys returned with a full briefing from resort security. Bringing with him new security insights—covering site activity, the surrounding area, resort access, vehicle movements, and any support available. Much more than the earlier CCTV.

"Rod. Rhys. What intel we got?" asked Crouton.

Rod laid out all they now knew and a plan was discussed. He remained in the penthouse, deep in strategic coordination with Nathan and Rohit.

"Chaiyala, Sienna, let's go find Alesandro." Crouton suggested Sienna could update he and Chaiyala on the way to the lobby, regarding her work with the missing historian.

"Affirmative," Chaiyala nodded.

Tim was preoccupied with the aforementioned piece of Atlantis. As always, he had a growing list of questions for Nathan. Increasing alongside that, was the peculiar feeling he was getting about his friend. Not that this deterred him in any way, from the long-standing pleasant and positive impression he had of the man. He'd always been equally as mysterious as he was agreeable, and where Nathan raised questions about himself, he never caused concerns.

What was it about Nathan that Tim could never put his finger on though?

It was like a whisper you could sense only in passing, but never grasp by listening.

Chad's expression suggested he figured the same as he stared curiously at his brother.

"Atlantium," Nathan began, "is phenomenally heavy. Even in very small amounts."

"What else is known of it?" Chad asked.

"Well that's the thing; that's where the trail seems to end, in terms of what is known," Nathan answered, "and where the assumption that it is nothing more than myth begins. Possibly because of its apparent properties leaning toward the fanciful."

Chad sensed an underlying complexity... he was pretty sure Nathan knew more than he let on, yet no one challenged him. Was there no need, or was Chad missing something? Perhaps Nathan played his hand carefully, concealing an agenda. But in this game, intent mattered more than mere strategy.

Since Nathan's arrival, Chad had studied his interactions. The man was flawless in nearly every way, yet oddly unconvincingly so... was he subtly controlling those around him, like a cult leader? Or was he truly as genuine, wise, and disarming as he seemed?

Chad's mind never rested. Each answer bred new questions, a relentless pursuit of deeper knowledge and understanding.

To Chad, Nathan was becoming too idyllic for the real world... *"But who's real world? And what kind of idyllic...?"* He wondered. *"How do we know that Nathan isn't in fact the completely normal one here and his speech and actions merely expose a very ancient and unchecked trail of abnormality?"*

"Shut up... goodness!" Chad blurted out without meaning to. He'd not realized it either, until he noticed Tim and Nathan looking at him, Tim slightly puzzled, Nathan returned to discussion with Rod.

The elevator doors had barely closed when Sienna began updating her father and Chaiyala on her work with Alesandro.

"As you know, when you asked me to be Alesandro's handler, he came to me before I even had a chance to contact him, sit down and speak with him about his family legacy. He said we came highly recommended by someone who'd known him as a child."

"Yup."

"And that he'd never actually met this person, but they'd been a very trusted family friend for a very long time and his parents and grandparents vouched for the person in question?"

"Yup."

"So, I've had my team trying to locate this individual. Until the other day, it might as well have been a cold case. I refused to give up, even if it nearly drove me crazy. This previously unnamed person has eight different names—none of them aliases..."

Chaiyala and Crouton both looked at her with raised eyebrows as any textbook go-tos vanished.

They exited the elevator and made their way along the Atrium towards the Grand Isle.

"...but also spans eight different life-times with no birth records or details of death, sorry, no real records of births or deaths."

"How's that even *possible?*" Chaiyala asked.

"You gotta be kiddin' me..." Crouton stopped in his tracks, frowning and looking straight ahead as he tried to grapple with that.

Sienna laughed, "I asked the same question of Cliff," her field partner "and he reckons the guy is an alien."

The expressions on the faces of the other two hadn't changed.

"Hmm," Sienna mused, brow furrowed. "An alien, ancient—nearly a millennia old. Gender? Unclear. But Alesandro insists it was a male voice on the other end of those calls. So, 'he' it is. All, of course from numbers that don't feature on any network and not a scrap of a record can be retrieved. We're also unsure as to how far back this guy's history actually goes, before he contacted Alesandro."

Crouton and Chaiyala looked at each other with questions in their eyes.

"My guess was an angel." Sienna suggested with a confident smile.

"Why an angel?" Crouton always began with why: why did they say that? Why did you feel that way? Why respond like that?

He taught Sienna to seek purpose first, settling for "what," "when," "where," and "how" only after. Why? Because every action has intent, shaping events directly or indirectly.

Sienna had learned to craft thoughtful, well-researched responses—not always immediate—but always outstanding. "There are far more documented accounts and historical records of angels than of aliens. Aliens may dominate pop culture and speculation, but they remain as unverifiable today as they were at Roswell. Angelic encounters, though often debated, have been recorded across millennia—many untouched by the dramatization and philosophical haze that clouds modern alien discourse."

By the end of Sienna's speel, Chaiyala was smiling—partly at Sienna's encyclopaedic knowledge, which she neither tried to match nor particularly wanted to, and the pace at which her friend could rattle all of that off.

"Very nice!" Crouton smiled.

Sienna smiled back with fondness of their almost private game.

They continued walking along the Atrium and around the corner along the Grand Isle to the lobby and the Entrance'd Café.

The three were able to trace Alesandro's path outside using CCTV footage.

"Cliff saw the chase unfold on the dashcam of his vehicle parked over there—from the main entrance to the bushes on that side of the car park." She pointed to the far western end, where her fellow agent had a clear view of both the entrance and the area where Alesandro evaded his pursuers.

"He'll fill you in on the finer details once he's back from working with local authorities on the home invasion and Alesandro's destroyed vehicle. But as he tells it," Sienna continued, brow furrowed but voice lively, "a third party emerged from that doorway—down the far end, just before the western tower where you've been staying—and stood there, watching it all unfold. Now this is where things start going full X-Files," she grinned.

Crouton gave her a mock look, as if wondering whether he should sit down for what came next.

He also wondered when things in their line of work hadn't been X-Files. Discovering Atlantis had already rewritten his definition of 'normal.' Now his daughter was talking aliens, angels, and ageless individuals.

"Only Cliff's RSS tech dashcam picked up the unknown figure. To the naked eye—nothing. From beyond the doorway, the figure intermittently waved or pointed in the direction of Alesandro and his pursuers."

"Right..." Crouton muttered, stroking his beard.

Chaiyala narrowed her eyes, absorbing every detail.

"That's nothing," Sienna said, lowering her voice. "Compared to how they floated—hovered—across the parked cars, toward where Alesandro escaped through the gardens. Then vanished. Like a ghost."

"Any signs of life?" Chaiyala asked.

"Heat signature, heart rate—all the usual distinctions between living and paranormal. Picked up by the scanner and recorded on the dashcam. Yet invisible to the naked eye."

"Only on the RSS dashcam," Crouton nodded, glancing toward the spot where Alesandro had disappeared. "CCTV don't have that kind 'o tech."

"We assumed he wouldn't go straight home." Sienna added "His pursuers knew his address. But he hardly lives there. He employs a cleaner and grounds keeper to maintain the place, but he only ever shows up well after the dust has settled."

"Go on," Crouton said, motioning for her to continue as they followed the path of the chase.

"In five years, Alesandro has faced twenty-eight hostile incidents—threats, calls, letters, and visits from thugs. All trace back to our adversaries in Egypt. No evidence of political or economic motives. These aren't senators or tycoons trying to shut down the Richat project for financial or historical reasons. They want to erase Red Sword—and all links to Atlantis, especially its technology. If they know about the Atlantis artefact, they may understand its past use as well as we do."

"Our hypothesis? Atlantis' destruction—this had something to do with it," Chaiyala said, revisiting the point.

"We need to find Alesandro," Crouton said, his voice urgent, "and make sure he—and the Atlantium—are safe and secure."

~~~~~~~

Earlier that morning at 5.50am...

Alesandro unlocked the door to the safe house, stepped outside, and immediately sensed someone nearby. He had a strong feeling he was being watched. *"Nathan?"* That was his first thought. Then— *"Crouton?"*

He caught himself off guard. Why those two? Why would they be following him—and hiding? The thought unsettled him. What if it wasn't
them? Still, his gut insisted it was Nathan and/or Crouton, though he had
no reason to believe it.

"What are they doing?" he muttered, confused. Yet the idea that it
could be someone else felt even less likely.

"Where are you? ...what are you doing?" he called out cautiously.

As he stepped several meters from the doorway, a sickening chill swept
over him. The sense that it might not be his friends returned—and with
it, his gut instinct vanished. Dread gripped him. He froze, exposed and
vulnerable.

Then came a strange sensation. He didn't hear the words, exactly—they
occurred to him, as if placed in his mind from outside himself: *"Do not be
afraid. Take the safe path down the hill and continue, as you intend, along the shoreline
toward The Caribbean Paradise Resort."*

He was no longer afraid. He felt relieved—yet utterly bewildered. How
did he know the words without hearing them? Was he losing his mind?
Voices in his head?

Yet an undeniable peace, with a sense of divine reassurance, kept him
grounded. Without it, he would've retreated back to the safe house and
waited for Sienna.

"Maybe that was God," he wondered suddenly. The thought felt safer—
easier to accept than something spooky—paranormal or the fear that he
was losing his grip. He looked heavenward. "I'm not a priest, though..."

He made his way down the dark, winding path, seeing it more in his
mind than visually—it was pitch black. As his vision adjusted, he shook
his head every few steps, trying to make sense of what had just happened.

He had nothing. Not a clue. Yet he felt as reassured as he did baffled—a
confusing combination.

Alesandro, dressed oddly but otherwise unremarkable, strolled the shore at dawn. He didn't look like a man who'd just fled pursuers. He was surprised by the number of early risers—fishermen casting lines—surfers prepping boards. Remnants of a bonfire party evident—bottles—and ashes still smouldering, one reveller slumped against driftwood.

A jogging couple passed as two men in black marched toward him. His pulse quickened. Could his disguise hold? The resort was near—he could see the dock and restaurants in the half-light—but could he outrun them in deep sand? The object in his pocket hindered his pace. Exhausted, he knew he couldn't.

The men closed in, silent and determined. His mind seized in panic, unsure whether to run. Then they walked past without a word, leaving him breathless and relieved. He wasn't cut out for this life, despite Sienna's training. His nerves frayed too easily—especially around confident women like Sienna, Charlotte, and Chaiyala.

Sienna, patient and perceptive, had gently earned his trust. She once joked he was like a stray cat. After a puzzled look, they both laughed, finally breaking the ice. He hadn't realized how much effort she'd put into making their meetings more than awkward silences, or filled by her words alone.

Alesandro was no more than fifty meters from the easternmost outcrop on the beach. Between the ocean and the Caribbean Paradise resort's pool precinct, he spotted the Shrimp and Marlin café—just as a creeping unease told him he was being followed.

He looked back. The shadowy figures he'd passed moments earlier were now trailing him, no more than ten meters away.

"Oh crap," he muttered, hot-footing it toward the Shrimp and Marlin, hoping to hide among others and discourage any violent intent.

Then came the distinctive sound of a silenced gunshot.

Survival instinct kicked in. Sienna's voice echoed in his memory: "When there's no choice but to flee in the open from an assailant with a firearm, stagger your line of escape. A moving target is harder to hit."

Alesandro, despite the weight in his pocket, picked up the pace. Running for his life, he didn't think about the difficulty of sprinting through soft sand in shoes. Adrenaline took care of that.

He was fifteen meters from the Shrimp and Marlin when he saw, out of the corner of his eye, two resort security guards running toward him from the resorts eastern tower. One was radioing for backup; the other aimed a handgun at the pursuers and shouted, "Stop! Stay where you are and throw your gun to the side!"

Two shots rang out—but not at Alesandro. Either someone was a bad shot, or his zigzagging was working.

First came the silenced shot. Then a much louder one. He didn't look back. He just ran—desperate to get away. Out of sight, and stay alive.

He leapt from the sand over a wooden rail onto the verandah dining area of the Shrimp and Marlin. The door was locked. Inside, two startled restaurant staff stared at him—wide-eyed.

Another silenced shot. This time, the unnerving thud of something embedding in the wooden cladding of the restaurant.

Two more unsilenced shots. Alesandro bolted through chairs and tables, vaulted the rail, hit the sand, and disappeared around the corner at the rear of the restaurant.

Shouting erupted behind him as he frantically searched for a place to hide. There wasn't anything suitable.

Then, more silenced shots. The sharp whack of small objects hitting wood. Followed by several louder gunshots.

A gate suddenly revealed itself—open a fraction—in a wooden wall that stretched ten or fifteen meters between the back of the restaurant and the rock outcrop. Alesandro didn't give it a split second's thought. He threw himself through the gate and kicked it shut as he tumbled along the boardwalk on the other side.

Spying a wooden staircase leading up through palms and the tropical bush cloaking the outcrop, he hurried in that direction. He was thankful for the first light of dawn giving him just enough visibility to see each step as he bounded up three at a time.

Winding around bends, ignoring the view, he was single-mindedly focused on putting distance between himself and the threat behind him. He eventually hit a dead end—but one with three outdoor sofas surrounding a large, low driftwood table, all under a canopy of banana plants and palms.

Alesandro looked down the snaking stairs and boardwalk he'd just sprinted up. He couldn't see a soul or hear a thing. He allowed himself a moment to catch his breath.

Then, utterly exhausted and drained, he collapsed into the cushions of one of the sofas—his body giving in before his mind could protest.

CHAPTER 20

Chaiyala traced Alesandro's frantic path through the resort gardens and into the reserve. He'd moved fast—probably for his life—leaving torn plants in his wake. In the dark, he could have seen little as he fled.

"Let's take a walk along the beach, shall we?" Sienna suggested.

They crossed the sand as gulls squawked overhead. Local kids tossed a Frisbee in the shade of tall palms.

Sienna planned to reach Alesandro's safe house unnoticed, blending in as beach goers before slipping into the bush. They looked casual, though an odd trio—Crouton in a grey singlet, black trousers, and army boots; Sienna matching, except for her Red Sword polo; and Chaiyala, still in her swim top and denim shorts, paused a moment, eyes fixed on footprints in the sand.

They suddenly became dramatic—three sets. One in particular looked as if the person had been startled, then took off running. "Strange. Right foot feels heavier," she said quietly. "The other two sets—they looked like they were chasing. All three moved fast." Chaiyala followed the trail, leading the others back along the beach toward the resort.

One set of footprints became wildly erratic and harder to track.

"Definitely chased. Shots fired. They knew... how not to get hit" she concluded.

"That has to be Alesandro," Sienna said, connecting Chaiyala's observations what she'd taught him during self-defence and survival training.

"Let's hope he got away then..." Crouton said, a mix of optimism and concern in his voice.

The trio followed the mess of hastily trodden footprints and arrived at the eastern side of the Shrimp and Marlin.

"Good morning," a waiter greeted.

"Hello..." Chaiyala looked up, momentarily surprised, her concentration broken by the unexpected voice.

"Hi there," Sienna added with a smile. "We're from Red Sword Security Services," she introduced, producing her ID—the other two followed suit. "Currently investigating suspicious activity on this beach earlier this morning. Is your manager available?"

"Yes, he is," came an older voice with a blunt Canadian accent. A man of average to short height, clean-shaven-headed, with a calm yet serious expression, stepped forward. "Neville Smith, manager of the Shrimp and Marlin. How can I help?"

The waiter left to greet other guests arriving from the beachside entrance. Sienna elaborated on their investigation with Neville.

"Security said you'd likely drop by to ask about this morning's events," Neville said, accommodatingly.

"What can you tell us?" Crouton asked.

"I wasn't here at the time, but my day prep staff gave resort security and the police a detailed account. I came in as soon as I was contacted."

"Go on..." Sienna prompted.

"They said a panicked-looking middle-aged man rattled the locked door—just over there." Neville pointed to a single door at the corner of the building, right of the larger ranch slider beach entrance.

"He vanished before they could let him in or understand what was happening. Seconds later, gunshots rang out—bullets ripping through the restaurant's wooden walls. A bit shaken, they later realized how lucky they were to have avoided the firing line.

Outside, resort security apprehended two men, soon joined by police. When asked about the man who'd nearly broken down the door, staff could only guess he fled along the shoreline around the outcrop." Neville glanced toward the rocky rise, its palm trees and tropical scrub thick with shadow.

"The only other way..." he began, then paused. He squinted at the wooden plank wall between the Shrimp and Marlin and the outcrop. A chain and padlock hung beside the gate to the backyard entrance behind the kitchen.

"That's curious. Didn't notice that earlier... the back gate looks like it's not—it's supposed to be chained up. Seldom ever unlocked," he said, puzzled, starting toward the wall.

They exchanged glances, then followed Neville to the close end of the back fence behind the restaurant.

To anyone passing by, it would have appeared the weathered wooden gate had been left ajar by mistake. But it should never open—and today, it no longer sat flush with the fence it was hinged to.

"It's unlocked," Neville said, unimpressed—and unsure why.

He pulled it open and examined the chain and padlock on the opposite side.

"What the..."

"A bullet passed straight through that thing, mate," Crouton observed as Neville held out a busted padlock in his palm, its twisted form resembling a doughnut. Its destruction had released the steel lock hook—and with it, the chain.

"No damage. Not to the gate, not the fence..." Chaiyala studied the scene. "Bullet went in through the hand-hole, hit the padlock. It let go—the chain... wrapped around the handle and bolt. But it came free..." She traced the trajectory, following it to where the pursuers' footprints vanished.

Neville looked at the broken lock, the other end of the chain, and the angle the bullet would've needed to hit.

"That's incredible," he muttered.

"Given the circumstances, I'm picking this one was sheer fluke—missing Alesandro as he ran this way," Crouton said.

"Where does that go?" Sienna asked Neville, now standing on the other side of the gate, staring down the boardwalk that ended ten or so meters ahead before climbing the outcrop via stairs disappearing into the bush.

Crouton and Chaiyala joined her, taking in the walled walkway lined with garden lamp posts, ferns, and cabbage trees. At first glance, it looked like an incomplete outdoor function area.

Neville explained, "This leads to several hidden private function areas and garden bars that ascend along the side of the outcrop."

They exchanged glances.

"We ain't heard jack-all from resort security about any progress finding Alesandro," Crouton said, looking at Sienna.

The girls shook their heads.

Crouton nodded, gazing up the boardwalk. "That's cos they haven't looked here—where the pursuit continued past the Shrimp and Marlin... or ended."

"Mind if we...?"

"By all means," Neville said. "Hopefully you'll find your guy. This morning's events were unnerving. But if you'll excuse me, I must get back to my staff and guests."

"Thank you so much—you've been very helpful," Sienna said.

Crouton shook Neville's hand. "We'll make sure your lock's replaced—with a top-of-the-line security system to boot."

Sienna pulled out her phone and noted it in her diary.

Neville nodded his thanks, quiet yet grateful.

They reached the function area at the boardwalk's end. Unlike the others, which had paths to sheltered platforms—suspended on cliffsides—this garden bar featured a spacious deck with stunning views of the Jamaican coastline. Attached, a larger wooden deck hosted guests beneath palms and vibrant tropical plants. To their left, Alesandro lay on a lavish outdoor sofa—his head nestled in an oversized cushion.

"There he is!" Crouton chuckled. "Ha!"

"That's our man," Sienna smiled, then added, "well done," directing her praise especially toward Chaiyala for her tracking skills.

Alesandro slowly awoke. Seeing the faces of his friends, he quickly came to, looked around cautiously, frowned, and asked, "What time is it?"

"It's a quarter to eleven," Chaiyala grinned. "You slept in."

"I—was chased—all night, it seemed."

"We know," Sienna smiled. "We watched as far as CCTV would allow us. Chaiyala tracked the rest."

"Thank you!" Alesandro dove his hand into his pocket—a sharp moment of anxious recollection—yes, it was still there!

He let out a sigh of relief, shook his head, and closed his eyes.

"Ya alright, matey?" Crouton asked. Chaiyala sat next to Alesandro.

He leaned back against the pillow, letting his heart rate settle. Then looked at the others again.

"It's okay," Sienna reassured, smiling. "No one's chasing you anymore. Your pursuers were apprehended by resort security and taken away by the police this morning. And we're here now."

Alesandro's nerves finally settled at that news.

Sienna sat beside him and placed a hand on his shoulder, then around him. "It's okay. You can take it easy now. You've done well."

"Really well," Crouton agreed, while Chaiyala scanned the area.

"Those people you were running from aren't easily avoided. You either got lucky—or had some form of divine protection."

"You followed your evasive action plan perfectly," Sienna added. She knew how much Alesandro hated confrontation and how hard this had been on his nerves.

Alesandro shook his head—marvelling at how well the others handled this kind of thing. He just wanted to be left alone by thugs.

"I have no home and no vehicle," he said, slightly mournful.

"You made it. You're breathing. You're free," Chaiyala reassured.

"And your safe house," Sienna added. "Your home is intact, just a mess. And compromised, for now."

"I know. I liked that place. I wish I could have spent more time there," he lamented. "It's just—these people never leave me alone."

"Don't worry about your home and ya car—we've already got that taken care of," Crouton said.

"Huh?"

Crouton was already planning to take Alesandro car shopping. He'd be invited to re-locate to the safety of the Richat Project camp for the time being, and have his Coral Spring home fitted with a security system worthy of the man and his work.

"Never mind. The point is, you're alive and safe—that's what matters. The material stuff? Easily replaced. Let's get you back to the penthouse. We can fuss over all that guff later."

Alesandro reached into his pocket and awkwardly pulled out the glassy prism, using both hands due to its weight.

Crouton and Chaiyala frowned.

"This thing is ridiculously heavy. It's... an enigma," Alesandro said, unsure how to explain.

"What is it?" Sienna asked, "—is that..."

"It's what I'm almost certain one of the people who attacked me referred to as a 'Piece of Atlantis.' I've heard it called Atlantium before. A very rare mineral, this is the only piece I know of. I don't even know what it's supposed to be, or why they were after it..."

"Aye... so this is the piece of Atlantis..." Crouton said, curiosity rising. He grunted as he picked up the small pyramid-shaped object— "Certainly heavier than it looks."

He handed it to Chaiyala, who was caught by surprise and quickly used both hands to stop it from falling. She adjusted to the weight and tested it a few times, curling it like a free weight.

"Oh yes! This is crazy heavy. Wow!" she exclaimed, then passed it to Sienna.

"We need to get this thing tested," Sienna said. "And you're sure it's Atlantium—possibly a piece of Atlantis?" she asked Alesandro again.

"That's my guess. I don't even know where it came from. It was in a box, among belongings that hadn't been touched for years."

"Interesting," Crouton muttered, stroking his beard.

~~~~~~~

Tim and Charlotte looked up from the laptop—greeting the others with a smile.

Crouton, Sienna, and Chaiyala had returned a rattled Alesandro safely to the penthouse suite, where Rhys cooked him a hearty meal of bacon, eggs, and hash browns.

Nathan, Rod, and Rhys gathered around, relieved to have their new friend back, safe and unharmed.

"Mate! You had us pretty worried for a while there," Rod said, placing a hand on Alesandro's shoulder.

"It's such a blessing you're okay," Nathan added full of relief.

As he spoke, Alesandro regarded him curiously—his voice, to be exact—with a pleasant uncertainty he couldn't quite place.

"Found him fast asleep, we did. Down at the beach on a couch," Crouton grinned.

Chaiyala propped herself on the corner of the table nearest Chad—the two of them exchanged a warm smile.

"There's been some interesting action over the last twenty-four hours," Sienna said, her tone inquisitive. "But I think it's over—for now."

They discussed the loss of Alesandro's vehicle, the trashing of his home, and what Red Sword could do to help him with a new car and protective measures.

Crouton, tired of holding the Atlantium, finally set it down with a thud on the hardwood table—carefully positioning it over a leg for support. He hesitated, eyeing it warily, half concerned the surface might splinter beneath its weight.

Alesandro wasn't sure either.

"So, this is it—the mysterious Atlantium," Tim observed.

"Hmm... a piece of Atlantis," Crouton replied.

"Yes—one of those pieces." Sienna began. "A very controversial one. It's what we suspect Alesandro's pursuers were after—and what all the early morning fuss was about."

"The legend of the Atlantium—it's true," Chaiyala said happily to Tim.

"Another 'myth' that wasn't so mythical after all," concluded Rod.

"In an increasingly long list of many," Sienna added.

The flood of ideas, discoveries, and questions was overwhelming. Chad wished he'd kept a journal of everything he'd learned—an old habit before his breakup with Sonia. Life had veered into chaos, and many routines had fallen away.

"It's so small—what, four square inches at the base," Sienna observed.

"And stupidly heavy!" Crouton remarked.

"It's made of Atlantium," Nathan said, eyes fixed on the prism—part observation, part confirmation.

"So, what is it, exactly? What does it do?" Alesandro asked, voicing the question lingering in the room.

"Now this is where the crazy really kicks in," Tim began, brushing aside the conventional pyramid-as-tomb theory. In its place, he laid out a compelling alternative—one backed by evidence and buried testimony. Pyramids, known in Atlantean terms as 'Carsakarisks', were not tombs at all. They were ancient power stations.

He presented data suggesting the Egyptians hadn't built the pyramids. That they had perhaps inherited and repurposed the structures. The prism of Atlantium sitting on the table was no mere artefact—it was the very tip of a pyramid—that lost technology, a fragment of a system designed to transmit energy wirelessly across vast distances.

Then, with deliberate intent, Tim revealed what he'd been holding back: the contents of two additional Solon diaries. Their pages didn't just challenge the tomb theory—they pointed to a civilization far older and more advanced than previously imagined. The pyramids weren't monuments to the dead. They were engines of energy, relics of a forgotten brilliance buried beneath layers of myth, sand, and silence.

Tim's voice had steadied as he laid out the next revelation. "Poseidon, stripped of myth, emerged not as a god but as a heavenly messenger—

grieved by Atlantis's descent into control and conquest. He withdrew to Alastragah, a sanctuary of restoration, and gathered loyal guardians. After his departure, Atlantis spiralled. They destroyed Hiva with weapons that bent the depths of the earth and the power of the sun to their will. Their might collapsed. Their pride undid them.

But Atlantis had been more than war—it had made incredible break throughs science and technology. They mastered matter relocation and wireless energy transmission through the Carsakarisks. When one failed in the north, it triggered a cataclysm that reshaped the world and ushered in the ice age. Only those in Alastragah survived."

Tim pressed on, the weight of Solon's final vision pressing into the room. "Solon had been entrusted with the path to Alastragah and the legacy of Poseidon's lineage. He'd dreamt of a gardener—an elemental figure who sifted creation, revealing a mosaic of time crowned by a Carsakarisk. At its centre stood a building with seven pillars. That was the key. A place that would reveal to them the location of the sacred halls of Alastragah.

And when the scarlet blade rises again, Atlantis will awaken."

Stunned silence.

"Of course, a great deal of this is brand-new information, translated from the Solon Diaries. I'm still getting my head around it myself," Tim clarified. "Legend has it that when the capstones of the Carsakarisks—pyramids—were removed, their tips were meant to be destroyed. When proven indestructible, the rulers of Egypt and other Atlantean sites had them transported as far away as possible."

"This was off the top of one of the pyramids of Egypt?" Chad asked, incredulous.

"Whether it came from one in Egypt," Nathan began, "or from any of the hundreds scattered across the old Atlantean empire—it's hard to say.

Legend claims they were all hidden, placed as far from the empire's heart as possible."

"Fascinating," Chad said.

"If this really is one of the fabled pieces of Atlantis—and definitely Atlantium," Tim continued, "then it's no ordinary artefact. According to legend, this little object can project hundreds of thousands of watts of energy into the ionosphere, bouncing it toward receivers—obelisks—across vast distances."

"My beard!" Crouton exclaimed.

"Of course, how the Atlanteans actually managed to achieve ionospheric bounce and return remains a complete mystery."

Chad raised his eyebrows. Charlotte was silent—both caught between awe and disbelief. At some point, seeing was enough. Scepticism became obsolete.

"Wireless electricity," Rod nodded, impressed.

"That's mad!" Rhys said.

Once Tim finished explaining the Solon Diaries and they'd concluded discussion about the Atlantium, Nathan declared, "Time for a break!"

He secured the Atlantium in a hidden high-tech safe behind the eighty-inch flat screen. As the TV screen slid across with a soft mechanical hum, it revealed a collection of extraordinary artefacts—each one stranger and more beautiful than the last. Crystalline objects pulsed faintly with internal light; metallic scrolls etched with indecipherable glyphs shimmered as if resisting translation.

The room fell into a hush.

Tim leaned forward—eyebrows raised—lips parted in disbelief.

Sienna blinked twice—her gaze flicking from one relic to another. It was as if recalibrating her understanding of history.

Crouton, visually bewildered, let out a low whistle.

Nathan aimed the TV remote control, pressing a few of its buttons. A coded sequence blinked to life, and an inventory screen unfolded like a digital scroll. He entered the Atlantium's details with practised precision.

"This is beyond mythic storage," he said quietly. "It's a map of what's been forgotten."

The screen dimmed, and the safe sealed itself with a soft click, leaving only the faint hum of the room's ambient tech. The artefacts were gone, but their impression lingered like the after-taste of something ancient and electric.

Nathan stepped back, brushing his hands together as if closing a chapter. "Well," he said, "that's another piece of Atlantis accounted for."

Sienna exhaled through her nose, half a laugh, half a recalibration. She didn't need more time to process—she needed a reason not to spiral. "So, we're just going to pretend that wasn't the most surreal five minutes of our lives?"

"No pretending," Nathan replied. "Just pacing."

Tim wandered toward the couch, still wide-eyed but visibly trying to re-anchor himself in the present. He picked up a coaster, turned it over, and set it down again. "I feel like I should be journaling or something." He looked in Charlotte's direction—they both laughed.

Crouton leaned against the wall, arms crossed, one eyebrow raised. "You know what this reminds me of? That time we found the fossilized eel spine in the freezer. Except this time, it's not frozen fish—it's history."

"History with a user interface." Nathan chuckled.

The group settled into a loose silence, not heavy, just thoughtful. The kind of quiet that follows a good story or a strange dream. No one felt the need to dissect it further. The artefacts had spoken in their own way, and

Nathan's system had logged them with clinical precision. Whatever revelations they carried, they were now part of the record.

Sienna glanced at the closed screen, then smiled at Nathan. "A good conversation for another time?"

"A *very* good one," he said. "And long. But nothing at all unusual."

"Good," she replied with a knowing smile as if they shared an inside joke.

"Yup"

"Well, that was educational." Chad concluded, gazing out to sea, then turned to Tim.

Rhys looked at Chaiyala, who shrugged, and shook her head with a wry smile.

With the artefacts secured, and the moment digested, the room began to feel less like a vault and more like a living space again. The tension dissolved—not dismissed, but folded neatly into the day's strange rhythm. They didn't need to solve it all now. They just needed to move forward.

Everyone seemed to snap out of it, turning their attention back to Crouton and Tim, wondering what to do next.

"I think we all need to get our heads out of Atlantis," Nathan suggested, "Atlantium, and pyramid controversy—and get some fun and relaxation in. Quite frankly, I'm starving. I could do with lunch."

"Absolutely!" Crouton agreed.

Tim, Charlotte, Chad, and Chaiyala decided to get lunch at the pools precinct and spend the afternoon in the water.

Rhys headed to the penthouse gym. Sienna would join him after speaking with her father about the morning's events.

Rod went to his room to call Kristie, after agreeing with Nathan's suggestion to order a few platters for lunch.

CHAPTER 21

T
im, exhausted, walked hand in hand with Charlotte, grateful for Nathan's perfectly timed escape. Behind them, Chad and Chaiyala followed, making their way along the Atrium toward the Splash Swim-up Bar at The Caribbean Skillet. They stashed their towels in a locker, then stepped into the water.

"Oh, that's so good," Chad said with pleasure, floating into the middle of the pool.

Chaiyala followed him in, with Tim and Charlotte close behind.

"I'm ready for a drink," Tim said as they made their way around the corner to the bar.

"Yes! Something cool and refreshing—and lasts forever!" Charlotte agreed.

Tim ordered a 'Tropical Chaos'—peach, pineapple, and cherry with a double shot of Appleton's White. Charlotte chose a 'Splash of Paradise'—passion fruit, banana, mango, pineapple, and Malibu. Chaiyala ordered the same. Chad, in the mood for something chocolaty and relaxing, asked if they could make him a 'Big Bad Wolf.'

"Fill me in, brudda," the bartender said with a big smile and a thick Jamaican accent. "Never heard o' dat, but if ya tell me da instructions and ingredients, I make it for you."

Chad crafted an indulgent chocolate cocktail—layering chocolate ice cream, Coruba, Kahlúa, Baileys, milk chocolate sauce, and chocolate milk into a massive glass. Topped with whipped cream and chocolate chips, it stunned onlookers. The bar owner was so impressed, he added the 'Big Bad Chad' to the menu.

As they swam, Chaiyala asked about its origins. Chad revealed it was inspired by a creation from back home—improved. They laughed, enjoying the moment and admiring Chad's creativity.

The pool precinct buzzed with relaxed energy—chatter from nearby diners blending with the sound of cascading water and tropical birdsong. Islands of ferns, palms, and exotic plants broke up the landscape, where macaws squawked, and capuchin monkeys clambered over rocks and tree trunks.

They slid into a horseshoe-shaped booth with underwater seating, tucked among towering yuccas and aloes in vibrant ceramic pots. One of many quiet corners scattered throughout the pools.

"Yup, this all does the trick," Tim said, easing into the serenity.

"This is fun! I could so get used to this place every day," Charlotte said.

"Nah... far too many people," Chad muttered.

"It's good—for a holiday," Chaiyala offered, "Just don't let it turn into too much of a good thing."

"Good point," Tim agreed.

"Don't get me wrong—I love it here," Chad added, nodding to Charlotte.

"Chaiyala," Charlotte said, remembering something she'd been meaning to ask, "have you ever been to the Outer Islands, the other times you've stayed here?"

"No, not me. But Rod, Crouton—and Nathan—they've been. Supposed to be chill during the day. Lively at night. Three islands. One's a party spot.

One has a lagoon—barbecue kind of place. The third? Overwater restaurant. Paddleboarding too."

"We should totally check it out!" Charlotte said enthusiastically.

"Keen," Chad nodded, glancing at Chaiyala, who agreed.

"Cool, let's do it then. I'll go make the booking?" Tim offered.

"Yes!" Charlotte beamed.

"Yeah man, count us in," Chad said, speaking for he and Chaiyala.

Charlotte and Tim got out and headed to the nearby booking kiosk.

She took Tim's hand as they exited the pool. Once retrieving their towels, they entered the palm-thatched hut—its layout resembling a travel agency. Four staff worked behind counters—two on laptops, one assisting guests.

One of the agents—Marcus introduced himself and greeted them warmly. He asked their names, and inquired about their stay before helping.

"We're wanting to book for the Outer Islands Experience," Tim said.

Marcus cheerfully pulled up a brochure and recommended the "All Day Island One" package—home to the Chill Out Bar by day and a lively Night Party after sundown. Charlotte and Tim were intrigued by the variety of options, including the Island Lagoon Barbecue, paddle-boarding, and the Over Water Paradise Restaurant. After some discussion, they agreed to start with Island One and consider a multi-island experience later.

Marcus explained the perks, including access to nearby islands and unlimited transport. Tim booked for six, hoping Rhys and Sienna would join, and asked to charge it to Nathan's tab.

"Oh, you're with Nathan? Wonderful!" Marcus said. "In that case, each ticket will be upgraded to the exclusive Caribbean Club option, which gives you access to all three islands' features for up to three days. You'll still have the come-and-go option, so you can return to the main resort any time within that window. And since you're with Nathan, your Outer Island

Experience begins now—normally it starts at 8 a.m. I'll email your exclusive VIP tickets now—one moment."

"Awesome! Thanks so much!" Tim exclaimed.

"You're very welcome. We like to look after Nathan and his friends," Marcus said with a warm smile. He paused with an afterthought. "Oh—when you're on the Outer Islands, ask about Brooke's Island... and how to get there." He raised his eyebrows, trying to sound confident—though he had no idea where the suggestion had come from. Internally, he scolded himself for acting on impulse but set aside the oddness in favour of professionalism.

Tim and Charlotte made a quiet mental note about Brooke's Island, then rejoined Chad and Chaiyala, having booked the tickets.

~~~~~~~

Rhys and Sienna appreciated being included in the visit to the Outer Islands. Nathan, Rod, and Crouton encouraged them to make the most of the experience. They thanked Nathan for his generosity before heading from the penthouse to the docks.

On the opposite side of the Shrimp and Marlin from its jungle gardens and function area, a boardwalk led them along the base of a rocky outcrop. A cliff face towered to their right, vines, wild grasses, and tropical plants growing from its cracks and crevices. To the left, a barrier of boulders and jagged rock shards lined the boardwalk, which ended at a palm-thatched hut with a checkout counter and guest lounge for charter boat passengers.

They arrived just in time, joining the queue as a host checked tickets and wished everyone a great evening. Tim scanned their electronic tickets, and each received a gold VIP wristband—granting them exclusive three-day access—before boarding the boat to the Outer Islands.

As the sun dipped low, they arrived at Island One's Chill Out Bar. A dusty path led them through palms to a sandy expanse beneath a shade sail, set with tables, bean bags, loungers, and a small library. That evening, it would transform into the Caribbean Island Night Party. A rustic bar nestled between the beach and jungle overlooked the ocean, waves lapping nearby. As they surveyed the scene, a DJ set up for the night's festivities.

"This is gonna be awesome!" Sienna grinned.

"Aye," agreed Rhys.

Tim nodded as they took it all in. Chad and Chaiyala were eager to explore.

"Let's go for a walk and check out the other two islands before we come back here later," she suggested.

"Yeah, keen," Tim agreed, and the others followed as Rhys and Sienna led the way. A sandy path took them through tall palms and tropical underbrush to the eastern shore of Island One, where a boardwalk stretched a hundred meters over the shallows. Schools of tropical fish and several turtles swam below.

A cheerful host in board shorts and a white rash shirt approached, his dreadlocks falling past his shoulders.

"Hail and welcome," he greeted in Jamaican Patois. "Would you care to try paddleboarding? Or would you prefer to enjoy the culinary wonders of our master barbecue chef, Enzo?"

"What are we doing first?" Tim asked, glancing around.

"I'm super keen for paddleboarding if you guys are," Charlotte expressed.

"I'm in," nodded Chad.

Rhys and Tim nodded in agreement. Sienna smiled. "Yah, this should be fun!" Chaiyala chimed in.

The host with the dreads and an easy grin stepped forward, "Great! I'm Agwe—one of the hosts here on the second of the three outer islands—and I will be your paddleboarding guide this evening. If you'll follow me..."

He led the group toward a small shed that looked like an extended bus stop—bench seating, a rack for coats and bags, and a tidy supply of paddles. Nearby, he rolled open the door of a second shed, revealing two dozen paddleboards stacked neatly inside. Tim, Charlotte, and Rhys exchanged glances—they looked like surfboards, only thicker.

"Any of you paddle boarded before?" Agwe asked.

Sienna and Chaiyala raised their hands.

"Perfect," he said. "We'll be using 'All Round' SUPs tonight. A SUP is a 'Stand Up Paddleboard.' They come in various sizes, but All Rounds are the most versatile—ideal for beginners. If you're more experienced, feel free to grab a shorter board."

"Charlotte, this—you get fast. You're dancer, it'll help," Chaiyala smiled.

"You're a dancer?" Agwe lit up. "Then you're halfway there! Paddleboarding is a slow, steady dance—with the paddle and the water."

Charlotte smiled and boogied playfully, already warming to the mood.

Chaiyala and Rhys unzipped their hoodies. Charlotte and Sienna dressed down to swimwear underneath. Tim and Chad ditched their shirts and footwear.

Agwe scanned the group. "You're all dressed appropriately—boardies and swimwear. The evening's warm, so even if you fall in, you'll dry off quickly. You can stash your gear on the rack," Agwe offered.

Once everyone was ready, he and the experienced pair helped the others choose the right SUPs and paddles. Agwe demonstrated how to carry both, then led them to a calm stretch of shoreline where they could launch easily.

"The lagoon's shallow—mostly a meter deep until about fifty meters out, where it drops off halfway to the resort beach precinct."

They placed their boards in water deep enough to keep the fins clear of sand. Agwe clapped his hands. "Three steps: stand up, paddle forward, turn left and right. Then you'll be masters. I'll be your employee, and you'll get rich running your own paddleboarding business."

They all laughed with him.

"When you're ready, climb onto your board on your knees first. You should feel stable—kneeling or standing. If not, switch to a longer board. A lot of people give up because they start on the wrong size."

Everyone seemed comfortable with their boards. Agwe nodded. "Good. Now watch me stand up—and hopefully not fall off."

He demonstrated with ease. The group followed, with Chaiyala betting Rhys he'd bail several times before finding his balance.

"Aye, and if I get it first go, you can swim back to the resort," Rhys teased.

"You don't make it, you swim back. That's deal," Chaiyala shot back, eyes narrowed, then smiled cheekily.

Agwe was about to explain what *not* to do when Rhys beat him to it—standing too quickly, celebrating too soon, and toppling into the water. Chad laughed so hard he lost his balance and fell in too. The rest burst out laughing.

"You swim back—I ride next to you, yes?" Chaiyala teased.

Rhys swore good-naturedly and made a mental note to drink too much later to attempt any swimming.

Agwe chuckled. "I was just about to say—feet shoulder-width apart—parallel. Don't stand like a surfer. As Rhys kindly demonstrated—yes, he meant to do that, of course—that stance will throw your balance."

Rhys grinned and shook his head as the group laughed again.

Eventually, everyone found their footing. Agwe moved on to paddling technique.

"There are a few basic ways to paddle forward," he explained. "All of them use the paddle as a lever. Don't grip it like a broomstick—that'll throw your balance and send you skyward like a witch. Well, not really. You'll just fall in again."

More chuckles.

"Top hand goes on the end of paddle—that's your driver. Bottom hand rests around waist height. Bury the blade in the water, and push the top of the shaft forward. That motion drives the blade and moves you forward."

The group practised, adjusting their grip and stance. The water was calm, the light golden, and the rhythm of movement began to settle into something fluid—almost meditative.

Agwe walked them through the final steps—how to adjust their stance, grip the paddle, and manoeuvre in straight lines and turns—then left them to explore. "Sing out if anyone needs help!" he called, moving between them—watching and guiding.

Tim drifted toward the eastern end of the lagoon, drawn by the quiet. The sun was beginning to set behind the palm-lined horizon of the Island. Hosts moved along the shore, lighting torches on stakes embedded in the sand, casting a warm glow that gave the place a 'survivor island' vibe. Across the water, the Caribbean Paradise Resort shimmered in the distance, backed by the lush Jamaican highlands.

Behind him, Rhys and Chad were laughing—Tim smiled, grateful. Chad had finally shaken off the weight of home and the noise that had plagued his headspace for too long. He was himself again, and Tim was stoked the others had welcomed him in so easily.

Rhys paddled up beside Sienna, who was lost in thought. "Hey," he said. "Hey," she smiled. "This is so beautiful."

They looked out over the lagoon. The air was warm, the water still. For a moment, everything felt right.

"I'm glad the others booked us tickets."

"Me too. Let's make the most of our time here."

She glanced at him, her eyes saying more— "...*our time together.*"

"We will. How long are you staying?"

"As long as you are. Nathan and my dad are planning to stay the full week."

"Seven nights."

"Good."

"Does your dad know?"

"Nope. Probably. Dunno. Nothing official to know yet, right?"

"I guess."

"Why? You worried?"

"Not really. I just want him to be okay with it."

"I don't see why he wouldn't be..."

Rhys smiled. They glanced around, checking if anyone was watching. Chad was grinning, paddling toward Charlotte and Chaiyala, who were skimming the edge of the lagoon. What was he up to?

Tim looked down at his paddle. *That's a lot of sound for one paddle*, he thought. Then—bam. A sudden thud from his right sent him flying off his board. He landed with a splash in the shallows, spun around, ready to tackle whoever had ambushed him.

He expected Chad. But it was Charlotte, grinning mischievously, with Chaiyala laughing nearby.

Tim laughed, distracted by his fiancée now trying to get him in a head-lock. Meanwhile, Chad snuck up on Chaiyala and gently nudged her into the water. Rhys and Tim cracked up—just as Sienna shoved a shocked Rhys off his board with a splashy "Woah!"

More laughter erupted. "Let's get him!" Sienna shouted to Chaiyala.

Sienna paddled hard toward Chad, who scrambled to escape the two experienced boarders closing in fast. She reached him first, shoved his shoulder, and sent him flying. Chaiyala wrapped her arms around him mid-fall, dunking him under.

"Woo-hoo!" Sienna cried, striking a victory pose. "Last woman standing!"

"Go Sienna!" Charlotte cheered.

Rhys and Tim laughed. Chad emerged, grinning menacingly at Chaiyala. They locked hands and wrestled in the water.

Tim and Charlotte climbed back onto their boards. "Race to the mouth of the lagoon and back to the shed!" Tim shouted.

"Last back cooks breakfast!" Charlotte added.

They all loved cooking—especially breakfast. Whipping up a meal for each other was more reward than punishment. But in the heat of the moment, the race was everything.

They scrambled to their boards, paddling hard toward the mouth of the lagoon. At least two of them were already masters at it.

The boys were all grit and determination, trying to pull ahead. But the girls had other plans. With a few exchanged glances and subtle nods, they agreed to sabotage the guys before take-off.

Chad and Rhys were just setting out when Chaiyala reached over and shoved Chad off balance. "No way!" he shouted, splashing in. Rhys swore as his foot was yanked sideways, and he tumbled in too.

Chaiyala and Sienna sped off, laughing. The guys, now fired up, scrambled back onto their boards and gave chase.

Tim dodged Charlotte's attempt to push him inshe nearly fell herself. He regained balance, saw what had happened to Chad and Rhys, and seized the lead. He'd picked up the technique faster than the other beginners, but he wasn't cocky. He knew Chaiyala's strength and grace could outmatch brute speed.

To their surprise, a host stood on a SUP at the mouth of the lagoon, marking the turning point. "Come around the back of me!" she called, playing referee.

Agwe and his team, along with other guests, had gathered to watch the chaos unfold, swept up in the competitive energy.

Tim rounded the stationary SUP, just as Charlotte's plan to knock him off was thwarted by the host's presence.

"Feet apart! Shoulder width!" Agwe shouted from shore. "Not the surfing stance!"

Chad and Rhys, desperate to catch up, had shifted into surfer mode—wrong move. Their boards wobbled, then dumped them back into the water.

Rhys cursed. Chad laughed, then narrowed his eyes at Chaiyala, who paddled past with Sienna close behind. She poked her tongue out at the two soaked boys.

They reached the shoreline near the equipment shed to cheers from guests and hosts alike. Agwe and his team clapped and laughed as Chad and Rhys finally made it back, this time staying upright.

Sienna hugged Rhys, smiling cheekily. He shook his head and smiled at her.

"You get beaten by me—again. It's becoming habit," Chaiyala teased, slipping an arm around Chad's shoulder.

"Shut up," Rhys muttered, grinning sheepishly.

They all laughed.

"Aww," she said, "we're still friends though."

"Yes, and I'm gonna prove it by cooking you breakfast. What ya gonna do?" Rhys shot back, grinning.

Chaiyala gave him a blank stare. They burst out laughing again. She rested her head on Chad's shoulder, smiling playfully at Rhys.

A host directed them to a table with two chillers filled with bottles of chilled water, ginger beer, and assortment of beers. Between them, a large bowl of Appleton's tropical punch awaited. They gratefully selected drinks and relaxed, taking in the atmosphere.

They were introduced to the island barbeque chef—Enzo, who moved meat around on a hotplate—creating a heavenly aroma.

Enzo's accent puzzled Tim, Chad, and Charlotte—it sounded Canadian, with hints of New Zealand and South African. When Chad asked, Enzo explained he was born in South Africa, moved to Christchurch at age ten, studied in Otago, and later immigrated to Canada.

As he grilled jerk chicken, Rhys revealed his Scottish-Māori heritage, proudly naming his iwi, Ngāti Tūwharetoa. Enzo recognized the region, and Rhys shared how he'd moved to New Zealand at nineteen to reconnect with his roots. His unique accent impressed and surprised Enzo.

They all laughed, sipped drinks, and joined the other guests at the tables as Enzo cheerfully announced the food was ready.

A lavish barbecue spread covered a massive sequoia table. Skewered king prawns in coconut and lime marinade, Caribbean-spiced tuna, towering Jamaican jerk chicken, Cajun pork steaks, and scotch fillet in sweet rum marinade, alongside pineapple chicken kebabs and jerk vegetables. Chilled desserts lined one end, salads the other.

Rhys enjoyed the jerk chicken, Chad and Sienna savoured pork with mango chicken salad. Tim loaded up on prawns and kebabs, while Chaiyala added Caribbean tuna with Jamaican rice and pea salad before tackling the scotch fillet.

Rhys and Enzo stood at a tall bar table with Tim, Chad, and Charlotte, continuing their conversation. While Sienna and Chaiyala chatted with a South African couple and two Australians touring the Americas from Alaska to Argentina.

Enzo shared with them "I spend winters at the Alpine Paradise Ski Resort in British Columbia and summers here at Caribbean Paradise—both owned by Maurice Chipolatto. I started with Paradise Hotels up there, and it's been the best season of my career."

The six friends spoke a little about where they were from, careful not to delve too deeply into the specifics of their work—for security reasons. Though their association with Nathan O'Conner was secure by design, with built-in safeguards, Chad and Charlotte moved through the dynamic with a quieter ease—less exposed, but still mindful. Their margin for error was wider, yet the expectation of discretion remained.

CHAPTER 22

A ll were grateful to Agwe for the paddleboarding experience and to Enzo for the food they'd enjoyed. Chad and Charlotte made sure to get selfies with their new friends from the Outer Islands before slowly making their way back along the boardwalk. The sun had begun to set, leaving a peachy glow in the sky slightly left of Island One. The view was now a tropical silhouette of palms, a thatched hut, and the shelter for the bar by day and the party by night.

Tim and Charlotte led the way across the boardwalk, leaving behind the paddleboarding island and its smoky Caribbean BBQ. They stepped back onto the party island, drawn toward the pulse of music rising beyond the palm trees.

Flaming torchlight illuminated the path toward the bar, and they found themselves in what was earlier the quiet, peaceful venue, had been completely transformed into a high energy party atmosphere. The DJ stood on a raised plinth behind twin turntables, mixing and jiving as he guided the crowd through the highs and lows of his musical creation.

Rhys, wasting no time, returned from the bar with his first two drinks and a couple of Sienna's favourites. She smiled gratefully as they let themselves get swept up in the terpsichorean mayhem spilling across the sandy dance floor. Charlotte stole the scene for a while and caught the DJ's eye, warranting a beat that matched her style and somehow managed to progress into some spectacular break dancing on the carpet at the centre of the crowd. Tim stood back and watched with excited admiration.

She concluded her display of dancing prowess to an applause from all including the DJ and joined Tim, Chaiyala and Chad at a low table between the bar and dance floor. They savoured drinks and an exceptional tropical cheesecake, a fortunate freebie from a catering mix-up—Chad happened to be in the right place at the right time. He insisted that if he'd been caught up in dancing instead of standing back, enjoying the music and observing, moments like this wouldn't come his way.

He pointed across the beach out to the water with his Jim Beam stubby, "What's that out over there?"

The others scanned the area he indicated, squinting or shading their eyes against the dance floor's bright LEDs and laser lights. In the distance, across the water, a flickering bonfire glowed in the darkness.

"Aye! It's a floating bonfire!" Rhys joked, feigning expert knowledge.

Tim, Chad and Chaiyala frowned and laughed.

"That's Brooke's Island, I think." Sienna remembered.

"Yeah... that'd be it," Tim said. "The booking agent, after learning that we were with Nathan O'Conner made the suggestion I ask about 'Brooke's Island' and how to get there."

Chaiyala gave Tim a look of warning. "Yah, Nathan's involved? Then, yeah. You'll need a seatbelt—and maybe a helmet."

Rhys and Sienna were torn between caution and adventure.

"Here we go..." Chad inwardly prepared himself for more crazy.

"That there's most certainly Brooke's Island," said a rustic voice with a Cockney accent from the end of the bar. "Named after the crazy lady who resides upon it. Loopy as you'll ever get, she is." The bar manager shuddered. "Gives me the shivers, she does."

"So, what's her deal?" asked Tim.

"Her deal? Who knows, most likely been there longer than this resort's been open. As long as I've been managing this island." He turned around and shouted some instruction to a staff member about a few boxes of RTDs.

"If it's the same person I'm thinking of," Sienna suspected, "I'd heard she was some kind of local witch doctor."

"Worse, and crazier." warned the bar manager. "Some go over there out of curiosity, but this crazy cat lady has used curiosity as a murder weapon to kill many a curious cat, so to speak. No one comes back the same." He told them, shaking his head disapprovingly. "No, I wouldn't bother with that nutter, that be for sure... so don't be askin' how to find passage across there."

"How do we get over there?" Tim asked, as if he hadn't been warned.

"Tim..." Chad sighed, shaking his head.

Charlotte giggled silently.

Chaiyala and Sienna observed the jaded, look of resignation on his face.

"Not happening, sorry." He shook his head. "I wouldn't take you over there for a grand!"

"What about two grand?" Tim produced a fat wad of cash.

There were frowns from more than just the bar manager.

"Three thousand." The bar manager looked at Tim as if he dared him to back down.

Tim produced another two thousand and called, "it's a deal!" He pat the bar manager on the shoulder and told him "Business is good tonight, my friend. Consider that a gift, fair payment for your troubles, a financial blessing—whatever you like." Tim got a curious response from his friends.

"A'right," the bar manager sighed, "Step foot on that island at your own risk though." He thought for a second then introduced himself as Sy.

"Yav been hanging around Nathan too much!" Sienna suggested.

"Bad inf'uence 'e is, on you lad!" Rhys slurred subtly.

Charlotte regarded him with a bewildered smile. "Why on earth do you have four grand sitting in your pocket like that?" she demanded.

"You're drunk." Tim told Rhys.

"Not yet, I'm not, just a little, having fun." He replied with a silly grin.

Sy had gone to organise passage across the three hundred-meter stretch between them and Brooke's island.

Chad was clearly at odds with the amount his brother had simply thrown away so flippantly.

"Dude, you just spent more on a boat ride to a silly island not even half a kilometre away than most people spend flying around the world." He looked at Tim, concerned.

Charlotte wasn't as hung up on it as his brother appeared to be, but was surprised none-the-less. She was also a fraction worried about Chad's attitude toward it.

Rhys was dancing away to the music in his own little world.

Sienna, no way near as tipsy as he appeared, yet was enjoying the atmosphere herself while keeping a cautious eye to make sure he stayed out of trouble.

Chaiyala rested her elbows on the end of the bar and facing the crowd politely but firmly declining offers from some male party-goers.

Chad'd noticed, but was preoccupied. While he was hung up on the money thing, he'd a vague awareness he was 'stuck' on it and could faintly hear someone yelling and banging on a door at the back of his mind trying to snap him out of it.

"Yes," Tim agreed, "and I paid pretty much double on two tickets from Auckland to Paris the other day. I'll do it again, no questions asked if someone needs it."

Chad was still frowning, remembering his gratitude for Tim's generosity. Alas, he couldn't get past the amount he felt his brother had thrown away like this.

"But, what about people in need? You just threw away four grand," he accused in disbelief.

"Who's to say that bar manager isn't in need?"

"What the hang?"

"Clearly, he's on a huge salary and can afford all he could want or need?" Tim suggested before his brother could argue it.

Chad's frown screwed up his nose, wondering what Tim was going to say next and if he'd missed something. There was still the banging and shouting in the back of his mind that kept up his awareness he was hung up and going nowhere with it.

"Chad," Charlotte said gently, "money's only an issue if you make it one." She and Tim both lived in a world free from the control, need, or dependence on it—and she knew he was still learning that.

"You never know who might be struggling financially, or who might need that kind of money to fix the car, get to a wedding, pay for an operation, or funeral they can't get to cos of cost. So, it pays, when you have been given much, to be generous with much."

"What if he's a druggy?" Chad had done it again, half of him was determined to keep pushing the envelope, the other half was mad at him for being so judgemental and presumptuous, once more, like his outburst in Mauritania regarding Nathan. But this one surprised even Chad.

Charlotte sighed quietly and looked away. She saw Chaiyala who'd heard that last part of the conversation but not the rest. Chaiyala could see Chad wasn't happy and looked his way with concern.

"Chad, brother," Tim held him by his shoulders and spoke calmly with a smile, "slow down... again, how would you know? I don't... sometimes you just have to go with your heart and be a blessing in someone's life and, just, leave it at that. I dunno... it's a faith thing. The thing you don't do, is get all hoo-ha and worry about all the risks and finer points, otherwise you'll never do anything worthwhile."

Chad exhaled a big breath and settled a little. What Tim had said, made sense to him, while it might not stand up in court, that was hardly the point. He still felt Tim had been irresponsible.

"Would it have made any difference if it hadn't had been money I gave him?"

"Yes." Chad replied almost instantly—surprising himself again.

"Hmm." Tim left it there.

"Forget it for now, Chad. Let's just enjoy the night," Chaiyala said, taking his arm with a kind smile.

"Yeah, you're right. Stuff... doesn't even matter eh. I'm sorry bro, I dunno... I just..." he apologized to Tim.

"It doesn't matter bro. You don't need to try and explain or make sense out of anything. Chaiyala's right. There's tonight, friends, all of this to enjoy."

Sienna had Rhys scull back a bottle of water a few metres away as Sy returned with a companion.

Tim observed the way Rhys was standing... he wasn't drunk, not *that* drunk. If he was, he'd have fallen over now on that angle.

Sy introduced his companion to Tim, "Gustefan here, will transport you across to Brooke's Island." He then saw Chad, Charlotte and wasn't sure if the other three were with them or not... "How many of you are there?"

"Six of us."

The bar manager paused momentarily—bewildered—shook his head "you're all crazy! I hope you're prepared for this woman. Regardless,

Gustefan will take you across in my dinghy." The bar manager pointed to where the craft sat on the sand a few meters from the water.

"Thank you so much, really appreciate it."

"Don't you dare tell her I sent you."

"Wouldn't dream of it," Tim replied warily. "Thanks again, Sy—you're a legend."

Gustefan got the six friends safely across the water in an LED-lit, motorised inflatable dinghy. He assured them he'd remain on shore for as long as they needed and added, with a note of caution in his voice, "If anything goes wrong, shout loudly, and I'll activate a flare... just get back here as fast as you can."

Once they were all on the sand, they made their way down the darkened beach toward a small group of people gathered near a large bonfire. It wasn't massive, but it was certainly no marshmallow-toasting camp fire either.

"We are going to be safe here, right?" Charlotte asked Tim.

"Hadn't actually given it a lot of thought," Tim admitted.

"Exciting," she laughed.

"We're all gonna die," Chad said with deadpan indifference.

Chaiyala smirked at his morbid humour.

"I thought so. That's why I brought the rest of my drinks," Rhys grinned at Sienna.

"Did you bring mine?"

Rhys handed her a bottle of Dragon Stout.

"Thank you," she beamed.

As they approached the seated gathering, a woman with long dark brown dreadlocks hanging just shy of the sand beneath her bare feet welcomed them to "The Free Island of Enlightenment." She introduced herself as 'Brooke the Liberator' and invited them to sit on one of several large, colourful cushions scattered around the space.

Tim dropped onto a huge pillow and placed his Corona in the sand. Charlotte snuggled up beside him. Rhys and Sienna did the same on cushions nearby. Chad leaned on half a large pillow, propped on one elbow, while Chaiyala, on the other half, lay back on both elbows.

Brooke sat and continued speaking as if they'd arrived late to a class the teacher couldn't care less about.

Rhys, half-asleep and in a silly mood, appeared drunk enough to feel it but not act on it. He rested his head on Sienna's tummy, gazing across the water toward the Outer Islands, wondering why they weren't still over there partying. But it was all part of his strategy. He'd had three drinks— he could triple that before getting tipsy. In truth, he was working. He and Chaiyala were on bodyguard duty.

They surveyed the island's eclectic group. Brooke might as well have been preaching Amish theology to stuffed toys.

To her left, near Tim and Charlotte, sat an unusual teenage couple. The boy, with metallic blue hair, nodded occasionally, eyes closed. He wore an oversized striped shirt and denim shorts that looked better suited to his girlfriend—the only one remotely grounded. She had long platinum curls in twin ponytails, white ribbons, and an outdated sleeveless white dress. Her stark white makeup contrasted with her tanned arms. A skateboard rested on her pillow as she leaned against him, the only person besides Brooke who acknowledged their arrival.

Beside them, a round-faced man in his fifties rocked back and forth, face covered in mysterious tattoos, tattered clothes and crudely stitched skin hinting at hard times. Nearby, a sun-drenched Crocodile Dundee lookalike in '70s zookeeper gear chuckled sporadically, lost in his own world.

Across from them sat a figure resembling Gandalf the wizard, clutching a Kahlúa bottle. Along from him, a wrinkled figure with long frizzy blond hair in a cream bathrobe, neither overtly male nor female, scowling with amusement as they inhaled from a bong every few minutes. Their presence felt curated—like a disguise meant to be forgotten.

"What an interesting group," Sienna thought. Harmless—yet on another planet.

Chad and Charlotte were mostly along for the ride. Though this pushed it—the bizarre little excursion was entertaining.

Brooke, likely in her early thirties, looked weary beyond her years. Her dark, exotic features and piercing eyes sparkled when she smiled—but chilled the heart when she scowled.

She launched into five minutes of disjointed rants. Barely finishing a thought before interrupting herself, she jumped between topics—they found her very hard to understand.

Chad, Tim, and Chaiyala wondered if she had ADHD—and found it a little spooky when, at that exact moment, she blurted something about vaccine needles causing aluminium build-up in the brain and causing ADHD.

Rhys tuned out—nearly dozing off—until his pillow moved as Sienna's tummy tensed with quiet giggles shared with Charlotte—mostly at Brooke's choice of words and complaints.

"None of them did a damned thing to help... stupid swine!" she ranted. "I'm glad I came after them—all of them. Stupid 'Edenites'. Stuffed up the world back then, they did! Fakes, the lot! Well, most of them. Some were just vague apparitions forged in the quarries of desperate minds—scrounging around in the desert in the shadow of those monstrous egg generators their forefathers used to ruin the world—again! Just like we had!" Her face contorted, and her eyes went black as she hissed.

Tim sat back and frowned. Chad did a double take. Charlotte and Sienna jumped. Rhys shot up to see what was going on, then lay back down.

"Osiris was up to no good, of course, and made a killing with his and Isis's peon games. The gods became deities, and they came up with all kinds of silly bedtime stories to entertain primitive minds."

Chad wondered where this was going. Chaiyala wondered why they were even there. Tim, however, was waiting for something.

He wasn't sure what. But if Nathan's hint—passed through the booking agent—had led them here, there had to be some relevance in the madness.

"All the gods came from the Orion star system," Brooke continued. "But the government covered it all up with religion!" She scowled. "Sports and politics should never be mixed in a pot! Otherwise, this is what you get!" She swore.

Rhys dropped the drunk façade. He and Chaiyala were now assessing the environment for threats.

Tim and Chad exchanged a glance. This woman was definitely unhinged.

"And never use the noodle-pigeon! Those things are completely stupid! All they do is fling spaghetti farts. They did it at the Berlin Wall, the Pyramids of Iceland, and Rugby Park in Hamilton in 1981! It's all tied to the tinfoil industry! They're making a fortune off pointy hats and rump steaks—take steaks, Rustabums! Dammit!" She was getting irate, struggling to find the right words. Apparently, she was trying to recall the name of the U.S. president.

Somehow, the teen girl in white figured that out— "Rutherford?"

"Yes!"

The others shook their heads.

"She might as well be speaking in code, or she's mad." Chad thought.

Brooke shot daggers at him and started to rise.

Chaiyala returned the look on Chad's behalf, ready for confrontation.

"Alimentary paste skirt chaser... sharks that eat spaghetti..." muttered the Gandalf wizard guy.

Brooke burst out laughing. So did the Crocodile Dundee lookalike, who fell over in the sand and stayed there.

"Idiot," Brooke snarled, then carried on. "God and the satan were among them—biggest egos of the lot. Both came from Orion's Belt."

"It gets better and better," Rhys muttered.

"One of the Orionite aliens looked human. The other, a serpent with arms and legs. All the racists descend from God, and all the slaves from the serpent—who God turned into a snake. And that apple story? Total fabrication! The whole Bible—an elaborate scam to control the masses! It has to be!" Her eyes were wild. "No human could conceive such mathematically strung-together hogwash with prophecies that all come true! It's a long-term con—ancient. Determined. Blinding them all like the Matrix! And they exterminated them all—the humanoid serpents, the giants— wiped out! Every government forbids their history in museums and textbooks!" She swore again.

Croc Dundee was now fast asleep in the sand. The round-faced man in rags still rocked back and forth—mind clearly elsewhere. The teenagers had vanished into the bushes. The mysterious character in the bathrobe had earlier gotten up, walked five meters, flipped the bird at Gandalf, then collapsed and now whined or laughed every few minutes. Gandalf himself had been asleep for most of Brooke's rant.

"You still haven't told me who you are and why you're here—you two... three." She pointed at Tim, Chad, and Charlotte with suspicion, almost accusation.

Everyone except Tim was caught off guard. Even he was slightly surprised—but focused on the fact that Brooke had singled out him, his fiancée, and his brother. He preferred it that way. Tim was working. Chad and Charlotte were his guests. Involving Sienna, Chaiyala, or Rhys would've required more explanation. Simplicity was best with someone like Brooke.

They exchanged puzzled glances. Tim took the lead.

"I'm Tim, an independent investigative historian. On a kind of working holiday." He gestured to Charlotte and Chad. "This is my fiancée, Charlotte, and my brother, Chad."

Brooke studied them, eyes narrowed. A slight smile played on her lips.

"You two are engaged," she observed.

They confirmed cheerfully.

"Oh, how lovely. That's so good," Brooke said, her tone sincere—at first. But her expression drifted into something unreadable. It was hard to tell if she didn't care or had remembered something sad.

"And you," she snapped, turning to Chad. "Your eyes tell me you have a million questions. But your body language says you're hurting. And your heart is burning—in *more* ways than *one*." Her voice shifted. "Not because of her... but because of her... who? Oh, where'd she go? She was right here..."

Tim and Chad exchanged a glance. Chad looked at Chaiyala, confused.

"There were three others! Where have they gone?" Brooke stood, agitated. "No, actually... there weren't," she corrected herself, sitting back down. "It was probably Leila and Tommy I'm thinking of. Those two promiscuous little parasites—off in the bushes coitusing on *my* island!" She was bitterly upset about that part.

"Oookay," Chad breathed.

Charlotte kept glancing at Tim, who remained focused. He and Chaiyala figured Brooke was referring to the two teenagers who'd left earlier.

"You are, are you?" Brooke said, returning to Tim.

"Sorry?"

"You're a historian."

"Oh—yes! Six years now," Tim replied. "Currently researching pre-Columbian civilizations in the Caribbean."

Brooke looked out across the water. It was hard to tell if she was listening or about to accuse him of lying.

Sienna wondered if the woman might be schizophrenic. Brooke's moods swung rapidly—pleasant one moment, creepy the next.

"There's definitely a lot of history in these islands," Tim offered.

"Most of it, I couldn't give a coconut for," Brooke snapped. "All madness and muppets, they who've been and gone and come back!" She swore. "That's why I stay here and tell the rest of those egotistical cockwombles to beggar off! They don't like me much." She grinned—a toothy, graveyard grin oddly in disparity with her pretty face. "That's why they don't come here. And I'm fine with that. They're all idiots for cursing the world."

She paused, suddenly despondent.

"But it leaves me lonely... which is why, I suspect, my brother keeps sending people here to keep me company."

Tim was caught completely off guard. He cocked his head and frowned.

"What?" she snapped.

"Ah, nothing. Go on..."

"You know him, don't you? You know my brother. That's why he sent you."

The others were puzzled beyond hope of reconciliation. Things had now illapsed into something stranger than strange. Of course, everything since stepping off the dinghy had been off-kilter—but Tim's reaction, and Brooke's in turn, made Chaiyala and Chad quietly confident there was more to this bizarre exchange than a mere suggestion from the booking agent. To the rest, it was just more discordant nonsense from the crazy lady's mouth.

"We have no idea who your brother is," Tim said plainly, glancing at the others for support.

They all shook their heads—equally confused and uncertain.

"Poseidon? Hippios? Neptune... whichever you like. All the same brother—or brothers. I don't know, I can't remember everything!" she snapped at Tim, as if he were demanding too much, trying to pry something from her.

All three names were familiar to Tim. He stared at her, puzzled by her accusatory tone.

Silence. The bonfire crackled five meters away.

Rhys got up, selected a few logs from the pile, and tossed them on the fire. Brooke gave him an appreciative smile, then returned her serious gaze to Tim.

He frowned, ready to move things along. Just as he was about to ask about her brother, she broke the silence.

"Never mind. Maybe you don't know him. It's hard to tell who he sends and who he doesn't..." Her despondent look returned, then shifted to a smile as she recalled something.

"Apparently, according to Samedi himself, my brother sent Baron Saturday to cheer me up one... Saturday!" She laughed, struck by the irony far more than anyone else. "Never saw where he arrived from, though," she added, narrowing her eyes.

Tim and Chad sensed she was about to say something important.

Chaiyala and Rhys remained silent and alert—intrigued, yet dismissive of much of what she said. Their focus remained on the safety of Tim, Charlotte, and Chad.

Sienna and Charlotte had drifted off—Charlotte resting her head on Tim's thigh, Sienna using Rhys's stomach as a pillow—

Having switched. A crab scuttled into the firelight, then vanished again into the shadows.

"Baron Saturday..." Tim echoed.

"Dresses like an undertaker—smokes cigars—twirls a cane. Face like a skull. When he's in graveyards, he's Baron Cimetiere—watches over cemeteries with a very grave expression." She grinned, waiting for the pun to land.

Tim and Chad offered polite smiles. Brooke narrowed her eyes at their disappointing response.

"Bashes grave robbers with a baseball bat and pokes out their eyes with his cane," she spat. "If they come near!" She glared grimly at them, then at Rhys and Chaiyala.

"We'll make a point of not robbing graveyards then, won't we, bro?" Tim said, maintaining eye contact with her.

Not that they ever had—or ever would.

"To be honest, I don't care," Brooke said flippantly. "Samedi was probably my brother's drinking buddy. Some say they've seen them together at the resort—filthy place of debauchery!" she spat. "Likes rum spiked with hot peppers, he does. Can't imagine my brother going for that, but anything's possible after enough of the stuff on a hot Caribbean Saturday night... even the odd chicken sacrifice."

"Sounds disgusting," Chaiyala thought.

"Saturday has a wife!" Brooke blurted, wide-eyed.

"Sunday?" Chad asked, grinning.

"No... no!" she snapped, shooting him a repugnant look. "Maman Brigitte. Daft woman, marrying a silly jungle of bones like Samedi."

You, and your fiancée, and your brother... no, not your brother... used to be?" Brooke shook her head. "Never mind. Not sure about you," she said to Chaiyala. "Probably. Actually, you're much like him," she concluded, nodding to Chad, who was as confused as ever. "Definitely not you—or her," she said to Rhys and Sienna. "Christians."

"Right!" Chad suddenly caught on.

Chaiyala gave him a puzzled look—until it clicked for her too. They both burst out laughing.

"Try and keep up, will you?" Tim joked, frowning.

Brooke grimaced, eyeing them with suspicion.

She continued, "It's way simpler for you two—one God, three persons. That's what you get when you don't let humans organise religion. There are over 2,500 so-called deities. In some parts of the world, it's a mess of who's who. But Christianity—just one God. What a refreshingly novel idea."

She scowled. "The idea that gods are meant to be worshipped is a stupid, irritating method of control. Governments and rulers made that up. Always been a conspiracy to manipulate thoughts, time and resources. You're being lied to!"

Tim felt a spark of recognition. Maybe they were finally getting somewhere.

Part of Chad wondered when this would all come together. Another part was certain there was something buried in the madness.

"He's a bit like Bondye, actually."

"Who is?" Tim asked.

"Jehovah. I'm pretty sure Bondye is the Caribbean equivalent. I lose track with that lot. That's the problem with not giving a Loa's ligature—you get out of touch with the madness."

"Oh, I'm pretty sure you're quite in touch with the madness," Rhys thought privately.

"How dare you! *Foolish* mortal!" she scolded.

Rhys looked startled. Tim stepped in. "Don't worry about him. What's the story with Bondye—and the gods not to be worshipped?"

Brooke calmed. Tim wanted to keep her on track—on account of a slither of hope they might be making progress. Finally.

"Bondye is uninterested. Away with the fairies. Always has been. No point bothering with that useless excuse for an administrator."

"So you call him an administrator, and say gods aren't meant to be worshipped?" Tim pressed.

This matched parts of the Solon Diaries.

Chad, Chaiyala, and Rhys had picked up on it too.

"They walk among mankind, you know—the gods," Brooke said.

Tim sighed. Was this going anywhere?

Brooke glowered at him.

He looked toward the bush, contemplating leaving. Maybe this was just one of those oddball moments one is meant to write off after all.

"Two thousand five hundred walking the earth, Tim. And none of them are deities. Never were. Never will be. There's only one who is—and that one comes three in one. I think we both know who that is."

Tim had no choice but to take her words as they came, sifting for relevance. Although, her tone had shifted however—no longer fragmented, but sharp and focused, even if still speaking in riddles.

"I also think," she said, looking across the water, "that you know—or have met—two or three of them already. Or will soon."

Tim furrowed his brow. What did she mean?

Her expression soured. She looked down at the sand.

"And they're all completely irritating," she muttered. "Like your politicians—carried away with their egos," she swore bitterly. "Civil servants, corrupted. No." She looked at Tim, then the others. "I want no part in that. They lost their way long ago."

Then he heard it: *"Ask her what she knows of Atlantean colonial activity in the area."*

"What?" he asked, looking at Chad.

"Ah... nothing..." Chad replied, confused.

Tim glanced at Charlotte, asleep in his lap, then at Chaiyala and Rhys—attentive—curious. No, the voice had come from Chad's direction, though he clearly hadn't spoken.

It was a whisper. Tim had heard it.

"Oh," he said casually. "What do you know of Atlantis? In particular, Atlantean activity in this part of the world?"

Rhys's eyes moved to Chaiyala. She smirked subtly.

"About time," Chad thought. His investigative mind mirrored his brother's. Though he hadn't thought of the question himself, he was relieved someone had finally asked the crazy lady something meaningful.

"Atlantis... hmm..." Brooke looked up into nowhere, as if the name itself stirred something. "Why do you ask me about Atlantis?"

"I've always had a passion for the idea," Tim said. "In my spare time, I research different theories and expeditions—anything I can find. I figured I'd put it out there, seeing as you sound pretty familiar with the old ways and lore of the region."

Brooke studied him carefully, glanced away in thought, then back with suspicion. Finally, she straightened—as if deciding Tim could be trusted, and began.

"Deep in the jungle—not far from here—in Cockpit Country, there's a toppled obelisk. What the Order of Kittim didn't realise was how much is buried *beneath* one of those things," she looked at Tim to ensure he was following.

Barely. He was applying educated guesses and waiting to see how far they'd get him.

"Most of the technology was underground, connected to the obelisk once it received energy. There was talk of copper ropes wrapped in fibrous carbon—powering lights, tools, machines. All the things the Atlanteans were going to bring with them... before they ruined the world." She sighed, "And that's all I know!" Her tone turned cynical, as if recalling that last detail soured everything.

"Do you know where we might find this toppled obelisk?" Tim asked.

"Kinloss. You'll need to go to Kinloss on the B10 highway, and find the Haddington New Testament Church. The pastor there is the steward of ancient archives that date back that far. Maybe he can help you."

Tim went to thank her—but they were interrupted by a splash in the shallows.

Brooke startled, wide-eyed, and stood. "He's here! Isn't he?"

"What? Who?" Tim was alert.

"You brought Poseidon with you! I can sense him!" Her eyes glowed white like headlights. Rhys and Chaiyala were already on their feet. Sienna stirred. Tim and Chad shifted uneasily—Tim hastily trying to wake Charlotte.

Chaiyala prepared to take Brooke, but the woman's wild—phantom-like rage made her hesitate. This was beyond her pay grade.

All hell was about to break loose. The wizard and Croc Dundee—suddenly sober—shouted and swore as glowing white waterfalls streamed from Brooke's eyes.

Chaiyala swore as Brooke levitated a foot off the sand.

"You fools!" she croaked.

Sienna jolted awake as Charlotte screamed. The group scrambled for the dinghy—kicking up sand as they ran.

"Hurry! Run!" Gustefan roared, firing up the outboard and launching a flare.

Brooke shrieked like something from another world—just as a ghostly figure emerged from behind the bonfire.

Rhys, Tim, and Chaiyala barely made out its shadowy form skipping along the sand—a skull in a top hat, grinning through lipless teeth, a cigar clamped between them. Draped in a tattered three-piece suit. It twirled a cane, chuckling before bursting into manic laughter.

Brooke spun toward the newcomer, screeching wildly—"SATURDAY!"

None of them wanted to see what happened next. It was hard enough sprinting through soft sand.

In one fluid motion, all six leapt into the dinghy, followed closely by Gandalf and Croc Dundee. Gustefan had them speeding full throttle across the water.

"What the hang happened?" Charlotte asked, still unsure if she was dreaming.

Sienna looked and felt like she hadn't fully woken—trapped in a living nightmare.

Rhys and Chaiyala glanced back. Brooke hovered above the sand, eyes blazing. The shadowy figure, bathed in bonfire glow, stared across the water—its hollow sockets filled with twisted glee.

They immediately regretted looking back.

Tim, Chad, Charlotte, and Sienna focused on the party island, where Sy and others had gathered, alerted by Brooke's shriek and Gustefan's flare. Security were already mobilising.

"Ha ha ha ha haa haa ha!" laughed Croc Dundee. He threw a wild gaze at Tim, then leapt overboard before they reached shore.

Sienna squealed as the man splashed through the final ten meters of water, coat tails flapping, top hat visible, cane swinging overhead. A spotlight caught him mid-stride. His laughter echoed into the night.

"What the blazes..." Tim shook his head. Chad did the same. Goosebumps rippled over them.

Gustefan grimaced. "That's the last time I ever take anyone over to that cursed island!"

"That, back there—that was next-level whacked," Rhys said as they climbed out of the dinghy.

"No kidding," Chaiyala muttered.

"Where's the wizard?" Chad asked.

Tim and Sienna looked around. "He's gone too," Tim said.

A dozen guests and staff, including Sy, rushed over—concerned, asking questions. Two burly men tried to chase the Baron—formerly Croc-Dundee—or so they'd thought—but he'd already vanished.

"That's crazy!" Charlotte said, still trying to process what she'd seen.

"I told you that was a crazy thing to do!" Sy greeted them, shaking his head. "I don't know what you did, but she's never lost the plot like that before. I hope you got your money's worth."

"Absolutely!" Tim said—ginning—slapping him on the shoulder.

"Your boyfriend is mad," Sy said to Charlotte.

She shook her head, finally settling. "Are you okay?" she asked Sienna.

"I think so," She replied as they hugged. "Are you?"

"Yes, now that I'm properly awake."

"So—we all saw that, right?" Chad asked.

"The crazy goat lady floating over the sand with bright white eyes and the spooky Skulduggery Pleasant lookalike puffing a cigar?" Tim grinned.

"You even got her to levitate?" Sy asked in disbelief—impressed—and a little concerned. "You've certainly added some excitement to the evening."

"MIDNIGHT!" someone shouted, and the beat of the music shifted to exotic Caribbean fusion—bongo drums, harmonica, didgeridoo, and pan flute.

"Ah, the midnight party with Kamakoa," Sy explained as a conga line formed. "Local band—bongo drums, an old guy with a harmonica, an Aboriginal lass on didgeridoo, a Cherokee fellow on pan flute, and usually a joker with bagpipes... but I can't hear him tonight."

The six friends were intrigued.

Tim leaned against the bar. Charlotte took his hand. Out of the corner of his eye, he spotted a tap labelled 'Baron Saturday'. He did a double take.

"No way," Charlotte grinned.

"Good grief—he even comes on tap!" Tim laughed.

"What? Who does?" Chad asked.

"Baron Saturday," Tim replied, shaking his head.

"Not bad, that. Good stout," Sy said.

"Alright, let's have it then," Tim said. Chad and Chaiyala were also keen.

The party was alive. The tropical night was warm and still.

"I'm shattered after all that," Rhys declared, holding a Corona with no enthusiasm.

"Same," Charlotte yawned. Normally, she, Rhys, and Sienna would be in the front of the conga line.

"Brooke's long been rumoured to be a sorceress," Sy began. "Messes with strange forms of Voodoo. She's all kinds of mad—depends on who you ask. Most who go over there are already intoxicated or come back that way. You six, are the exception... though," he looked at Rhys, "I've never known anyone to do it the other way around."

They laughed.

"All things considered, tonight's excursion sounds like the most dramatic so far—with the least casualties."

"Sorry?" Chad asked.

"It's been getting worse. People come back messed up—not always physically, but mentally. I don't know if it's worth the risk anymore."

"Fair enough." For the first time, Tim wondered if they should've gone at all. Still, his adventurous side—and confidence from above—reassured him.

At 12:15 a.m., Rhys noted the ferry would leave in fifteen. The friends strolled the sandy path through palms, agreeing they'd loved the Outer Islands experience—though Brooke's island had delivered far more than expected.

Chad and Tim wrestled with unanswered questions. But Tim couldn't stop thinking about the fallen obelisk—especially what it might mean for wireless energy and Atlantean colonization.

Meanwhile, Sienna's thoughts drifted to the night's eerie events. She remembered the ghostly figure captured on the Red Sword's dash-cam during Alesandro's chase.

They spoke softly of the unseen as they crossed into the resort, the hush of water and lantern light guiding them through the pool precinct toward the penthouse.

There was much more yet to see on this adventure.

~~~~~~~

They stepped into the penthouse suite to find Nathan, Crouton, Alesandro, and Rod scattered across the sofas, the movie had been paused upon their arrival.

The conversation flowed toward the Outer Islands. And—almost inevitably—found its way to Brooke's island.

"So, you met Brooke Russo then?" Nathan asked, his enthusiasm carefully restrained. "Sy, the manager of the party island, was happy to have you escorted across?"

"Yes. Mate! That's gonna be an experience we'll never forget," Tim said, still buzzing.

The others nodded in agreement.

"After a small fortune was paid," Chad reminded.

"A small blessing—for a man who needed his mind put at ease, now that I think on it," Tim replied thoughtfully.

"He made the arrangements," Chaiyala added. "But he didn't want to."

"Hmm, yes indeed," Nathan looked away. "Meeting Brooke Russo is an experience for strong, sound minds. That's for sure..."

Tim and Chad exchanged glances.

Charlotte thanked Nathan for the VIP upgrade.

The others echoed her gratitude. Tim shot Nathan a curious look. "At the booking office, the agent suggested we ask about Brooke's island once we got to the Outer Islands. And yes, the bar manager was very reluctant."

"Pretty much tried to talk us out of it," Chad added.

"What do you know of Brooke?" Tim asked, cautious but curious.

Nathan leaned back, reflecting on the early days of their Atlantis research over twenty years ago. The Caribbean had emerged as a focal point. They were led to Brooke Russo—rumoured to hold knowledge of Atlantean connections in the region. But she'd proven elusive, as unpredictable as she was intelligent, and reluctant to share anything useful.

"She's feared as a witch doctor," Nathan explained, "but I don't think that's the reality. She plays a role—manipulating perception, keeping people off balance. You never quite know where you stand with her."

Charlotte frowned. "So she's not actually dangerous?"

Nathan shook his head. "Not in the way people think. She thrives on mystery, shaping rumours to her advantage. She distrusts most, but if you agree with her—or at least appear to—you might get somewhere. Still, it's hard to predict what will set her off."

"Schizophrenia? Mental illness?"

"No," Nathan said. "She lets people believe that, but she's cunning—a master illusionist. Brilliant, creative—wasted potential."

The group fell into thoughtful silence. As the night stretched past 1:30 a.m., and once the visitors to Brooke's Island had shared what she'd revealed to them of the obelisk in Cockpit Country, Nathan called it a night. Tim and Charlotte went separately to their rooms, Rhys and Sienna settled on a couch on the deck leaving Chad and Chaiyala in the kitchen. Nathan went to his private deck, quietly contemplating his sadness over Brooke's legacy.

CHAPTER 23

I t was late in the morning when Chad and Chaiyala made their way into the living area to find Tim, Charlotte, Sienna, and Rhys eating breakfast. No one had a clue what time it was—no one cared—and phones were scarce. Nathan was in the kitchen making smoothies and chatting with Tim.

Good morning greetings were exchanged, and Nathan handed them smoothies.

Rhys and Sienna had polished off a large helping of scrambled eggs and streaky bacon on toast. Tim and Charlotte, surfacing after them, opted for fruit salad, cereal, and yoghurt.

Chaiyala moved toward the kitchen, still waking up, working her hair into one long plait.

"Tim is heading inland tomorrow with Rod," Nathan began, addressing her and Rhys, "to meet with Pastor Reo Richie at the Haddington New Testament Church near Kinloss on the B10. I take it you have the particulars?"

"We do," she confirmed.

"Crouton and Rod are off with Alesandro at present. Organising a few things regarding Alesandro's replacement vehicle and repairs to his home," Nathan added as they ate.

"When everyone's back," Tim said, "Rod and I will run through the plan—starting with today and what we hope to achieve. If all goes well, we'll locate the obelisk Brooke mentioned. Or at least gather enough intel to send a secondary team in while we head back to Mauritania."

"As far as I'm concerned," Nathan interjected, "you've only been here a few days. So, take your time adventurising in the jungle—or, relax and enjoy the resort. Might as well savour the experience while we're all here."

"Sweet! I'm good with that," Tim smiled.

"You are the boss man," Chaiyala said.

"We go wherever you, your brother, and your lass go," Rhys added.

"That's actually a pretty sweet job," Charlotte decided.

"For the most part..." Sienna agreed.

"It is—until you run into black ops and militia," Nathan cautioned. "Whilst Miss Ninja Warrior and the Maori-Scottish Hulk here find such encounters a walk in the park and tend to show off, it's still more often than not a life-and-death situation," he added light-heartedly.

"We are not show-offs," Chaiyala protested, flexing with a wry smile.

"Aye! You are but a midget lady," Rhys mocked, striking a similar pose.

Sienna grinned fondly.

"Oh please—six-foot-three, built like a tank, and suddenly we're all midgets? You're show-off, Rhys... Meat head, behave." Chaiyala joked.

"Look who's talkin'."

"You guys are hopeless," Tim dismissed with a smile.

The others laughed.

"Whatever they are, they're my top agents and the best bodyguards you three could ask for," Nathan said. "Regardless of their egos, they're more down-to-earth and professional than they let on."

Chad and Charlotte laughed again, then finished their breakfast.

"Do I really have an ego?" Chaiyala later asked Tim and Sienna.

"Wouldn't have thought so," Tim said.

"No, hun," Sienna reassured. "Rhys has both his and your shares of that kind of thing."

Rod, Crouton, and Alesandro returned just shy of midday.

Rod joined Tim, Charlotte and Sienna for a beach run. While Chad craved solitude. As he headed to his room, something caught his eye—a faded black top hat and weather-worn cane—oddly out of place. They stirred a memory, but he couldn't quite grasp it.

After a shower, he wandered to the kitchen, planning to raid the fridge before heading to the beach. Alesandro and Nathan were chatting about the safe house.

Then déjà vu hit—what truly caught Chad's attention was Alesandro's careful handling of a chilli pepper, just as the top hat and cane came back into view. He finely chopped chillies, adding them to a glass of Appleton's.

"...likes rum spiked with hot peppers, he does," Chad recalled Brooke mentioning of Baron Samedi the night before.

He stared at the chillies going into the rum. His expression must have looked disconcerting, because Nathan asked, "Everything okay?"

"Ah... yeah, fine," Chad nodded. "Just trying to figure out what you were doing with those chillies. Looks familiar..."

"It used to be a popular additive to rum here in Jamaica," Alesandro explained. "Doesn't seem so common nowadays."

"Might've seen it served at a bar downstairs, perhaps?" Crouton suggested.

"Would you like?" Alesandro offered.

"No—no, thank you," Nathan declined.

"Can't imagine my brother going for that though..." Chad recalled Brooke's words. He shook his head, dismissing the weirdness. He had more than enough on his mind already.

He turned and opened the fridge—pleasantly surprised.

Half a dozen squealers of Tim and Chad's favourite Hamilton craft beer sat on the shelf in front of him.

He helped himself to one, stashing it in a chiller bag, then made his way down the elevator.

Barefoot, Chad walked across the sand that had crept into the pool precinct.

He scanned for anyone too close—his bubble feeling unusually large. A dozen guests lounged on beach beanbags nearby, sunbathing or reading. One—comically oversized for their small blue beanbag, resembled a rhino. His face obscured by a massive sombrero as they dozed.

Chad settled against a driftwood log buried in tussock-dressed dunes—placing his rucksack, with the cooler bag inside, beside him. His mind felt like a congested city again, disheartening him. He'd thought being with his brother on the other side of the world would leave his struggles behind. Distance had brought distraction—the incredible, the otherworldly—but once the novelty faded, his depression remained. It wasn't about Hamilton, past events, or a place. Maybe the place was him.

He pulled out the squealer, unscrewed the cap, and took a long swig of Hazy. The tropical rush pulled him back to summer—deck side at his parents' Hamilton home, their pool glistening. The better memories of the Waikato.

He was still with Sonia back then, and they were going strong. She was about to compete at the ASB Classic in Auckland. They were in love, high on life.

In dull sequence, those memories faded to the chill of separation, rejection, and betrayal.

He held the bottle in one hand and used the other to pull his legs closer. He sculled some more.

Here he was, in a tropical paradise, drinking his favourite tropical craft beer—yet he felt nothing. A dark cloud cast a cold shadow over his reminiscence, his self-worth, and everything he touched.

"What the hang am I thinking? Chaiyala is way out of my league. Probably on with Rhys or someone anyway. I don't deserve her..." Chad told himself. "I don't even have a remote chance... she's probably just like Sonia. Face of an angel—body of a Greek goddess—with a stone-cold heart. Girls like her are like that—superficial as dust. All aesthetic bait and skin-deep magnetism—they use and abuse."

He was plummeting, and he knew it.

He needed to put the beer back in the chiller bag and zip it shut. He didn't. His fast-inebriating state overtook him. Even as he thought otherwise, he took another long swig.

"What a damned fool you are, Chad," he sobbed.

Twice now, since the gym, he and Chaiyala had let things go too far. And while it hadn't felt wrong in the moment, something about it lingered—unsettling, unresolved.

And what of everything he'd witnessed since arriving in Africa? And now Jamaica?

"Nathan and Crouton don't know me! Why are they doing this for me? What do they want? They're up to something," Chad shook his head in anguished confusion. Profanities echoed in his mind as he mouthed each foul word—wiping tears escaping from beneath his sunglasses.

His internal monologue sank to the depths—a murky blend of stagnant sludge and discarded remnants of worthlessness. A cesspool reserved for losers like him.

He decided he'd made a huge mistake travelling to Mauritania. He was going to get in the way. And he still couldn't figure out why he was in Jamaica at a luxury resort with all expenses paid.

"What a waste, that all is! This place! The rich elite!" Chad's hang-up about wealth and wealthy people poked its crooked finger into his heart.

He went rigid. He felt extremely vulnerable and unsafe.

Since they'd been in Jamaica, Alesandro had nearly been killed, his home broken into and his car blown up. Last night they'd encountered some kind of crazy, demon-possessed woman, whom Tim was taking seriously for details about Atlantis in the Caribbean.

"Even Tim's gone. My own brother is caught up in this madness..." He shook as he thought about it—yet stayed as still as he could.

Chad wished he could pull the blankets over his head so whatever was moving in the darkness of his bedroom—whatever had climbed out from under the bed—couldn't see him. Maybe he'd wake up safe in the light of dawn.

This wasn't a bad dream. It was a waking nightmare. Crushed by a panic attack, silent tears fell as he longed to vanish beneath the sand—free from pain, rejection, and the weight of himself.

"Finish the bottle. Smash it. Slam its shards into your throat, you worthless..." a voice snarled from the pit of hell.

But another voice. Powerful. Tranquil. Beautiful, cut in: ***"Silence."***

Chad's soul, like a drowning man grasping a lifeline, drifted into suspension—utter serenity. For a few seconds, he felt nothing. No peace, no pain, no thought—no need of any. The world faded—waves, seagulls, distant voices—gone.

He free-fell, emotionally. Subconsciously. Metaphysically. Then, seated motionless against driftwood, he landed in a sea of bliss.

"Peace, Chad... peace," the second voice said. *"Peace... peace... peace."* It repeated soothingly, yet with authority. With each word, a layer of hatred, sadness, darkness, depression, and anxiety peeled away.

"Peace!" the voice said with rising enthusiasm. *"Let there be peace... Chad—be free!"*

He felt the most bizarre combination of utter liberation and sheer agony, as if something toxic was being wrenched from within him. Pure freedom and peace rushed in to fill the void.

His only response was to cry out loud as his chest lifted upward—the rest of him trying to follow.

Something sinister had departed him. Now he was left with an ocean of peace within.

Chad sat up and breathed a huge sigh of relief.

"What on earth was that?" he asked inwardly, staring at the bottle still in his hand. Nope. Was sealed tight. Not spiked.

"I've lost it... that's it. I've truly lost it. Everything's gotten too much, and I've lost the plot," he said aloud, not realizing it.

That's when he noticed a family—mum, dad, and three girls—had witnessed the whole thing. From the vocal theatrics to his last sentence.

"Hey... are you okay?" the dad asked awkwardly with an American accent. The girls stood nearby in swimsuits—towels clutched to their chests—their faces drawn with concern. Mum looked like she was trying to figure out how to help the disturbed stranger sitting against driftwood.

"Ah... yes," Chad replied, wondering if it was true. "Yes—I think I am," he smiled warmly. "I'm sorry if I startled you... I dunno—I might've nodded off and... I think I was having a bad dream. But I'm fine now. Thanks for asking."

"Okay, that's good," the dad said. "Long as you're okay."

"I am. I'm fine. Thanks again." Chad felt awkward and was keen for the exchange to end.

"Riiiight," one of the daughters said—unconvinced, then gazed down the beach.

Her mum shot her a look as they carried on.

Once again left to his own devices, Chad felt peculiarly relaxed.

It had nothing to do with the beer. No, there was more to it than that.

This was a sensation he'd not experienced in a long time—something forgotten. A peace of mind that surpasses understanding. A kind of peace that made anxiety irrelevant.

Chad's thoughts drifted to a conversation he and Tim had years ago with their friend Lawrence—a disillusioned returned missionary they'd met through church circles and mutual friends in Paeroa.

They'd been sitting outside Lawrence's rural Morrinsville home, sipping Lemon Lime and Bitters and eating scorched almonds. Gazing out over the rolling hills of the Waikato landscape, Lawrence shared how he'd found his way back to Christ after years of bitterness and avoidance.

"Ironically, it was all kind of simple," Lawrence had said. "There was the car accident—lucky to have survived—even to be having this conversation with you. There was the stress of losing ninety percent of my investments when the company collapsed, and a close friend's daughter was kidnapped—thankfully rescued. But all of it left me shaken. Vulnerable—nothing felt stable.

Counselling had been recommended, but the counsellor was weird—talked about strange stuff that triggered my anxiety. I couldn't stick with it," he laughed, though it was tinged with weariness."

Instead, Lawrence had relied on the stress and anxiety medication, and later accepted an invitation from friends to join a week-long trek through Fiordland—down in the South Island and Milford Sound. "It felt fantastic," Chad recalled Lawrence sharing, "refreshing, freeing—but it didn't last. Triggers would still set me off, and I'd spiral, bouncing between bliss and anxiety."

Lawrence shook his head. "I'd spent years building a bubble of wealth, success, reputation—aiming for perfection. But for someone who rejected religion, I'd become awfully religious about wealth and security. And the truth? I'd been running ever since I turned my back on my faith."

His so-called prosperity was relentless—high maintenance—fragile. A single misstep could unravel it.

Lawrence had stopped mid-sentence, his gaze drifting toward the distant hills. The conversation had gotten meaningfully deep, but something deeper still, had tugged at him.

"You know," he said quietly, "I was sitting out here a few weeks ago... just me, the wind, and a sky full of silence. And I realised—I couldn't remember the last time I felt genuinely okay."

Tim and Chad'd waited, sensing something important was surfacing.

"I've had good days," Lawrence had continued. "Moments of laughter, success, even clarity. But peace? Real peace? That's different. That's rare."

He stood, glass in hand and moved toward the edge of the deck—voice low. "I've chased it in all the usual places—career, travel, relationships, and wealth. But it never sticks. It's like trying to hold mist in your hands."

He'd paused, then looked back at them with a faint smile. "But then it hit me. The last time I felt truly secure... was when I stopped trying to earn it. When I stopped running. When I let God be enough."

The silence that followed was sacred. Complete.

Lawrence exhaled slowly. "I think I've spent years trying to build a life that didn't need Him. But the truth is... I do. I really do."

Chad remembered Lawrence saying, "The thirst for something bigger than the world and mere existentialism became too big to ignore. And whatever it was had to be greater and more stable than anything I—or anyone else—could make up. That's the thing that says to me, God is for real. He's the only deity you can't fully understand—so He can't be made up, and the only one who doesn't require anything more than me just being me."

Chad sighed at the last recollection—the words echoing in his mind like a distant tide.

"Therein lies the never-ending dilemma though," he whispered to himself. "If God doesn't require anything other than just me... why does religion seem to ask for more?"

~~~~~~~

Rhys's 'sniper-eyes' checked in for the fifth time. A hidden Red Sword agent—stationed in an ocean-facing room—kept Rhys and Chad in sight—scanning the area, updating Rhys every ten minutes or if security changed. So far, all was neutral.

Rhys kept a close eye on Chad after his unexpected outburst fifteen minutes earlier. He wondered what that'd been about. He figured the odds of finding out were slim. More often than not, things like that remained unknown. Unless Chad'd choose to share later.

Rod and Chaiyala weren't far off, with Tim and Charlotte jogging back along the beach toward Chad's position. Chaiyala knew Rhys's proximity. He'd remain undercover until Chad was no longer exposed.

~~~~~~~

Chad needed to figure something out—and soon. His mental health struggles were searing evidence things had gotten too much. The weight of confusion and hurt from his breakup with Sonia had set off a chain reaction. Insecurities and hangups were surfacing and burdening him in debilitating fashion.

"I can't run from this stuff... can't even fly across the world to escape it," he thought. *"I need something that's going to blast this out of my headspace properly... maybe if things eventuated with Chaiyala..."* that would settle his emotions and mental state.

"Don't even go there, Chad. You know full well it doesn't work that way," he corrected himself.

He knew enough to know putting all his hope in that basket ran the risk of having it all shattered. *"Nah—can't go trying to find security in people—most people can't guarantee their own. That's foolish. And unfair on Chaiyala. Don't even know her well enough anyway. And you were just labelling her like Sonia less than half an hour ago."*

He searched his mind and heart—sidestepping the real issue—an overwhelming, unstable external world. It was taking a toll on his mind. He needed to find lasting peace within.

"...but there's less peace within me than rain in a desert," he lamented.

He knew full well where this was leading him. But if he went there—it was all or nothing.

His values wouldn't allow him to go half-heartedly—picking and choosing like a spiritual band-wagoner.

Chad was stuck between a rock and a hard place.

And that place—was the same spot Lawrence had arrived at all those years ago.

CHAPTER 24

Lost in thought, Chad was pleasantly surprised when his brother, Charlotte, Rod, and Chaiyala suddenly appeared—he'd been too distracted to notice them arriving from his right.

They'd completed a decent run along the beach—all dressed in gym gear fit for the tropical warmth.

"We did bouldering too!" Charlotte told Chad excitedly.

Rod couldn't fathom how she remained so bubbly despite their relentless pace. He and Chaiyala had raced, despite her trying to take her time—her competitive streak wouldn't let her slow down.

Tim having trailed just behind, had been amazed he'd kept up at all.

Rod leaned back against Chad's driftwood—hands behind his head—eyes closed, catching his breath. Tim sat beside his brother. Eventually, Charlotte stopped bouncing around and settled across from Tim—her back to the sea.

Chaiyala rested her head on Chad's shoulder after asking how he was and sitting down close to his left.

"I'm good. Lot on the mind, though," he replied.

"Yeah?" she asked kindly.

Chad paused. "Anxiety's sorta come back... not too surprised. I think... a lot of unresolved things lingering in the background—with a whole new world of overwhelming questions piling on top."

The others listened respectfully. Rod faced the ocean, yet nodded attentively.

"I came down to the beach to be alone with my thoughts. Long and short of it: my mental health challenges have followed me to Jamaica. I had a panic attack about half an hour ago and then... somehow..." Chad still wasn't fully sure what had happened, "I snapped out of it really quickly. Actually, way more forcefully than I ever have. I kept hearing the word 'peace' in my mind. It repeated. The more I heard it, it's like... I dunno, something left me."

"Like a burden lifted?" Charlotte suggested.

"Yeah," he agreed, still perplexed but at ease.

Tim noticed a distinct difference. Normally, Chad wouldn't have been able to talk about this without breaking down.

"That's good," Tim nodded, smiling.

Chaiyala rubbed his shoulder affectionately.

Tim checked in—was Chad still taking his medication?

"Yeah, always," Chad confirmed he was—they were helpful along with other crucial habits. There'd be no way he'd stop without proper consultation with his doctor and counsellor.

The Nectar of The gods café was about a hundred meters behind them, facing the beach—situated at the bottom of the eastern tower. Having caught Charlotte's eye, she suggested they head there for smoothies to cool off.

"Keen for that!" Tim agreed.

They arose from the sand. As the friends made their way across the beach from the dunes to the resort, the big guy on the beanbag stood, lifted his huge colourful sombrero, and smiled cheerfully.

"Rhys! Come join us," Tim called.

"Sleeping on the job, I see," Chaiyala teased, knowing otherwise.

"Nearly. The most exciting thing that happened was four attractive females in swimsuits spoke to Chad, then left."

Chad frowned, clueless. "What? Where exactly were you?"

Rhys laughed—clearly amused at his own cunning.

"Sitting on this beanbag, 'round ten—twelve meters away from you. You strolled right past me, then sat down."

Chad pieced it together as they walked. Rhys and Chaiyala joked about Chad's unknown 'girlfriends'.

Tim and Charlotte were in stitches. Chad shook his head at their cheap humour, though he conceded a grin.

"You're all eggs and I don't like none of ya!" Chad retorted with theatrical flair.

They laughed.

Tim thumped him in the arm as they neared the café. "Love ya, bro."

Chaiyala got him in a headlock-turned-arm-around-the-shoulder, affectionately.

Once at the café, Tim and Rod each ordered an elaborate iced chocolate. Charlotte got a berry smoothie. Chaiyala chose a mango-berry iced tea that looked like it had been attacked by a fruit salad—refreshing and chaotic. Chad ordered a large bowl of fries to share and a tall glass of Coke.

They found a seat in the sand under a canopy of shade sails and palms. Chad paused, as if he'd heard something—someone calling his name. It felt like a conversation was being had about him—somewhere nearby. They were smiling. He felt warmth. Nothing unnerving, but he still looked around—wondering where the feeling came from.

"... Chad!" Tim called for the third time.

"Eh?" Chad looked at his brother—snapping out of it.

Tim frowned.

"You okay?" Charlotte asked.

Chaiyala regarded him with heartfelt concern.

"You got a bit on your mind, alright," Rod agreed.

Chad took a seat next to Chaiyala. She placed a hand on his forearm.

"I, um... oh man," Chad smiled and shook his head. "I got no idea..." He sat back chuckling—struggling to find words. "I'm either losing my marbles or something else is going on." He tried to piece together what he'd experienced—earlier, and just now—but came up empty.

"What do you mean *starting* to lose your marbles?" Tim joked.

Chad looked at him blankly. "Given the circumstances so far, you probably don't have any of your *own* left to lose."

Rod and Rhys laughed.

"Bro, that's old news. I've been lost as a dog since before I began my classics degree... then discovered the world's been nutty since way back. Figured I'd join in and have some fun," Tim said with a shrug.

They all laughed.

There was a pause, then Chad continued. "Before I heard the word 'peace,' I went to a very dark place. I heard..." He winced. "Something evil and nasty told me to... end it."

Chaiyala took his hand, grimacing empathetically.

"Chad..." Charlotte looked at him sorrowfully.

"It's okay, though," he continued. "What happened immediately after that was where things got *really* interesting. Another voice—clear, kinda... I dunno—angelic spoke with the power to overrule the other. It kept repeating 'peace,' and it was like I was being restored... ah, it's friggin' nuts, eh!" He shook his head—smiling—still feeling freer than usual.

Tim and Rod exchanged a look. Chaiyala and Rod did the same.

"Hmm. Sounds a bit paranormal," Rod suggested.

"Good," Chad grinned. "I'm not going nuts after all. Just ghosts."

"I think what stands out," Tim said, "is you clearly had a real experience. Suicidal thoughts, yes—but something positive and more powerful overruled them. And you're alive to tell the tale."

The others agreed. The girls reiterated they were always there for him.

"To be honest, Chad," Rhys said, "nutty is probably the last thing anyone would assume, given recent events."

"There's been a wee bit of that going on while we've been here," Rod added, sipping his iced chocolate.

"That Brooke Russo chick," Rhys muttered.

"And Baron Saturday," Charlotte added.

"Yeah, you ain't gonna catch me on Brooke's island," Rod said. "She's one freaky piece of work. If she's summoning things like Baron Samedi—sheesh. That's crazy voodoo. I'm keepin' my distance."

Rod was no stranger to the paranormal—Red Sword agents dealt with it periodically. But some things unsettled him more than others. Classical deities like Zeus and Osiris felt like relics—long gone. But modern pagan practices—voodoo, witch doctors, tribal rituals, even speaking in tongues—unnerved him.

The group chatted about such things for a while—swapping eerie stories, including Alesandro's strange experiences. It was the kind of subject you could spend the rest of the day on, then continue around a bonfire with drinks in hand into the small hours.

But Chad remained distracted. He pondered the experiences of Lawrence.

Lawrence had told Tim and Chad his extended family and close friends had never stopped praying for him. Unexpectedly, he found himself asking about church and maybe coming along.

"You good, bro?" Tim asked, detaching from the group conversation.

"Nah, bro... I'm a complete mess," Chad replied, deadpan—then smiled. "Egg."

"Nah—I'm good. Still got my marbles," he joked.

"Silence. Both of them looked out to sea—thoughts unspoken. Along from them, the others kept talking—ghosts, spirituality, the paranormal. Charlotte was deep in theology—tracing the parallels between hermeneutical nuance and eternal context."

Staring across the ocean, Chad asked Tim, "You remember that day we called in at Lawrence's in Morrinsville—right after he'd gotten his stuff sorted with God?"

"Yup."

"Hmm... might be in a similar predicament myself."

"True?"

"Yeah, bro... crazy times, eh?"

"Just a normal day in paradise," Tim smiled. "Crazy is a normal way of life—working with Crout and Nate."

"Is it hard to tell the difference between surprises and normal events?"

Tim stopped to consider— "Come to think of it, I haven't been surprised for a while..."

They both laughed.

"Must be quite nice—not being surprised by the unexpected," Chad wondered. "I mean, good surprises are fine—that's different. But I dunno, not being shocked by stuff—that gets old—I reckon."

"A wise man once said to me," Tim began, "Being shocked by the mess of sin contradicts the heart of the gospel—a gospel of love and grace that meets people in their mess, not after they've cleaned it up, and calls us to love as Christ loved—without flinching at the mess."

"Oh, that's good," Chad said, pleasantly caught off guard, "smooth, sharp, and exactly what I need."

Tim grinned silently.

"Yeah... I didn't realise how deeply those words would take root—how much it would shape the way I see people, and the way I carry myself in the day-to-day."

Chad nodded thoughtfully... "So yeah, Lawrence had been accused of financial fraud after he went off to missionary work, right?

"Yeah. They pulled support before anything was verified. He felt betrayed—said they shafted him. That's what drove him away from God and the church in the first place."

Chad nodded. "So, did he ever commit the crime then? I dunno if I ever heard the whole story of that aspect of his life..."

"No, he was in the clear." Tim thought back to conversations he'd had with Lawrence about it. He remembered "he said it was complicated—it took years to get the full picture. The whole thing was handled badly, and by the time clarity came, bridges were already burned. Communication had broken down with the very people who could've told him he was no longer under suspicion."

"I see."

"Thing is—he never received an apology. And, the way it had completely thrown his life right out of whack—the lack of justice and never being able to get any closure—that took a huge toll on him."

There was a reflective silence between the two of them. The others continued chatting down the other end of the table.

Tim continued, "Over time, Lawrence's experiences and perspectives shifted. Like he said when we were both with him—he found himself needing assurance and stability from God, and returned to church."

"Yeah." Chad nodded thoughtfully, pensively. He seemed caught in a paradox—at peace, yet unreconciled.

"He simply knew God loved him," Tim concluded, "and in the church he'd joined, he saw that love in action—real and unconditional. He said he was still guarded—had a long way to go with trust and getting back to where he'd once been in church life. But he set those hurts aside—because his relationship with Jesus mattered more."

"Well that's good then. I'm glad he's not stuck in some perpetual cycle of bitterness getting him nowhere..." Chad looked distantly out to sea.

Tim regarded his brother with care and curiosity. "Ultimately, who we are and what we do pales in comparison to who God is and the redemption Jesus accomplished for us. Stereotypes and rigid religious expectations mean little against His boundless grace. His power and love surpass human reason. When we truly grasp that, no identity, struggle, or perceived flaw can separate someone from God's love. His grace reaches deeper than our brokenness. With the gospel centred on love, everything else loses its weight."

That resonated with Chad. His heart warmed to the notion, but his mind searched for rebuttal.

"Isn't that compromising though, as far as what's acceptable in the sight of God?"

"Chad, I'm gonna be frank. If you were in a court of law on this one, the defence attorney would be Jesus Himself—that's the whole point," Tim said plainly. "If God's nature is perfect love, then what's acceptable in His sight is always consistent with that love—holy, just, and redemptive. There's no compromise—or fear, for that matter—in love. But when there is fear of compromise, it's hard for love to shine out of us. Again though, God is still bigger than that. His perfect love casts out all fear."

Chad nodded, the connection clicking into place. Playing devil's advocate with the truth of Ultimate Love was as futile as the defeated devil itself.

If Tim argued that God's grace outweighs judgement and covers all human error, he'd be biblically correct. Though such a view might be controversial among more rigid theological traditions. While they, too, claim biblical accuracy, their emphasis on rule-keeping can sometimes obscure the heart of grace... and the very purpose of Jesus' death on the cross.

"Chad," Tim said, serious but kind, "people debate endlessly about what's 'acceptable' to God—but often, that debate isn't really about Him. It's about religious systems, and human standards, or fears. The truth is: empty religion knows little of love and grace. So why let it define what matters most?"

Rod overheard—narrowed his eyes and studied Tim carefully. *"This has gotten seriously deep,"* he thought. He'd heard similar rhetoric from non-or ex-church types, but never knew why it was argued so intensely. He was beginning to get a better idea.

Rhys was more or less on the same wavelength—listening closely.

"How about judgement and grace being the same thing?" Chad asked. It wasn't a new idea—he'd heard it before—but he was curious to hear Tim's take.

"Grace and judgement being the same thing... that takes us all the way back to creation. God's whole reason for creating human beings was to pour out His love on them. Cut out all the debating, all the convoluted religious stuff and the mess of sin, and you have a God who, despite our unworthiness, chooses to pour out grace—chooses to love. That should've been obvious with His self-sacrifice on the cross. But no, religion and humanism had to cloud it five ways from Friday."

Chad wasn't unfamiliar with the logic, or, the message of the gospel—however one chose to perceive it. He had to be honest with himself: he was desperate for a way out. Accepting the truth meant confronting what he'd long refused to believe—even as his heart screamed for him to do otherwise. It wasn't the truth itself that terrified him, but the discomfort it would bring. And yet, deep down, he knew: whatever forced him to face the music had to be the real thing... it *needed* to be the real thing.

This was it—the heart of the entire saga. His world was being pushed beyond its limits, forcing him to consider what lay past his fears, doubts, and the limitations that had kept him trapped in narrow thinking.

"You're on a mission with this one, aren't you?" Tim asked, realizing Chad's theological probing and earlier comment about being in a similar spiritual journey to Lawrence were both a path and a destination. One he was painstakingly making his way along.

"Yup, sure am," Chad confirmed, taking another long sip of his Coke.

He called the waitstaff over and ordered another

Figuring it was lunchtime, he also ordered a chicken burger and asked if the others were hungry too.

Rod, no longer distracted by Tim and Chad's dialogue, noticed how famished he was and ordered tortellini. Rhys went for a beef burger, inspiring Chaiyala and Tim to do the same. Charlotte opted for a seafood basket.

As the wait staff stepped away to relay orders, the others leaned in—drawn to the exchange—where contention and purpose collided in a conversation too charged to ignore.

Chad had no issue with the Bible, its claims, or principles. A law student with an investigative mind, much like his brother's pursuit of historical authenticity, he'd explored the staggering world of facts that validated Scripture.

Yet, between Chad and undeniable truth stood his perception of the church. He didn't like what he saw—irritated by a perceived failure to be what it claimed to be.

A question was going to burn a hole in Chad's mind, and Tim could sense the frustration building.

"Spit it out, bro. Don't sugar-coat it trying to dress it up as something PC."

"Church!" Chad spat. "Dammit. Why does God require so little, but the church requires so much more? Why is it always asking for money, and why does it spend so many millions on buildings when people in the same neighbourhood are going hungry? And why do so many people get hurt by the church, leave, and then no one ever talks about it?"

Rod and Rhys sat stunned. Chaiyala was curiously unsurprised—intrigued, but not shocked. Tim and Charlotte were no strangers to this debate.

Tim paused, hearing the echo of a conversation from a decade earlier—around the time Lawrence had been wrestling with the same questions.

"If I recall," Tim began, "Lawrence asked the exact same questions. Then he ended up throwing them out the window and deciding they didn't matter anymore... why did he do that, I wonder?"

Chad glowered at his brother, at ease now that he'd gotten it off his chest. But it was clear he wasn't throwing anything out the window.

"The thing is, Lawrence is not here—and your questions do matter. I'll do my best to answer them. But first, where did the questions come from? Are they yours, or someone else's? Did someone leave you with a burden that was never meant to be yours, then walk out and leave you in a heap?"

That was typical of Tim. Chad should've known he'd play that card. He cursed under his breath for letting emotion get the better of him. Then something strange overcame him—something of the mind... and spirit, perhaps? It reminded him of where counselling often led. It came with the distinct feeling that the burden of confession had been taken on by someone else.

But initially, he figured he'd blind side Tim with what he thought he wouldn't expect.

"Sonia's questions." He bit his lip—looking away—then back at his brother with welling eyes. "She came into my life with all her baggage, stole my heart, filled my head with everything wrong about church... and we both walked away. Now they're my questions. They might not have been at first, but now I can't see anything else but the cursed things!"

He swore, pushed himself roughly back from the table, digging his chair into the sand. He looked out toward the horizon.

Now he didn't even know if what he was asking were legitimate questions—or just speaking from a dark legacy Sonia had left him with.

Chaiyala put her hand on his. She smiled at him, and he smiled back, briefly. There was too much swirling in his head. It needed to stop.

"What happened when you walked away?" Tim asked.

"That was it. I turned my back on church, they turned their back on me, and so did..." He was about to say "so did God," but it didn't feel right. He snapped out of it. "I was shafted and judged. That was it."

Tim nodded thoughtfully. "By whom, exactly?"

Half a dozen names came to mind—guys he'd been mates with since kids' church who'd always stood by him. His life group leaders had invited he and Sonia to dinner, to watch rugby, then just Chad for coffee. Each time, he'd made excuses—Sonia had encouraged them. The last he'd heard from them was a Facebook message: *"You're awesome, buddy! Keep in touch if you can. Always keen to hang out. Always thinking of you and praying for you..."*

Chad swore inwardly. "It was me. I was the one doing the judging."

Anger tried to override guilt. "Everyone stopped talking to me..." But the memories were being called to the witness stand. They were being interrogated—and no names came to mind to fit the role of the shafters or the perpetrators of judgement.

"Chris and Vicky..." Tim said gently.

Just their names—his life group leaders—were enough. The memory of their invitations and that last message betrayed him.

Chad sobbed, putting his hand to his forehead, closing his eyes and waiting for the tears.

Chaiyala embraced him, her strong heart breaking for the genuinely lovely guy she was growing in admiration of.

"Grant, Kaylan, Sven, Zach, Shakeel..." Tim listed the five guys who'd kept in touch with Chad. The ones he certainly didn't feel judged by. They were the real deal—stood by him when the vomit hit the fan over Sonia Tallay and through his struggle with depression and anxiety.

Charlotte knew each of the seven individuals well. The others were putting two and two together.

Chaiyala was juggling a handful of significant personal sentiments. Mostly her concern for Chad. Acutely aware of his struggle and discomfort. Yet the topic had brought into the spotlight a number of similar questions about her own spirituality, lifestyle, and heritage.

Chad was a mess of mixed emotions. A growing freedom now shared the stage with anger toward Sonia—for dragging him into her bitter world, and for leaving him with questions that were never his to answer, or ask.

"Bro, I am truly gutted and deeply sorry that you experienced feelings of rejection and being shafted. Some people stopped talking to you. What you probably don't know, is that for a lot of them, it wasn't out of judgement, but uncertainty. They simply didn't know what to say—or if saying anything would help."

"Actually, thinking back," Charlotte interjected, "I recall most of the conversation around you and Sonia leaving being about how important it was that you *weren't* made to feel judged. That you were to be loved—no matter what. Tom and Vicky, even Pastor Ryan and Pastor Megan, were very adamant on that."

Chad sobbed again, knowing that now. He thought of Ryan and Megan—their senior pastors—and only the fondest of recollections arose. The consistent friendship of Chad's tight five, Chris and Vicky's text, and the way Tim and Charlotte cared for him all corroborated that truth.

"The other thing worth considering," Tim continued, "is that this is a human issue—not a church one. It applies to any group or institution made up of people. It's seldom 'the church' that hurts people—it's individuals, with their own baggage, who make mistakes. Sure, they may not represent Jesus well, but their actions aren't a true reflection of the church He founded."

"Isn't it though?" Chad challenged. "They are the church. So, when they do bad things, they're representing it."

"What about us?" Tim countered, gesturing to himself and Charlotte. "Don't we represent the church too? What about Chris and Vicky, Grant and the guys?"

Chad paused, nodding. "Good point." He appreciated getting these unchecked ideas out into the open. It helped narrow things down to what mattered—what was real.

"If an entire church supported ostracising someone, that's a serious issue—even if only half did. But Ryan and Megan actively worked to counter negativity toward you and Sonia. That has to matter. It sets Abundance City Christian Centre apart from any legalistic churches full of self-righteous judges."

"If I may," Rod added, "if Tim—and I think the same goes for Charlotte—are representatives of the church, then my opinion of the church has become pretty darn high. In the short time I've known Tim, he's the real deal when it comes to being what a Christian is supposed to be."

"Cheers, man." Tim thanked.

Charlotte beamed. "Beyond that, if those representing the church aren't also embodying Christ, then what's their purpose? Just representing themselves? That contradicts the very essence of the church."

Rhys nodded... that was it. That's what he'd always hoped the church could be. Charlotte's words put language to something he'd felt but never articulated.

"Regardless of rumours and stereotypes, a representative in the flesh is better than a story in the tabloids," Rod concluded.

"Chad, this isn't to deny that some churches hurt people—far from it," Tim continued. "But those are often cults or rigid, legalistic groups that misrepresent Jesus and should be avoided. Plenty claim to be Christians, yet through judgmental words and actions, fail to reflect Christ's Spirit. They may grasp theology, but when they act as judge, jury, and executioner, they overstep their calling as Christ's hands, feet, and voice. Their delivery of the gospel is downright appalling."

Tim shook his head, gazing out to sea.

"Shat the bed, to be completely blunt and real about it," Rod added. "Empty religion gives true Christianity a bad name," he recalled Tim saying once.

Tim continued, "Our church in Hamilton is built on the grace and redemptive truth, freedom, love, and acceptance, Christ offers. People's struggles are met with kindness and resolved in the beauty of community and God's goodness."

"No one is forced or coerced into anything—God's love simply draws them in," Charlotte added.

"That is how it should be," Chaiyala smiled.

"People get hurt, and injustice exists everywhere—but so does kindness," Rhys noted.

Chad realized the church is often scapegoated for human hypocrisy across society. He hadn't seen it before—not clearly. But now, it was obvious: the church hadn't failed him. People had. And people could heal, too.

"I'll be honest with you, man," Tim said. "Choosing to go against what you knew—your values, your convictions, what Scripture teaches—by dating someone who didn't share your faith, who opposed it, even... that was your decision. And any fallout from that? That's on you. It wasn't the church's doing, and it sure wasn't God's."

He paused, letting the words settle. "But none of that changes how much you're loved. Not by me, not by Charlotte, and definitely not by Him."

Tension peaked. Tim had built up to this moment, drawing out the issue like poison from a wound.

Chad didn't speak right away. The words had landed—not like a slap, but like a mirror. He let out a breath, somewhere between a sigh and a laugh. "Okay... fair."

Rod looked between them, half-relieved, half-impressed.

Charlotte gave Tim a look that said, *You pulled that off better than I expected.*

Any tension at the table deflated like a pricked balloon.

"People get distracted by irrelevant specifics. What matters most is your relationship with your Creator. That's between you and Him. The only business anyone else in the church has is to make sure you and Sonia are cared for and treated with the dignity and honour every child of God deserves. No matter what anyone else has said, bro, no one has the right to condemn. The Bible—despite all its so-called ambiguities—is clear on that.

The only one with the right to judge is the God of the universe—because only He can judge perfectly, and still choose to love and redeem us."

A beautiful silence and stillness settled over the group.

"Woah..." Rod nodded reflectively.

Rhys felt unexpectedly at ease, as if he'd been let off hooks he never knew he'd been on.

It hit Chad—he'd misjudged everything. While dwelling on perceived injustices, he'd condemned himself and blamed 'the church' for judging him—when no one had.

"Goodness!" He shook his head, relieved to let go of the misplaced burden.

Chaiyala was deep in thought. Tim's words had answered questions she hadn't known how to ask—questions that'd lived quietly in her heart for years. She felt a reassurance about God, and a longing to explore this side of Him—one that felt both unfamiliar and deeply rooted in the heritage she'd only partially understood.

Meanwhile, Chad's mind was combing through everything—searching for problems to address, while his heart rolled its eyes at the cynicism.

Then another question surfaced, "What about the issue of money in the church? Why is it always asking for money?"

"Same reason everyone does—it's a means to an end. To put food on the table, pay bills, etc."

"Yeah, that's not really my point," Chad said, trying not to get annoyed. He didn't know why he kept getting hung up on money.

"No, it's not. There's more to it than that," Tim clarified. "I'm not going to leave a million-dollar question with a ten-cent answer. Your point being:

why does the church ask for money when God should be able to provide everything?"

"Exactly."

Rod frowned. Rhys and Chaiyala were also curious about Chad's fixation on finances. Rod recalled a conversation they'd had in Mauritania about Nathan O'Conner's wealth and generosity—how it wasn't about quantity, but heart.

Tim thought for a moment. Chad had nudged a deeper frustration— one Tim had wrestled with for years: why isn't the completed work of Christ emphasized more in theology? It'd clear up so many of the issues people get stuck on.

"It's the same issue," Tim muttered. "People fail to grasp the finished work of the cross and fall back into man-made, ultimatum-driven religion.

Because God has already provided everything anyone could ever need—in the hands of *everyone*."

Chad looked at him blankly, waiting for the unpacking.

Rod and Charlotte got it straight away. For Rod, Chaiyala, and Rhys, it echoed Nathan's philosophy around finances.

"People keep getting it backward. God already provided the resources. Chad, if He valued humanity enough to send His Son, He also entrusted us to steward the world's wealth and work together. The Church, alongside organizations like World Vision, Tear Fund, and The Salvation Army, advocates for this divine provision."

"Aye! Nathan would say the same thing," Rhys chimed in.

"Love it," Rod nodded.

"How do you mean?" Chad asked, eyes searching.

"Let's use our church, Abundance City Christian Centre in Hamilton, as an example," Tim said. "With 5,000 members, over a hundred are millionaires or very wealthy. The church isn't just its leaders—it's the people. The church already possesses financial resources. The conversation is about directing them toward agreed-upon projects and missions that glorify God and bless people. That's not even including the tithe—that's a separate topic."

Tim felt the same profound relief he'd once experienced defending his faith at university. He looked out at the sea, overwhelmed with gratitude.

Charlotte was thinking, *"That was brilliant."* She'd never thought of it that way.

Rhys and Chaiyala were impressed—intrigued by the idea of collective stewardship.

Chad was happy with the explanation, but still had questions.

"That's awesome, bro. It really is," Chad said. "That's how it should be. But is that actually how it goes? In our church? In any church? Or is that just a lovely dream that never really happens?"

Rod found himself saying, "It'd depend on individual perspective..." unsure if he was stating or asking.

Chaiyala looked like she was about to say something similar—then nodded in agreement and stayed quiet.

"Well, yeah..." Tim began, acknowledging Rod's point. "It's a fair query nonetheless." He looked at Chad, then down at the sand, weighing whether to list examples or just get to the point. He chose both. "It happens all the time—weekly—sometimes daily. And throughout the year, there are dozens of significant examples."

"Really?" Chad asked. He wanted to stay aligned with true north on this—clarity mattered.

"So, here's what I'll do," Tim said, leaning forward. "I'll draw from conversations I've had with Pastor Kane, Robin Tainui, and Dr. Alaina Gibson."

Tim, Charlotte, and Chad were familiar with them—though Chad less so—having been less involved in church lately. Tim gave context.

"Ps. Kane Kardinai is one of our pastors back home. He handles pastoral care for the young adults ministry, teaches, and has a passion for social and political sciences. He does an obscene amount of research into church sociology, politics, trends, and stats. He co-founded the Compass Foundation with former Chief and All Black Austin Rawlenson. It's a think tank that connects individuals, businesses, schools, churches, and philanthropists to identify needs and coordinate community-driven solutions.

Robin Tainui, is on more boards than a house and has more letters after his name than a book," Tim introduced.

Chad and Charlotte laughed knowingly.

"Sounds like someone we know," Rod said, nodding toward Rhys and Chaiyala. They grinned.

"Robin wears many hats. He's a church elder and lectures in theology and leadership at Horizons College—the Bible college attached to Abundance City Christian Center in Hamilton.

He also teaches business studies at the University of Waikato. And when he's not immersed in church or academic life, he quietly oversees several community initiatives with steady dedication.

Alaina Gibson—Chad's and my aunt—is a gifted sociologist and political scientist. She serves on the board of the Meridian Institute, which advises the New Zealand government on social and political dynamics and policy making."

"These three are key people in our church. Their expertise helps shape how we respond to community needs. So yes," Tim said, looking at Rod, "perspective plays a big role in what the church does and how it's perceived."

Chad felt at ease. He'd nudged Tim into a discussion that played to his strengths—big-picture thinking. He trusted Tim's insight.

"To use another figure of speech," Tim continued, "if you can't see the forest for the trees, you'll get stuck in a rut and hung up on the wrong things."

He paused, then added, "From what I've learned from them—and my own, limited research—the global evangelical church is in a good place. It's doing its job. Its positive impact on society is at an all-time high. You won't hear that in the news, but despite human error, false doctrine, infighting, and corruption, the body of Christ is doing what it's meant to do."

"At Abundance City, the sixteen-million-dollar Eastern Suburbs campus was paid off ten months ago. Last year, twelve-million-dollars went into community ministries—poverty reduction, youth work, food banks, shelters, and the Genesis Project—which helps people transition into stable jobs and housing."

Chad, feeling steadily encouraged, felt a mental burden lifting.

"Now free from debt, the church is channelling twenty-two-million into ministry work. While also partnering with the Eden Initiative to fight human trafficking across Southeast Asia. The church has also joined forces with NZ Prison Ministries to support inmate rehabilitation and reintegration.

Next year, projected funding will rise to thirty-two-million dollars. By 2021, the goal is forty-five-million—invested in blessing the city and expanding outreach across the region."

"Mate! These are massive numbers!" remarked Rod.

"For sure!" Chaiyala concurred.

Rhys and Charlotte nodded slowly.

"Celesta recently shared a new project unfolding in Hamilton high schools. Using heartfelt, innovative approaches to reach youth at risk and strengthen ties between the church and those on the margins.

"That's hard-core legit!" Rhys shook his head. Gripped by the concept of a church operating in such large realms to impact the community at this level.

Chad looked out to sea, feeling bewildered, encouraged, and inspired.

"That's phenomenal," Rod said. "Nathan'd fit right in."

"Aye, bro! That'll be Nathan's church—has tae be," Rhys said, grinning. They all cracked up.

"I've got the two of you to thank for flying me out from under the rock I've been living under," Chad said.

"Funny, isn't it?" Chaiyala began, narrowing her eyes at him.

He frowned.

"...what happens when you live under a rock."

"Yeah, the church turns out to be completely legit—and Atlantis is discovered!" Chad laughed. The others joined in.

Rod chuckled after a moment. "You'd think I'd be used to it by now, but every time I hear 'Atlantis has been discovered,' I'm still gob smacked. Feels like a dream."

"I hear ya," Tim agreed.

Everyone nodded.

Tim continued, "Earlier, I listed a few negatives about the church—but not the dozens of positives. I haven't even touched on the fact that the negatives are few and far between when you look at the big picture. You've heard of mindfulness in counselling, right?"

"Yup," Chad nodded.

"Factfulness, like mindfulness, is a vital thinking skill. It promotes clarity by reducing over-dramatization and focusing on fact-supported perspectives. It helps you step back, manage emotional reactions, and ask better questions: Why do I think this way? What's the evidence?

If I highlight six problems but ignore thousands of good things, I'm not giving a fair report of the whole picture."

Chad nodded. "I like that—that's good. Now we're reading from the same script."

"Gapminder.org," Rod said with a knowing smile. "You should check it out."

"This lines up with a lot of what you've shared before, eh?" Chad said.

"Pretty much."

"All that stuff you shared on the sky hill—did you get it from Kane, Robin, and Alaina?"

"Mostly, yeah. Honestly, those three are a blessing!"

"I'm actually looking forward to seeing them again and having a proper chat," Chad said, feeling encouraged.

"It's all about who you surround yourself with. They've got to be the right people, or you'll get led up the garden path," Tim said.

"And before you know it, you're stuck in a compost heap," Rhys added with a mock-wise expression.

There was a beat of silence, then laughter.

"True!"

"You'll do well to catch up with them—and check out Gapminder.org," Tim said.

"That'll rearrange the way you see the world," Rod added, as if speaking from experience—then his phone buzzed in his pocket.

He glanced at the screen. His expression shifted instantly.

"...oh come on! For real? You've got to be kidding me." He stood up, eyes wide. "Yup—on our way," he hung up.

Everyone looked at him, alert.

"That was Crouton," Rod said, voice low but urgent. "Egypt's declared war on Mauritania."

The table froze.

Chad blinked. "Wait—what?"

Tim leaned forward, stunned. "Pardon me?"

Charlotte was already pulling out her phone. Rhys and Chaiyala exchanged a look—half disbelief, half readiness.

Chad rose slowly, the weight of the moment pressing in. The spiritual clarity he'd just gained now had to coexist with the reality of a world on fire.

He glanced at Tim, "guess the world doesn't wait for us to finish our conversations."

"Nope. But maybe that's why they matter," Tim replied—giving half a smile.

They made haste toward the eastern tower. The serenity of the beach was already fading. The sun still shone, the waves still rolled—but the world had shifted.

And they were walking straight into it.

CHAPTER 25

T he sudden, unexpected news changed the subject in no uncertain terms.

Rhys swore under his breath. He and Chaiyala moved quickly, in a certain sense of being unsurprised.

Rod led the way—cutting a beeline through the pools precinct toward the western tower. Tim, Rhys, and Chaiyala followed, propelled by instinct more than decision.

Chad and Charlotte trailed behind, still trying to register what was happening.

Tim's jaw tightened. He hoped to God there'd been some mistake. They'd made real progress—and there was still so much left to do.

Charlotte broke the silence. "So—what happens now?"

"I've got no idea, Angel... probably means we're on the next flight back to New Zealand, in the other direction from Africa—and that's gonna be the worst."

Chaiyala was sceptical. She'd need to see something—or hear a clear explanation from Nathan or Crouton—before she'd believe it. The suddenness of it all smelled fishy.

~~~~~~~

Rod and Rhys led the way—hot footing it out of the elevator into the penthouse suite—Chaiyala on their heels—Tim, Chad, and Charlotte close behind.

Sienna stood with her hands resting on the back of the three-seater, leaning forward.

Alesandro sat on the edge of the same couch. Both looked at the new arrivals, then at the eighty-two-inch screen.

"Nathan's on the phone with President Aziz Ahmedou of Mauritania, and I'm pretty sure Crouton's speaking with President Amani Darafed of Egypt," Sienna informed them. "Both calls sound the same—full-scale damage control."

"Right, okay. What do we know?" Rod asked her.

"Our agents are on it, but everyone's been caught on the hop."

"Well, what are Amani and Aziz saying?" Rod pressed.

"That's the best part. They haven't a clue either—they're in the dark too."

"Sorry?" Chaiyala asked, confused.

Rod frowned, leaning in as if he'd misheard.

Chad and Charlotte exchanged uneasy glances.

"Check this out," Tim said, joining Alesandro in front of the screen.

"Tensions between Egypt and Mauritania are escalating rapidly," the news anchor reported, *"following a wave of corruption allegations against the Mauritanian government and unresolved disputes over historical assets and antiquities earlier this month. Details remain unclear, and no official statements have confirmed the nature of the conflict. At this stage, it's difficult to pinpoint exactly what's driving the unrest between the two Saharan nations."*

"Hmm..." Chaiyala narrowed her eyes. "I do not buy that. Someone is playing games."

"Albarad," Rhys suspected.

"Guarantee it's Albarad," said Rod.

"Wouldn't put it past him," Tim agreed.

"... *Mauritania's military has been put on high alert after Egypt's Minister of Egyptology—Hamet Albarad—stated that if Mauritania doesn't stop what it's doing, Egypt will be forced into armed conflict. That the time for sanctions and talks with their Saharan neighbour is over...*"

"Sanctions and talks, Hamet?" Nathan smirked, fresh off the phone with the Mauritanian president. "That's news to me."

"Ha!" Tim laughed. "There ya go."

"Oh, my goodness, why am I not surprised?" Chaiyala muttered. "Who does he think he is? What has he got to do with such decisions?"

"*...Egypt's President Amani Darafed and Minister of Defence have publicly renounced any threats of war against Mauritania. They've also condemned recent remarks made by Minister of Egyptology Hamet Albarad, calling them gravely out of line.*"

"Typical," Chaiyala said through gritted teeth, still itching to knock Albarad into next week after their last encounter.

She partly resented Nathan for holding her and Crouton back.

"The man's a complete salmon," Rhys muttered, shaking his head.

"This is really not a smart move," Tim said, also shaking his head. "Is he trying to commit diplomatic suicide?"

"Or does he have something else up his sleeve?" Chad asked. "This comes across as foolish and desperate. I just hope he's merely that stupid— and not playing a hand he thinks he can't lose with."

Chaiyala looked at him, narrowing her eyes—both impressed and bothered.

"*Political correspondent Marissa Le Grande describes the Sahara stand-off as a clash between politicians wielding power they believe they have—without offering clarity on what's really going on. Here's Marissa now.*"

The face of the French political reporter appeared on-screen.

"The situation between Egypt and Mauritania remains unclear," Marissa began. *"It looks like a public dispute between high-ranking officials, but the true cause is anyone's guess. There's speculation about ancient artefacts, historical sites, and contested assets—but without evidence, it's hard to separate fact from noise. So far, nothing concrete has emerged. No one in either country seems to have a clear grasp of what's unfolding. And the central figure—the Egyptian Minister of Egyptology—has yet to respond.*

One thing is clear: the fact that this has surfaced suggests something volatile exists within Egyptian politics, aimed at Mauritania, and it needs to be addressed. The more likely scenario may involve a very secretive large-scale archaeological dig currently underway in central Mauritania. This is important to note: based on the Egyptian President's and Defence Minister's positions, it could be a personal issue rather than a matter of state policy."

"What archaeological dig?" Rhys feigned puzzlement. "Aye, there's nothing going on there... just camels and sand. Camels and sand..."

The others laughed.

"And elephants that look like giraffes!" Tim added.

More laughter.

"I've never even been there. You?" he asked Rod.

"Nah," Rod shook his head. "Didn't even know Mauritania was a place till now."

A few sides were starting to hurt.

"...but any information on the dig site has dried up," said the correspondent. *"No one can get a straight word from anyone involved. The last we heard was an exclusive interview via New Zealand's TVNZ, when chief historian Tim Harison explained a little about the discovery of an ancient city predating Ancient Egypt, Rome, and Greece by tens of thousands of years."*

"Right then," Tim sat bolt upright. "So that actually happened? I thought it was all a strange dream."

The others laughed again.

"So—I guess we just hold tight—and wait to see what comes of this," the CNN anchor concluded, glancing at her colleague. *"Unfortunately, we don't have much more than that,"* the political correspondent replied. *"Just arguments between politicians within the Egyptian government and between Egypt and Mauritania—along with the Mauritanian military preparing for the worst, which may not even come."*

"This is certainly an interesting turn of events..." Rod remarked.

"Yeah... sounds weird though...," Tim frowned—still waiting on further comment from Nathan and Crouton, who were now, both off the phone with the presidents of Egypt and Mauritania.

Chad and Charlotte weren't sure what to think, or how to feel, about 'rumours, or threats of war.'

The other Red Sword agents watched Nathan and Crouton closely, awaiting their take.

Crouton shook his head, half wishing his chief nemesis was within arm's reach.

"Blasted cabbage," he muttered, referring to Hamet Albarad. "What in blazes is he trying to achieve by this? If Darafed doesn't throw him out on his keister after this stunt, I'll be shocked." Crouton was filthy with frustration.

"What'd Aziz say?" Rod asked Nathan.

"He's livid. Confused and concerned. 'Preposterous nonsense' were the English words he used—along with a flood of expletives in French and Arabic. Mauritania's defence force isn't preparing for war, and Aziz hasn't heard a thing about this from Amani's side. He wants an emergency meeting between heads of state and defence ministers—and he'd like us present."

"Will Albarad be there?" Chaiyala asked.

"He's AWOL. At least he had the sense to disappear after this stunt," Crouton grunted.

"I can count on you two not to fall over each other trying to send the Egyptian Minister of Antiquities flying out the window if we end up in the same room?" Nathan asked Crouton and Chaiyala.

He was confident they were beyond doing anything brash—but he needed to know they knew it.

Tim chuckled.

"Absolutely," Chaiyala replied with a devilish grin that excited Chad—much to his own surprise.

Charlotte looked quizzically at Sienna, who grinned and shook her head.

Later, Sienna would explain the history between Albarad and both her father and Chaiyala—filling in what Charlotte didn't already know.

"What did Amani say?" Rod asked, brushing past the moment.

"He's in the same boat as Aziz," Crouton replied. "Angry as a flicked hornet. His Defence Minister is just as volatile. He feels set up—falsely accused—and," he glanced at Nathan, "he's eager to meet Aziz to straighten things out ASAP. What stood out was everything President Amani Darafed didn't say."

"Okay...?" Rod prompted.

"Amani's hands are tied—or Egyptian politics is caught in something uniquely dysfunctional and dangerous," Crouton muttered. "His words—his tone... it all suggested as much."

Yeah, I don't like this," Chad admitted.

He and Chaiyala exchanged a look, silently affirming their mutual suspicions.

The CNN political commentator continued: *"When Egypt supposedly made threats of war against Mauritania, France and the United States were quick to step in and attempt mediation. But like everyone else, they were caught off guard—surprised to learn no real threats had been issued.*

To make matters worse, Egypt has abruptly cut off communication with the mediating nations—many of whom were already uncertain where to begin. In a written statement, Egypt's Minister of Defence accused the United Nations of being 'clueless and naïve' about Mauritania, its leadership, and its President. He went on to claim that the UN had enabled what he called a nation of 'corporate criminals' responsible for Egypt's suffering.

That's all we know for now. The situation is murky, and we're completely in the dark. What's clear is that military activity in both Egypt and Mauritania looks like a disturbed wasp nest—though no one knows anything for certain. Egypt's commanders are awaiting orders, Mauritania is bracing for defence, and early suspicion is falling on Egypt's Minister of Antiquities."

"What? That's just confusing," Charlotte said—frowning frustrated by the contradictions.

"I'll tell you what's going on!" Crouton snapped. "Albarad is s bluffing his way to the international court with this desperate new tactic!"

"None of that would have actually come from the top, in Egypt," Rod dismissed. "Not from the Egyptian defence minister..."

"No. You're correct," affirmed Nathan, "that directly contradicts what we know from them personally."

"We knew he'd try something drastic eventually," Rod reminded. "I just didn't think it'd be this brash—or this poorly put together."

"Well, if he is trying to confuse the hang out of everyone, looks like he is succeeding," Chaiyala said.

"Typical Albarad," Tim added. "He's never been known for making much sense."

"It's okay," Sienna reassured. "Rod's right—we anticipated a major hit-out, just not this," she shook her head, amused. "Regardless, we're prepared. My team's already on it—executing protocol, revising contingencies."

Charlotte felt reassured, as did Tim and the others.

Chad, however, was caught in mental turmoil. Questions about what he'd gotten himself into bounced through his mind like restless gargoyles. Unease threatened to slip into anxiety. He realized he was on a psychological roller coaster—shifting from peace to neutrality before plunging into uncertainty. He needed to hold onto peace, to keep from being swept up in the chaos around him.

Tim and Charlotte focused on how Nathan, Crouton, and the Red Sword agents were responding, while Rhys and Chaiyala kept their eyes narrowed on the TV.

"This is the biggest load of rubbish I've ever heard," Rod said, shaking his head at the screen. "Honestly, how do you drag out a dramatic twenty-minute news piece with nothing more than a supposed 'declaration of war' and 'no one really knows what's going on?' Trust modern news media."

Tim pointed at Rod without a word, silently agreeing.

The anchor continued: *"...we now have political scientist Dr. Guion Spaezee from Georgetown University with us in Washington, alongside political analysts and the Egyptian ambassador to the United States. They're trying to piece together what triggered this kind of action from Egypt toward Mauritania. Guion, what can you tell us?"*

"This should be interesting..." Tim muttered. He shook his head wondered how an Egyptian ambassador could be so out of the loop on his own country's political activity and foreign policy.

"Obviously, the apparent—or supposed—military activity in both states is our only certainty. But it's long been suspected that something in Mauritania has ruffled feathers high up in Egypt—bitterly so. The details remain a mystery, but questions are now

being raised about a large-scale archaeological excavation in the northeast Adrar region of Mauritania. We understand that a city the size of central New York, predating Ancient Egypt, may have once existed there. At this stage, that remains the only confirmed detail of significance"

"Oh for goodness' sake, you've already been over that!" Rod protested.

Tim hoped Celesta wasn't watching—she'd be spitting tacks at the awful excuse for journalism. She probably was.

"Egypt's claim that Mauritania has somehow wronged them also remains unclear—especially given the alleged link to an archaeological dig on the far side of the continent. One theory, currently stirring heated debate, suggests the ancient city in question may have housed a technology capable of wiping out civilization before the last ice age—an engineering science more advanced than anything known today.

Experts, however, are dismissing the idea as far-fetched. They point to basic historical facts, including the timeline: for such a city to exist, it would have to predate the Bronze Age.

Leading historian Paula Walovyeis..."

Tim shut his eyes and sighed—resisting the urge to curse.

Rhys and Rod laughed at the name, while Chad and the others exchanged looks—barely following the report but catching the blatant pun.

Nathan nodded along, as if this was all par for the course.

"Come on! Seriously?" Rod shook his head with a grin—looking at Tim and Crouton.

"...has dismissed the concept as entirely fictitious—problematic, implausible, and rooted in the wild imagination of conspiracy theorists."

"My beard," Crouton muttered, grinning now too.

"There we go!" Nathan laughed—finally breaking his calm. "Works like a charm every time. You can hide behind the truth and shout, 'Here I am!'—and they still won't believe a thing—yet."

"Oooh I wish someone could please just tell us what's actually happening?" Chad requested—his voice tight—the confusion and dread finally spilling over.

Charlotte, Chaiyala and Rhys were looking lost.

"Paula Walovyeis—or 'Pull-the-wool-over-your-eyes'—is no more a historian than the idea that she even exists," Tim said flatly. "There's no such person. Despite her name being quoted every time some pseudo-authoritative—reassuring dismissal is needed for public comfort. It's like the darn Matrix..." He glanced at the screen. "She doesn't exist."

"Are you sure about that?" Sienna asked, a little too casually.

"What? Yes. Any self-respecting historian worth their research knows this. I've checked and rechecked. Sure, she might have a website, Facebook, LinkedIn, even an itinerary—but she never shows up. Always some excuse. A lot of people in the field are fed up with it. No one's ever actually met her." Tim looked at Sienna, a little more sternly than intended.

"I'm pretty sure she's real," Sienna grinned—nodding.

"Oh, and you've met her?" Tim shot back.

"Hmm, not quite..."

"Then..."

"...but you have," Sienna teased.

Tim narrowed his eyes. "What do you mean?"

Crouton burst into laughter. "No way!" He looked at his daughter—no response—then laughed again.

"You're looking at her," Sienna smiled.

Tim stared. "What...?" He didn't know whether to scream or laugh. "You're kidding me..."

Sienna shook her head.

The others were all an exchange of puzzled expressions, and an odd mix of amusement and disbelief.

Crouton had known of Paula Walovyeis and her ties to Red Sword. But as Nathan's contact, he'd never questioned her role.

The revelation that Sienna was the fictitious historian stunned him.

"Paula Walovyeis is a smokescreen," Nathan said. "Her job is simple: present a credible media voice that shuts down anything outside the usual intellectual and historical frameworks. Sienna's team manages her—she gives us cover."

"She's a distraction—more, a pressure valve," Sienna continued. "While the public debates her dismissals, we move quietly beneath the noise. We don't stand with the system—we use its blind spots to finish the work it would never allow. And when it's done, the veil lifts."

"Buys us time, and keeps things looking reasonable while we work behind the scenes," Rod nodded—reflectively.

"Take Atlantis," Sienna added. "The idea of a lost, high-tech city buried beneath the Sahara—older than Egypt—rattles anyone tied or committed to conventional timelines. Worse, it suggests history's been tampered with for generations. Paula helps manage that tension. She reinforces the idea that conspiracy theories come from ignorance, while experts like her calmly dismiss them with logic. Most people are happy to leave it there."

"Ayeee..." Rhys was impressed.

"You give the media what they want to hear," Chad said. "The lowest common denominator—accommodating society's comfort zones."

"Exactly," Nathan said. "We're not preserving illusions—we're buying time to expose them."

Sienna nodded. "Paula keeps the spotlight off the cracks in the system, so we can work without interference."

"Goodness!" Tim shook his head with a grin. "And to think how annoyed I've been with this woman... who doesn't exist."

Nathan, Chaiyala, and Sienna laughed.

"Till now, I've found her to be an infuriatingly dismissive know-it-all who can't think outside the box to get all the facts—not just the comfortable, conventional ones," Tim confessed, arms folded. "Well played, though," he conceded.

"That's hilarious!" Rod said, and the others agreed.

"Obviously, the construct serves its purpose effectively," Nathan concluded. "Even you were none the wiser."

For some reason, Chad was craving rugby. He'd never cared for sports—that was Tim's domain. But after the CNN broadcast, the Red Sword agents' reactions, and the chaos unfolding in Africa, something in him ached for home. Rugby—any game, any team—felt like comfort.

He'd been silent—rattled by the news, and the confusing tension and speculation on TV. Then, out of nowhere, he asked Tim about Super Rugby. Tim blinked, caught off guard. "It ended weeks ago," he said. "Crusaders took the final—bit of a let-down, really. Argentina's Jaguares made it in."

Charlotte looked at them both, recognizing the unexpected nature of Chad's enquiry.

Tim explained, "while the Super Rugby season's done, the Rugby Championship—New Zealand, Aussie, South Africa and Argentina has just commenced."

Chad stood. "I'm gonna get some space. Back in a while." He figured he'd head to the Round Robin Sports Bar, see if any All Blacks matches or any rugby was playing.

"All good, bro," Tim smiled—making a mental note to check in later.

Chaiyala rose a moment after Chad, glanced at Tim, and gave Rhys a subtle signal to follow in two minutes. She wasn't about to let anyone wander off alone—not after what happened with Alesandro.

Tim was relieved and gave her a grateful smile.

Chad entered the elevator and turned to press the ground floor button when Chaiyala slipped in beside him. She gave him a confident, reassuring look that said, *"Don't argue—I'm coming with you, and I've got your back."*

Chaiyala liked Chad. She was cautiously letting herself explore that— guarding her heart, yet ready to test the waters.

Chad had wanted solitude, but her quiet presence was comforting. He didn't mind her company if she insisted.

"You are okay?" she asked.

"Dunno... just outta sorts. Part of me wants to go home."

She nodded kindly.

"And I get sick of people after a while..."

She raised her eyebrows understandingly. They exited the elevator and proceeded to the Round Robin Sports bar.

"But not of you," he added, realizing it as he said it.

"I get it. I need space too—sometimes more than half the time."

They exited into the leafy lobby and made their way toward the Round Robin Sports Bar and Grill.

"You and your brother are introverts, yes? But Tim—I don't know, sometimes he feels more like an omnivert."

"An omnivert?"

"It's like a people-oriented introvert. Or not really introvert, not extrovert. Somewhere in between. I get energy from both—people and quiet. That's me."

"Interesting," Chad nodded thoughtfully.

His mind was miles away as they approached the bar. It felt like the sun had set inside him—as if everything else was asleep in his inner world.

Chaiyala felt eyes on her. Not the usual admiring glances she ignored—this was different. She scanned her periphery, assessing everyone within a few meters of Chad.

Rhys was seated at a tall table with two men and a woman—each undercover Red Sword agents. Beers (non-alcoholic) in hand, a jug in the middle. The illusion: Rhys had been there all along, just returned from the bathroom.

Chad felt a flicker of normalcy seeing four people in All Blacks jerseys. The crowd—Rhys and co. included—were gathered around tall tables and on sofas in front of a big screen. A Rugby Championship match between New Zealand and Argentina was about to kick off.

"Great timing, Chaiyala. I think we got here just in time. I'll get us drinks—what are you having?"

"Tropical smoothie. Dairy free," she smiled, momentarily distracted from her scan.

He turned to order—but froze. Ten meters away, a man was staring at him with a hostile gaze.

"No way," Chad breathed.

Chaiyala snapped to attention. "What is it?"

"That guy—he looks like the one from the airport in Paris. The armed guy. Red Sword agents took him down."

She followed his gaze and knew instantly. She rose from her stool, ready to approach.

She'd just reached the end of the bar when a group of officious-looking men entered from the Grand Isle. They didn't fit in. And there in the midst of them—surrounded by the others as they moved...

"No way," Chad mouthed, hand on the bar.

Hamet Albarad.

They'd just seen his face on the news twenty minutes ago. And now he was here—in Jamaica. At the Caribbean Paradise.

Chad's next thought: *"All the wrong people are in the same place."*

Chaiyala positioned herself between Chad and the group as they neared.

"Ms. Mizrah!" Albarad snarled, his voice oily and unwelcome.

"Albarad. What are you doing here?" she asked coldly.

Flanked by bodyguards, Albarad looked smug. Chad figured these were the infamous black ops grunts people regarded with disdain.

Chad was tense, but less so with Chaiyala in front of him—and Rhys nearby with backup.

"I heard Father Christmas and his elves were here on holiday," Albarad sneered. "Thought I tell him to get back to the North Pole—get back to work—Christmas is coming!"

His entourage snickered.

Chaiyala tilted her head, grinning menacingly.

"Who is this?" Albarad asked, eyeing Chad. "Your new boyfriend?"

A quiet tension crept through the room—unease settling in. Some had just recognized who the Egyptian politician was.

"Yes. Where is yours?" Chaiyala shot back, taking Chad's hand and holding her ground.

Albarad scowled and stepped forward, stopping a meter and a half away.

"If we were not surrounded by witnesses, I'd slit your throat, you filthy tomb-rat," he hissed. "Your kind are scavengers dressed in sentiment—unworthy of history."

Chad's stomach turned. He braced for a fight.

Chaiyala's eyes went wild. She clenched her fists—nearly crushing Chad's fingers. She let go—he wasn't worried. Rhys and the other agents arrived behind them.

She stepped up to Albarad.

One of his men raised an arm to push her back. Mistake. She gripped his wrist without breaking eye contact with Albarad.

"How fast you run, old man?"

No response. The tension was electric.

"Ten seconds. That's all I need for your monkeys. Then it's your turn."

The bodyguard twitched.

"Want me to break off your arm, knock you out with it?"

He froze. Albarad gestured sharply for him to back off, his impatience barely masking reluctance.

Albarad hated her. He feared her. But his pride wouldn't let it show.

Chaiyala smirked, stepped back, and stood close to Chad. She took his hands, wrapped them around her waist, and gave Albarad a triumphant look.

Albarad's eyes shifted left—and so did his expression.

Chad instinctively held her at her side as she leaned into him.

"Hamet is here to see me. Are you not?" Nathan said, arriving with Rod, Tim and Charlotte. Rohit and Maurice with two resort security arrived, and Sienna entered with Alesandro. Crouton stood beside Nathan—towered, more like—looking utterly livid.

"Nathan. What a pleasure," Albarad said flatly.

He extended his hand to Nathan, Maurice, and Rohit—but not Crouton. He wanted to keep that hand. Losing it to Chaiyala would be bad. Losing it to Crouton would be suicidal.

Rod, Tim, Rhys, and Sienna suppressed smirks. Charlotte and Chad watched with interest. Crouton was seething. Chaiyala fantasized about pinning Albarad to a wall like an insect and beating him senseless.

"How's the bed, Albarad?" Crouton asked.

"What?"

"Bet it's pretty fragrant right now," Crouton grunted, referring to Albarad's war declaration stunt.

Chad was torn. He found Chaiyala incredibly appealing for so many reasons—but that was not the plan. His heart was racing.

"Welcome to the Caribbean Paradise Resort. It is an honour to host you, sir," Maurice said diplomatically—masking his disgust with a sugary smile. He made a mental note to rinse his mouth out later.

Rohit was relieved he didn't have to say anything. Nathan looked as bothered as a rhino with a finch on its horn. And Crouton shook his head—privately annoyed that Nathan kept putting him in rooms with this man.

Rohit, Rod, and Crouton escorted Albarad and his entourage to a lavish conference room above the Caribbean Skillet. The venue offered sweeping ocean views. Nathan and Maurice followed.

The others remained at the Round Robin, now fully immersed in a physical but entertaining All Blacks vs. Pumas test match. Tim ordered a first round of drinks after the tension eased. Sienna and Rhys ordered a towering platter of wedges, chicken nuggets, prawns, and fish bites.

After the game, Alesandro disappeared for a nap while the rest gathered in the twin-share suite Rhys and Rod were bunking in at the penthouse .

"So now you've met Hamet Albarad," Tim said to Chad and Charlotte. "Bogus Minister of Egyptology, for the Egyptian government."

"The man is poison," Chaiyala said, her tone silk and steel. "A wolf? No. Even that's too noble. Jackals have more grace."

"Not gonna lie," Chad muttered, "I was half-expecting you to go postal on him and his crew after what he said."

"I could have," she admitted. She paused, exhaled. "But I had to dig deep. If I hadn't... the political damage would have been worse."

"So, what exactly did he say?" Charlotte asked—then instantly regretted it.

Chaiyala obliged. Her voice was low, her gaze fixed out the window. "That kind of venom doesn't come from nowhere. He's a dirty piece of work."

Shock and disgust rippled through the group. Charlotte and Sienna reached for her, arms wrapping gently around her shoulders. Chaiyala didn't pull away. Her breath shook, close to tears.

The silence stretched—until Tim finally spoke—voice tender. "Let's not let his rudeness ruin paradise. We've always got your back. The map to the fortunes of Atlantis is in our hands, now the Solon diaries are translated. We're heading inland... sometime soon..." he paused. "It's just a matter of time, now, until Atlantis is revealed to the world and things will roll into motion to put the likes of Albarad behind bars for a very long time."

"Aye," Rhys agreed. "Nathan's briefed us on the plan."

"This is true," Chaiyala added thoughtfully.

"So let's make the most of our time, then, eh?" Chad smiled.

Chaiyala gave him a look that caught him off guard—warm, entrancing, quietly appreciative.

"What?" he asked.

"You two should do something about it," Tim said, as if it were the most obvious thing in the world.

"About what?" Chad frowned, still preoccupied.

Charlotte grinned, clearly on board.

"Oh man, how jealous would that make Rick?" Rhys said mischievously.

"Ooh yes! I so want to make him jealous! I want to make him squirm!" Chaiyala said dramatically.

They all laughed.

"You know he won't, though," Tim said. "He's a pain. Always acts like he couldn't care less. Carries on like he's king of the world."

"Hmm, I don't know," Chaiyala joked. "He can only resist me for so long. I bet he dreams about me and cries in his sleep—poor guy. What can he do?"

Tim snorted. "You're unbelievable."

Chaiyala winked. "I know."

She burst into hysterics—and so did everyone else.

"Oh my goodness, someone's a bit confident," Charlotte grinned.

"I think cocky is the word you're after, babe."

"I am both," Chaiyala said with a smirk.

"You're such a show-off," Rhys grinned.

"Look who's talking, Mr. Walks-Around-With-No-Shirt."

"I get it," Rhys said, gesturing to his torso. "It's hard to behave normally when you're around this all the time."

"Yeah, okay—shut up is a good idea right now," Chaiyala said, giving him a look.

The others were in hysterics.

"No need for that—jealousy's not a good look," Rhys teased.

"Do you know who you sound like right now?" Chaiyala grinned. "Rick."

"I sound like the man!" Rhys declared.

"Rhys, you are forgetting—I can beat you at arm wrestling," Chaiyala said.

"No way! Seriously?" Sienna asked.

"Yup. She can beat Rhys at arm wrestling," Tim confirmed—throwing Rhys under the bus.

"She cheated," Rhys muttered.

"Now you definitely sound like Rick," Tim and Chaiyala said in unison. More laughter.

Chad's mind drifted back to the suspicious figure he'd seen before Albarad arrived. He couldn't shake the feeling that the man was connected to something else.

"Before Albarad showed up," he began, "there was this guy who caught my eye. Looked a lot like the two we saw in Paris—before we met Rod at Charles de Gaulle."

"Oh yeah, what happened?" asked Rhys. He and Sienna hadn't been present when she and Chad had shared previously.

"We were minding our own business," Charlotte began, "looking for Rod, when two men approached us aggressively. It all happened so fast, but I managed to take one of them down before Red Sword agents intervened."

The others looked impressed. Charlotte's petite frame hadn't prepared them for that kind of story.

"Go Charlotte!" Chaiyala cheered.

"I'll say!" Sienna added.

"That's my girl. She's tougher than you'd think," Tim said proudly.

Charlotte did a little shadow-boxing. "He had no idea what hit him. It was funny. Then, a bit scary."

"You're saying that guy today reminded you of one of those men from Paris?" Chaiyala asked gently. "That's... strange, no?"

"Correct," Chad confirmed.

"Do you know anything about them? What did Rod say?" Rhys asked.

"Rod thinks they're connected to a Sudanese billionaire who opposes Red Sword's work in Mauritania," Charlotte explained.

Sienna, Rhys, and Chaiyala exchanged knowing looks.

"Al Cardinal," Rhys said.

They recorded Chad's statement. The potential threat was too serious to ignore. Resort security and Red Sword agents began searching for the man for questioning.

Later, Rhys and Sienna headed out for lunch at Trattoria Italia, leaving Tim, Charlotte, Chad, and Chaiyala back at the penthouse.

"So then," Charlotte said, "you two—what's happening?"

Tim wrapped his arms around her, grinning as she put the other two on the spot.

Chad looked at Chaiyala. She met his gaze—warm, kind, strong. He'd never met anyone like her. His cautious side wrestled with his adventurous streak. Was he ready for another relationship? Was he over Sonia?

Yes. That much was clear.

But had he healed from the pain she left behind? There was no proof he hadn't—nor any that he had.

Why did it have to be so complicated?

His cautious side reminded him his taste in women had been terrible— Sonia turned out to be a druggy.

"Chaiyala's not a druggy. Rack off," the internal argument went on.

His adventurous side begged him to go for it.

"Oh for goodness' sake, shut up."

Around Chad, Chaiyala felt free. She could be herself. He wasn't fazed by her athleticism—unlike others. A gymnast since childhood, she'd always embraced her strength. It filtered out those who admired her beauty but couldn't handle her defiance of stereotypes.

Chad was sweet, sincere, and unphased by the superficial. He seemed to see what really mattered. Like her, he knew what he wanted—because he also knew what he didn't.

Tim and Charlotte loved the idea of them together. Tim knew Chaiyala well and thought she'd be perfect for his brother. Charlotte agreed—she was already growing close to Chaiyala.

"You two are seriously cute together," Charlotte said. "No pressure—but seriously, you'd be great."

Chad chuckled at the contradiction but appreciated the sentiment. "And you'd have a built-in bodyguard," Tim added. "With her ninja skills, you wouldn't need a security system. You'd be the safest bloke around."

Chad and Chaiyala laughed.

CHAPTER 26

Hamet played his cards carefully, having woven Egypt's leadership into a web of subtle deceit over decades. Yet even he knew there were limits—push too far, and his adversaries might gain the upper hand.

Hamet walked a treacherous path, always dodging fallout while others paid the price. In politics, ruthlessness wore the mask of diplomacy. Yet every move he made served one purpose—power, wealth, and dominion over Egyptology and antiquities.

Yet he lived in constant fear of an ancient secret, known only to a few trusted allies—less treacherous, but no less complicit. The world remained blind to the truth he'd buried: myths of Egypt's gods, narratives shaped around pyramids and lost cities, scholars manipulated to think within his boundaries—usually non-the-wiser. Anyone who questioned too deeply was swiftly expelled from Egypt's academic field.

His mastery of persuasion rivalled history's most infamous figures. He had once viewed Hitler as a threat—not for his politics, but for his obsession with the occult and alternative history. Under a former alias, Hamet had worked tirelessly to keep Germany from unravelling the grand deception he'd spent centuries perfecting.

Ironically, the forces of darkness had risked exposing the very truths he feared Nathan O'Conner and Red Sword Security were pursuing now.

He despised the name 'Red Sword' and its ancient significance. To counter their investigations, he had to be more calculated than ever.

For years, he refined his methods—deep pockets silencing opposition, while alliances formed quietly with the CIA, politicians, journalists, archaeologists, and experts. Many aided his cause without knowing it—blind to the truths they were helping suppress.

Few grasped the true science behind Egyptology. Only the occasional physicist, historian, or investigator slipped past his controls—poking holes, asking uncomfortable questions, exposing inconsistencies. Among them were investigative journalists: persistent thorns in his side.

Hamet had perfected concealment, but he knew the dangers of exposure. And now, the threat loomed closer than ever.

For a time, these were lone operatives—easy to dismiss as conspiracy theorists. Their reputations were swiftly dismantled by Hamet's far-reaching grip. His control remained unchallenged until the rise of the Scarlet Blade and the era of revisionism—two separate and opposite forces—both a threat.

Revisionism had begun to confront established narratives head-on. It introduced evidence that unsettled scholarly consensus. Unlike the Third Reich, which reshaped history to serve ideology, this new force operated through decentralization. By disrupting accounts, ethics, and events without ever correcting them. In the digital age, it spread unchecked, making history more fluid, and more fragile than ever before.

It ushered in a post-modern age where truth fractured into a thousand competing versions of itself—fluid, shifting with the teller, not the tale. Conspiracy theories—both fabricated and legitimate—spread like wildfire, creating an uncontrollable surge of scepticism. This was the last thing Hamet needed.

Recognizing the threat as more insidious than Nazi-era occultism, Hamet took drastic action. He raided dig sites and museums, stripping them of controversial artefacts. Anything that might expose his deception was concealed, or quietly destroyed.

Enter Nathan O'Conner and Collin Ericson. With their legal team behind them, they secured Albarad's conviction for antiquity theft and vandalism. But the verdict went nowhere—Hamet paid no fine, served no sentence, and walked free. It was enough to deepen Crouton's contempt for Albarad, and for what he called Egypt's "idiotic Egyptology."

To Hamet, Red Sword was far more dangerous than revisionists. It was methodical, well-prepared, and traced its roots to what he feared most. Again, and again, it had undermined him—buying out, undercutting, dismantling his influence. Given the chance, he would have eliminated Nathan, Crouton, and their entire network.

But Red Sword had anticipated every move. His grip on Egyptology, the Sahara, and the shadowed realm of parahistory was slipping—unravelling thread by thread.

And of course, three questions remained: Firstly, what exactly is Hamet Albarad afraid of Red Sword revealing? Secondly, who is Hamet Albarad, really—and how has he controlled Egypt's government for so long? Finally, how is he old enough in 2019 to have a personal beef with Adolf Hitler eighty years prior?

The atmosphere in the conference facility above the Caribbean Skillet was taut with tension. On one side of the expansive boardroom table, Nathan and Crouton stood alongside their associates and resort representatives—united, alert, and bracing for whatever came next.

Opposite them, Hamet and his silent, watchful security team formed an unnerving presence. Confusion and tension filled the room. No one knew what to expect, but everyone braced for confrontation.

Maurice, Rohit, and their security personnel, unfamiliar with Red Sword's volatile history with Hamet, remained uneasy. Handhelds at the ready—they kept worst-case scenarios in mind.

Crouton had a simpler solution—thrash Albarad's men and hang the corrupt politician by his crown jewels from the rafters. He smirked at the thought, then reconsidered. If he acted without Chaiyala, she might never speak to him again.

Hamet's group consisted of six officials, three in his inner circle. His chief of security, a man of violent repute, was ready to strike like an ill-tempered Doberman. Another, a creep with a greasy presence, had stared at Chaiyala at the Round Robin. She'd already resolved to rearrange his face if he tried anything. Then there was a gaunt, exotic-looking rapscallion, scanning the room with smugness. Crouton shot him a glare, breathing heavily to avoid saying anything.

Nathan waited, savouring the moment. Then, with a loud snap of his fingers, everyone took a seat—except Hamet, who looked annoyed but eventually sat across from Nathan.

To Maurice's surprise, wait staff emerged with platters of seafood, sweets, and tropical fruit, followed by plates and bottles of fine wine on ice.

"Right then..." Nathan began. "Let's put aside our ancient, tedious differences and pretend to act like civil human beings."

Hamet chuckled quietly.

"Even you can manage that," Nathan added, like a parent expecting better behaviour.

Hamet ignored the jab.

"No one's going to beat the daylights out of anyone or hang them by the jewels," Nathan said. The room chuckled, then looked puzzled.

"For goodness' sake, eat, drink. Let's talk, then go our separate ways without making a scene."

Rod led the way. Crouton eagerly followed, determined not to miss out on the spread. Hamet's men slowly followed suit.

Maurice silently wondered how Nathan had arranged the feast so quickly, especially since Hamet's arrival had been a surprise.

"I'm not here to see you, Nathan," Hamet said coldly.

"Of course not. You're here for the piece of Atlantis," Nathan replied—waving his hand over the room.

Time stopped.

Everyone froze—indoors and out. Seagulls hung mid-air like pictures on a wall. Only Nathan and Hamet remained in motion.

Hamet looked around, then glared at Nathan.

"You can't do that anymore," Nathan said. "Your abilities are dying with your long-expired privileges as an administrator."

Hamet hated Nathan for many reasons, but most of all, for reminding him that his power was fading.

"Don't talk to me about responsibilities!" Hamet shouted, slamming his fists on the table.

Nathan waited.

"You abandoned your people! You let them bring about the flood, the ice age, the destruction of the world! Don't lecture me!"

"Responsibility..." Nathan mused. "A concept dark lords like yourself twist to justify selfish ambition..."

Hamet snarled.

"...We were charged with educating and aiding—not controlling. But you overstepped—corrupted your purpose, and separated yourself from the Creator."

"Damn the Creator!" Hamet croaked, his voice distorted.

"If you wish to side with Lucifer, be my guest..."

"Damn him too!"

"...you know how that ended last time."

"You accuse me of corruption? We were set up to fail! The Creator gave them free will—what did He expect would happen?"

"The Creator loved you, Hamet. As He loved me. As He loved all of us."

"Loved?" Hamet scoffed. "He played with us like puppets!"

"That kind of blasphemy emptied Paradise of a third of its population. Before the war, we had free will too. It was us the Creator enjoyed fellowship with. Then Lucifer spoiled it. We were assigned to show these people how not to make the same mistake."

"And yet they did! Which makes the Creator a fool!"

"No. It's not the Creator's fault. It's not on Him—for ruining their world, twice. With free will comes responsibility."

"So it's their fault?"

"In part. But not entirely."

"Rubbish! You'll say we partnered with Lucifer to turn them against the Creator."

"Hamet, that's exactly what happened. Even if you didn't mean to, Lucifer did. It was always about control."

"You fool! Freedom leads to destruction! Give people choice, and they choose ruin. We tried to stop that. We've been misrepresented!"

"Oh, Hamet. Don't you know who you sound like?"

"Who? Speak the name!"

"Lucifer. You speak his words. You share his spirit."

"How dare you!" Hamet's voice distorted again as something dark stirred within him.

"Silence!" Nathan commanded, with the authority of the Creator. "You shall not make your presence known. You will remain Hamet until the time appointed."

Hamet's body stiffened. The entity within him was restrained, forced back into dormancy. Unwillingly, he calmed.

Nathan sighed, gazing out the window. Time remained frozen—silent, unmoving—while two men of old argued over the fate of humanity.

"And," Hamet continued bitterly, "you speak of deception, yet which of these"—he gestured toward Crouton and Rod— "know who *you* really are?"

"You've forgotten what matters most," Nathan replied.

Hamet ignored him. "Not even your closest friend, Collin. He knows nothing, does he?"

"The difference between us is that you hide the truth for power. I will reveal it—when the time is right."

"When you intend to rebuild Atlantis," Hamet said, disapproving.

"You're afraid of the truth, Hamet. Afraid of failure. That's why you hide behind mythology. It's a masterpiece, I'll admit. But if you operated from love and respect, you'd see the same results I have."

"Atlantis turned on you!" Hamet snapped.

"That was Atlantis of old. People deserve a second chance."

"And then what? Relive the same nightmares? I won't let you use the Atlantium that broke the world twelve millennia ago!"

"There's your problem—you always assume the worst. You're the eternal cynic. But you and I both know the Creator has His creation under control."

"Ah, rubbish again!"

"History backs it up. The world is improving—slowly, yes—but steadily. The pace is deliberate, so people can keep up without being overwhelmed."

Hamet's expression softened slightly, "that much, I'll give you."

"I don't know why you're still clinging to this Hamet persona. You have no real ties to this realm."

Hamet was silent, thinking.

"Make Hamet disappear," Nathan said gently. "Come back as someone else. Reveal the truth. Spare yourself the media storm that will come with Hamet's public crucifixion."

"No. I know what you're suggesting." Hamet's anger returned. "Do you think I'm that stupid?"

Nathan leaned back, weary.

Hamet continued, "as soon as people learn what the Carsakarisks and Obelisks were for—and what Atlantium can do—they'll go to war trying to rebuild the same energy system that nearly destroyed the world. Stopping that is my purpose now."

"Hamet, that's never going to happen."

"Ahh! You're so stubborn and naïve! Curse you!"

"What do you think I've been doing for the last several decades? I've been building a counter-system—one that's invulnerable to the current world order, which right now is fragile. Take away its utilities, its precious internet, and it collapses. Unless... unless you have people, who put truth and others before fear, before ideology—even before their own version of truth."

"What are you talking about?" Hamet shook his head.

"The fact that you have to ask—there's your first problem!" Nathan dragged a hand down his face, exasperated. "You should understand history's patterns. The quiet mechanics of reality. But you're still caught up in theatrics."

"I don't care what you say, Nathan. I will have the Atlantium—whether I take it from a corpse or bring war to Mauritania to stop you from resurrecting a people of death."

"You're not the only one who can play with words, old friend. You're like a man who arrives at a duel only to find his sword has no blade. Your threats are meaningless."

"We are not friends."

"Then go. Leave us. Pursue whatever it is you're trying to achieve."

"So be it."

Nathan tapped the table twice. Time resumed.

Everyone in the room continued eating—awkwardly, though the quality of the food helped. If nothing else, the spread was excellent.

To the others, the only noticeable change was Nathan's mood. In an instant, he'd gone from upbeat and diplomatic to distant and drained.

Crouton thought he looked uncharacteristically spent. More like a man who'd just endured a fruitless negotiation.

"You alright?" Rod asked.

"Yes... I am now. I have to be."

Rod and Crouton exchanged a glance, unsure what he meant.

"Come!" Hamet barked, standing abruptly. He looked across at Nathan and added, "We leave. We have matters to attend to."

"What?" Crouton grunted.

Rod frowned, trying to figure out what he'd missed.

Rohit and Maurice looked puzzled. Hamet's men were irritated—they'd barely started eating.

Crouton was fuming. "Ya friggin' moron! Turn up, sit down for a few seconds, then get up and leave without a blasted explanation!"

Hamet looked at him coldly, said nothing, and stormed out with his entourage.

"Take your blasted bad attitude with you, ya daft, pig-headed excuse for a leader!" Crouton shouted after him. "I hate that guy so much," he muttered once they were gone.

"What the heck was that about?" Maurice asked, looking around. "No one said a thing..."

"Hamet," Nathan said with a sigh, "is an infuriating individual. I try my best with him, and he never listens."

"I sincerely do not understand why you bother," Crouton said, returning to his food. "Why waste your time with that rooster?"

Rod was suspicious. There was more to this than they'd witnessed.

Rohit raised an eyebrow. "You liken him to several farm animals?"

"It's cos he is one."

"Never mind, Rod," Nathan said, regathering himself. "Let's eat and enjoy the food and wine, regardless."

Crouton looked at Rod, confused by his expression.

Rod shook his head and decided not to overthink it. He went back to his food, letting the weirdness slide—for now.

CHAPTER 27

Tim and Charlotte, Chaiyala and Chad spent the hours before sunset swimming, then freshened up at the penthouse and returned to the atrium, settling on The Caribbean Skillet for dinner.

Chaiyala had brightened up after her clash with Albarad, while Chad wrestled with growing feelings for her and the weight of political turmoil he wasn't prepared to face. His thoughts bounced between gratitude for recent blessings and the stress of being far outside his comfort zone, with the prospect of venturing further still.

He sat gazing across the pools precinct from the Caribbean Skillet's outdoor sofas. Chaiyala leaned over the opposite arm of their two-seater, fervently discussing the next day's plans with Rhys. Chad had finished his fish and chips and now sat perplexed by a strange inner current—foreign, vivid, and beyond his control. It felt like a waking dream, as if he were remembering something that wasn't his.

At first, it concerned him. But the clarity and timing of it all felt too precise to be madness. He was increasingly suspicious it was something divine—yet he needed assurance he wasn't losing his mind.

The sun had set—the sky now a beautiful blend of peach and aqua cyan. Soft ambient lighting, glowing reflections from beneath the surface of pools, and flickering ember torches ushered in the hush of a calm tropical evening.

Sienna, seated next to Rhys with a view of the ocean, had just finished her meal. Adjacent to Chad and Chaiyala sat Tim and Charlotte, happily chatting with a couple Charlotte's fans from Wellington—fellow Kiwis on holiday who'd recently seen her in concert.

"Chad." He snapped out of it. Sienna had appeared on a bean bag below his line of sight.

He looked at her—softly dazed—still half-lost in his daydream.

"Hey!" he raised his eyebrows and smiled—hoping his shift in tone would reassure her.

"You okay? You've been off in space since you finished eating. And you downed that pretty fast without a word."

"Yeah... I'm good. I think. Actually, I'm certain." He nodded, as if finally convincing himself. "Feels like my brain's been running overtime... and it's persistent."

She nodded thoughtfully. "Had a hunch."

Chad had no idea how to explain the peculiar nature of his introspection.

"I need another drink," he decided. "You want anything?"

"Yes, sounds good."

They both ordered drinks and requested dessert menus. Chad moved to a bean bag behind the end of the sofa.

Their drinks arrived, and after placing dessert orders, Chad began with a quiet tone. "I'm gonna go out on a limb here. If this sounds crazy, forgive me."

"Hello! Crazy is half my job," Sienna grinned. "Most of it, some days." She sipped her Guinness and looked across the luxurious outdoor scene.

"How could I forget." He smiled. "Okay, our time with Brooke the other night—the more she spoke, the more I felt like she was speaking in code. Like there was a hidden message in her ranting. I agree with

Nathan—she's not the 'crazy goat lady' she pretends to be. It's gotta be all an act—for reasons I've no idea."

Sienna gave him her full attention.

"I'm not sure when you fell asleep, but eventually she started speaking logically—about Atlantean colonial activity in the Caribbean. That's when we found out about the toppled obelisk. And here's the thing: it wasn't until Tim and Charlotte mentioned Nathan O'Conner at the booking kiosk that the agent changed his approach. Not just upgrading us, but suggesting we ask about Brooke's Island once on the Outer Islands."

They sat in silence for a moment.

"What's the connection between Nathan and Brooke's Island?" Sienna wondered.

"That, I'd love to know... my gut tells me none of the people we saw on the island were random. Sy was crystal clear—he wasn't sending anyone over there unless his arm was twisted or his wallet overflowing."

"He was about as reluctant as you could get."

"Exactly."

"Then how did the others get over there?"

"I wondered that when we first arrived. That teen couple... where did they disappear to?" Chad paused. "This is the thing—I can't shake it. I have these concepts in my head about those people, Brooke, and everything she said. And in my mind, they're solid facts. Like, I know, with certainty, if we investigated tomorrow, the outcomes would match exactly what I'm thinking. That makes no sense. I've been trained to follow evidence, not gut feelings. But here I am—convinced."

"Who do you think the teens are?"

"They work for someone. Possibly spies. Especially the girl—she's deep in something. Feels like a covert corporate initiative. American. The boy's just tagging along."

Sienna narrowed her eyes, weighing Chad's words. She'd dealt with nutters, con-artists, even occult deception. Chad didn't fit any of those. Despite his recent struggles, he was grounded.

"This sounds like a sixth sense kind of thing."

"Certainly what it feels like."

"And you've never experienced this before?"

"No—not before Brooke's Island. And that weird spiritual experience on the beach the other day. Croc Dundee—I'm positive he's a shape-shifter. Possibly one of the deities of the Caribbean. The round-faced hobo guy with the tats—no idea. But I'm convinced none of the others were there by conventional means."

"And the Wizard and the one in the white bathrobe?"

"The Gandalf guy, he's the Wizard of Dunedin. Bathrobe—he's posing as a climate change activist. Like the younger blondie, he's connected to something hidden—more admirable than the teen girl's affiliation."

"You think Bathrobe is a he?"

"Yes. The look and lifestyle are a ruse."

"Okay." Sienna considered. "What do you reckon is the connection between all six?"

Chad thought. "The teens were there to see Brooke. Bathrobe is tracking the teens. Croc Dundee is with... Brooke—possibly Baron Saturday. Hobo's a mystery. The Wizard... he's peculiar, but I think he's legit."

"And he really is the Wizard of Dunedin?"

"That's the one." Chad thought some more, "if you look into his history, being on Brooke's Island isn't even the weirdest thing about him."

"Okay."

"And yeah, like I said, I don't know how I know any of this. But I do. Without a shadow of a doubt. And it doesn't feel like something I've deduced. That's what throws me."

"Are you feeling unsettled? Anxious?"

"Unsettled, yes. But more curious than uneasy."

Their desserts arrived. Sienna, momentarily absorbed in her berries and honey yoghurt, gave Chad space to reflect. He was stunned by the clarity of his recall—like a mental playback, able to fast-forward, rewind, even pinpoint details on a timeline.

"She rambled about gods—Edenites from Orion's Belt... I assume that's a reference to Sumerian texts and conspiracy theory circles. I think she suspects the teen couple are up to no good—her words designed to confuse them. That might explain why they left."

"She didn't seem too fond of them."

"Right. Then she said 'sports and politics shouldn't be mixed in a pot.' Her phrasing, tone—it all felt like codewords. I'm pretty certain."

Sienna opened her phone's notebook app. "Sports and politics should never be mixed in a pot," she recited, typing.

"Add 'This is what you get'—emphasis on 'what.' Might be relevant."

"Got it."

"She also said, 'Never use the Noodle Pigeon. They fling spaghetti farts at the Berlin Wall, the Pyramids of Iceland, and Rugby Park, Hamilton, 1981.' Then something about the tin-foil industry making a fortune off pointy hats and rump steaks... Rustabums. I don't think those last two are keywords, but note them anyway."

"Jackson Rutherford."

They both frowned.

"I must've been asleep by then," Sienna said. "This is crazy!"

"Oh, that's right!" Chad remembered. "At that point, I started wondering if she was speaking in code. And as if reading my mind, she stared at me like she was going to lunge at me. Chaiyala looked ready to pounce."

"Bet you love having that hottie for a bodyguard."

"I'm not complaining."

"Bet you're not."

Chad smiled. "Alimentary paste skirt chaser and sharks that eat spaghetti."

"Way to change the subject, Chad!"

"The Wizard said it. And it has significant meaning—no idea what."

Sienna corrected the spelling. "Alimentary with an A, right?"

"Correct. She mentioned the Orion alien concept again—two beings, one human-looking, one serpentine. That's ancient serpentine theory."

Sienna nodded knowingly.

"You've been down that track?"

"Oh, it's a highway to another world. Thousands of years older than Atlantis. Another story for another time."

Chad shook his head. "Good grief. Should've stayed home."

"Sometimes ignorance is bliss. Not nearly as exciting though," she added with a grin.

"The first half of Brooke's rant echoed the Sumerian conspiracy theory—God and Lucifer as equals until God seized control and banished His rival. She aimed that at the Hobo, Leila, Tommy, and The Wizard. The elder two—I've no clue. But with the teens, she was playing a long game. Stringing them along, sowing confusion. I think she suspected who they were and what they were up to. We joined the story already in motion."

"Interesting."

"Definitely. Then she shifted from ancient conspiracy, to apologetics. First calling the Bible a grand scam, then praising its infallible wonder. She highlighted fulfilled prophecy, intricate mathematics, supernatural precision... a divine plan only an infinite mind could devise. The contrast with the Sumerian ideas was brief but striking. I think she leans toward the biblical view."

Sienna nodded, typing notes into her phone. "Any contradictions were strategic."

"Likely... there was someone else with us on the island," Chad said suddenly—a chill in his voice. "Someone no one could see."

"Invisible?"

"Yes. We had no idea they were there. I don't think Brooke could see them either."

"Who?"

"No idea. But there was a point where she was talking about me—how I had heaps of questions, how she could sense I was hurting, and my heart was burning... something about 'because of her. ' I thought she meant Sonia, but no..."

He paused, eyes intense.

"Chad? What happened next?"

"She couldn't see you, Rhys, or Chaiyala from that point on. At least not until the end. I'm sure Chaiyala was about to take her on, then reconsidered when Brooke went all paranormal. Whoever that unseen presence was, they somehow, shrouded you guys from Brooke's vision. I wonder why."

"Weird... is that why she got mad about us bringing someone with us? Oh my goodness! That would explain the splashing in the water, mentioned, when no one was there."

"Probably. And she knew I was hurting from Sonia... and that I'm keen on Chaiyala."

"Oh, that's spooky." Sienna shuddered, then smirked.

"What? It's hard not to be keen." Chad smiled, heart swelling at the thought.

"She mentioned 'they who have been and come back.' She swore bitterly about them. I think she meant her brothers—and all the Caribbean history she didn't care about when Tim told her what he did for a job."

Sienna took another sip of her Guinness, then resumed typing.

"She's going back home... she's lonely," Chad said, frowning.

They looked at each other. "Where's home?" Sienna wondered.

"I thought she was a local," Chad said.

"Maybe not. I haven't been able to track down much about where she's from—let alone where she calls home."

"She has two brothers. The eldest is Poseidon, the younger is Neptune. And Brooke Russo isn't her real name."

"Her real name coming to mind?"

"Not yet."

"I thought Poseidon and Neptune were the same god—just Greek and Roman versions?"

"That's where it gets confusing. In antiquity, there are often multiple names for the same thing—Greek, Latin, Egyptian, Persian. But now that ancient history and mythology are being 'proofread,' who knows what we'll end up with."

"Baron Samedi—or Saturday—he's not a person, in the context of her brother's drinking buddy," Chad said, narrowing his eyes. "More like a thing. Or an event. I wonder if it's the stout—the beer that was on tap at the chill-out party island."

"Maybe."

"See if you can find anything about a local event or festival featuring the Baron. I don't know if it's significant... or if chicken sacrifices are involved."

Sienna grimaced. She watched Chad's expression shift from frown to wide-eyed.

"What is it?"

"Baron Samedi doesn't exist anymore. He was devoured by another demon."

"Baron Samedi was a demon?"

"Apparently. And the one we saw—the skull-faced figure with the top hat and cane—that wasn't Samedi. It was the one who devoured him. A shape-shifter. A fallen archangel. Basically, a demon on par with satan."

"Oh great," Sienna muttered, typing it down.

"Midway through her rant, Brooke had leaned toward monotheism—viewing belief in one God as a refreshing alternative to man-made religious constructs. She claimed the 2,500 gods worldwide weren't true deities but human inventions. This was aimed at the Wizard—likely in hopes he'd incorporate it into his public speaking back in Dunedin."

"That probably ties into the Solon diaries," Chad said. "Tim would've picked up on that."

"She claimed Bondye is the Caribbean equivalent of Jehovah, which is absurd. Only a distorted understanding of both could lead to that conclusion. There must be a hidden meaning—otherwise why'd she say it?"

"And Tim would've figured the same and ignored it as off-topic?"

"Exactly. He was trying to steer the conversation back to why we're in Jamaica. She kept getting sidetracked—likening gods to egotistical politicians. He was working hard to keep her on track."

Sienna finished typing and looked back at Chad, who frowned, deep in thought. She gave him a quizzical look.

"Things changed when Tim thought I'd said something. He gave me an odd look, glanced at Rhys and Chaiyala, then down the beach toward Gustefan. I didn't know what he was doing. Then, out of nowhere, he asked her about Atlantis."

"I was asleep by then."

"You were. And she gave us all the info we needed about the obelisk—Pastor Rio in Kinloss, everything. She went from fragmented riddles to focused and logical. Then she lost it—accused us of bringing Poseidon with us."

"Lost it? She turned into a monster!"

"Rudest awakening ever?"

"I thought I was having a nightmare."

"Craziest night. I'll never forget it."

"None of us will."

"What's odd," Chad continued, "is how Croc Dundee jumped into the dinghy with us, along with the Wizard. And we all saw Baron Saturday come out from behind the fire as we sped away. Brooke shrieked his name. Then Croc Dundee leapt overboard, splashed through the waves, and turned into the Baron."

"Definitely odd. Shape-shifting?"

"Yes. Or one of his accomplices—Cimetiere—assuming they weren't all the same."

"Okay, so we know Croc Dundee—Baron Saturday—left Brooke's Island. But the Hobo and Bathrobe were still there. And where did the Wizard go?"

~~~~~~~

It was midnight. Tim, Charlotte, and Rhys had gone to bed a couple of hours earlier.

Chad was the only one left in the living area. A quarter bottle of red remaining, a little cheese and crackers on an oak board. He debated whether to go to bed or relocate to the balcony.

Sienna and Chaiyala appeared from the elevator, greeting him cheerfully.

They looked a sight for sore eyes.

Chad remembered—they'd gone back out after dinner. He welcomed them and offered cheese and crackers. No drinks—they sounded like they'd had enough.

The three of them polished off the snacks. Sienna went to bed, leaving Chad and Chaiyala alone.

"Good night?" Chad asked.

"Yes, thank you. The best! So good to catch up with Sienna—just us, besties. Relaxed and lovely," she smiled. "Oh, and that man you saw outside the Round Robin before Albarad showed up..." Chaiyala remembered, snapping into focus.

"Yes?" Chad gave her his full attention.

"He's one of Al Cardinal's men—connected to our adversary in Sudan. He refused to say why he was here. He's not a guest. Other than working for the bad guys, he's no real threat. He's been removed from the Caribbean Paradise."

"So, he's been evicted?"

She poured herself a small glass of red.

"Yes. He won't get back in. And if Rhys or I are with you, there's nothing he can do."

"Okay. Thank you—for everything."

The space between them was warm and intense. Chaiyala smiled, walked over, confident, finishing her wine in one smooth motion. She eased onto his lap, the closeness both comforting and charged.

"I'm not going to let anything happen to you," she whispered, her voice filled with determination and affection.

Chad's hands found her hips. Hers rested on his shoulders. Their connection deepened as they leaned in and shared a long, passionate kiss.

CHAPTER 28

The following morning, Chad found Chaiyala, Tim, and Rhys in the kitchen and dining area of the suite. Crouton was checking logistics with Rod and Sienna for sentinel deployment prior to arrival in Kinloss.

"Mornin'," Chad greeted.

Charlotte and Chaiyala smiled warmly at him, exchanging greetings. Chaiyala smiled, took his hand affectionately, and pulled him in for a hug.

She joined, Rhys, and Charlotte again, prepping GPS gear, compasses, a glossy map book of Jamaica, first aid kits, hand-helds, and ammunition. Chad noticed a cell phone that looked like it could survive an eight story fall from the balcony, or being run over by a freight truck—one of seven, ready for those heading inland.

"Ever used one of these?" Chaiyala asked, handing him a SIG P320 firearm. Tim slid Chad a cold black forest chocolate breakfast smoothie along the counter.

"Once or twice," Chad replied. He thanked Tim and took a sip. "Did a few rounds of clay bird shooting at a mate's stag do. Slightly different to this though," he added, frowning as he examined the gun.

"I don't like them. I prefer close combat—disabling, not killing. But I carry one. Protocol—last resort."

She smirked, lining up the unloaded gun through the ranch slider, aiming at some distant point over the sea. "So, I tie Rick to a fence, put a can on his head, and have target practice. He just hopes I'm not getting slack."

Rhys grinned and shook his head.

"Hope Rick has a decent supply of clean underwear," Chad said, placing a hand on her shoulder and sipping his smoothie.

"I would never actually do that to anyone. Even if I imagine it because he drives me insane."

Chad and Charlotte laughed. "So you've thought about it at least?"

"Oh, many times I would happily shoot Rick. He'd shoot me back though—from a distance."

"Ninja warrior versus master sniper," Tim chuckled.

Tim and Charlotte packed lunches—chicken salad rolls, nut bars, apples, dark chocolate, and super-juice—into their backpacks. Chad admired the military-grade lunch boxes.

"These trusty boxes are great for so many purposes," Chaiyala said.

"Including lunch."

"The indestructible lunch menu," she joked.

Once the packs were checked and rechecked, Crouton briefed them on the next couple of days. They'd be staying in Kinloss with Pastors Reo and Alini Richie of the Haddington New Testament Church and their children, Taneil age fourteen and Malanda age twelve. Rod and Sienna, having coordinated with local RSS agents, had quietly secured the site—hidden surveillance, satellite coverage, and fallback routes all in place. The kit-out was complete: not just gear, but groundwork. Undercover units were already embedded, the location fortified without drawing attention. Every detail was tuned for a silent, seamless operation.

Chad and Tim finished their smoothies while the girls braided their hair—a practical choice for the unknown, as Sienna and Chaiyala had explained to Charlotte.

"Red Sword agents will be present, though covert. The main objective is to locate a toppled Atlantean obelisk with the help of Pastor Reo, based on information from Brooke Russo. Tim will lead the site examination. Rod and I will lead the expedition into Cockpit Country with the Pastor and one other. Chaiyala and Rhys, you're sticking with Tim and co.?"

"Copy that," Rhys replied.

"Always," Chaiyala smiled.

"Ho, ho, ho, merry Christmas!" Crouton bellowed, handing Chad and Charlotte a shoebox each.

Laughter followed as everyone appreciated his Santa act.

Chad and Charlotte laced up their brand-new, ultra-comfy steel cap hiking boots—built for adventure.

Nathan and Crouton reviewed final details, answering questions. Charlotte listened intently, aware of the real dangers ahead. She took cues from Tim, trusted Chaiyala and Rhys, and appreciated their protection.

Chad, meanwhile, found himself instinctively drawn to Chaiyala's presence, trusting her depth of experience and skill. His scepticism faded, replaced by a quiet logic: *"Why would I ever want to be apart from this extraordinary woman?"*

Nathan, Sienna, and Alesandro bid them farewell as they filed into the elevator. They made their way through the atrium to the Grand Isle, and exited via the VIP entrance at the Entrance'd Café to the secure basement car park where a couple of Humvees had been parked.

"Good morning," one of three Red Sword sentries greeted Crouton as he led the others toward the Humvees.

"All's ready, prechecked, and fuelled up. Good to go."

"Good to go," Crouton nodded appreciatively, as the agents helped load gear.

"Chaiyala," he called. She looked up. He tossed her the keys.

Crouton, who would drive the second Humvee, grinned his strange cheerful grimace.

Chaiyala narrowed her eyes and smiled back.

"Oh dear," Rod sighed. "At least get out of the basement without smashing anything, a'right?"

Tim shook his head, grinning, and followed Rhys and Charlotte to Crouton's Humvee.

Engines roared to life, echoing around the basement.

"I hope you're going to be a gentleman," Charlotte said to Crouton, raising an eyebrow.

"Of course I am," Crouton replied, as if questioning her doubt.

Tim frowned. Crouton was unpredictable. The others assumed he'd race Chaiyala on the A1—and even she expected it.

She eased the throttle, calm and deliberate—defying the urgency in the air. The two Humvees rumbled out of the basement behind her, tires gripping onto cobblestone. Crouton followed last, unusually quiet, his usual bravado replaced by a watchful stillness.

Chad sat in the front with Chaiyala driving. Rod sat behind, poised for action.

"Crouton won't race me," she said as they neared the A1. "He'll be gentleman—he'll let me lead."

Rod and Chad weren't sure if she was being sarcastic.

"And you'll beat him up otherwise?" Chad smirked.

Rod laughed.

"You want to see me take on a grizzly bear?" she grinned.

"He's a big teddy bear," Rod chuckled.

At the last moment, Crouton did nothing, letting them believe other-wise—until, without warning, he floored full throttle.

Chaiyala grinned and floored it, shifting gears rapidly—heel and toe, dancing the accelerator and clutch with furious precision. Crouton, with-out warning, tried to pass her.

Rhys sat shotgun in Crouton's Humvee as it tore down the A1.

"So, if a cop sees this, who gets the ticket?" queried Rod.

"What happened to being a gentleman, Crout?" Tim asked.

"Dude, give up—she's too fast for you," Charlotte teased.

"What?" Crouton barked.

Chaiyala used her lead to block him at corners, forcing him to back off.

Outside the Ocean View Resort, flashing blue lights appeared behind them. Both Humvees pulled over.

A Jamaican officer approached Chaiyala's window. She rolled it down.

"Do you know how fast you and your friend were going?"

"No... I was going quickly?" she said sweetly. "Officer, with respect, I know what you plan to do..."

"And what is that?" he asked, opening his ticket book.

"You're going to ask me to be your date to the police ball."

Rod looked away. Chad stifled laughter.

"Lady, police do not have balls," the officer replied, dead serious.

Chaiyala smirked. Rod and Chad lost it, laughing uncontrollably.

The officer sighed, shut his ticket book, and walked to Crouton's win-dow. He noted the Red Sword logos on their shirts and the sides of the humvees, and sighed again.

"Slow down. Please. Both of you. And tell your pretty, smart aleck friend to slow down too."

He returned to his car. They all laughed. Crouton called Chaiyala.

"Let's take it easy from now on, shall we?"

"Copy that."

"Isn't Chaiyala a former cop?" Charlotte asked.

"To think you used to be a police officer," Chad grinned.

"I know, right? So funny!" she replied.

Crouton and Chaiyala drove more civilly along the A1. Beyond the Ocean View, the landscape shifted—fewer resorts, alternating between urban pockets, scattered shops, gas stations, and tropical bush as they approached the town of Duncans. They left the A1 and headed inland along the B10, which forms Cockpit Country's eastern border after passing through Kinloss.

Rod was unusually quiet for most of the half-hour trip. He barely registered Chad and Chaiyala's non-stop chatter in the front. He was content to watch the scenery—green paddocks, plantations, farms, and bush pockets flash past.

Halfway along, before skirting the western end of Clarkestown, they passed a sugar factory.

"You all good, Rod?" Chad called.

"All good, thanks. Just a tad tired. Processing the last few days—meeting Albarad, chief among them."

Chaiyala narrowed her eyes and growled subtly at the mention of the man.

Rod returned his gaze to the countryside. Something about that meeting had unsettled him—not just mentally, but deep within. It didn't add up. And what bothered him most was not knowing why.

Crouton pulled into a rough concrete driveway that served as a courtyard between a few small homes on the left and a modest church hall on the right, overlooking the road from a rise. It was about eleven o'clock when they arrived at the edge of Kinloss and were greeted by a crowd of children and a handful of adults.

"Hail," Crouton greeted warmly as they exited the Humvees. "We're looking for Pastor Reo Richie."

Half the children pointed toward the church hall entrance. They'd been playing basketball, cops and robbers, or making things in the front yards—now all gathered around the newcomers and their large vehicles.

"Come this way," said a cheerful, stocky man in a white singlet and blue boardies. "Pastor Reo is inside."

He led them onto a wooden deck in front of the church entrance. "I believe he's been expecting you."

Inside, the church was spacious yet simple—white and cream walls, gleaming tiles, red doors, and yellow-framed windows. Three steps led to a blue lectern draped with a yellow cloth, flanked by choir seating and a modest PA system. Nearly a dozen pews lined either side of the central aisle.

At the front, two men and a woman sat chatting. A tall, well-groomed man with short black hair stood and smiled warmly, extending his hand.

"Hail! Welcome!"

The gesture directed at Crouton, whose Santa Claus resemblance matched Nathan's description. Pastor Reo recognized him instantly, along with the others.

"I'm Pastor Reo Richie. Welcome to Kinloss and to Haddington New Testament Church."

"Thank you, Pastor," Crouton said kindly, introducing the team.

"You are most welcome! This is my wife, Alini."

A stunning Jamaican woman stood and embraced the guests with a kind hug and a big smile. Two children soon arrived through a side entrance and ran to join their parents.

"And these are our children—our son, Taneil, and our daughter, Malanda."

"You have a beautiful family, Pastor. It's an honour to meet you all," Rod said on behalf of the group.

"This is Mathesius, my youth pastor and good friend," Reo added, introducing the second young man, who smiled and nodded respectfully.

Mathesius left with the first man they'd met—warmly bidding the visitors farewell and wishing them an enjoyable stay. He hugged Reo and Alini, fist-bumped the kids, and promised to see them Saturday night for basketball and a barbecue.

"Come, our home is right next door," Reo invited.

They crossed the grass to a modest three-bedroom home with a wooden deck. Inside, the open-plan living space was filled with seating—clearly a hub for Bible study and gatherings.

Tim explained their visit as Reo poured homemade lemonade for his guests.

"We've learned of a toppled obelisk," Tim began, "hidden in the jungle near here."

"How did you find out about that?" Reo asked, then corrected himself. "Actually, the question is—what, or who, led you to that knowledge?"

Tim glanced at Crouton. "Brooke Russo," he said, recounting how the conversation had been cut short, and they'd been thrust into a supernatural escape. It was all a blur.

"Hmm," Reo said, staring out the window. Alini ushered the children out—Taneil went to join friends, and Malanda joined her mother to gather Reo's lunch and gear.

"Brooke Russo... she is not Brooke Russo," he said flatly—shaking his head—a distant look in his eyes.

"Okay... who is she?" Tim asked.

Crouton frowned, glancing between them.

"I don't know," Reo admitted.

The others listened intently. Charlotte got goosebumps.

"We were all there when the crazy goat lady flipped out all phantom-like," Rhys said. "If she's not who we thought..."

"I don't know who she really is," Reo said. "Some say she's full of demons. Others claim she is one. Some believe she's a powerful witch doctor who's discovered the fountain of youth or used voodoo to delay death. In Jamaica, spirituality often feels like a mix of intoxicated camp-fire stories that grow and change."

Silence settled over them.

Those who'd been there the night Tim learned the obelisk's location wondered what they'd truly witnessed. Rod leaned against the doorway, gazing out at the deck. Crouton, still frowning, waited for Reo to continue.

"Alas, none of this is anything to worry about. My apologies," Reo said, realizing he'd unsettled them. "I didn't mean to trouble you... we should move," he added. "If we're to reach the obelisk and return before dark, we mustn't waste time talking here."

Alini passed him his backpack, and he found his tramping boots.

"We arrived in two Humvees. We've room for at least two more passengers," Crouton said.

"Good. It's eleven-thirty. We'll take the B10 south to Spring Garden," Reo said, considering the logistics. "The B5 is simpler but takes over an hour. The B10 gets us there in under forty-five minutes. We'll have lunch at the home of Kristian Phillips—a close friend and skilled bushman. He works as a tour guide through Cockpit Country."

Reo hugged and kissed Alini, embraced his kids, and joined Chaiyala, Chad, and Rod. Tim and Crouton thanked Alini and the children for the loan of their husband and father.

Once the Humvees were on the road again, Crouton called Rod, who set his phone on speaker.

"Kristian has a dozen quad bikes," Reo explained. "I've arranged for some to take us deep into Cockpit Country—a forty-minute ride. From there, it's a tough two-and-a-half-hour trek to the obelisk. The terrain is tricky, but we've cleared a decent path. Keeping it visible is a challenge. Then there's the humidity—you'll be drenched by the time we arrive. If you're comfortable, wear what you would for swimming. It'll feel like walking through a downpour."

"I hate humidity," Rhys groaned.

"You'll be fine, son," Crouton encouraged.

"Sounds challenging," Chad said.

"It is. But once we get there, the site is in a cool spot—windy and shaded. What you'll see is something from another world."

"Oh, this is gonna be good!" Tim exclaimed.

"What you're going to see, my friends, you'll never forget. There's a lot yet to discuss."

"We've got several hours," Crouton said. "Let's catch up, get to know each other, and get on the same page."

Pastor Reo came from a long line of local archivists. Unlike Alesandro, though, he didn't trace his roots from an ancient Greek figurehead. His interests went beyond historical record keeping. He was drawn to the strange and sacred, where theology and the supernatural met in forgotten corners of history and philosophy. He was fascinated by their hidden overlaps. These topics were often taboo, but Reo had a gift for timing and discretion. Having learned how to navigate such terrain with care, he knew when and where to explore them without provoking academic or religious controversy.

Tim and Rod placed their phones in charging docks and on speaker.

"Crouton can attest to my knowledge of Red Sword Security and its global work. I've been a friend of Nathan O'Conner's for some time and enjoy catching up on the projects he's involved in. Tim, the Lechaion harbour discovery in 2017—Corinth, Greece—that must've been the experience of a lifetime?"

"Absolutely! It was the realization of a dream—to document part of one of the most important biblical cities of antiquity. Now, it feels like a lifetime of incredible experiences is unfolding. It's been both breath-taking and exciting," Tim beamed.

"So, what's your story, Pastor? How does a small-town Jamaican minister become an archivist of para-historical records?" Crouton asked.

"I've always been passionate about God's work in Jamaica. From a young age, I felt called to be a shepherd—senior ministry was a natural outcome. Ten years ago, before passing into the presence of his Lord, my grandfather took me aside. He had something important to share—something he wanted me to consider taking responsibility for. He'd followed my research into theology, ancient history, and the supernatural, and had quietly prepared me for a role as an archivist in the Order of Kittim."

"Kittim..." pondered Chaiyala. "Some say the name echoes through Greek myth as Kronos. It's speculative—but the overlap between ancient names and legends is hard to ignore."

"Yes," Reo affirmed.

An odd silence followed.

"Ahh... what?" Tim frowned. "This is different..."

"Kittim, in Hebrew," Reo continued, "before modern approches to mythology blurred and twisted history into spectacle, was also Kronos, in the Greek, and was a grand son of Noah—as was Poseidon."

"Sorry?" Crouton blurted.

Tim's expression shifted. "I hadn't considered that before..."

"That detail doesn't appear in the biblical account," Chad noted.

"Neither does the books of Noah, or Enoch" Reo added.

"I didn't know any of this until the other day," Chaiyala said. "My cousin Mordechai explained it while we walked along the beach."

"What? When were you going to tell me this?" Tim's voice came through the phone.

"Girl, you got me curious now too!" Crouton barked. "What's with the withholding of significant developments?"

Chad gave her a look of mock betrayal.

"I don't know... give me a break! I've got a lot on my mind. I'm special tactics, investigation and security—para-history is not usually my thing."

"Yup, I can appreciate that," Rod said. "And to be fair, there's a lot of, 'different', going on. It's a wonder any of us can keep up."

"Being a bodyguard is nice and simple," Rhys chimed in.

"Is it?" Chaiyala challenged.

Charlotte smirked.

"Nice for some," Rod added light-heartedly.

"I thought being a historian'd be straight-forward," Tim joked. "Then I met Nathan O'Conner."

"I hear you, brother," Reo grinned.

"Yup, the man has 'at effect," Crouton agreed.

Chaiyala and Ps. Reo spent the winding journey through Cockpit Country tracing the link between Kittim and Poseidon—both aboard the Ark and in the echoes beyond. Chaiyala sifted through her cousin's insights, setting aside the tangled threads of Israel-Atlantis diplomacy.

Ps. Reo's research focused on lineage—mapping Kittim's descent into Atlantean history. He traced the line to the Talakanis. The Atlantean navy vessel said to have carried curious descendants of Kittim across Central America and the Caribbean during Atlantis's expansion.

Tim nodded, excitement rising, "The Triremes of Atlantis—massive warships with a single sail and three tiers of oars. Thousands, hidden underground, waiting..."

"Yup!" Crouton exclaimed. "Within the Richat Structure itself—around the third ring of land."

"Goodness, imagine that," Charlotte said in awe, picturing a naval base the size of Hamilton's city limits.

"That's insane eh? We've driven around the city limits of Hamilton countless times—we've felt that scale!" Tim shook his head.

"An incredible engineering marvel: 1000 subterranean docks spaced every 163 meters around a 163 km perimeter," Ps. Reo added.

The team in the two humvees arrived at a sprawling single-storey house constructed of weather boards, with a corrugated iron roof that gleamed in the midday sun.

A smiling man with tussled greying hair and a weathered look—not too dissimilar to Crouton's, yet a few years younger—came out to greet them. He and Ps. Reo embraced each other with a hug of brotherly friendship.

"Kristian, meet my new friends..." introductions were made accordingly. "They're good friends of Nathan O'Conner's."

Kristian welcomed Reo and his guests to his raised, rustic home, situated on a terraced hillside on the edge of Spring Garden. The view stretched across southern Trelawny Parish, revealing the rugged beauty of Cockpit

Country. Kristian had lived there half his life, drawn to the Caribbean after emigrating from Canada with his wife. They'd married young, built a jungle tour business, and raised four children—two now back in Canada—the younger two working in Jamaican tourism.

After losing his wife in a Bermuda Triangle plane crash, Kristian held onto her memory, honouring the legacy they'd built together through Quad-Bike Jungle Tours. Chad studied him—tough yet vibrant, fifty-something with the energy of a young man, deeply passionate about forgotten history.

Kristian Phillips downed a second chicken salad roll as he explained the origin of the name 'Cockpit Country' to the group.

"Cockpit Country is a unique geological formation—deep hollows and jungle-covered conical hills. It was the battleground for the Maroon Wars in the 1700s. Escaped slaves used the terrain to resist British forces, forcing a treaty. The name 'Cockpit' comes from its resemblance to the cramped, humid, bloodstained space below decks on warships. The British, overwhelmed by the terrain and guerrilla tactics, coined the term."

"Consider yourselves educated," Crouton said. "Myself included—very interesting."

"But wait," Kristian continued, "there's more! Off-track its wild. The heat presses in like its alive—thick, wet, relentless. Every breath feels borrowed from the jungle itself—heavy with moisture and the scent of rot. The gullies twist and fold—limestone, slick with moss and shadow. There's no breeze, no horizon—just green walls and the drone of insects. Sweat pools at the base of ya spine, and there's a lotta ducking under fallen branches, crawling over jagged stone—it'll test you. It's more of a reckoning than a hike. The Cockpit Country doesn't welcome visitors, it endures them."

"You're not selling this to us at all, are ya?" Rhys protested.

"You are such a sook," Chaiyala teased.

Rhys groaned.

"This is why I can beat you at arm wrestling... you're weak."

Rod and Tim laughed. Chad shook his head—looking forward to tackling the jungle regardless.

"You're never gonna let him live that down, are you?" Rod grinned.

"Never," Chaiyala giggled.

Kristian looked at Rhys, shirtless as always, then at Chaiyala, trying to make sense of the exchange.

"You're clearly good friends. A lotta fun and laughs."

"Right on. Practically family," Crouton nodded.

Kristian chuckled, finishing his roll. His gaze drifted to the rugged expanse of Cockpit Country.

He led them from the deck down to a corrugated barn where a fleet of quad bikes were parked. Helmets and tour kits hung along one wall. Most of it unneeded—his guests had come well-prepared.

With Reo, Rod, and Crouton's help, Kristian got the crew comfortable with the bikes and helmets. Once sorted, they lined up in convoy. They passed through a tall wooden gate adorned with indigenous carvings and unlit torches.

Kristian led the way, followed by Reo and Crouton—Rod taking the rear. After half a forty-minute ride, they reached a clearing where the bikes had to be dismounted.

The air was thick with humidity, carrying a musty, botanical scent. It smelt like something between compost and a sun-baked inner-city alleyway, tangled with tropical vegetation.

Kristian and Reo removed their shirts and tied them around their heads.

"Feel free to do the same," Reo advised. "We've done this a few times—the sweat pours off you like a waterfall."

Kristian opened a box of 'Jungle Tours' bandanas and held it out. "Helps keep the sweat outta your eyes."

"When we get back," Reo added, "we'll jump straight into Kristian's pool."

"Absolutely!" Kristian agreed with a grin.

Tim peeled off his shirt and tied it loosely around his shoulders, the fabric already damp with sweat. Charlotte and Chaiyala followed suit, shedding their outer layers to reveal practical swim tops—functional, breathable, and better suited to the heat. Together with Tim, they tied bandanas snugly around their heads, keeping sweat from their eyes and focus on the trail ahead.

Rod and Crouton rolled up their Red Sword trousers, mud streaking the hems.

The girls had stopped trying to stay dry—skin glistening, hair damp, expressions resigned but focused. Chad had drunk half his water, using the rest to cool his eyes, questioning why they were even doing this.

"It's ridiculous, huh?" Reo asked Rhys.

"You're right, Rev. We might as well be swimming to the obelisk!"

Tim, Charlotte, and Crouton remained silent, conserving energy in the brutal heat. The forty-five-minute hike felt like hours.

Crouton, seasoned in tough expeditions, found the challenge familiar. Tim and Charlotte, used to New Zealand's cooler bush treks, had also faced extremes even-so—Tim in the Sahara, Charlotte under blazing stage lights—but nothing quite like this.

Relief came when Kristian and Reo stopped beside a small pole leaning slightly to the left, appearing to be made of a dark red ore.

Its unique design and markings caught Tim and Crouton's attention.

"Fascinating..." Tim said, his face lit up, examining the ancient carvings. He pulled out his phone and began taking photos.

"We found this half-buried nearby," Reo explained. "Now it serves as a marker—possibly from a race predating the Inca and Mayans, with ties to the Amazons and Olmecs."

Before Reo explained the final climb, Charlotte held out her hand for Tim's phone. "You'll want more shots—I can handle the photos while you explore."

"Thanks," Tim said, handing it over.

Reo advised that the steep track upward was marked with red ropes for grip. Though taxing, it gradually levelled off at the top. "Hard to gauge scale with the trees, but this knoll is roughly a football field—seventy by a hundred meters. Only a few have been up here. This is probably the largest group ever, and I must ask you to keep its location secret."

"Most definitely," Tim said sincerely.

"Absolutely," Crouton added. "If we can help secure the site, we'd be happy to assist. No strings attached."

Reo and Kristian exchanged a grateful glance. "That would be deeply appreciated," Reo said.

They passed between two large stone pillars, weathered by twelve thousand years of wind and rain. Vines and creepers clung to the ancient uprights. At the summit, they stood in a narrow clearing—two meters wide stretching left and right out of view—beneath a canopy of treetops.

They entered a larger glade—concealed beneath a man-made canopy of camouflage netting.

Chad stood in awe. Crouton, Rod, and Chaiyala spread out, taking in the surroundings.

"Nice stuff," Tim breathed.

They stood in quiet awe before the massive horizontal stone structure—ancient beyond reckoning, yet strangely out of place.

"So, this is it then." Rod examined, intrigued.

The overgrown jungle had nearly swallowed it, vines and foliage creeping across its edges, but the stone itself remained pristine. It looked as if it had been placed there only months ago. The toppled obelisk lay half-buried in the jungle floor, its presence echoing the otherworldly mystery that had become the hallmark of the Atlantis they were uncovering.

"This is incredible, Rev," Crouton said.

"This is, what, maybe thirty, forty meters?" Rod guessed as they beheld the massive obelisk.

"Not bad," Reo replied. "It's thirty meters long with a base of four and a half square meters. The clearing around it is twenty by forty-five."

Charlotte and Chad studied the canopy above, where vines wove through the netting. Rhys and Crouton exchanged glances, savouring the cool breeze. Dressed for the beach, with bandanas and shirts tied around their heads, they welcomed the relief from the suffocating humidity.

"The canopy," Reo explained, "is made of high-grade military flecktarn netting."

Tim examined the two massive wooden poles supporting it. "When was this place discovered?"

"Recovered, more so," Reo said. "Though the golden age of El Dorado expeditions had passed, whispers of lost cities of gold, the lost continent in the South Pacific, and ancient relics of great value still lured explorers into the jungle well into the 1700s. British Royal Navy soldiers—covert members of the Order of Kittim, descended from explorers aboard the Atlantean Talakanis—had come here. They'd tracked expeditions with a singular purpose: to abandon their posts, vanish from record, and become guardians of this place. Earlier attempts to infiltrate Spanish galleons under Columbus and Turkish fleets led by Piri Reis had failed. But hidden within the ranks of the British Royal Navy, they succeeded.

"The obelisk was found using an ancient form of GPS—star navigation. They cleared the bush, built huts, workshops, gardens—everything they needed to live here. Along with the obelisk, they became stewards of an old prophecy..."

"At last two brothers will reunite. At last, survivors of the deluge will walk together and bring together that which will reveal the garden of Epoptes Asphalius."

"Righteo... what's that mean?" Crouton asked.

"Two brothers..." Tim mused. "Epoptes and Asphalius are both functional names for Poseidon— 'watches' and 'gives safe voyage across the sea'... and the garden?"

"Oh!" Chaiyala said suddenly. "Would the two brothers be Poseidon and Eber?"

"Very good!" Reo encouraged. "So far as we know, the two brothers— or cousins—are Poseidon and Eber. The 'survivors of the deluge' part is still a mystery..."

"Not anymore," Chaiyala interrupted again. "The deluge would be Noah's flood. They both survived."

Reo paused. "Of course! They were both on the Ark."

"Nice stuff!" Tim commended, impressed with Chaiyala's new-found knowledge of the para-historical.

"Pardon me for getting theological," Chad said, "but where does this talk of Poseidon and his other names sit with the Bible, for you, Pastor?"

He expected a certain answer—and was surprised.

"Back on the ride to Spring Garden," Reo recapped, glancing at Chaiyala, "we touched on something the Order of Kittim holds deeply.

Before religion—pagan or otherwise—those called gods, goddesses, even extraterrestrials, were actually administrative angels.

They were assigned to guide humanity—each responsible for aspects of life, society, and geography. Their role was to impart wisdom, skill, and understanding—always in alignment with God's will."

Crouton gave a slow nod, eyes fixed on Reo. "Still wild to think about."

A knowing look of mutual recognition passed between them.

"As far as the Bible is concerned," Reo continued, "those details are peripheral—like the apocryphal books in Catholic tradition. Insightful; even factual, but not central."

"Because all scripture points to Jesus," Chaiyala said—catching on.

"Exactly," Reo confirmed. "His life, His Lordship, His example. Everything else is context—valuable, but not foundational."

"So believers can explore the fringe stuff—as long as it doesn't pull them off-centre." Chad concluded.

Reo smiled. "That's the idea."

CHAPTER 29

Two questions played around in Tim's mind. First: Ps. Reo and Kristian knew of the Talakanis—but how much did they know? Second: Where did the prophecy the Order of Kittim held originate, and was more known of it? He shelved both for now. Something else had captured his attention.

Tim could not get past the obelisk's pristine condition—so unlike the weathered ruins he was used to. Chad, noticing the same, asked Ps. Reo and Kristian about its upkeep.

"Preservation's never been a priority," Kristian said. "Despite occasional visits to maintain access, the obelisk remains untouched by moss or lichen. It seems to maintain itself. The Order of Kittim has always focused on safeguarding it, but not studying it."

"Kinda wishin' we brought an archaeologist with us now," Crouton said.

"Hmm, yeah." Tim nodded, eyes fixed on the surface. "It's magnificent. A beautiful finish, even with all the questions it raises. Definitely unlike anything else I've seen. So, no preservations ever been done?" Tim double checked.

"None," Ps. Reo confirmed. "My grandfather only provided its location."

"Our focus has always been secrecy and the preservation of this site," Kristian added. "We're not experts in ancient artefacts—just passionate about the preservation of forgotten history."

"*There is nothing new in the world except the history you do not know.*' - Harry Truman," Crouton quoted.

"Tim, is just me," Chaiyala asked, "or this obelisk—it doesn't look toppled? No scratch, no dent. Maybe the Atlanteans placed it here, but never stood it up, yes?"

"I think you might be right," Tim replied. Their gaze lingered on the obelisk as did their thoughts on the suggestion. What had begun as Chaiyala's quiet speculation, now pressed with a kind of certainty neither of them could ignore.

"Have a look at this..." Charlotte called. She and Chad had been examining the base, searching the weeds for anything significant while Rhys and Chaiyala explored along the top of the structure.

Tim, Crouton, and the others gathered around Charlotte.

Until now, the base had appeared smooth and pitch-black—closely matching the rest of the obelisk, which was only slightly lighter—deep black or darkest grey.

"The sunlight's shifted," Rod observed. "The bottom's hollow!"

"You're right!" Charlotte agreed.

Chad waved his hand through the darkness. Rod did the same, then ran his fingers along the edge—revealing a thick wall. Crouton shined a torch inside, revealing a chamber stretching five metres along the obelisk's length.

"Goodness! It's like a small room," Charlotte said.

"Check those out!" Tim pointed at two thick copper rods, maybe half a meter long, protruding from the farthest wall in the chamber.

"Never seen any of this before," Kristian admitted. Both he and Ps. Reo were amazed by what their visitors had uncovered—details they'd never considered, nor noticed.

"Yup, I'm gonna go with this thing was placed here, as opposed to toppled over," Rod said, nodding toward Crouton.

Chaiyala led the way along the sloping obelisk, noting its dark grey and black hues with a faint green sheen. As they progressed, patterns emerged—resembling the foreign script found in ancient Mauritanian ruins.

"The end closest to the base must be about three or four meters wide," Rhys suggested.

"Yes, tapering on all sides... until it's maybe one meter at other end." Chaiyala added—then stopped short. She and Rhys observed the tip of the obelisk, where it ended in a right-angled pyramid formation—something intriguingly familiar.

Back at the base end, Chad stepped back, his heel pressing into something unusual—like solid ground sinking underfoot. The ground gave way slightly, nearly throwing him off balance. As he steadied himself, a grinding, snapping sound echoed—stone shifting, something darting through the bush. Charlotte, thinking fast, reached toward him. They locked wrists before he toppled into a newly formed opening, while Rod and Ps. Reo jumped aside to avoid the same.

"What in blazes?" Crouton swore.

"Woah!" Rod gasped, peering into a small black chasm.

Rhys and Chaiyala returned from their exploration.

"Nice!" Tim said, putting an arm around his surprised fiancée to check she was okay.

"This just went all Indiana Jones!" Chad grinned.

"Does that, from time to time," Crouton said casually.

A few inches from the base of the obelisk, an opening had split the jungle floor—revealing dark stone stairs descending into blackness.

The entrance felt deliberate, as if a hidden structure had been designed to part. The steps—pristine like the obelisk—descended into a void that whispered of secrecy, depth, and something ancient waiting below.

"What have you gone and done?" Chaiyala teased Crouton as she jumped down with Rhys.

"Nuthin'. Was ya boyfriend who found this," Crouton shot back.

She gave him a blank stare.

Tim and Crouton turned to Ps. Reo and Kristian for guidance.

"This is all very new to us, my friends!" Ps. Reo expressed. "We had no idea this was even here!"

"Righteo then. Shall we check gear and head on down?" Kristian suggested.

Rod tied a labyrinth cord to a sturdy root while Crouton, Rhys, and Chaiyala checked flashlights and headlamps.

Kristian led the way, torch in hand. Ps. Reo followed, then Crouton, with the others trailing behind into a dark chamber. They came to the centre of a narrow passage.

"Where to now?" Rod asked, eyeing the passage as it turned ninety degrees at both ends.

"This is so cool," Tim said, taking in the sparse architecture.

"It's black. Pitch black," Chad muttered. "Everything's black."

"Looks like polished black granite," Crouton said. It reminded Charlotte of Tim's parents' bathroom tiles.

"Incredible," Crouton remarked, quietly.

Tim shook his head, awed by the craftsmanship. The structure had to be Atlantean—it looked it—but they needed proof.

The granite blocks here mirrored the Tetris-like interlocking technique seen in Mauritanian ruins. Even the floor matched, though its coarse surface lacked the polished finish of the walls.

They split up—investigating left and right of the stairs that'd led them down. Kristian, Ps. Reo, Rod, and Crouton met the others around the far side.

"Interesting," Kristian said, glancing at Tim.

"Yup... definitely," Tim agreed. "So this wall continues around in a full square—or, rectangle..."

Kristian nodded. "Yes, appears so."

Rod and Crouton pondered what else might be hiding. Tim, uneasy about the chamber's shadows, knew poor lighting concealed whatever lay beyond the light of their torches.

Charlotte looked up, wondering if the interior wall met the ceiling. "Tim? Can you give me a boost?"

"Okay..." Curious, he bent his knees, cupping his hands.

They all looked up, trying to see what Charlotte had noticed—a gap between the wall's crest and the ceiling.

Tim boosted her. She gripped the top—three and a half meters up—and hauled herself over onto a square floor.

She pulled out Tim's phone—switched on the torch.

"What can you see?"

"Apart from two thick copper rods disappearing into the ceiling? Not much. They go straight up" She snapped photos of everything she could.

"Anything like the rods comin' outta the obelisk?" Crouton called.

"*Exactly* like them," she replied. "They stand in the middle of a granite floor—about, eight by six meters. There's maybe two meters to the ceiling."

"There has to be more below the rods," Crouton said. "That square Charlotte's standin' on's hidin' something."

"I agree," Tim said.

"Definitely points to the obelisk being prepped for install," Rod added.

"Installation that never happened. But if it had..." Tim began.

"...the copper rods mighta' been connected," Crouton finished.

Ps. Reo and Rod nodded as they all searched for an entrance. After twenty fruitless minutes, Rod leaned against the stone, weary.

Now it was his turn to accidentally trigger a hidden mechanism.

As Charlotte stood atop the stone square, the structure beneath her began to shift. Walls and ceiling panels slid inward—folding into themselves with a coarse, subtle rumble of stone moving against stone. Within moments, the entire square retracted into the ground, revealing a vast chamber below. The narrow passage they'd followed vanished, replaced by a cavernous space. At its centre, dark cubes, angular surfaces, and protruding rectangles emerged—silent and waiting, artefacts from a forgotten design.

Charlotte had leapt down just before her perch vanished, landing with cat-like agility. As the stone shifted, a mysterious light flickered to life—its glow like amplified firelight.

"Woah!" Chad, Rhys, and Charlotte said in unison.

"This is the stuff!" Tim declared.

"My beard!" Crouton gasped.

"All this time..." Ps. Reo breathed, looking at Kristian, who returned his gaze, eyes wide.

Rod straightened up, regaining balance.

Lights flickered to life across the chamber, adding to the glow on the surrounding surfaces. Screens emerged from the walls and benches, displaying shifting diagrams—obelisks, pyramids, and geometric patterns pulsing with quiet energy.

"That's the exact same script we've found at the Mauritanian sites!" Tim exclaimed observing the screens with the others.

"Damn straight it is, boy!" Crouton grinned. "That's evidence to back Solon's tales—the Talakanis and Haskalaran explored the Caribbean. They were expanding their empire."

Charlotte rejoined the others as they approached the strange, ancient equipment.

Its surfaces were as if brand new, etched with symbols and seams that hinted at hidden mechanisms.

"I worked as an electrical engineer in Vancouver for twenty-eight years," Kristian said, eyes scanning the setup.

"To me, this is electrical—no doubt about it. The instrumentation's familiar, even if it looks alien. I'd say it's built to distribute energy... and not just locally. This is large-scale."

He examined the cables closely.

"Some of these parts look like they're built for resistance control," Kristian suggested. "Could be regulators or load management. The whole thing roughly resembles a modern electrical system."

"Good grief," Chad whispered, goosebumps rising.

"That is truly incredible," Rod nodded, eyes wide.

Tim stood speechless—a grin spreading across his face.

Everything they'd suspected—Atlantis's expansion, its rumoured use of wireless electricity—was no longer theory. It was real. Tangible. Confirmed in the quiet hum of ancient systems awakening beneath their feet.

"Yes! Albarad, you sucker! Oh, this is SO good!" Tim couldn't contain himself. "Thank You, Jesus! And, thank you so, so much for bringing us here!" he said to Ps. Reo and Kristian.

"You're very welcome," Ps. Reo replied warmly. "Thank you for discovering all this—for letting us witness history being made."

"We're not trained explorers or archaeologists," Kristian added. "Your expertise means a lot."

"Never mind archaeologists," Crouton said. "Your electrical insight—identifying all this—is just as valuable, especially with what's going on in the field."

Tim and Chaiyala nodded and smiled.

Rod pat Kristian on the back. "Of course, this'll need proper testing by our teams," he added, "but I think it's safe to say—we've found exactly what we were lookin' for."

Chaiyala gave Crouton a wry smirk, eyes glinting with mischief.

"What're you lookin' at me like that for? That's the same darn look Sienna gives me when she wants something—like a pony or... I dunno. You two are bad as each other."

She fought back a full smile—letting the moment linger.

Rhys stepped in, shaking his head at the pair. "There's something you need to see—up near the top end of the obelisk, sir."

Tim's eyes widened. "Of course!" He nearly kicked himself for not thinking of it earlier.

They hurried back to the surface, pushing through weeds and scrub until they reached the far end of the obelisk.

"Would ya look at that, eh!" Crouton beamed, seeing what Rhys and Chaiyala had found earlier.

"Awesome!" Tim grinned. A small, glassy aqua-blue prism attached sideways at the obelisk's tip.

"Another piece of Atlantis, yes?" Chaiyala asked, wonder in her voice.

Tim, Chaiyala, and Crouton moved closer to the softly glowing object, while Rhys and Chad leaned against the obelisk and Charlotte peered past Tim's shoulder.

"Certainly looks like it," Tim said.

Ps. Reo shook his head. "This keeps getting better and better!"

"How many times have we walked past this and never noticed?" Kristian asked, running a hand through his silver hair.

"What do you know of the lost pieces of Atlantis, Rev?" Crouton asked.

"They were rare, with immense value," Ps. Reo replied, "hidden by the ancients to prevent greed and conflict. Beyond that, details are scarce—virtually untraceable."

Tim was about to respond when a coin-sized circle, made of the same material as the Piece of Atlantis, caught his eye. Pressing it unintentionally, the obelisk released the artefact.

"Tim! What is this, ah? What the hang you doing?" Chaiyala protested, lunging forward a split second ahead of Crouton to catch the unexpectedly heavy relic before it landed—sinking the dirt.

"Yup, definitely a piece of Atlantis," Crouton said, accepting it from her. He sighed. "Now we've got that to haul back."

With Rhys' help, they moved it near the obelisk's base and wrapped it in makeshift fabric from shirts and bandanas, securing it with rope.

"We'll take turns carrying it," Crouton offered.

"Sorry." Tim smirked. "Lightning reflexes though!"

Chaiyala glowered, then gave him a playful shove.

Kristian checked the sun's position. "Best we head back before navigation gets tricky."

"You'd think the humidity would ease by now," Rhys grumbled.

Kristian laughed. "A sweet dream—but no cigar, son."

Two hours at the obelisk site ended with a humid, punishing trek back to the quad bikes. Drenched but grateful for the breeze whipping past during the forty-minute quad bike ride—and for clean clothes waiting at Kristian's—they arrived by 6:35 PM and dove into the cool pool, washing away sweat and jungle haze.

Kristian, in his quiet spirit of generous hospitality, returned with freshly sliced watermelon. He wheeled out a chiller brimming with ice-cold beers and fruit juices—offering refreshments with the easy grace of someone who found joy in serving others. He and Ps. Reo settled at one of three octagonal wooden tables near the pool, opposite twin staircases leading to the raised deck and house.

"So, Alini's not expecting you back tonight?" Kristian asked.

"That's correct," Ps. Reo confirmed. "If we didn't make it back before the evening, she's expecting us mid-morning tomorrow."

He glanced at Tim and Crouton. Both nodded—happy to stay the night.

"Well then," Kristian announced, arms wide, "since this was the last tour of the day, dinner is included: Wild Pork Spit Roast!" "Aye!" Rhys' eyes lit up. Crouton lifted his stubby in silent approval, while Tim, Chad, and the others nodded in agreement.

Below Kristian's house sat a garden shed, the pool shed, and a storage area big enough for two trailers and an '88 Mercedes-Benz. At the yard end, a spa pool nestled among river stones and tropical ferns. Against another staircase, a workshop stood, with the land sloping sharply back toward street and foundation level.

"Need a hand with the spit roast?" Tim offered.

"Won't say no," Kristian said, heading under the deck toward a massive chest chiller. "Thanks."

Crouton had dried off and pulled on a singlet top and clean Red Sword trousers. Tim still had a towel wrapped around his boardies. Both joined Kristian at the chiller.

Crouton grinned—impressed at what he beheld.

"That's awesome!" remarked Tim.

"Nothin' by halves here, son. Could I get ya to grab two boxes of hash browns?"

Inside were four massive wild boars, stacks of T-bone steaks, boxes of hash browns, big bags of chicken drumsticks, hoisin-marinated spare ribs, and wherever there was room—lamb shanks.

"You're my kind of people, Mr. Phillips," Crouton smiled, helping lift a spit-ready hog from the chiller.

Kristian thanked them as they walked to the centre of the yard, where two cast-iron A-frames flanked a stone-rimmed fire pit lined with cricket-ball-sized rocks.

Surrounding the pit in a half-circle, four hollowed logs served as rustic wooden sofas. Kristian stepped onto a fire pit stone on the rim of the stricture, triggering a steel pole to rise from a hidden socket near the A-frame.

"Look at that!" Tim and Crouton watched, fascinated. Ps. Reo smiled, having helped build the system himself.

"Hold this steady..." Kristian said, removing a 2.5-meter pole and feeding it through the pig's hollowed centre. "Once it's through your end, you'll have about 200 mil sticking out. Then we fit the ends into the pivot holes atop the A-frames."

Crouton followed his lead. Kristian continued, "Each A-frame has a spacer and T-bar handle to lock it in place."

He found the pieces—secured to the frame with magnets—and copied Kristian's movements at the other end.

"Nice," Tim applauded.

Crouton nodded, impressed.

"Ah, but wait—there's more!" Kristian twisted the T-bars, lowering both ends into place until they rested on a centre bar. Another twist, and the pig began to rotate.

Kristian stepped onto a second stone.

Soft blue gas flames hissed to life beneath a pit of heated stones, glowing red-hot. The air shimmered with steady, radiant heat—perfect for the slow-turning roast suspended above.

"I'm impressed!" Crouton said. Kristian smiled.

"My own invention—Reo helped install it, and a local gas fitter at Haddington New Testament took care of the rest."

"The mind of an engineer. Very nice," Rod added—strolling over—towel around his waist.

"Not bad at all," Tim agreed.

"That's so cool," Charlotte complimented from the pool.

"Definitely!" agreed Chaiyala.

"I like it. I want one," Chad declared.

"Aye—you and me both," Rhys added, grabbing his towel.

"Now we wheel out the barbecue. In about forty-five we cook the hash browns, then it's time to eat. For now, enjoy the refreshments and relax," Kristian smiled.

Solar-powered party lights and citronella candles lit the relaxed, warm atmosphere.

Rod and Tim rolled out the barbecue, placing it nearby.

Dusk settled over the hills, Chad and the girls moved from the pool to the upper deck, where warm torch light bathed six cosy sofas arranged in a half-circle. He and Chaiyala lugged the drinks chiller to the centre, then dropped onto a couch facing the shadowed sweep of Cockpit Country. The view was vast, quiet, and alive with the hush of evening.

Charlotte settled beside Tim—legs draped over his—handing him another glass of peach, passion fruit, and pineapple.

Chad passed corn chips to Chaiyala, while Rhys munched fresh coconut with Kristian. Ps. Reo and Crouton prepped salads in the kitchen, and Rod disappeared to video-call Kristie.

The evening was warm and tropically serene, filled with crickets chirping and the heavenly aroma of roast pork. Laughter floated on the breeze as they relaxed on the deck, sipping chilled drinks and sharing stories.

Playful banter soon turned into teasing when someone made an offhand comment about Rhys and Sienna. Rhys chuckled, deflecting the attention, but the nudging continued.

"So, when's the wedding?" Tim joked, grins spreading. "News to me!" Crouton grunted, sipping his drink, a smile sneaking through. Rhys hesitated, a grin flickering. Was he playing along—or was there something more?

Rod leaned back, amused. "Well, mate, if you're serious, better start taking notes from Chad and Chaiyala."

Chad frowned, while Chaiyala's look mixed warning with amusement.

The conversation bounced between laughter and speculation, never landing on a conclusion. Was it just banter—or did Rhys have a secret? The question hovered, wrapped in laughter and curiosity.

Dinner was divine—spit-roasted wild pork, its skin crisped to perfection, served with a trio of sauces: homemade apple, Jamaican-style sweet chilli, and a fiery mango habanero.

Crispy hash browns and vibrant tropical salads rounded out the feast, each bite a serene experience of flavour and warmth.

Afterwards, they gathered around the now-cleared fire pit. Laughter rising with the smoke as they indulged in seconds and passed around drinks—the night settling into a rhythm of contentment and friendship.

The fire pit, once used for cooking, now glowed as a crackling bonfire. Its flickering light cast warm shadows as the group shared stories into the night.

"This is fantastic, Kristian," Crouton said. "More than we expected—cheers."

"Aye, it's a pleasure. You've given Reo and me a unique experience—unlocking everything at the obelisk site. Still wrapping my head 'round it. After all these years, neither of us knew what was hiding down there."

Ps. Reo asked Tim and Crouton to walk him through their theory and what they knew. Though he'd seen signs of it at the obelisk site…

This was the first time he'd heard it laid out fully—how the artefacts might function as ancient, high-tech conduits for wireless electricity.

Kristian and Ps. Reo exchanged glances, floored by the enormity and implication of what they were hearing. Excitement flickered across their faces as the pieces began to click into place.

Tim asked the Pastor, "Do you know much about the ship's origin? The Talakanis?"

Ps. Reo sat forward. "The Order of Kittim traces its origins to late 1097, when knights—descendants of Kittim—among their ranks infiltrated Antioch during the city's siege in the First Crusade. Beneath the ancient stronghold, they discovered hidden tunnels, secret chambers, and books filled with mysterious writings. Smuggled out under cover of night, they were later translated—revealing journals about wars between ancient kingdoms, battling over lost technology and power.

Tim nodded, asking— "Any clues about whom those kingdoms were?"

"Strangely," Ps. Reo said, "all names and places—except one—were redacted. It's as if someone wanted the records preserved, but identities erased."

Rod and Crouton exchanged a look. "Why hide such crucial details?" Tim asked. "And where are those journals now?"

Ps. Reo smiled. "In my office safe. Preserved in archival containers—they're incredibly old."

Tim lit up. "Part of me wants to read them now... but it's late," he sighed.

"Aye," Rhys agreed, stretching. "This evening's prime storytelling weather too."

Tim nodded—Rod and Crouton agreed.

"There was one name left unredacted," Ps. Reo continued. "Among the commanders who refused to participate in conflict, one stood out: Britannia."

Tim narrowed his eyes.

"Okay... who's that?" Chad asked.

Reo looked thoughtful. "That's the mystery. It's unlikely to mean Britain or the Roman goddess. 'Britannia' entered records around the fourth century AD, later becoming a Roman province in 43 AD. The classical Britannia was Rome's invention—after they invaded the British Isles, which were once called Albion.

But the redacted texts speak of Britannia as a warrior princess—revered by all. She had military authority, commanded respect, and led three ships—one of which, as we now know, was the Talakanis."

"The others are the Haskalaran and the Serenea," Tim added—voice low with thought. "But the Talakanis... it seems especially significant here in the Caribbean."

A silence settled, reverent and heavy. The fire crackled softly—stars peeking through a velvet sky, and somewhere beyond the yard, the breeze whispered through the tropical foliage. Some mysteries could be chased with reason. Others had to be waited on. The Talakanis, Tim felt, was one of the latter... his thoughts spun, the pieces shifting and aligning, forming something... not yet complete, but undeniably important.

Fatigue set in after a thrilling day deep in Cockpit Country. It's jagged limestone terrain, echoing sink-holes, and the hidden obelisk chamber below.

Now, with muscles aching and minds still reeling, they felt the weight of discovery settle into their bones.

Kristian bid the others a good night. "See you in the morning. I'll get breakfast going 'round eight or nine-ish."

Ps. Reo retired to his usual guest room, texting back and forth with Alini before goodnights.

Charlotte stretched out across a wooden sofa, her head in Tim's lap.

Upstairs—inside, Chad, Chaiyala, and Rhys set up their sleeping spots in the lounge. Chad and Chaiyala prepared the bed settee, fluffing pillows and laying out the duvet.

Rhys wrapped up a text conversation with Sienna—longing but content. He rested his head—one arm behind—gazing beyond the partially opened ranch slider.

Chaiyala loosened her long blonde braid—tossing her hair back as she toyed with it. Chad admired her—her quiet strength, kindness, and the power tucked behind reserved composure.

Rhys glanced up and caught the silent exchange.

Chaiyala smirked, stretching languidly. Her shoulder lifted—slow, deliberate—a silent invitation woven into the curve of her posture. Both arms rose in a fluid arc, the gentle tension in her frame hinting at strength beneath ease, a quiet display folded into grace.

Rhys smiled to himself, thoughts drifting back to Sienna. Their connection was unmistakable, even if not official—perhaps they were more subtle than Chad and Chaiyala's unfolding spark.

The three spoke late into the night about their adventure and what felt like history in the making. Eventually, Rhys nodded off.

Chaiyala glanced sideways at Chad, half-reclined beside her. She leaned in as their lips met. The kiss deepened, blooming into slow passion before she eased back, catching her breath.

"What if..." Chad began.

"I will hear if someone is coming," Chaiyala assured him. "Your brother, Rod, and Crouton—they are deep in discussion. They won't finish before one, maybe two a.m. We have plenty of time."

"How do you do that?"

Chaiyala tilted her head—focused—listening, "they are talking with someone—on the speakerphone..."

Chad frowned at her in awe.

"What was it you said to me, the other night?" she asked, tilting her head.

"You have the face of an angel and the body of a Greek goddess," he recited.

"Hmm. And this goddess, she has powers—naturally."

"Of course."

"Or maybe," she teased, "you are falling for a luscious ninja, eh?" Her smile dazzled—bold, playful, and just shy of daring.

"I love your confidence."

"I am not usually so cocky," she said with mock seriousness, eyes narrowing just enough to tease. "You bring out the worst in me... but also the best, eh?"

Chad reached out, tracing the back of her hand with the gentlest touch, as if grounding the moment before it drifted too quickly into memory. "Then I'm doing something right," he replied softly.

Chaiyala leaned into him again, her forehead resting gently against his. "You are doing more than that," she whispered. "You make me forget how guarded I am... usually."

There was something unspoken between them—no rush, no expectations—just a hush that let clarity settle in. Chad's hand came to rest at her side, firm but reverent, as though he wasn't claiming her, but simply being present with her. She responded with a softness that didn't ask to be praised or pursued—only received.

~~~~~~~

Crouton, Tim, and Charlotte relaxed beside the fire pit, sleepy and wonder struck by the day's discoveries. Rod passed around chilled drinks. They sipped and talked—about Tim and Charlotte's wedding, Rod and Kristie's pending holiday, the obelisk's mysteries, and progress at the Underground Docks in Richat.

Bon Jovi's 'Living on a Prayer' broke the quiet—emanating from Crouton's pocket. He hummed absent-mindedly to the tune as he fished out his phone and answered.

"Nathan! Good evening, brother! One sec, I'll put you on speaker— Tim, Charlotte and Rod are with me."

"Charles is here on conference call."

Greetings were shared, along with stories of the day. Nathan recounted his meeting with UN reps and officials from Mauritania, Egypt, France, and the USA. Charles and Sienna had attended; Hamet Albarad was absent.

Crouton wouldn't have been any more surprised than if his nose had sprouted wings, flown off, and returned as a cheeseburger. Tim and Rod agreed it didn't matter—Mauritania and Egypt aligning meant the volatile misunderstanding was defused. War was starting to feel like the manufactured illusion it'd been all along.

"Glad you're dealing with all that hoo-ha, Nate," Crouton said. "Like sortin' out fights in a playground."

Rod chuckled, "Makes you wonder."

"It comes down to keeping the main thing the main thing," Tim reflected. "Not getting distracted by theatrics and smokescreens."

"Exactly," Nathan replied.

"That's almost like defying human nature," Crouton mused.

"Well, yes..." Nathan's reply carried a strange weight—subtle, elongated—like something more lingered beneath it. Tim felt it stir something he couldn't place. A stray thought of Chad surfaced unexpectedly. Since meeting Nathan, Chad'd noticed things—quiet signals, half-formed thoughts behind Nathan's words—Chad's expression suggesting his investigative mind was processing more than it said aloud. But this time, Chad wasn't there to catch it.

"Tell me about the toppled obelisk!" Nathan asked eagerly.

"Where do we begin?" Tim laughed.

"We don't think it toppled," Crouton clarified. "More likely, it was never erected."

They described the obelisk's material, condition, and the second piece of Atlantis found at its tip. Rod sent Nathan photos as they spoke, and Tim shared Ps. Reo's insights on the Order of Kittim and the ancient journals beneath Antioch—their connection to the Talakanis and Britannia.

Nathan paused—silence...

"Nathan? Still there?" Crouton asked.

"Hmm... yes. Britannia. Incredible... You're making serious progress on Atlantis in the Caribbean."

Tim didn't need Chad to be there to notice that one.

"We're nearly certain," Crouton said. "The obelisk reveals proof of electrical tech. We just need experts to verify. Mind you, Ps. Reo's good friend Mr. Kristian Phillips—an experienced electrical engineer was able to shed light on that already."

"That's fantastic," Charles said over speakerphone. "The Florida team arrives within the week."

"Great," Nathan replied.

"Ps. Reo with you?" Charles asked.

"Nah, he's called it a day," Crouton answered.

"Not to worry. We'll finalize things in the morning."

"Hypothetically," Rod began, voice low but charged, "if this really is a piece of Atlantium—if it's capable of receiving energy—could we get it to connect with Alesandro's? I mean... wireless electricity?"

He paused, the implications settling in. "Not just a power source, but a receiver. A conduit. If they are designed to resonate across distance—like tuning forks, or ancient relays?"

The others exchanged glances. Even Crouton stopped mid-sip, brow furrowed.

Rod leaned back slightly, the firelight catching the edge of his face.

"In theory, yes," Nathan said. "And today's tech might not need something as massive as a Carsakarisk."

"The last real attempt was Tesla," Crouton noted. "1891. Never fully realized."

"His ambition deserved better," Rod sighed.

"Human nature takes time to absorb major leaps—in tech, theology... or the fusion of myth and truth," Nathan said.

A silence followed. They absorbed the weight of his words.

"To Rod's point," Nathan resumed, his voice steady, "if the obelisk's tip is a receiver, then testing starts immediately. We'll need synchronized readings, energy mapping, and a clean channel between the devices. If they're truly Atlantium—if they're designed to resonate—we'll know within hours."

He paused, letting the weight of possibility settle.

Crouton nodded slowly—impressed, wordless.

"Magnificent work, team," Nathan said.

Charlotte and Tim hugged.

"There's a lot to process," Tim admitted.

"You're not wrong," Rod agreed. "This is jackpot-level intel."

"Exactly," Tim nodded. "But I vote sleep—we're deep in wee small hour oblivion."

"Agreed," Nathan said.

"Plenty to tackle soon," Crouton added, snapping back to the moment.

The call ended, leaving everyone satisfied and a little blown away.

Tim scooped Charlotte into his arms, regretting not doing so earlier. He carried her to the bed settee, barely navigating the dim light. Under the duvet, she curled against him, soon asleep.

~~~~~~~~

Rod was first to stir, jolted by the obnoxious cry of a macaw. Sunlight radiated around the yard.

Grimacing, he shifted between the lingering fire warmth and the log sofa. Crouton blinked at the empty Dragon Stout bottle he still held. He glanced at Rod, then Kristian's backyard.

"Morning, boss," Rod yawned.

"Howdy squire," Crouton nodded and trudged inside—first in line for a hot shower.

After breakfast and showers, Kristian embraced each farewell with quiet warmth. Pastor Reo and the team offered heartfelt thanks—words laced with gratitude, laughter, and the gravity of shared discovery. Crouton pressed a business card into Kristian's hand with a wink and a promise: "For when you're ready to upgrade the perimeter."

They drove Pastor Reo to Kinloss, the road winding through jungle hills and quiet farmland. At the reunion point, Reo's family waited with open arms, their joy radiant and grounding. The others returned toward the Caribbean Paradise.

The trip back was quiet, reflective. The journey had ended not with fanfare, but with gratitude—woven into every mile, every memory of the experience enjoyed.

CHAPTER 30

Rod gazed out to sea, seated with Crouton, Nathan, Alesandro, and Sienna to his right. Chad, Chaiyala, Charlotte, Tim, and Rhys enjoyed their meal across the table at Poseidon's Garden, marking their final night at the Caribbean Paradise Resort in Jamaica.

Halfway through his spicy Moroccan lamb salad, he paused—distracted by a nagging, unidentified notion pressing at the edge of his mind. It had been inching closer all day, drifting within the hidden parts of his curiosity, barely visible yet oddly persistent. It was distracting him from his meal—or perhaps the meal was distracting him from working out what was troubling him.

Crouton long since buried his frustration from another fruitless encounter with Albarad the other day—reluctantly moving forward. That was, until their next inevitable clash, when fury would rip the hinges off that frustrating cupboard and explode. In that scenario, reality would grab Hamet by the crown jewels and swing him around like a screaming cat—and Crouton would laugh with delight.

It was a sadistically amusing thought, though it failed to bring any lasting joy.

Nearby, Sienna, Rhys, Nathan, and Alesandro were deep in discussion about the Solon Diaries. They discussed the intricacies of hidden history and how it differed from pseudo-history. Their conversation wove through ancient sources, suppressed accounts, and the fine line between myth and manipulation.

The others chatted casually about resort attractions. How they enjoyed the lighter moments of their Jamaican adventure and the laughter shared between the more unusual events that had shaped their journey.

Rod, lost in thought, was momentarily distracted by Chad and Chaiyala's body language and proximity—directly across from he and Crouton. They looked amazing together. Chad in particular had moved beyond his scruffy, insouciant look to a still-casual yet more refined style—for reasons he could probably guess.

He smiled, then returned to trying to pinpoint what was really bothering him—or whether anything was, or if he simply didn't know what to think any more. Whatever the case, it was hard to tell.

Chad finally drifted out of his quiet admiration for the beauty seated beside him when she and Charlotte slipped into a moment of girlish chatter. Noticing Rod's distant expression—his eyes locked in thought, Chad considered checking in.

Rod spotted the younger man's attention and smiled, returning briefly to his lamb.

"You all good, man?" Chad asked.

"Always," Rod replied with an air of mystery... "Always good... often intrigued or curious."

Chad nodded. "Bit on your mind?"

Rod chuckled. "Always that too. Definitely a *bit*." He had a couple more mouthfuls of lamb before setting his fork down. Pausing, he glanced out toward the ocean, then back to Chad.

"It's been an odd few days," he began. "First we find Alesandro—then this Atlantium crystal. Small as a fist, but heavier than it should be. Near-mythic stuff... watching Egypt-Mauritania tensions flare in the news. All standard in this line of work. So are tense encounters with Albarad. But while trekking Cockpit Country, something about our impromptu meeting with him keeps nagging at me."

"What's the deal?" Chad asked.

"We arrived at the conference-room above the Skillet—food and wine already arranged. Like someone had planned the meeting with Albarad. The atmosphere was tense; Nathan navigated it diplomatically.

Then Albarad scowled, barked at his men, and walked out without explanation. Everyone—except Nathan and Albarad—were baffled. Even Albarad's own team, barely into their meals, looked annoyed and confused."

Rod hesitated. "I felt like I'd lost half an hour—something was off. But that's not uncommon in this job, either."

He described strange time glitches: the sun jumping across the sky too quickly, shadows shifting without warning, or memory gaps—moments that simply disappeared. Yet this time, the questions haunted him more than usual.

"It comes up often," he admitted. "The sheer scale of what we've found—especially Atlantis—is overwhelming. Our wellness supervisors say it's pushing the limits of how much we can mentally absorb. History, geology, physics—they're all colliding with what we've uncovered. The contradictions are coming fast, and it's exhausting."

"That's one theory. But some say if they didn't know better, it'd feel like a cover-up."

He paused. "But the other day... I don't know. Something feels different."

"That's interesting," Chad replied— "what do you mean?"

Rod tapped the table, "For starters, no one knows what it is. It's never happened before. It's like, a brand-new field in psychology."

"No, I meant the cover-up bit," Chad clarified.

Rod nodded, recalling previous discussions.

"Let me play devil's advocate," Chad said softly, leaning in to speak discretely. "What if something *is* going on? Something none of you are aware of—and there's a mind-altering method of covering it up. As crazy as it sounds... has that possibility been explored?"

Rod nodded. "Yes, it has."

"Nathan and Crouton assembled a team of experts—psychologists, investigators, former detectives. Their task: protect Red Sword Security from anything that could erode trust. They weren't taking chances. Not with what was coming.

The team was vetted like a jury—any hint of bias was eliminated. The irony is that their role feels both unnecessary and redundant, yet it exists to prove just that, if the question ever arises.

They're re-evaluated regularly—along with their methods—to ensure everything remains fit for purpose. Other than Nathan and Crouton, we don't hear from them. They're silent oversight. If something seems off, they speak up—first to Nathan and Crouton. If either of them is ever implicated, the matter defers to Charles and myself."

Rod leaned back. "They quietly ensure our integrity holds firm. While we trust one another, you can't always expect the same from the outside."

"Good grief!" Chad sat back, half stunned. "That's brilliant. Countries should model their governments off that."

"Ironically, it wouldn't work in government. Too many flaws. Too much self-interest. Finding enough unbiased people every term would be like searching every haystack in a massive barn for one needle each term. But yeah—it'd be a refreshing change."

"So based on all that," Chad pondered aloud, "you eliminate any chance of dishonesty or secrecy. You'd need supernatural powers to pull off a cover-up that consistent."

Rod raised an eyebrow. "Hmm. Yeah..."

Then he shook his head. "Forget it. If it matters, I'll figure it out. Right now, I don't even know what the questions are, so I'm shelving it."

He glanced at Chad with an amused frown. "I can't even figure *that* out."

Rod and Chad finished their meals and joined the broader conversation as dessert menus circled the table.

"...it was downright macabre. A sorry scenario you'd expect in a Stephen King novel," Crouton continued—sharing the eerie tale of Edward Mordrake. "A nobleman born with two faces—one his own, the other that of his twin sister. The second face couldn't speak, but was said to whisper demonic things. Surgeons refused to remove it, fearing it would kill the man. It'd cry when he was happy, and grin when he was distressed—driving him insane. Took his own life at twenty-six, requesting his body be burned to prevent the face from haunting him in death."

"That is creepy and twisted," Rhys remarked, enjoying the yarn.

"The medical term is craniofacial duplication," Nathan explained.

"And so sad," Charlotte added—sympathetic.

Sienna and Rod shook their heads in dismay.

"Though the 1895 Boston Post claimed it was factual," Tim began, "the story was later revealed to be fiction—misrepresented in medical journals."

"Victorian history presents challenges," Sienna noted. "Narratives often reflected imperial and social biases. The push for truth gained traction in the mid-20th century, but ironically, today's era faces misinformation and pseudo-science at full speed."

She explained that the condition, though real, is often fatal due to neurological conflict. Rhys winced, the weight of it sinking in.

"Bit of a fail, eh?" Crouton quipped.

"Frustrating," Tim sighed.

"Weird," Chad breathed. Restless for something familiar—yet grounded by Chaiyala's steady presence.

"Weirder than the man from Toured?" Crouton asked, eyes on Tim.

Tim raised a brow. "Hmm, the man from Toured... now *that's* beyond weird. Practically a whole new project for Red Sword."

"Crows teeth! I ain't takin' that on," Crouton scoffed. "Beyond my pay grade. Nathan maybe—not me. That sort of crazy carry-on'd do my head in!"

Nathan grinned.

Their waiter returned and took dessert and drink orders.

The sun had set, and the restaurant and pool precinct buzzed with life—guests laughing, swimming, and savouring the flavours and experiences that defined the resort's charm. The heat had softened, easing from a humid mid-thirties to a gentle mid-twenties, as the Jamaican evening unfolded—lush, lingering, and suspended in time once more.

"So, what's the story?" Chad asked.

"Who exactly was the man from Toured?" Charlotte echoed.

"He arrived at Tokyo's Haneda Airport in 1954," Rod began "carrying a passport from a country that didn't exist—Toured—supposedly located between France and Spain. Authorities detained him for questioning. Guards were posted outside his hotel room... but by morning, he was gone. No trace. Not even his documents."

"Very peculiar..." Chad said, frowning. "But what happened after? Were there similar cases—anything overlooked or buried?"

It unsettled him—nudging thoughts of truth versus fiction.

The others focused in, drawn to the mysterious tale and the thoughtful exchange between Chad and Rod.

Nathan smiled. "Your curiosity will make you a brilliant lawyer—always digging past the surface."

Chad smiled, appreciating the encouragement.

"Most cases had to be documented quickly before they vanished," Crouton said. "The phenomenon seems tied to high-altitude airspace—possibly parallel dimensions."

Nathan nodded. "I support the theory, but it's too vast to fully chase."

"We're standing at the edge of an ocean of mystery," Rod added, "with no vessel to explore it."

Crouton continued, "We've got footage showing travellers arriving—yet some hadn't even stepped off a plane. Others had no idea anything was strange until stopped at customs."

"Some passengers booked for New York," Rod interjected, "landed in Sydney—set off teleportation debates. Over two-thirds came from forgotten or fictional regions: Toured, Nurari—a stretched Mongolia from Turkey to New York.

Then there was Kilimanjaro—listed not as a mountain, but as a city-state. Sareihaan—an Ottoman-European state long erased from maps. Ibungali—a precolonial version of modern Australia.

Other names surfaced too: East Germany, Persia, Rhodesia, Tawantinsuvo—the Inca Empire—and Mesopotamia, Antioch, and Assyria. States and empires long extinct, or historically incapable of air travel."

"These events seem to fix themselves," Nathan said. "As if reality knows when something's off. Our scientists call it dimensional correction. A theoretical fail-safe."

Chad's expression shifted—wide-eyed, breath taken. He finally grasped it. Nothing was hidden. It didn't retreat into shadow or secrecy. It simply ceased to exist.

Not erased. Not concealed. Just... undone.

Like reality had folded in on itself, quietly, without protest.

"Did we miss anything?" Crouton asked.

"Nope," Sienna replied. "Though some religious texts do hint at time travel—in more obscure corners."

Charlotte recalled her and Tim once discussing parallel dimensions—just as Rod turned to Tim with a similar query.

"Tim, what are your thoughts on this... from a religious point of view?"

"Very unorthodox," Tim replied—smiling at Rod.

Chad was intrigued. He often resonated with Tim's take on theology—finding it refreshing and feeling at home with the way he aligned his thinking with the person of Jesus—relational, mysterious, and resonant.

He named the moments that defied explanation—Jesus appearing out of nowhere, Enoch vanishing without a trace, Philip reappearing miles away. Tim nodded, pointing to echoes in the Qu'ran and the Bhagavad Gita—stories where time and space bent in ways that felt eerily familiar.

Tim wondered why belief in creation and the miraculous couldn't extend to multidimensional theories or time travel. He speculated that such movement might influence destiny and free will. They agreed—science and the supernatural held mysteries deeper than most were willing to admit.

"Come to think of it," Tim pondered, "nearly everything Jesus did was obscure. Proceeding him, many of the Apostles miracles and some of the more bazaar miracles of classical and medieval history."

"For example?" Chad asked.

"The Seven Sleepers," Tim said. "Seven Christian youths fled Roman persecution in 250 A.D.—hiding in a cave sealed by Emperor Decius. Centuries later, a farmer opened it and found them alive. Christianity had become the state religion, and their ancient coins baffled locals. The story is well-documented and regarded by many as more than myth."

"Back then," Nathan added, "miracles were taken at face value. Fiction hadn't advanced enough to blur lines. Without scepticism or technology to mimic wonder, miraculous events were simply accepted and woven into tradition."

"Is a good point," Chaiyala said quietly.

Chad nodded, deep in thought—so much to absorb... or reconsider.

"It's important to understand," Nathan began, addressing Chad, Charlotte, and Alesandro, "Red Sword doesn't engage in conspiracy theories or take sides. If something we uncover happens to confirm or disprove one, it's simply because the evidence speaks for itself. Chasing agendas or jumping on bandwagons doesn't serve our purpose."

"We always have a different agenda," Crouton summarised.

"One that deals in matters beyond politics, land, resources, or truth vs. human philosophy," Nathan finished.

"Which is why we haven't blown the whistle on Hamet and the pyramids," Rod added.

Hamet Albarad's misdemeanours are just one thread in a vast web of historical deception—set to unravel with the revelation of Atlantis. That discovery will ignite a global chain reaction. Each breakthrough will peel back another layer, exposing a history far more complex—and far less familiar—than we've ever known.

Rod had had enough of the circus of enigmas and oddities. He retired to the penthouse suite, determined to clear his head with bourbon and a line-up of action movies—or at least until fatigue called for sleep. But not before his nightly video call to Kristie—an unmissable part of his Jamaica routine.

After coffee at the Skillet, Nathan, Crouton and Alesandro took a brief moonlit walk before turning in.

~~~~~~~

The others all headed to the beach precinct where fire pits had been lit—resort staff occasionally stoked the glowing flames. Guests either sat around in loungers or bean bags and Rhys and Sienna headed to the Shrimp and Marlin's beachside bar to order snacks and drinks.

Tim, Charlotte, Chad, and Chaiyala remained at the fire pit they'd claimed and dragged bean bags to sit around.

Chad was quiet—clearly out of sorts.

"You okay, man?" Tim asked.

"Yeah... just processing. Dinner was weird—a lot to process, on top of everything. But I'm holding up."

Tim nodded, sensing it best not to press.

Chaiyala, also distant, drifted into her own thoughts her gaze fixed on the dancing flames of the fire.

"Fire's easy to get lost gazing at, especially late at night." Sienna mused.

"Like moths to a flame," Tim said, almost without thinking.

"Maybe Chad and I—we are part moth," Chaiyala joked—her grin flickering in the firelight.

"Who knows?" Tim shrugged.

"Stranger things have happened," Rhys added.

Their drinks arrived in two ice-filled chillers, along with steaming curly fries and bacon-crumbed chicken nibbles.

"Nicely done!" Tim praised.

"This way, no need to return to the bar." Sienna explained.

"We are so sorted. Thank you!" Charlotte expressed, reaching for chicken.

"When we get back to Mauritania," Rhys declared, "I'm raiding the deep freeze and eating the rest of the New York steaks."

"All by yourself?" Tim raised an eyebrow.

"Like heck you are," Chaiyala cut in.

"Oh, no, you can all help. I just want a Crouton sized slab of meat!"

Everyone laughed.

"The steaks here are tasty, but two-fifty grams at a time doesn't cut it. I need double."

"Why didn't you just order a double?" Chad asked.

Rhys blinked. "Brilliant idea. That, I like. I'll remember it for next time." He raised his stubby. "Cheers."

"Not just a pretty face after all," Tim joked.

"Not at all," Rhys agreed, winking at Chaiyala.

"He's prettier and smarter than you," she teased, poking her tongue out.

Chad frowned, exaggerated and theatrical. "Look what you start," he said, pointing at Tim.

Tim and Charlotte burst out laughing. Chad shook his head.

"Oh now, that's just rude," Rhys protested, trying not to laugh. "Cheeky punk," he muttered at Chaiyala, taking a swig.

"You two are hopeless," Sienna said with a sigh.

"When we get back to the Richat," Tim said, "I can't wait to see what the pieces of Atlantis can tell us when put together and properly examined."

"Yes," Sienna nodded. "Nathan and my dad want them tested immediately—soon as you guys step out of the plane."

"It's going to be fascinating, no doubt," Tim said.

"Definitely," Chaiyala agreed, her gaze flicking from the fire to the stars.

"What else is news from the project?" Rhys asked.

"Ooh, cool stuff!" Charlotte beamed, recalling how Crouton had briefed her, Tim, and Nathan on the latest developments.

"During the chaos of finding Alesandro," Tim began, "Crouton got a call from Charles. Excavation uncovered a massive chamber beneath the third ring of hills in the Richat. To begin with they fired flares into the darkness to get a visual—one struck stone, the other hissed into water. The chamber is vast, layered, and eerily precise. It matches the ancient schematics almost perfectly. This is the site—exactly where Atlantis's underground naval docks were believed to be."

"Nice!" Chaiyala said, snapping back into the moment.

"Charles confirmed it's even larger and more intact than they'd hoped."

Everyone quieted.

"Sonar mapped hard stone walls, vast water-filled chambers and in two of them—enormous ships. Though nearly twice the diameter Plato described, the concentric rings of the formation mirrored the Atlantean naval schematics in proportion—down to the spacing between the outer docks and the central island."

"Where the triremes were housed?" Chad asked.

"Exactly. The speculation's behind us now. We've got physical structures—chambers carved deep into bedrock—flawless symmetry—intentional flood design. This is the kind of evidence you dream about. And now it's right in front of us."

Sienna exhaled. "Twelve thousand years untouched..."

"There's more," Tim added. "Scans suggest adjoining rooms. Purpose unclear—but nothing natural forms with that kind of precision. It's the strongest archaeological evidence for the Triremes we could have hoped for. This isn't mythology any more. We're dealing ancient infrastructure and maritime history."

"This is super exciting!" Charlotte beamed.

Tim nodded, grinning.

Rhys grinned wide. "Atlantis is only the beginning."

Eventually, Rhys, Sienna, Tim, and Charlotte disappeared off toward the dance party between the Shrimp and Marlin and Hot Rocks and Roast.

Chad and Chaiyala stayed behind, basking in relaxed nighttime beach atmosphere.

"It's a weird, weird world out there," Chad said quietly, as if thinking aloud.

"Yes, definitely," Chaiyala replied. "Mystery—paradox—everywhere."

"I don't always like it eh," Chad said. "My head's full of all things from the sublime to the ridiculous... feels like that Star Wars scene before they blow up the Death Star."

"Which one?" she chuckled.

"Huh? Which—what?"

"They destroy Death Star again and again. Is always same," Chaiyala said, amused.

Chad chuckled. "Fair call."

"Was never into Star Wars," she said. "But I take it over Star Trek."

"Good," he said approvingly.

"But Stargate SG-1—it's my favourite," she said.

Chad lit up. "Mine too."

They high-fived.

"This space battle in your head—what now?" she asked—tilting her head.

"Unsure... I hate living in a world of secrecy—the cloak-and-dagger stuff, people disappearing."

"Try not to dwell too much—it wears you down," Chaiyala cautioned, sitting up and meeting Chad's gaze. "Is last thing you need now."

Chad hesitated. Could he really just ignore it? It mattered to him—deeply.

Silence lingered. Then Chaiyala spoke. "All this crazy—you treat like books on shelf. You choose what to open, what to leave. No need to decide—fact or fiction."

"Hmm. Yeah, that works."

Chaiyala finished her cider. "Chad, we don't hear full story—only one side, limited. Important angles missing. Not always cover-up or people vanish—sometimes facts just not there. You know this. You have investigative mind—don't let emotion, fear, or drama cloud it."

Chad sighed, taking in her wisdom. As their eyes met, the tension in his thoughts eased. His admiration for her grew quickly—his earlier reservations, and her resemblance to Sonia, vanished long since.

She was stunning, grounded, quietly funny, and fiercely intelligent—with a captivating Israeli accent. Tougher than most guys he knew. She was nothing like Sonia. She was herself.

"You are good guy," she said, looking at him kindly. "Genuine. Thoughtful. Loyal. You protect your peace, okay?"

She quoted Nathan: "Few things truly matter. Most are neutral. But freedom of the mind, the soul, and friendship—that's everything."

Chad's heart skipped. *Marry me'*, he thought. That was it—he'd fallen for her.

"That's awesome," he said aloud. "I really like that."

She smiled. "Walk on beach?"

"Yeah. That sounds perfect."

They stowed their shoes in a nearby locker, then wandered barefoot along the moonlit shoreline. Waves washed over their feet, drawing them away from the resort festivities.

Chaiyala nudged him. "Look down."

Bioluminescent algae sparkled beneath the surface—bright with every ripple.

"This is seriously cool!"

"Beautiful, huh?"

"I've only ever seen this in pictures."

They walked toward the bushy peninsula where Alesandro's safe house lay hidden. Chaiyala spoke of it discreetly, close enough for their hands to find each other's. Once they connected, they walked on in blissful silence, getting used to the feeling of togetherness.

The romantic silence broke as they began splashing each other. Glowing water scattered like sparks and liquid light. Laughing and dodging the sprays, Chaiyala tried to get Chad in a headlock—but he ducked, grabbed her waist, and lifted her into the air as she squealed happily.

He gazed up at her, and she looked down into his eyes.

"I'm heavier than you expected?" Chaiyala teased, reading his expression.

"You're solid!" Chad grinned.

She smirked and squared her shoulders with exaggerated pride as he gently lowered her onto the wet sand.

Chad was overflowing with admiration for her—and she felt exactly the same about him.

They stood hand-in-hand—her head resting on his shoulder—gazing out across the ocean. Moonlight splashed across drifting clouds, casting haunting shades of black, grey, and silver above the glowing sea. The scene resonated deeply—electric and serene—a reflection of everything they'd been through, and everything unfolding between them. It was peace they could feel and understand, even if no words could fully describe it.

Chad placed his hands gently on Chaiyala's shoulders, caressing the silky warmth of her arms. She followed his touch as his hands explored, then wrapped around her in a quiet embrace, settling against the contours of her taut stomach.

They lingered in quiet bliss for several minutes... then, with his heart racing, Chad took the plunge. He asked Chaiyala to be his girlfriend. She turned her head, then her whole body as he held her close around the small of her back.

"Yes!" she said, eyes bright. "I would love very much."

She smiled wide—and then they kissed, long and unhurried, a moment that stretched on like the night itself.

Hand in hand, they walked back to the resort, debating when to share the news—tonight or morning. Stepping off the elevator, Rod's thunderous snores greeted them. The menu screen of Armageddon looped on the 82-inch above a scatter of bourbon bottles. Rod lay sprawled on the couch, clutching one mid-snore.

Suppressing laughter, Chad gently removed the bottle while Chaiyala draped a blanket over him. As they slipped away, Rod muttered in his sleep, "No, don't... a good amount will do. Santa Claus... and a bad sandwich... terrible," followed by "a goat, and spaghetti who can do this..." he did something funny with his fingers—eyes still closed, then began snoring again.

Chaiyala pulled Chad into the kitchen before they lost it in hysterics. Chad eventually turned off the TV—effort still needed to suppress laughter.

Tim and Charlotte slipped out of the elevator in the early hours, careful not to wake anyone. In Tim's room, they gathered a few blankets and retreated to their shared balcony, sinking into a giant bean bag.

"Ooh!" Charlotte whispered, spotting Chad and Chaiyala on the balcony opposite.

"What?"

Charlotte pointed, and Tim's eyes widened—his brother and Chaiyala were wrapped in a moonlit embrace. Charlotte hugged him, thrilled for their friends. Tim, hesitant to assume too much, felt quietly relieved. Chad had clearly moved on—and to Tim, Chaiyala seemed right for him.

CHAPTER 31

It was shortly after 5 a.m. when Crouton, Rod, and Sienna arrived at the scene at Nathan's request.

Multiple zones had been cordoned off—the Grand Isle, Atrium, Entrance'd Café, and the main lobby. Security, police and Red Sword agents were everywhere. The bomb squad we busy, securing explosives and sweeping for residuals.

The trio hadn't expected anything like this.

"What in the world...?" Rod muttered, confusion overtaking him.

Sienna instinctively checked her phone—no missed calls, no alerts, no dead battery. Had she allowed last night's distractions to interfere? Still, nothing had come through.

"Boss? What's going on?" Crouton frowned.

"An attempt to level the resort—with us inside. That's the short version," Nathan replied.

All three stared, stunned.

"Don't worry—it's under control. All happened very fast, which is why you weren't notified until now."

Nathan briefed them as three Red Sword agents arrived.

"I'd returned from an early morning walk when I discovered the resort swarming with security. Six individuals had been caught trying to rig explosives at critical support zones. The response had been immediate. Whatever they were planning, they'd somehow botched it up. And apparently had been caught fighting."

Shackled and defiant, the failed terrorists occasionally glanced blankly or dirtily over at Nathan and co. They were led away for processing.

"Albarad?" Crouton asked, furious.

"Of course."

Crouton scowled. Nathan didn't flinch. "Albarad's actions qualify as terrorism and violations of international law. He'll face trial for all of it. He won't see freedom again."

"What, are we talking site-wide evacuation?" Rod asked Nathan and Crouton, then looked toward where Maurice and Rohit were speaking with police and other agents.

"Sir, if I may," one of the agents who'd joined them interjected, "we've completed the full sweep—sound infra-red across every cubic meter of the resort. No anomalies. No heat signatures outside expected thresholds or locations."

"We ran a full examination—every corner of the resort. No hostiles, no weapons, nothing suspicious. We pushed the scan fifty meters beyond the perimeter. All clear."

"Management's seen the report. They're satisfied—glad we locked things down without spooking the guests or triggering an evacuation."

"Excellent!" Crouton smiled.

"Yes, that's absolutely fantastic!" added Nathan.

Rod and Sienna looked at each other with relief.

Curious all the same, Crouton and Sienna questioned how they'd missed such a major move.

"We're usually ahead of these guys—or at least quick to counter," Sienna mused.

"This time, we were the latter," Nathan said. "Albarad staged a distraction at the Skillet, while his team installed explosives. Some Resort security had been compromised. The bombs were set for remote detonation—but one of the compromised staff, working against Albarad's crew, kept them inactive."

The others exchanged puzzled looks.

The Red Sword agents who'd arrived filled them in on more details. Relief replaced shock—the outcome could've been devastating.

"So—I don't understand," Rod began, "why didn't they speak to Maurice or Rohit..."

"From what we gathered," one of the agents said, "the men who pressured resort security may have instilled enough fear that compromised staff felt they couldn't risk their families—or whatever consequences they imagined might follow."

Crouton frowned. "Don't removin' the detonation components count as risking?"

"Yes. But whoever did it, made sure it couldn't be traced."

"We've got no idea who it was?" Rod asked, baffled.

"I assume every measure has been taken to protect the compromised security and their families?" Crouton asked.

"All covered. The resort workers are in high-security detention, and their families either have Red Sword protection or have been relocated."

Crouton nodded. "Good."

"Well done—excellent work," Nathan added.

"What about CCTV?" Sienna asked.

"Not much," the agent admitted. "The optics cables were sabotaged. Cameras were disabled during their movements."

Crouton sighed. "Once this mess is behind us, I'll speak to Maurice about a full security overhaul."

Rod pieced it together—"They tried to set it off, nothing happened, and came back to check?"

"Exactly."

Crouton chuckled. "Forced to finish the job, risk exposure, or leave evidence behind. That'll teach 'em."

Nathan continued, "Their camera sabotage didn't help at that point—we got to them before they could flee."

"Fools," Crouton muttered.

"Caught red-handed," Nathan confirmed.

"And there was serious infighting," the agent added. "Two offenders ended up dead. The rest looked battered—total chaos."

"Interesting..." Sienna said thoughtfully, her mind connecting the dots. This wasn't just a botched escape—something bigger was unravelling.

"No wonder they looked like they'd fallen off a truck," Rod remarked.

"Plenty of questions," Crouton said, scanning the area.

Rod shook his head, aware of how close they'd come to disaster.

"We need to find out who pulled the detonators," Sienna stressed. "They deserve recognition—how many lives did they save?"

"Thousands..." Crouton guessed.

"Over three thousand," Nathan confirmed.

They glanced around at bomb techs, agents, and resort security in serious discussion.

"Alright... where do we go from here?" Rod asked.

"I want to know who sabotaged those bombs—who threw the wrench in the works," Sienna declared. "My team will get right on to that."

"Agreed. Thank you," Nathan said.

Crouton nodded. "We'll check in with Rohit and Maurice... once we can pull them away from their briefings."

Maurice and Rohit balanced talks with authorities and technicians. Then prepared to face the press under the watchful eyes of resort security.

Confident things were under control, Nathan chose to head back to the penthouse suite and check on the others.

Crouton, Rod, and Sienna approached the press. Sienna expertly managed the swarm, delivering polished sound bites the media could digest.

Rod was impressed. Sienna kept the message simple: "Terrorists failed, security prevailed."

"You're a show-off," Crouton teased.

"Not bad for someone who's been awake twenty minutes," Rod added.

"Fair point," Crouton admitted.

"I look pretty good for first thing in the morning, huh?" she smirked.

Rod chuckled and shook his head.

"Bet Rhys'd agree," Crouton muttered.

"You be nice to him, Daddy. I like him—a lot."

"So do I," Crouton assured her. "And I fully approve. I'm still gonna have my fun though."

Sienna narrowed her eyes. "No, you are not!"

"You remind me of your mother when you do that."

"Does that rattle you?" she teased.

"Anyway, I'm proud of you," Crouton said, sidestepping the banter. "You do a fantastic job. I'm impressed by the way you carry yourself and represent Red Sword Security Services."

"Thank you," Sienna nodded gracefully.

Rod shook his head again, smiling.

Nathan stayed behind briefly, taking a walk with Maurice before returning to the suite, while Rod and Crouton continued speaking with Rohit.

Sienna requested a delay in transporting the terrorists—she wanted to meet them first. After handling formalities with Rod, Crouton, Rohit, and Maurice, she headed to the lobby's loading bay.

Police cars, Red Sword Humvees, and armoured sedans packed the area. Officers clustered everywhere.

Two fellow agents recognized her and greeted her.

"Good morning," she replied. "How many suspects total?"

"Eight hostiles confirmed, including the two dead," one said, motioning to six armoured sedans parked between Humvees.

"There are at least five resort security in custody," he continued, "but possibly eight. Three haven't shown for their shifts. Two are being actively searched for. The one that stands out is the third—Leonard Kesemalu— new to the payroll. And here's the weird part: it's like he vanished off the planet, "he gave her a troubled look, "background checks show nothing."

Sienna stared into space, then smirked. "I knew it..."

"Kesemalu's probably your priority," the agent concluded.

Sienna nodded. "Yes,and thank you."

She paused, weighing her options. Then insisted on meeting the suspects before transport.

Led by the two agents, she assessed the detainees. Four were familiar from their pursuit of Alesandro down the Grand Isle a few nights prior. Reviewing their profiles, she dismissed them quickly.

"Nope. Thank you, you can take them away," she instructed.

Engines roared as the convoy left the Caribbean Paradise car park.

Despite hours of relentless digging, Sienna found herself staring at a void. No fingerprints. No records. No traceable background. Kesemalu was as if a ghost.

"Who are you?" she muttered—not to the screen, but to the silence it kept offering.

The other detainees had no answers; they barely knew why he was involved. No financial trails. No off-the-books payments.

Frustrated but composed, Sienna held steady. Her patience set her apart, for now.

She focused on the bigger picture—answers would come.

She decided to check in later with investigators.

For now, she headed off in search of proper breakfast... and Rhys.

~~~~~~~

Little sleep was had by Tim, Charlotte, Chad, or Chaiyala on their final night at Caribbean Paradise. Between an electric storm—thunder rumbling, lightning flashing across the sky—and the new romance between Chad and Chaiyala, the night was unforgettable.

With another beanbag dragged onto Tim and Charlotte's deck, the four spent the night lost in excited and reflective conversation.

They woke at eight—too early after an almost-all-nighter. The Caribbean sky was mostly sunny, the last clouds parting to make way for a fine day. The air hung muggy but pleasant.

Across from, Crouton, Nathan, and Rod leaned on the main balcony railing, quietly watching the younger four as they began to stir. Alesandro joined them as Nathan called out, "Good morning! Enjoy the storm?"

Tim groaned, "Yup—morning," stretching under the blanket he shared with Charlotte, who refused to open her eyes.

Chad waved wordlessly. Chaiyala blinked, disoriented, then hugged him. They smiled, savouring the warmth of the moment.

"Those two...?" Crouton asked Tim, nodding at Chad and Chaiyala with a knowing grin.

Tim nodded, smiling. "Yup," then yawned.

The older men smiled.

"We leave in one hour!" Crouton declared.

The beanbag dwellers glowered in his direction.

Crouton laughed. "...after a long hearty breakfast!"

Tim and Chad grinned. Chaiyala smiled through narrowed eyes—a look Crouton caught and chuckled.

Charlotte stood. Tim hugged her, lifting her into his arms—they shared a smile.

Chaiyala offered Chad a hand; he accepted, rising with a yawn. As they stretched, they embraced the morning, unsure what came next, captivated by the Caribbean view.

Later, Rhys surfaced, wondering where Sienna was, as the others showered and Crouton prepared a cooked breakfast.

Rod read the morning news, focusing on Sienna's press interview.

Nathan and Alesandro discussed the trip to Mauritania and asylum at the project camp.

Rhys, shirtless as usual, nearly dozed off at the table.

"Good night?" Crouton asked while cooking.

"The best. I love this place," Sienna replied, arriving from the elevator.

Once everyone had eaten, she, Nathan, and Crouton shared details of the failed resort attack—met with shock and relief.

Chad, sipping orange-mango juice, stood on the balcony, gazing over the resort and sea.

He and Chaiyala had packed, as had the others. Now, she assisted Sienna in a video call with Maurice, Rohit, and a local detective.

Rod, Tim, and Crouton reviewed the latest from Mauritania.

Chad was experiencing a new-found peace, sleeping better and eating healthier than he had in months. He even noticed his breathing had changed.

"It's the free air," Nathan said, arriving quietly.

"Sorry?"

"It's a freedom thing," Nathan said. Chad still looked puzzled.

"Your body language. The way you hold yourself—it's changed. You breathe like someone who's found peace... free air."

Chad nodded slowly, impressed. But his expression made Nathan frown.

"You seem surprised."

"Uh... no... I'm good. That was an excellent observation. It means a lot, thanks."

Chad appreciated the sentiment—but wasn't prepared for how unexpectedly, or perfectly Nathan delivered it. He'd done it again. Somehow, Nathan knew what Chad had been thinking before he'd said a word. *"How does he do that?"*

"You're welcome," Nathan smiled. "Not bad for a trip to Africa to see what your brother does for a job, eh?"

"Yeah... that's seriously all I thought it was going to be. Maybe a bit of a relax and a getaway."

"I'm guessing you got way more than you bargained for?"

"Something like that."

Nathan chuckled. "Everything happens for a reason, Chad."

"It's funny how that works..." Chad's reply was layered—part test, part question, even irony. A challenge.

They'd been staring out to sea. Now they looked at each other.

Nathan's gaze was intense, as if he understood Chad's every thought.

Chad was beginning to wonder.

Nathan took a short breath, thoughtfully. "When you get back to New Zealand... your law studies are on hold, right?"

"Yes."

"Do you intend to resume?"

"Absolutely." Chad hadn't had time to focus on, let alone think about all of that, but his plan remained.

"Good. How much more do you have to go?"

"Two and a half years."

"And your student loan?"

"Nearly ten grand now, closer to twenty when I finish—interest-free."

Nathan calculated. "If you're overseas, it won't stay free..." He paused, then turned to Chad.

"Regardless, it's covered—your debt and the rest of your education," Nathan said warmly.

"Nathan, that's incredibly generous—but I can't accept that. My family's loaded."

"I know."

"Then you know I don't need charity."

Nathan didn't respond immediately. He glanced out to sea.

"Look," Chad back-pedalled. "That didn't come out right. Please forgive me—you caught me off guard. I don't deserve or need anything..."

"Chad, are you saying that because your family's wealthy, you don't deserve gifts? That only certain people qualify for blessings?"

Chad was caught off guard again.

Nathan gazed out over the Caribbean. "If wealth is a disadvantage, I must be the most unlucky bloke on this backward upside-down planet," he smiled. "Chad, I'm so absurdly rich that Elon Musk and the Rothschild's combined wealth'd be pocket change to me. But money? I neither love nor hate it—it's a tool. A blessing and a curse."

Chad couldn't believe what he was hearing—he couldn't register it.

Nathan shook his head. "It's one of the simplest ways to get things moving. 'He who has the most toys wins'? No. He who shares the most— who's the most generous—wins."

He glanced at Chad, then looked back to the horizon. "True prosperity lies in generosity, not accumulation. There's enough money in the world for every person to earn $700,000 a year, yet inequality prevails."

Chad frowned.

Nathan chuckled, shaking his head knowingly. "Forget the maths. The real mythology is the economics of the world—not Atlantis. That's a whole other conversation for another day. What I want you to remember is this: giving leads to receiving—but only when the motive is pure. Selfish intent unravels the power of generosity."

Chad narrowed his eyes, caught in thoughtful tension.

"Money," Nathan continued, "is a smokescreen—mistaken for happiness or success. Mammon... are you familiar?"

"No."

"Look it up when you get a moment. We're getting off-topic."

Shifting gears, Nathan revealed "your student debt is already cleared— not an offer, it's a done deal. I don't do charity or hire employees. I give financial gifts to trusted associates, affirming their partnership in Red Sword Security Services."

Chad was now included. His future funded. "No strings Chad, just a gift," Nathan smiled warmly.

This guy is unbelievable... on a completely different level," Chad thought.

"And what level might that be, Chad?"

Chad went pale—he hadn't breathed a word.

"Calm, Chad. Peace. Don't be afraid." Nathan reassured, "are you okay?"

"Yeah... I think so. Pretty sure." Yet part of him whispered to himself, *"You're a lying sod."*

"Chad, be honest with me now—are you okay?"

"Oh for crying out loud—I have no idea what I am or what's what anymore! I got on a plane to a country I didn't even know existed, then I'm in the Sahara with whale bones and shipwrecks, then I find out Atlantis is real—what? You guys discovered it in the Sahara! Then I'm being shot at! Then I'm in Jamaica at this obscenely luxurious resort in what resembles an Indiana Jones movie, and I'm falling in love with a drop-dead gorgeous, ninja-trained ex-cop from Israel... the resort was going to be blown up!

And all I thought I was doing was visiting my big brother!"

Chad swore like he was in pain. He and Nathan stared at each other, half stunned.

"Oookay..." Chad exhaled, surprised but oddly relieved.

Crouton, Chaiyala, and the others had gathered, drawn by raised voices and tense expressions.

"Is... everything okay?" Crouton asked cautiously.

"Nathan, don't break my boyfriend, okay? We only just started dating—I need his brain working."

Tim, Rod, and Charlotte exchanged bewildered glances.

"Chad's broken? I think Nathan's broken," Crouton muttered. "Boss, I've never seen that look on your face. Tell me everything's okay."

Nathan hesitated. "Chad?"

"Yes, actually." Chad checked himself, then smiled. "Now that I got that off my chest, I feel way better."

"Thank God for that!" Nathan sighed—relieved, nearly needing to sit down. "I'm so sorry—I didn't mean to freak you out."

"Still not happy," Crouton frowned. He'd never seen Nathan this rattled.

"What exactly were you two talking about?" Tim asked.

Rhys shook his head. "I'm confused."

"Yeah, I think we all are," Sienna agreed.

Chad and Nathan exchanged a look—time to exit. "It's okay," Chad said. "I'm just overwhelmed. A lot of crazy stuff's been happening, and I've got a myriad to process. Nathan's incredibly kind and generous. He offered to pay off my student loan and fund the rest of my studies. I kinda freaked out. I'm sorry for the fuss."

"Oh wow!" Charlotte said, pleasantly surprised.

"Nice!" Tim nodded, grateful for Chad.

Chaiyala smiled admiringly at Nathan.

"Yup, that's our Nate," Rod smiled, "most unbelievably generous man I've ever met."

"Right..." Crouton nodded, still unsettled by Nathan's rare demeanour. "If that's all, then good. You're a good man, Nate." He clapped Nathan's shoulder and glanced out to sea. He headed inside, still processing, unable to shake a feeling. He knew Nathan well—Chad, not enough. But his gut-feeling maintained Chad was no concern.

"You are, Nathan," Chad agreed. "I truly appreciate your generosity." He hugged him warmly.

"You're very welcome, my friend. And, we can talk more on the flight back to Mauritania," Nathan added. "There's something else I'd like to discuss with you. An offer—something you can choose to accept or pass up." He placed a hand on Chad's shoulder.

~~~~~~~

After a packed week at the Caribbean Paradise resort, they all prepared to depart. Time had felt strangely suspended—especially for Chad and Tim—while Rod and Crouton had unknowingly experienced that literally.

Amid Hamet Albarad's disruptions, key meetings had still gone ahead. Tim and Charlotte's lunch with J-Mac, and the meeting with Alesandro achieved all they could have hoped for.

After farewelling Maurice and Rohit, the Humvee drive to Sangster International was quiet, but charged. The kind of silence that follows wonder—windows down, minds replaying moments they still processed. Sienna drove with focus, Caitlyn scanned the horizon as they wound along the coast. No one said much, but the weight of what they'd seen rode with them all the way to the terminal.

The pieces of Atlantis were transported with serious care, under close watch from Rod and Crouton in an impenetrable sealed, light-proof case.

Nathan secured high-level clearance required to transport the kind of unique and interesting luggage they had, out of the country. Rhys and Chaiyala coordinated personal security. Tim, Chad, Charlotte, and especially Alesandro, remained their top priority.

Rhys and Sienna shared a heartfelt goodbye before he boarded, already longing for when they'd meet again.

~~~~~~~

Mid-flight, Chad woke to find Chaiyala asleep beside him. Tim and Charlotte resting, and Crouton dozing, while Alesandro immersed himself in Solon's translated diaries.

Nathan shut his laptop, following an online meeting with North African heads of state. He smiled at Chad.

"You wanted to discuss something with me as we travelled back to Africa," Chad said, leaning forward.

Nathan set aside his laptop. "I'd like you to consider joining Red Sword Security Services as one of our lawyers."

Chad raised an eyebrow, nodding slowly.

"It's a different kind of legal work. The firm operates independently by design—morally required—but Charles and I own it. Once you've finished your studies, the three of us would form a partnership—we can sort out the details together."

"Wow, thanks." Chad considered. "I appreciate it. I'll think it over, talk to Tim and Chaiyala first."

"Take all time you need—the offer stands indefinitely."

"I'll likely say yes, but experience tells me to sit on it first."

"Wise."

Lost in thought, Chad pondered the Richat, the pyramids, and Nathan himself—unsure where to begin.

Nathan caught the vexed expression. "There's a great deal turning over in your head."

Chad smiled. "So much."

The others remained asleep.

"What else is there to know about Atlantium.?"

Nathan paused. Few knew of its existence—let alone its significance. "Atlantium is one of several dozen ancient, near-mythical elements—so rare, they're not on the periodic table or found in pseudo-science. Not to be confused with rare earth or endangered elements. Atlantium as well as a few other minerals and substances have been around... more to the point lost or forgotten, well before the creation of the periodic table."

Chad's expression demanded more.

"Atlantium is different. If the world knew its worth, gold and diamonds would look worthless in comparison. Scarcity alone could spark chaos.

It's dangerously volatile—like a nuclear-powered magnifying glass. Alesandro carrying it around won't matter, but if one of those bullets had hit it?" Nathan shook his head. "There'd be no trace of him—or Montego Bay. We'd not be here, having this conversation."

"Wow... goodness!"

"Which makes it, for all intents and purposes, a weapon of mass destruction."

Chad fell silent, disturbed. "How the heck did you get it through customs?"

"They didn't know what it was. It just looks like a heavy glass trinket."

Chad shook his head—wide-eyed.

"Atlantium only reacts to energy or friction," Nathan said. "Some believe it powered ancient civilizations—concentrated light, maybe even early weapon tech. But there's little proof. It has to be stored in a dark, static-free, fireproof container. Mishandling it could be catastrophic. Alesandro, without knowing, could have vaporized his safe house."

Expose the prism's sides to electricity or focused light and you'd get a fire. But from the base up—it becomes a laser, cutting through 200 kilometres before fading."

The gravity of the pyramids presence in the world had fully settled. Monumental machines, designed to transmit energy. And the tech they'd uncovered, the geopolitical unrest—a convergence. A chilling possibility had surfaced: what if someone tried to weaponize the Atlantean systems? The fallout wouldn't just be technological. It would ripple through power structures, secrecy, and global stability.

"It must be studied—then left alone..."

"...because unless Atlantis's full history and tech are confirmed, revealing this could trigger global hysteria and risk." Chad finished.

"That, my boy, is why I want you working for me." Nathan smiled, impressed by Chad's sharp deduction.

Chad leaned back, a myriad of thoughts swirling. Nathan gave a quiet nod, returning to his laptop. Outside, the day stretched beyond the horizon—past the edge of dreams and destiny, of awe and quiet contemplation. The hum of the engines softened as the haze of the African coastline came into view. A soft chime echoed overhead.

Rod flicked on the 'fasten seatbelt' sign as two fighter jets—bearing the gold star and crescent moon on green—flanked the Lear jet. Their Mauritanian escort had arrived to guide them safely to Nouakchott.

"Ladies and gentlemen, clowns and ninjas—we're about to descend into the land of sand, the madness we call home, and the end of the world as we know it."

He earned a round of laughter.

"I hope you enjoyed your flight with Air O'Connor. Time is 8:35 p.m. local in Nouakchott, and it's a pleasant 45 degrees with zero humidity."

~~~~~~~

Sienna had spent three days chasing shadows. Leonard Kesemalu—the mysterious Caribbean Paradise employee—possibly a double agent—had disappeared after the failed attack. Not a single trace.

She dropped manual tracking and switched to Red Sword's automated systems—designed to scan every known global database. Including rare access to the Vatican archives.

The web of mistrust and global fragility wasn't lost on her. She understood it intimately.

She awaited intel from off-grid agencies too, decoded using software similar to Tim's translation tech. The system scanned, collated, and analysed. With each passing day, the mystery deepened.

Suddenly something—her eyes locked onto the screen. It froze: 'Josiri Gilbert. Jamaican-born.'

"Yuss! Finally!" she hissed—then gasped as the screen vanished and flickering resumed.

"Noooo! You've got to be kidding!" Her voice cracked a new octave.

Two colleagues burst in. "Everything okay?"

Sienna's glare spoke volumes—then she calmed, serene.

"I have a name."

Confused, one said, "Yeah... Sienna?"

She laughed, explaining the name she'd seen, before it vanished.

They shared her frustration.

The room went quiet. "Have we been shut out?"

"No way... that's never happened before," Sienna muttered. But it sure looked that way. If someone had flagged the search, access would be revoked instantly.

"That's bad..." They all grasped the gravity. Had someone outmanoeuvred Red Sword's advantage?

Sienna shook her head. "Highly unlikely. To stay hidden this long, they'd have to exist in another dimension."

"Regardless," a colleague returned, "what is Gilberts connection to Kesemalu?"

Sienna re-entered the name: "Josiri Gilbert..." The system scanned—then froze again. "Who, exactly are you? And do you have anything to do with Leonard Kesemalu?" She asked softly, mostly thinking aloud.

"Oh, come on!"

"Tech support?" someone asked.

"Nope—T.A.S.D. (Tech Anomalies and Special Dynamics)."

Sienna nodded, dialling to put in a request. Her eyes narrowed.

~~~~~~~

Chad walked into his room—the same one he'd been staying in before their Jamaica trip—and felt instantly at home. Chaiyala stood in the doorway behind him, watching silently, thoughtfully.

He turned to face his new girlfriend. How quickly everything had changed. Here he was, caught up in something unexpected: a new relationship that made him feel freer and happier than he had in years.

They took each other's hands and held a gaze of mutual admiration. Chad knew, deep down, Chaiyala was the one—something he'd never felt with Sonia. Their connection felt fated; once the realization hit, it was as if they'd known each other forever. He chuckled, thinking back to how blindly he'd accepted Tim's invitation to Mauritania—never imagining it would spark a love story between a Kiwi law student and former Israeli cop turned elite security specialist.

"You laugh—why?" she asked.

"A few weeks ago, I had no idea how different life was about to become. How free I'd feel—how in love I'd be."

Chaiyala gave him a sultry look, pushed him onto the bed, and shut the door with her foot.

Later, the two joined Tim and Charlotte on their way across the terraced deck to Rhys and Crouton's place, where Rod and Kristie were already waiting.

Warm greetings were exchanged before Kristie lit up, diving straight into conversation with Tim around the Solon diaries.

Crouton had been slowly coming to terms with a fatherly paradox. It was a strange sensation—knowing that one of his closest friends, despite being twenty-odd years younger, had grown extremely close to his daughter. It stirred a storm of emotions and quiet quandaries.

Sounds in the wee hours had been unmistakable. While the young couple hadn't officially announced anything, they certainly weren't hiding their rendezvous or dates at Caribbean Paradise.

Crouton adored his little girl. She and her brothers were all he had after losing their mother—his beloved Natalie. He wanted Sienna to be with someone who truly respected and cherished her—someone who'd treat her with the honour she deserved.

Unexpected as it had been, he'd come to know that Rhys was perfect for Sienna. Her choosing Rhys Harvey—the self-described 'Maori Scotsman'—a man Crouton trusted above all. Rhys had earned the admiration of everyone who knew him, and Crouton had made peace with the idea. More than that, he was glad Sienna was in good hands.

Still, he was Crouton Bull. A reputation to be upheld none-the-less—a bit of fun was required.

Tim, Charlotte, Chaiyala, and Chad joined the lively gathering, where, Rhys, Rod and Kristie lounged while Crouton and Alesandro prepped dinner.

The mood shifted when Crouton asked bluntly, "Rhys, what are your intentions for my daughter?"

"Passionately intimate ones, sir," Rhys replied politely, straight-faced.

Without looking up, Crouton slammed a cleaver into the chopping block.

"You'll have to chuck that out now," stated Rod, a hint of lamenting for the board in his tone.

"What?" Crouton barked.

"It's ruined," Rod replied, feigning annoyance. "You carved the Grand Canyon of kitchen tools into it—no point keeping it. Toss it. There are plenty more."

Without pause, Crouton flung it out the window. It landed in the pool with a splash.

The others were all exchanging puzzled glances. A strange and unusual mix of caution, curiosity and amusement filled the atmosphere.

"Admirable ones, my friend," Rhys clarified, shifting gears with sincerity.

"Good," the response matching the clarification.

Crouton stayed alert, emphasizing commitment. "I'd prefer you put a ring on her finger if you two are going to 'engage,'" he said, raising a brow.

Confusion flickered across the room. All were intrigued with a wondering of what might have been missed. Chaiyala narrowed her eyes at Crouton, then at Rhys.

Rod frowned, asking, "Is this your way of saying, 'Yes, Rhys, you may marry my daughter'?"

"You need a ring for this kinda thing," Crouton grunted.

"Yeah, well, Frodo had a ring too. Nearly killed him," Rod muttered.

"Rhys'd best be careful then—do you have one?" he asked Rhys.

"I do... but I ain't tossing it into no mountain of fire," Rhys said, deadpan.

Crouton sighed, stared out the window, then nodded. "Good then," he smirked, returning to dinner prep.

The odd exchange settled. Curiosity lingered, but laughter softened the moment.

Alessandro stood at the other end of the bench, cautiously hiding behind a jar of pickles.

"Welcome to my family, Chad," Chaiyala smiled warmly. "You too, Alesandro."

"Mad bunch o' nutters, we are," Crouton admitted with a grin. "Rod should've warned you."

Rod raised his brows, then smiled.

Dinner was Crouton's Caribbean Chicken—a dish he'd enjoyed in Jamaica and had been itching to recreate for everyone.

Perfectly seared jerk chicken, grilled pineapple, corn kernels, diced cucumber, and cherry tomatoes over coconut rice, all drizzled with lime mayo. At first bite, satisfied expressions and gratitude erupted around the table.

"This is so good," Rod said, satisfied and impressed.

The others whole-heartedly agreed.

"This'll be a regular dinner from now on," Tim declared—he and Charlotte had first tasted it at the Shrimp and Marlin in Jamaica.

The evening unfolded gently—laughter rising around the brazier flames, stories traded between dips in the softly glowing pool. The water shimmered with an otherworldly light, casting reflections that danced across nearby faces.

Rick and Antonio arrived late, dust still clinging to their boots after three days in the Adrars above Chinguetti. Their mission had been a success: a mercenary camp, quietly funded by Iranian billionaire Mohammad Saurashan, had been neutralized.

"Saurashan's one of Red Sword's nastiest adversaries," Antonio said, settling in beside Chad and Charlotte. "If the Richat Project goes through, he's in serious trouble."

Crouton stood on the top deck near his room, texting. He leaned against the rail, watching Charlotte, Jacqui, Rhys, and Rick play cards, Rod and Charles chatting near the brazier, and Chad and Chaiyala immersed in the private conversation at the far end of the pool.

Tim approached, handing Crouton a Corona with a wedge of lime.

"Cheers."

"All good?"

"Yeah, mate. Just texting my Sienna," Crouton said, thumb hovering over the screen. "She's stuck at that NATO Security Policy Round Table— room full of bureaucrats and government suits, trying to run countries like corporations and stop tyrants from wrecking their portfolios and weekend plans."

"Sounds exciting," Tim teased.

"They'd have a suicide to deal with if I were there. But my girl's got patience and diplomacy second only to Nathan's. Gotta admire that."

"She's a neat girl. You must be proud."

"Words don't do it justice, son."

Crouton sent the message dropped the lime into his beer.

They sipped, watching the gentle chaos below.

"So, about the ring comment... before anything else happens?"

"You mean Rhys proposing to Sienna?"

"Figured that's what it was..." Tim gave him a curious grin. "The whole marry-the-girl-before-sleeping-with-her thing's mostly a religious thing. Admirable, sure—but... your interesting exchange with Rhys earlier's got me curious about your take on things."

Crouton raised his brows, nodding thoughtfully.

"Given how ya pushed for marriage, the way you did," Tim added.

"Marriage is mysterious and underrated," he said, then paused... "and possibly misunderstood at times. The principle runs deeper than many appreciate. It's the ideal foundation for intimacy, kids—much of life concerning a man and woman."

Tim was intrigued—not by the topic itself, but by its speaker. Hearing this from rough-edged, irreligious Crouton Bull made all the difference.

Crouton took a swig.

"Funny ol' world. I've spent half my life chasing truth, digging into my family's origins—never gave God or religion much thought. Not that I've ever been against em—far from it. But somehow, it led me to Atlantis and a forgotten world... knowledge that's both comforting and mind-bending.

There are countless principles—originating in the Bible—that work whether people'r religious or not. They transcend opinion. Generosity, *marriage*... you don't have to be religious for them to work."

He waved off the depth. "Philosophy's Nate's thing. But sound study and evidence don't lie. Sex, intimacy, kids, finances, mental health—they flourish in strong marriages. The numbers are staggering."

"Divorce is a different beast," Crouton continued. "At's about people—baggage, unresolved stuff—*not* the principles. When you've got selfless love and grit, marriage works. The studies prove it."

He cursed under his breath. "I'm no saint—you know that. Yeah, yeah, you always say I'm closer to God than I think. More Christian than some who sit in church every Sunday."

He paused, eyes narrowing.

"But Scripture? Not just old stories. Anyone who reads it and skims the surface is missin' the point. I believe in the supernatural. I don't have a neat framework like you and Charlotte, but I've seen enough—quiet things, wild things—that pretending it's not real would make me a liar."

He straightened, voice sincere and firm.

"And when those supernatural principles line up with hard facts—again and again—you don't get that anywhere else."

He looked out across the evening. "I want the best for my daughter—like any honest father. Rhys is the best for Sienna. But if she's meant for something bigger—I'd fail her if I didn't nudge them toward it."

Tim nodded, genuinely impressed.

They let the moment settle into the warm breeze and clinked bottles.

"What's Charlotte's father like? Did you ask for 'er hand?'"

"I did. He's very Latin American. Catholic by heritage—not rigid in practice. He appreciated that I asked. We get on well—Salvator Espanzia, Assistant Principal at Pakuranga High in Auckland."

Crouton chuckled, "Did it feel like walking into the principal's office?"

"Absolutely! He poured me a whisky afterwards and said, 'Here, looks like you need this.' I calmed down eventually."

Crouton roared with laughter.

The two stood in silence for a moment, the breeze drifting softly through the portico. Music and chatter floated below. A warmth lingered—friendship, hard-earned love, and the kind of respect forged through challenge and purpose alike.

Crouton turned, clinking bottles with Tim's. "To marriage, mystery, and good mates."

Tim raised his drink with a smile. "And stubborn fathers who mean well."

The both laughed again.

CHAPTER 32

- -

Rick flipped pancakes while Tim grilled bacon and banana, with Charlotte perched at the breakfast bar. As breakfast sizzled, Rick launched into a wild dining tale from Manly Beach, Sydney. He, Chaiyala, and a few friends, dared his cousin Scott, to order the infamous Flamin' Mayhem burger at The Greedy Wombat.

"I swear," Rick laughed, "he looked like a bloke in labour—sweating, squirming in his seat."

They all cracked up.

"We egged him on, told him he'd never make it and should hand it off to Chaiyala. But he was determined. The burger was epic, mate! Jalapeño cheese that looked like guacamole, a 200-gram beef patty loaded with chilli flakes, cracked pepper, red and yellow chillies, *more* jalapeños, and sweet chilli-marinated bacon glazed in more sweet chilli sauce—plus guasacaca."

"Yeyah! Venezuelan hot sauce!" Charlotte grinned.

"Oh, I didn't know that," Rick smiled.

"Yah—that's home territory."

"All crammed into a chilli powder bun," Rick said.

"A chilli powder bun?" Tim frowned.

"Yeah, mate! More chilli powder than flour—apparently."

Tim and Charlotte laughed.

"It came with a tub of ice cream, a six-pack of beer, tissues, a bandage—and a chocolate frog."

Tim blinked. "Recovery kit?"

"Exactly."

"A bandage and a chocolate frog?" Charlotte laughed, puzzled.

"No idea—he gave the frog to Chaiyala."

"How'd Scott handle the beer and ice cream?" Tim asked, thinking of a bourbon and banana-choc-chip disaster witnessed years ago.

"Scotty was wrecked," Rick said, chuckling. "Sculled half the beer, downed the ice cream, then lost everything into a bin down the road. He was a bit subdued for the Sea Eagles game."

"And did Chaiyala try the burger too?" Charlotte asked.

"No," Chaiyala said, entering with Chad. "Eh, I dared Scott to order it—if he couldn't finish, I'd take it from there."

Tim laughed, slapping another pancake onto the pile in the warming drawer. "Very clever."

"Heeey! Blondy! You're late for breakfast duty!" Rick stirred.

Chad frowned, confused.

"Not you—Rapunzel here."

Tim shook his head, smiling. Charlotte grinned.

Chaiyala gave Rick a dirty look, then smirked. "You took it very well, that I have a new boyfriend... but I know inside, Rick, it burns you. Like lava."

"Oooo!" Tim stirred.

"You're Chad's problem now, not mine," Rick grinned.

"Ricky boy, don't worry—I'm not going anywhere. I'll always be your problem."

Laughter rippled through the group.

"And you'll always want my babies," Rick added.

Chad grinned but said nothing. He and Chaiyala exchanged a loaded glance—part hesitation, part calculation—as if weighing something unspoken.

"Oh my—what?" Charlotte gasped—wide-eyed, then looked confused.

Tim chuckled, anticipating what was coming. Chad smiled.

"Well..." Chaiyala said cautiously, weighing how to break the news. She looked to Chad.

"Shall we tell them?"

"Tell us what?" Tim asked, still grinning.

Chad nodded, hoping he'd read her right. "Might as well. They're gonna find out soon anyway."

A pause.

"Oh wow," Tim said, blinking—yet, unsure about timing.

Chaiyala turned to the others, composed but clearly bracing for reactions.

"Seriously? That fast?" Tim asked, puzzled.

Charlotte frowned, exchanging a look with Tim.

Rick looked up, distracted—still catching up. "Didn't expect this..." he muttered.

"It wasn't exactly planned," Chad added.

Chaiyala smiled. "In nine months, I am moving to New Zealand. I've taken assignment on the new project Red Sword is preparing—and I will be closer to Chad."

Charlotte's expression flickered—surprise, curiosity, a hint of amusement.

"Wha—wow! Okay... that's fantastic news!" Tim laughed.

Tim laughed, shooting Chad a mock glare for the cheeky build-up. He grabbed the pancake pile.

"That's so cool!" Charlotte said.

Rick shot Chaiyala a dirty look—she'd had him teetering on a cliff's edge, then pulled him back at the last second.

"I do love you, Rick," Chaiyala said softly, "just... not in the way you want."

Rick shook his head. "You're such a piece o' work," he grumbled, smirking as he grabbed the bacon.

"You'll get over me—eventually. I'm taken now," she said, cheekily over her shoulder as Chad led her outside.

"And a rotten snot," Rick muttered.

"Who's a rotten snot?" Tim asked, returning in time to hear.

Rick smiled. "The madness continues, brother."

Tim chuckled, knowing. "Yes, it does. Never ends with you and Rapunzel. Just keeps going like a ridiculous energizer bunny."

Chad and Chaiyala found seats at one of the wooden outdoor tables, eyeing mouthwatering pancakes, seared bacon, and grilled bananas split lengthwise—skins still on.

She leaned back into Chad, who wrapped his arms around her.

Tim brought out cutlery and a jug of deep maple syrup to drizzle over Rick's and his pancake masterpiece.

Chaiyala chatted quietly with Charlotte and Tim about her relocation plans. Nathan arrived, followed by Rhys and Crouton.

"Good morning! Smells amazing!" Nathan greeted.

"Cheers," Rick replied.

"Aye! Looks amazing too!" Rhys agreed.

"Who's thirsty?" Crouton asked, thumping two big jugs of juice on the table and pouring as Rod, Kristie, Charles, and Jacqui arrived and morning greetings were exchanged.

Over breakfast, they shared stories—Jamaican adventures and Richat updates. Nathan and Crouton announced Chaiyala's upcoming transfer to New Zealand for a new project. Nathan also revealed plans for an open presentation at the Hub, followed by a visit to the newly opened entrance to the underground docks within the Richat's third ring.

~~~~~~~

Nathan and a technician reviewed final cues at the front of the Hub presentation theatre. Tim lingered with Charlotte, Rod, Jacqui, and Alesandro before they took seats near the front, then Tim joined Nathan on stage. Charles and Kristie arrived with Chad and Chaiyala, just as Andrew Herald—head of Archaeology—and his team settled across the first two rows. Nearby, Crouton joked with Rick and Rhys about Albarad's antics in Jamaica, filling Charles and Jacqui in as the theatre steadily filled with department reps.

The house lights dimmed. Spotlights lit Tim and Nathan. A long LED screen came alive:

The Richat Project Presents:
THE PIECES OF ATLANTIS

Animated artefacts and vibrant graphics flickered across the screen. Tim stepped forward, greeting the crowd in multiple languages, nodding to the project's multicultural mix. When he threw in a cheeky "Gudday mate," the Aussies and Kiwis erupted in laughter.

Tim stepped forward and introduced 'The Pieces of Atlantis'. He explained how their discovery had shifted from fiction to serious science.

"I'm excited to confirm that, at least two of these pieces of Atlantis—possibly among many—were uncovered during our recent expedition to Jamaica," he announced.

As he spoke, two technicians wheeled in a secure case. Tim continued, outlining current theories about Atlantium: how "pyramids (Carsakarisks as known by the Atlanteans) and obelisks may have formed an empire-wide network for wireless energy transmission. This idea is what has sparked heated debate between Red Sword Security and critics of the Richat Project."

The screen lit up with schematics and simulations, revealing how the system might function across the empire.

Nathan then took the stage. "Knowledge of The Pieces of Atlantis has been even rarer than knowledge of Atlantis itself," he said. "Now, recent discoveries have prompted researchers to classify artefacts as either 'Verified' or 'Fabled'.

Among the verified pieces were the tips of the Carsakarisks. Small glassy blue prisms believed to project energy into the ionosphere. Along with the tips of the Obelisks, thought to receive and redistribute it.

These findings reinforced prior speculation that the Atlantean system operated through a dual-phase energy exchange—initiated by the Carsakarisks and completed by the Obelisks. With evidence pointing to 122 pyramids and over 2,450 obelisks across the region, further testing is underway to understand how the system truly functioned. The 'how', remains to be discovered.

The Crimson Sword is another piece of Atlantis—first owned by Poseidon, then gifted to his son Atlas." Nathan looked directly at Chad.

Chad froze. The name echoed too closely to 'Red Sword'. Why wasn't anyone reacting... at least noticing? Not Tim. Not Charlotte. Not even Rhys.

"Why did Nathan look directly at me?" Chad wondered. *"Is this a coincidence—or something more?"*

He scanned the room. No one else seemed affected.

"Is Nathan brainwashing them? No... that's not him. Or is it?" This was going to mess with him *"Why'd he look directly at me when he mentioned the Crimson Sword? Like I was the only one here."*

Chad was caught between curiosity and caution. In his mind's eye, he could see anxiety begging to be triggered—for airtime. He ignored it.

"Stay focused. Keep composure."

Nathan continued listing the Verified Pieces: The Crown of Atlas, The Prophecies of Atlas, The Book of Zeus, The Wings of Carbolate, The Geminon Tablet, and The Axylon Screen. Most were familiar to Chad from dinner table discussions—but the Crimson Sword felt... different.

"Was this all just a dream? No—it was happening. No mind games. I need answers. But how?"

First, he'd talk to Tim, Chaiyala and Charlotte, then Rod. Then, if needed, he'd approach Charles.

As Tim wrapped up, Chad's thoughts drifted to the Fabled Pieces—artefacts once confined to legend and pulp science fiction: The Bull of Atlantis, The Five Twins, Pandora's Box, The Spear of Hercules, The Virgin's Shield, The Enchanted Gold of Zeus, and The Sword of Aries. Pandora's Box rang a bell. The rest sounded like a movie pitch.

~~~~~~~

Tim woke with a start, unusually refreshed. He reached for his phone—5:45 a.m. He considered texting Charlotte but paused when a message from Chad popped up: *"Hey bro, up on the Sky Hill... you keen for a chat when you're up?"*

Tim replied: *"Mornin man. Sure thing! Give me a mo and I'll be right up. You all good?"*

"Yeah... got a few questions."

"Cool. See ya in a minute."

He tossed on boardies and a long-sleeved hoodie and sent a quick text to Charlotte: *"Good morning Angel! Heading up to Sky Hill with Chad. Come up in an hour if we're not back. Bring Chaiyala if you want. Love you!"*

Tim wound his way up the narrow dirt track through rocks and tall grass to where Chad sat at the wooden table, leaning back on the bench and taking in the view.

"Good morning," Tim greeted.

"Morning," Chad replied, a trace of tension in his tone.

"What a view, eh?"

"It's awesome."

They sat quietly a moment.

"I keep thinking of the view from Mum and Dad's deck—looking toward the Raglan hills," Chad said.

"Yeah—often think that eh."

"Yet, there are twelve millennia between the views."

"It's greener back home—less sparse."

"I feel like I just woke up, like I'm still processing everything," Chad began. "Not freaking out, but seriously... the Sahara? What the hang? Never even knew Mauritania existed before you came here!" Chad gestured toward the Richat hills. "Then I find out you guys discovered Atlantis— *here*, in the desert!"

Tim laughed. "Who'd a' thought?"

"I sure didn't!"

"The last place on Earth."

"Feels like a strange joke—but far from it."

Tim smiled—explorers had always assumed Atlantis was underwater. "That's why no one found it—until we looked outside the box."

"My whole world's now '*outside*' the box."

Tim understood—Chad's life had flipped upside down in mere weeks.

"First, we're getting shot at, then we're in Jamaica, meeting Jacob McKenzie. And now I've met the girl of my dreams! Fifteen days, brother! Fifteen days..." He shook his head, a trace of a smile.

Tim nodded.

"The wildest part, though? All of it—none of it compares to the mystery of Nathan O'Conner."

Tim's face subtly shifted—nose wrinkled, gaze distant. No need to say it—they were on the same page.

"I'll go first," Chad said. "Who exactly is Nathan O'Conner? *Really?*"

"Trust you to be abrupt."

"Law student," Chad reminded.

"Of course."

"Seriously, he seems too good to be true. But unless this is some grand performance, what you see is what you get—he's a humble genius and a solid guy."

"But that's not enough," Tim replied. Something deeper was bothering Chad.

Chad shook his head, wordless.

"Something's bothering you?"

"I'll be completely straight with you... and, I kinda want you to tell me I've gone nuts from the heat."

Tim frowned.

"Nathan's been reading my mind. And other strange stuff—as if speaking just to me in a crowd, and no one else hears it."

Tim felt goosebumps. Chad continued, trying to make sense of it.

"Being around Nathan feels like hanging out with someone who spent *a lot* of time with Jesus—like it rubbed off in the wildest ways. And sometimes it goes beyond that."

Tim nodded, sorting through thoughts—keeping them in check.

"I'm trying to reconcile what I know about the mind and the paranormal with what I'm feeling—but it's starting to go beyond crazy."

Tim let the silence sit. "Well, I can't exactly say you're losing it," he said, looking toward the Richat.

"Darn. I could've handled crazy—but what is this then?"

Tim wasn't challenging his concerns.

"To some extent, I've had questions too. He's remarkable, but some things don't add up—gaps in time, odd feelings. Like in Jamaica, when Nate and Crout were with Albarad... the meeting ended before it began."

"Rod noticed."

"Really?"

"Yeah, he said it felt like half an hour just—disappeared."

Chad recounted Rod's version: Nathan started calmly, but then, in a blink, became distant—Albarad stormed off, meeting over.

"Yeah, I'd heard it was all a bit odd..."

"And then," Chad added, "there was that moment on the penthouse balcony. Nathan responded to a thought I had—like I'd said it out loud. Freaked me out."

Tim nodded, recalling Chad's sudden outburst.

"He calmed me—too fast. Then I lost it."

"That's when we thought it was a panic attack. Crouton said he worried you'd triggered Nathan a similar way."

"I didn't mean to."

"Figured. The strange part—Nathan never seems fazed. Crouton later told Sienna and I it seemed too odd. Like Nathan *wanted* to appear rattled—for some reason."

Chad hesitated, "but why?"

"No idea."

"Another unanswered question."

"Typical..."

Chad sighed, "no kidding."

"He's also asked me..." he began, then stopped at a rustling noise.

Crashing sounds came from the bush below Sky Hill's north side.

Tim stood and peered over the rocky edge. Chad joined him, scanning the dense foliage.

"Hey!" Tim called out.

No response.

They exchanged glances, then plunged down the slope, weaving through palms and undergrowth toward the sports fields.

"Sounds like more than one person..." Chad said.

They paused near the bush's edge, listening. The crashing seemed to lead toward the field.

Tim guessed the intruder would emerge at the road ahead.

"Oi!" a familiar voice rang out.

"That's Rod..." Tim said as they stumbled onto the gravel road, "Is he chasing someone?"

~~~~~~~

Fifteen minutes earlier, Rod and Kristie had just surfaced.

"You know what I love about life here at the Project Camp?" Kristie said. "Every day begins with a perfect sunrise and ends with an equally stunning sunset."

Rod held her close. "And the heat doesn't matter when we've got air-con."

Their morning serenity ruptured without warning. A hooded figure stood motionless on the back deck, face hidden, watching them through the ranch slider. The cloak it wore—so black it seemed a tear in the world—a portal to darkness itself.

Kristie gasped as Rod instinctively moved between her and the stranger.

The shadowy spectre flinched, then darted toward the edge of the backyard without hesitation.

"Go to Tim and Chaiyala's—stay with them. Call Crouton," Rod said, sliding the door open before bolting outside.

"Rodney!" Kristie called after him. Then reason kicked in—she'd been trained by Chaiyala, she knew what to do.

Rod watched as the figure glided over the fence, vanishing into the palms without touching the ground.

He vaulted the fence, crouching between two trees. The figure moved effortlessly through the foliage.

"Who the hang is that?" he whispered.

Excitement and caution surged—he was chasing what felt like a ghost.

Barefoot, he barely registered the stones biting his soles as he sprinted across the cul-de-sac. Tim and Chaiyala's place behind him, he passed between the Sky Hill, Charles and Jacqui's. The figure slipped into the bush near the edge of the camp.

Rod crashed through ferns, adrenaline pumping. By the time he'd reached the north road, the figure was halfway across the sports field.

"Oi!" he shouted, watching them vault the fence and slip into the desert sands. "Dammit!" he muttered.

Tim and Chad appeared, alert.

"You a'right, man?" Tim asked, noting Rod's boxers and bare feet.

"Did you see that?" Rod asked sharply, pointing across the distance.

"There *was* a second person," Chad said.

"How does someone move that fast?" Rod puzzled.

Tim and Chad followed his gaze, unable to see anyone.

"We heard crashing below the hill," Tim explained.

"I was chasing someone," Rod said. "Some freaky-looking wraith was standing on the deck watching us."

"Serious?" Tim's eyes widened.

Chad frowned—scanning the flats—uneasy. "I don't like this."

"Neither do I," Rod agreed.

"Weird!" Tim said. "Let's get back—Kristie okay?"

"She's fine. She'll be with Chaiyala now."

Chad shivered as Tim bent down, picking up a decaying cane.

"What's that?" Rod asked.

"Baron Samedi..." Chad whispered.

"Pardon?"

"Why Baron Samedi?" Tim asked.

"Because the last time I saw that, was in Jamaica."

"This?" Tim frowned.

"Oh man!" Chad's stomach tightened. He'd seen a top hat and lice-ridden cane in the penthouse while Alesandro chopped chillies and talked with Nathan.

He recalled Brooke Russo's words: *"Likes rum spiked with hot peppers, he does... Can't imagine my brother going for that though...'"*

"Yeah, I remember that," Tim said.

Rod sensed more to this.

"Well, as Alesandro chopped up chillies to put in his Appleton's at the penthouse, I spotted the hat and cane in the corner. And *this* cane looks exactly like it."

Tim hesitated—puzzled, he frowned— "Spooky coincidence..."

"True... but spiked rum isn't unheard of in Jamaica," Rod added.

"Still—the cane and top hat?"

"Largely circumstantial. It was Jamaica—could have been part of a festival, or maybe a previous guest left it behind."

"You're right—it's circumstantial," Chad agreed. His tone grew thoughtful. "But even so... what are the odds?"

Tim shifted the cane in his hand. Something caught Chad's eye.

"Wait—what's that?" Chad lifted the tip.

"It's paper," Rod observed.

Chad carefully peeled off a damp parchment wrapped tight around the end. He unfolded it: an A5 sheet. Scrawled across it:

"Let my brothers know I am here. Anubis is on the move again."

Chad and Tim locked eyes, both pale.

Rod sighed, half naked and holding his breath. "And the questions and weirdness keep on commin'."

"Welcome to my world," Chad said—

"How is that unusual?" Tim said—both speaking at once.

An awkward pause hung in the air. Tim suggested Rod find some clothes so they could meet with Nathan, Charles, Chaiyala and Crouton somewhere private to discuss the note—and the cane.

Just then, Crouton, Charlotte, and Alesandro arrived.

"There you guys are!" Crouton boomed. "Morning, gentlemen."

Tim and Charlotte hugged. Chad handed the cane to Alesandro, watching closely. Alesandro hesitated, examined it, then glanced between Tim,

Chad, and Crouton. Crouton frowned—something about it tickled the edge of familiarity.

"W-what's this for?" Alesandro asked.

Chad studied his every reaction—eyes, posture, voice, searching for something.

"What are you doing?" Tim asked.

Chad grinned. "Sweet—all good."

Tim and Charlotte exchanged glances. Chad wasn't explaining—not yet.

Alesandro looked genuinely lost. Chad gave a reassuring smile—he'd seen what he needed.

"Right..." Crouton said, impatient. "So, what's the deal? Kristie said there was an intruder on your back deck—and you chased them over the fence? ...why are you half-naked?"

Rod shrugged. "We'd literally just got out of bed."

Crouton nodded. "Gotcha. So—what's with the stick?"

"No idea," Tim replied. "Could've been deliberately dropped by whoever Rod was chasing."

"You lost them? Do we have a security breach—or was it just some strange local?" Crouton asked—trying to understand.

"Let's go with strange local for now—keep things simple," Tim sighed.

Rod wasn't having that. The figure had moved like something unhuman. He insisted a remote visual recon and described the encounter to Crouton, whose eyes widened.

"My beard..." Crouton muttered.

"Where are Kristie and Chaiyala?" Rod asked Charlotte.

"Sorting breakfast when we left." Charlotte informed reassuringly, "Kristie's fine."

Rod exhaled. Kristie was strong and sensible. And with Chaiyala nearby, she'd be more than fine.

He made a mental note: *"Thank Chaiyala properly—as soon as I've got pants on."*

The group moved together, energy shifting from urgency to quiet concern. The cane lingered like a strange centrepiece, its message still rattling beneath the surface.

"I'll call Internal Surveillance," Crouton muttered. "Let's see what the team can pull."

"Good," Tim nodded. "They'll have tracked movement beyond the perimeter."

Rod exhaled. "Could be nothing," he said—hopeful, yet unconvinced.

Chad watched him, remembering Rod's unease with things paranormal.

They began walking back toward the houses. Gravel crunched underfoot as the early sun painted the desert in copper and peach.

"So—Anubis?" Crouton's query broke the silence.

"Symbol of judgement and passage," Tim said quietly. "In Egyptian myth, he guarded the threshold to the afterlife."

"Fitting." Crouton nodded, his tone dry. "If someone's sending cryptic notes, they're either clever... or theatrical."

Tim led the way up the steep path that wound across the sky hill, linking to the summit track and down toward the opposite side of the road from their accommodation.

Before they all reached Tim's place, Rod ducked off to get dressed. When he returned, he hugged Kristie and filled her and Chaiyala in on the encounter.

Breakfast was eaten over heavy discussion about the mysterious black cloaked figure, and its unnatural speed. More questions were raised than answered. Afterwards, Rod, Crouton, Tim, and Chaiyala, joined by Nathan and Charles, made a beeline for the Red Sword Hub.

~~~~~~~

Rod took a call from Internal Surveillance and received the review code. "We've got footage from this morning," he said, placing his tablet on the boardroom table with purpose.

"Let's see what happened before this thing showed up in ya backyard, then," Crouton said.

A wide view of Rod and Kristie's backyard appeared on-screen, timestamped five minutes before the cloaked figure was first seen. They fast-forwarded slightly.

"Wow," Tim breathed.

"Okay," said Chaiyala, wide-eyed.

The spectre appeared suddenly—just before the deck, standing on the grass, facing the ranch slider. A moment later, it turned and moved quickly toward the perimeter fence.

"My beard!" muttered Crouton.

They watched, baffled, as the figure lifted—not jumped or climbed— cleanly over the top of the fence. Seconds later, Rod—barefoot and in box- ers—darted after it, scaled the fence, and disappeared off-screen in pursuit.

"Simply appeared out of nowhere..." Tim said, frowning—needing to hear it aloud.

Rod shook his head. He and Kristie hadn't imagined it.

Another angle showed the chase continuing behind the fence, skirt- ing Rod's and Tim and Chaiyala's places. A cul-de-sac camera across from Charles and Jacqui's caught the figure darting across the road—Rod trailing behind, slower.

Rod chuckled quietly at the sight of himself bush-bashing in nothing but boxers. Tim and Chaiyala smiled with him.

Nathan had the look of someone weighing more than just what was on the screen.

The feed switched to cameras between Sky Hill and Charles's residence, tracking the chase through dense foliage. Then came the final, startling view: well before Rod emerged from the bushes flanking the north road, the figure accelerated unnaturally—racing over gravel, down the slope, and across the events arena at vehicle speed. It cleared the north fence effortlessly and vanished into the desert dunes.

They sat in stunned silence.

Rod finally spoke. "I'm definitely in doubt it was one of the local Tuaregs."

"This—whatever they are—moved with incredible speed," Crouton said—still processing.

"I could keep up through obstacles, but once in the open? They were doing fifty k's tops—easy."

"That's really not normal," Chaiyala stated.

"They were gliding more than running. Right over fences—no jump, just... smooth," Tim observed.

He and Charles exchanged a sharp look.

"If this isn't a local," Charles said, "and they're of unusual nature or origin, I'd suggest they're meant to be here."

Nathan nodded thoughtfully.

Crouton stroked his beard, considering.

All eyes were on Charles, encouraging him to elaborate.

"There's no evidence of anyone breaching our boundaries. None of the 982 grid sensors register unknown activity. No stowaway on the flight back from Jamaica. "So, it has to be either local—or one of our own. But with that kind of speed?" He paused. "That narrows it down... to no one."

"Reminds me of that spectre on footage," Crouton recalled, "hoverin' over the cars at the Caribbean Paradise the night Alesandro was chased. We've still got as many answers for that one as Albarad tells the truth."

Chaiyala and Tim grinned.

"And so, you're saying they're meant to be here? That this is... purposeful?" Tim reflected, his gaze settling on Charles.

"Indeed."

"What would be the purpose, I wonder?" Chaiyala asked quietly, eyes narrowed.

"What's the grid sensor status report say?" Crouton asked.

"All functional—no errors," Rod confirmed. "Updated every 2 hours."

"No breach," Chaiyala recapped. "No stowaway. No movement underground—the satellite imagery—it rules that out."

"I'm at a loss... what's your take, boss?"

Each of them privately entertained the same farfetched idea—hesitant to voice it.

After a brief silence, Nathan finally spoke. "I'm inclined to agree with Charles."

He explained, "It's not always about logic," Nathan said. "Sometimes the heart must lead. When every avenue's exhausted and the mind runs in circles, faith is what remains. I believe—wholeheartedly—that if our systems insist this person shouldn't exist... then maybe Charles is right. Maybe they're here for a reason."

Tim unwrapped the cane and handed Nathan the note formerly attached.

Nathan gave the cane a long look, similar to Crouton's earlier reaction. He read aloud:

"Let my brothers know I am here. Anubis is on the move again."

"Hmm." He examined the cane more closely. "I've seen this before."

"Chad'd spotted it at the Caribbean Paradise," Tim explained. "Along with a tattered top hat. It sat in the living room of the penthouse suite. Alesandro was chopping chillies at the time... right after Brooke Russo shared some strange stories.

'Dresses like an undertaker, smokes cigars, twirls a cane... Samedi was probably my brother's drinking buddy. Likes rum spiked with peppers,' she'd said."

Nathan nodded, taking it in. "Given what Brooke said—and what you witnessed—I understand Chad's concern."

"Right... so that's why Chad handed Alesandro the cane!" Rod said.

"No. Alesandro Karahalios is not the Barron in disguise," Nathan assured. "If Barron Samedi were playing a double game that deep, he'd need an Oscar. Chalk and cheese, those two—more than you and Chad," he said to Tim.

"Wait—Chad thought Alesandro was Samedi?" Chaiyala asked, brows raised.

"Stranger things have happened," Tim said, recalling the shape-shifting antics in Jamaica.

Nathan moved on. "Anubis, is our lovely friend, Hamet Albarad."

Crouton rolled his eyes.

"Oh, he just delightful," Chaiyala muttered sarcastically through gritted teeth.

"Why Anubis?" Tim asked.

"He's been called that—mostly in Egyptian politics—by allies and adversaries alike."

"Because the cretin's got the charm and people skills of a jackal," Crouton said.

"So, the god of the grave—very fitting," Chaiyala said with a smirk.

"The Egyptian Canid," Charles corrected.

"Yes, the African golden wolf," Nathan added. "Originally it was mistaken for a jackal."

Chaiyala scoffed. "A wolf's too majestic for that slug, no?"

"Well, Hamet's never cared for historical accuracy," Tim shrugged.

"The nickname's mostly derogatory—defender of the buried past," Nathan added.

"Put him in his own grave," Crouton grumbled.

"Let me smash him first," Chaiyala said, too casually. "He deserves the honour."

Tim refocused. "So, he's trying to shut down the Richat Project. We know this, but what's new? Is there something we don't know?"

"Nothing new, far as we know," Rod said. "I've got a video call with Sienna—we'll go over any intel on that level for sure—see if there are any relevant developments."

"And who are the brothers?" Nathan frowned. "Who's the message for?"

"No idea... but on the island," Tim glanced at Chaiyala, "Brooke spoke of Poseidon as her brother. So, we do need to consider whether this note came from her."

"Are you suggesting the intruder was Brooke, or just the note?" Charles asked.

"Either—or both. Who knows?"

"Fair enough. This whole thing's bizarre," Crouton sighed.

"Like I said—there's no end to the weird—questions keep piling up," Rod reminded.

"At least you're dressed this time," Tim smiled.

Rod grinned. The others laughed.

"Where to from here?" Nathan asked. "Rod, you're due to check in with Sienna on Albarad. Let's get clarity on his activity and keep tabs."

"Sounds good," Rod replied.

"Rick and Rhys are heading up a tracking team," Crouton reported. "Twelve agents on the move. Satellite updates are now half-hourly. Bart has briefed the Richat's oasis village to stay alert for any suspicious wanderers. All subproject sections are now on watch as well."

"Very good."

~~~~~~~~

Chad sat alone at an outdoor table, staring past the pool. His eyes were distant—locked not on the scenery, but on the paradox of Nathan O'Conner and the surreal buffet of strangeness laid out before them.

He didn't notice her until he heard the splash of Charlotte diving into the pool. She swam laps, surfaced, pulled her long hair back and called out:

"Heya!"

"Howsit?"

"Good! You coming in?"

"Hmm." He stretched and yawned. "Maybe... dunno."

"You seem pensive." She lifted herself out of the pool, resting on her hands. Her shoulders rose with the effort, quiet and deliberate.

"Quite a bit."

She climbed out, dripping as she reached for her towel. She sat opposite Chad, facing him.

"crazy way to start the day, right?" she said.

Chad chuckled. "You never know what to expect around here."

"Nope." She tucked her wet hair behind her ears. "What was the deal with that stick? You guys were talking about a note?"

"Yeah..." Chad recapped the cane and top hat, describing how he'd spotted them in the penthouse suite in Jamaica—then the same cane turning up at the camp with a note attached.

"And you're sure it's the same one?"

"Positive. It was way out of place in that tidy suite. I'd know it anywhere."

"That's mad. Like—what the actual heck? So—is this intruder Barron Samedi?"

"Better not be. I'm pretty sure he's nastier than people realize."

"Who then?"

"Well, the note says 'tell my brothers...'"

"Brooke?" she suggested cautiously.

Chad nodded slowly.

"Noooo. But how?"

They unpacked the eerie possibilities, which led to what had Chad truly puzzled.

"At first I chalked it up to stress. Memory gaps, maybe... there's a lot I'm sifting through. A lotta mystery around Nathan—that's part of it. But it kept happening. Even when I was calm and composed. That's how I knew it wasn't me—or stress."

"Go on," Charlotte said, her eyes narrowing with focus.

"I notice it tends to happen when the topic of conversation is about to veer into something disruptive or distracting—as if the dialogue itself was being... skipped."

"And you think Nathan's involved?"

"I've seen him tap his pen or click his fingers—and suddenly everything's changed. Topic shifts. People move differently. Once, I checked the clock and nearly ten minutes had jumped."

Charlotte blinked. "That's pretty serious. Now that you mention it, I do remember moments like that. I usually pass things off—trust Tim,

Rod, Chaiyala. They're better at the puzzle stuff. Crouton, though... he's an expert on Nathan—knows him better than anyone. But you're right."

"Reckon there's such a thing as being an expert on Nathan?" Chad asked—half-joking.

Charlotte gave a tired laugh— "Who knows?"

"Tim's noticed things too. He confirmed I wasn't imagining it. Honestly, thinking I was going crazy might've been simpler. Instead, we're stuck with... this."

"Oh yes, he was telling me about it last night, actually." She twisted her hair to one side, recollecting.

"Rod had suspicions, too. That meeting with Albarad in Jamaica—time went sideways. They were in there an hour, but people talked like it ended before it began, like literally—a fraction of that."

"You're right... I hadn't thought about that," Charlotte said, her voice quieter now.

"What I'm about to tell you—I've only shared with Tim," Chad added. "I don't fully understand it myself, but I'm convinced Nathan's read my mind..."

Charlotte stared at him.

"... Not often. But there've been moments when he's responded to thoughts I hadn't voiced."

"What?"

"Sometimes it catches him off guard. I don't think he always means to."

"You mean he's only meant to pick up certain things?"

Chad paused. "I hadn't thought of that. But... yeah. I've seen subtle surprise in his eyes. Like he heard something unexpected; unintended?"

"How many times?"

"Half a dozen, maybe."

"You're unsettled about it?"

"I've questioned it endlessly. But I'm not anxious. I don't think Nathan's doing anything sinister. Still, when someone replies to a thought you haven't spoken... it shakes you."

Charlotte nodded. "That's wild."

"He's kind of like someone who's been so close to Jesus... that something's rubbed off. Even the supernatural."

She smiled. "Actually, that's a pretty great way to describe him."

"He's not perfect—not God. But... he's too humble, too kind, too generous, too selfless to be playing some double game. I've tested every angle. He's not too good to be true. I'm convinced."

Charlotte watched the pool shimmer in the sunlight. Then looked back at Chad and said, "I'll definitely be keeping a closer eye now. On what stacks up strange when Nathan's in the mix."

Chad nodded.

"I totally agree—Nathan's trustworthy. It's just the unconventional stuff around him that mystifies..."

"Yup. That's it."

Charlotte stood. "Too hot to stay out of the water."

Chad threw off his singlet.

"Race ya!" she bolted toward the pool with a splash.

Chad followed—a split second behind.

"I won!" she grinned.

"You yelled 'race' after you started running!" he laughed.

"Whatever, dude. Is that what you say every time Chaiyala beats you?"

"What!"

"Kidding," she smirked. "Messin' with ya."

"I'll mess with you!" he splashed water at her as laughter filled the air.

CHAPTER 33

Tim bounced out of bed like a kid on Christmas morning—wide awake and grinning. He went straight to Charlotte's room. His lovely fiancée already awakening, already looking better than anyone should, first thing. Tim loved that about her—among countless other things. He couldn't wait to marry her, to wake up beside her every day.

Today would mark the unveiling of what Tim and the historical and archaeological teams were certain was the fabled lost navy of Atlantis. He'd barely slept, consumed by possibilities. How many ships had survived? Would they uncover the three sister vessels Solon described in his hidden journals, passed on by the man in the scarlet robe? And what happened to the three most significant of the legendary warships during the twin conflicts with Athens and Hiva?

"Hey you," Charlotte greeted sleepily.

"Good morning, Angel."

They kissed—both whispered, "I love you."

Charlotte sat up, blinking, gazed toward the long hills of the Richat through the trunks of palm trees.

"You excited?" she asked, smiling wide.

"Oh, I can't even describe! This is gonna to be incredible."

"It's so exciting... I can't wait to see what they look like."

Tim agreed, beaming with anticipation.

Charlotte leaned back on her hands... then, after a stretch and a yawn, she rose and wrapped Tim in a grateful hug. "Go pour ice-cold orange and mangos for us," she whispered. "I'll get dressed and join you."

Tim stepped into the living area just as sunlight broke the horizon. Outside, Chad, Chaiyala, Rhys, and Rick were already in the pool. He poured two tall glasses of juice—set Charlotte's on the bench, and sipped his own.

Today was going to be monumental. Not just witnessing one of the greatest archaeological finds in history—but having those he loved with him. His brother happier than ever, Charlotte by his side, and their New Zealand wedding on the way. Life was unfolding like a dream come true. He quietly thanked God—eternally grateful. Smiling, he went outside before Charlotte arrived.

"Good after morning, brother!" Chad called.

Tim laughed. "After morning!"

"After morning?" Chaiyala asked, puzzled.

Her, Rhys and Rick awaited clarification.

"First thing we used to say each morning—back in high school," Chad explained.

Chaiyala grinned.

"Good after *mooorning!*" Rick chuckled.

Laughter rippled through the group.

"Today's going to be awesome!" Tim declared. "And wow—it's already hot!"

The air-conditioned house masked the early heat—stepping onto the terrace made the contrast startlingly clear.

"Hence why you guys are in the water," Tim said, tossing aside his shirt.

"Aye," nodded Rhys.

"It will be great day. You are excited, yes?" Chaiyala asked.

"Nah—not really. Just another hole in the dirt," Tim dead panned.

"Whatever," Chad shot back.

Chaiyala narrowed her eyes at Tim's dry humour.

"Jokes! If I could fly a chopper myself, I'd already be there," Tim added seriously.

Charlotte stepped onto the deck, casually braiding her hair—dressed in a sleeveless white hooded tee, relaxed cargo shorts, and bare feet. "Heya," she greeted.

"Good after morning!" Chad and Rick greeted her, cracking up.

Charlotte paused, glancing at Tim. "Haven't heard that in a while," she said with a sleepy smile, sitting down to enjoy her drink.

A Humvee pulled up. Out jumped a monument of a man with a reddish vintage hairstyle and a matching bushy beard. He opened the gate, climbing the terrace with another of his team.

"Morning bro!" Tim greeted.

"Mate! Today's the day!" the exuberant man beamed, arms wide.

"That it is, my friend."

Tim and the big man clasped hands with a pop—pulling into a quick one-arm hug.

Nathan, Crouton, then Charles and Jacqui arrived. Rod, Kristie and Alesandro close behind.

Tim introduced Chad and Charlotte to "Andrew Herald, who is lead archaeologist for the Richat Project."

Andrew smiled, shaking their hands as Tim added, "He and lead geologist Jacob Mendoza oversee the Underground Docks and Exploded Carsakarisk sections, primarily."

Chad and Charlotte were especially eager to learn more about the Atlantean underground docks.

Rhys, now wrapped in a towel, joined Crouton and Rod at the grill. Crouton slapped down rashers of bacon and hash browns while the others cooked eggs and grilled tomatoes.

"First, we feast! Then, adventurise underground!" Crouton boomed.

They settled into a hearty breakfast."

"Dig in, Andrew if you haven't eaten," Rod invited.

"Don't mind if we do! Mmm—glad we'd never got around to brekky—this looks so good."

"These hash browns are melt-in-your-mouth," Tim said. "Crispy outside, fluffy inside."

"Gettin' em like that," Crouton began, "takes the right oil and the right heat. Leave 'em too short, they flop. And *no-one* wants a floppy hash brown."

Laughter broke out.

"Celesta makes them perfect like this in the toaster," Tim quipped.

Crouton nodded, impressed.

After breakfast, Charles, Rick, and Rhys remained to hold down camp. Jacqui and Kristie wished Charles, Rod and the others all the best—then proceeded to the village. Those remaining prepared to head toward the outer ring of the Richat.

"The dig sites about fifteen minutes' drive across what was once suburban Atlantis," Andrew explained. "North-northwest, flat gravel roads—no choppers needed. The merchant harbour floor, though, it's quad bikes through rocky terrain."

"Sounds like fun," Tim said.

"All set inside the cavern?" Crouton asked.

"Techs wrapped up the electrical and system checks yesterday morning, right after construction signed off," Andrew said.

"There's a ton of water down there. Some of the old stone docks are either gone or falling apart. But temporary access is solid, and the structure's holding. Lights, power—everything's good to go. Dinghies are ready for recon. That's phase one of the subproject done and dusted."

Andrew turned to Tim and Nathan, beaming with controlled excitement. "The drone gave us a glimpse of Phase Two. Footage is limited, but we've spotted two Atlantean Triremes. They're enormous—magnificent."

Nathan, mostly silent, nodded with a satisfied smile.

"You have footage? Awesome!" Tim asked—his expression practically shouting: "Where is it!"

"It's in the Humvee—come! It's gonna blow ya mind!" Andrew grinned.

Chad helped Rhys and Chaiyala load gear into the back. Nathan and Crouton were chatting with Red Sword team leaders, and Rod made a quick phone call.

Charles discreetly whispered something to Tim that made him frown. Chad and Charlotte caught Tim's lip movement: *"Like what?"* They couldn't see Charles's face, but Tim looked a mix of intrigued and perplexed. Charles patted his shoulder and wished them well.

Tim's excitement about the drone footage was distracted slightly.

Crouton climbed into one Humvee. Rod already in the front passenger seat—deep in emails and subproject briefings.

Chad and Chaiyala rode with Crouton and Rod. Nathan, Tim, and Charlotte with Andrew in the second Humvee.

Andrew placed his license and credit card on the dashboard tray.

"Where's your wallet?" Nathan asked.

"Down between the seats," Andrew replied, reversing out and following Crouton.

"Right..."

"It keeps slipping down the gap between the seat and console," Andrew muttered. "I'm done fishin' it out—can stay there. I'm teaching it a lesson."

Nathan chuckled.

Charlotte laughed. Tim grinned, shaking off distraction and turning his focus back to Andrew's tablet.

They drove around the base of the palm-cloaked hill, past the grassy events arena below.

~~~~~~~

Ten minutes later, the hills marking the Richat's outer ring came into view.

"This is amazing," Chad marvelled.

"Truly something else eh," Crouton remarked.

"This all would've been homes, shops, gardens..." Chad shook his head.

"Everything. Gone in minutes," Chaiyala added, her tone clipped and shadowed with disbelief.

Rod explained, "evidence shows the giant wave carved out three to six vertical meters of earth as it tore through. Atlantis's complete destruction took about 24 hours—but the city itself? Minutes."

"That's incredible," Chad said.

"Frightening," Crouton added.

Rod continued, "Early researchers struggled to grasp how entire buildings were hurled distances of fifty to a thousand kilometres—yet remained intact. That government building, we visited? It travelled over sixty kilometre then buried in mud. The wave didn't destroy it. The mud should have. Atlantean engineering was extraordinary."

"Not what we expected," Crouton said. "Plato made it sound simple. But surviving structures from such violent displacement? Their design was clearly advanced."

They arrived at a long building, similar to the Chinguetti site. Crouton and Rod hopped out, followed by the rest. Nathan seemed unusually quiet and peaceful.

The setup of this site resembled their last subproject visit—minus the high security fencing.

"Because the terrain near the third ring of the Richat structure is unstable, instead of transporting down a cliff road, heavy machinery gets airlifted in by those two helicopters." He pointed toward a clearing.

"Mil MI 26s," Chad nodded, recognizing them.

"Got 'em second-hand," Crouton said. "Modified for excessive lift."

"Boss One! Boss Two! And friends!" called a Red Sword agent with exuberant energy and a thick African accent.

Chad and Charlotte admired the man's pearly smile—striking against his dark complexion—and the warmth in his easy, enthusiastic presence.

The man shook Crouton's and Nathan's hands before turning warmly to the rest, making a point to welcome Chad and Charlotte as Tim's guests.

"Chad, Charlotte," Nathan said, "this is Metemameni Nayala and Anastacia Keselov."

A tall, slender woman stepped forward—jet-black ponytail, sharp nose, and eyes that gave nothing away. Her pert smile barely registered, a stark contrast to Metemameni's warmth and easy energy. She and Tim smiled warmly.

"Metemameni oversees security and logistics at the Underground Docks," Nathan continued. "Anastacia is our lead historian here at the docks. She works closely with Andrew and reports to Tim."

"Come," Metemameni said, beckoning with a wide arm. He halted, eyes catching Chad and Chaiyala's closeness. His smile widened. "Look at da energy 'tween you two... mm! That's good. Very good."

Chad didn't catch his meaning at first, then smiled, wondering if Metemameni was just perceptive—or if he and Chaiyala were less discreet than they'd assumed.

They'd gone over boundaries—more than once. The need for focus, professionalism, and subtlety wasn't just a guideline; it was a condition for being there. According to Crouton, they'd kept things tight. Just enough to stay engaged, not enough to give anything away.

Metemameni and Anastacia handed out light Hi-Viz jackets, hard hats, and gloves. Tim helped Charlotte attach her headlamp, while Chaiyala explained the gas detectors they'd be carrying. "You may keep the jackets as a souvenir," Metemameni added. Charlotte noticed the logo: *"Richat Project — Underground Docks Section."*

Metemameni led the way toward the building's far side, joined by Andrew and Anastacia. They retrieved three large cases—first aid, food, and supplies for the cavern expedition.

Tim stepped onto the verandah, gazing out across the outer Richat ring. He walked a few meters, then stopped at the edge of a slope that fell into a ravine of cracked mud. Scattered rocks and sweeping bands of white crystalline sediment formed a striking tapestry—ghostly remnants of what had once been Atlantis's bustling merchant harbour.

Chad and Charlotte spotted gravel roads cut through the boulders, leading across the wide valley.

Rod explained it was roughly two and a half rugby fields wide, spanning about 163 kilometres around. Beyond that, steep, craggy cliffs—weathered and fractured—marked the remnants of what had once framed the harbour's edge. Their jagged faces bore the scars of time and collapse, jutting like broken teeth from the ravine below—the outer circle stretching into the sandy haze. In some places towering fifty to sixty meters.

To the left, the Adrar Highlands loomed.

"It's massive!" Charlotte gasped.

"And the whole structure had underground docks housing thousands of warships..." Chad reflected, stunned. "Nothing today comes close!"

"Correct," Rod said.

"Above it—barracks, stables, war machines, command centres," Tim added.

"That's insane..." Charlotte said. Now that she observed the sheer scale of it, the weight of the past settled deeper—heavier, more real.

"Like a giant Pentagon..."

"Nearly a hundred times the Pentagon's size," Crouton clarified. "And this wasn't just a base—it circled the whole city's heart as a defensive measure."

"It's hard to fathom," Nathan noted.

"Exactly," Tim agreed. "Another question is whether this was all of Atlantis's military, or if they had outposts elsewhere."

"There had to be," Rod suggested. "Atlantis wasn't just an island—it was a vast empire."

"That's the thing."

"How did Atlantis lose to Athens and Hiva?" Charlotte pondered out loud.

"They should have won," Crouton said.

Tim nodded. "They should've—arrogance made them complacent. With tech, tactics... everything."

"I could not have put it better," Nathan said, shaking his head. He stared across the outer ring, his expression shadowed with disappointment. Crouton missed it. Rod didn't catch the nuance. Tim and Charlotte weren't sure what he meant—maybe passion for the history. The loss of millions.

But Chad saw it—something personal. A flicker of guilt? He studied Nathan, sensing a grimace. Recollection of something deeper, perhaps?

They descended onto the dusty ground where the third body of water once lay—desiccated ancient harbour, now lost to time.

Chad's thoughts drifted, caught on Nathan's paradox—brilliant and mysterious, yet warm and generous. An open book of authenticity and a locked vault of enigma.

Then there were the mind-reading moments. Jamaica. *What the hang was with that?* Chad wondered. Or maybe Nathan got lucky. Heightened intuition? Still... it was hard to ignore. *He knows people. Knows how to read them.*

Four large quad bikes sat beside the deck on the northwestern face of the building. Shade fading as the sun crossed from the east.

"We need four drivers—three carry six passengers, one takes the gear." Metemameni said.

"Yup. I got the gear," Rod volunteered.

Metemameni tossed him the keys.

Crouton preferred Humvees, but the terrain told him otherwise. The craggy harbour floor ruled them out—built for quad bikes... maybe horses.

Chad and Chaiyala settled onto the back of Metemameni's bike as he led the group down the slope. Anastacia followed with Tim and Charlotte. Andrew rode behind with Nathan and Crouton. Rod brought up the rear, three bags strapped to his tray.

The winding ride through rocky harbour twists took as long as the journey from camp.

"This place is fun!" Charlotte grinned, taking in the alien scenery.

Crouton eyed two massive rocks fringing a natural passage, the road climbing up between them before curving left and down sharply.

Anastacia called instructions—urging drivers behind to lean left as the road snaked again. The slopes weren't steep, but caution was key.

Beyond the labyrinth of rocks, their next concern was whether the road had held—despite the region's environmental threats: sink holes and underground tremors.

Near the satellite site on the far side of the ravine, boulders grew larger—fragments of fallen cliff faces.

"Some... but only few broken rocks," Anastacia began. "'Round zis side of outer ring... dey were once foundations of wall around military ring of land," she told Chad and Charlotte. "Some of my team... spent much time looking for remains, working close with geological team."

The gravel road climbed slightly near the base of the cliff, ending in a flat clearing. A marquee stood, flanked by repurposed shipping containers—admin, storage, science labs.

They parked. The scene unfolded: helicopter pad at one end, a steel-and-timber gateway to a shadowed cavern at the other. Towering between, a reinforced retaining wall stretched fifteen to twenty meters, backing into the rugged cliff.

"Hard hats—extremely important," Metemameni warned. "Falling rocks—real risk. Anastacia, Andrew, and I—we all been hit before—rocks, ten centimetres across. Dis not a small thing."

Charlotte glanced around, craving a roof.

Tim and Rod exchanged looks—it was now clear why the marquee and helicopter pad sat at the harbour's edge of the flat.

"I fully appreciate the need for the Mil MI 26s," Tim observed.

"The stability of this cliff—if you can call it a cliff..." Andrew started, eyeing the crumbling boulders and eroded terrain. "...building any kind of access—a haul road from the top, down to the docks here would've been a disaster. Too risky, too expensive."

"Took long enough to pinpoint a suitable construction site," Crouton muttered.

"We still don't know how many Triremes survived," Andrew continued. "According to Atlas's writings, we're lucky if the grandest—The Haskalaran, The Talakanis, The Serenea—are what the drone picked up."

"That so?" Chad muttered under his breath.

Tim caught Chad's sceptical look just before Metemameni moved them on. Charlotte glanced at Tim. "What?"

"Not sure..."

Nathan knew exactly what they were thinking but gave no sign.

Inside the marquee, techs greeted them. Andrew introduced Chad and Charlotte to a team of archaeologists before leading them toward the underground docks.

A steel-and-timber edifice framed a vast gap in the boulders—an entry to the Richat structure's interior. The surrounding stone and sand seemed frozen in time, yet fragile.

They stepped into the substructure of Atlantis's naval ring—a colossal 163-kilometer band of land. At least a kilometre wide, it encircled the middle harbour—the second ring of water according to Plato's description.

The overhead framework felt stable. Beneath its surface lay a thousand docking chambers, each roughly one and a half times the size of a rugby field, arrayed outward in radial formation. The chambers faced the ringed harbour beyond, sealed now in silence and ruin.

Inside the shade, the air was much cooler and surprisingly fresh for a space sealed up for twelve millennia.

Chad and Charlotte had expected a musty smell, like the Auckland Museum—dense with ancient artefacts.

"This place has a unique and unexpected smell," Andrew mused. "During the breakthrough, we anticipated a rush of foul air... like a giant finally farting after twelve thousand years." He smirked.

Tim and Charlotte chuckled.

Anastacia frowned.

"Int'resting..." Crouton muttered. "N' what'd ya get?"

Chad tracked every word with quiet intensity, noting more than he let on.

Tim and Rod, exchanged looks—fresh air? Here? Given the location and everything they knew about the dig's specifics, it made no sense.

The short tunnel, lit by overhead LEDs, led to a makeshift timber dock. Eerily still, dark water lay beyond—as if hiding some creature in its shadows.

Charlotte and Chad hesitated to approach.

"'Woah... it's like the water becomes the darkness behind it," Chaiyala said, peering across the disconsolate liquid into the pitch-black nothingness.

"This place is awesome!" Tim grinned.

"What, these two containers and the truck?" Crouton joked.

The stone landing, lined with newly built wooden docks, was wide enough for a small truck. Steel trusses supported overhead lights. Two stacked containers featured a timber staircase and balcony. And a door and window on each faced the water—light glowed inside.

"I'm dying to see these things!" Tim exclaimed.

Charlotte smiled sharing his contagious excitement.

Nathan scanned the area curiously. Chad observed him.

"You okay?" Chaiyala asked Chad, noticing his expression.

"Yeah... I'm good."

"You look distracted. Should I distract you more?" she looked at him—eyes dancing, flirty, mischievous, and far too enchanting for Chad to concentrate.

"Huh?" Chad snapped out of it, they grinned.

"The drone footage gives a rough idea... but no more than a glimpse," Andrew said, heading to the containers.

A man descended the stairs to meet Andrew, Anastacia, and Crouton while Metemameni guided the group to the docks. He flipped a switch on the steel truss frame around the dock—a series of lights came to life.

Four illuminated a jetty with moored dinghies. The rest lit up the water's edge before it vanished into blackness.

Nathan and Crouton climbed into a dinghy, steadied by Andrew and Anastacia. Tim, Charlotte, Chaiyala, and Chad followed. Rod and Andrew secured another as Anastacia and Metemameni boarded, passing in boxes of gear. Techies loaded the third craft with lights and film equipment. The archaeology team took the fourth. Spotlights mounted, motors humming—they slipped into the black.

Andrew led—followed by Rod, the techies, then archaeologists.

"This first cavern's empty, and the next one too. At this stage, we think the ships meant to occupy them were likely away—sailing abroad or engaged in oceanic combat," Andrew explained.

"Ahaa—this is awesome!" Tim celebrated. "That'll help us understand Atlantis's naval campaigns."

Crouton shone a spotlight toward an opening in the wall. It revealed a collapsed ceiling, tilted thirty-five degrees, resting on boulders and an interior wall.

"Nothing left of dock in zis chamber," Anastacia said. "But next one—plenty artefacts. To your left, rocks support ceiling; beyond dat lies outer ring. Merchant harbour."

Crouton swept the light over a thick stone wall—red, white, black rock—like the government building site visited upon Chad and Charlotte's arrival.

A massive crack in the partition between chambers—wide at the top—narrowing where it met the water, like a pizza slice perpetually dipped into the dark abyss.

The dinghies squeezed through.

Andrew led the way, veering right. The spotlights swept across a series of docking structures—an esplanade, a mezzanine, a staircase, and what appeared to be an elevator shaft. Each element emerged from the shadows like fragments of a forgotten freight hub, half-buried in dust and silence.

A large arched doorway featured on the interior wall, flanked by smaller access-ways and cube-shaped objects.

At the centre of the lower dock, a sloped stone ramp extended five meters before abruptly stopping.

"This could mean ships were boarded from stern," Andrew suggested.

Tim nodded, surveying both detail and the space.

They docked. Two techies and an archaeologist disembarked. The others assisted them in unloading some of the gear. While the archaeologist reviewed the drone footage on a tablet—brows furrowed, eyes scanning for anomalies.

Once the generators roared to life, floodlights bathed the ancient dock in a harsh white light. The stark contrast carved out a visual intrigue, drawing the eye beyond the immediate vicinity as the others continued on, their figures drifting deeper into the shadows.

The drone footage revealed a third dock, exposed by damage like the last. A larger breach—twenty-odd meters wide—provoked curiosity, opening into eerie darkness.

The ceiling, stabilized by clustered rocks, held firm.

The cliff face had come down in the quake and wave that destroyed the city, sealing the harbour-side entry. Now, everything was still. Silent. Near the buried entrance, a jagged breach had been torn in the dividing chamber wall—just wide enough for the dinghies to pass through.

While visual data had confirmed safe clearance between the ship and the chamber wall, it revealed almost nothing about the vessel's design. Its true structure remained hidden in shadow.

Crouton eyed the black space beyond... certain something was hidden there.

As Andrew neared the gap, Crouton lifted the spotlight.

Andrew's eyes widened. Tim and Chaiyala's jaws dropped.

Chad and Charlotte—stunned—did a double-take.

Crouton trembled with excitement. Nathan smiled—oddly proud. Rod shook his head in disbelief.

The ship emerged like a ghost—immense, beautiful, and menacing.

Andrew slowed the dinghy. Spotlights illuminated the bow: a soaring eagle, its exaggerated head and gleaming golden beak frozen in flight.

The port-side wing vanished into shadow, carved with intricate hardwood feathers. Golden claws at the base of the bow formed a brutal battering ram.

The shifting spotlights made the feather edges sparkle. Once within a meter of the hull, each hardwood plume shimmered with turquoise light.

"This is... this is..." Rod couldn't finish.

Tim, Crouton, Andrew were glassy-eyed. Others sat speechless.

"Truly magnificent," Nathan said.

"This is unreal..." Chad breathed.

"I've never seen anything like this!" Andrew said, steering carefully.

As they passed through the gap, the stone wall revealed a rare cross-section—its construction—intricate and interlocked. The archaeologists erupted with excitement. They began snapping photos and marvelling at the design beneath the surface.

"First time we've seen a cross-section of an Atlantean-built wall," Crouton said, astounded.

"Until now, they've all been soundly intact," added Rod.

Chad leaned in to study the stonework.

"It's no wonder why too. The stonework interlocks inside, as well as out!" Tim observed.

"That's why the buildings didn't break—even when they were thrown across land and sea," Chaiyala remarked.

"Wow, the colours are crazy... and pretty!" Charlotte said.

The dinghies continued through the gap, gliding along a ten-meter-wide channel between the chamber's eastern wall and the Trireme.

"Ayeee, this is fun," Andrew grinned, steering steadily along the ship's enormous 200-meter length. There was only a meter to manoeuvre on either side, relying on Crouton's spotlight.

Above them, the pale hull glistened—seemingly coated in white carbon fibre. Oar port lids came into view. Tim gave up counting when his neck protested the angle he was looking up at.

Tim, Crouton, and Rod barely contained their exhilaration.

Charlotte beamed at Tim's delight.

Chaiyala and Chad soaked up the magnitude of it. They snuck glances at Nathan—his quiet awe and unwavering smile piquing their curiosity.

Nathan, aware of their looks, remained unbothered. He knew they trusted him—even as their questions multiplied.

They reached the dock, untouched by light for millennia. Spotlights revealed timber piles—ordinary at first glance. Tim and Andrew hesitated, puzzled. Anastacia and the archaeologists exchanged looks. How was it so well-preserved?

Andrew stared at the 12,000-year-old timber—perfectly intact.

Turning to Tim and Crouton, he smiled. "I've a feeling this is going to be more than fascinating."

With raised eyebrows and a grin, he followed the others onto to the stone dock.

Lamps were set up, flashlights guiding each careful step. Then, without warning, flames erupted along the chamber walls high above, racing around near the newly visible ceiling from the rear of the dock along the sides—except where the northeast corner had crumbled.

Behind the flames, something reflective amplified the glow. It cast light across the entire chamber—unveiling the full Trireme from stern to bow.

The technicians exchanged stunned looks. The lamps hadn't so much as been connected to the generators, much less been switched on.

Tim and Charlotte, mid-crate lift, froze. They turned toward the ship.

Chad had been staring toward the direction of the stern end of the Trireme. Barely able to make out its faint shape in the sparse, misaligned flashlight glow—until the entire vessel materialized before him, sudden and dreamlike.

Crouton, Rod, and Chaiyala sprang to alertness. Eyes darted. Escape routes, potential threats—assessed in silent haste.

But nothing came. Only awe. Silence.

"Wow... *wow!*" Tim breathed.

"Oh... it's so beautiful," Charlotte gasped.

"You got that right..." Chad whispered.

"Would ya look at that," Crouton muttered.

"The size of it," Rod gasped.

Chaiyala and Anastacia agreed.

"I don't understand... what the...?" one of the techs began.

Nathan rejoined them, emerging from behind a scatter of crates and bulky equipment near the back of the chamber.

A few wanted to ask where he'd gone.

Rod ignored the obvious query, and asked, "You alright, boss?"

Nathan stared at the Trireme. Focused. No eye contact. After a pause, he nodded. "Yes."

The ship gleamed—its white hull adorned with vibrant patterns: dolphins leaping, octopuses unfurling, eagles mid-swoop, and tigers in motion. Across the stern, Manuscrat script shimmered in a gradient of royal, cobalt, and deep navy blue, the letters glistening under the golden light.

Its trimmings mirrored the marbled hues. The mesmerizing aqua aphlaston—soared fifteen meters above the upper deck.

It was an intriguing paradox—otherworldly craftsmanship shaped with the elegance of ancient Greek maritime design. As it met the water, it did so with quiet grandeur, its contours both familiar and foreign...

Chad, Tim, and Charlotte watched Nathan. His reaction wasn't awe—but strange familiarity, as if studying a creature. He moved to the edge of the dock, emerging from shadows.

Andrew and Rod exchanged looks—quietly concerned. Nathan was paradoxical. Open, enigmatic. Sound mind, yet cloaked in mystery.

Trusted. Commanding. Transparent. Yet something remained elusive. Crouton and Chaiyala now felt it too.

What was going on with Nathan? The question lingered—not alarming, but... perplexing. A flickering mystery just out of reach.

Nathan sensed their thoughts, unbothered. He'd reached a precipice, resting in the trust he'd built with those closest—even if his ways felt 'otherworldly.'

Nathan's gift was rare—an ability to nudge memory without force. It was delicate and precise... yet risky. One nudge could protect a mind from trauma. But repeated use? That risked fracture. The subconscious might rebel, the conscious mind lose grip, and reality itself begin to shimmer like a half-remembered dream.

He used it sparingly. No one ever knew. No one was harmed. But each intervention was a gamble, demanding precision that bordered on divine.

Human minds are fragile. Early neglect, or the absence of compassion, can seed damage that never heals. In a world fractured by Eden's fall, even the gentlest touch carries the weight of ancient loss. Nathan understood this. Every choice required restraint. Every act, discernment. The consequences were rarely visible—but always there, waiting.

Then, seemingly half self-aware, Nathan looked around and frowned gently. "Is everyone okay? You all look like you've seen a ghost, and that ghost is me."

Silence.

Crouton broke it. "Nah, nah—we're all good. Just... more than a fraction dumbfounded by everything." He smiled. "Not you," he lied, keen to preserve the group's stability. "This is simply incredible—in ways we never imagined."

Nathan raised his eyebrows and nodded, as if 'incredible' barely scratched the surface.

He moved toward the sloped dock beside the ship's stern, admiring the height of the aphlaston.

Aware his companions needed to discover their own way aboard, he looked up again. "So, where do we go from here?" he asked—not as leader, but as mentor. A prompt for understanding. Yet from their view, he was simply deferring to the experts he'd hired for the challenge ahead.

They were all thinking the same thing. Andrew, Crouton, and Anastacia had been the first to wonder—if not immediately—how the Trireme could be in such pristine condition.

"Why... how is it possible? A ship like this still looks so perfect?" Anastacia was stumped.

Tim, Rod, and the archaeologists exchanged glances, their silence echoing the same quiet wonder.

As procedural tasks wound down, Andrew broke the ice. "This doesn't seem right... something's really off."

"This ship is in perfect condition," stated Chad.

"And everything else," Tim added, glancing around the dock—echoing the thought, though his focus was lost in disbelief.

Chaiyala, Chad, and Charlotte exchanged uncertain glances. Their expert guides were now hitting walls of logic.

Rod, drawing on his background in logistics hesitated, "Why... exactly... how?"

Nathan finished "...does a ship twelve thousand years old, sealed in a cavern for just as long, look freshly cleaned? Brand new, even." Nathan's gaze returned to the stern of the massive vessel, anchored by two obscenely thick steel ropes jutting from iron housing embedded in the stone dock.

Charles had given Tim a quiet warning earlier that day. *"Remember Solon's seventh journal,"* he'd said before they departed. *"Especially Atlas's cryptic remarks about keys and vessels—things that don't fit, easily dismissed. I believe once the deeper Richat is entered, the rules will change. Be ready. This is uncharted territory. Up until now it's been ruins and wonder. But now? It's about to come alive—with very different rules."*

Tim had wanted to ask more, but Charles just smiled, placed a hand on his forearm, and walked away. Now, floating near the Trireme, Tim exhaled slowly. What had he gotten himself into? He'd asked that often since meeting Nathan O'Conner. Each time, it felt less like history and more like adrenaline. Reading journals was one thing. Being here—with impossible truths pressing in—felt like dreaming while fully awake.

He'd speak with Charles again. There was more to say. Why had he spoken to Tim, specifically, and with such conviction?

Charlotte's puzzled expression snapped Tim out of his thoughts as Andrew continued. "...so maybe the whole place shares that same... whatever it is. Explains the fresh air. No stale mustiness. Nothing we expected."

"The same what thing?" Tim asked, realizing he'd missed the start of a conversation. Nathan stepped in. "Either someone's cleaned up before us... or the Atlanteans had methods of preservation—tech or techniques—that kept this ship and the dock intact. Such that we do not know about according to any of our scientific discoveries."

"I'll go with the latter," Crouton said, tone resolute.

Tim and Andrew agreed, and others nodded along. "We know the area was sealed under tons of mud and rock before excavation," Andrew added.

"So," Chad began to ask—careful thought etched in his expression, "when it was opened and lacked that stale, enclosed smell... did you suspect another access point?"

"Yes," Andrew confirmed.

"And you searched thoroughly?"

"We did—went back east, searched the outer ring—nothing. Several Ks each way."

Nathan beheld the Trireme, docked several meters away. Not as a scholar or commander, but as a quiet revelator—bearing witness to something long buried and newly alive. Its discovery marked the beginning—one of several magnificent, mysterious finds that would help bring Atlantis into reality, both technologically and culturally. He stood still. Thoughtful. Absorbing its presence. The ship was a revelation as much as it was a relic. A convergence of myth and engineering, memory and meaning.

"Gather in," Nathan called.

Crouton and Andrew pulled others into a huddle. Nathan addressed the full team.

"Some of you have been here since the beginning. Others joined months—or even weeks—ago. Together, we've built more than a team of experts. We've built a culture: loyalty, transparency, authenticity.

We've stayed clear of political entanglements. We don't chase trends or make decisions driven by fear—we act with purpose, not reaction.

When we talk about economics or diversity, we mean it—no tokenism, no empty gestures.

And when the tools we needed didn't exist, we built them. 'New and improved' isn't always better. So—we created our own manufacturers. Our own services. We made what others couldn't deliver.

From day one, Red Sword have operated with precision. Every idea, belief, or assumption—no matter how controversial—has stood trial in reality's crucible. Conspiracies, theories, facts—all assessed fairly. Some outcomes have stunned us. Others remain mysteries.

At our core, we are conservative open-minded thinkers—free of prejudice or corruption—both grounded and diverse. From that, trust and unity have flourished. And now, we move forward with clarity and momentum."

Nathan turned toward the stern. "Clearly, this is an archaeological anomaly. If the legends are true, we're facing countless unknowns. If Atlantis belongs to a 'para-historical' era, and its tech could be 'para-normal'—functionally beyond current science. Look around. This site, this ship... it's preserved like nothing we've seen."

Andrew and Anastacia nodded.

"Everything's different," Tim added.

"The woodwork and metal designs don't match any ancient culture," Andrew observed.

"A different age, with different tech," Crouton mused. "Maybe even different rules o' physics."

"I wouldn't doubt it," Tim said.

"I'd *expect* it," Crouton furthered.

"I doubt there's room left for surprise," Chad muttered.

"Exactly," Nathan said. "Prepare yourselves. What's onboard might not make sense—not at first—it may rewrite what you think is possible."

"So, weird and whacked-out hoo-ha?" Rod summarized.

"Good. I'm ready," Crouton said.

"Anyone else?" Nathan asked.

"Let's do this," Chaiyala responded.

"Good, I'm itching to get on board this thing." Andrew stated.

Nathan nodded with gravity. "We're entering unfamiliar territory. Not just new—but deeper, more complex than anything we've encountered."

Chad remained deeply thoughtful... clearly this was something unprecedented. Yet he couldn't get past the way Nathan spoke—suggesting he had an already organised understanding of how much so...

Crouton, Rod, and Chaiyala moved to check gear while Tim and Chad pondered Nathan's warning. Did he know what lay aboard... or was it genuine uncertainty? Both leaned toward the latter—the former lingering in their minds. He looked at Chad—who was already looking at him, wondering the same.

Andrew, Anastacia, and Rod opened a crate of gear: ropes, ladder guns, lights, brushes, markers. With techies and an archaeologist, Andrew took a dinghy to the left of the stern and dropped anchor. They fired ladder guns, steel hooks gripping the rail twenty or so meters above. Andrew climbed up, joining the others for recon.

Nathan, Crouton, and the rest followed. Once aboard, Tim turned to assist his fiancée—only to step back as she leapt over the rail with a smile.

Chad and Chaiyala joined them. Andrew led the team of archaeologists across to the starboard side while techies began setting up camera and electrical gear.

Nathan and the core group explored the stern's top deck—a vast hardwood expanse stretching way ahead of them. A sleek and modest gold cube structure stood near the stern, its surfaces gleaming as Crouton tapped it for texture.

A dark glass window-surface wrapped the front and sides, with double doors at port and starboard—one at the stern side.

"This... it looks incredible. Solid gold?" Chad admired.

Chaiyala and Charlotte were awestruck.

"So cool... truly amazing!" Tim remarked, examining turquoise-bound beams across the deck.

Crouton, Rod, and Nathan explored the back and far side of the gold structure. Chaiyala joined them, stunned by the view surrounding: the eagle's wings and head rose in the distance at the bow. The deck stretched like a wooden football field. "What did they need all this space for?" Chad asked.

"There's enough room for marshalling troops, Tim suggested. It was also possibly used for parking and stationing large weapons—ballistae, catapults,"

"Check this out!" Chaiyala noticed. A large opening with stairs stood hidden until now, leading beneath the bow end of the gold building. The wide mahogany stairs disappeared below. Above them, the dark glass of the gold cube-like house-sized building held watchful intrigue. "The ship's bridge, maybe?" Crouton guessed. "Probably," Tim nodded, as Nathan led them below deck.

Andrew joined them, eyes puzzled. "Boss," he said, bewildered, "I'm not qualified for this—need to go back to school. Though, nothing they teach will help me explain this. It's so far outside the box, we shouldn't even be having this conversation."

"Different world, different rules," Crouton grinned.

"You're not wrong." Andrew laughed. "This is what I'd expect on a 20th-century ocean liner—or one a hundred years from now."

"Alrighty then," Rod acknowledged—curious.

"Everything's immaculate. My crew don't even know where to begin! Techies are just as lost..."

"We're all in the same boat then," Chad said deadpan.

Charlotte groaned and leaned into Tim. They smirked.

"Would've expected that from Rick or Rhys," Crouton smiled, shaking his head.

"Should I thump you?" Chaiyala smirked at him menacingly—teasing.

Chad shrugged. "Had to say it."

They burst out laughing.

Rod grinned, slapping his shoulder. "Nicely timed comic relief."

"Cheers."

"Lemme guess," Tim began, "was on the tip of your tongue? Just itching to jump overboard?"

Charlotte buried her head in Tim's shoulder, laughing softly.

"Wow," Chaiyala muttered, turning away with a grin.

"My beard!" Crouton added, joining the chorus of laughter.

Nathan smiled. "Let's take a look around—see what we're dealing with and where we go from there."

Andrew and his crew soon discovered curious electrical systems near the bow, just beyond the stairwell. He pulled in Nathan and Crouton for input.

Rod, Tim, and Charlotte explored the starboard corridor, while Chad and Chaiyala took the port-side passage. The surreal weight of their surroundings settled in—feeling as if they'd stepped into science fiction, only it was undeniably real. They paused often, adjusting to the staggering truth: this place had remained sealed and untouched for twelve thousand years.

The corridors—three meters wide with dark hardwood floors—were now lit, likely activated by Andrew or the techies. Soft lighting ran along the tops of the walls, casting a clean glow across both ceiling and floor.

Soft greys and blues wrapped the walls, adorned with dolphins, eagles, tigers, and octopus in mystifying, almost three-dimensional designs that drew the eye with otherworldly artistry. Gold-plated doors with turquoise handles lined one side like a luxury hotel corridor; fewer doors faced them from the opposite wall.

Tim turned the handle cautiously and peered inside. Warm orange light spilled through a large bay window, cast from the fire-lit docking chamber beyond. As they stepped in, the room brightened fully—light rising from the wall skirting and tracing the ceiling borders.

"Woah..." Rod breathed.

"Seriously..." Tim said, shaking his head. "Use of sensors."

The space was simple—seven bunk beds with bare mattresses. A large single-paned window faced port side, and the wool-like carpet resembled modern design. But the true mystery wasn't the furniture—it was the impossible fact before them: this ship predated the Bronze Age... even the Stone Age. Yet here it was—sealed, intact, and unmistakably real. For the first time—or so history had always claimed.

CHAPTER 34

- -

C had and Chaiyala counted twenty doors along the port side corridor, checking every few to confirm they were all sleeping quarters. It certainly seemed that way.

"Too bad we do not have one of these rooms, just for ourselves—and locked," Chaiyala said with a smirk and a mischievous glint in her eyes.

"We'd get caught," Chad cautioned. "But we can still take a quick moment... to do this." He smiled, nudging her inside and pulling the door shut behind them.

They moved closer, eyes locked, forgetting the ship, the Richat, and everything else. Chaiyala was stunning—beyond her tough exterior, her eyes revealed compassion and care. Chad radiated kindness, rugged charm, and a disarming presence.

Quiet freedom moved between them. Peace and reassurance came easily, and they relaxed into it, falling further for each other. They kissed once, then again, and finally locked lips for several moments. Chad gently ran his hands across her shoulders and arms, then embraced her lovingly—before the door clicked open.

Crouton's blank expression turned a wide, indecorous grin. "Booh!" he said, a little too late.

"I already look at you..." Chaiyala muttered, unimpressed.

Crouton chuckled. "Knew it! Soon as the door shut."

Chad grinned sheepishly.

"Shut up, Crouton!" Chaiyala scolded—smirking, eyes narrowed.

"You're s'posed to be working, not snoggin' your boyfriend."

"I am on break."

"Oh, that's alright then! As ya were," Crouton dismissed--grinning—his mischief complete.

Chad and Chaiyala followed Crouton back into the passage.

He relayed that Rod and Tim were investigating the interior rooms. They'd found the armoury, which held hundreds of metal spears tipped with crystal, feather-light shields, intricately crafted composite bows, and ornate swords and daggers.

Intrigued, Chad and Chaiyala considered checking it out until something else caught their attention. At the passage's far end, a doorless entrance led to a small room at the ship's bow. A soft red glow emanated from within, illuminating a massive, oddly shaped window on the port side. The strange light and window design drew them in—but something else lingered, an unsettling mystery in the air.

The room's floor tiered upward toward the far wall, narrowing to four meters at the back, or stern end. It had two entrances—one where they stood and another near starboard. Angled windowed sides framed a meter-wide front, confirming they were at the bow's furthest end. Two elliptical windows dominated the port and starboard walls, their thick, convex panes featuring a shimmering black circle near the bow.

"We're inside the eagle's head," Crouton realized as he and Chad observed the dark disks embedded within the glass eyes of the massive wooden bird. "It's shimmering without any obvious light source," Chad remarked, trying to understand its strange glimmering quality.

Chaiyala studied a machine about a foot and a half wide and a meter tall, shaped like an elongated pyramid and set upon a dark marble plinth at the back wall between the two entrances.

"You must come see this...." she beckoned, examining the strange object's detail. A system of mirrors, prisms, and gold rods surrounding a huge red jewel—the source of the glow. It was cut with angles that matched several small mirrors and glass pieces facing it.

"This thing's fascinating," Chad said in wonder.

"Certainly is," Crouton nodded, inspecting each angled component.

"And if it is what I think... it might be," Chaiyala said slowly, tracing the line from one prism to the black disk inside the eagle's eye, "Tim and Andrew—they will want very much to see this."

"Right!" Crouton realized. "You reckon this has something to do with that ancient laser weaponry Tim's mentioned?"

Chad crouched beside them, frowning. "You're suggesting this machine shoots lasers out of the eagle's eyes?" Part of him felt silly saying it—but most of him wouldn't have been surprised.

Crouton stood and chuckled. "Crazy, eh."

Chad shook his head, bewildered.

He recalled Tim had mentioned Atlantis had experimented with light— and other technologies in ways that defied convention. The other night the concepts had come up, of harmonic shielding, resonance-based propulsion, crystalline data storage. Topics no textbook dared to name, had been discussed. And so, the idea of laser weaponry seemed to fit within the vast bounds of Atlantean wonders.

Chaiyala and Chad discussed it as they followed Crouton toward the open doorway on the other side of the room.

"Exactly the same as the port-side corridor," Crouton observed, opening a door to reveal another sleeping quarters.

"It is mirror image. Just... opposite direction." Chaiyala added.

Adjacent to the long row of doors on the port wall were others, fewer and spaced further apart. Chad opened the nearest one.

"How's it going?" Rod greeted them as Nathan, Tim, and Andrew looked up.

Charlotte smiled, adjusting her ponytail as the others glanced her way.

Tim and Andrew were examining long glass-like objects stacked on racks, marked with Atlantean script. Surrounding them were machines and contraptions that felt strangely familiar.

"It is gym," Chaiyala noted with certainty.

"We kinda figured," Rod nodded. "Makes sense," Tim agreed, scanning the room.

Tim and Andrew moved from the gym's centre to the double doors at the stern-end wall, with Charlotte and Nathan following. Beyond the doorway, they entered a short corridor lined with doors.

Tim opened one to the left, Andrew to the right—both revealing bedroom suites with large stand-alone beds, drawers, cabinets, and shelving. Opposite each bed was a large black screen in place of windows. Below it sat a desk with empty drawers and a leather chair. "Fascinating," Andrew said.

"These were likely the officers' quarters," Tim suggested.

"Same layout," Charlotte confirmed, opening the next door.

They passed ten rooms—five on each side—investigating three. Charlotte moved further down the corridor, Nathan following casually. "Wow, look at this," she exclaimed. The corridor opened up into a larger room. She approached a large wooden table surrounded by thirty leather chairs. "Goodness!" Andrew gasped as he and Tim caught up.

"Looks like the officers' mess and administration," Tim speculated.

"I'd say you're right," Nathan agreed, running his hand along a marble bench top with built-in beverage faucets and unfamiliar kitchen components.

Tables and chairs filled the remaining corners. At the stern-end centre, a second passage mirrored the first, lined with ten more doors. At its end, another open area appeared—walls lined with sleek dark screens, half a dozen sofas at the centre, and a large square glass coffee table. "These smooth, glassy surfaces—could they pass for LED screens?" Tim speculated.

"Wouldn't surprise me," Andrew said, examining what resembled a lounge.

"We've got the lights on," Nathan noted. "I'm sure whatever powers them will reveal the function of these screens."

Tim and Andrew exchanged excited looks.

"Tim! Guys! Check this out!" Charlotte's voice called from a room at the stern end.

They rushed in. Nathan followed, not with urgency, but with a calm curiosity. This was the largest suite they'd encountered. Every wall was smooth, dark glass—identical to the suspected screens. A massive bookshelf lined one side, packed with books, ornaments, and unidentifiable objects. A large double bed rested against the stern wall.

Charlotte stood before a spacious oval desk, where a single sheet of paper bore inscriptions in Atlantean Manuscrat. She didn't touch it. Tim and Andrew joined her, staring at the paper and the golden pen lying across it. "It... doesn't look old enough," Tim uttered, frowning.

Andrew narrowed his eyes. "This looks like it was written... in ballpoint pen?"

"And recently," Charlotte added.

Andrew removed gloves and a sterile plastic bag from his tool belt.

"If you expect things to follow conventional rules and time, that won't work," Nathan said as the others stepped aside.

He paused, examining the note. "Hmm." He looked up, then to the side, thinking. He put on gloves no one knew he had and carefully placed the paper into a sterile bag. "I'll take care of the note; the pen is all yours." He smiled at Andrew and returned to exploring. Andrew frowned at Tim, who glanced at Charlotte. She gave him a quizzical look. She didn't speak, but her eyes lingered on the pen. Something about it unsettled her—at first. Then, scanning through earlier clues in her mind, she quietly began to realize: this was only the beginning.

"Things that don't fit in time," Tim recalled softly, thoughtful.

"What's the significance of that artefact?" Andrew asked.

"I've a feeling about it, I can't place," Nathan replied, scanning the bookshelf.

He pulled out a book written by Neptune on horse riding in battle. He shut it, gazed into nowhere.

"Nate, you okay?" Tim asked.

Nathan delayed. "Yes. Sorry. I'll get this note seen to... I need to—never mind. Nothing to worry about."

He snapped out of it. "This quarters was likely the fleet admiral's," he said, looking around.

"Hmm, yes, that'd be my assumption," Andrew agreed.

Nathan returned to the bookshelf.

Tim joined Nathan, examining book spines while Andrew studied the pen.

He studied the spines until he felt Charlotte watching him. Andrew was preoccupied with the pen. She glanced at Nathan, absorbed in the book, then looked back at Tim. He peered at the older man, noting how he seemed to be reading fluently—in Manuscrat —, not English.

"What's in there?" Tim asked.

Nathan paused. "Hmm... trying..." he stopped short. "No. I was trying to see if I could make something out of the characters, but no. It's not there. More of a hunch." He shut the book, returned it to its shelf, and left the room.

"Interesting..." Charlotte said.

Tim sighed, wide-eyed. "I've known him for years. He's reliably transparent and good-hearted... but he still leaves me wondering. I trust him because of that."

"I see why they call him a mystery man," Charlotte added.

"Yup," Tim nodded.

They rejoined the others, exploring the lower deck—bathrooms, saunas, hot tubs near the gym, an entertainment room, the mess hall, and the galley.

Andrew called for Nathan and Tim, with Charlotte close behind, to examine strange ceramic cylinders and units resembling batteries or computer hubs. Tim and Andrew were blown away by the implications. "You know they'll call us nut cases when this goes public?" Andrew grinned. Tim and Nathan chuckled.

"That'd be," Nathan replied, "if we lacked substance or if access to that substance were contrived. But it's not. We've spent decades ensuring it's beyond reproach."

Rod, Crouton, Chaiyala, and Chad spent half an hour exploring the galley—an advanced culinary hub built for long ocean voyages.

"None of this looks twelve thousand years old," Chad mused.

"It's like the furniture and electrical equipment are some unique blend of retro... I dunno—nineteen-twenties, then past twenty-twenties."

"Technology—very similar to what we have today," Chaiyala began.

"...and yet different," Crouton finished.

"Like a parallel dimension," Chad speculated.

"Or a forgotten one," Rod suggested.

Crouton's spoke quietly, "A civilization like ours—just as advanced. And then... wiped clean."

"Fascinating," Chad said, deep in thought.

Tim appeared suddenly, grinning. "You have to see this! It's awesome!" He disappeared before they could respond. They hurried after him.

He descended the port-side stairs to the lower decks. The others followed down a narrow steel platform with balustrades. Joining Andrew, Charlotte, and Nathan, they reached a viewing terrace flanked by stairs.

The sight before them rivalled the grandeur of the bow eagle. Overhead lighting revealed a vast chamber filled with hundreds of enormous oars, three levels deep. The top layer—easiest to see—sat retracted at an angle, blades pointing port or starboard. Below, glimpses of the lower levels hinted at scale.

Stairs descended to suspended steel walkways running the ship's length. Tall, dark units resembling engines and motors lined the platforms—complete with switchboards, screens, and lights.

The pristine condition defied logic. What method—what unknown preservation tech—could have kept it untouched for millennia? The mystery lingered, impossible to ignore.

"The size of these oars is incredible!" Rod exclaimed.

"You're not wrong," Nathan said.

Crouton stood speechless at the sight of the oars disappearing into the distance beyond suspended walk ways.

"No human could operate these—no wonder they're mechanized," Tim said.

"Let's take a closer look," Andrew suggested.

They descended from the upper level of three walkways. Below, more steps revealed breathtaking views of the triple-layered rows of oars stretching port and starboard.

"My goodness! Unreal!" Charlotte exclaimed.

"This is something else," Tim breathed.

"Definitely like another world," Chad said.

"It is another world," Nathan said. "A forgotten one, hidden beyond the horizons of history and our current understanding."

"Remarkable," Rod shook his head.

"*There is nothing new in the world—except the history we do not know*'," Tim quoted.

"Harry Truman," Nathan recalled. "Thirty-third U.S. president."

Each oar blade would have been five by two meters, and was attached to thick twenty-meter hardwood shafts. They were fastened to steel grips on elliptical pivots, secured to metal units mounted on oval tracks. Behind those, under the platform and protruding past the walkways, were larger motor components powering the motion.

"Imagine being in here while the ship was mid-voyage!" Tim said with an excited grin.

"Watching this, it would be something incredible," Chaiyala said with a breath of awe.

"That wa-would've been—quite something to behold," Nathan stammered, emotion slipping through. Tim and Chad noticed, though the others remained focused on the mechanical wonder.

"I'm struggling to grasp this level of technology," Rod said.

"Mate, I've given up. This world o' hoo-ha would hurt my loaf if I tried wrapping my head 'round it," Crouton laughed.

"Fair call!" Chad agreed.

In the armoury, Andrew and Tim found Metemameni and Anastacia recording items. Nathan, Crouton and the others soon joined them.

They discussed the magnitude of the discovery—each of them bewildered and blown away by how such an anomaly, far beyond conventional science, could actually be real. They were experiencing it in real time, there in person. History was shifting, and the rules had changed. The field's approach had to evolve. But most of all, every person there—hand-picked guests, close allies—held a pivotal role now.

They'd all ventured far past the comforts of familiarity. Even the convenience of distance—removal from their immediate experience and point of view. They had to square with the reality of bold new ideas and bewildering facts. The challenge now was to process this world-altering truth, with professionalism and composure.

"Clear, careful communication will be key in presenting what we've found," Nathan affirmed. His voice was steady, but beneath it lay urgency. "Not simply to explain it—but to protect it. To ensure the truth isn't lost in disbelief, or twisted by those who fear what it means. We're shaping how the world receives it. Far more than merely presenting a discovery."

Later, back on the upper deck, they all stood in stunned silence, absorbing the sheer scale of their surroundings—and the weight of what they'd uncovered.

"Still, I cannot believe we are here," Chaiyala beamed, her excitement radiant.

Rod shook his head, searching for words. "How do you even come back from this? Until now, it's been regular digs—exciting discoveries to share with the world..."

"But this? This is next level," added Tim.

"Way beyond that," Chad agreed.

"This is truly something else—unequivocally from another world" remarked Rod.

The others echoed their agreement.

Crouton crossed his arms, nodding slowly. "We be in foreign territory now, my friends. Make no mistake—this is unheard of. You wouldn't read about it! This is new... out of this world in more ways than one."

Nathan's gaze drifted across the vast docking chamber. "And the most exciting part?" his voice held a quiet certainty, "this is barely even the beginning. Alastragah is next. And that... oh, that is going to eclipse everything we've seen here."

"Even leading up to it," Tim's eyes gleamed with anticipation, "the implications of finding the sacred halls, the puzzle pieces coming together—it's monumental" He and Charlotte exchanged a thrilled embrace.

All of them were abuzz with excitement. Anastacia included—her usual reserve broken.

Chad turned slowly, taking in Haskalaran's massive deck. The megalithic docking chamber walls, the distant ceiling overhead, and the firelight glowing where they met. "Who would've thought we'd ever see something like this?"

Charlotte nodded, eyes wide. "I know!" The sentiment rippled through the group—a shared, wordless sense of awe and gratitude. Andrew placed a hand on Crouton and Nathan's shoulders, pulling them into a hug. "What a day. What an adventure—well done!"

"Thanks, brother," Crouton smiled, shaking his hand firmly.

Nathan nodded, his expression warm. "And thank you—for everything. For all you've done in the northern sections, and the wider project. Tim, Anastacia... all of you—for every part played, large or small, that got us here."

"Thank you, Nathan!" Tim high-fived him, then pulled him into an embrace.

They took a moment to savour the reality of it all—sharing thoughts, laughter, reflecting on the journey so far, and the untold discoveries still ahead.

TO BE CONTINUED...
Book Two: Secrets of The Sahara

ACKNOWLEDGEMENTS

All glory and honour to my Lord Jesus—for the passion, the inspiration, and the opening of many doors. You enabled opportunities, sustained the journey, and breathed life into this project. Ultimately, Beyond Our Horizons is for Your glory and for the blessing of those who pick it up.

This work would not exist without the generosity, wisdom, and presence of many. It was shaped by a community of voices, silences, and shared thresholds. I'm deeply grateful to those who walked beside me—friends, mentors, and readers—whose insights, questions, and quiet presence helped refine both the craft and the courage behind these pages.

Family and Foundational Support. First, and most gratefully, to my incredible, supportive, loving and encouraging wife Amanda, and our three beautiful children—Kaylee, Ester and Michael. Amanda—thank you for your patience and sacrifices, and for walking this creative journey with me. Your meticulous reading, honest feedback, and deep understanding of the heart behind this story made all the difference. I couldn't have done this without you. Thank you for allowing me the time and space to write. Your presence is woven through every page.

To my parents, Hylton and Ruth, and my in-laws, Gerald and Gill—thank you for your unwavering support, encouragement, and generosity. Your belief in this work, and in me, helped carry it from dream to reality.

To my brother Aaron, and to Krissy, Derek, Josh, Sarah, Doug, Nathan, Bex and Simon—thank you for your time and support, your feedback, and your faith in the process. Your insights helped shape and enhance this work in ways I'll always treasure.

Creative and Practical Contributors. To Ryan, who sourced the laptop PC that became a faithful workhorse—and for connecting me with Sean and Craig from the Palmerston North City Library.

Thank you, Sean and Craig—your wisdom and experience is so appreciated.

To Nick, our neighbour down the road, who found the aforementioned workhorse when it fell off the roof of the car—and for clearing things up with the Police when they lost track of it after you'd handed it in.

To Robyn, Anne, John, Dave. H, Lynley, David and the team at Manawatu Writers Hub—my community of local fellow writers who brought experience, insight, encouragement, and practical tips to my creative process.

To the team at NZ Christian Writers—for the wealth of creative inspiration, spiritual and industry insight, know-how and expertise.

To the guys from Trade Staff Hamilton—Tom, Zack, and all the amazing staff I worked alongside. Your support, humour, and wild ideas added unexpected colour to this journey.

Publishing Partners. To the incredible team at Ark House Press—John, James, and Nicole—thank you for welcoming me into the Ark House family. You've been a pleasure and a blessing to work with, guiding and advising the way ahead with grace and professionalism.

Church and Community. To my ever faithful, curious and encouraging friends and whānau at Hope Vineyard and Cross Roads Church—thank you for your support and enthusiasm for this project.

Special thanks to Pastors Shane and Lydia, Grant and Heather, John and Wendy, Mike and Lauren, Sam and Grainne, Steve, Chris, Richard (Dickie), Debs and Jonny, Tawhai, Sharon, Tim and Helenka, Helen and Ian, Sam and Ruth, Isaac and Tamra, Claire and Luke, Nathan, Tyler, Chris and Mel, Robyn, Scottie and Basha, Jacob, and Eran.

Friends and Extended Family. To Jeremy and Michelle, Anna, Cody, Sam and Jess, Pairama and Levi, Peter. D, Andre—who thought I was kidding when I said I was a writer, then worried I might turn him into a character.

To Tony, Jason and Sarah, Joy and Bevan—for the most valuable and insightful two hours of wisdom, tips, and industry prep at the beginning of this journey.

To Andrew and Zoe for opening up your home to me for a week's writing retreat.

To Phil Strong—for your insight, experience, and inspirational podcasts on writing and Christian life.

To Christine, Clem and Andrew, Vasanthy, Glenn, Caroline, Dianne, Heather, Glennis, Deanne, Chris, and Marilyn—thank you for your constant support.

To Hamish—for your love and creative journeying as we shared progress, highs and lows.

To Vaughan—for our enthusiastic and encouraging chats on the road back from New Wine Festivals.

To the team at Park Road Play Centre—thank you for your support and curiosity during our time there. Your encouragement and interest in the progress of this project meant more than you know—Kathryn, Steph and Mark, Vanessa, Amanda and Lance, and Ellie.

Inspirational Sources. Special thanks to George S. Alexander and Natalis Rosen for the initial inspiration—your amazing documentary Visiting Atlantis—and to Jimmy Corsetti for catching my attention and directing me to it via your Bright Insight presentation linking the Richat Structure and Atlantis.

Special thanks to Alex Marestaing, whose sessions on story arcs at New Wine Festival (2024/2025) helped crystallize key narrative rhythms in this manuscript. Your insights and advice were a timely gift.

Ethical Transparency and Pastoral Gratitude. To those whose stories echo through these chapters—whether through direct inspiration or thematic resonance—I honour your journeys. Where privacy was paramount, I've reimagined scenes to protect relational trust while preserving transformational impact.

SOURCES AND INSPIRATIONS

Author's Notes and Ethical Transparency

Narrative Mental Health and Faith-based Dialogue

Faith-based coping strategies appear throughout the manuscript in character dialogue. These reflect personal beliefs and lived experiences, not clinical recommendations. Mental health journeys are deeply individual, and while faith plays a central role for some, others may find strength through different means. Readers are encouraged to seek professional support when needed and to explore what brings peace, healing, and hope.

Narrative Theology and Sacred Reality

Theological themes are embedded as sacred realities within the story's metaphysical framework. When characters speak of divine preservation or scriptural inerrancy, they are voicing truths that, within the world of this narrative, are real and active—not doctrinal positions, but revealed constants. This dual approach honours the sacred without imposing it, inviting reflection without demanding agreement.

Fictionalization and Real-World References

Beyond Our Horizons is a work of fiction. Real locations, institutions, and historical references are used for narrative purposes only. All characters, organizations, and technologies are fictional unless otherwise noted. Where privacy was paramount, scenes have been reimagined to protect relational trust while preserving transformational impact.

Theological and Spiritual Inspirations

- Saint Irenaeus: "The glory of God is mankind fully alive" is quoted in theological discourse and used to anchor themes of divine purpose and human flourishing.
- Scriptural Echoes: The title "Ancient of Days" (Daniel 7:9) and references to Jehovah and other spiritual and divine preservation reflect symbolic and spiritual layering.
- Christianity's Historical Impact: Works by Rodney Stark (The Rise of Christianity) and Diarmaid MacCulloch (Christianity: The First Three Thousand Years) informed depictions of early Christian transformation and moral reform.
- The Seven Sleepers: This legend, found in both Christian and Islamic traditions, inspired themes of miraculous preservation and time displacement.
- Faith and Healing: Scenes involving spiritual renewal and relational grace are fictional, inspired by pastoral care and the transformative power of forgiveness.

Historical and Archaeological Echoes

- Plato's Atlantis: Timaeus and Critias (Penguin Classics, trans. Desmond Lee) are foundational texts. Solon's journey to Egypt and the Temple of Sais are reimagined throughout the narrative.
- Richat Structure: The idea of the Richat Structure as a possible site of Atlantis was inspired by Jimmy Corsetti's Bright Insight presentations and the documentary Visiting Atlantis by George S. Alexander and Natalis Rosen. Their research and storytelling encouraged and championed global curiosity and shaped the mythic foundation of this narrative.
- Lake Chad and Sahara Paleogeography: Research by Drake et al. (2008) and Coe (2001) shaped the depiction of ancient African landscapes.
- Egyptology and Pyramids: Sources include Flinders Petrie, Mark Lehner, Ian Shaw, and Toby Wilkinson. Fringe theories from Christopher Dunn and Graham Hancock are reimagined mythically.
- Crusader History: The siege of Antioch and hidden chambers beneath the city are based on First Crusade events, woven into the fictional Order of Kittim mythos.
- Occultism and Revisionism: Chapter 28 draws on literature about Nazi occult interests and politicized archaeology to dramatize historical suppression.

Speculative Science and Para-History

- Tesla and Wireless Energy: Historical works by Cheney and Seifer inspired fictional technologies like Atlantium and the Carsakarisk.

- Quantum and Cognitive Psychology: Concepts like inattentional blindness, perceptual shock, and dimensional correction draw from neuroscience and speculative physics.
- Para-Historical Constructs: Terms like "para-historical" and "para-normal" describe speculative technologies and cultural phenomena within the Atlantis Universe.
- Dimensional Correction: A fictional concept inspired by quantum speculation, used to explore memory gaps and reality distortion.

Real-World Locations and Fictional Constructs

- New Zealand: Paeroa, Hamilton, and references to Super Rugby and V Energy drink anchor parts of the story in Kiwi culture.
- Jamaica: Dragon Stout, Appleton's, Montego Bay, and the University of the West Indies are real; Caribbean Paradise Resort is fictional, inspired by the Royalton White Sands Hotel in Falmouth, Jamaica.
- Cockpit Country and Kinloss Church: Real locations used fictionally; the portrayal of the pastor and Atlantean archives is entirely invented.
- Ngâti Tûwharetoa: Rhys's heritage is included with respect and admiration for Mâori culture.
- Abundance City Christian Centre: Loosely inspired by LIFE Church in Auckland; all portrayals are fictional and imaginative.

Cultural and Pop Culture References

- Ben Boyce & Jono Pryor: Referenced as inspiration for a fictional prank; a nod to Kiwi comedy culture.

- Doctor Who, Star Wars, Stargate SG-1, Armageddon: Used conversationally to reflect character personalities and emotional states.
- Bon Jovi's "Livin' on a Prayer": Evokes mood and character levity.
- Edward Mordrake and The Man from Toured: Urban legends used to explore psychological distortion and dimensional anomalies.

Mental Health and Narrative Psychology

- CBT Techniques: Thought compartmentalization and grouping are inspired by cognitive behavioural therapy, used to explore emotional regulation.
- Gapminder.org and Factfulness: Inspired dialogue around balanced thinking and global awareness.
- Mental Health Portrayals: Chad's journey and Lawrence's reflections are fictional, honouring themes of healing and grace without offering clinical advice.

Creative Homage and Personal Influences

- TobyMac and Goatee Records: Jacob McKenzie and Mountain Goat Records are fictional, inspired by Toby McKeehan's music and ministry.
- Aiden Holiday: The phrase "Philosophy Breeds Methodology" is attributed to his teachings at Vision Leadership College and A.H. Frontiers.
- Phil Strong and Christian Podcasts: Influenced spiritual and creative reflections throughout the writing process.

www.ingramcontent.com/pod-product-compliance
Lightning Source LLC
Chambersburg PA
CBHW030920020726
47498CB00001B/39